WHAT *PASSIONS* "INSIDERS" ARE SAYING ABOUT TABITHA LENOX'S DEBUT BOOK

"Absolutely bewitching . . . Lenox is a clairvoyant seeing things in the human heart all too often missed by the naked eye . . . She's a force of nature destined to change the literary landscape forever."

NOSTRADAMUS

"*Hidden Passions* is a sumptuous romp through the den of propriety—this well-heeled community called Harmony . . . A sinfully delicious romance."

NERO

"If it's true hell hath no fury like a scorned lover, then Tabitha Lenox has taken romance to an all-time low to prove it. She has dug so deep, the pages of this tell-all book melt with temptingly hot details, if I do say so myself."

HECUBA

HIDDEN

PASSIONS

Secrets from the
Diaries of Tabitha Lenox

HarperEntertainment
An Imprint of HarperCollinsPublishers

This is a work of fiction. Names, characters, places, and incidents are products of the author's imagination or are used fictitiously and are not to be construed as real. Any resemblance to actual events, locales, organizations, or persons, living or dead, is entirely coincidental.

HARPERENTERTAINMENT
An Imprint of Harper CollinsPublishers
10 East 53rd Street
New York, New York 10022-5299

ISBN: 0-06-102084-2
www.harpercollins.com

Special thanks to James E. Reilly, the creator of *Passions,* for his collaboration on this book.

Written by Alice Alfonsi

First HarperEntertainment paperback printing: January 2002
First HarperEntertainment hardcover printing: February 2001

HarperCollins®, 📖®, and HarperEntertainment™ are trademarks of HarperCollins Publishers Inc.

Printed in the U.S.A.

10 9 8 7 6 5 4 3 2 1

For Timmy

FOREWORD

By Timmy

If you happen to live in the picturesque New England
town of Harmony, then you know what an amazing soap
opera its residents' lives have become over the years!

If you do not live among us, then perhaps you are one
of our frequent visitors (this is, after all, a tourist
town, attracting millions every season!). Maybe you
have enjoyed the sunrise over our little harbor or have
even gotten to know some of our citizens—the powerful
Crane family; the respected Dr. Russell and her husband; Police Chief Bennett and his wife.

Timmy can assure you, however, that no matter how
many times you have visited Harmony, you know only a
fraction of what has gone on beyond the shuttered windows of its stately old colonials.

There is but one person who knows the scandalous past
histories (not to mention private passions) of our upstanding residents. That person, dear reader, is Tabitha
Lenox.

Often dismissed by her neighbors as a batty, eccentric old character who carries around an exceedingly
adorable and dashingly handsome doll (no other description of Timmy will do!), Tabitha has more charm (or

should Tim-Tim say, charms!) than she likes to let on.

Her Harmony diaries document her clever handiwork at manipulating the lives and hearts of those around her (Timmy should know—he's read more than three hundred years' worth of entries!). And she's drawn from them to create the revealing tell-all you now hold in your hands.

Tabby came up with the idea for *Hidden Passions* twenty years ago. With her abundance of supernatural skills, she saw no reason why she couldn't conjure up a romance as breathless and satisfying as any of those written by Jacqueline Susann, Danielle Steel, or one of those Collins women (and so she has, Timmy must admit!).

As she worked on the book, Tabby was certain she'd be joining the ranks of all those other rich, glamorous, bestselling authors. But after Tabby completed her masterpiece, she decided that she'd made a terrible mistake. She could never allow *Hidden Passions* to be published—even anonymously—because the risk was too great.

Not the risk to others, you understand, but to herself.

You see, Tabby never had a problem exposing people for who they really are (the great ones never do!), but her own secrets—well, that was another matter entirely!

Tabby was not ready to tell the world that she has been a sorceress, a spellcaster, a woman of untold powers who has been causing trouble around Harmony for centuries!

Timmy really can't blame Tabitha for her little "identity" issues. After all, the last time her true nature became public, the Harmony townsfolk burned her at the stake (in 1693, sentencing guidelines for witches were not yet fashionable!). And it appears that Tabby will never forgive the town for this heated event (would you?)!

It was only through the latent publishing genius of her enchanted elfin doll, Timmy, that this manuscript was discovered in Tabby's attic; a well-timed call was

placed to a most influential party at HarperCollins in
New York; and the manuscript was subsequently printed
in the form you now hold in your hands.

While Timmy would love to state that his bold action
was a selfless attempt to benefit the great literary
canon, the truth is, Tim-Tim needed the money for Mar-
timmies. This uniquely uplifting beverage—one of
Timmy's finest creations—requires secret ingredients
that are a tad costly. And to Tim-Tim's horror, Tabby's
monetary reserves had suddenly run dry.

Once the book contract was signed, Timmy convinced
both Tabitha and her editor to supplement this nearly
complete work with entries from Tabby's diaries as well
as insightful Timmynotes (just keep your eye out for
the little Martimmy glass throughout). The words
spilling forth from them will shed further light for
you, dear reader, on both the history of our town and
the creative choices of our author (surely the most enchanting literary goddess of the new millennium!).

Finally, Timmy must compliment Tabitha for the risk
she is taking here in exposing herself to the world at
large and to Harmony's townspeople in particular. (Even
in this day and age, one must not rule out the public
frying of those who air their neighbors' dirty laundry!).

Then again, the only reason Tabby is taking this risk
is that she has thought up a clever way to cover her
posterior. You see, a marvelous spell has already been
cast upon you with the simple act of having opened the
cover of this book.

You shall forget that everything you read herein is
true. You will think of it only as fiction—a conjurer's
fancy and no more. Or, as Tabby herself has put it—

"Like a dream you won't recall / all my secrets you
read here / they will fade from memory / keeping my neck
in the clear!"

                                              —Timmy

HIDDEN

PASSIONS

ONE

The Cranes

Above the crashing waves of the New England coastline, crowning the top of Raven Hill, the Crane mansion stood overlooking the small town of Harmony like an imposing monarch.

Inside this vast estate, not so very long ago, an innocent pair of eyes searched the face of a refined, mature woman.

"Read to me, Mummy!" cried two-year-old Sheridan Crane, tucked beneath the covers of her miniature canopy bed.

Katherine Barrett Crane was forty-three. Though her blue gaze was no longer as clear as her daughter's, her hair not quite as golden, her features still reflected the aristocratic beauty that had descended from mother to child for generations.

The high, smooth forehead, sharply defined cheekbones, and natural slenderness were all part of the reason she'd passed the Cranes' careful scrutiny to become the bride of Alistair, the handsome heir to the Crane fortune, almost twenty-five years earlier.

Katherine could still recall her first weeks in Harmony as a young newlywed. Raised among the privileged members of high society, she'd been accustomed to the brilliant bustle around her family's elegant town house on Boston's exclusive Beacon Hill. In comparison, the sleepy harbor town of Harmony felt secluded—almost rustic.

Fearing she'd die of boredom, Katherine had urged her new husband to travel the globe with her. But their jet-setting life had abruptly ended when her slight body became pregnant with her son, Julian, and her doctors warned her to stay put.

Forced to remain in her new marital home, Katherine finally began to explore it: the cobblestone streets lined with quaint colonials; the lush town green; and the crowded little harbor, where fishing trawlers were moored next to racing yachts.

Harmony, she discovered, had a heartbeat. Now that she was a few years older and the anxieties of her difficult pregnancy were pressing down upon her, she found a surprising comfort in listening to its faithful, steady rhythm.

There was dawn's flotilla of fishermen heading out to sea, then early morning's gaggle of children skipping toward school. Noon triggered the cannery's whistle and the raucous lunchtime break for town workers. Then came the baby stroller brigade, circling the Little League ball field like a tiny wagon train.

Sunset brought squawking gulls, trailing the returning boats, and the reliable turning of the old lighthouse beacon, which had safely guided Boston-bound ships along the coastline since before the Revolutionary War.

How could she not have loved Harmony from the start? It was a New England dream, tempting tourists to turn off the Coast Road and shop for marine relics at the antique store, snack on fried clams at the Lobster Shack, and become entranced by the spectacular streaks of scarlet that painted the horizon every evening.

Through spring, summer, and fall, the deep blue waves of Harmony's shoreline perpetually glistened in the bright sunlight, and laughter could always be heard bobbling atop the salt sea air.

It was only in winter that Katherine felt the gloom set in. Clouded skies hung over the slate-gray ocean like a weighted tent canvas, threatening to suffocate every living thing beneath. The streets and roads were icy and deserted, and Katherine felt cut off from the universe.

After Julian's birth, she had learned to cope with her cold-weather depression by jetting off to Aspen for skiing, Paris for shopping, or the Crane resort in Bermuda, where summer's vital glow never ebbed.

But ever since little Sheridan's difficult birth two years ago, however, Katherine could no longer escape the oppressive sadness, which now clouded her spirit the whole year through.

Most days her poor health had kept her a prisoner inside the Crane mansion. And Alistair was no help. His usual preoccupation with the family businesses left Katherine to fight her bleak periods of internal gloom all alone.

Perhaps that was why she clung to the only ray of light left in her daily existence—Sheridan. Absolute joy filled Katherine at the sight of her daughter's chubby cheeks and golden curls. But it was gazing into her bright blue eyes that cheered Katherine the most.

Unlike what she saw in the eyes of her grown son, Julian, Katherine could still see nothing but blissful innocence in Sheridan's eyes. And that's how Katherine wanted her to remain—unspoiled, untroubled, and unaware of the blemishes on the Crane family's past.

She prayed that Sheridan would never learn from Alistair what Katherine had over the years: How the Cranes had burned "witches" in the 1690s, shipped and traded slaves during the 1700s, and engaged in the murderous business of rum-running during Prohibition.

Nor did she want Sheridan to learn how, in the 1930s, the Cranes had treated their own Depression-stricken neighbors like dirt, instructing the bank to foreclose on any mortgaged farm that bordered their property—so the Cranes could expand their estate's riding trails and build four tennis courts.

For now, thank heaven, Sheridan knew only the tastefully decorated world of her nursery, tucked into the mansion's luxurious interior—and the smile of her mummy, which seemed to warm her more thoroughly than the soft pink blanket covering her custom-designed canopy bed.

Hearing the howl of the February wind outside, Katherine shivered a bit as she crossed the room and picked up Sheridan's favorite storybook. The masterfully preserved volume of fairy tales had been published in the nineteenth century and given to Sheridan on the day of her birth by one of the Harmony townspeople, an odd woman who hired herself out to tell fortunes at society parties. ⌐

"Once upon a time," Katherine began to read, "there lived a king and queen who had a handsome son, but when he grew up, he left the palace, and the queen felt all alone. She longed to have another child but could not, until a powerful fairy heard her wish and put a magic spell on her so she could give birth to a golden-haired princess—"

Little Sheridan squealed with delight. She knew this story by heart—how another magic spell put the poor princess into a sleep for a long time, and then a handsome dark-haired prince chopped his way through and woke the sleeping beauty with a kiss!

Mummy was almost done with the story when a man's voice interrupted. "Katherine, it's late. I'm sorry, darling, but you know you need your rest."

"In a minute, Alistair, I still—"

"*Katherine.*"

This fortune-teller is, of course, our own dear authoress, Tabitha Lenox! By the way, according to Tabby's diary, this little Sleeping Beauty fairy tale that Sheridan Crane likes so much—let's just say that as it applies to Katherine Crane's life (not to mention little Sheridan's), the story is far from fictional!

The voice was calm but firm. It was *Daddy's* voice, the little girl knew, but she never heard it more than once or twice a day. Like her mother, the little girl reacted to it by growing very quiet and wishing in her heart, with a sad sort of yearning, that she could hear it more often.

"Go to sleep now, my sweet girl," soothed Mummy, whose smile had disappeared.

"What about the story?" whispered Sheridan.

"You know it by heart, don't you? Good night, love."

Sheridan didn't like the dark, even with the dim yellow glow of her kitty night-light, so she closed her eyes tight.

"And they lived happily ever after," she whispered, determined to finish the story, even if she had to do it all by herself.

TWO

Julian

"Pleasure is an art form. Something the underclass fails to understand."

To punctuate his statement, twenty-four-year-old Julian Crane raised his martini glass and indulged his lips in one of their favorite nighttime pleasures—the bright numbing sting of alcohol.

Sitting at the bar of the Blue Note, Boston's hippest new jazz club, Julian knew very well to what class *he* belonged. *Breeding is in the genes*, his father, Alistair, often told him. *The Crane genes*.

And Julian felt certain this was true. After all, any impostor could put on an impeccably tailored blazer or toss off a haughty, erudite manner. But not just anyone carried Julian's god-given strand of Crane DNA.

Yes, Julian knew his well-muscled, athletic build could attract many an admiring female stare, but it was his patrician intellect and ruthlessly sharp hazel eyes (father's side), as well as his aristocratic brow and squared-off chin (mother's side), that made him look like a member of the *ruling* class. And since the invention of the television, *looking* the part was over half of any battle—JFK had discovered that little advantage when he'd run for the presidency six-teen or so years ago.

"Julian, *everyone* understands pleasure," challenged Tommy Biddles from an adjacent bar stool. "Class has little to do with it."

Like Julian, Tommy was a fellow Harvard law student and a dyed-in-the-wool WASP—from the top of his strategically tousled blond hair to the soles of his hand-tooled leather loafers.

"Tommy, you have a lot to learn," replied Julian.

"You mean *earn*, don't you? My trust fund is handsome, but yours looks like a Greek god."

"Cash flow has little to do with imagination. On the other hand, what good is money if you aren't spending it on *pleasurable* pursuits?"

Such sentiments were typical of Julian. After all, he had been raised to think of himself as American royalty. And by most accounts, he possessed the same prerogatives as any son of a monarch.

With both his father's and mother's bloodlines reaching back to the *Mayflower*, Julian's social position was assured. And with a bank account that rivaled any Saudi prince's, Julian knew very well that he would one day be influencing world trade—and world leaders.

Indeed, on some future date, Julian fully expected to begin taking over the reins of power from his prominent father, Alistair. Until then, however, his main concerns were one, enjoying himself, and two, graduating from law school in the next few months—and in that order of priority, to be sure.

A hollow *ching* resounded as Tommy Biddles touched Julian's raised glass with his own. A notorious Boston play-boy himself, Tommy understood precisely Julian's meaning in the words *pleasurable pursuits*. In fact, Tommy had joined the club that Julian had formed to do nothing but pursue pleasure.

He'd formed it during their hellish first year at Harvard Law when the pressures became overwhelming. Julian and his friends needed some sort of outlet, and whacking a tennis ball around on the Harvard courts every morning just wasn't cutting it. So Julian formed a private club out of his study group and introduced them to a new game.

All the members of Julian's "Sack Pack" were young men of privilege. Handsome, wealthy, and of dubious moral upbringings, they had each learned well—from the cutthroat business strategies of their fathers and backstabbing social tactics of their mothers—that anything was possible, as long as one did not get caught.

Julian told them he'd been inspired by the playboys of history—from Sir Francis Dashwood and his Hellfire Club (of which Ben Franklin was a satisfied member), to Lord Byron's acclaimed sexual escapades with his fellow poet Shelley, to the more recent role model of John F. Kennedy, whose Rat Pack cronies helped him into the boudoir of more than one glittering Hollywood starlet.

The object of Julian's club was to seduce as many young coeds as possible—and everyone knew that Boston, with its surfeit of colleges located within a few cozy square miles of each other, was more famous for coeds than baked beans.

He'd begun the game himself by bedding a healthy string of undergraduates, few of whom ever suspected that they were sleeping with Julian during the same weekends, and sometimes the same nights, as their friends and classmates. Feeling charitable, Julian often passed along discards to his friends.

Each "score" was counted by the Sack Pack in the form of what Julian liked to call "love photos." The game had become quite exciting over the last few years, with points racked up in every conceivable venue—from five-star restaurant bathrooms and art gallery closets to private study rooms in college libraries and the carpeted floors of Harvard faculty offices.

Julian himself had lost count of his scores last fall, after his friends declared him the hands-down winner. Since then, he had grown bored with the game. When you were as young, rich, and well built as Julian Crane, females fell into your lap before you even crooked your finger to summon them across the room.

Now, with well over three months to finals and graduation, Julian's law school tensions were at a lull, and he was in the market for a more interesting diversion. Cheap beer and quick shots had their uses in a pinch, but Julian's tastes were quickly maturing.

Julian smiled to himself as he nursed his dry martini— "shaken, not stirred." He'd had a new private fantasy of late. Fancying himself a young James Bond, he'd taken a trip to London over the holidays, buying himself some suits from Savile Row and the essential Bondmobile—a silver Aston Martin DB5 convertible. He'd even indulged in a few romps with English debutantes for the hell of it, but found them rather tepid between the sheets.

The fact was, Julian liked sexual games, and the English girls he'd encountered didn't have a clue. Then again, when you'd bedded as many women as Julian had, straight sex no longer thrilled. At the tender age of twenty-four, he could see where this might pose a problem.

Years ago, his mother had tried to warn him about disciplining himself. Eating chocolate-hazelnut *gâteau* every day at every meal made one sick of chocolate-hazelnut *gâteau* before long. Julian well remembered *that* lesson.

And he remembered more lessons as he'd grown older, watching others of his class—cousins and friends—become so bored with their lives that only the most dangerous behaviors allowed them to feel anything at all. Tragedy occasionally resulted, as he recalled: foolish drug overdoses, smashed sports cars, rookie pilot errors, gruesome plunges off Nepal mountain peaks. The list went on . . .

Of course, Julian refused to see himself stumbling into

such cliché pitfalls. Instead, he told himself, he was simply a man who knew how to enjoy himself. A connoisseur of pleasure. In his case, the pleasure preferred was sexual.

Arriving back in the States after Christmas, Julian quickly began to yearn for something different to savor, something sultry . . . maybe even darkly exotic.

That was the main reason he'd chosen the Blue Note as his spot to prowl. This hot new Boston club was sure to provide much spicier dishes than the usual white-bread fare he'd consumed back in the manicured squares of Cambridge, and he'd been right.

Just last week he'd met one of the Blue Note's songbirds. Eve was a tasty morsel with luscious cocoa skin and eyes like pools of coffee liqueur—mmmm, chocolate-hazelnut *gâteau* indeed!

The moment he first saw her, Julian held her gaze for the longest, most thrilling moment, and then, to his absolute satisfaction, she'd looked quickly away, as if she had no interest at all in a handsome, well-groomed heir to billions.

Fabulous, my little songbird, Julian had instantly thought. *Make it sporting for me*.

He'd bought her a bottle of champagne and enticed her into drinking it with him. Still, she resisted his charms, while he became more and more entranced with her sultry curves and satin-smooth voice. Even thinking about her now, a full week later, was making his body tighten with the need to possess her.

"So where's this singer you've been salivating over for days?" asked Tommy.

Julian checked his watch. "She'll be starting her first set soon. Only sings one or two nights a week, so when she finally shows, get lost, won't you?"

Tommy smirked with haughty amusement. "Feeling lucky, Julian? I thought you said she turned you down last week?"

Julian's eyes narrowed on his friend. "Just part of the game. But I assure you, a Crane *never* loses."

His father had taught Julian that well enough—well, actually, *taught* was too tame a word. Alistair had pounded this idea unmercifully into his head since the day Julian was born.

Tonight, Julian would put that lesson into action. Eve had slipped away from him once; she wouldn't again. He had devised an imaginative plan that included the Crane jet, the infamous Studio 54, and a sunrise flight toward tropical breezes.

"A Crane never loses, eh?" goaded Tommy. "Want to stack the deck a bit, just in case?"

"Stack the deck? *Please*, Tommy, don't you know me by now? How do you *think* a Crane never loses?"

"Okay, so you've already got some tricks up your sleeve. But you don't have what I can give you. Foolproof insurance."

At Julian's raised eyebrow, Tommy reached into the breast pocket of his jacket and pulled out a little plastic bag filled with yellow oblong pills.

"One of these is all she'll need," insisted Tommy.

Julian recognized the pills. They were what some of his Sack Pack pals liked to refer to as "tools to party with." Julian himself hadn't resorted to them before; he never had to. And, frankly, he'd never wanted to. Just wasn't sporting as far as he was concerned. Just wasn't his style.

"Thanks but no thanks, Tommy. I do believe Eve will be more than willing to party with me tonight," said Julian smoothly. "It's just a matter of turning on the Crane charm."

"Maybe so, but why not take the insurance anyway?" asked Tommy, proffering the pills.

Julian stared at the small plastic sack, which Tommy was casually swinging back and forth, back and forth. Perhaps it was the strength of the martini, but Julian began to see images of his father's face swimming on every one of the little pills—a dozen miniature Alistair Cranes staring out at him, echoing his often repeated litany: "*Cranes get what they want. When they want it. A Crane never loses . . .*"

Julian blinked, set down his martini glass, and met Tommy's gaze.

"Well?" Tommy prompted. "What will you do if she tries to bolt again?"

The very idea made Julian's heart stop.

For days he'd been dreaming about her, fantasizing. Tonight lust was pulsing in his veins—and not lust for any girl. Lust for Eve.

He wanted her. *Primally*.

"Okay, I'll take them. But only to shut *you* up." Julian glanced away in disgust as Tommy transferred the bag to the breast pocket of Julian's blue blazer.

"Just remember the Sack Pack motto," Tommy said with a superior smirk. "Never take *no* as her answer."

With a dismissive wave, Julian raised his martini glass and swiveled his bar stool to face the brightening spotlight at the front of the club.

THREE

Eve

Eve Johnson appeared onstage dressed in red. Her gown was a valentine of velvet, seductive yet sophisticated, with halter straps that bared her light brown shoulders, a soft bodice that caressed her hourglass curves, and a high slit in the long scarlet skirt that gave a tantalizing glimpse of smooth, shapely leg.

For two hours she sang jazz and blues. The Scat Perkins Five backed her natural skill in bringing the room up, then down, then up again. How she relished using her voice to seduce the crowd.

Glad to see my classical vocal training hasn't gone to waste!

Tossing her dark brown curls, Eve smiled to herself, amused by the idea of peddling that training in a smoky nightclub.

She could only imagine how shocked her uptight parents would be if they ever saw her here. But they *never* would. The Blue Note was Eve's little secret.

From the stage, her dark gaze scanned the audience. Then she saw him, sitting on a bar stool in the back—that guy who'd introduced himself last week as "Julian."

Oh, the way he looks at me!

Hungry hazel eyes devoured her in sizzling tingles of electricity, bursting bubbles of heat . . .

For the entire past week, she couldn't stop thinking about him. On the surface, he wasn't really her type. He was a bit more arrogant, more aggressive, and definitely more white than she usually fancied. But there was something about him . . . the sexual predator beneath the polished veneer.

It excited her.

This must be what prey feels like, she thought with a nervous giggle, feeling both repelled and attracted by his intense interest.

Yes-yes-yes!

Sexuality was an exquisite new rush for Eve—heady and powerful. She let the sultry feeling fuel her last song of the night as her mind replayed how Julian had advanced on her the week before . . .

He'd bought her champagne, the best in the house; and as the bubbles went to her head, she'd allowed him to flirt then dance with her.

She'd been touched when he tenderly took her hand and kissed it. Then she'd tentatively run her slender fingers up the sleeve of his blazer, resting them on his broad shoulder, delighting in the arousing evidence of male strength beneath her delicate hand.

He'd leaned in close, his expensive aftershave tickling her nostrils as he dipped his head to nuzzle her neck with warm lips. The champagne, the male attention, it had felt wonderful—

But at the end of the night, when he'd invited her home, whispering promises of passion, she'd fled like Cinderella out the back-alley door.

Eve hated to admit it to herself when she'd returned to her dorm room that night, but for all her sexual posturing, for all her seductive gowns and sultry delivery of Billie Holiday blues, she was still a sheltered little girl inside. And she was damned tired of feeling that way. Tired of living in a gilded cage, hitting only the notes she'd been told to.

I'm only eighteen years old, and I'm already sick of myself!

Ladies and gentlemen meet Eve Johnson, the always perfect, oh-so-well-behaved daughter of too-busy Harvard history Professor Warren Johnson and journalist Tanya Lincoln Johnson, whose award-winning work covering the volatile political climate of the 1960s had regularly taken precedence over raising her young daughter.

Since the age of eight, Eve had pretty much been brought up by a succession of elderly baby-sitters. Tanya and Warren had claimed it was their only alternative after Eve's beloved maternal grandmother—the woman who had raised Eve up to that point—had died of cancer.

But who cares, right? thought Eve.

It didn't matter that her parents had no time for her. She made sure to always be Warren and Tanya's perfect little girl, anyway. Just in case they might look her way for an hour or two one week.

White-glove church socials, singing and ballet lessons, and private girls' schools had been Eve's whole life. Because *that* was the life Warren and Tanya had wanted for her.

But now that she was a sophomore at Radcliffe with excellent marks in her premed major, Eve was beginning to wonder what *she* truly wanted out of life.

The trigger came just after Christmas break when her parents invited her to a Sunday dinner, neglecting to tell her they were setting her up with the son of one of her father's friends. The man was a buttoned-down, bespectacled academic—a guy without a hint of sexuality in his demeanor and, as far as Eve could determine, barely a heartbeat.

The stiff, formal evening—capped with the man's cold, clammy handshake—sent Eve back to her women's dorm feeling like a walking corpse. Did she truly want a marriage as passionless and cerebral as her own parents'?

In two words: *No way.*

The whole world seemed to be breaking free around her, and she wanted to break free, too, find a little wildness inside her before it was too late and she'd become trapped in a life of polite routines.

Time for some changes, Eve had decided. *Time to stop playing the game of life by Warren and Tanya's rules and decide what it is I truly want.*

That weekend she'd auditioned at the Blue Note.

She'd had this secret fantasy for over a decade, ever since she saw the Supremes on television as a little girl. What would it feel like to own the spotlight? Hold an audience spellbound?

It was time to spread her wings, try a new identity on for size, Eve had decided. Besides, it would be *fun* to play at being bad—like Diana Ross playing Billie Holiday in *Lady Sings the Blues.*

Of course, Eve hadn't grown up like Billie—or Diana, for that matter, who'd spent her childhood in a housing project.

Eve hadn't lived anywhere near "the streets," and she knew very well that as the sheltered daughter of a respectable black family, she was far from equipped to.

Deep inside, she knew she was just playing with an image. And even when she *was* onstage, acting the part of the sultry bad girl, she still felt like that child of the 1960s, using a Coke bottle as a microphone in front of the TV and mimicking the moves of Diana Ross.

But I don't want to feel like a little girl anymore, Eve decided tonight on the Blue Note's stage. And this guy was going to help her, because in his hungry eyes, she could finally see the seductress she wanted to be.

As she held Julian's gaze from the stage, Eve let one cinnamon-frosted eyelid fall closed. It was a wink of invitation she knew a man like Julian would not miss.

C'mon, honey, she told him with a sly little slither of her velvet-wrapped body. *Make me feel like a bad girl tonight!*

* * *

Hours later, Eve was giggling as she drained yet another flute of champagne and glanced out the small oval window of the Crane family jet. The lights of Manhattan flickered in the distance, and Eve felt like a kid on Christmas morning.

"So, Julian, if you're a law student, what's your area of concentration?"

"The seven deadly sins."

"Is that so?"

"Yes. And do you know what that makes you?"

"What?"

"Homework."

When Julian had approached Eve after her set, she didn't doubt that he had money. Eve had been raised with money herself and could spot a custom-tailored jacket from twenty paces. But she'd never expected the kind of wealth that could arrange for a private jet to fly them from Boston to New York with only thirty minutes notice.

And she would never have guessed in a thousand years that Julian's last name was Crane. Everyone knew about the Cranes. Their reputation was surpassed only by the Kennedys, or maybe the Du Ponts.

Eve couldn't believe her luck. It was February 13th, Valentine's eve, and here was her billionaire Prince Charming right on time!

Julian seemed like a genuinely nice guy, too. He even took the trouble to toss the Blue Note's house band leader, Orville "Scat" Perkins, his personal card, promising some high-paying gigs.

"Ring the Harmony Country Club and use my name," Julian had offered. "The bands they book are atrocious compared to your smooth sound."

Scat had smiled and tipped his hat in thanks.

Eve was impressed with Julian, and there was no way she was going to turn down his invitation to visit the famous Studio 54! *Everyone* knew about *that* club. All the heavy hitters in the entertainment industry went there—directors, actors, club owners, and record company execs.

Record deal, record deal, record deal!

The idea didn't just echo through Eve's mind, it vibrated through every particle of her being. Julian even claimed he could get her into the super-exclusive celebrity subbasement where stars like Stevie Wonder and Donna Summer sometimes partied!

When the small jet finally landed, a Mercedes stretch limo met them on the tarmac. Eve felt like a movie star as they pulled up to the club. The door of the limo opened to a red carpet. Julian stepped out first, gallantly holding out a hand for her.

What a gentleman!

A huge crowd waited to enter the club. But all Eve had to do was take Julian's extended arm and waltz right in. Dozens of faces gaped as this white man of wealth escorted a gorgeous light-skinned black woman in a stunning gown of scarlet velvet past the burly security guards. Every face in the crowd registered the same thought: "Surely they must be famous!" As they passed, lightbulbs flashed, testifying to that belief.

Eve threw her head back and laughed at how intoxicating getting the star treatment felt. In the club's entrance they waited in line to pass into the main room, and Julian pulled her close.

"You are such a luscious beauty," he growled in her ear.

Eve laughed again and ran her hands along the soft material of his blazer.

"Like what you feel?" asked Julian.

"Can't complain."

"Tennis. It's my passion. Or *was*. Now that I've found you. You're my *new* passion, Eve, what do you think of that?"

"I, uh, I don't know, Julian. This is all too much . . ." Eve wasn't used to sexual banter, and she wasn't sure how to play this game. But Julian didn't seem to care. Before she knew it, he was brushing her lips with his own.

The kiss was sweet and tender at first, and Eve enjoyed it,

responding in kind. But then the kiss changed. Julian's tongue began to push hard against her lips, forcing them to part for him.

His arms were holding her so tightly, she could hardly move as his tongue plunged deeper inside and began to ravage her mouth. This moment of unvarnished sexual aggression in such a public place unnerved Eve. She broke away and stepped back.

"Let's go inside," she said quickly.

Eve's eyes grew wide at the spectacle that greeted her in the huge main room. The place was packed with gyrating bodies—many of them in outrageous costumes, their faces and limbs painted in silver and gold. A mirrored disco ball spun high above, shattering the wildly moving spots into dancing light while confetti and bubbles fell on the pulsating crowd like stardust.

On one wall of the room a huge spoon filled with white powder swung toward the nose of a man-in-the-moon sculpture, and on a balcony just above the dance floor, half-naked couples were moving to the beat of Donna Summer's "Love to Love You, Baby."

"C'mon!" shouted Julian over the blasting speakers.

He pulled her toward the bar, where a shirtless bartender with a black bow tie winked as he poured her more champagne. Suddenly, though, Eve felt she should slow down.

"You look a little nervous, Eve, my darling," Julian murmured in her ear as he handed her a champagne flute. "Drink up."

"Thanks but I think maybe I've had enough for a while."

"Nonsense." Julian pushed the bottom of the flute, forcing the edge to her lips.

Feeling silly about protesting, Eve drank a little. Still, she couldn't shake the feeling of unease. The club was certainly a shock to her system. She'd expected it would be hopping, but not out of control.

Cocaine was being consumed around her as freely as alcohol, and some of the couples were so high they began to have sex on the dance floor.

Julian pulled her along through the twisting bodies until they found a spot of their own in a shadowy corner of the floor. He spun her around with one hand, then pulled her close to him and began to sway her with the other.

"What an exotic creature you are," he whispered, pressing intimately against her. "From the moment I heard you sing, I knew I had to have you."

His lips caressed her neck, then moved lower to sweep across her cleavage, coquettishly displayed in the sweetheart cut of her velvet gown's neckline.

"Julian, I think you better slow down—" As politely as possible, Eve tried to separate the lower half of her body from the hard evidence of his arousal.

Julian didn't react well to Eve's resistance. He brought his head up to face her, and, for a moment, a glittering chill flashed over his features. But then he blinked, and the look was gone.

"I think you need to relax," he purred as he dipped two fingers into his blazer's breast pocket, then pulled something out. "This should help."

"What is it?" she asked, eyeing the strange oblong pill.

"Just a little downer. A 'lude."

"I don't do drugs—"

"It's not 'drugs.' Good lord, it's just a little pill to help you feel better. My mother takes such things, for heaven's sake—though her doctor calls them Seconal."

"I don't know, Julian—"

"You know, maybe I was *wrong* about you, Eve. I shouldn't have brought you here. A pity, since you haven't seen the subbasement yet or met any real celebs—like Stevie and Donna and—"

"Wait!" Eve exclaimed as he began to pull her toward the door. "I didn't say I wanted to go!"

"But you're way too uptight to meet anyone. You've got to *relax*," insisted Julian, presenting the pill again.

Annoyed, Eve snatched it from his hands and gulped it down, chasing it with the rest of her champagne.

"Good girl," Julian murmured in her ear after pulling her body against his again. "You know I've told our pilot to keep the plane ready. In a few hours, my darling, I'm whisking you away to Bermuda—"

"What!"

"That's right," Julian went on. Eve tried to pull away again, but he held her firmly in his arms. "No need for us to make love in this wretched winter cold. When I take you, my dear—and I intend to take you over and over again—it will be on a tropical breeze—"

"No, Julian, you're moving too fast . . ."

But the lights were swirling around her now as she slowly felt her anxieties falling away. The little pill was changing her world . . . and her mind was riding the wave . . .

This is what you wanted, wasn't it? whispered a voice inside her mind . . . or was it Julian's voice in her ear? *Something different, something wild . . . stop being such a little girl . . . don't be afraid . . . just let go . . .*

The pounding throb of the disco became a part of her pulse, the mirrored ball above a hypnotic jewel. Suddenly she began to think that maybe the voice was right.

"Yes," she murmured in Julian's ear. "Perhaps a tropical breeze would be heavenly at this time of year . . ."

She didn't even feel the need to protest when Julian backed her against the wall and tugged her velvet gown high above her bare thighs.

"That's right, my dear, open your legs for me," coaxed Julian as he pressed himself into her. "Yes, darling, the party's just beginning . . ."

FOUR

Alistair

The next morning was exceptionally bitter on Harmony's Raven Hill, even for the middle of a New England February, but Alistair Crane thought the cold invigorating. As was his usual practice, he rose from his warm bed with the dawn.

By nine he'd completed his tai chi, skimmed the *Journal*, *Globe*, and *Times*, and had already taken two conference calls with his new associates in Asia.

Sitting in his richly paneled study, Alistair was never more aware of his family's history—and never more proud of its accomplishments.

More than three centuries earlier, this mansion was nothing but a rustic New England cabin. With the passing decades, however, the Cranes had amassed a fortune that allowed them to add room upon room, then wing upon wing, until it resembled an American palace.

By the late 1800s, the sprawling estate boasted riding stables and a comfortably furnished guest house. By the 1940s, the Cranes had added tennis courts and a ten-car garage. And by the 1960s, a sauna and whirlpool were installed along with a luxurious indoor-outdoor pool, heated to an agreeable 82 degrees in summer and winter.

The surrounding property had also grown with time. Like sharp-eyed predators who understood when to strike at weak prey, the Cranes always found ways to take over the land of their Harmony neighbors, often the very day that promissory notes became overdue.

Alistair was well aware that Harmony's residents began to dread each new generation of Cranes. But that was not a bad thing to Alistair.

Fear brings respect, his father had taught him, *and respect bolsters power.*

In these modern times of the 1970s, Alistair knew the Cranes had achieved a level of wealth far beyond any family in the surrounding region. He himself had acquired for his family a private jet and for Crane Industries two skyscrapers in Boston.

But Alistair had learned a very important lesson from his late father—a lesson that he would soon impart to his own son, Julian. As time marched on, it took with it the stability of any given industry, and thus the security of any family's fortunes.

Alistair could still hear his father's deep, booming voice, vibrating through his being: *For three hundred years, since we came to this country, none of we Cranes have ever taken our security for granted. It is up to you, my boy, to carry on our traditions. Grow the business, son. Any way you can.*

And Alistair had.

Crane Industries, which dealt in shipping, fishing, tourism, and various other commercial entities, had already expanded from regional to national concerns. And as the current patriarch of the family, Alistair had now set a new personal goal—to see Crane Industries go global.

These near-dawn conference calls with Asia each morning were the start of that very process.

Alistair was on his second cup of tea and about to begin his third conference call when the phone rang for him first.

"Good morning, Mr. Crane, sir."

"Go ahead."

"He took the small jet at midnight from Boston to La Guardia, then flew to Bermuda at dawn."

"Bermuda? Whatever for?"

"To impress a woman, sir. One of *color*, I might add."

Alistair paused a long moment. "I see," he finally replied tightly.

"He's checked into one of the Crane resorts with her, Hotel Tropic. The bridal suite."

"*Bridal suite*. My god, they're not—"

"No, sir. Not married. Your manager told me it's Presidential Class, best in the resort, the one honeymooners usually take. But Julian didn't get married to the girl. He just wanted to—"

"Yes, I get the picture. Keep an eye on him, then, and continue your daily reports."

Entering the breakfast room, Katherine Crane stared in silence at her husband.

"What, Katherine? *What?*"

"Is it really necessary for you to spy on your own son?"

"Every generation of Cranes must be protected, Katherine. You have no idea how many gold diggers would love nothing more than to contaminate our line with a little blackmailing bastard."

Katherine sighed at the harshness of her husband's words, the steely determination in his eyes. A shiver touched her skin despite the crackling fire in the nearby hearth.

Her years with Alistair had given her many worldly benefits—trips to Europe, balls at the White House, movie premieres with Hollywood stars—but with the passing decades, she had become increasingly less impressed with such things.

Katherine hated the idea of saying they bored her, because at first it had all seemed so beguiling, so incredibly glamorous. But the truth was, she was tired now. Too tired to even think about eight-hour flights to Paris or even short hops to Broadway for opening-night orchestra seats. And she'd been married too long to a man who treated his personal relationships as little more than business transactions with estimated gains and losses, resulting from a series of implemented strategies.

Katherine observed her husband. His forceful features were still sharp, his aristocratic profile as powerful as his steady gaze. He was, it seemed to her, as handsome in these middle-age years as he'd been in his twenties when she'd first laid eyes on him. When she'd first fallen in love with him.

Of course, he was more distinguished-looking now, with his hair graying at the temples and the edges of his eyes displaying subtle signs of crow's feet, tiny wrinkles that only added an air of rugged character to his face.

Katherine loved Alistair still.

But she knew now, with his ever-present remoteness, how much that love had cost her. And would continue to . . .

He had been a generous man over the years, generous with money and lavish gifts, but never with himself. And Katherine had eventually learned that even his gifts came at a price. Total and complete control.

Sheridan had become Katherine's only true joy now. The only reason to rise in the morning.

For a short time, she had felt like that with Julian, when he was very little. But Katherine hadn't understood Alistair's plan to twist Julian until it was too late.

These past few years, especially, Katherine saw that Julian had truly become Alistair's boy—a Crane, body and soul. Perhaps a trace of herself was left in him, but no more than a trace; and the truth was, Katherine knew she had not worked hard enough to make that difference in her son's life.

She wasn't proud of her weakness—that she'd never been able to fight her husband's will. What hurt the most was the knowledge that Rachel surely would have.

Even years ago, Katherine's spirited older sister had known exactly how to manipulate Alistair. But then Alistair had fallen head over heels for Rachel. She had been his first love. His *first* choice to wed.

Unfortunately for all of them, Katherine's sister had died young, drowning in a sailing accident off the Cape two weeks before the ceremony, and leaving Katherine an inescapable legacy.

In Rachel, Alistair would always have his eighteen-year-old raven-haired bride. She would always be beautiful, never grow old, never be anything but perfect in his memories. And, the most important thing of all—she would always be beyond his reach, ensuring that Alistair would always pine for her.

Katherine realized all of this much too late, of course. As a young bride herself she'd never considered what drove men like Alistair . . . and what bored them. Things might have been different if only she had understood what to withhold from her husband to keep him interested.

But these days, Katherine was too tired to even try with Alistair anymore. Ever since Sheridan's birth . . . the complications, the hemorrhaging.

Doctors couldn't help her, just said her body had been weakened, that she never quite recovered. Bed rest and lots of it had been her life for two years now . . . but she felt sure things would change for her. Someday soon she'd get her health back . . . her strength back . . .

Katherine wanted to protest again to her husband, get him to admit it was wrong to spy on their son. But his iron-cold look killed the words in her throat. And, as she had so many times before, she simply slipped away.

Alistair watched his wife leave, but his mind was not on Katherine or her concerns about spying on Julian. Katherine was naive—but then, what could one expect from a woman?

No, Alistair's mind was still on his son—and the unsettling news that he had taken a woman of color to a Bermuda bridal suite.

My god, thought Alistair, even the *chance* that Julian would marry such a woman made his flesh grow cold. His firstborn would become a social outcast in their circles—and how could Julian inherit and run Crane Industries when he had not properly developed either the social or business contacts to do the job?

The modern marketplace and world economy were never more unpredictable, and Alistair knew it would take a great deal of vigilance to successfully maintain the family's fortune—vigilance and, when necessary, ruthlessness.

Alistair had learned that from his father as well.

No, this affair could *not* be permitted. And yet Julian was a grown man now. Alistair had to be very careful in how he chose to influence his son. There was no room for error. The strategy must be foolproof.

And it wouldn't hurt to kill two birds with one stone, thought Alistair.

After mulling it over for a solid hour, Alistair picked up the phone and called an old friend and business rival, Governor Harrison Winthrop.

"Harrison? Alistair. How is Helen? . . . Good, good . . . And what about that lovely daughter of yours, Ivy. She's in college now, isn't she? . . ."

FIVE

Ivy

That evening, just outside of Harmony, flurries began to fall, dusting the moonlit grounds of Rutland Women's College with a layer of silvery white.

Glancing back to make sure no one was following her, Ivy Winthrop darted off the well-lit sidewalk that led to the college's library and crunched through the shadows of the snow-covered lawn.

The back drive was slippery when she reached it, and Ivy nearly lost her footing as she walked to its end, where a locked gate was supposed to separate the young women of this exclusive school from the world that lay beyond it.

Brushing back a stray lock of curling white-blond hair, she peered through the bars and saw the rusting Pinto with the Harmony Pizza Shop logo spray-painted on its side. For a moment, she couldn't stop herself from cringing at the pathetic little vehicle.

But when she moved closer to the locked gate and saw Sam Bennett's dazzling smile shining at her from behind the windshield, her legs went as shaky as the first time she'd seen him bare-chested on Harmony's shoreline almost two years before.

It was always like this for Ivy.

Sam made her whole world disappear, with all of its demands and expectations. He drew her magically into a perfect cocoon of romance. As she gazed now at his handsome, square-jawed face, a flood of cherished memories washed over her . . .

Starlit summer nights making love on Harmony's beach, the waves lapping close in a sensual rhythm . . . fall picnics on horseback, gazing at the turning trees, kissing for hours on a blanket of fallen leaves . . . winter getaways to his father's rustic fishing cabin, moonlit snow framing the glistening ice of the mountain lake . . .

That's where they were heading tonight for their special Valentine's date—to that tiny one-room log cabin in the woods just west of Harmony, where Ivy could shut out the rest of her world and Sam's hard body would make love to her for hours on that soft fur rug by the crackling fire . . .

Suddenly Ivy blinked her sky-blue eyes and willed herself to remember where she was—and how careful she needed to be.

Warily, she looked behind her, making sure yet again that no one from the college was watching her slip through the bars of the back gate.

She could almost hear the nasty laughter from the girls of Alpha Alpha Alpha, the most exclusive sorority in the country. Every last one of them would be wildly amused at the sight of her climbing inside Sam's sorry little car.

For an awful moment, Ivy relived the tricky ordeal it took to get here—fifteen endless minutes that began with three little words:

"Valentine's Day sucks!"

The words had reverberated like Greek thunder through Alpha's campus home, rising up the curving marble staircase and striking Ivy's delicate, diamond-studded ears with irritating force.

A *vulgar pronouncement*, Ivy had thought upon hearing it. *From an even more vulgar girl*.

Ivy's one goal this evening had been to flee through Alpha House's ridiculously ostentatious stone foyer—*impossible* to heat properly during the New England winters—and slip free of Rutland's high stone walls without being grilled like a war criminal.

This, Ivy knew, was an unlikely prospect now that the raven-haired terror by the name of Clarissa Morton had come tramping through the great arched doorway below, stomping slush off her Austrian-made snow boots with the delicacy of a Nazi storm trooper.

"I mean it. I hate V-Day," Clarissa continued to rant. "All that forced sentimentality. Drugstores full of cheap perfume and candy hearts. The entire freaking idea of sending valentines was cooked up by some cretin on Madison Avenue!"

To Ivy, whose father had once served as governor of the state and counted the Kennedy and Crane families among his prestigious list of acquaintances, it seemed that Clarissa had a lot in common with her statements. She was rude, tacky, and tolerated in Ivy's social sphere only because an international food conglomerate had bought her parents' silly little ice cream company with stock options that had split ten times in three years. As a result, Clarissa had built this drafty rendition of an English manor for Alpha's housing needs the very year she had pledged.

Now a senior at Rutland, Clarissa, an exotic-looking girl with a flowing mane of black curls and piercing green eyes, was also the head of this year's membership selection committee. "Greek thunder" described her pronouncements to a tee.

I just want to get to my Sam! Ivy silently lamented. But the only path to her secret boyfriend was down Alpha's marble stairway and through its great oak doors, now effectively guarded by Clarissa and Rebecca Osburn, who had just joined Clarissa's snow-be-gone clogging dance.

Rebecca was a girlhood friend of Ivy's. But she was also a slippery little freshman pledge, ready to do or say *anything* to finally be accepted as an Alpha girl.

"You're so right, Clarissa. I never liked Valentine's Day," lied Rebecca, nervously twirling a strand of her strawberry-blond hair. "Makes you feel like you're a leper or something if you don't have a date."

"A *date!*" shrieked Clarissa. "Nobody has *dates* anymore! Get this through your head, will you, Rebecca, *Happy Days* is not a television show, it's *historical fiction.* I mean, for god's sake, how did you get your head stuck in 1950s sand?"

Rebecca's wide blue eyes blinked rapidly in a state of obvious panic. "I blame my parents," she covered quickly. "I mean, *they* think like that, not *me*—"

"Well, I *don't* think like that," said Clarissa. "When Jonny and I get it on, it's good straight sex—"

Jonny was, of course, Jonathan Hotchkiss, Clarissa's half-English boyfriend—yet another reason the Alphas were so impressed with her.

Hotchkiss, although born near Harmony, was the nephew of a bona fide English earl. He was now finishing up his last year of higher education across the Atlantic at Oxford.

Jonathan claimed Clarissa was "cheeky" and "colorful." But Ivy had heard some gossip that suggested his family's aging dynasty was strapped for cold hard cash, and they'd put up with anything—even a vulgar, badly bred American in-law—to gain solvency.

"I say screw sentimentality," Clarissa continued to advise Rebecca. "Haven't you read that new Erica Jong book yet?"

"She's sort of pornographic, isn't she?"

"Rebecca, you are so out of it. Come to my room and I'll lend you my copy."

Ivy sighed in disgust. Although she'd never say so out loud, her views on sex were far different from Clarissa's. Ivy well knew that the hip and fashionable trend these days was to trash romance. But for Ivy, sentimentality was a wonderful thing. In fact, she had guarded her virginity until she'd found a boy who truly loved her—and whom she truly loved in return.

Having sex and making love were two very different acts in Ivy's mind, and she had vowed never to have sex or marry for any reason other than love. Although sometimes Ivy secretly wondered if her mother would agree . . .

"Your father is a good man," Ivy's mother often told her. But Ivy never once recalled hearing her mother talk about *loving* him.

Ivy's mother, Helena Revere-Mott-Beaton Winthrop, was a straight-laced DAR and a well-bred woman of taste and intelligence. Her family, which was distantly related to Revolutionary War equestrian Paul Revere, once boasted a fabulous fortune and friendships with the likes of Franklin Roosevelt, Scott Fitzgerald, and the Duke of York. ▼

Unfortunately for Ivy's mother, much of her family's money was lost in a single hand of Monte Carlo baccarat. Romantically enough (or tragically, depending on how one looked at it), the wager had been placed by Helen's uncle a week before his wedding, to impress a breathtakingly beautiful Danish countess he had just met.

After a passing fancy had fleeced the Revere-Mott-Beatons of their fortune, the family limped along on credit for a few years. Then Ivy got the distinct impression that her mother, a natural bombshell with lavender eyes and flowing white-blond hair, had been sold to the highest bidder.

It's not that her mother had ever expressed unhappiness at marrying the heir to the Winthrop Marine shipping fleet. Ivy's father, Harrison, was a charming man. Of course, his fortune couldn't be compared to the hundreds of millions

DAR, of course, refers to the Daughters of the American Revolution, a group that actually rejected Tabby's membership application. "I just can't understand it!" Tabby wrote in her diary. "I told them there was no need to produce a relative who lived during the Revolution when I saw the whole thing myself!"

controlled by the Cranes, but Harrison Winthrop did have nearly ten million to his name in addition to his fleet of ships—and he had distinguished himself by holding the office of governor for two terms during Ivy's childhood.

Still, it seemed to Ivy that some days her mother would stare off into thin air, a wistful look on her face. Maybe it was just Ivy's childish imagination, but she could not shake the feeling that her mother was daydreaming about another life. An alternate life. A life she would have lived if her uncle hadn't been quite so drunk on champagne at a Monte Carlo card table in 1952.

"Hi, Ivy. And *where* are *you* going?" The voice of Rebecca Osburn startled Ivy back to the present, instantly reminding Ivy of her secret Valentine's night date. Sam Bennett's lantern jaw, granite body, and tenderly passionate kisses were almost within reach!

"Just stepping out," said Ivy breezily, trying to slip by.

"But it's so late," said Rebecca, appearing concerned.

"Not for the library," Ivy lied smoothly—an art she'd learned well over the last two years of seeing Sam. "It's open all night."

"The *library?*" Clarissa's eyebrow lifted, and her critical gaze settled on Ivy's fur-lined, cream-colored coat and matching silk and cashmere scarf, which Ivy had strategically selected with her mother at Saks to make her long, silky blond curls appear angelic.

"*Look*, Rebecca, our little Ivy has magically transformed from social butterfly to dreary bookworm. Can you believe it? I *can't.*"

"Just be careful out there," Rebecca warned. "There's some pizza delivery car at the back gate. Whoever the driver is, he's been parked there an awful long time."

Ivy's heart nearly stopped when Clarissa cast a knowing gaze at Ivy and said, "Don't be so paranoid, Rebecca. The delivery guy's probably hoping he can score some action, since we're overloaded with estrogen around here. I'd even let him service me if it weren't *beneath* me."

Ivy's kid glove stilled on the latch of the half-open door, her face flinching from the typical bite of New England chill. Against her better judgment, she answered back, "You know, Clarissa, my mother always said that some people can amass all the money in the world. But no matter how many replicas of English manor halls they build, it still won't buy them class."

Behind Clarissa, Rebecca's eyes widened in shock as her mouth went slack. *Nobody* insulted Clarissa—not to her face.

But Ivy stood her ground, trying not to look completely unnerved as Clarissa's thin lips pursed and her green eyes narrowed.

"Why defend some silly *pizza boy*, Winthrop?" Clarissa finally replied in a voice as chilly as the drafty rooms of the ostentatious hall she'd built. "After all, don't you feel the same way? No self-respecting Alpha girl would waste time with a townie loser."

Ivy was speechless for a moment. She hadn't expected Clarissa to zero in so sharply on the truth.

"If you're feeling the itch," continued Clarissa, "there are plenty of Harvard and Yale men who come sniffing around our weekend parties. We have *standards* to maintain. It would disgrace the sorority to stoop any lower. And if you don't agree, maybe you ought to *rethink* pledging Alpha."

Ivy bit her bottom lip. She hated to admit it, but if Clarissa could prove Ivy's destination tonight, she could easily sink her final acceptance into the exclusive sorority—an inconceivable disgrace for Ivy with every last one of her friends pledging.

Dropping out was no option, either. Her father had refused to release control of her one-million-dollar trust fund until she'd completed a four year degree. Ivy had no choice but to imprison herself within these vine-covered stone walls. And enduring Rutland Prison for four years would be tolerable only as an Alpha girl.

Besides, Ivy had to admit that her beloved grandmother

would be devastated if Alpha dumped her. The Winthrop women had all been Alpha girls since before the first World War.

Don't push it, thought Ivy, eyeing Clarissa's sour gaze. *Just bolt.*

"Well, I really *must* get to the library," sang Ivy, whisking into the night before Clarissa even knew the conversation was over.

SIX

The Wish

Slipping at long last through Rutland's back gate, Ivy cast a final worried glance behind her and prayed that none of the Alphas could see her climbing into Sam's rusting car.

Closing her eyes, Ivy sighed in frustration. For a moment, she just couldn't stop herself from whispering a wish into the frigid New England air. A wish that things could be different . . .

If only some magic wand would transform Sam's Pinto into an Aston Martin and Sam into a man as filthy rich as Julian Crane. I'd give anything for that.

With the Crane millions, Sam could have joined Ivy and her sorority sisters at Mimi Higgenbotham's Swiss ski chalet over their last winter break, or raced a yacht in the Harmony Country Club regatta that everyone who was anyone attended every August.

But Ivy didn't have a magic wand. All she had was an antique locket with the face of the boy who loved her inside it. For almost two years that had been enough magic for Ivy—and in her heart, she knew it still was.

What was she anyway? A rich brat? Scarlett O'Hara before the war? Suddenly ashamed, Ivy reminded herself that she'd just die without Sam in her life. She was a woman in love. And that's what she would be—for the rest of her life.

I will love Sam Bennett forever.

As she opened the car door and slipped inside, the warmth of his brilliant smile enveloped her.

Despite the bitter winds outside, the car's interior was quite comfortable. The vehicle had been idling so long with the heater on full blast that Sam had taken off his Castleton College football jacket and tossed it into the backseat. He sat now behind the wheel, his broad chest wrapped in a ivory fisherman's sweater and his strong legs encased in worn blue jeans.

Ivy loved how he looked—rugged, earthy, masculine, and as hot as any of Harmony's young fisherman's sons whom she and Rebecca used to drool over from a distance in their early teen years.

"Hi, baby," he said, his low voice tender. "God, you look beautiful."

He reached out and brushed at the silvery flakes of snow still clinging to her white-blond curls.

"Happy Valentine's Day, Sam," she whispered, overjoyed to finally be with him again.

"You too, honey. C'mere."

He pulled her against him and her hands splayed on the thick ivory sweater, feeling the rock-solid chest beneath.

Oh, yes . . . thought Ivy, *how I adore those eyes . . . those smoldering, passionate, deep blue eyes . . .* That hungry look inside them was all she needed to reassure her that she was a woman in love.

Now she just needed to get through three more years of Rutland and graduate. Then her father would release her generous trust fund, and she and Sam would live well off her million for a few years. That's all the time she'd need to convince her father that Sam would be the best man to take over the helm of Winthrop Marine. Then, finally, she and

Sam would be living the life of multimillionaires, as she knew they were meant to.

Ivy's plan was foolproof. In a few short years she'd have Sam, the money, and the social position. She'd finally get everything she wanted, and with very little sacrifice, really. She and Sam just had to be very careful, and continue to keep their relationship a secret for a while.

Watching Sam's strong jaw descend, Ivy felt her heart begin to race. Not just from the feel of his soft, warm mouth reclaiming hers, but from the fear of getting caught.

She couldn't be too careful, really.

In another few minutes, the worry would be over. Sam would break the kiss and start the engine and they'd be on the road toward their cozy fishing cabin. Then, for a little while anyway, they'd rekindle their perfect romantic bliss . . .

Never once did Ivy suspect that the little wish she'd so sincerely whispered to the frigid night air had floated across town to the doorstep of a woman with the powers to grant it—Harmony's very own Duchess de Rune, a sorceress with powers beyond compare . . . ☞

"Well, well, well! Did you hear Miss Ivy's little wish?"

Duchess de Rune! A sorceress with powers beyond compare! Please, she's a witch! Timmy finds it wildly amusing that when Tabby first wrote these pages, she really thought she could hide behind such flimsy literary devices as these!

Dear reader, Timmy knows you would easily recognize the identity of this person; therefore, Timmy convinced Tabby and her publisher to forgo the coy pretense from this page forward and simply call this "character" by her real name—Tabitha Lenox!

Harmony's attractive young enchantress, Tabitha Lenox, asked her longtime companion, Fluffy the cat. ▼

"She says she'll give anything for a man 'as filthy rich as Julian Crane.' *Anything!* Well, my old friends *down below* will certainly want to take her up on that little whispered bargain, and I must say, I'm sufficiently amused by the delightfully cruel possibilities up here! So let's get started, shall we?"

Jumping onto Tabby's kitchen table, Fluffy meowed with approval.

"I'll be looking in on Julian and the rest of the Cranes, of course," Tabby mused as she reached into a cupboard for a large crystal bowl, then filled it with water.

"My scrying bowl has always served me well, conjuring lovely clear visions for my crosstown spying. But what about young Mr. Sam Bennett? Perhaps we should try disposing of him right away. How about a car accident? Yes, that should start things off with a bang!"

Like a specter, the doe appeared out of nowhere.

Bewitched by the girl sitting next to him, Sam Bennett had allowed his attention to recklessly stray from the road ahead. Ivy was an irresistible vision tonight, a snow siren in a cream-colored coat with a white fur collar, icy flakes sparkling like tiny diamonds in her cloud of long, white-gold curls.

Distracted, Sam had no time to react when he finally saw the deer leap into the Pinto's headlights. Jerking the

Did you catch the word attractive and young in Tabitha's description of the witch? Timmy will admit Tabby is his princess and therefore beautiful in his eyes, but young?! Please! Timmy thinks Tabby was showing signs of senility when she wrote that one!

steering wheel, he swerved the little car enough to narrowly miss the animal, but the resulting spin on the slick road sent the vehicle careening toward the surrounding forest.

Ivy screamed in terror as the back of the car swung into a wild arc, shooting the driver's side toward the five-foot-wide trunk of a hundred-year-old oak.

I'm dead.

The son of Harmony's police chief, Sam had seen enough gruesome car wrecks off these winding rural roads to instantly know the results of his own impending crash. Ivy would survive with injuries. He would take the crushing death blow to his left side, spine, and skull.

Sam closed his eyes, grateful at least, in that split second before the end, that the deadly impact was on his side and not Ivy's.

He waited.

But, miraculously, no crash came.

The sudden stillness confused him. He glanced at Ivy. "Are you—"

"I'm fine," she rasped, her throat dry from the exhausting screams, her breathing quick and shallow.

Sam reached out and pulled her into his embrace, but he could feel her stiffen. *I scared her to death*. He knew it in an instant. And he felt just as shaken.

Letting her go, Sam popped the door and stepped out of the car, mumbling something about checking for damage, which was a lie.

Sam didn't care about the damage to his piece-of-crap car. He just didn't want Ivy to see his hands trembling. He'd been her iron-jawed hero for almost two years now, and he'd be damned if he'd let her see him shaking like a little girl.

The New England air was frigid as Sam stepped around the bumper, looking for some reason the huge black oak had not become his grave marker.

But there was nothing. No damage, nor any evidence of

why their merry-go-round ride had halted three feet before impact.

"What in heaven's name stopped us?" he whispered to the forest air.

As if in answer, the tree branches above him began to violently sway. A moment later, a strange warmth brushed his cheek, like a gentle kiss in the subzero cold.

"What the hell—?"

Sam blinked. Was he hallucinating? Having some kind of attack?

Suddenly a brilliant vision of the purest white light appeared on the limb of the hundred-year-old tree.

Sam stepped back.

The unearthly light should have scared him, but it didn't. Instead, it somehow comforted him.

Sam touched his head, but he knew this wasn't fever. And it wasn't a concussion, because he hadn't hit his head. And the strange white light, which was now fading away, wasn't lightning, either.

Sam almost called to Ivy, but stopped himself. This warmth blossoming inside him, calming his shaking hands, reassuring him, had nothing to do with Ivy. He didn't know how he knew this, but he did.

It was coming from . . . someplace else.

"Hell's bells!" screeched the enchantress from her kitchen table, sending Fluffy running for cover.

Tabitha had watched the accident play out just as she'd planned. Her spell over Sam kept his eyes on Ivy and off the road. The doe leaped out in front of him as she'd prescribed. But something had stopped the car from crashing into the tree with the delightfully shattering impact she'd arranged.

Jumping up, Tabby ran to the living room to consult her *Book of Black Arts*.

"I don't understand it, Fluffy! The 'tragic accident' spell was perfectly cast. I made no mistake."

Returning to her scrying bowl, the sorceress closed her eyes and concentrated. "Show me who put a protection spell over this man. Who *dares* to interfere with my dark powers . . ."

Over one hundred miles from Sam's near-fatal accident, outside a small New England logging town, an old farmhouse sat in a snow-covered clearing.

On this snowy February night, a home-schooled girl of seventeen with long, sand-colored curls and wide blue eyes lay quietly on her bed, her lips moving silently.

Across the room, her identical twin sister asked, "Who are you praying for, Grace?"

Grace Standish smiled. "My husband."

Faith smiled at her twin. "Guess that's appropriate for Saint Valentine's night. Who's the lucky guy? Do you know?"

"Don't know his name yet," said Grace. "But he's somewhere out there. I'm just asking my guardian angel to keep him safe until he can find me."

"Damn my soul," muttered the witch. "It seems those wretched Standish twins have grown quite a bit since I last tried to destroy them. And they've grown quite a bit in their powers, too, if one was able to send an angel to protect Sam Bennett!"

Tabby began to pace the kitchen, her cat's tail twitching with interest.

"If the Standish twins are already starting to challenge me, then I'd better keep an eye on them from now on."

"Meow!" protested Fluffy.

"Oh, don't worry! Watching them won't sidetrack me

from my little hobbies here in Harmony. Nothing could keep me from that much fun! But killing the young Bennett simply isn't going to work now. Not with Grace's angel watching over him . . .

"I'll just have to find some other way to grant Miss Ivy's secret wish!"

SEVEN

The Party

Winter thawed to spring, and Julian Crane, to his surprise, had failed to grow bored with the enigmatic Eve.

Part of the obsession, he suspected, grew from her mystery.

Every other female with whom he'd creased the sheets had talked mainly about the trivialities of her life. But Eve refused to reveal details about her past or present. She even forbade Julian to meet her anywhere but the Blue Note.

As a result, Julian began making up elaborate fantasies about her, believing her to be some kind of tragic Jazz Age–type heroine with a sordid past, maybe even wanted by the law.

Perhaps her mother had been a lady of the evening, her father a musician who'd skipped town. Perhaps she'd been a kept woman of a wealthy older man—like the beautiful quadroons of the antebellum South.

Perhaps her mature lover had schooled her in her impressive grasp of music, art history, and political science. Perhaps she had this lover even now, waiting at home, or perhaps there was a jealous husband in the wings.

The possibilities excited Julian all the more, bringing him back to the Blue Note again and again for more doses of Eve's coquettish voice and sensuous body, which, with his continual supply of cocaine and 'ludes, became ever more willing to do whatever he asked of it.

Weekends were filled with gourmet dinners, impromptu shopping sprees, and round-trip flights to the Crane's Bermuda resort. Studio 54 became a weekly ritual. Eve wasn't always willing to part her legs for Julian, but he'd gradually become a master at finding ways to manipulate, control, and overcome her resistance.

Julian liked to tell himself that Eve had become addicted to his lovemaking as much as the lavish recreation and the free-flowing drugs he provided. But the truth of precisely why she'd become hooked didn't really concern him. As Alistair had taught him, *Cranes get what they want. How they get it is of little importance*.

Despite the lure of Eve's pleasures, however, final exams eventually pulled Julian back to reality. By the end of April he was immersed in round-the-clock law studies, and by the end of May he was looking forward to his graduation.

Because Julian's commencement ceremony fatefully coincided with the blooming of the award-winning Crane Lavender Roses—created by Alistair's own grandmother through a hybrid of English tea and Fantin Latour varieties—Alistair insisted on throwing an elaborate garden party for Julian at the Harmony mansion.

A white tent was erected on the rear grounds, a string quartet was shuttled up from Juilliard, and twenty Dutch copper skuttles were arranged on a bed of seaweed to create a fashionably rustic-looking raw bar.

Guests arrived at noon and feasted on eighty pounds of boiled gulf shrimp, ten dozen rock crab claws shipped in from Maine, and three hundred fat Louisiana oysters, sliced to order by an expert shucker, specially flown in that morning from Baton Rouge.

Two hundred lobsters were ordered poached and split, and bowls of caviar were placed on ice along with frosted bottles of vodka and a seemingly endless supply of Dom

Pérignon. And, finally, a dessert table was assembled with practically every French pastry known to Julia Child. And if you were watching your waistline, then the bowls of fat, ripe strawberries with splashes of *créme de fraises* and dollops of *créme fraîche* would do nicely, thank you very much!

"Delightful spread, Katherine," complimented Alistair, spooning a generous helping of beluga on a thin slice of baguette toast. "Vodka's iced just right."

"Used a new girl for the catering," said Katherine, elegant as ever in a Laura Ashley sundress, hair in a chignon, a delicate string of pearls at her throat. "From Westport, Connecticut. Helen Winthrop highly recommended her. Martha something-or-other."

"Keep her in mind for Julian's wedding."

"Excuse me? Julian's *what?*"

Alistair sipped at his iced vodka and took another bite of the beluga. "Time he got married."

"To *whom*, Alistair? The boy didn't even bring a date to his own party."

"That's of no consequence."

"Well, of course it is. Julian is still sowing his oats—"

"That's what concerns me, Katherine. I'm quite aware of this 'free love' sensibility among the young people today, but sowing enough women will reap something we, none of us, will want, I assure you."

"Don't be crude."

"It's the boy's behavior that's been crude. He needs a wife."

"He's too young for marriage."

"He's older than I was when I—"

The silence went on for heart-stopping seconds. Katherine fingered her pearls and drained half her champagne flute.

"When you proposed to my sister," she finally finished for him. "Rachel."

"Yes," said Alistair with the slightest vocal tremble.

To a casual listener, nothing would seem amiss, but to

Katherine, that tiny tremble represented a shockingly rare revelation of Alistair's vulnerability.

With an imperceptible sigh, Alistair turned his patrician profile toward the ocean's treacherous waves in that melancholy way he sometimes did—as if he could still see part of Rachel's submerged sailboat, a torn piece of her bright yellow slicker.

Alistair was older now, but to Katherine he was still as handsome and powerful as the evening she'd first glimpsed him. For a moment she was back there again, hearing the front door chimes, exactly on time, to escort Rachel to Harmony Country Club's Christmas ball.

Fourteen-year-old Katherine, in ponytail and braces, had been perched on the front staircase when the twenty-two-year-old Adonis in his sleek dinner jacket had winked and flirted with her, leaning rakishly on the banister beside her as he'd waited for her tardy sister to descend from her bedroom.

Katherine's older sister had always hated fashion. Dressing up in ball gowns and twisting up her unruly mane of raven curls was akin to torture for a girl who much preferred tennis, riding, and sailing—the latter of which had brought about her tragic end.

Even now, thought Katherine again. *Even now I'm still paying for my terrible wish.*

After falling head over heels for Alistair that night, the teenage Katherine had pledged anything, even her own soul, to switch places with her older sister.

Little did Katherine know that such wishes could be heard—and be made to come true. Or that getting what one so vainly and selfishly wished for would become its own punishment in the end. ⟩

 Well, dear reader, Timmy is sure he doesn't have to tell you who in Harmony heard and granted that wish!

Turning away from her husband, Katherine now looked to her son.

Handsome and relaxed in beige khakis, a white polo shirt, and blue blazer, Julian stood on the manicured lawn chatting amicably with another Harvard grad. Katherine noticed the great number of young women who had posted themselves all around him, each pretending to be chatting with another, yet constantly glancing his way, hoping to attract his attention.

The scene brought back memories of her own girlish days, waiting to catch the eye of a Crane. And just like his father, Julian was truly gifted at acting casually oblivious to the desperate longing that lived around him.

"Whom did you have in mind?" Katherine suddenly asked Alistair. "For Julian's wife. What young woman?"

"You know very well who."

Katherine's eyebrow rose. "If you mean Ivy Winthrop, she's far too innocent for Julian."

"She's a lovely girl."

"Of course she is, Alistair. I never said she wasn't. Class begets class, and Helen and Harrison are the best people we know, not counting Jackie and Aristotle—God rest his soul. But it doesn't mean Ivy, and Julian for that matter, are ready for such an important step."

"*We'll see.*"

The words were said with the sort of steely finality she'd heard a thousand times before. Draining her champagne flute completely, Katherine turned back toward the caviar station. Suddenly she needed to sample the iced vodka herself.

Then perhaps she'd let Alistair make her apologies so she could slip away to her bedroom for a rest. It was a miracle she'd made it this far into the party without her usual fatigue settling in.

Thank goodness the Stewart woman had handled the details of the party preparations. Since giving birth to Sheridan, Katherine no longer had the energy for such things.

* * *

"Careful, Julian, sounds like you're falling in love."

"Lust, my friend. Both are 'L' words, never to be confused."

"Fine, you're in *lust* with her, then. What I want to know is . . ." Tommy Biddles paused a moment and lowered his voice. "Do you have *evidence* to share?"

"What? You mean photos? Tommy, that Sack Pack game has been over for months."

"Hobby is habit, and I can't imagine you're not adding Eve to your collection. Come on, I've been hearing about the girl for weeks now. Give me a peek, at least."

"Well . . ." Julian glanced about to make sure no one was close enough to see. Then he pulled out his wallet and extracted a snapshot of Eve, naked and sated, her long form stretched out like an ebony feline on a bed of red satin. "I took this one in Bermuda," he said, staring longingly at the picture.

Tommy pulled it from his hands to examine it.

"She's got a very prudish outward manner," Julian continued, "but that's part of the turn-on. When the girl's ice melts, she's a volcano."

A long, low whistle came from Tommy's lips, and Julian snatched the photo back. Tommy chuckled. "A bit possessive, aren't we?"

"Don't even think about it."

"Why not? You've always shared your toys—"

"Not this one."

"So where is she, then?" challenged Tommy, making a show of looking around. "I'd like to meet her."

"Are you *insane*? Do you know what my father would do to me if I brought a woman of *color* to a party like this?"

Tommy shrugged. "She's not so black, really. And besides, she's gorgeous."

"Don't tax my patience. She's also a jazz singer with a dubious background."

"Have her investigated."

"Believe me, I've considered it, but . . . I don't know, learning the details could spoil everything. I'd rather enjoy her with the mystery intact, while my interest lasts, anyway."

"Suit yourself," said Tommy with another shrug. "So who's looking good on the grounds today?"

Together, Tommy and Julian casually turned to survey the sea of young blondes and brunettes and one raven-haired girl, Clarissa Morton.

"I see Clarissa and her troupe of Alpha girls have already arrived." Tommy raised his glass in their direction.

"So . . . *Clarissa's* here. Intriguing girl, that one. With all her jabbering about sex, I've often wondered if she'd be the best lay in New England or the worst. Wish I'd had a chance to find out, but Jonny Hotchkiss has already proposed to her."

"Clarissa's all right, I suppose, but everyone knows what precipitated that proposal, and it wasn't Clarissa's alleged acrobatics on a mattress. She's loaded and Hotchkiss's family is strapped."

"Not for long, I expect. I had dinner with him in London last winter break. Everything may turn around with his father stepping in to manage the family finances. That's why he's back here for the summer."

"Oh, I see. So he's not here just for Clarissa?"

"No," said Julian. "He's learning the business from his own father—the member of the family who knows how *not* to screw it up. Anyway, I heard him bragging about entering the Harmony regatta, so I'd get the yacht out of dry dock soon, if I were you."

"Oh, is that so? I better take a minute to intimidate him."

"Good luck. You'll need it. Jonny's a cocky SOB."

"Where is the half-English bastard, anyway?"

"Over there, by the pool—"

Julian and Tommy turned to find Jonathan Hotchkiss engaged in an intense conversation with a lovely blond girl.

Clarissa Morton, Hotchkiss's fiancée, was nowhere in sight.

"Hmmm, looks like Clarissa shouldn't have stepped out to the ladies' room—not with that Alpha vulture circling," remarked Tommy.

"Oh, but what a pretty little vulture she is. What's her name?"

"Rebecca Osburn. Another Alpha, just a freshman."

"She works fast, this beguiling Rebecca—soon to be Hotchkiss, I'll bet. Too bad for us she's staked out our boy Jonny already. She's quite a fox. Of course, that may leave *Clarissa* free again, which is good news for me. She and I do seem to see eye to eye on many things. But with Jonny in the picture, I'll just have to wait my turn."

"Yes, well, don't despair, Julian. There are enough Alphas here for the picking today, and some are quite ripe."

"Oh, really?" asked Julian, smoothly looking around. "Like?"

"Like little Miss Ivy over there."

"Who?"

"Ivy Winthrop."

EIGHT

The Proposition

"Ivy Winthrop, did you say?" Julian asked Tommy Biddles. "She's the daughter of the former governor, isn't she?"

"Right you are."

"I haven't seen her in years, not since I started law school. Which one is she? Point her out, won't you."

Tommy gestured toward the dessert table, where a slender young woman stood.

"Braces are off now," said Tommy, "or she got a nose job—or something must have happened to her in the last two years. The girl's turned into a very pleasant distraction."

Julian studied the young woman spooning a fluffy little cloud of *crème fraîche* onto a half-dozen strawberries. She wore a short pink-and-white sundress that showed off her temptingly tanned legs in strappy heeled sandals. Her mane of long blond hair spilled freely down her back—luxurious gold, just waiting to be touched.

"Can't argue there," murmured Julian.

"Think I'll have a go—" said Tommy, starting toward her, but Julian's arm barred the way before he could take another step.

"*My* party, Biddles. And as the host, I have a duty to greet each and every one of my guests."

Julian sauntered over to Ivy with practiced nonchalance, stepping softly up behind her until his lips were almost touching her ear.

"I can think of *much* better uses for that whipped cream." Julian's voice was low and bemused, far from the tone one might use to discuss pastry techniques.

"Julian Crane!" blurted Ivy, nearly jumping out of her sandals. "You startled me."

"Did I?"

Ivy swallowed nervously. She'd known of Julian Crane, of course. Their parents had been friends for a decade, ever since her father had served as governor. But Ivy certainly couldn't call him a friend.

Usually distracted by older girls or fellow tennis pals at the Harmony Country Club, Julian had always kept his distance from Ivy. And that had been just fine with her, especially after meeting Sam two years ago.

Ivy didn't trust Julian, and, notwithstanding his outrageously forward whipped cream comment, she certainly didn't know him well enough to consider whether she even liked him.

"Sorry I startled you, but I do believe that was the secret of the big bad wolf," murmured Julian with a sly half-smile. "*Startling* little girls, before *devouring* them."

Julian then passed the tip of his middle finger over Ivy's desert plate, stealing a fluffy white curl of *crème fraîche*.

Ivy was appalled. She watched, incredulous, as he pulled the *crème* across his parted lips, then unfurled his tongue to lick it clean with an exaggerated flourish.

"Who gave you permission to do that?" she snapped, trying her best to achieve her mother's chilliest tone of propriety.

"Let me give you a little tip, darling. Cranes never *need* permission to do much of anything—especially on their own grounds. And we prefer to consume only *the best*."

Ivy's eyebrow rose. "Am I supposed to take *that* as a compliment?"

"Glance around, Ivy. Take a little tour of your girlfriends' jealous expressions. Can't you see that my selecting *you* to flirt with, among all the other maidens, is the highest compliment you could ever receive?"

Ivy wanted to smash the entire plate of strawberries into Julian's smug, smirking face, but she hesitated—not only would her mother and father be completely mortified, but her sorority sisters would think she'd lost her mind.

Despite Julian's arrogance, Ivy knew quite well that he was *the* most sought-after bachelor in their social circle. She hated doing what Julian suggested, especially in front of him, but Ivy couldn't help herself. She glanced around to quickly verify that every last one of the Alpha girls who'd been lucky enough even to be invited to the Crane party was now staring directly at her and Julian.

Ivy was tempted—very tempted—to take advantage of the situation. A part of her wanted to string out this moment of glory and make the Alpha girls die with envy.

But she refused.

Ivy knew where her heart and loyalty lived—and it wasn't in the gaze of this smug jerk.

Without giving it another thought, Ivy politely excused herself, then turned on her heel and walked away, leaving a completely flummoxed Julian Crane behind her.

When she reached a secluded lawn chair, Ivy set down her strawberries and pulled out a piece of paper from her sundress pocket. It had become slightly dirty and somewhat worn since she'd picked it up that morning from beneath the secret loose stone in Harmony Park's garden wall.

After carefully looking around to make sure no one was watching her, she unfolded it for the tenth time that day and read the words, her gaze caressing every flourish, every loop and letter of the bold, masculine hand.

"I'll be there, Sam," she whispered, glancing at her watch and knowing she'd been counting every second until she saw him again.

Then she kissed the note and lovingly folded it back up.

* * *

"Mr. Crane, would you like me to tell your fortune?"

Alistair Crane, after observing the prickly encounter between his son and Ivy Winthrop, had wandered into the mansion's garden to brood.

Perhaps Katherine is right, Alistair told himself. *Perhaps pushing Julian and Ivy together won't work—*

No sooner had Alistair considered these thoughts, however, than he'd glanced up to find a very attractive young woman in flamboyant gypsy clothing staring intensely at him, asking to tell his fortune.

Alistair knew little about the woman, just that she was a popular entertainer at high-society parties around New England. She performed palm and tea leaf readings, tarot card fortunes, and all that sort of hogwash.

The woman was a fruity eccentric making money on balderdash, as far as Alistair was concerned, a hired actress, nothing more.

Still, there was something about her that seemed offputting. He knew it was a ridiculous notion for an accomplished man of his status, but he felt uneasy, even nervous, in her presence—as if he understood on some strange subconscious level that this was not a woman one should cross.

"Thank you, no," he said quickly, but politely, to the offer of a fortune.

"Suit yourself," said the woman brightly, then turned her lovely face to the Crane garden, where orchids, irises, and

Let's see now. In describing herself, Tabby's gone from "attractive" to "very attractive." Seems to Timmy the old girl got carried away with her fictional face lift. Unless, of course, she's got a little crush on Alistair here—and secretly wants *him* to consider her this way! Hmmm . . .

the famous Crane lavender roses blanketed the grounds in a scheme of royal purple.

"How well your gardeners have kept *out* the *weeds*," remarked the woman before turning to go. "Of course, Mr. Crane, as carefully as you try to *control* your little garden, *seeds* aren't always *planted* where you want them."

The cryptic words haunted Alistair after she left, disturbing his very spirit. *What the hell does she mean by that?* he wondered.

Then he suddenly recalled the private investigator's reports on Julian over the past three months and the boy's rather intense affair with that black jazz singer in Boston.

What will happen if Julian gets her pregnant? My god, is that what the gypsy's remark meant? Has he gotten her pregnant?

Unsettled and in a panic that this gypsy woman might know something, Alistair decided to find her again, but when he searched the party, strangely, she'd vanished.

"Katherine, have you seen the fortune-teller?" he asked his wife, who appeared exhausted as she headed toward the mansion for a short nap.

"What fortune-teller?"

"The one you hired for the party."

"I hired no such person. Perhaps the Stewart girl arranged it."

Alistair thought of tracking down the caterer, but decided to drop the subject, for fear of looking ridiculous. Still, he couldn't shake the disturbing feeling that his fortune had been told to him whether he'd liked it or not.

And he didn't like it. Not one bit.

This, more than anything, was what led Alistair to a new line of thinking about his son, and a new guest to chat with—Ivy Winthrop's father.

Alistair crossed the lawn with a purposeful stride and approached the former governor and owner of Winthrop Marine, one of Crane Industries' chief competitors on the New England coast.

Close to fifty now, Harrison was a tall man with a hefty build. His love of golf had done little to preserve the athletic body he'd once had as a college track star, and he now had a penchant for overdressing to compensate for his middle-age spread.

"Harrison, how goes it?" asked Alistair.

"Not well, Alistair. I must confess, I've had bad luck lately. The business has taken an even worse turn since we last spoke."

"Goodness, that's a shame." Alistair noticed that his rival's sandy-colored hair was peppered with more gray than it had been the last time they'd met. Forcing his lips *not* to curl with pleasure, Alistair asked, "Then have you reconsidered my offer—for an alliance?"

"Yes, I have."

"And?"

"And you might be interested to know that I've made some arrangements. Ivy will be *free* for the summer. *All* summer. Tell Julian there'll be nothing to stand in the way of his courting her."

"Very good news." Alistair was relieved beyond measure.

"I tell you, Alistair, I can't begin to imagine what is in my daughter's mind. That boy she's been seeing is absolutely unsuitable for a girl with her background—working-class sort, you know. Roughneck type."

"Goodness, that must be upsetting for you and Helen."

"Helen doesn't know. It would break her heart after all the care she's put into Ivy's upbringing. That's part of the reason I've stepped in behind Ivy's back. I mean, I don't feel good about hoodwinking my own daughter, but what can I do? I thought for sure she would have given up on this little girlish crush of hers by now. You know young people today—they flit from one to the next like bees in a garden."

"But she hasn't given the boy up?" asked Alistair, intrigued. "Even after a year at Rutland?"

"Doesn't matter what she *wants*. I know what's *best* for her future. This is all for her own good."

"I like the way you think, Harrison. You're a man of action, like me."

"And men of action leave nothing to chance, am I right, Alistair?"

"You are indeed."

Hours later, the sun came down, along with the billowing white lawn tent. Most of the guests had either departed or were asked to come inside the mansion for silver service and sorbet.

Julian looked in on his tiny sister in her nursery, then found his mother with the remaining guests and kissed her good-bye. He was asking one of the servants to retrieve his Aston Martin from the mansion's ten-car garage when his mother approached him in the hallway.

"Julian, did you look in on your little sister?"

"Yes, of course, Mother. But she's very busy, you know. Having her own little tea party with her nanny and two china dolls."

Katherine smiled. "Did she pour you a cup?"

"Oh, yes. I pulled up a chair and got the inside scoop on the machinations of the entire doll world. Mrs. Cricket is wildly jealous of Miss Bun-Bun's dresses, it seems."

"Thank you, Julian."

"My pleasure, Mother. And I *mean* it—that young nanny of Sheridan's is quite fetching—"

"Oh, Julian!" Katherine shook her head, unable to keep from laughing. "Do you *ever* behave when it comes to women?"

"Of course! In fact, I did just now. 'Hands off the help!' Isn't that what you used to tell me—ever since I turned fifteen and you caught me with that shapely little catering assistant—"

"Let's not go down memory lane with your indiscretions, Julian. I know you're still sowing your oats. But your father and I would like to see you settle down soon."

Julian shook his head. "Long way off, Mother. *Long* way."

Katherine took her son's hands in her own. "Son, now that you've graduated law school . . . are preparing to move on with your life . . . I'd like you to promise me something . . ."

"Anything, Mother. Just ask."

"I want you to make an effort to remain close with your sister, Sheridan. And I want you to *promise* to look after her. *Protect* her—"

"Oh, Mother, you've been doing a perfectly fine job of that already—"

"But if something should happen to me—"

"Stop it. I won't listen to such talk. You've got years and years—"

"Please, Julian, *humor* me. Just promise—"

"Okay, don't get upset. I promise, all right? I promise I'll look after my little sister. Protect her. No matter what happens."

Katherine's face relaxed with relief. She leaned forward and kissed Julian's cheek. "Thank you, son." ✝

Checking his watch, Julian strode easily out the door. Chalking up his mother's worries as baseless female anxiety, his mind swiftly shifted to the night ahead.

Eve had a late set at the Blue Note, and he couldn't wait to pull her into his arms again. He hated to admit it, but that bitch Ivy Winthrop's public rejection of him had left him harder than a pimply schoolboy with an open *Playboy* centerfold. A part of him wanted to kill her, and another part wanted to tame the foxy little spitfire—in bed, of course.

Hmmmm . . . Reading this over twenty years later, Timmy truly wonders if Julian still remembers that he made this promise.

He'd settle for venting his lust with Eve tonight. But he vowed to have another go at the feisty little Winthrop girl before summer's end.

"Julian!"

The unmistakable sound of his father's voice still put as much fear into Julian as it had when he was an awkward prepubescent brat. Instantly, he halted in the front drive, his hand on the roof of his beloved silver Aston Martin.

"Now what," muttered Julian, eager to be on his way.

Thirty minutes ago, Julian had passed by his father's study to wish him a good evening, but Alistair had looked too busy to interrupt. He and former governor Winthrop were discussing some sort of business arrangement, and Julian knew better than to bother his father when he was sealing a deal.

He just wished his father had included him in the meeting. It was a sore point for Julian. For years, Alistair had excluded him from the family business dealings. Now that he had gotten his law degree, Julian had hoped things would change. But it appeared that Alistair's throne room was going to remain off-limits for years to come.

"Where are you going?" asked Alistair, stepping under the high-columned portico that covered the front drive.

"Back to Boston."

"No. I need you here."

"Why, Father? I have plans, and—"

"It's important, Julian. Stay at home tonight, and in the morning I'll tell you all about it."

As usual, Alistair expressed himself in commands, never requests. Still, Julian was surprised by his father's words— and a little spark of hope ignited within him.

Perhaps the apprenticeship to power wasn't so far off after all. Now that he'd graduated from law school, his father might finally want, even need, his involvement in the family business.

Julian suddenly felt elated. Despite all the energy he put into his diversions, he well knew that idleness was no asset.

History was full of princes who had been doomed to live out their lives in the wings, forever waiting for the chance to wear their fathers' crown, growing older but never maturing.

Dilettantism of the worst kind could be his fate—a life of utter uselessness, filled with nothing more weighty than pleasurable yet pointless pursuits.

Could his father's request be the beginning he'd hoped for? The path to taking over the kind of power and influence he'd watched his father wield all his life?

Julian certainly hoped so.

"Of course I'll stay, Father. You know I'm more than happy to do whatever you wish."

Besides, thought Julian, glancing at his watch, if he stayed the night, he could call his tennis coach first thing in the morning and get a good workout on one of the Cranes' courts.

The regional men's singles tournament was coming up in a month, and he was far from ready for it.

Eve wore blue tonight, a sequined gown that hung off her bared shoulders on thin spaghetti straps and shimmered in the spotlight like a star sapphire.

At the close of her set, she nodded her thanks to the Scat Perkins Five, then stepped off the Blue Note stage.

Her brow creased with apprehension as she scanned the smoky, dimly lit room. She checked every table, every booth, but he was not in the club.

Where are you? thought Eve, annoyed. He'd promised to make it tonight.

With a sigh, Eve approached a shapely blonde in a lime-green mini-dress and matching headband who was sitting at the bar in the back of the club.

"Hey, Crystal."

"Great set, honey." She smiled and winked. "Always a pleasure to hear you sing. You're the best."

Crystal was in her mid-twenties. A salty, streetwise woman who always spoke her mind, she and Eve had become fast friends since Crystal began singing at the Blue Note six weeks before.

They shared everything from vocal techniques to clothes, jewelry, and gossip about the recording industry. They saw eye to eye on just about everything—except one man.

"Uh . . . Crystal . . . you haven't seen Julian tonight, have you?"

"No, sorry, I haven't."

"Good evening, sweet thing."

Eve jumped. A masculine arm snaked its way around her waist and jerked her against a barrel chest covered by a cheap polyester disco shirt. Glancing up, she found a rough-looking white guy drooling over her. He had a day's stubble on his jaw and five cheap gold-plated chains around his neck, his breath reeked of whiskey, and his eyes were glazed and bloodshot.

He's high.

Recognizing a user was a new skill Eve had mastered since meeting Julian. Unfortunately, she had yet to master the trick of getting rid of bothersome mashers. God, she hated these clumsy, sometimes frightening passes that happened to her almost every night she sang here!

Julian Crane had been the one gentlemanly exception. Since the night they'd met, he'd been romancing her in champagne style. All the others were like this creep—a borderline violent drunk who treated her like she was a piece of meat. Eve felt her heart race in fear every time one of them approached.

"Get your hands off me."

She tried to infuse her voice with as much outrage as she could muster while still keeping the volume low. Eve hated scenes.

He laughed, rubbed his nose. She noticed bits of white powder clinging to the stubble on his face. She licked her lips. Needed the hit. But the very idea of getting it from this creep revolted her.

"I said let me go." She tried to push away.

"I got what you need, baby. A little toot. Right over there with my friends. We can go someplace private to enjoy it—"

Eve glanced over to his table. Two more guys, just as rough-looking, stared back. Their eyes were glazed, tinged with the promise of violence. A shiver ran through Eve. *Party with these thugs in private? No thanks!*

"That's what you want, baby, isn't it?" he slathered in her ear, pressing his lower body into her. "A little white root for your brown sugar—"

Eve felt her stomach turning.

"Hey, jackass!" came the loud voice next to them. Half the bar turned to look their way. "Shove off or I'll call our bouncer to break your arms!"

The man looked up, into Crystal Harris's hard blue eyes. They communicated one thing. She had actually seen a man's arms broken, and she'd take great pleasure in seeing it done again—to him.

The guy released Eve instantly.

"Chill out. Chill out. Just wanted to extend the invite to the brown baby here."

"Get lost. *Now,*" Crystal demanded.

And the guy did.

With relief, Eve sat down on the stool next to Crystal.

"Thanks."

"You're welcome, honey. But you've got to learn how to deal with these creeps if you're gonna keep singing in clubs."

"I guess." But Eve didn't care to learn Crystal's dubious skills. Why should she? It wouldn't be long before Julian got her a recording contract. Then she'd be in a nice safe studio and out of this nightclub.

Eve checked her watch. "I wonder what's keeping Julian?"

"Looks like he's standing you up again."

"No. He'll be here—"

"Eve," said Crystal firmly, "haven't I warned you *not* to

trust him? He's the sort who'll tear your world to shreds without missing his cocktail hour."

"You are dead wrong about Julian," Eve replied, pride adding a slight sharpness to her tone. "He's got real feelings for me. He's told me so. He's even going to help me get a record deal—" Crystal's eyebrow rose skeptically at that, but Eve ignored her. "And you have no idea how *sweet* Julian can be. How generous . . ."

Eve touched the diamond choker at her throat, but her fingers were shaking.

"Expensive jewelry isn't the only thing he's hooked you on, is it, honey?" asked Crystal softly, eyeing Eve's slight tremors.

Eve turned away and motioned to the bartender. "No . . . it's not that . . . it was that Disco Johnny. He scared me. I just need a drink."

She had too much pride to admit that Crystal was dead right about the tremors. Ever since she had started sleeping with Julian, her life had been unraveling. Her grades had plummeted from cutting classes, and drugs had become more than recreation.

At first she had relied on partying with Julian to satisfy her needs, but during this last month she hadn't seen him as regularly. Now one of the Blue Note's bartenders was hooking her up: cocaine to keep her flying during the evening gigs, Quaaludes to help her come down afterward.

All along, Eve kept telling herself that it didn't matter, that she was in control. That this was what she wanted. She was smart. With it. She could handle anything.

Of course, she'd also been lying to her parents for the past few months. And that had worked for a while, too. But then, just two weeks ago, her final grades had been mailed to her family's home.

The truth was right there on paper—and now her parents knew it—she had failed her sophomore year. The furious phone call came first, then the checks stopped, all in an effort to get Eve to come see them. To explain. To ask forgiveness and beg for another chance.

But Eve couldn't. Her pride wouldn't let her.

Her parents would take one look at her bloodshot eyes, her shaking hands, and that would be it. They would grill her, then lecture her, then demand that she move back home.

Eve would never do that. At the school year's end, she'd moved out of the dorm and into a tiny apartment a few blocks from the Blue Note.

She'd made up her mind to live her own life. She just wished Crystal would stop needling her. And that this queasy feeling would go away. She'd been plagued with it for a few weeks now.

Turning from the bar, she headed for the bathroom, continuing to scan the crowd for a sign of Julian as she went.

"Hey, Eve," called Scat as she passed him. "With the club closing for the July Fourth holiday, I got the band a high-payin' gig in some little town called Harmony. Fat cats are throwin' an Independence Day ball. You want to be our canary?"

Eve needed the money now more than ever. "Yeah, sure, Scat," she called, then rushed for the door of the ladies' room, bile rising in her throat.

"Well, Fluffy, my incantations worked fabulously, if I do say so myself!"

"Meow!"

Harmony's spellcaster extraordinaire proudly polished her fingernails on her chartreuse caftan, her dozen jade and copper bracelets jingling with the movement.

"It was quite simple to pull off, really. Two little 'slip in the shower' spells and *poof!* Harmony Country Club's regular band had its pianist *and* drummer in traction!"

Tabby laughed at the memory of Tiffany Biddles flying

into a tizzy at the news. It was her first year volunteering to head the Red-White-and-Blue Ball's entertainment committee, and she had little time to begin searching and auditioning new bands for the big July Fourth event.

That's when Tabby's second incantation kicked in—a standard "suggestion spell" she could practically throw off in her sleep—

Remember Julian's offer, Scat? The night he picked up Eve . . . remember how he tossed you his card, and told you to call the Harmony Country Club and use his name? Pull that card out now, Scat . . . and be sure to ask Eve to sing with you that night . . .

"Yes, Fluffy, having Eve appear in Harmony to entertain an exclusive gathering at the country club should be just the ticket to giving Julian a nice little heart attack!" cried Tabby in delight. "Oh, how I love to see Cranes suffer!"

"Meow?"

"What's that, Fluffy? You think I should have a little fun with Eve and her parents as well? Perhaps I will. Yes, perhaps a little missive to the upstanding Professor Warren Johnson and his wife, Tanya Lincoln Johnson, is just the thing to create an evil bit of fireworks."

With a devilish smile, the witch began to swirl her hand in the air . . .

Dear Warren and Tanya,
I cordially invite you both to the Blue Note in Boston to hear its hottest new jazz singer. Her name is Eve . . .

Tabby cackled with delight. "Yes, Fluffy, and I think I shall sign it 'a fan.' That's rich, isn't it?! . . . Though I think I'm going to bide my time before posting it . . .

"You see, Eve isn't yet certain that she's pregnant. She's at least two months along. But with all of her partying and problems, she's been oblivious to her body's changes.

"By the end of summer, she'll be showing. When it's more than apparent that she's carrying Julian's child, I'll send my little note . . .

"Oh, Fluffy! Can't you just see their faces? Imagine *Alistair Crane's* face, too, when he hears of his coming grandchild! I'm sure he'll just be pleased as punch to welcome this newest Crane into the world!"

NINE

Tabitha's Diary

ENTRY: *Timmy & the Witch-Hunt*

Timmy Introduction: As you can see, Tabitha is not a fan of the billionaire Cranes—or any of the townspeople of Harmony. Her vow to forever bring heartache into their lives was made hundreds of years ago. To show you why she made that vow, Timmy interrupts this story to share these entries he found in Tabby's diary of 1693. Not a good year for the old girl!

September 25, 1693

Dear Diary,

Here I sit in the Harmony town jail, watching the menfolk pile up kindling in the middle of the town green. Yes, William Ephraim Crane, the town magistrate, has given them the recipe for my redemption: Two days hence, place Tabby on an upright spit, cook flesh until medium rare, no basting necessary.

Death by fire. Canst thou believe it, Diary? How's that for sentencing guidelines! Fire is such a complete horror to rejuvenate from. I haven't done it since the Middle Ages.

Meet the New World. Same as the Old World.

Who knew? I mean, the Mayflower was no party, but at least they had a goal! Pioneer a new land. Start fresh with religious freedom (which I took to include witchcraft, thank you very much!).

I was ready for a change, after hundreds of years of the same old king-and-country dung. War upon war—first this one wants the throne, then that one beheads this one because the other one wants it.

I had my fun, of course, casting my spells for one side, then the other, but ultimately it felt the same, century after century.

Mortals really need to get some new ideas.

Take this witch-hunt lunacy. The whole thing actually started over yonder in Salem Village when a few little prepubescent brats accused some innocent people of practicing my craft. If you ask me, it's those little girls who ought to be strung up!

Just like that Prudence Standish waif—for what she did to me here in Harmony! I mean, what an exaggerator! There she is, barely sixteen years old, leaping to her feet at the church meeting to declare she'd seen me in the woods, "communing with a pack of demons."

What pack, is what I want to know?

It was one little evil spirit!

I suppose this is the downside of my particular career track, especially in an era of Puritan lunacy. I mean, if kissing in public, wearing the wrong kind of boots, or falling asleep in church can land one in the stocks, what did I think these dogmatic crackpots would do to a woman accused of conversing with agents of the devil?

No surprises here—the town of Harmony put me on trial. And, of course, there is no such thing as a public defender in this muddy little settlement, unless you count my pig farmer neighbor who said, and I quote, "I do not dissemble in the giving of testimony that with mine eyes I did never witness on the lands of Miss Tabitha Lenox anything unnatural in particular."

So much for competent defense counsel.

What vexes me is that in Salem they're hanging their witches. Or rather, they're hanging the poor mortals accused of being witches by the aforementioned little brats.

So why don't they just sentence hanging here in Har-

Remember those Standish twins (Grace and Faith), who vexed Tabby earlier in this story? Do you want to know why she hates them with such passion? Well, they happen to be the descendants of Prudence here! And when it comes to taking down evil, let's just say the Standishes have made it a family affair.

mony, is what I want to know? Hanging is easy to rejuvenate out of, just a simple spell and the rope mark's gone.

But no! There'll be no hanging for Tabitha Lenox.

Hanging's been done.

Executions around these parts must have that original
Harmony flare! So the contemptible magistrate William
Crane decides to top the Salem show by sentencing me to
burn.

That scourge, I'll get him.

I swear it, Diary.

And the little Prudence Standish girl, too. I'll get
them both if it takes all my unnatural years.

September 26, 1693

Tonight's the night. The big breakout.

I meditated for hours for a solution, and voilà! I even
managed to summon up the right spell from memory
(without my Book of Black Arts and potion bag, it's
rather rough going).

At sunset, I'll begin to chant these words: "Little doll
so sweet and small, eyes will open, knees will crawl.
Hands will flex, mouth will talk. Come alive, stand up
and walk! Find the door and come to me; I have your
task—to set me free!"

Once the spell is chanted three times, if all goes as
planned, that little Voodoo doll I sewed to vex Timothy
Parris will come to life and walk across town to the bars
of my cell's window.

What shall I call him? I wonder. Well, I suppose,
since I sewed him to look like Timothy Parris, I ought to

call him Timothy. No, that's too formal. Perhaps Timmy. Yes, that's perfect! Timmy! ❦

It should be nice and dark outside by the time my little Timmy arrives, and I'll immediately send him off to steal the cell door keys from James Bennett, the town jailer. ❦

Once Timmy comes back with the keys, I'm out of Harmony. Gone, gone, gone, thank you very much!

Wish me luck, Diary!

September 27, 1693

Well, Diary, we almost made it.

But, alas . . . here I am again, sitting in this dreary, decoratively challenged jail cell.

My spell worked, so don't blame the magic. Timmy came to life, as planned, and got me out of the cell. We ran as far as the edge of the Harmony woods, but the pollen count's been higher than usual, and who'd ever guess that a sod-stuffed rag could have allergies?

Anyway, Mary Fitzgerald's twin boys were camped out in the treehouse, keeping watch for demons and spirits, when they heard Timmy's nonstop sneezing.

Seeing a living doll sneezing in the arms of an accused witch fleeing into the woods in the dead of night sort of gave them a clue to send up a general alarm. Menfolk

Timmy finds it fairly shocking that a TIMMY existed before ME! After all, present-day Timmy is a one-of-a-kind sort of guy!

That's Sam Bennett's great-great-great-great-great-great—well, you get the idea!

with torches came running, and what can I say? Now I'm back in my cell, but at least Timmy managed to escape.

I've cast another spell, instructing Timmy to steal one of William Crane's wigs and come to the site of the burning. With any luck the town will believe he's a little magistrate from another town, come to speak in my defense.

Of course, time is short. The kindling's being prepped as I write this, and the Timmy defense is a pathetic last hope. But I swear to you, Diary, I'll make my rejuvenation work.

I'll be back.

And I have a long memory.

When I return to Harmony, hell itself will become my new ally, and I will exact revenge on this town for centuries to come. The Cranes, the Bennetts, the Fitzgeralds, and all of their descendants will regret the little parts they played in my puritan demise.

But my sharpest vengeance will be reserved for Prudence Standish, the little brat who first accused me and continued to witness to the town, urging my burning. For her, and all the Standishes who come after, death by fire will be their fate.

It will be my new mission in life.

And death, as it were.

As evil is my witness, I do swear it.

Addendum: In continuing to read Tabby's diary,
Timmy discovered:

1. Puritan Timmy did manage to steal a wig and
brilliantly defend his princess, but the sim-
pleminded townsfolk of Harmony were already
sold on their bonfire idea, and Tabby went up
in smoke;

2. Puritan Timmy suffered a similar fate a few
days later when one of the Fitzgerald boys accused him of being the enchanted doll they'd
seen sneezing in Tabby's arms;

3. Tabby did indeed rejuvenate from the ashes
within weeks, with her powers restored. She returned to the town as Margaret Good, a cousin
of the accused who'd come to assume control of
Tabitha Lenox's property.

As Margaret, Tabby attempted to kill Prudence
Standish by setting fire to the church where
she was being wed to a young Fitzgerald man.
The groom died, but Prudence escaped, fleeing
the town with all the Standishes.

Relieved to be rid of them, Tabby finally took
back her original name.

Oh, but there's one more thing . . . a very important thing that Tabby eventually learned!
After Prudence Standish fled from Harmony, she
settled in a New England town far away called
Mill Valley. She married another man and had
many children.

Since then, every succeeding generation of
Standish women has become more and more powerful in their psychic ability to combat evil.

Tim-Tim told you the Standishes were going to
be a pain for poor Tabby! Believe Timmy when he
tells you that back in 1693, her troubles were
just beginning!

TEN

Sam and T. C.

There is a scenic two-lane highway near Harmony that travel writers love to cite for its ocean views, historic lighthouses, and quaint local eateries.

"Coast Road is your gateway to seaside splendor," gushed the 1976 edition of *A Guide for New England Day Trippers*. "Hugging the Atlantic shoreline, the route winds past a number of picturesque harbor towns, including one aptly named Harmony. Without doubt, the road is an oasis of tranquillity . . ."

On the day of the Crane garden party, however, that tranquillity was up for grabs. The aggressive strains of Strauss's *Wein, Weib und Gesang* barely rolled off the strings of the Julliard Quartet and down Raven Hill before they collided with the raw beat of Cheap Trick, Alice Cooper, and a bootleg recording of some new bar band called Van Halen.

The latter were the preferred orchestrations of the Castleton College students, who'd assembled across the Coast Road, on Harmony's public beach, to enjoy a raucous clambake.

Near sunset, as the Crane party began to disperse, the Castleton crew pumped up the volume for the night ahead.

But not everyone was planning to party till midnight on the dunes.

Checking his watch, Sam Bennett casually rose from the sand, pulled his blanket and athletic bag off the ground, and waved good-bye to his friends. More than a few young women actually sighed with disappointment as they watched Sam's hard body and blue eyes depart.

The sky was blushing brilliantly with streaks of maroon and pink. It was the perfect romantic evening for cuddling up with a handsome Harmony lifeguard. But the boy of Castleton girls' dreams was instead heading off into the twilight.

Their wide-eyed gazes tracked Sam as he hiked down the curving shoreline and toward the rocky cliffs that everyone under the age of fifty knew as The Lovers' Beehive. A dozen secluded coves provided privacy for couples too young and poor to afford a hotel room—or too fond of nature to do it in the cramped backseat of a Gremlin.

Back at the campfire, the gossiping began the moment Sam left. Over the past year, many of the young women at school had tried to lure Sam into their beds. He was always polite, always a gentleman, but he always refused.

Speculating on Sam's love life had now risen to the level of professional sports betting. No one knew who Sam was seeing, although the rumor definitely got around that he was delivering more than pizza to some lucky girl inside the exclusive walls of Rutland College.

Sam himself remained as silent as the grave, even as he walked away from his friends on the beach. To his surprise, however, not all of his friends were content to be left behind.

"Bennett! Hold up!"

Hearing his name above the sound of the surf, Sam wheeled to find a handsome African-American man jogging easily toward him. Thornton Chandler Russell was Sam's oldest friend. Their families had been close since before the boys were born.

"I don't suppose if I ask where you're going, you'd actually tell me this time?" asked T. C.

His smile was as dazzling as Sam's, and his dark, muscular body just as well developed from years of dedication to athletics. The difference was that Sam played football for fun, a passing school hobby, but T. C. played tennis with the passion of making the sport his entire life.

"Where am I going? I've got a date," replied Sam flatly.

"Right, *no kidding*, Bennett. Look, man, you just turned and walked away from about a dozen *very nice*—not to mention *nice-looking*—young ladies. Any one of them would be a great match for you because they'd be happy to spend time *openly* with your family and friends, which is more than I can say for this mystery chick you've been seeing. So why don't you just turn around and come back with me?"

"T. C., why are you even wasting your breath with the same old argument?"

"Because this hide-and-seek routine ticks me off. What's the issue with bringing her around, man? Are you *ashamed* of your buddies? Are we not *good enough* to meet this girl?"

"You know that's a load of crap."

"Well, then, why don't you bring her around?"

"She's . . ." Sam sighed, dropped his bag softly on the sand, and remained silent for a moment, considering what to say. "She's asked me to keep our relationship a secret. Her family objects to my seeing her, and if I tell anyone, even you, then I'll be breaking my word to her."

"Okay, don't *tell* me. But I'll just have to guess, 'cause I've been hearing plenty of rumors."

"What *sort* of rumors?" A dangerous look of fierce protectiveness slammed over Sam's features like a curtain of steel.

"Whoa, man, take it easy. Nothing nasty about the girl, just that she probably goes to Rutland."

Sam looked away, his jaw twitching unhappily.

"Well, doesn't she?"

Reluctantly, Sam nodded.

"Then I've got to say this. You are sailing straight into heartbreak reef."

"That's my business, T. C."

"I'm your friend, Sam, and I don't want to see you crash and sink—"

"You know what they say—if you don't want to see it, then when it gets to the scary part, *hide your eyes.*"

"Come off it, man, you're not part of their world. Listen to me, because I know. My pop worked around those people all his life at the country club. He knows what they're like—and you don't want to mess with them. It's like jumping into the shark tank. So come on and turn around with me now. Come back to your own little pond. There's plenty of fish who'd love to swim with you tonight—maybe even skinny-dip if you flash them that razzle-dazzle smile of yours."

"Thanks for the clue, but I'm not going back to catch the other fish in the sea because I'm not *in love* with any of them. But I've got a brilliant idea—how about *you* take your own advice?"

"What's that supposed to mean?"

"I mean, why don't you turn your butt around and go reel in some willing catches for yourself?"

"Sorry, but you know my rule: *Women weaken legs.*"

"Man, that's just some bogus philosophy your coach picked up watching *Rocky* a dozen times. The truth is, you are so focused on turning pro that you're missing out on the best part of being alive—"

"And that would be?"

Sam shrugged. *"Love."*

"Heaven help me!" cried T. C. to the sky. "My jock best friend's turned into Dear Abby. Man, you *know* my sole passion in life is *tennis* and it will remain *tennis* until I play Ashe at Wimbledon. I mean, can't you just see it? Two brothers battling it out for the top tennis title in the world!"

Arthur Ashe was T. C.'s ultimate hero. He'd become the

first African American to win the men's national singles championship in the United States, and just last year, T. C. had gone totally crazy in front of the TV watching Ashe become the first black man to win at Wimbledon.

T. C. swore then and there that he was going to be the second black man to win in England, and his dearest fantasy was to win it by playing the final match against Ashe himself, proving to the world once and for all that black men could play the elite games just as well as anyone.

And it would prove something else.

It would prove to T. C.'s father, Reggie Russell, that all of his bowing and scraping had been worth it. And he'd never have to do it *ever* again.

Since T. C.'s father was sixteen, he had worked at the Harmony Country Club, as a caddie and a maintenance man. T. C. never understood why his pop stayed in a demeaning job like that at an all-white club.

A part of T. C. was actually embarrassed by his dad—so eager to please men who didn't have a fraction of his pop's strength of character. But T. C. dearly loved his father, and ever since T. C. had been a little kid, fishing expensive rackets out of the country club trash bins and waking at dawn every summer morning to grab a public court, T. C. had known his old man had been pinning all his hopes on T. C. bringing glory to the Russell name.

Just last month, T. C.'s tennis coach at Castleton had told him he was ready for the NCAA fast track this fall; and T. C. himself was going to prove it by winning the regional men's singles title on July 5. The tournament was scheduled to be played right here, too, on the Harmony Country Club courts.

T. C. was so looking forward to that tournament. It would be his second chance to beat the shorts off Julian Crane, who now held the regional title.

But then, Julian had held the junior title, too. He'd held it for five solid years when T. C. had shocked the entire town by defeating him.

Yeah! Reggie Russell's boy had actually beaten Alistair Crane's son!

T. C. would never forget the look of pride on his father's face, and the look of rage on Alistair Crane's.

Suddenly the Cranes' genes weren't so hot after all. They were *second* best—*after* Russells'. And in a few weeks, T. C. would prove it again!

"You know, T. C., dreams of glory are all well and good," said Sam. "But I don't see why you can't fit a girlfriend into your big pro plans. Maybe you ought to take a closer look at those pretty ladies back there."

"I'll look. I'll even flirt. But once they agree to hitting the sheets, I always tell them the up-front score. Tennis is *everything* to me. She's my one and only love. She will *always* come first."

"Okay, then, I'll make you a deal," proposed Sam. "I'll leave you to your love if you leave me to mine."

With a sigh of defeat T. C. waved Sam off, then turned to jog back to the clambake crowd. "Just be careful, okay?" called T. C. over his shoulder. "Those Rutland girls are rough on guys without trust funds. I'm spelling trouble with a capital *T.*"

"You're wrong, T. C. And someday you'll understand why!" Sam shouted over the pounding surf. "Someday you'll meet a girl who's worth taking on all the trouble in the world!"

ELEVEN

The Beach

"Sam! Are you here? Sam!"

With nervous anticipation, Ivy Winthrop crossed the deserted sands on the very edge of Harmony's public beach. Following the violent curve of the shoreline, she braced herself when the jutting landscape forced her out into the night tide.

The waves were chilly as they washed over her bare feet and ankles, but she pushed forward, hiking around the natural jetty, then up the rise that led to a network of rocky coves.

Only a few Harmony residents actually knew the history of Harmony's rugged shoreline— ▼

Thousands of years before, a destructive tidal wave had slammed into Harmony's rocky cliffs, gouging out chunks of soft earth at their base. When the water finally receded, a network of natural coves remained behind, situated far enough from the Atlantic shoreline to remain dry, even during high tide.

Tabitha Lenox of course, being one of them!

In the 1700s, roving bands of pirates used the coves to hide booty they'd stolen from cargo-laden ships venturing into Boston and New York. Much later, during Prohibition, bootleggers used them to smuggle alcohol down from Canada.

Such illicit activity had created a strange sort of eerie karma around the dark, craggy rocks. Ivy didn't know much about the coves' history, but she felt the weird aura and always shivered when she neared them.

It wasn't until she saw the small fire inside one of them, and noticed the folded blanket and large athletic bag sitting nearby, that her nervousness eased.

When her gaze finally fell on the Harmony Lifeguard windbreaker, all trepidation was replaced by a warm wash of affection. Ivy sighed, knowing this windbreaker was the one Sam had worn the summer they'd fallen in love.

It was still hard for Ivy to believe that she and Sam could be so in love now; during most of their high school years, they'd never met.

Of course, back then they were traveling in very different circles. Sam's world was public high school, football, and hanging with his working-class Harmony buds, while Ivy's was private school, horse shows, and helping her mother with local Junior League events.

On the other hand, since she'd turned thirteen, Ivy had been utterly fascinated by a less refined sort of male. She smiled at the memory of how she and Rebecca Osburn used to salivate over the hunky local fishermen's sons they'd see around Harmony's harbor and Lighthouse Park.

Ivy herself had never done anything more than giggle over the steamy possibilities at a slumber party—fantasize from a distance. What other options did she have? With a politically prominent father and socially connected mother, Ivy had been handed a life full of imperial expectations.

Winthrops must maintain a respectable image. She'd practically learned that from the crib. And from the day she reached puberty, her life had been packed with formal fund-raisers, charity auctions, and political picnics. She'd learned to float through difficult social situations without even thinking, like a young swimmer who'd learned complicated strokes by watching her parents cut through the water for years.

When she finally turned seventeen, Ivy was more than prepared for her coming-out ball. Her mother and grandmother had bred her to understand the expected protocols of the debutante ritual—what to wear, what to say, how to act. And Ivy was determined to emerge triumphant at her debut.

Over a dozen girls in their region were presented in Ivy's year, including two daughters of congressmen, three daughters of state senators, four daughters of important corporate executives, and a distant relative of Jacqueline Bouvier Kennedy. *Town & Country* even covered it.

All the other girls were pea green with envy when the magazine ran Ivy's photo a half-size larger and posted the caption: "Miss Ivy Winthrop, presented by former Governor Harrison Winthrop, daughter of Helena Revere-Mott-Beaton Winthrop, DAR and Harmony Junior League president. The most captivating belle of this ball."

Her mother had been so deliriously proud, she'd cut out the magazine page, laminated the thing, then matted it, framed it, and displayed it on the mantelpiece beside her most precious antique—her great-great-great-great-grandfather's glass-encased musket from his days raising hell with the Minutemen.

One little *Town & Country* caption as good as declared her the most eligible young lady in the region. Droves of young men were sent by their parents to call on her. All were the "right" sort, according to Ivy's mother and father. But Ivy found the lot of them conceited and tiresome. Not one appeared capable of loving anyone or anything more than their own reflections.

Her mother tried to give her some gentle advice. The

kind you'd find in a 1950s dating pamphlet about "listening" to the boy and "reflecting back" to him how interested she was in everything he was interested in.

Mirror, mirror on the shelf, Ivy used to mutter to herself on the most dreadful of those dates. *Look in my eyes to see yourself.*

When summer came around, she was relieved to decline the dates with the excuse of throwing herself back into her riding lessons. After one particularly hard jumping workout, she decided to refresh herself with a swim. She'd biked alone down to Harmony Beach and dived into the Atlantic surf without a second thought.

Ivy was a good swimmer, and quickly kicked far away from the shore. When her limbs began to stiffen, however, it hit her how stupid she'd been. She'd already exhausted her body with the strenuous riding workout, and now her abdomen was cramping and her legs and arms were giving out.

She immediately turned around to swim back, but with an undertow working against her, every painful stroke now seemed useless.

Ivy had never felt the kind of stark fear that overcame her during those agonizing minutes. A few pathetic cries for help were all she could manage before the waves smashed painfully into her face, sending salty seawater into her mouth and up her nostrils.

She fought to stay afloat, but the ocean's unforgiving current dragged her down, closing a curtain of black over her head.

The next thing she knew, the sun was in her eyes and a lifeguard's mouth was sealing itself over her own. A moment later she was coughing up what felt like a gallon of seawater.

Sam Bennett had saved her life that day. She'd never forget the lantern jaw and stunning blue eyes looming over her. But, more than that, it was the *look* in those *eyes*. The *expression*. Concern and fear and something more.

Sam hadn't just saved Ivy from drowning, he'd fallen instantly in love with her while doing it, and she'd seen it right there in his honest, open eyes. Eyes filled with the kind of fearless courage and loyal devotion she'd never before encountered.

From that moment on, Sam had become Ivy's hero.

"I'm here, Ivy!"

Finally hearing the deep, firm voice she knew so well, Ivy shook her mind clear of her memories and stepped beyond the dark cave wall to find Sam moving along the shoreline. He was carrying a huge armload of driftwood.

Ivy laughed, knowing he must have walked more than a mile to have gathered that much. But it meant their fire would now last till dawn. A stirring tension touched Ivy's body at the thought of all the hours now in front of them.

Hours and hours to lie in Sam's arms.

The sky's twilight blue was deepening, but the full moon's ivory face was large and bright, hanging just above the indigo waves and giving Ivy plenty of light to admire the approaching man.

His red swim trunks revealed thighs corded with the heavy muscles of an active football player. A worn gray Castleton College athletic shirt was stretched tightly across his hard torso. The tightness of the cloth revealed the attractive bulges in his upper arms and the thrilling breadth of his chest.

Ivy licked her lips in anticipation.

"Shake a leg, Bennett," she called playfully, "the fire's going to die out by the time you get your butt in here!"

"Can it, Winthrop! Or I'll put your skinny little limbs on the fire instead."

"*Skinny!* I'll have you know I've been doing push-ups. I'll lay odds I can arm-wrestle any Alpha into the ground."

"Arm-wrestle Alphas? Don't make me laugh!" Sam smiled as he approached her. "They'd be too afraid of breaking a nail!"

"To hell with you, Bennett, I'll take *you* on. I'm not afraid!"

"Oh, is that so?" Sam teased as he dropped the wood and moved toward her. "Not afraid?" he asked, looking down. She could feel the warmth of his breath on her cheek.

"Well, maybe you *should* be."

This kiss was hard and possessive. Ivy delighted in the knowledge that Sam was as hungry for her as she was for him. His large hands pulled her closer to his body, and she curled her arms around his neck, eagerly pressing her soft breasts into him.

He groaned with the feel of her. Suddenly her tongue slipped out to taste him with a teasing lick. The intimate touch undid him. Sam broke away, his arms gently holding Ivy a few inches from him, his lungs taking in short, shaky breaths.

"Let's slow this down," he whispered. "I can barely control myself around you—"

"You don't need to control yourself, Sam. I love you. I want you."

And with that, Ivy reached for the edges of her T-shirt and pulled it over her head. The yellow bikini top hit the sand next.

Sam swallowed, his knees feeling weak as he gazed at the beautiful girl in front of him. The long curls glistened in the firelight as they spilled over her bare shoulders and naked breasts, dusky pink nipples peaking through the lustrous strands of white-gold silk.

"You look like some magical, unearthly thing," whispered Sam. "Like a mermaid. Too beautiful to touch."

"Don't say that," Ivy told him, reaching out for his hand. "All I want is for you to touch me."

Sam moved closer, his eyes fastening on hers as she guided his large hands to her body. His fingers absently brushed the antique chain of the locket she always wore close to her heart—the one he had given her. The one with his picture inside it. He smiled.

"Yes," she whispered encouragingly as his rough fingers

moved over the full, ripe swells of her breasts, then slowly swirled, teasing the tender halos at their tips.

With a delicious playfulness, Sam held Ivy's gaze as his fingers stilled a moment. Then he flicked his callused thumbs across her sensitive nipples. With deliberate slowness he inflicted the exquisite torture, listening with triumph to Ivy's throaty moans and ignoring his own body's shuddering response.

Ivy felt herself growing almost dizzy with the sweetness of the sensations, the intimacy of Sam's penetrating blue gaze. Tilting her head back, she parted her lips, then moistened them with her tongue, inviting Sam's kiss.

But Sam didn't kiss her.

"I *said* we should slow this down," he teased, his thumbs moving once more over the aroused nipples, which had already tightened into hard little buds.

"Oh, you think so?" Ivy asked, her voice unsteady as she reached for Sam's shirt and tugged upward, unveiling the sculpted male muscle beneath.

Now it's my turn, she decided, tossing the shirt aside.

Using a feather-light touch, her slender fingers moved slowly over the contours and grooves of Sam's torso, tracing a path from his broad shoulders to his heavy collarbone, then down his smooth, tanned pectorals and abdomen, hardened from a disciplined weight-lifting routine.

Ivy watched his face carefully, taking satisfaction in the sweet torment she was now giving him.

"Careful, Ivy—" Sam warned tightly as her hand dipped lower.

She responded with a nymphlike laugh and an even bolder reach. Snaking along the front of his swim trunks, her fingers delicately traced the evidence of his arousal.

Sam's eyes closed at the incredible shudders her touches were creating. Suddenly his hand moved over hers and closed firmly around her fingers.

"You're an *impatient* girl," he scolded.

Ivy's lips pursed prettily. "So sue me, Sam Bennett. I've waited long enough."

Sam laughed as he gently tugged her down on the sand and pulled her beneath him. "You need a lesson in patience."

"And you think *you* have enough patience to teach me?"

With a growl of defeat, Sam yanked a small plastic square from the pocket of his swim trunks and tore it open with his teeth.

Ivy's eyes twinkled with gleeful triumph. *If Sam Bennett wants to give me a lesson in patience, it's certainly not going to be tonight!*

In less than a minute, the rest of their clothing had formed a pile next to the fire, and Sam was again covering Ivy's body with his own.

TWELVE

The Promise

Hours later, Sam held Ivy against him as they reclined on the beach listening to the lapping surf and eating chocolate-covered strawberries—Ivy's favorite. Sam had lovingly packed them, along with a bottle of wine, into a small basket that he'd hidden in his athletic bag.

The fragrance of jasmine perfume tickled Sam's nose as he studied Ivy's beautifully shaped mouth. His lips curled automatically with the memory of where she'd used that sweet mouth last on his body.

The delicate skin of her throat tempted him to dip his head. With his lips and tongue, he explored the length of it, ending at the vulnerable hollow above her collarbone.

He felt her hand begin to stroke his chestnut hair. Sam kept it short for the summer—for ease, he'd told Ivy. By the end of fall's football season, however, she'd once again be needling him into letting it grow into a shaggy style more in keeping with the modern 1970s fashions.

He smiled as he felt her hand move down his body, tracing the contours of his chest, heavily muscled from his daily workouts . . . his years of playing football . . . and the constant training in dangerous ocean currents to remain a qualified Harmony lifeguard.

Sam would always value that lifeguard training. Especially when it came to Ivy . . .

He could still see that image of her, so lost and vulnerable, the day he'd pulled her from the water and laid her gently on the sand.

Can you breathe, miss? Can you breathe?

He'd never before saved anyone's life.

The emotional impact of it had stunned him. He'd never forget her wide blue eyes, so innocent, searching his face with gratitude and affection. In an instant he'd become her knight, her savior, her protector.

It was a role he'd never before experienced.

His father had, of course. Ben Bennett was an army veteran, chief of Harmony's police department, and the undisputed man of the house.

Up to that moment, the only way Sam had ever seen himself was as his father's boy. But on the beach that day two years ago, after diving into the chilly Atlantic waves and pulling Ivy out, Sam had sloughed off his boyhood skin.

In Ivy's eyes, he'd become a grown man.

And weeks later, on the very same beach, they'd lovingly pledged themselves to each other. With their hearts, minds, and bodies . . .

Sam's fingers stroked Ivy's long blond hair and felt her fingers dipping down, below his chest, below his abdomen, between his legs . . . for a moment, the air left Sam's lungs.

"Can you breathe, Sam?" she whispered with a mischievous smile. "Can you breathe?"

"Yes . . . barely," he answered, his voice slightly shaky as he closed his fingers around hers and gently tugged them free.

They'd get back to the lovemaking soon enough, but for the moment, he wanted to talk to her about his news — that he'd been offered a job on a Winthrop Marine fishing boat for the summer.

"You read my note?" he asked her.

"I read it, Sam."

"And?"

"And if you want my reaction, I don't like it. A fishing boat could keep you away from me for weeks at a time. That's not what we planned."

"I know, Ivy. But it's a great opportunity. I couldn't say no."

"There's a lot going on this summer. I'd hate for you to miss it. I'm on the Junior League's planning committee for Harmony's Independence Day celebration, and Alistair Crane is actually flying in fireworks experts from Hong Kong," said Ivy excitedly. "That man is so generous!"

Sam sighed in barely veiled disgust.

"What's wrong?"

"The *Cranes*."

"What about them?"

"Don't be too impressed with them, Ivy. They're not what they seem."

"I admit Julian is far from a candidate for sainthood, but then again he's not all that different from a lot of the guys I used to date. And my parents are close friends of Alistair and Katherine Crane. What do you mean, they're not what they seem?"

Sam wanted to tell her, but he just didn't know how. The truth would only point out to Ivy just how different their two worlds were.

Few of Sam's friends even knew that the Bennett farm, which had been in their family for generations, had been foreclosed on by the Crane Bank during the Great Depression.

Sam's grandfather had been barely overdue with a payment when the Crane lawyers descended like vultures. Grandpa Bennett had begged and pleaded, called upon the Cranes at their mansion, asking them to be good neighbors and friends, to do the right thing.

They didn't.

The Bennetts lost everything. Sam's grandfather had been forced to move into town and work in the Crane's cannery—while the Cranes had built four tennis courts.

Sam's father, Benjamin, left without a farm to inherit, had eventually joined the local police department.

But that wasn't Sam's only lesson in the Crane way of doing business . . .

The summer before Sam turned fifteen, he was pedaling his bike home one evening from his after-school job at the Pizza Shop when he came upon a strange sight.

Two other teenagers, well dressed in sharply creased khakis and immaculate knit shirts, were monkeying around with a stop sign at one of Harmony's intersections.

"Hey, what are you two doing?" Sam demanded, pedaling up to them.

"Get lost," snapped one, a skinny blond.

"Yeah, beat it," said the other, who was darker haired and better built, with forearms that were so well developed it looked like the guy played golf or tennis all day, every day.

Sam recognized both the young men. The skinny one was Tommy Biddles, and the better-built guy was Julian Crane. Everyone in Harmony was impressed by Julian—he was the eldest son of Alistair and heir to the Crane fortune.

But Sam knew another side of the guy. Ben Bennett's police cruiser had been pulling over Julian's new Corvette all summer, warning him to slow down and stop running lights.

Sam remembered how angry his father had been one night, railing to his mother, Margaret, "You know what that cocky kid said to me? 'One does not issue *tickets* to a Crane.' Can you believe that crap? That boy's gonna put somebody in the hospital if he's not careful."

Sam watched Tommy and Julian working. They had some sort of metal-cutting saw and were trying to cut through the stop sign's post. Sam knew he had to do something, but what? Swallowing nervously, he glanced around.

There was nobody else on the street. He could run home and get his father, but by that time the sign would be down.

No, it was up to Sam himself to handle this—

"Hey! Don't mess with that sign!" Sam commanded loudly, still straddling his bicycle while trying to imitate his father's voice. "That's public property!"

"Hear that, Julian?" asked Tommy, laughing.

"Listen," Julian replied, "in *this* town 'public property' just means the Cranes own it. So beat it."

Sam was a strong kid, but this was two against one. Still, he remembered his father saying that part of police work was taking command of a situation.

Even when a suspect is bigger or there's more than one, an officer can get them to back down. The trick is getting them to understand the consequences of their actions—and to respect your authority.

"Somebody's going to get hurt or killed with that sign down!" Sam asserted in his most authoritative tone. "You know who I am, don't you? I'm Police Officer Bennett's son!"

At once, Sam knew he'd said the wrong thing. Julian Crane dropped the saw and turned toward him.

"Hey, Julian, isn't that cop the jerk who keeps giving you speeding tickets?"

"Yes, it is."

Sam's eyes narrowed on Julian. "My father's not a jerk!"

"What are you?" challenged Julian. "A mini version of your stupid flatfoot father?"

Sam's fists clenched. He had never before heard *anyone* insult his dad. Everyone in town respected Ben Bennett!

"Look at this, Tommy," goaded Julian. "That jerk cop Bennett has gotten so lazy he's sending his son out to do his job for him—"

"Yeah, he must be too busy eating doughnuts—"

"Or banging some Harmony housewife—"

Sam's bike fell to the ground as he flew like a guided

missile straight into Julian Crane's stomach. The impact sent both boys backward into the grass.

The rest happened too fast for Sam to remember much. Julian and Tommy were both on him at once, sending blows to Sam's face that knocked him out cold.

When he'd woken up, with a black eye and a sore jaw, his head was pounding and lights were flashing.

Julian and Tommy were long gone—along with the stop sign.

And, in the fifteen minutes that Sam had been left unconscious on the side of the road, two cars had collided in the middle of the intersection.

Sam still remembered the giant silhouette of Ben Bennett approaching him in the flashing red and blue lights of his police cruiser. His father always did cast a long, tall shadow, and Sam felt then—as he did now—both nervous and proud to be in it.

He'd told his father everything, of course—except for the insults. Sam worshipped his father and could *never* repeat those awful things the boys had said about him.

After his son and the accident victims were given medical attention, Sam's father finally ascended Raven Hill.

When he knocked at the door of the Crane mansion, Ben found a summer party in full swing. Apparently one of the night's party games had been a treasure hunt. Someone had come up with a list of items around town that three teams of partygoers had to retrieve. One of the items on the list was a "sign."

Julian and his friend Tommy had decided that stealing a stop sign would be a funny gag.

"A prank. An unfortunate prank, but one that can be rectified."

Apparently Alistair Crane himself had given that explanation to Sam's father. And, in the privacy of the mansion's library, Alistair gave Ben Bennett something else . . .

Officer Bennett came back down Raven Hill that night,

not with Julian and Tommy in handcuffs, but with a fistful of cash for the accident victims—and Sam.

"I don't want it," said Sam. He was humiliated, angry.

"Son, it's two thousand dollars."

Sam looked up at his father. That was a hell of a lot of money in the Bennett house, and they both knew it. Sam would have to deliver pizzas part-time for six months to earn that much.

But Sam was furious over what had happened.

"It's a bribe," he whispered, holding his father's hard stare. "I don't want it."

His father thrust the thick wad of bills into Sam's hands. "Take it. They took it from us."

"But—"

"Put it in the bank. For college."

"College?"

"You've told me that you want to be the best police officer Harmony's ever had. Well, to become the best, Sam, you need to get an education. A degree in criminal justice. Then use your knowledge of the law to take the Cranes down. You hear me? Be a *better* man than me."

Sam couldn't see how he could ever be a better man than his father. Sam had loved and admired the man from the day he was born. All he ever wanted to do was make the man proud.

Sam agreed to take the money, and eventually he applied to Castleton College, just as his father wanted.

That night, Sam went to bed thinking he'd heard everything his father had to say. Then later, lying awake, he overheard Ben's voice. It wasn't loud. But it was angry.

Quietly, Sam crept to the half-closed door of his parents' bedroom . . .

"I know it was wrong to accept the money, the promise of a promotion to chief when Fletcher retires, but don't you see? I want Sam and the boys to have a better chance than I did. There'll come a day, Margaret, when the Cranes will never again be able to rip off or buy off a Bennett. I won't be seeing that day. But Sam will. I swear to God he will."

Sam didn't quite understand what his father meant that night, but as he grew older, the picture became clearer. Alistair Crane controlled everything in Harmony. He sat at the head of every board—education, banking, commerce, even the board that determined the police budget.

Crane held the livelihood of Sam's father, and the fathers of Sam's friends, in the palm of his hand. And he seemed to enjoy playing with them all like pieces on his own private chessboard.

"Sam? What about the Cranes? Sam?"

"Oh, sorry."

The light, feminine voice brought Sam back to the present, to the private little beach co.e and the vision of Ivy's naked curves reclining in his arms. The earlier pounding of high tide had now gentled to a soothing rhythm. Sam echoed that cadence with each stroke of Ivy's long, soft hair.

"Forget it, sweetheart," said Sam softly. "It's not important. Not anymore. And certainly not to us."

"Okay, so let's talk about what is important to us. I want to know how you got this job with my father's company. I mean, I've been very careful about talking to my father about you. He knows I'm seeing a 'wonderful young man,' but I've never mentioned your name. I'm sure he thinks I'm seeing one of those bozos who came calling on me after my coming out. So how did Winthrop Marine get your name?"

"Chance, honey, that's all. I filled out an application at Castleton College's Summer Jobs Network. I guess some supervisor of your dad's saw that I was a young, strong guy with lifeguard experience who was capable of manual labor. So they called me."

"Right, a coincidence." Ivy's voice was unhappy and suspicious.

"A lucky one. This work pays very well. It'll be the beginning of our nest egg for the future."

As far as Sam was concerned, this summer job on a

Winthrop Marine fishing trawler was their future. It would earn Sam enough money to take Ivy away from Harmony and start a new life elsewhere—away from her family, her sorority, and all the social pressures that Ivy seemed to be ruled and intimidated by.

Ivy shifted uneasily, clearly still digesting Sam's news. "Sam, you know my trust fund will be free as soon as I complete another three years at Rutland."

"Ivy, I've told you before, I don't want us to live off your trust fund—or anything else that's a handout from your family. We can make it on our own. I just need to graduate from college first, and I'm a year ahead of you, which means we can get married in just two years."

Unless I can come up with the money to set up a home for us first, thought Sam. And he honestly believed this chance to work one of her father's trawlers for the summer could do it for them.

A good month of hauling could yield a crew member as much as ten thousand dollars—and Sam hoped they'd keep him on for the entire summer. With that kind of payoff, Sam could afford to marry Ivy and set up house with her as early as the coming fall.

Sam wanted to tell Ivy his plan, but he wasn't sure yet about the money he was going to earn. It all depended on how good the fishing was. He knew it would be better to wait these few short months, earn the money, then surprise her with an engagement ring in September.

"Sam, I know how you feel about my trust fund, but it's so much money. You *can't* just turn your back on it—"

"Ivy, please, let's not argue. Like I said, we can make it on our own. And we will."

Ivy was silent for a moment, studying the stars. Then a thought seemed to occur to her and she shifted to face him. Her eyes were wide with excitement.

"Listen, Sam, my father gets reports on all of his boats. I'll bet if you do an outstanding job, the captain will write you up and my father will see it!"

"And?"

"And don't you see? Then he'll understand what a great guy you are. I can finally introduce you, and maybe he'll begin to consider that you're the kind of guy who can take over the family business someday."

"Ivy, you're dreaming! You know how your father feels about anyone who's not a card-carrying member of Harmony's country club set—"

"It's *possible*, Sam."

"I don't want it to be. Listen to me, honey, *really* listen. I'll say it again—we can make it on our own. *I can support us.* We don't need your father's money."

"Let's not argue," Ivy said quickly. "Not tonight."

"Yeah, you're right. It's our last night together for a long time." Sam pulled her close and smiled. "You can think of better things to do with those soft lips of yours than argue. Can't you?"

Ivy's mouth was on his before he'd finished the last word.

By the first light of dawn, they were sated and exhausted.

"Promise you'll write to me, Sam," whispered Ivy as they gathered their things and prepared to part.

"Every day. I promise, Ivy. I'll send my letters out every time we dock."

"I'll cherish them all, just as I've cherished the notes you've left me in Harmony Park."

"And you'll write to me, too?" asked Sam.

"Of course!"

"We'll be following the fish, but I understand this captain likes to dock every two weeks or so. You can send them to me care of the harbor master's office in Halifax. Okay?"

Ivy nodded, too emotional to speak.

"Don't cry, honey. I shouldn't be away for more than a month, six weeks at the most. We're sure to head back home by then, and I should get a week or two off before we go out again. I have to tell you, though, there's a slim chance—*very* slim—that we'll be chasing the fish straight out, as far north as Newfoundland. In that case, I might not see you for *three* straight months, but I honestly doubt that'll happen. The waters up the coast are teaming with good catch."

Ivy nodded again, silently drinking in Sam's loving smile as if it would be her last drop of fresh water for years.

"Kiss me, honey," whispered Sam, seeing the longing in her eyes.

And Ivy did kiss him, with all her heart, more certain than ever she would be in love with Sam Bennett for the rest of her life.

Up on Coast Road, Harrison Winthrop started the engine of his luxury-class Lincoln Continental and pulled away from the sandy shoulder that bordered Harmony's public beach.

He had to get out of here fast, before his daughter noticed him.

Exhaling in disgust, Harrison tried to banish the disturbing image he'd just witnessed of his innocent Ivy emerging from the secluded cove where he'd watched her disappear the night before.

Seeing the passionate way she'd thrown her arms around the Bennett kid left no doubt in Harrison's mind what had gone on inside that cove all night.

Harrison's hands were wrapped around the Lincoln's steering wheel, clenched so tightly his knuckles turned white.

"I hope you enjoyed my daughter, you young bastard," he muttered. "Because I promise, when you come back from that fishing trip I've arranged, she'll never want to see you again."

THIRTEEN

The Bargain

A few miles away from Sam and Ivy, Julian Crane was tightening the tasseled belt of his red silk robe as he strode into a glass-enclosed terrace.

"You wanted to see me, Father?" asked Julian, doing his best to hide a wide yawn.

Alistair was seated before a perfectly steeped pot of green tea, watching the dawn break through the floor-to-ceiling windows.

" 'Rising to see the sun in all its glory brings glory to those who rise to see it,' " the Crane patriarch announced, quoting one of his ancient Eastern philosophers.

"Mmmmm." Julian sat down. The hour might have been fine for a man indulging personal Japanese warlord fantasies, but it was horrifically early for an Ivy League playboy.

"Would you care for a cup of green tea?" asked Alistair, waving over his personal valet.

"God, no. Espresso and plenty of it," Julian tossed to the valet. "And have Cook toast some brioche for me, won't you?"

"I don't believe Cook has risen, yet, Master Julian," replied the valet.

Julian simply stared.

"Yes, of course," the valet muttered with a sigh. "I'll wake her."

"So, Father—" Julian paused to yawn again. "What did you want to discuss?" *At this ungodly hour,* Julian wanted to add, but was careful to put the brakes on his tongue before the words passed his lips. His father was a mercurial man with little patience, and Julian had too much to lose not to obey his every word.

"I know it's early for you, my boy, but now that you've graduated from law school, you should discipline yourself to keep the hours I do."

"Well . . . perhaps at summer's end . . ."

"Asia is thirteen hours ahead of us, Julian. Get used to it if you have any illusions about *ever* taking over the family business."

"I don't think I understand. We have no interests in Asia. Do we?"

Julian tried not to flinch under Alistair's withering glare. "Why do you think I've been studying Sun-tzu and reading *Shogun?*"

Because you've gone off the deep end? Julian thought as he watched the valet place the steaming cup of espresso in front of him. Julian practically pounced on the black brew, desperate for the caffeine to jolt him alert enough to face what was clearly shaping up to be another one of Alistair's little "tests for Julian."

"In war, one must understand the mind of one's opponent," explained Alistair.

"But you're running a business, Father, not fighting a war."

"In business, Julian—and, one might argue, in life—*everything* is war."

"Yes, I see, Father. Brilliant philosophy. Just brilliant."

Alistair sighed in disgust. "Don't try to humor me, Julian. I know you don't yet grasp what I'm talking about—but if you have any expectation of controlling the Crane empire, I *do* expect you to have the sense to watch and learn."

"Yes, of course, Father," said Julian quickly and as sincerely as he possibly could at five o'clock in the morning. "Of course."

"Listen carefully, then. The world economy is shifting. Japan is rising as a powerful market force, one we must invest in. And Hong Kong is another area of untapped profit. It's time the Crane Industries' shipping arm established a steady trading route to Asia."

Julian shook his head, grateful that he was finally feeling the effect of the espresso's caffeine. "Forgive me, Father, but our fleet is taxed to its limits now, and building more ships is hardly a practical investment with the current tariffs on new steel."

Alistair nodded. "Very good, Julian. Now you're using your head."

"Thank you, sir. But I still don't understand your plans. You just said you wanted to expand our shipping to Asia. How do we do that without new ships?"

"We do it with *more* ships. Not necessarily new ones."

"I see."

"No, you don't. Not yet."

Julian's eyebrow rose. The valet brought his brioche toast, and Julian wasted some time buttering, then chewing, so he could think. His father wanted something from him, Julian could sense it. *But what could it be? And, more importantly, what will it end up costing me?*

Alistair remained silent, simply waiting for his son to ask. Finally, Julian did.

"*What* don't I see, Father?"

"You don't see how you can help me, son. You do want to help me, don't you? And the family? And our business concerns, helping us broaden our global interests with the least possible capital risk?"

"Yes, Father, of course, but how can I—"

"With an *alliance*, my boy."

"I don't understand—"

"Winthrop Marine has a fleet of ships valued at over eighty million dollars. Quite an asset. Unfortunately, my old friend Harrison, though he was quite capable of running the state government, can't quite get the hang of running his family's company—unless, of course, it's into the ground. His own wife and daughter don't even know it, but even his personal finances are a shambles and he's in danger of losing everything. So I've made him an offer."

Julian's eyebrow rose. "You want to buy his business?"

Alistair shook his head. "Outright buying would be a disaster. There's nothing but debt. Anyone who tried to buy his business at this point would have to sell off every ship to pay that debt. But there's another way to keep Harrison out of bankruptcy and still control his ships."

"And this involves me?"

"I want you to become Harrison's son-in-law, Julian. And so does he. It will assure a smooth alliance of our two family businesses. Within a year, maybe two, my global market plan will erase the Winthrop Marine debt and Crane Industries will double its worth *and* have its international foothold."

"*Son-in-law?*" Julian had stopped listening from the moment his father had spoken the word. "You mean, you want me to marry—"

"Harrison's daughter. It's time you settled down, son. I really must *insist* you follow my advice in this."

Julian took another slice of toast, buttered, chewed, and, with great difficulty, swallowed.

"But, Father, really . . . I hardly even know this girl—"

"*Get* to know her. This summer, take a few months to court her. I know the ritual sounds old-fashioned, Julian, but I think you'll find that she's a lovely young woman, well bred, with good taste and good looks. She'll give you attractive children, raised well, and, as far as your personal peccadilloes—you're a grown man of the upper class. The middle class likes to cling to its little narrow-minded moralities, but for men like you and me, Julian, indulging in affairs with other women is an expected practice—as long as they're discreet."

"Father, really, I'm not so sure I'm ready for marriage."

"Julian, this isn't a marriage; it's an arrangement. I'll be frank, I had the same words spoken to me at your age."

"What? You mean about—"

"I didn't love your mother, but her family's business was something my own father wanted in the Crane portfolio. It allowed our local concerns to broaden to national ones. And now *you'll* help the Cranes go global. Do you see, Julian?"

Julian was still reeling from his father's announcement that he didn't love his mother.

"Son, listen to me. If you ever want me to leave you in control of the Crane fortune, then you must prove yourself worthy of the reins of power, just as I did. Start showing some maturity. This business alliance between you and Ivy must take place, and I expect your full attention on this merger all summer."

"But father—"

"*Enchant* Miss Winthrop. It's not difficult to pretend you love a young woman, Julian. There are tricks—believe me, I know. I used them on Katherine. And incidentally, the Crane jet and Bermuda resort are *off-limits as of now.*"

Julian nearly gagged on his brioche. "But Father, you know how much I make use of the jet—"

"You use it to seduce young women, Julian, and I forbid you to see any woman *but* Ivy until she accepts your proposal."

"*Ivy . . .*" repeated Julian, rolling the name around on his tongue.

He *had* enjoyed making a pass at the little blonde during his party yesterday—*until* she publicly rejected him, he reminded himself. And he'd vowed to tame her in his bed.

"She *is* quite attractive," admitted Julian.

"Yes, Julian. Quite. Even so, it's only right I offer you the same perspective my father offered me: What you do *after* your marriage is your affair—or *affairs*, as the case may be."

"Mmmmm."

Julian contemplated his predicament by weighing his own lust for the Crane fortune against his father's stubborn will. The process of consideration might have taken longer, but when Julian factored in his own lust, it wasn't so difficult to agree to his father's bargain.

"More espresso," Julian said with a crook of his finger at the valet.

"You'll agree?" asked Alistair.

"Oh, well, I suppose so. Anything for you, Father."

Besides, thought Julian, the quicker he persuaded Ivy to marry him, the quicker he would regain his access to the jet, the Bermuda resort—and, most especially, Eve.

Katherine Crane stood as still as a statue.

"It's not difficult to pretend you love a young woman, Julian."

She had risen early when she'd heard the men stirring and followed their voices to the glass-enclosed terrace, stopping just outside the doorway to eavesdrop.

How she wished she hadn't.

"There are tricks . . . I used them on Katherine . . ."

She should have been devastated, standing there in the chilly hallway of the Crane mansion, her fisted hands jammed into the pockets of her thin silk robe. But she wasn't. Just cold. And numb with the realization that Alistair's secret didn't surprise her enough.

"I love you, Katherine."

How many times had he said those words in the last twenty-five years? Hundreds? Thousands?

But in her heart, had she ever *completely* believed them?

Katherine knew she could always pack her bags and leave Alistair. But she also knew the consequences such an act would likely bring. A Crane would never stand for the shame of being abandoned. Alistair would destroy her for it—frame her for child abuse or adultery or some other awful thing.

And if Alistair used Sheridan as a weapon, Katherine would never see her beautiful child again. Katherine couldn't risk that under any circumstances. She loved that little girl with all her heart and needed to be around to protect her from "the Crane way" of twisting every new generation.

She had failed with Julian. She vowed she wouldn't with Sheridan.

You did make your choice twenty-five years ago, Katherine reminded herself.

She'd willingly entered into an alliance with a Crane, and now she was strapped to it like a puppet tied to its master's crossbars.

Overwhelmed with regret, Katherine wanted to rush in and tell Julian the inheritance wasn't worth it. She wanted to call Helen Winthrop and tell her to make sure her daughter Ivy chose what truly mattered in life.

But Katherine knew what she had to say wouldn't matter—not to Julian or to Helen. Katherine's own mother had tried to warn her about the Cranes, but Katherine had wanted it all. Wanted to believe in the fairy tale of wealth and power coming with love and passion, too, and none of it with strings attached.

Of course, nothing would change now that she knew Alistair's true feelings. The marriage would go on as it had before. Just as civil. And just as empty.

No difference would be evident as they played their parts—and it was that sad fact that depressed Katherine the most.

Sighing softly, Katherine swiped at her dampened cheek. She had risen this morning *wanting* to join her husband and son for breakfast, but now she turned back in the direction of her bedroom, wanting simply not to *want* anymore.

Perhaps she'd take a Valium to calm her nerves—and in

the afternoon, when she woke again, there'd be little Sheridan to love.

Yes, my angel, Sheridan, thought Katherine with a numb smile. *Perhaps today we'll go to Harmony Park.*

Julian showered after breakfast and a hard workout with his tennis coach on one of the Cranes' private courts.

Then he went to his closet to select his clothes for the day. Spying the Gucci shoe box on a high shelf, he couldn't help but pull it down and gaze at the photos of Eve he'd taken in Bermuda.

"Truly a shame," he whispered, gazing at her lustfully. "Too bad, my Lady Day. Guess I'm forced to shelve you— for the moment."

A voice inside Julian, a considerate mother's voice, urged him to write Eve a letter, telling her he'd been called back to Harmony on family business.

But another voice in his ear—one with the ruthless tone of his father—told him to think better of it, deciding she'd get the idea when he'd stopped sniffing around the Blue Note for her.

Finally, a third voice seemed to manifest itself inside Julian's head: it was his own.

"'To hell with it. I can easily yes Father to death and still find some way to see Eve. Not right away, of course, but later in the summer. I'm sure I'll be bored to tears with that prickly little Ivy by then."

FOURTEEN

The Girls

"Winthrop residence."

"I really must commend you, Pilar. That time you picked up after *barely* one ring."

Pilar Lopez-Fitzgerald's dark eyebrows rose. The twenty-four-year-old Hispanic maid knew who it was the moment she heard his voice. He'd been calling the house almost every day for the past two weeks.

"Tell me, Pilar, is she there?"

Pilar bit her bottom lip, and her free hand began to fiddle with the end of her long black braid. Raised in a strict religious home, Pilar hated to be put in a position of lying, but that's what Ivy had asked her to do.

"I'm sorry, Mr. Crane, Miss Ivy is . . . ah . . . not in the house." *There*, thought Pilar, *that is the truth*.

"She's *around* the house, then," guessed Julian. "On the lawn or by the pool. Isn't she, Pilar?"

"Well . . . I . . . do not *see* her, Mr. Crane . . ."

On the other end of the phone, Julian laughed with genuine pleasure.

"I don't think I've ever encountered a person who was so very *bad* at lying, Pilar. I truly look forward to the day I meet you. You have a sweet accent. I'll bet you are quite exotic.

Sable hair, flashing dark eyes . . . *muy linda*—you are beautiful. Am I right?"

"*Por favor*, Mr. Crane, do not say such things! I am a *married* woman."

"Then you *must* take pity on me. I'm all alone, don't you see? In need of female companionship."

"I—I don't know what to say to that."

"Say you'll tell Ivy that it's me calling again. Don't worry, I take rejection well. I've heard it from her for two solid weeks now. Come on, Pilar, *por favor* . . . for old times' sake . . ."

Pilar sighed, unable to believe how determined Julian Crane was to get around her defenses. But she refused to give in.

"I'm sorry, Mr. Crane, but I'm hanging up now—"

"Wait!"

"What?"

"I know you want to do what Ivy asks of you, Pilar. But remember that Ivy isn't really your boss. Harrison Winthrop is."

"So?"

"So *he* wants me to see Ivy, and I assure you that he wants my calls put through to his daughter."

"He does?"

"Yes. So you'd better at least *tell* Ivy that I'm calling."

"I'll tell her, Mr. Crane. But it does not mean she will *take* your call. Just a moment, please."

Pilar put down the phone and walked toward the back of the house.

The Winthrops' large colonial was far from the size of the vast Crane mansion up on Raven Hill; nevertheless, it was a huge place to care for—easily three times the size of the small cottage Pilar shared with her husband, Martin Fitzgerald, and their two little boys, Antonio and Luis.

Pilar was still so grateful to Mr. and Mrs. Winthrop for trusting her with this job two years earlier. She'd never worked as a housekeeper, yet they gave her this chance, telling her that her youthful energy would likely make up for her lack of experience—and it had.

Pilar took as much pride in the Winthrop home as the Winthrops themselves—more so, since she was responsible for its well-kept state, everything from the gleaming shine on the tasteful Chippendale and Hepplewhite furnishings to the freshness of the brocade draperies and the spotless polish of Mrs. Winthrop's antique pewter and silver, two pieces of which had been made by Paul Revere's own hands.

Mr. and Mrs. Winthrop had also asked Pilar to serve as a personal maid to their daughter, Ivy, whose entrance into society required many special attentions to her clothing, makeup, and hair.

Pilar was only too happy to oblige. There was a bubbling energy about the girl that Pilar admired, and the two had learned to laugh together over the latest town gossip. In fact, she and Ivy were so close in age that Pilar began to think of Ivy as more like a younger cousin than the daughter of her employers.

Without any sisters to confide in, Ivy was soon trusting her maid with her most heartfelt secrets—including her undying love for Sam Bennett. This was partly why Pilar felt almost as uncomfortable as Ivy with these sudden attentions from Mr. Julian Crane.

On the one hand, Pilar felt flattered for Ivy by all of Julian's fuss. The Cranes were a powerful, important family in Harmony, and such attentions were a great compliment. But on the other hand, Pilar knew very well that Ivy's heart belonged to Sam.

There was only one problem. Since Sam had left to work on a Winthrop Marine trawler, over three weeks ago, he'd failed to write Ivy as he'd vowed he would.

It pained Pilar to see Ivy so unhappy about Sam's careless forgetfulness.

"Miss Ivy," called Pilar as she stepped through the

French doors of the spacious family room and onto the stone patio. "You have a phone call."

It was a glorious cloudless day of sunny summer weather, and Ivy was sunbathing with three of her friends by the Winthrops' pool, a glistening blue rectangle surrounded by the lush, manicured grass on the property's rear grounds.

A short distance beyond the pool, a small private dock stretched like a welcoming arm into the swirling currents of the beautiful Atlantic shoreline. Mr. Winthrop had built it for family friends who enjoyed paying visits by way of their pleasure yachts.

"Miss Ivy?" Pilar called again, stepping closer. "Phone call."

Wearing a sky-blue bikini that matched her eyes, Ivy put her hand across her brow and squinted. "Who's calling, Pilar?"

"Julian Crane."

"*Again.*"

"Yes, miss."

Pilar couldn't help but notice the reaction of Ivy's three sorority sisters, all of whom had been reclining on cushioned lounge chairs with their eyes shut.

There was Clarissa Morton, a green-eyed girl with a mane of crow-black curls whose outspoken manner at times was almost rude; Rebecca Osburn, a slender, blue-eyed strawberry blonde whose gaze ran up and down everything as if she were appraising its market value; and Mimi Higgenbotham, a petite young woman with a heart-shaped face, short, curly brown hair, and a funny sort of laugh that reminded Pilar of that little woodpecker her sons Antonio and Luis liked to watch on television.

At the mention of Julian's name, the girls' eyes simultaneously snapped open and their heads turned toward Ivy as if they were synchronized swimmers performing a practiced routine.

Pilar had to bite her lip to keep from laughing out loud.

"Did you tell him I wasn't here, Pilar?" asked Ivy.

"Yes, miss. But he seemed to know that you were. I apologize, but Mr. Crane is a *very* insistent man."

"Yes, I've gathered as much," affirmed Ivy. "Please tell him I can't talk right now."

"Are you *crazy?*" Clarissa Morton cried, sitting bolt upright. "Ivy, it's Julian Crane. Julian *Crane!*"

"I know," Ivy said with a shrug. "And I've been turning him down for weeks, so this should be no big shock to him."

Seeing the gaping mouths and startled expressions of her three Alpha sisters, Ivy couldn't help but laugh. "You three look about as dignified as Moe, Larry, and Curly."

"Winthrop, you *are* crazy," shrieked Clarissa. "Absolutely mental. Hey, Pilar, give Julian Crane a message for me. Tell him that Clarissa Morton will go out with him. *Anytime.*"

Pilar's dark eyebrows rose in unhappy surprise until Ivy spoke. "Tell him no such thing, Pilar. Just do as I ask and that will be all for now."

"Yes, miss," said Pilar, who swiftly turned and left.

"Clarissa, how *could* you throw yourself at Julian Crane?" challenged Ivy. "You're engaged to Jonathan Hotchkiss, for heaven's sake!"

Clarissa sank back into her lounge chair and closed her eyes. "Not anymore."

Ivy and Mimi both turned their gazes on Rebecca, who seemed awfully uncomfortable all of a sudden.

"When did this happen?" Ivy asked Clarissa.

"Last week. No big deal. It was a mutual thing."

"*Was* it?" asked Ivy pointedly.

Rebecca shifted again and bit her lip.

"Yes," said Clarissa. "We *mutually* agreed that he's a shit. And if I ever find out the name of the little tramp who lured my Jonny away from me, I'll wring her neck."

Ivy glared at Rebecca, who was looking awfully terrified all of a sudden, then instantly tried to change the subject.

"Ivy!" blurted Rebecca. "Why *don't* you like Julian?"

Because I love Sam Bennett, Ivy wanted to shout from the rooftop. But, of course, she couldn't. So she said, "Because . . . just *because* . . . he's no gentleman."

Now it was Clarissa's turn to laugh. "That's ridiculous, Ivy. He's a *Crane.* He doesn't *need* to be a gentleman."

"Of course he does—" returned Ivy, but was cut off by Mimi and Rebecca talking over each other.

"I heard he's always accidentally-on-purpose bumping into Ivy all around Harmony—"

"And he sends Ivy flowers every day—"

"And expensive jewelry—"

"And sails his yacht by the Winthrop dock all the time, shouting hello—"

"And inviting her to sail with him to the Hamptons—"

"And Newport—"

"But Ivy just ignores him—"

"Enough!" cried Ivy, as if she were exasperated, but a part of her was secretly pleased. For the first time since she'd pledged Alpha last fall, Ivy was enjoying the respect— and envy—of her sorority sisters.

Wow, it felt good!

But it was just a game, really. A silly game.

Ivy knew very well that Julian Crane had no chance with her. She loved Sam Bennett. Case closed.

"Miss Ivy," called Pilar, stepping toward the pool again. "This just arrived for you."

Ivy accepted the package and read the return address. "It's from the Crane estate."

She tried not to smile at the raised eyebrows on her friends' faces. With care, Ivy opened the box and pushed aside the white tissue paper. Inside was a gourmet box of chocolate-covered red cherries and white chocolate truffles.

"Read the note!" exclaimed Mimi, reaching for the box of candy. She popped a truffle into her mouth, then passed the box to her friends.

Ivy sighed as if this sort of gift came every day, which it practically did.

" 'Red is for your beautiful blush. White is for your willowy skin. Blue is for your enchanting eyes. Please share them with me next week.' "

"The ball?" asked Rebecca.

"Of course!" snapped Clarissa. "What do you think!"

All the Alphas were going to Harmony Country Club's Red, White, and Blue Ball next week. It was the most exclusive July 4th celebration outside of Boston, and the highlight of the summer social calendar—with the August regatta a close second.

"Where's the *blue?*" asked Mimi suddenly.

"Blue?" asked Ivy.

"That's right," agreed Rebecca. "You've got *red* cherries and *white* truffles, but there's no blue—"

"Look under the rest of the tissue paper," advised Clarissa.

Ivy rooted around until her hand hit something hard.

All three girls sucked in their breath when Ivy pulled out a deep blue velvet box that was clearly made to house some sort of jewelry.

"Open it!" urged Mimi.

Ivy lifted the lid of the beautiful box, and all three Alphas released a swooning moan that seemed a combination of shocked admiration and desperate jealousy.

Ivy's slender fingers lifted the gorgeous necklace of blue sapphires, white diamonds, and tiny red rubies—clearly a custom-made piece that Julian wanted Ivy to wear for him the night of the ball.

"Fifty thousand at least," blurted Rebecca without thinking.

"You're going with him, *of course,*" bullied Clarissa.

Ivy shook her head. "No, I'll send this back. It's ridiculous. I didn't ask for his attention—"

"You mean you *have* a date?" asked Mimi. "*Who?*"

"No," said Ivy, shifting uncomfortably and biting her lip. "I don't have a date."

She loved Sam and wished she could tell her girlfriends

that *he* was the reason she didn't have a date for the ball. But if she told them the truth, Ivy would be exposed to terrible ridicule in the eyes of every Alpha at Rutland, not to mention her own parents.

"You do *want* to go, don't you?" asked Rebecca.

"*We've* all got dates," said Clarissa. "Jonny may have dumped me, but I've got a half-dozen guys waiting to take me out, I assure you."

Ivy sighed. A part of her did want to go to the ball. But it just wasn't right to go out with another man when she loved Sam!

"You know, Winthrop," Clarissa started in, clearly sensing Ivy's internal struggle, "I'm beginning to suspect you've got some *secret* boyfriend on the side."

"Really?" asked Mimi, leaning in closer.

"That's got to be it," Clarissa needled. "Or else why won't you agree to go to the ball with Julian?"

"Is that true, Ivy?" asked Rebecca.

Ivy swallowed, her heart beating like a jackhammer. *Sam, help! They're backing me into a corner!*

"C'mon, Ivy," urged Mimi. "Do you have a secret boyfriend?"

"No," said Ivy softly, her eyes downcast. She hated being forced to lie like this!

"Then *why* won't you say yes to Julian?" asked Mimi.

"I . . . well . . . I want to play hard to get, you know?"

"Any harder and he'll be using a cane by the time you decide to see him," said Clarissa.

"That's right," agreed Rebecca. "There's no reason for a girl to play those old-fashioned games anymore. It's the seventies, for heaven's sake! Break free! Explore your female power! Go after what you want!"

Ivy stared wide-eyed at Rebecca, shocked at the once-conservative girl's change in attitude since she started hanging around Clarissa. *Must be the Erica Jong book,* decided Ivy.

"Well?" prompted Clarissa.

"Okay, okay!" Ivy finally blurted. She felt terrible giving in to her friends and betraying Sam. But since she didn't feel a thing for Julian anyway and intended to keep things platonic the whole night, maybe Sam would understand and forgive her once he got back from his fishing trip.

I'll just explain to Sam that I really went out with Julian to throw off everyone's suspicion, Ivy told herself. *It's actually sort of a sacrifice on my part.*

That thought brightened Ivy's mood. "I'll go to the ball with Julian. I'll call him tonight."

"Which reminds *me*," said Clarissa, "I better get my butt in gear and say yes to one of the guys who've been asking me. With Jonny out of the picture, I'm a free woman again, which means, of course, I've got to waste time going on damned *dates*."

"I thought you said dates were outmoded? '*Happy Days* historical fiction' was the term I believe you used," said Ivy, unable to resist needling the big-mouth right back.

Clarissa reclined and closed her eyes again. "I only said that because I already had a fiancé lined up to keep my sheets warm at night."

Ivy met Mimi's eyes, and they both rolled them skyward.

"But dates *are* a true pain," Clarissa insisted. "It'll take me months to find someone who's as good in bed as Jonathan Hotchkiss. And I swear, when I find out *who* lured my Jonny away . . . I'll kill her."

Instantly, Ivy and Mimi let their gazes drop to Rebecca's face.

"Got to use the loo!" sang Rebecca before bolting for the house.

After a long, terribly silent pause, Clarissa finally spoke. "Did she say *loo*?"

"Uh, yes. She did," said Mimi.

"That's *British* slang," realized Clarissa, rising slowly to a sitting position, her green eyes narrowing. "Now *where* in the world would Rebecca Osburn be picking up *British* slang in Harmony?"

"Coincidence?" Mimi tried.

"Right," Ivy agreed. "Coincidence. So just let it go—"

But Clarissa was already on her feet and making a beeline for the Winthrop powder room. "That little bitch. *She's* the one. She's the one who seduced Jonny away from me!"

FIFTEEN

The Trick

Hours later, Ivy bid farewell to her unhappy friends and plunged headfirst into the crystal-clear water of her family's swimming pool.

She couldn't believe the crazy circus her house had become. It had taken three of them—Mimi, Ivy, *and* Pilar—to pull Clarissa off Rebecca.

Clarissa had stormed off in a huff, and Mimi and Ivy had been forced to deal with a tearful, hysterical Rebecca.

They'd sat her down in the kitchen and let Pilar ply her with Mexican hot chocolate and cinnamon *galletas* until she'd calmed down enough to babble that she "couldn't help it" if Jonathan Hotchkiss had fallen desperately in love with her!

For the next two hours, Rebecca had alternated between blotting at her tear-stained cheeks, hiccuping between theatrical sobs, and brushing *galleta* crumbs from the edges of her mouth as she recounted the details of their love affair . . .

How she'd approached Jonathan at Julian Crane's graduation party—because she'd heard so much about him from Clarissa and wanted to meet him . . .

How she'd driven over to his family's seaside mansion

the next day to drop off a book of her father's about the history of the America's Cup—because they'd discussed it at the party, along with how much they both adored Newport, and she thought he might want to read it right away . . .

How she'd asked for a tour of his house—just out of politeness . . .

How, in his bedroom, she'd remarked that his aftershave smelled like something she'd want to buy for a boyfriend, *if* she had one, which she didn't, but could she have a closer sniff anyway? . . .

How her lips landed on his neck, and they just sort of ended up making love for hours . . .

How she suggested they see each other secretly until . . . well . . . until Jonathan "had just all of a sudden up and decided" that he loved her instead of Clarissa!

Ivy, Mimi, and Pilar exchanged glances during the tale, clearly thinking the same thing. Jonathan Hotchkiss had fallen desperately in love with Rebecca for one reason— she'd *thrown* herself at him!

Ivy silently prayed that Clarissa would find another man quickly and forget the whole mess with Rebecca before the school year started again. Otherwise, Rebecca was absolutely dead meat.

"Best you stay away from Clarissa," Mimi had advised.

And Rebecca had nodded her head in agreement before departing.

Now Ivy swam lap after lap in the refreshing water of the Winthrop pool, wanting to clear her head of the day's unhappy events.

If she were honest with herself, however, she would admit that today was no less trying than every moment of the last three weeks.

Face it, Ivy, you've been miserable since the day Sam left . . .

Every night she tossed and turned, twisting her sheets into a tangled mess. She couldn't stop dreaming of his touch . . . his kiss . . .

And listening to Rebecca's heated confession all after-

noon had done little to relieve Ivy's own desperate longing
for Sam. Even now, as her arms and legs sliced smoothly
through the water, she could still hear his tender words
from their last night together . . .

*"You look like some magical, unearthly thing. Like a mer-
maid. Too beautiful to touch."*

"Don't say that. All I want is for you to touch me . . ."

Ivy burned for Sam . . . for his arms to hold her again, his
body to make love to her for hours . . .

"Promise you'll write to me, Sam."

*"Every day, I promise, Ivy. I'll send my letters out every
time we dock."*

But he hadn't.

Not *one* letter had come in three agonizing weeks.

Ivy had been so worried that she'd called Winthrop Marine yesterday afternoon, pretending to be Sam's sister. The
supervisor had assured her that *Yankee Hope*, Sam's boat,
was just fine. It had docked twice over the past three weeks
in Halifax. He'd also assured her that any letters to him
should be addressed to the harbor master's office up there—
just as Sam had told her.

Ivy couldn't understand it. She'd sent at least a dozen letters. Yet he hadn't answered one!

"Pilar," she called, after emerging from the pool and
toweling off. "Could I have a word with you out here?"

"Yes, Miss Ivy," said Pilar.

"Tell me, please, have you seen anything today . . . letters or messages . . . *anything* at all from—" She lowered
her voice dramatically. "*Sam?*"

Above Ivy and Pilar, in a richly paneled den that overlooked
the pool area, Harrison Winthrop unlocked the top drawer
of his mahogany desk and dropped Sam Bennett's latest
batch of letters into it.

There were quite a few in there now, realized Harrison.
Almost thirty. *Good lord, the boy writes fast!*

"Why do you think Sam isn't answering my letters, Pilar?" Ivy's voice was now asking below Harrison's window. "Why is he breaking his promise to write?"

It saddened Harrison to hear the pain in his daughter's voice. He loved Ivy with all his heart. But he knew that the little bit of pain she was feeling now would be over soon—and then there would be nothing but wedded bliss.

After all, Harrison told himself, this Sam Bennett character couldn't give Ivy the life she deserved. Harrison had encountered enough of his sort on the Winthrop Marine fishing crews. They were a low-class type of man. Drifters, adulterers, wife-beaters, alcoholics . . .

Harrison knew very well that Sam was Chief Bennett's son, and he had to admit that the chief was a good man. But that didn't mean his son Sam wasn't using Ivy for a cheap thrill.

Sam was the kind who'd likely discard his little girl after he grew bored, as men of that class sometimes did. The very idea made Harrison's blood boil!

His Ivy deserved better. An educated, well-bred gentleman like Julian Crane was the kind of man who could give her lasting happiness—not this working-class Sam, who wouldn't understand the true nature of a gentleman's code.

Furthermore, Sam could never understand the intricacies of running a business like Winthrop Marine, especially now that the business was in so much financial trouble.

Julian Crane, on the other hand, was a Harvard Law graduate. He and his father would provide the perfect stewardship for the Winthrop business. Together they would turn it around so that Ivy, her children, her grandchildren, and even her great-grandchildren would have a secure financial future.

Harrison hated to admit it to himself—nor had he *ever* planned to confess it to his wife and daughter—but without the Cranes' help, everything the Winthrops had built over the last hundred years was likely to be lost.

Gazing out the window, Harrison's eyes fell on the glistening waters of the heated pool he had built over eighteen years ago, the same year Ivy was born.

Harrison had never told Ivy *why* he'd built this pool.

As a young father, he spent dozens of sleepless nights worrying about the rocky shoreline along the edge of his property. The swirling currents were far too treacherous for a child to swim in, and Harrison began to have unsettling nightmares about Ivy being caught in the ocean waves, calling for help.

It unnerved him. Desperately worried for his little girl's well-being, Harrison had ordered the pool built so Ivy would have a safe place to swim.

What he was doing now, with Sam, was not unlike that same protective net. Only this time Harrison wasn't merely building a pool, he was building a future.

With a sigh, Harrison closed and locked his desk drawer. On Monday, he'd stuff the pile of Sam's letters into his briefcase and destroy them at the office. He couldn't risk tearing them up at home, since Pilar might notice the pieces in the wastebasket and alert Ivy.

Rubbing his neck, Harrison sighed again. This entire plan had *seemed* simple when he'd first hatched it, but now it was practically becoming an episode of *Mission Impossible*.

Intercepting Sam's letters had been easy on his end. Harrison held the only key to the lock on the Winthrop mailbox, which meant he could hide Sam's letters before Ivy or Pilar ever saw them.

At sea, Ivy's letters were also being intercepted—of course, *that* part of the plan had been much harder to arrange.

All Winthrop Marine fishing crews received their mail through their captains. And the captain of Sam's ship had at first objected to violating federal postal laws and destroying any letters to Sam that carried a return address from the Winthrop home. But when the captain understood that he'd get a *very* healthy bonus for his effort—and get to keep his job—he'd agreed.

The captain had also agreed to warn Harrison, through a relayed radio message, when their boat was about to dock. The boat docked every two weeks, and stops were rarely more than three hours, which meant Harrison could dismiss Pilar and stand ready to pick up Sam's calls.

Whenever the phone rang, and the male voice on the other end identified itself only as "a friend of Ivy's," Harrison was ready with the same lie: "My apologies, but Ivy is out with a young man . . ."

Someday Ivy would understand why he had done all this. When she was happily married to Julian, with children of her own, she would understand what lengths a parent might go to in order to protect his child—to ensure her happiness.

Below his window, Harrison could hear Pilar trying to defend Sam to Ivy. He leaned closer to the window and listened . . .

"Perhaps Sam is very busy on the boat. Too busy to write."

"Pilar, you don't really believe that?"

"I believe Sam loves you," said Pilar reassuringly.

"Yes. I know he does. I just . . . don't know why he'd break his promise to me. Why won't he answer my letters? Do you think maybe . . . up in Halifax . . . he met someone else?"

"No, Miss Ivy. Not when he has you. Perhaps tomorrow he will write."

"Yes. Tomorrow," said Ivy, but the tone of her voice betrayed a very sad doubt that he would. "Are you sure about today, though? That there was nothing at all in the mail?"

"I'm so sorry, Miss Ivy. The only thing that came for you today was that package . . . from Mr. Crane."

In the window above, Harrison Winthrop sighed with relief. *It won't be long now, honey,* he silently whispered to his daughter. *Your happiness is just around the corner . . .*

SIXTEEN

The Fourth

"You awake?" asked Scat.

For a moment, Eve Johnson wasn't sure.

When she'd closed her eyes earlier to grab a nap, Scat's van was just pulling out of the hot, dirty congestion of Boston. Opening her tired eyes now, she felt as though she'd entered a New England dream, one she didn't want to wake from . . .

Stately colonial homes stood along tree-lined streets like proud old women, their white picket fences flashing toothy smiles of welcome. Red-white-and-blue banners fluttered cheerful hellos from old-fashioned lampposts, and the doors of the quaint little shops and eateries seemed thrown open just for her.

The busy little harbor was crowded with bobbing boats and snow-white sails; the baseball field was packed with players of all ages; and over at the town green, families of all races were spreading their blankets next to each other to enjoy a July Fourth concert . . .

"Scat, I think I must be dreaming."

"You *look* awake."

"But this town . . . it's unbelievably perfect!"

"Ain't it, though," Scat agreed as he turned down another tree-lined street, this one with a white-steepled church on the corner.

Eve closed her eyes and breathed in the tang of the salt sea. It felt cool and fresh and cleansing.

"I could live here for the rest of my life," she whispered.

Scat Perkins laughed. "I think the Harmony Country Club only wants us for one night, honey, but I'll see what I can do."

Scat's band wasn't scheduled to play until eight o'clock, but he'd wanted a few hours to set up, rehearse, and relax. When he'd picked Eve up, she'd grumbled about facing the holiday traffic so early, but now that they were here, she had to admit that the little town's cheerfulness lifted her troubled spirits.

She knew, of course, *why* the Blue Note's band had gotten this high-paying gig in the first place. According to Scat, Julian Crane had suggested he drop Julian's name with the Harmony Country Club's party planners.

Knowing that had given Eve an added reason to anticipate this singing gig. This was her chance to confront Julian.

Almost five weeks had gone by without so much as a visit or phone call—just a cryptic note that said he was "wrapped up in some important family business for the summer" but that he'd "see her again soon."

What the hell does "soon" mean to Julian Crane? Eve wanted to know!

Over and over, she had rung his Boston apartment—the only phone number he'd ever given her—but there was never an answer from Julian, just an answering service; and two weeks ago, he'd even disconnected that.

Eve wanted an explanation. Julian owed her one. And now that she was here in his hometown, she intended to get one before this day was through.

* * *

"Well, Fluffy, here we are again, another Independence Day celebration in good old Harmony, U.S.A. How many have I been to now . . . two hundred or so? Of course we can't count the first one, no one in these parts even knew the Founding Fathers had *declared* independence until July Fifth!"

Holding Fluffy's red rhinestone leash, Harmony's resident seductress of the supernatural strode across the chaotic town green with her cat trotting happily beside her.

"And speaking of those Founding Fathers, I really cannot help but recall what a charmer Benjy Franklin was! Not much in the looks department, I grant you, Fluffy, but the man certainly knew how to warm up a girl on a feather mattress!" ⍭

As she moved through the crowd, Tabitha Lenox stepped around the patchwork of blankets, quilts, and old table-cloths that littered the lawn.

Every Harmony family seemed to have turned out for the free concert. Unfortunately, they'd all brought their annoying, Frisbee-throwing offspring, who to her looked more like a hostile tribe of unruly pygmies than the sons and daughters of the town's residents.

Ducking one of the wildly thrown plastic discs, the sor-

Tabby often admits she's a few hundred years old, but that's just girlish vanity talking. She's not nearly so young! The truth is, Tabitha's got more mileage on her than a NASA space probe! Sleeping with Benjamin Franklin is nothing! You want dirt? When she really lets her hair down she talks about what a party animal Genghis Khan is. Now that's old!

ceress headed for a nearby bench to take cover with her sweet-natured cat. ᛋ

"Oh, look, Fluffy, there's Martin Fitzgerald with his wife, Pilar, and their two boys, Antonio and Luis . . . and Chief Bennett with his wife, Margaret, and his boys picnicking with Reggie Russell and his son, T. C. . . . Isn't it a shame that the chief's eldest son, *Sam*, is missing all of this?" said the sorceress with a little cackle.

"But, of course, you know I can take credit for that little situation! My spells over Ivy's father and Alistair Crane are working out just perfectly . . ."

"Meow?" Tabitha's cat yawned.

"Good idea, Fluffy. I'm hungry, too. Let's get us *both* a nice snack!"

Lunch came specially delivered, floating nicely away from the Bennett's picnic basket—three pieces of homemade fried chicken and a slice of chocolate cake.

"Look, Fluffy, it's Katherine Crane chatting with Pamela Osburn," remarked Tabby as she finished licking her fingers free of chicken grease. "But where is Katherine's daughter, Sheridan?"

The next moment, her eyes spotted the little girl just a few feet away from her mother, playing on a patch of green lawn with a small red ball.

"Ah, the perfect lure," she murmured, then crooked her

"Sweet-natured"—ha! Timmy finds it laughable that Tabby would describe her devil-cat Fluffy in such glowing terms, not to mention speak to the lame-brained animal as if it cared about a word she said. Of course, Tabby had yet to sew modern-day Timmy, so what choice did she have but to confide her thoughts to that nasty little puff of prickly clawed fur!

finger. Instantly the red ball rolled away from the two-year-old.

With a quickly murmured second spell, Tabby made sure Katherine Crane would overlook her young daughter, trotting after the red ball as it rolled across the town green.

"Funny lady!" squealed the golden-haired child when she found the ball at Tabby's feet.

"Yes, dear, you have *no* idea."

The little girl laughed as the funny lady picked her up. The red ball was instantly forgotten, dropping to the ground and bouncing away, as the child reached instead for a new object of desire—the pretty, sparkling crystal that hung from the funny lady's neck.

As Sheridan's tiny fingers closed around the stone, Tabitha felt a warm energy flow through her, and she began to witness some very entertaining visions . . .

"Well, well, Fluffy. What do I see here?"

Splendid lights flashed through Tabby's mind—memories upon memories—a stockpile too extensive to have come from one little two-year-old girl! At record speed the visions slipped past, too fast for the sorceress to pick up any significant detail.

"Hell's bells, Fluffy, I'm on to something here . . . but what?"

With a deep breath, she concentrated her psychic powers and was gradually able to slow the girl's subconscious memories to a point where she could read some of the visions more clearly.

There were the expected images of her mother, Katherine, the little nursery in the Crane mansion, her favorite stuffed animal hugged up close to her chin, but then the pictures began to shift and change . . . and Tabby began to see visions from another life . . .

"Here it comes, Fluffy . . . will you look at this! Our little Sheridan has lived out quite an interesting collection of lifetimes . . . and some of them right here in Harmony—as a *Crane!*"

Tabby tried to get some coherent details from these life-times—the sort of juicy tidbits she could make valuable use of in her future meddlings with the girl and the Cranes—but the only lifetime she could get any sort of psychic hold on was the one connected to the anniversary of this day, America's Independence Day.

"*Sarah*," murmured Tabitha. "Two hundred years ago, Sheridan's name was *Sarah* Crane . . . and it seems she became involved with another Harmony soul . . . the little boy playing across the lawn right now with his family . . . little Luis Lopez-Fitzgerald . . . but back then his name was *Luke* . . . Luke Fitzgerald . . .

"Yes, I remember Sarah now . . . and some of this tale. Oh, this should be entertaining to relive!

"So why don't you show it to me, little Sheridan," the sorceress whispered into the little girl's mind. "Let me see what you saw . . . feel what you felt . . . all those many years ago . . ."

Dear reader, if you would like to see what Tabby saw in Sheridan Crane's mind—and take a revealing trip back in time to her past life with Luis Lopez-Fitzgerald during the Revolutionary War—then you need only turn to the Tim-myAppendix Tim Tim snuck in on page 357.

Enjoy your trip!

SEVENTEEN

The Lopez-Fitzgeralds

Tabitha had finished viewing a significant portion of Sheridan's past life in Colonial Harmony when the two-year-old's tiny fingers suddenly released the pretty crystal amulet hanging around the witch's neck.

Tabby blinked as her psychic visions vanished.

Gone were the dusty streets filled with horse-drawn wagons, the harbor of tall-masted ships—and the Redcoats.

"Thanks very much for the look back, Sarah . . . I mean, *Sheridan*," whispered Tabitha as she set the child down and waggled her finger. "Now be off with you, my dear."

With a happy squeal, Sheridan ran after the wonderful red ball as it once again began to magically roll itself back across the lawn of the town green, still crowded with the picnicking families celebrating Harmony's Independence Day.

"Hell's bells!" Tabby cried a moment later, ducking a whizzing plastic disc.

"Excuse me, ma'am," called a dark-haired man in his late twenties. "Would you mind handing that Frisbee to my son?"

Tabby's eyes narrowed in annoyance until she turned and realized who had spoken to her. It was Martin Fitzgerald, and the son he was speaking about was Luis Lopez-Fitzgerald!

"Of course!" she called to Martin as she bent to pick up the irritating toy.

"Here you are, Luis," she cooed.

The little dark-haired, dark-eyed boy ran up to the witch on fast little legs. "*Gracias!* Thank you!" he cried as he reached out his tiny hand to grasp the red disc.

Immediately, Tabby focused her power.

Using the plastic Frisbee to bridge a psychic connection, she began to read the child's subconscious memories. But a split second later the boy was tugging the disc free—and the witch got nothing more than a glimpse of his past lifetimes.

"Well, that one was a wash," the sorceress told her cat as she watched Luis run across the lawn to rejoin his father. "But at least I got to confirm for certain that Luke Fitzgerald's soul is back . . . reincarnated as Luis Lopez-Fitzgerald!"

And that wasn't all that Tabby had confirmed.

"It appears that Luis's soul met Sheridan's in other lifetimes after the Revolutionary War. But that's all I had time to read."

The witch then cast one final glance at Martin Fitzgerald, who was rejoining his wife, Pilar, on a picnic blanket.

"I understand Martin is working for the Cranes," the witch told her cat. "A shame . . . but if what happened to poor Luke Fitzgerald is any indication . . . when a Fitzgerald works for a Crane, it's truly a *bad* idea."

"Pilar, I've been waiting to tell you some good news."

"Good news is always welcome," said Pilar, wiping little Luis's mouth with a paper napkin. The family had just finished their meat-and-vegetable *empanadas*, and Pilar was about to unpack dessert, Mexican chocolate brownies made from her beloved grandmother Teresa's special recipe.

"I got a raise!" announced Martin proudly.

"Oh, Martin, that's wonderful!"

Pilar threw her arms around her handsome young husband. "Did you hear that boys?" she asked her two sons. "Now Daddy can buy you both the bicycles you wanted!"

Five-year-old Antonio grabbed his little brother Luis's hands, and they yipped and hollered and danced around the picnic blanket.

Martin lifted an eyebrow at his wife. "I didn't say a thing about bicycles, Pilar," he scolded quietly.

"Oh, Martin, what do boys so young understand about a 'raise'—but *bicycles* they understand. I know you've been saving for that."

"Okay, you're right." Martin gave in with a sparkle in his eye. "So what about you? What can 'Daddy's raise' buy you, sweetheart?" he whispered teasingly in her ear.

"I want a *niña*. Another baby, a little girl this time, so I can name her after my grandmother, Teresa. And another boy, to name after my father, Miguel."

"Aw, Pilar, I'm sorry . . . I want us to have a daughter, one as beautiful as you . . . and another boy, but the raise isn't enough for us to afford a third child, let alone a fourth. Not yet . . . but soon."

"How soon?"

"Things are going *very* well. Alistair Crane himself called my supervisor at Crane Industries. Got me promoted. I'm not a junior executive yet, but at least I'm off the factory floor and into the back office."

"*Alistair Crane?* How in heaven's name would a man like that know *you*, Martin? It seems so strange—"

"No, honey. Nothing strange about it. Mr. Crane heard about some new ideas of mine that saved Crane Industries a lot of money. He was happy to hear they came from me, and he said that the Fitzgeralds have been working for the Crane family for a very long time. He remembered my grandfather working for his grandfather, and he told my boss that I should be promoted."

Pilar's smile faded as an unsettling chill slowly seeped into her system.

"Come on, Pilar, why the frown?"

"I don't know . . . I just don't trust the Cranes. It is a feeling I have. I cannot explain it."

"You worry too much, sweetheart. Why not just remember that old saying: Don't look a gift horse in the mouth."

"Martin," Pilar replied firmly, "that saying comes from the famous story of the Trojan horse. And do you know what my grandmother Teresa once told me? 'If the Greeks had *looked* in the mouth of that gift horse before they'd rolled it into their fortress, they would have seen a legion of Trojan troops waiting inside to slit their throats.' "

Martin laughed. "I've met your grandmother, Pilar, and I know you love her, but she's a suspicious, superstitious old woman. Stop being so suspicious yourself and just be happy for a minute over some good news. The Cranes are going to bring us good fortune, I'm sure of it."

Pilar wasn't so sure, but she didn't want to argue with her husband on such a fine summer day.

"Come on, sweetheart," he whispered, leaning close. "Kiss me."

Pilar did, and her chilling, troubling thoughts quickly warmed, as they always did, when Martin's lips brushed hotly across her own.

How she loved him!

He was so kind and tender as a husband, so thoughtful and attentive as a father. And his eyes still carried the same spark of passion from the day they'd met six years ago.

Martin had been in the army then, stationed in New Mexico, near the small town where her uncle Carlos lived. One of Martin's army buddies turned out to be a cousin of Pilar's, and he'd invited Martin to attend a Lopez family wedding with him.

She'd been a bridesmaid, dressed in pale pink lace with fresh blossoms in her upswept hair. And in Martin's dark gaze, she saw such a thrilling combination of fascination and tenderness, she could not help but respond to him. He was so handsome and fit in his military uniform. So gallant and kind when he'd approached her uncle to ask permis-sion for a dance.

Pilar had come to America at fourteen for one reason—to get a better education in order to become a doctor. Her uncle Carlos and aunt Marta had taken her in and become her second family, and she'd worked hard to become one of the top students at the local American high school. She had just finished her first year of college at the time she'd met and quickly fallen in love with Martin.

It had not been easy for Pilar to leave her native country at fourteen—to kiss her mother, father, brothers, and sisters farewell. She found it equally difficult to say good-bye to her uncle, aunt, and grandmother in New Mexico. But Pilar could not bear to see Martin leave New Mexico without her.

When, after six months of intense courtship, he had asked her on bended knee to become his bride and follow him back to his New England hometown, she'd readily agreed.

Never for one day did Pilar regret her decision to marry Martin. Never for one day did she regret the unexpected pregnancy with Antonio. With two beautiful boys laughing nearby, she was certain she'd been truly blessed. That life could never be happier.

And she was confident that once she and Martin had fin-ished creating the big family they talked about having, she could again return to her studies and her girlhood dream of becoming a doctor. Martin had promised to support her in pursuing that dream one day. And she knew that was part of the reason he was working so hard to increase his salary now.

"Oh, I almost forgot," said Martin softly when their kiss finally ended.

"Forgot what?" asked Pilar.

"Mr. Crane. When he heard about my ideas and that I was a Fitzgerald, he took the time to stop by the office and shake my hand. He asked about my family, of course, and when he discovered what you do—that you work for the Winthrops—he asked me for a favor."

Pilar drew back, and the slight chill of suspicion crept back into her system. "A favor? What sort of favor?"

"It's something you can do for his son, Julian."

"Julian?" Pilar was stunned. "What could Julian Crane want from *me*?"

EIGHTEEN

The Ball

"Ivy, honey, I hear a car door!"

Ivy was fully prepared to die of embarrassment.

Her poised and refined middle-aged mother had just skipped across the bedroom like an excited schoolgirl and was now hanging out the second-floor window, giving her daughter a play-by-play of the action on the ground below.

"Look at the shine on his sports car, Ivy . . . Oh, isn't that nice, he's putting the top down for you! . . . Here he comes . . . he's so handsomely dressed . . . Honey, I'm so thrilled for you . . ."

Sitting at her antique Chippendale dressing table, Ivy sunk her head into her hands and sighed. She had never missed Pilar more. Her young maid had taken the holiday off, and Ivy's mother had taken over the role of personal maid.

For hours while she helped Ivy with her clothes and hair, Mrs. Winthrop had chattered on about the Cranes until Ivy wanted to scream. She loved her mother and didn't have the heart to disappoint her, but she desperately wished Pilar were here so she could confide how she really felt about Julian Crane!

Mrs. Winthrop selected Ivy's ensemble herself, insisting

that every facet of her appearance be dictated by the extrav-
agant Crane necklace.

For the gown, she chose a Dior white chiffon they'd
bought last month at a Boston boutique. It was elegant but
simple enough not to take away from Julian's jewels at her
daughter's throat. Then she swept up Ivy's hair to further expose the girl's neck.

Gazing now into her bedroom's antique mirror, Ivy
numbly acknowledged that her mother's strategic mission
was a success. She had prepared her daughter to become
the belle of yet another country club ball.

If only Sam could see me . . .

Her fingers automatically reached to open the small antique locket on her dressing table. Sam's handsome photo
smiled lovingly out at her.

It's so you'll never forget me, he'd told her when he'd put
it around her neck last Christmas. *As if I ever could,* Ivy had
promised him. And she'd refused to take the locket off ever
since.

Until tonight.

"I'm going downstairs to greet Julian with your father,"
said Mrs. Winthrop when the doorbell rang. "You look
lovely, dear. Come down whenever you're ready."

Ivy was ready. But not for Julian.

*Why can't it be you coming for me tonight, Sam? . . . Are
you even thinking of me tonight? . . . Why haven't you answered any of my letters?*

After grabbing her beaded evening bag, Ivy moved toward the staircase and comforted herself with the fact that at
least Pilar would be happy that she was going out.

"Miss Ivy, you will make yourself ill with your sadness,"
her maid had advised her last night. *"For your own health,
you must get out. Try to have some fun . . . I cannot bear to
see you so sad . . ."*

Halfway down the steps, Ivy paused to observe the scene
in the Winthrop's foyer. Julian *did* look good tonight, Ivy
had to at least admit that. He wore a black tailcoat and

matching slacks, white vest, shirt, and bow tie. A classic ensemble, tailored to perfection to hug his very fit build.

Ivy overheard her father complimenting Julian on his clothes. In an easy tone, Julian replied that he'd had them custom-made in London by Prince Charles's own tailor.

"Of course, the tailor claims Charles needs a few extra pockets in his trousers—for the crown jewels."

Ivy's father laughed with delight.

"Julian, would you care for a cocktail?" asked Ivy's mother, her face beaming as she approached him.

"So good of you to ask, Mrs. Winthrop, but I feel I must decline. After all, I'll be driving your very precious daughter around Harmony tonight, and I wouldn't dream of taking a chance on being less than fully alert behind the wheel."

"How very responsible of you, Julian," complimented Mr. Winthrop.

"It's just that I do care for your daughter, sir—and, more importantly, I wish to show you that I can take care of her. And, if I may add, not just tonight."

"Well! Goodness! Did you hear that, Helen?" asked Mr. Winthrop.

"Yes," she answered, looking even more bowled over than her husband.

Standing quietly on the staircase, Ivy was not so much impressed as confused. She had exchanged barely a few words with Julian at his law school graduation party, yet suddenly he appeared completely smitten.

Certainly, Ivy understood love at first sight—she'd felt it herself the day Sam Bennett had rescued her from the ocean. But could a young man as jaded as Julian fall in love that way?

Ivy started down the stairs again, and saw at once that Julian was now looking up. From the moment he spotted her, his gaze never left her face. Silently, he watched until her delicate evening slippers stepped from the carpeted staircase to the gleaming parquet wood of the Winthrop's foyer.

"Ivy," he finally breathed, a touch of awe in his voice, "you're enchanting."

Good lord, thought Ivy, a bit startled when she finally looked into the forceful planes and angles of his handsome face. This wasn't the Julian she remembered at all.

Tall, strong, and dashingly handsome, Julian suddenly seemed an overpowering regal presence in the modest entryway of her family's colonial home.

Gone was the smirking boy from the party nearly two months ago. Standing before her now was a confident, well-dressed gentleman, gazing at her with the poise and maturity of a grown man—one who gave the impression that he knew exactly what he wanted.

Heaven help her, he actually seemed sincere, and with that look of open admiration in his eyes, she couldn't stop her icy armor from melting just a few degrees.

Eve Johnson had to admit, she hadn't enjoyed singing this much in months!

Scat Perkins and his band were hotter than ever tonight, and her voice was in top form, skipping like a smooth stone over the sea of pastel gowns and black dinner jackets.

The Harmony Country Club's penthouse ballroom was elegantly designed with floor-to-ceiling French doors and a wraparound balcony that gave spectacular views of the town and harbor.

Within the first hour of the Red, White, and Blue Ball, the sun began to set. As twilight overtook the sky, lights began to twinkle in the town and harbor, making the ballroom feel to Eve like a midsummer's dream.

How she loved seeing the happy crowd swarm to the dance floor when she began to sing a new number. And what a kick to watch her sultry love songs melt stiff-armed couples into passionate embraces.

With soaring spirits, Eve searched the room yet again for

any sign of Julian Crane. She had actually talked herself into the idea that he had personally arranged this gig as some kind of surprise for her.

He must know I'm here, Eve told herself, *which means he probably pulled strings to get me here—so he could see me again. He'll be surprising me anytime now. I'm sure of it.*

An hour later, he did.

Eve and the band had taken a short break and were sitting at a table beside the bandstand when she spotted Julian arriving on the other side of the crowded ballroom.

He looked incredible in white tie and black tails, and a wash of emotion flooded Eve's system at seeing him again. Until that moment, she hadn't realized just how much she cared for him.

She smiled with excited anticipation. *Wait until you hear me sing tonight, Julian! Wait till you see how much this crowd loves me!*

How proud he was going to be to take her in his arms after he saw that she'd gained instant acceptance in his world . . . that she held this crowd—*his* crowd—in the palm of her hand!

She was just about to rise and ask Scat to play one of Julian's favorite numbers when she noticed something . . .

Julian wasn't alone.

A beautiful blonde was stepping up to him. The young woman turned too quickly for Eve to see her face, but it was clear enough that she was no mere acquaintance. Julian's arm wrapped itself possessively around the girl's tiny waist—and his mouth began to whisper in her ear in an obviously tender way.

A vile knot formed in Eve's throat as she watched Julian and his date move toward a cluster of club members in the corner of the room.

She glanced at Scat and saw him staring at her. Obviously, Scat had seen Julian, too.

Crystal was right all along, Eve realized.

Despite her best efforts to control her emotions, Eve felt her eyes filling with tears.

Dammit, she cursed silently. *Don't you cry over him. Don't you dare!* . . .

Rising quickly, she fled out a side door. Her head was spinning and she knew she needed either some fresh air— or a loaded gun.

But the sad truth of it was, if a gun were placed in her hands right now, Eve honestly didn't know whether she would point it at Julian . . . or at herself.

"Ready for tomorrow's rematch with T. C. Russell?" asked Tommy Biddles, swirling the gin and tonic in his hand.

"Of course," answered Julian, his arm tightening around Ivy's chiffon-covered waist. "Ivy here will be my good-luck charm. Not that I need it. Russell may be good, but I'm far better, I assure you."

Julian had arrived late to the ball because he'd first taken Ivy for a romantic drive along the Coast Road. The summer night was quite pleasant, and she actually seemed to enjoy the relaxing ride in his convertible, taking in the spectacular sunset and the fresh sea air.

He was actually sorry they had to end their private time together by coming to the crowded country club. The second he'd stepped through the ballroom doors, he'd been swamped by a gang of fellow members, many of whom had lost badly to Julian's superior skills on the tennis court.

Julian could see how eager they all were to play him in tomorrow's regional men's single tournament. This year it was even going to be locally televised.

"What's that I hear, Crane?" asked Darius Webster, a twenty-eight-year-old banker, as he strode up to the small group around Julian. "You say you'll beat T. C. Russel, do you? You know, there are quite a few members betting otherwise—"

"Then I suppose they'll *lose* their bets, won't they, Darius? Just like the Russell kid is going to *lose* tomorrow. I hold the title, don't forget."

"I haven't forgotten," countered Darius. "But neither have I forgotten the day the great Julian Crane, undefeated on the Harmony tennis courts, was trounced by the son of a caddie! Do you remember that match five years ago, Biddles? Quite an upset, wasn't it? I'll never forget Alistair Crane's *face!*"

Julian had to work hard at keeping his rage under control at the very mention of that humiliating match. His body stiffened, and his fist clenched at Ivy's side.

"T. C. Russel will *never* beat me again," Julian insisted through gritted teeth. "No *caddie's* son can make a streak of luck last *that* long."

"I should hope not," insisted Darius. "I mean, really, the kid trained on rackets we threw away! It was quite humiliating for the club, if you recall—"

"Oh, stuff it, Darius," cut in Tommy. "Russell simply caught Julian on a down day. So stop trying to get a rise out of him and go suck down another pitcher of martinis."

Julian nearly burst out laughing when he saw Darius's face turn redder than the stripes on the decoration committee's Independence Day banners. With an arrogant sniff, the man turned on his heel and headed off—straight for the bar, Julian noted.

"Thanks, Tommy," said Julian, feeling his blood pressure ease a little. "And you're quite right, I *won't* be losing to T. C. a second time. I guarantee it."

"I *certainly* hope not," said Tommy, rolling his eyes as he mocked Darius Webster's ridiculously serious tone. "The club's *reputation* is on the line now!"

Julian laughed with Tommy, but deep down he knew that, in fact, those sentiments were true. And he was heading for disaster tomorrow. He had not practiced long enough or hard enough to retain his men's singles title. Losing it to another club member might be tolerated by Alistair, but if Julian dared to lose it to T. C. Russell, his father would likely slice and dice him with his newly purchased samurai sword.

"Julian! Julian!"

Relieved to have a reason to stop thinking about tomorrow's match, Julian turned to find Tommy's sister, Tiffany Biddles, rushing up to him.

"I just wanted to thank you, Julian, for finding the new band! The entertainment committee is just thrilled with the crowd's reaction!"

"What new band?" Julian asked.

"The Scat Perkins Five, of course. They were on a break, but look, they're just about to start playing again —"

"The Scat Perkins Five?" Julian murmured with dread. He couldn't believe it. He vaguely recalled telling Scat to mention his name at Harmony's Country Club, but he had no idea the man would take him up on it!

When Julian finally turned and looked up at the bandstand, his breathing completely stopped. The Scat Perkins Five was up there all right, but that wasn't the only surprise —

"Ladies and gentlemen," announced Scat, "please welcome back our lovely songbird."

The warm applause bolstered Eve's courage as she climbed the bandstand and approached the microphone. With her trembling hands hidden behind her, she nodded to Scat, then closed her eyes and began to sing.

"I see you there . . . across the room . . . with her you dare . . . to play your tune . . . you done me wrong . . . oh, you done me wrong . . . tonight . . ."

Eve opened her eyes and met Julian's stunned gaze.

He stood at the back of the room, oblivious to the people chatting around him, his jaw slack.

Couples packed the dance floor and swayed back and forth, listening to this singer's heartrending blues. Eve let every note tremble with her bittersweet emotions, every phrase shake with her devastating disappointment. The moving power of her song actually put tears in the eyes of some of the women listening.

"I trusted you . . . you lied to me . . . I cared for you . . .

you sighed to me . . . your loving words . . . your loving lies . . . now go to her . . . and break all ties . . . with me your song . . . is over now . . . 'cause you done me wrong . . . you done me wrong . . . tonight . . ."

Julian appeared shocked, clearly comprehending Eve's message. He didn't seem to know what to do, beyond standing and staring, never breaking his hold on Eve's gaze.

The rest of the room continued to dance, oblivious to the crackling arc of communication between the two lovers.

Hearing the beautiful music, Julian's pretty blond date began to tug at his sleeve. From across the room, Eve watched this interplay with curiosity.

She couldn't see the girl's face, but it appeared she was asking Julian to dance with her.

Julian's response was to shudder in obvious horror. Then he took the girl's arm and practically dragged her away from the ballroom.

He's running, Eve realized. *Fleeing from my song.*

That was how she'd targeted him, of course. Not with a gun, but with a set of loaded lyrics aimed straight between his eyes.

And he was running away . . .

That was his return volley to her. And from the stage, Eve felt its impact like a bullet. It hit her hard, somewhere in the middle of her chest, forcing her to finally see Julian for what he was—a coward and a cad.

He was willing to dance with Eve *only* if they remembered their places, only when she was up here on the stage and not down there as a member of Julian's club.

Clearly, she was nothing more than a plaything to Julian—an anonymous entertainer to his wealthy friends. The pain of that realization put an emotional power in Eve's voice that no one in her audience had ever before heard in a singer. Couples actually stopped dancing to stare in awe at the stage and whisper their praise.

Eve refused to stop singing. Refused to give up her last bit of dignity. She was the best damned jazz singer in New England right now, and she was going to finish this song . . . and this gig.

Unaware of Eve's turmoil, the couples ripped into deafening applause after she finished.

This was the most amazing singer some of them had ever heard. Utterly entranced, her audience felt certain that, whoever she was, this woman was a brilliant star in the making.

Julian had never in his life experienced a more powerful emotional moment.

Eve had stripped raw her feelings and laid them bare right here in this crowded ballroom . . . for him!

My God, realized Julian. *I cannot lose this incredible woman!*

"What's wrong?" asked Ivy, still standing wrapped in his arms. "Why don't you want to dance?"

"My most precious romance . . ." he murmured.

"What?"

Rubbing the back of his neck, Julian tried like hell to pull himself together. *I have to obey Father—I must. But I cannot lose Eve!*

A painful band of stark fear began squeezing Julian's heart, his lungs. Suddenly he was having trouble breathing.

"Julian? What precious romance? What are you talking about?"

"I . . . uh . . . I meant that I want *us* to enjoy a precious romance tonight, Ivy—"

"Julian, I already told you in the car, I came out with you as a *friend*, that's all—"

"We need to be *alone*," Julian suddenly insisted. Ignoring Ivy's protests, he rushed her out the ballroom doors, taking one last glance back.

Eve was gorgeous tonight in a red satin gown that shimmered over her sweet curves, his diamond collar wrapped gorgeously around her lovely throat.

You're mine, Eve, and you're going to stay that way.

No matter who Julian had to marry to please his damned father, he would not risk losing Eve as his mistress. Of that he was certain.

Like preserving the finest cognac he'd ever tasted, Julian knew, he had to do whatever he could to protect the vintage of his affair with Eve.

He didn't know *how* he was going to do that yet, but he'd find a way. Getting Ivy out of the club was the first thing he could think of to do. As for the second, he'd keep thinking—he'd come up with *something* before the night was through . . .

NINETEEN

The Fireworks

"Happy Fourth, Ivy. Wherever you are."

Sitting on the open stern of the *Yankee Hope*, Sam Bennett tilted his head back and sighed, wondering if Ivy was gazing at the same billion-star sky he was.

The Atlantic was glassy tonight, a flat black mirror. Light foam lapped the side of the steel-hulled fishing trawler and Sam's fingers felt a little numb. After folding up the letter he had just finished—the thirtieth in four weeks—he stuffed his hands into the pockets of his heavy wool football jacket.

Ivy's probably warm back home, thought Sam.

July was always hot in Harmony. Nothing like the chill Sam felt tonight. But what else could you expect sitting two hundred godforsaken miles off the Newfoundland coast, in what felt like the middle of an Arctic jet stream?

Sam found life at sea to be tedious and hard. When he wasn't hauling nets or baiting lines, he was helping the seven-member crew repair equipment and sharpen hooks. Some days were slow, giving him a chance to enjoy the whitecapped waves and passing schools of dolphins. But other days were physically exhausting, filled with sixteen hours of hard labor.

When he collapsed into his bunk at the end of those

harder days, Sam often closed his eyes and tried to conjure the sensations of Ivy's featherlight touches. He could almost feel her slender fingers moving slowly over the contours and grooves of his tired body, trailing a path from his broad shoulders to his heavy collarbone, then down his hard pectorals and abdomen.

How Sam missed those incredible shudders her touches gave him. And the look in her eyes when he thrust into her, the blue color darkening with her unleashed desires, like the sea when she releases her spectacular storms.

Ivy was like the sea to him now, realized Sam. Beautiful and limitless . . . full of life and promise . . . yet dangerously unpredictable.

With his own hands, Sam had literally rescued Ivy from the water . . . yet she still felt as elusive, as unwilling to be caught, as a wave receding from the beach.

Why hadn't she answered any of his many letters? *Why?*

Yankee Hope had docked in Halifax three times so far. Each time, Sam had mailed off a new batch of letters, all of them telling Ivy when he'd be docking again, so she could wait by the phone.

Yet he'd never received one letter from her. And she wasn't even bothering to stay close to the phone whenever he called.

For the last month, Ivy's father had picked up. Sam refused to identify himself, of course, beyond saying he was a friend of Ivy's. And Mr. Winthrop would always tell him the same thing: *Ivy is out with a young man.*

Finally, when they had last docked a few days before, Sam got the courage to ask Ivy's father who this "young man" was that Ivy was seeing. When he heard the answer, Sam wished he hadn't asked—

"Julian Crane."

Sam couldn't believe his ears.

There must be some explanation, he kept telling himself. Ivy wouldn't betray him, and certainly not with Julian Crane.

And yet . . .

Sam couldn't stop replaying Ivy's words before he'd left. *Alistair Crane is actually flying in fireworks experts from Hong Kong. . . . That man is so generous!*

Ivy was obviously impressed with the Cranes. But was she impressed enough to have started dating Julian behind his back?

This was Sam's worst nightmare, that Ivy would choose some jerk's cold hard bank account over the heat of his own unshakable love.

"C'mon, honey, hang in there. Don't give up on me," Sam found himself calling out to the night sky.

"Keep it up, son, maybe the stars will relay your message."

Sam didn't have to turn around to know who had spoken—the smell of the applewood pipe tobacco easily gave the man away.

"Evening, Blackie," called Sam over his shoulder.

"You know, there's an old South Pacific superstition, says if a sailor sends a message through the stars, his true love, wherever she is, will always feel it. She just needs to look up."

Blackie Coombs was one of the trawler's fishing crew. Close to fifty, he'd been at sea almost thirty years now. His hair was more gray than black these days, but the other fisherman said his nickname hadn't come from his hair color anyway—it had come from his love of morbid nautical folklore.

The "true love" superstition was actually a change of pace for him. He'd usually pipe up with some old saw about ghost ships, sea sirens, or legendary killer storms. The guy just loved to wax on about the sea's "dark side."

"Well, I wouldn't need to send a message through the stars if I could just get off this tub and get back to Harmony for a few days."

Blackie laughed. "Haven't you heard the old sayin',

Sam? Goin' to sea is like goin' to prison. With the chance of drowning besides."

"Well, there's no need for anyone to drown on this trip. Haven't you heard I'm a certified lifeguard?"

"You'll save my life, will you?"

"Maybe," Sam teased, his teeth flashing white on the dark deck. "On a good day."

"Then let me return the favor."

"Excuse me? Last I looked I wasn't in the water."

"Nope. But you're sure as hell in over your head with this girl of yours, whoever she is."

"With all due respect," Sam told Blackie, "you don't know what you're talking about. My girl is special. Very special."

"Special. Right. In other words, she's the prettiest girl who ever gave you the time of day."

"I wouldn't put it that way."

"But she *is* pretty, isn't she?"

"Yes," whispered Sam. "She's beautiful."

"Son, in my experience, the prettier the flower, the more watering it needs."

"Do me a favor, will you? Stow the riddling-old-sailor routine and just tell me what you're getting at!"

"I'm getting at the fact that this girl isn't married to you. Hell, you've told me she isn't even officially engaged to you. And she's probably not going to wait around all summer doing needlepoint. So stop the tortured-boy routine, son. You're drivin' the entire crew to drink."

"*I'm* driving the crew to drink? Yeah, right. So they wouldn't be drinking otherwise?"

Blackie smiled as he puffed on his pipe. "Figure of speech."

Sam just shook his head. In the past month on this trawler he'd watched a small group of men drink more alcohol than he and T. C. had *seen* consumed during their entire two years of college parties.

And yet, with all the drinking around him, Sam refused

to give in to the bottle—even with his anxieties over Ivy—because he knew it would feel like defeat, like he'd given up. And he wasn't about to give up.

Blackie seemed to be the only other crew member, besides Sam, who didn't see much sense in getting drunk every night. Maybe that's why the guy kept trying to reach out to him, thought Sam. Maybe he saw something of himself in Sam—or, at least, something he admired.

"Well, anyway, son," said Blackie, a plume of pearl-gray pipe smoke encircling his head as he turned to move below deck, "happy Fourth."

"Same to you, Blackie," replied Sam as he checked his watch. It was nearly ten o'clock. Time for the big Crane fireworks display in Harmony.

Well, Ivy, I guess you're surely watching the sky now, thought Sam. Then an ugly question reared up in Sam's mind—*But who are you watching it with?*

Heading toward the wheelhouse to take his turn at watch, Sam spotted a half-empty beer bottle on the steel deck. The men were usually good about keeping the deck clear, but they'd been drinking especially hard tonight with it being a holiday and most of them hating to be away from their friends and families.

Sam picked up the bottle, tempted to polish is off. But he didn't. Instead, in a sudden act of rage and painful uncertainty that surprised even himself, he heaved the bottle with all his might.

It flew up into a high wide arc, then hung for a few seconds in the thin cold air before disappearing soundlessly into the sea.

"How's that for a July Fourth rocket, Julian?" Sam found himself railing to the ocean. "Rivals the Crane extravaganza, I'd say."

"Grace, will you look at that one!"

"Wow!"

"These fireworks finales get better every year!"

"Sure do!"

Grace Standish sat cross-legged beside her twin sister, Faith. The seventeen-year-old girls had hiked about two miles from their remote farmhouse to a high hill overlooking the nearest town, a small logging community, where the public fireworks display was just ending.

"Why do they save the best rockets for last?" asked Grace, tossing back her long sand-colored braid and finishing off her apple.

"Gets you to watch till the end, I suppose."

The twins applauded the spectacular finish, then rose to fold their blanket, pack up their knapsack, and brush the grass off their jeans.

"Well, that's it for this year," said Faith. "Head back?"

"Yeah, let's," said Grace, deciding on a strange sudden whim to throw away her apple core by heaving it toward the sky in a high, wide arc.

That's when she saw it. From out of nowhere.

"Hey, Faith, look! There's one more—"

"One more what?" Faith turned.

Grace pointed at the shimmering beacon of white light. "Rocket."

"What? Where?"

"There! That one! It's brighter than any of the other rockets we saw all night! Wow!"

Faith stared at her sister. "I don't see anything, Grace," she whispered.

Grace glanced at her sister, then back to the single soaring rocket.

"You *really* don't see it?" asked Grace, who suddenly felt warmth flush her skin and a slightly uncomfortable band tighten around her heart . . . as if someone close to her was in distress and sending up a flare.

"No, I don't see it," said Faith softly, eyeing her sister with concern. "But it doesn't mean *you* don't."

Grace glanced worriedly at her sister. This kind of strange occurrence had happened to Grace before.

Faith, too.

But neither of the twins knew what it meant.

"You know, my father spared no expense this year—went all the way to Hong Kong to fly in experts."

"Yes, Julian, I heard."

"So why aren't you enjoying them?"

Ivy sighed. From this remote parking spot on Raven Hill, Ivy knew she had the best seat in all of Harmony to witness the Crane fireworks, which were being launched this year from a barge in the harbor.

Unfortunately, Ivy didn't want to be here.

Well, maybe she wouldn't have minded being here—in the butter-soft leather of Julian's luxurious silver convertible—if only Sam were sitting next to her instead of Julian.

Oh, Sam, where are you tonight? Why can't we be on the beach again, in each other's arms? And why haven't I heard from you in all this time?

A deafening boom split the sky, and Ivy suddenly jumped.

"Take it easy, Ivy," soothed Julian. "Listen, I swear to you . . . I'm not going to do a thing you don't want me to."

"Thanks," said Ivy softly. At least Julian was acting like a gentleman tonight, she thought. And for that, she was grateful.

"Hey, I know what will make your day," said Julian, suddenly turning around.

Ivy glanced behind her and saw Julian reaching into a small cooler in the backseat. She expected champagne or a vintage wine to come out of it—something typical of a Crane—but instead Julian retrieved two frosted bottles of root beer.

"Berkshire Crowns! Julian, where on earth did you get those!"

"Had them shipped in," he said with a smile as he uncapped the chilled bottles and handed one to Ivy. "Your refrigerator back home is now full of them."

Ivy couldn't believe it. This brand of root beer could only be bought in a remote mountain inn over one hundred miles west of Harmony.

"Your favorite, right?"

"I haven't had one of those since I was a little girl. How in the world did you know about Berkshire Crowns?"

Julian shrugged. "I asked your father what would make you happy. What would surprise you. He said you all used to vacation in the Berkshire and . . . well . . . you still sometimes talk about missing this homemade root beer."

"I can't believe it. That's so thoughtful of you . . ." she whispered, incredulous.

"Drink up, Ivy. Maybe it will cheer you."

Ivy sighed. "I'm sorry. I guess I've been a pretty disappointing date."

"No, not at all." Julian's voice was surprisingly tender. "You've made it clear that you want to be just friends. And that's what we'll be. It's okay. Cheers—"

Julian smiled, and Ivy was startled for a moment by how open and kind his hazel eyes looked tonight. And she could hardly believe how understanding he was being about her feelings.

For the first time since they'd parked here, Ivy smiled back.

"Cheers," she said.

The root beer bubbles tickled her nose, and she laughed.

"There you go," teased Julian as he sipped his own root beer. "First you smile, then you laugh. Next thing you know, you might actually want to be sitting here with me instead of throwing yourself under the wheels of my DB5."

"Oh, god, Julian. Have I really been that gloomy?"

"No. Not at all. Not if we compare you to, say . . . Morticia Addams."

Ivy laughed again. "You know, you're not so bad after all."

"Gee, thanks."

"Well, your reputation *is* awful, Julian. And you were beyond obnoxious to me at your graduation party."

"Too much champagne and caviar. Went to my head. That's my only excuse. That and . . . well . . . I can be a real jerk sometimes, Ivy, I know that. But I do like you. And that's the truth, I swear to God."

"I like you, too." Ivy was surprised she'd said it, but it was the truth. She was actually beginning to enjoy herself.

"Friends, then?"

"Sure," said Ivy. "I can always use a friend."

"Because you already have a boyfriend?"

Ivy nearly choked on her root beer. "What made you say that!"

Julian's eyebrow rose. "You're actually going to deny it?"

Ivy stared nervously at the windshield, pretending to be interested for a moment in the rockets that burst, one after another, in midair, then fell to the harbor waters in trickling streams of vanishing light.

"Ivy," said Julian, his voice deep and knowing. "I've been around the block. I know when a girl has another guy on her mind. You do, don't you?"

Shifting uneasily, Ivy dropped her gaze to the root beer in her hands.

"It's okay," whispered Julian. "I'm not asking you *not* to like this guy, whoever he is. I guess I'm just asking for a chance . . ."

"What sort of a chance?"

"A chance to show you that I'm a good man, too. That I can be good for you. A friend . . . and maybe . . . if and when you ever want it . . . maybe more . . ."

"That's very generous of you, Julian, but why am I the lucky girl?"

"Oh, Ivy, don't you know?"

Silently, Ivy shook her head, disarmed by the vulnerability Julian was so smoothly able to expose to her.

"You're special, Ivy Winthrop."

Ivy swallowed nervously as Julian reached out a hand and touched her cheek. His fingers were chilled from the root beer, and she shivered . . . though a part of her feared the shiver came less from the cold than from the slight tingling thrill of his touch alone.

"Julian, I . . . I don't know what to say."

"There's nothing you have to say, Ivy," he whispered. "This isn't about what I want to take *from* you. It's about what I want to give *to* you."

The words touched Ivy, and she found herself gazing at Julian for a long moment . . .

This wasn't the first time Ivy found herself thinking how handsome this man was. How forceful his features, how fit his build. But it was the first time she didn't try to hide her thoughts from him.

With an uneasy openness, she allowed Julian to read her admiration on her face, in her eyes.

He leaned closer then, and she felt enveloped by his warmth, the subtle, sophisticated fragrance of his elegant aftershave. Her head felt light, and an age-old curiosity made her wonder . . .

What would it feel like to kiss this man?

The brushing of his lips was respectful, almost reverent. It was the kiss of a friend . . . yet, beneath it, Ivy felt the slight trembling, the crackling heat, the desire for something more.

His eyes stayed on hers as he pulled slowly away. The hazel hue was glistening in the evening's light, burning openly with how much he wanted her.

The effect was a powerful drug. And Ivy had to close her eyes and mentally shake herself to get clear of it.

Sam. Sam, she reminded herself. *I love Sam.*

But with Sam out of touch for so long, she knew she was becoming vulnerable.

"Julian, I'm sorry, but I think I'd like to go home now."

* * *

"Come on, Eve, come out and see the fireworks."

"No, Scat. No thanks."

Scat Perkins was worried. The rest of the band and most of the couples attending the ball had stepped out onto the ballroom's wraparound balcony as soon as the fireworks had begun. But Eve refused to enjoy them. She simply sat by herself at the band's small break table, sucking down the complimentary champagne as if it was water.

Scat stepped back into the nearly empty ballroom. He'd been watching Eve closely all night, ever since Julian had skipped out with that pretty little blonde.

Sitting down beside Eve, Scat glanced back at the sky. Outside, the booming rockets of red, white, and blue streaked through the night, one after another, illuminating the blackness above Harmony with umbrellas of temporary brilliance.

"You know, honey, the thing of it is . . . sometimes the hotter it burns, the quicker it dies out."

"Scat, I don't care about the rockets," said Eve irritably, pouring herself another drink of the complimentary champagne.

"I'm not talking about the fireworks, honey. I'm talking about the way things can sometimes go between men and women."

Eve looked up at Scat, her eyes brimming with unshed tears.

"I know, I know . . . ' 'T'ain't nobody's business' if it does," said Scat, quoting Billy Holiday with a wink. "Just be wise to the truth that them kind of hot rockets nearly always burn. But even the most painful burns will one day heal."

He put a hand on Eve's shoulder, and Eve finally broke down and sobbed. Scat held on to her like a father.

"It's okay, honey. Have your cry out. Then forget him."

Outside, the rockets continued their heated trajectories. Eve watched them through her tears . . . firing hotly, delighting the crowd, then falling to the silent dark ground . . . used up and burned out.

* * *

Small steps, thought Julian forty minutes later as he took Ivy's hand and walked her to the Winthrops' front door. That's what his father had advised him. And so far it was working like a charm.

"Good night, Ivy."

Julian flashed her a simple but playful smile—one that seemed to say, *Aren't I going to at least get a good-night peck?*

Ivy bit her bottom lip and hesitated.

Julian raised his eyebrows and gently tugged her closer, careful to do no more. He knew that Ivy had to be the one to initiate this.

"Let's try that again," he said with a wry tone. "*Good night, Ivy.*"

Clearly disarmed by Julian's teasing approach, Ivy lifted herself up on her toes and put her lips to Julian's cheek.

But Julian wasn't about to settle for a mere peck.

In an easy move, he turned his face and brushed his lips against Ivy's for the second time that night.

Ivy wanted his kiss. Julian knew it the instant their lips touched. He felt it in her response—the small movements of her jaw to achieve a better angle, the slight pressure to deepen the connection, and then the opening of her mouth.

Ah, yes, the invitation of his tongue. He was just about to oblige her when—

She broke it off.

Obviously she felt guilty or embarrassed or afraid. Whatever it was, though, within seconds she was pulling back and turning away.

"Good night," she sang out, clearly trying to sound unaffected as she sailed through the front door.

But Julian had heard the slight tremble in her voice, and he knew he'd breached her first round of defenses. Yes, he was certain that Ivy would be thinking about that kiss for the next few nights.

"Well, Father, looks like you were right," whispered Julian as he strode back down the path to the street.

Women don't like to be pushed too hard or too fast by a man, Alistair had advised him this morning. *Make her believe she's in control—even though she's not. It's like a business transaction, son, let the other party get comfortable with you. Solicit their trust first. And everything else will quickly go your way . . .*

With a sigh of relief, Julian climbed into his DB5.

"Finally, work is over for the night," he muttered.

Not that it was *hard* work. Ivy was a gorgeous young woman. It would be a pleasure to slowly seduce her into his bed. But Julian's mind wasn't focused on bedding Ivy at the moment.

Right now Julian wanted nothing but pure pleasure.

Checking the clock on the dashboard of his Aston Martin, Julian fired up the engine and peeled out, turning the car toward Harmony's country club.

When it came to pleasure, there was only one woman who could satisfy him now . . .

Eve.

TWENTY

The Lie

"She hated him . . . hated him . . . hated him . . .

"Yet wanted him still . . ."

The bottle of tequila sat one-third empty in front of her. She'd flirted it, along with a fistful of lime slices, out of the bartender an hour ago as she'd watched him lock up the liquor for the night.

This bottle was full when I got it. Wasn't it?

Eve knocked back another burning shot, squeezed the lime into her mouth, and felt her eyes about ready to close. It was after midnight now, and the crowd had gone. But Eve was still singing. Making up her own lyrics as she went . . .

"The party's over . . . over . . . over . . . over . . . but that ain't all that's over . . ."

The band was packing up across the room, and Eve was waiting for Scat to pour her into his van and drive her back to Boston.

Despite it all, she hated leaving Harmony behind. Notwithstanding her devastation at the hands of a fool named Julian Crane, this pretty little town was like a picture postcard to her—a paradise with picket fences . . .

"A song . . . a cloud . . . a lover's dream . . ."

Eve couldn't seem to stop making up songs!

Then she blinked, wondering if she was also making up visions. *I'm not that drunk! Am I?* Rubbing her eyes, she looked again. But he was still there . . .

"Can't be him," she whispered to herself.

But it was.

Julian Crane had pushed through the closed ballroom doors, his bow tie undone, his dinner jacket slung over his shoulder.

The sight of his handsome form walking toward her in an easy, confident stride sent sharp emotions slicing through Eve: rage, pain, devastation . . . and finally, though she hated herself for it . . . hope.

Leap to your feet, Eve . . . Tell him off . . . Do it!

Crystal's voice and her own blended together in her head, advising her to cling to her anger. Use it like a shield. A weapon.

"Like the threads?" he asked her teasingly. His voice was deep and strong. "Got them in London. The name's Bond, Julian Bond."

A wry smile crossed his lips as he sat down next to her.

Eve sat there, frozen for a moment, still less than entirely certain he wasn't some sort of drunken delusion. Then she realized he always had been . . .

"Forgive me, Eve—"

Her eyes narrowed with those words, and she finally found a way to communicate all the things she felt.

The splash of stinging tequila flew quick and straight out of Eve's shot glass. It hit him right in the eyes, making him cry out, then sputter in disbelief.

The moment the glass hit the table again, Eve was on her feet, ready to bolt.

"Dammit, Eve! Wait! Listen to me! *Listen!*" pleaded Julian, closing his fingers around her arm with one hand while trying to wipe away the burning tequila with the other.

"My father has pressured me into entertaining the daughter of an important business associate this summer. That's who you saw me with tonight. I couldn't say no."

Don't you dare listen to a word he says, Eve. Don't you dare!

"You bastard. You're two-timing me. You think I don't know what I saw tonight—"

"Forgive me, Eve—"

Again she answered him without words. The sharp crack of her hand to his cheek rang out in the empty ballroom, shocking both of them for a moment into stunned silence.

The loud, violent sound made Scat Perkins and the band glance up from their pack-up work at the other end of the room.

"Hey, Eve! You okay?" Scat called from across the dance floor, the ominous tension evident in his tone.

Every last member of the band appeared ready to jump on Julian with one word from Eve.

"She's okay, Scat," Julian answered, recovering first. "It's *me* that got that slap."

"Oh," muttered Scat. "Well, that's all right then."

Unhappily rubbing his cheek, Julian sank to one knee before Eve while firmly taking both of her hands in his—an act of self-defense as much as one of romance, Eve decided.

Then Julian looked into Eve's dark, luminous eyes. They were red-rimmed and full of hurt, her lower lip trembling. It truly pained Julian to see her like this—and he swore to himself that he'd make it up to her.

"I don't love her, Eve," he pledged. "I don't want her. I want you. And that's the truth. I *swear* it."

Eve blinked, hearing the words and wanting, wanting, wanting to believe them.

She stared at the angry red imprint of her hand on the flesh of Julian's face. "I should tell you to go to hell," she whispered.

"You should? But *will* you?"

Eve inhaled, then exhaled in frustration, trying to clear her fuzzy brain. The truth was, she wasn't brave. And right now she felt all alone in the world—not to mention trapped in a condition she was terrified to face alone.

With Julian on his knees here in front of her now, saying the right words—well, she just didn't see how she could turn him away. Neither did she see how she could tell him the truth. That she was a little more than three months pregnant with his baby—

What will he say? What will he do?

If he ran again, she didn't know what would become of her . . .

"Eve?"

Eve blinked once more, paralyzed. Wanting yet not wanting this reconciliation. Wanting yet not wanting to tell him about their child.

Using her indecision as a crack in the door, Julian decided to act. Picking up the tequila bottle, he gently told her not to think about it anymore, but to just come with him.

"We'll finish this together at a more private location. You'd like that, wouldn't you?"

The ploy worked. Eve numbly followed Julian, letting him slip his arm possessively around her waist.

She wanted it there, Eve realized. Wanted him next to her tonight. And every night. But was *he* willing to stay? Now, and more importantly, *after* he learned the truth?

That was the ultimate question—and Eve knew the answer wouldn't be coming tonight. Because she was too much of a coward to ask it.

"Scat!" called Julian. "I'm giving Eve a ride back to Boston."

"Eve? You sure that's what you want?" asked Scat, appearing worried.

"Yes, Scat," she replied, weakly nodding. "It'll be okay. Julian will take care of me."

At least, she prayed that he would.

"That's right, pet," he murmured in her ear. "I'll get us a penthouse suite at the best hotel . . . we'll set the bed on fire."

Julian knew, of course, that he could not stay more than this one night with Eve. His father would kill him if he knew he was seeing her again, but Julian couldn't be expected to withstand the tepid courtship of Ivy without some sustenance along the way. A man like himself needed to bury himself in real heat. And Eve was a volcano.

In the morning, he'd gently tell her that he needed to return to Harmony for the regional men's singles tournament. Then he'd call her from Harmony and explain that he had to fly to Europe on family business. A few gifts shipped straight from Milan and Paris would surely hold her over for the summer.

And in the fall, after the wedding to Ivy, he would set Eve up in a luxurious apartment in Boston, and she would become his mistress for good.

Once Eve finally saw what he was offering, she'd know it was worth the wait!

Julian felt good. He always did when he got what he wanted.

He would get little sleep tonight, but so what? All he really needed to do was save face by knocking T. C. Russell out of the running.

T. C. Russell, thought Julian. *Now there's a guy I'd love to run into tonight and make disappear. That's a wish I'd like to see granted.*

Well, dear reader, by now Timmy is sure he doesn't have to tell you that someone in Harmony did indeed hear that wish of Julian's. And, in the interest of evil, was all too willing to grant it.

T. C. Russell yawned and checked his watch. It was after midnight, and he was driving home along the dark Coast Road from the tournament players' beach party.

At this hour his father was probably already fast asleep. *Pleasant dreams, Pop*, he thought. *I know I'll be having some . . .*

T. C. smiled as he thought about all the fresh faces he'd met tonight—the fresh female faces. Whoa, those girls were lovely. Many of them were tennis fans from other area towns. They'd come in to watch tomorrow's regional tournament—to cheer on a brother or a friend.

But, of course, now that T. C. had personally charmed so many of them, he figured they'd be rooting for him, too. Especially after he knocked their brother or friend right out of the competition!

T. C. smiled to himself with the confident knowledge that he was ready to win. The title was as good as his.

As he drove along the twisting road, T. C. became aware of a high-performance engine behind him. Probably an expensive sports car. He glanced in his rearview mirror and saw a convertible's headlights speeding toward him.

As it passed under one of the few streetlights along a bend in the road, T. C. got a fleeting glimpse of the car.

Wow, that thing is moving like a silver bullet!

"Ease up, fool!" whispered T. C. in the dark interior of his junker. He had a bad feeling about this. The Coast Road was winding and dangerous, with unexpected drops and hairpin turns. But this jerk, whoever he was, didn't seem to care in the least.

In seconds the sound of the encroaching sports car's engine grew louder in his ears, as if it were right on his tail. Uneasily, T. C. tightened his grip on the steering wheel. *Don't you tailgate me, you bastard—*

In the next moment, he felt a slight tap to his bumper.

"Hey, jerk!" T. C. cursed out the open window, his heart beating now with real fear. "Back off!"

Again T. C. glanced into the rearview mirror.

What happened next would haunt him for the rest of his life.

Reggie Russell wondered why his son wasn't out of bed yet. He'd knocked on T. C.'s bedroom door a half hour ago.

"T. C.! Get up now, son!" he called through the small house.

Reggie checked his watch against the kitchen clock. The boy barely had time to eat some eggs before he was due to start his warm-up practice at the country club courts.

He himself had to get a move on, too. He was due to start tending the golfing greens in an hour—and then Alistair Crane wanted him as a caddie for a ten o'clock round.

"Damn . . ." The soft curse escaped the fifty-year-old man's lips as he stretched his sore back. Lord, he was looking forward to the day he could quit his job.

Suddenly the sigh became a chuckle.

That day was coming soon. Very soon, thanks to T. C. Reggie was sure of it. *Yeah, I'll tote your heavy golf bag for you, Mr. Crane, sir. Be glad to today. Just so I can remind you not to miss this afternoon's tournament—the one that my son, T. C., is playing in. The one T. C.'s gonna win!*

"T. C., you hear me? Get up, now!"

All his life, Reggie had known how his son had truly felt about him. Sure, T. C. loved him well enough, but Reggie also knew that T. C. was secretly ashamed of the way he made his living, fetching and carrying for the snobby members of a restricted club.

Someday, though, Reggie knew it would all be wiped out—every snide remark, every lowly look, every menial task. None of it would matter after T. C. won this regional tournament today.

"T. C.!"

Reggie headed for T. C.'s bedroom door again, figuring his son had stayed too late at that tournament players' beach party. A damn fool thing to do the night before a match. But T. C. was hard-headed—and Reggie suspected, a little lonely for some female company.

As he passed through the small but carefully dusted Russell living room, he glanced at the collection of tennis trophies that held a place of honor on handmade shelves above the mantel.

Those trophies were nothing. With Ashe breaking down color barriers, the way was all clear now for Reggie Russell's boy. T. C. would conquer the NCAA titles this school year, then the U.S. Open and finally Wimbledon. T. C. and Reggie had talked about it for years now—planned for it all of T. C.'s life.

The only sad note was that his late mother, God rest her soul, wouldn't be here to see it.

Reggie knocked once more on the door, then opened it. "What the hell . . ."

T. C.'s bed was empty. Made. It had never been slept in.

Just then, the living room phone rang.

The news on the other end of the line was something Reggie could barely comprehend—it struck him hard, like a physical punch, and he stumbled backward into a chair.

T. C., his son, his pride and joy, was in the hospital.

He had never come home last night because there'd been a terrible accident on the Coast Road.

While his boy was driving home, it looked as though someone had deliberately slammed into him . . . and sent his car over a cliff.

TWENTY-ONE

Tabitha's Diary

ENTRY: *Timmy & the Underground Railroad*

 Timmy interrupts the story again because inquiring minds will surely want to know how the Crane and Russell families have gotten along in the past. How shall Timmy put it? Let's just say that they were never really on friendly terms. In fact, the present-day Russells might be very interested to know about a little sideline business one of the Crane ancestors once had. Tabitha Lenox, of course, knew all about it . . .

September 20, 1859

Dear Diary,
  A shady parade of characters has been making their way up Raven Hill lately. So I pulled out my crystal

bowl, filled it with water, and did a little scrying on the Cranes . . .

My clairvoyant visions showed me that Nevil Crane has gone and hired his own private band of bounty hunters to search the state for runaway slaves. That's who those shady characters are, Diary, bounty hunters!

Of course, Nevil believes he is quite right in doing this. Says the Crane family lost a fortune when Congress outlawed the transport of slaves into the U.S. in 1807.

Now Nevil wants some of the money back by running this new business on the side—capturing runaway slaves and collecting the bounties from their owners when he returns them in chains.

I'm going back to my scrying to see if I can learn more!

September 21, 1859
Morning . . .

Dear Diary,

I had so much fun last night, I cannot wait to tell you!

While I was spying on Nevil Crane through my crystal bowl visions, a scruffy bounty hunter by the name of Bo Ward entered Nevil's study and dumped his grubby knapsack on Nevil's elegant desk. Out of the soiled sack fell something Bo called a "freedom quilt."

Apparently, Diary, these quilts are sewn by slaves, with a secret map hidden in the design. This particular map showed runaways how to escape north through a part of the Underground Railroad system that included our own town of Harmony!

By the way, Diary, the Underground Railroad is not really a railroad with a train and tracks. It is a system of safe houses, shops, and farms that the slaves are using to make their way north to Canada, where they can live freely. Both whites and free blacks are helping the runaways by providing food, shelter, and transportation.

Nevil Crane knows he stands to make a fortune capturing runaways if he finds out who in Harmony is operating a stop on the Underground Railroad.

As I watched Nevil and his bounty hunter try to decipher the map's clues, I immediately told Timmy that I saw a smashing fine way to have fun with another descendant of William Ephraim Crane!

I closed my eyes and sent my powers through the visions in the crystal bowl. Nevil and the bounty hunter quickly grew sleepy and retired for the night.

Then I took Timmy over to the Crane mansion and sent him in with needle and thread to sew a few extra-special little clues into the quilt.

I'll get back to you later, Diary, to tell you what happens!

September 21, 1859
Evening . . .

Another Timmy! Good heavens, it's beginning to look like Tabby's got a little Timmy franchise operating right out of her sewing closet! Well, at least it's for a good cause!

Dear Diary,

What a ripping good time!

This afternoon, Nevil and his bounty hunter came to only one conclusion from the quilt clues: The Underground Railroad could be found by following Harmony Creek two and one half miles west of town.

Nevil insisted on camping out with his bounty hunter tonight. He said he did not wish to miss the fun of capturing unsuspecting runaway slaves.

What Nevil doesn't know, of course, is that Timmy and I had a little fun with those quilt "clues" already!

Timmy finally asked me today where we actually sent them to camp out for the night.

"Far, far away from the real railroad stops at the Bennett and Russell farms," I told him.

"But where exactly did we send them, Tabby?" he asked.

"The town dung heap, Timmy dear!"

TWENTY-TWO

Unhappy Surprises

Sitting at his large mahogany desk in his dark-paneled den, Harrison Winthrop took a fortifying sip of brandy as he sliced open the fat white envelope, embossed with the silhouette of a cargo ship.

Anxiously, he pulled out the pile of papers and riffled through them, passing over the monthly managers' reports and separating out the stack of log summaries filed by the ship captains in his fleet. Slowly, he leafed through them until he came to one particular fishing trawler—

"*Yankee Hope,*" he whispered at last.

He held his breath as his eyes scanned the captain's remarks on crew performance. When he read the notation about Sam Bennett, Harrison released a heavy sigh of relief. Then he grabbed his brandy and headed downstairs.

Harrison was no actor, but he did his best to appear nonchalant as he sauntered into the family room. Smiling hello to his daughter, who was on the phone, he took a seat in his large leather armchair and leaned back, pretending to be engrossed in the stack of papers in his hand.

"No, Julian, I don't think Tommy Biddles has a chance of beating Jon Hotchkiss. Jon's won the regatta for three straight years . . . What's that? He said *what* to Tommy?"

Ivy paused, listening, and began to laugh.

"Well, maybe Tommy shouldn't have insulted Rebecca in front of Jon!"

From behind the stack of reports, Harrison smiled. He was delighted to hear the sound of his daughter's laughter floating through the house again.

For the past four weeks, ever since the night of the July Fourth ball, Julian Crane had been doing his level best to make his daughter happy. And Harrison was grateful.

The young Crane heir had already taken Ivy on countless outings with his friends, escorted her to formal dinners, played golf with her, given her tennis pointers, and sailed her over to the Hamptons for a weekend party thrown at the mansion of some big television star.

Don't worry, sir, I'll win Ivy's heart, Julian Crane had promised Harrison. *She says we're just friends, but I know women. There'll come a day when she'll need a shoulder to lean on. I'll be that shoulder. And when she leans on it, well . . . let's just say I'll be ready to inspire her to feel more than just friendship for me —*

"What's that, Julian?" Ivy continued on the phone. "You want me to join your crew? At the regatta?! You're kidding, *really*? No one's ever asked me to sail with their crew before —"

Harrison lowered his stack of papers and looked over at his daughter. Her blue eyes were wide with surprise and bright with pleasure.

"But you know I'm not a very good sailor. I'll ruin your chances for a top finishing spot —"

Ivy listened intently for a quiet moment. Harrison watched as the expression on her face became vulnerable, moved.

"That's so sweet of you to say, Julian."

Harrison smiled. Obviously Julian had made it clear that Ivy's enjoyment of the day meant more to him than a regatta trophy.

Well, young man, Harrison thought to himself, *you may*

lose a placing trophy, but you'll certainly win my daughter. I'm sure of it.

And Harrison was ready to help.

With a casual glance at his watch, he rose, stretched, and placed the stack of Winthrop Marine reports on the coffee table, taking great care to make sure one particular ship's report was right on top.

Then he mouthed "good night" to Ivy and headed out of the room.

"Yes, Julian, I'd love to join you for a sail tomorrow," continued Ivy as she waved good night to her father. "Newport sounds fabulous. Can we breeze by Hammersmith Farm? . . . Great! But you must let *me* bring lunch aboard . . . No. I insist. You've been so generous and thoughtful toward me over the last few weeks, it's the least I can do . . ."

After a few more minutes of conversation, Ivy yawned and checked the clock. It was after eleven and she was tired. Her morning foursome on the club greens with Julian, Tommy, and Tiffany Biddles had gotten her out of bed before seven, and she was beat.

She said good night and hung up, ready to turn in for the night, when she noticed the stack of Winthrop Marine paperwork on the coffee table that her father had left behind.

"That's not like him," she murmured.

He'd been very guarded, especially lately, when it came to his business paperwork. Curious, Ivy glanced at the stack—

"Yankee Hope," she read across the page, and her heart fluttered.

That's Sam's ship.

Ivy closed her eyes, her entire being filled with love at the mere thought of him. Of his big blue eyes and granite jaw, his dazzling smile and broad shoulders. His deep voice telling her he couldn't wait to make love to her again.

Even though, in the last few weeks, Ivy *had* allowed herself to become distracted from missing Sam by having fun with Julian, it didn't *mean* anything.

Julian was just a guy to hang out with, like a brotherly companion—a convenient date for the social functions that her parents or his parents had asked them to attend over the last four weeks.

Sam Bennett was the man who held her heart. And he always would.

Now joy filled Ivy with this chance to read his captain's report. Sam was such a hard worker, such a selfless, good man. Surely the captain would have seen that and sung his praises to her father.

And maybe there would be some sort of explanation for why a crewman like Sam wouldn't be able to send out letters or place a call. Maybe they hadn't been able to dock at a place with mail or phone service—*something!*

With extreme care, Ivy stepped to the archway of the family room. The hall was empty and the house was quiet, so she rushed back to the coffee table and picked up the report.

What she read there made her knees weaken.

With the paper clutched in her hand, she felt her body sinking to the sofa. Tears swam in her eyes until finally the page blurred before her and she could no longer reread the awful words that pulled her down, dragged her under . . .

Why, Sam? Why? How could you do this to me? To us?

She was suddenly drowning all over again, drowning in pain, in hurt, in betrayal—and this time there was no way for Sam Bennett to save her.

Many miles away, in the heart of Boston, Eve Johnson had just arrived at a hopping private party, a stash of drugs in her purse—drugs she hadn't touched for almost a month.

What Eve needed now was money. Not a high.

And since she'd given up all drugs nearly four weeks ago for the sake of her baby's health, she wanted to sell this cache back to the Blue Note bartender who'd been supplying her since May.

The party was in full swing, and every conceivable narcotic was flowing freely throughout the large luxury apartment. Cocaine lines covered the big mirrored coffee table, pills and tabs of acid filled the crystal candy dishes, and pot smoke could be smelled everywhere.

Eve had just spotted her dealer across the room, crowded with well-dressed mingling bodies, when she heard a sound like booming thunder above the pounding beat on the stereo speakers—

"Everybody freeze, police!"

Eve turned and gasped. A dozen armed, uniformed men had burst into the place and were now swarming through the crowd.

"Up against the wall, now!"

People were screaming and shouting. Some were trying to flee. The cops were pulling out their batons, turning people to the walls, frisking them.

"Please!" Eve cried to a female officer who demanded she put her hands up. "I'm not a part of this! I was just leaving—"

"That's fine, honey. You can go. But I've got to insist on giving you a nice pair of bracelets to wear on the way. Now turn around and spread 'em!"

"I'm going to jump ship, Blackie. I've decided."

"What!"

It was past midnight, and *Yankee Hope* was steaming out to sea again after a quick return to Halifax.

Sam had been alone on watch in the wheelhouse for the past two hours. Watch duty entailed nothing more than keeping an eye on the radar and weather bulletins and occasionally punching numbers into the autopilot. It was easy.

Too easy.

It had given him way too much time to think.

Two months had gone by now without a word from Ivy. Not one letter answered, not one phone connection made.

And this morning, after they'd pulled out of port, the captain had shared with the crew a recent Harmony paper that the home office had sent up to them.

That's when Sam saw it. Evidence impossible to deny any longer.

Julian Crane and Ivy Winthrop were smiling out at him from the society page. Julian was in a dinner jacket, Ivy in an evening gown, and they'd been snapped, arm in arm, at a local charity fund-raiser.

"When we pull back into Halifax in two weeks, I'm flying home to Harmony."

"Sam, you can't do that."

"Oh, yeah? Just watch me."

"You'll lose everything, son. Didn't you read the contract you signed with Winthrop Marine? I mean, the fine print?"

"What fine print?"

"If you jump ship before we return to Harmony, you forfeit your entire wage."

"But won't the captain make an exception?"

Blackie shook his head. "The captain's under the same Winthrop Marine contract. It's not up to him, Sam."

"Dammit!"

"You'll lose two months of good hard-earned wages, son. At least ten thousand dollars."

Sam rubbed the back of his neck. That money was supposed to be his nest egg for Ivy and him to get married, set up house. He couldn't lose it now!

"Told you already, Sam. Goin' to sea's like goin' to prison—"

"With the chance of drowning besides—I know."

"Just hang in there. A few more weeks, and you'll see her soon enough."

"How do you know this is about *her?* I didn't say that."

Blackie stared at Sam as if he'd just asked how he knew the world was round.

"All right," said Sam with a sigh. "I'll stay. Guess I don't have much of a choice now, do I?"

He'd just have to trust Ivy and pray that when he returned, she would have some reasonable explanation for what felt like the worst stab in the back Sam had been given in his life.

TWENTY-THREE

Courtship

"Miss Ivy, you have confided much to me over the last two years. And now I must confide something in you."

"Certainly, Pilar. You know you can tell me anything."

The spotless Mexican-tiled Winthrop kitchen was drenched with sun this morning. Bustling around the bright yellow space had lifted Ivy's spirits—and after last night, they definitely needed lifting.

The Winthrops' wicker picnic hamper was almost full now. For the last two hours, Ivy had been helping Pilar shop for, wrap, and pack into it some of Julian's favorites—Brie and chilled grapes, lobster salad, country pâté, caviar, crusty warm baguettes, and chocolate-hazelnut *gâteau*.

"Miss Ivy, you know my husband, Martin? He works for Crane Industries, and last month he asked that I talk to you, but I did not think it was right to interfere . . ."

"Interfere? With what?"

Grabbing a chilled bottle of German Riesling from the fridge, Ivy turned to face her young maid.

"With you and Mr. Julian. But now that I see you are becoming more serious with him—"

"Serious with Julian? Oh, no, Pilar. I may see a lot of him now, but he's just a friend. You know I still love Sam," whispered Ivy, though it was hard to say those words after what she'd read about him last night.

"I know you cry about him, Miss Ivy. I know you write to him, but he does not write back. And I know what you told me this morning about the awful things you read about him last night in that terrible report from the Winthrop Marine captain. How it kept you up crying half the night—"

Ivy put up her hand.

"Please, let's not talk about it. I've had my cry and I've already decided to put it out of my mind until Sam comes back. I love him, Pilar. I have to trust there's *some* explanation for what was in that report. I just . . . I just hope he comes back soon."

"As do I, Miss Ivy."

Ivy sighed. "In the meantime, I've decided the best thing I can do is try to keep myself occupied. Keep my mind off all this agonizing about him—"

Glancing up, Ivy noticed the top of a tall triangular sail floating by the kitchen window, a fluttering white wing against summer's cloudless blue.

"Look, Pilar, that sail must be—"

"Ivy!" called the deep voice of Harrison Winthrop from the back. "Julian's here!"

Ivy moved quickly to the open window for a better look at the Crane yacht. She was a gorgeous two-masted schooner, big yet sleek, and Julian guided her expertly in beside the Winthrops' dock.

"Julian's racing in Harmony's regatta in two weeks. Did I tell you he asked me to sail with his crew?"

"No, you did not tell me. But you sound excited, Miss Ivy."

"Yes," said Ivy, turning back from the window with a smile. "I guess I am."

Ivy had to admit she was looking forward to spending the day with Julian on the water. It would be nice to get away, at least for a little while, from her anxieties.

"I'll see you later, Pilar!"

"Miss Ivy!"

"Yes?"

"What I wanted to tell you . . . well . . . seeing you so happy to go out with Julian now . . . I think . . . I think I should say this to you anyway. And just let you be the judge of it."

"Oh, okay. Tell me then," said Ivy, tapping her foot. She wanted to be patient with Pilar, but she didn't have a clue what her maid was trying to say, and Julian was waiting!

"Mr. Julian asked his father to ask my husband to ask me to persuade you that he is the perfect husband for you."

"Pilar!" Ivy laughed. "What in the world does that mean?"

"Miss Ivy, I do not know Julian Crane, and I could never advise you about a man that I do not know—other than to say that I do not approve of such a method of trying to influence another in such an important matter. Do you see what I am trying to say?"

"Yes, Pilar. Of course," Ivy said, humoring the woman. "I've got to go now. I'll see you later, okay?"

Picking up the hamper, Ivy moved quickly out the back door and over the Winthrops' rear grounds. It was only when she saw Julian expertly lasso the Winthrop mooring with a heavy rope from his yacht that Pilar's words really hit her . . .

The perfect husband for you, Ivy repeated to herself as she admired the yacht's gleaming teak deck, bobbing next to the rough wood of her family's simple little dock.

Pilar had not liked the Cranes' "method," as she put it, but Ivy could not help feeling flattered and impressed that Julian would go to such lengths in his courtship of her— imagine, going through her maid's husband to get to her!

Could Julian truly love and want me that much?

Suddenly she saw the envious faces of her Alpha sisters all lined up in a pew, forced to watch Ivy walk down the aisle in bridal white, the star of a spectacular Crane wedding.

Ivy blinked, and the girls' faces vanished.

In their place was a smiling Julian, standing right in front of her.

"You know the Crane remedy for boredom, don't you, Ivy?"

"Let me guess. Shopping?"

"Ah! I see you know my mother very well!"

"Not that well, but I know mine."

Julian laughed. "Well, the Crane way of doing it is not at Saks or Neiman Marcus, I assure you. We go to the source, the top design houses in London and Paris. And when shopping becomes a bore it's partying in Rio at Mardi Gras, tanning on the Crane beach in Bermuda, mingling with the Hollywood stars at Oscar time."

Ivy's eyes widened, and she made a show of glancing at her watch. "Fairy-tale time already, Julian?"

He laughed. "Not a tall tale, I assure you. The Crane life is a good life . . . Now come here. Sit closer to me."

Ivy did. The wind was easy today, and the ocean calm. She watched Julian work the wheel with his strong forearms, the muscles of a serious tennis player.

She remembered how fabulously he'd played in the regional men's singles tournament last month. The title was his again, of course, although he'd very nearly lost it to another competitor.

Ivy vaguely recalled some news about a tragedy the night before. A promising young player had been run off the road, or something like that. What a shame it was for that player, whoever he was, thought Ivy. The papers said that his knee was completely shattered, along with his tennis career.

"Are you okay?" asked Julian.

"Sure," said Ivy, but her smile was halfhearted.

"Let's try that one again—*Are you okay?*"

"Oh, Julian . . ."

For the past few hours, Ivy had been fine. Julian had given her racing lessons and they'd eaten a pleasant lunch, but now Ivy's mind was beginning to swing back to the thoughts she'd been avoiding all day . . . those terrible, awful words in that captain's report that had set her crying into her pillow last night.

One minor crew problem to report . . . Sam Bennett . . . classic "girl in every port" has turned into two and three in any given liberty period . . . almost missed ship twice . . . keep having to pull him from hotel rooms . . . excessive drinking from the start . . . cannot recommend we rehire . . .

Ivy tried to block out the words she'd read. But she couldn't.

She had wanted so badly for her father to see Sam as a great guy, a hard worker, someone who could learn the business and run it for him as a son-in-law . . . but that report had dashed all her hopes.

Why, Sam? Why have you done this?

Despite her vow to put it out of her mind until Sam could return and explain himself in person, Ivy felt tears welling up in her eyes again.

"Oh, no, Ivy," said Julian as she began to sob. "Whatever it is . . . can it really be that bad?"

It *was* that bad. Everything was falling apart with Sam, and she didn't even understand why.

"Shhhh. It's okay. Just put your head on my shoulder," said Julian gently, putting his arm around her and coaxing her to relax into him.

Ivy did.

His body was sturdy and warm, and by now his expensive aftershave had become a familiar scent to her, one she'd automatically begun to associate with security and comfort.

Ivy had to admit, Julian had been true to his word of a month ago. He'd been the perfect gentleman. Never pushing her physically, yet always there for her as a friend.

Sometimes, over the last four weeks, when Ivy had felt bad about missing Sam, Julian would hold her, stroke her hair, tell her how hard relationships could be sometimes.

Julian didn't know Sam's name, of course. Ivy refused to reveal any details. He knew only that there was some man far away whom Ivy longed for terribly.

It was precisely because Julian knew about the existence of her secret boyfriend that Ivy felt comfortable with him. *Funny*, thought Ivy, *but Sam is the very reason I feel closer than ever to Julian*.

"You're a sweet girl, Ivy Winthrop. I don't know why you're so sad today, but it hurts me to see you in so much pain . . . Is there anything . . . anything at all I can do . . ." He put his lips to her ear. ". . . to make you *feel* better?"

Nestled in the warmth of his arm, Ivy sighed and looked up to meet Julian's hazel eyes.

They were dark with desire . . . and for the first time since their date on the Fourth, Ivy let her body respond to it. Her lips parted in invitation and her tongue slipped lightly out, making them moist and ready.

When his hungry mouth descended, she did not protest.

Two weeks later, Ivy found herself on Julian's gorgeous yacht again, but this time she was not alone.

Kenneth Cutter and Stan Sumner, whom Julian said were friends from law school, were assisting Julian with the rigging, the sails, and the maneuvering tactics.

Ivy had never seen such expert sailors!

The blue waves had been rough all day, the wind tempestuous, but the young men were undaunted. With smooth athletic prowess they worked the sails, legs balancing their bodies, biceps and backs cranking the fully loaded winches, arms pulling lines taut to keep them from jamming.

At times during their last hour at sail, Ivy felt in the way of their expert handling of the yacht; clearly, she wasn't needed on board, but just the same, she was thrilled to be here—to see it all firsthand.

"Tack her to port or she'll end up in irons!" cried Julian at the wheel.

"Tally-ho! On your windward side, Julian!" exclaimed Kenneth, working hard at the winch with Stan to adjust the sail's angle.

"Who is it?!"

"Hotchkiss!"

"He's going to take our wind!" warned Stan.

"Dammit!" cursed Julian.

"Don't let him luff us!" advised Kenneth. "Run, Julian! We're almost home!"

The Harmony regatta wasn't a serious race, but most of the competitors certainly treated it that way. There were really no rules. A sailing ship of any shape or size could enter, and every year the race course was changed.

This year, the starting line for the fleet launch was just off Harmony's Lighthouse Point. The ships were to sail to Turtle Island, thirty miles north of Harmony, circle the tiny spot of land, and then head back.

The first vessel to return across the launch line won.

Julian had explained to Ivy that his schooner, while not as fast as John Hotchkiss's sloop, could potentially move faster if handled right. Julian's schooner had more sail, for one thing, and downwind could harness that power to greater effect.

Hotchkiss had gotten hung up with the high chop today. And because Julian's schooner was a larger boat, it heeled over a lot less in the rough waves, allowing his crew an even bigger advantage in working the rigging.

"All in all, I'd say Mother Nature is giving us a hand today!" cried Julian early on in the race.

Now it was neck and neck between Julian and Jon Hotchkiss. Tommy Biddles was a close third, and the rest of the fleet far behind him.

"All right, Ivy!" called Julian. "We're going to run with the wind before Jonny-boy puts his ship between us and the

Julian is only half right, as you might have guessed. He's getting a hand with the weather, but not from Mother Nature. Timmy must confess that some townspeople think of Tabby as full of hot air. In this case they are quite right.

breeze. That would put us dead in irons for sure. Raise the spinnaker like I showed you!"

Ivy quickly ran to the halyard that lifted the spinnaker, and began to pull the line taut. Excitement bubbled through her as she felt the cold spray on her face, then watched the colorful balloon sail billow out.

Don't let it luff! Don't jam it! Do it right, Ivy!

She felt Julian expertly turn the yacht downwind, and Ivy's raised spinnaker was now filling with full-on gusts, the load on the line pulling it as tight as a guitar string.

Instantly she felt the power of the sails propel the ship forward. The strong, stinging salt of the sea breeze tapered off, and the warmth of the sun returned to her cheeks.

Glancing back, she watched the road of ocean widen further and further between their yacht and Jonny Hotchkiss's.

"Julian, we're doing it! We're winning!"

Ivy was so glad to be here for this. No other Alpha had been invited to serve on a crew for the regatta—not even Jonny Hotchkiss would let Rebecca join him!

Pride filled Ivy as she cleated the spinnaker's taut halyard, making sure it was locked into place before she left the position. Her rubber-soled deck shoes squeaked as she raced across the dampened teak boards to stand by Julian's side at the wheel.

A broad grin split his face as he glanced into her eyes. Then together they watched the red buoys that marked the launch line rush closer and closer—until finally they sailed through them.

"We've won! We've won!"

A loud air horn blew, signaling the end of the race, and Ivy was so excited, she threw her arms around Julian.

"Your spinnaker did it for us, darling," he told her, then pulled her to him and fastened his lips to hers.

The moment was incredible.

And so was the kiss!

Maybe it was the joy of experiencing something new and

thrilling. Maybe it was the sun-dappled waves and shouts of the crowd . . . maybe it was simply Julian himself . . . but whatever it was, Ivy felt overcome with emotion.

She couldn't seem to stop her lips from parting, her slender body from moving toward him. He didn't waste a moment. One hand still on the wheel, he used his free arm to drag Ivy's body harder against him.

His lips moved over hers so passionately, so masterfully, that she felt her legs weakening beneath her.

"I love you, Ivy," he whispered against her mouth.

Ivy pulled back, eyes wide. "What!"

"You heard me."

Ivy blinked.

Julian's hazel eyes were fastened to hers. They were bright with excitement, passion—and expectation.

But what is he expecting? What does he want?

"Did you hear me, Ivy?"

Speechless, Ivy nodded.

"Good."

Julian turned the boat and Ken and Stan adjusted the sails again. The yacht slowed considerably, and began to parallel the shore. It would be a few minutes before they reached the moorings by Lighthouse Park.

"I love this woman!" he cried to Ken and Stan at the other end of the boat.

They laughed.

"I love Ivy Winthrop!" he cried to the crowd on the shore.

"Julian! Stop!"

"No! You can't stop love, Ivy. It just happens."

In one fluid motion, he sat down beside the wheel, pulling her into his lap. Before she could take another breath, he used his lips to communicate his feelings another way.

Ivy accepted the second kiss. Felt it spur her passion—

"You care for me, too, Ivy," he growled against her mouth. "I can feel it."

"Julian, I do care, but—"

"Shhh . . . don't say any more. Not with your voice. Use your lips. Your body—"

The distant yips and yells of the crowd skipped over the waves to her cars, spurring her to lock her hands around his neck and lean into his strong body.

He growled softly with the feel of her, used his tongue to pleasure her, and she let him.

It was an incredible ride, and Ivy couldn't seem to stop herself from enjoying it—body and soul.

TWENTY-FOUR

Release

Later that day, up on Raven Hill, Alistair was sitting at his desk in the richly appointed study of the Crane mansion, toying with a letter addressed to his son.

"Eve Johnson," he read on the return address.

Alistair knew very well who Eve Johnson was. Many weeks ago he'd instructed the servants that if she ever called for Julian—*ever*—they were to take a message and give it *only* to Alistair.

He had received a few such messages over the course of the month—all of which he'd torn to pieces. Then, two weeks ago, Miss Johnson had placed an urgent call for Julian from the Boston jail.

Alistair tore up that phone message, too, of course, and hoped that it would be the end of it. And Miss Johnson.

But it obviously wasn't.

This letter had arrived with today's mail.

Walking to the window, Alistair contemplated his son's future. The regatta seemed to seal it today, from what Harrison had told him in a phone call earlier.

Alistair hadn't actually watched the Harmony yacht race. He hadn't in some time—couldn't bear to. Not since he'd seen Rachel tack her little sloop across the finish line well over twenty-five years ago.

God, that girl loved to win. And how I loved her for it!

"Rachel. My Rachel." Just saying her name caused a bittersweet knife to slice through Alistair Crane's heart.

He hated that feeling. It made him feel vulnerable. Weak.

Better not to feel.

Turning from the window, Alistair forced his mind to turn as well, back to the matters at hand . . .

Julian was certainly right about hiring Cutter and Sumner.

Alistair had to admit, today's investment had achieved the desired result—and it had only cost him thirty thousand. Checking his watch, Alistair knew that Kenneth Cutter and Stan Sumner, two of the world's finest yachtsmen, were probably just now reboarding the Crane jet. It would take them back to Australia, where they were training for the next America's Cup.

Julian had certainly benefited from the expert crew. The win put Ivy in his son's arms, and soon they'd be walking down the aisle.

But they weren't there yet.

Striding back to his desk, Alistair picked up the letter from Miss Johnson with one hand and the knife-sharp letter opener with the other.

Alistair had instincts like a shark near a slaughterhouse, and he was certain this letter from Eve Johnson spelled trouble. With one quick slice, he ripped it open. Then he scanned it swiftly and let out a sigh of uncommon distress.

Trouble all right. Trouble in the worst way.

Issuing another distress-filled sigh, Alistair picked up the phone and began to dial. He actually punched in the wrong numbers once before he was able to calm his temper enough to see the phone pad clearly.

After punching the correct number this time, he listened to the tinny ringing on his private investigator's line.

"Wilkes here."

"I need you to verify a touchy situation with a young woman in Boston—one of my son's very, *very* stupid mistakes."

Alistair was almost through with his instructions to Wilkes when he saw his wife in the doorway of his study, wringing her hands.

"Alistair?"

"What is it, Katherine?"

"Police Chief Bennett is waiting in the library."

"What does he want?"

"He says he's investigating that terrible hit-and-run accident last month—the one that involved that young black man . . . you know, the son of your golf caddie?"

"Yes, dear. *What* does he *want?*"

"The young man, T. C. Russell, finally pulled out of his coma this morning. He released a statement to the police about the car that hit him. His description fits *Julian's* car, dear."

"I don't know how to thank you, Crystal. I've never been in this much trouble before. Never . . ."

Eve was so ashamed, she couldn't even look her friend in the face, but Crystal didn't care, she just hugged Eve close.

"No thanks needed, honey," she said softly. "Let's just get you the hell out of here. Scat's got the van running at the curb. C'mon . . ."

Choking back tears, Eve nodded and followed her friend across the grimy green floor of the Boston jail's women's release area.

After her arrest at the party, she'd been forced to spend almost two weeks behind bars. It was so unfair! She hadn't been buying drugs at the time—just trying to sell them *back* to him. She'd stopped using drugs a month ago and had badly needed the money for her prenatal care.

"It was so humiliating, Crystal. They cuffed and booked

me like a common thug. Took my mug shot and fingerprints. Locked me up . . ."

How could I have sunk this far? How?

Eve closed her eyes, but she knew she'd never erase the
images of the dirty jail cell from her mind. The open toilet
in the corner. The hooker in the next bunk muttering ob-
scenities. Shouts and screams and profanity bouncing off
the dingy walls all night long.

"It was a horror show."

Eve shuddered. Her hair was a rat's nest. She was dirty,
hungry, and cold. Touching her gently rounded stomach,
she vowed then and there that she'd do whatever it took to
climb back out of this sewer she'd tumbled into.

Whatever it takes, she pledged to her unborn child, tears
welling in her eyes. *Whatever it takes*.

When she'd been arrested, she had tried to contact Julian for help. But he was traveling in Europe for the summer and the housekeeper at his family's home in Harmony
would do no more than take a message.

Eve then tried her parents. But their answering service
said that Professor Warren and his wife, Tanya, were on a
two-month tour of South America. *"Do call us back in September,"* commanded her mother's no nonsense voice.

It finally hit Eve just how long she'd been avoiding her
parents—not returning calls and ignoring invitations to
come see them.

They were busy people, wrapped up in their own lives
and careers. And they always had been. Obviously, without
any contact from their daughter for months, they had decided to simply return to their own plans with gusto.

Eve had never felt more abandoned, more alone.

Crystal and Scat had been the only ones there to help.
She'd asked them to empty her bank account for bail
money. And when that wasn't enough, Crystal used most of
her own savings, too.

"I have the money to pay you back, Crystal."

"No, you don't, girl, so just don't even worry about it."

"I *do* have the money," said Eve. "Julian gave it to me."

"Oh, he did? Well, okay then . . ." said Crystal.

It's not entirely a lie, thought Eve. The pawn shop downtown would give her at least three thousand dollars for Julian's diamond choker. And there were some gifts he'd shipped over from his European trip. A gorgeous vase from Milan, a gown from Paris—

She'd sell them, too.

What choice did she have? The last time she'd even *seen* Julian was a month ago, when she'd blacked out in his car on their way back to Boston. She'd woken up the next afternoon in the penthouse suite of a hotel room, but Julian had already left.

All she'd found was a note by her pillow inviting her to watch him on some televised tennis tournament that was already finished by the time she got out of bed.

Two days later, he'd called from the airport to tell her that he was heading to Europe for the rest of the summer on family business—

"But don't worry, my pet," he'd told her. "I'll be coming straight to you just as soon as I return."

During that brief good-bye call, Eve had considered telling him about the baby, but he'd sounded like he was in such a rush, trying to catch his plane. And at that time, Eve didn't think she could bear to just blurt it out and risk him never coming back to her.

But she could bear it now, she told herself angrily.

Since he'd left her with no contact address or phone number in Europe, the only thing she could do was try to reach him through his family home in Harmony. But clearly that hadn't worked. The Harmony housekeeper had never heard of her, refused to give her a forwarding number, and the messages she left there went unanswered.

Maybe his family would forward the letter she'd mailed from jail a few days ago. It told Julian everything—from the baby to the arrest to her need for money fast. But she knew she couldn't count on that, either.

It's up to you alone now, Eve. This baby needs you. So you better start counting on yourself.

She decided then and there to start singing seven nights a week at the Blue Note to earn as much as she could. And she would sell off every piece of jewelry she owned to pay for the rent, the food, and the prenatal care.

After climbing into Scat's van and settling into the backseat, Eve fished her hand into the plastic bag of "personals" the prison matron had given back to her when she'd left the jail. She touched the cold hard metal of her twenty-four-karat gold cross and pulled it out.

Grandmother Eve had given her this cross when she'd been baptized. A beautiful diamond sat at the center of it, sparkling like the Christmas star.

Eve had loved this cross all her life. Worn it next to her heart. It had always been a reminder of her late grandmother's fierce belief in her faith. In all things good.

Turning the cross around, she read the tiny inscription: *Virtue is its own reward.*

The tears in Eve's eyes spilled down her cheeks.

She'd just have to sell it, too, that was all there was to it.

Touching the cross to her stomach, she knew she'd sacrifice *anything* now to support and protect her baby.

She'd already given up the drugs, and from this moment on she vowed to give up the alcohol, too. She had tried once already but had weakened and failed, going right back to the bottle in her depressive state over Julian.

Now she was ready, finally, to swallow her pride, to grow up and do what needed to be done—even if it meant releasing her last precious fantasies about Julian Crane—because with or without that man, with or without her parents, she was going to resurrect her grandmother's spirit and do the right thing in her life again.

And I'm going to start by doing right by this child, she vowed as Scat's van pulled away from the prison.

No matter what it takes.

TWENTY-FIVE

Homecoming

By early September in Harmony, the hot nights were bringing out the fairylike flickering of lightning bugs; the town's summer baseball leagues were heading into final playoffs; the local schoolteachers were preparing classrooms for the fall term; and Sam Bennett's boat was at last pulling into Harmony's harbor.

Sam came home to find that life in Harmony was the same as it ever was. But his own personal life had taken a turn for the worst.

His best friend, T. C. Russell, had been in a terrible car accident. At first Sam was angry with his father for not putting that news in any of his many letters.

Chief Bennett had apologized, but said Sam couldn't have done anything for T. C. anyway. "I assure you, son, we're doing all we can for T. C. and his father. I just didn't want your mind to be troubled for weeks at a time out there in the middle of the Atlantic."

Sam understood, but he was still unhappy. After greeting the rest of his family, he tore over to see T. C.

His old friend had checked out of the hospital a week before, but he was still undergoing outpatient therapy—and would be for months to come.

T. C.'s shattered leg was still in very bad shape. But it was his spirit that had taken the harder blow. Bitter anger had enveloped him like a morbid death shroud. And seeing Sam didn't help in the least. He'd been diagnosed as clinically depressed, and was on medication and in the care of a psychiatrist.

Everything T. C. had hoped for in his life—his rise to professional-level tennis, his deliverance of his father from a demoralizing job, his own dreams of glory—all of it had been shattered along with his leg.

And that wasn't all. The health of T. C.'s father had declined badly since the accident, too. He'd had a heart attack watching his son lie in a coma for a month, and his blood pressure now had to be regulated with heavy medication.

After his gloomy visit with T. C., Sam had asked his dad about suspects. "Who did this? Who ran him off the road?"

"I've got nothing on anyone that will stick, Sam. T. C. says that he only got a glimpse of the car that hit him."

"Where did it happen?"

"Coast Road, late at night."

Sam nodded, understanding Chief Bennett's problem. Coast Road skirted a lot of towns along the shoreline. Plenty of expensive hot rods flew back and forth along that scenic route, to and from Boston. Even tourists used the route on their way up to Main or down to New York.

Chances were that T. C. was hit by a complete stranger to their area—not necessarily someone from Harmony. Likely a drunk driver. And without witnesses or any hard evidence, Sam's father had no case.

The news about T. C. wasn't the only thing that hit Sam between the eyes the day he came home.

After seeing T. C., Sam sat down with a cup of coffee in the living room, hoping to distract himself with the day's paper. After nightfall, he planned on going to Harmony Park. He would secretly leave a note for Ivy under their special rock—letting her know that he was finally back and wanted to see her, wanted to put this crazy summer behind them and get on with their future.

Page 12 of the *Harmony Herald* made Sam's trip unnecessary.

It was the society page. Engagement announcements.

The sight of the photo was revolting to Sam—and what shocked him even more was the wedding date they'd set. Early October, just five weeks away.

"What's their hurry?" he wondered aloud, crumpling up the paper as he headed for the door.

Sam's rusted Pinto pulled up in front of the Winthrop home to find the driveway packed with Mercedeses and BMWs.

He stepped to the window and peered in.

Ivy was there. The sight of her beautiful face after so many months away from her sent Sam back a step. Through the disbelief and confusion, he still felt love . . . and desire for her . . .

She sat on a sofa, surrounded by a gaggle of giggling sorority girls. Presents were piled up around her. Streamers and balloons. A cake sat in the corner.

Ivy was in the middle of her wedding shower!

Shaking with rage and the pain of betrayal, Sam wanted nothing more than to burst in and demand an explanation. He strode to the door and knocked, but Harrison Winthrop met him there and pushed him outside.

"I'm here to see Ivy, Mr. Winthrop. I just want a few words with her—"

"I know your voice. You've called the house all summer."

"I'm her friend, and I want to talk to her—"

"I know who you are, Sam."

The words took him off guard. Had Ivy told her father about him after all? Why? After she'd tried so hard to keep their romance a secret from him—had she changed her mind about *that*, too?

"Listen to me, Sam, Ivy is happy. And if you care about

her, then you'll leave here now." Harrison Winthrop pulled Sam back to the front window. "Look. See for yourself. See how happy she is. Do you want to ruin it for her?"

Sam found that he could do little more than gape in shock at the sight of Ivy opening gifts with her girlfriends, looking as happy as she did in her page 12 engagement photo, beside Julian Crane.

Mrs. Winthrop sat down next to Ivy and began to show off the sketch of Ivy's wedding dress. "Isn't it beautiful, girls! It's being especially designed for Ivy by a top Paris house!"

Sam turned away, unable to take anymore.

As she passed by the open front door of the Winthrop home, Pilar Lopez-Fitzgerald noticed Harrison Winthrop stepping back inside, an agitated look on his face.

Curious, the young maid stepped to a small window off the entryway.

Pushing back the curtain, she saw a young man heading toward the street, hanging his head like a little boy who'd lost everything in the world he ever cared about.

The sight stabbed at Pilar's heart.

On a small farm over one hundred miles away, a young woman collapsed as she moved through the family's back-yard flower garden. The girl's twin quickly ran to her side.

"Grace! What's the matter?"

"I don't know," Grace told her sister. "All of a sudden, I felt such terrible pain. In my heart."

"Should I call an ambulance?"

"No. It's not that kind of pain. Just sadness. Terrible sadness."

"Oh. Then it's—"

"Yes, it's coming from . . . somewhere else . . . you know."

Faith nodded, understanding without another spoken word what her twin meant.

TWENTY-SIX

Last Chances

Early that evening, Ivy was in her bedroom. She was looking over the caterer's suggestions for wedding reception appetizers and the floral designer's options for possible bridesmaids' bouquets when she heard a soft knock on her half-open door.

"Did you enjoy the shower, honey?"

"Yes, Mother. It was very nice—"

"Sweetie, is something wrong? You were so quiet at dinner."

"I'm just . . . a little tired, I guess . . ."

Her mother had changed out of her Laura Ashley summer flowers and into comfortable white slacks and a sleeveless white blouse. She'd taken the pins out of her hair, and it hung down around her shoulders. She almost looked like one of the Alpha seniors standing there in her bedroom doorway.

That's when it hit Ivy how much younger her mother had been looking these past few weeks.

It's because she's so happy.

"Honey, I know there's not much time to plan, but I don't want you to worry. Everything will be perfect. You can trust Katherine Crane, too. She and I will see it all runs beautifully for you—"

"I know, Mother. I know you love this."

"I love *you*, honey! And I'm just so happy for you! And so happy to help you plan this event. I mean, marrying a *Crane*. I've dreamed of this for you, Ivy, and now it's coming true. And your father! Oh, my god, Ivy, your father is just in seventh heaven! I haven't seen him happier since you were born!"

Ivy nodded, doing her best to affix a smile to her face. But after four weeks of forcing those muscles to work nonstop—through dinner after dinner, party after party, photo after photo—it felt as though her cheeks had finally been strained to their limit.

Tonight she was all out of smiles.

This crazy whirlwind had all started a month ago—the day of the August regatta. She'd ridden across the finish line with Julian and he'd begun shouting to the world that he loved her.

The thrilling win had made her giddy, and Julian's kisses made her melt. Then the champagne began to flow and she'd consumed quite a lot by sunset when music filled Lighthouse Park.

Couples began to dance barefoot on the manicured lawn. Ivy kicked off her deck shoes and socks and invited Julian to do the same. The fast music slowed, and Julian pulled her close. She let him. Let her body melt against his again.

If Sam can forget me, she repeated to herself firmly, *then why shouldn't I forget him, too?*

After reading that report of his womanizing two weeks before, Ivy had, at first, promised herself to wait for him to come home. She'd even told Pilar she was going to wait.

But in the wee hours of the following morning, she couldn't stick to that resolution. She'd scribbled an impassioned letter, pleading with him to write or call. She'd told him that she'd learned of his awful behavior. The other women. The drinking. And she'd demanded he answer her.

The next morning she'd sent the letter to Halifax.

She'd waited for two weeks, but heard nothing.

Not a word.

His silence was her answer. She'd figured that one out clearly enough. And by the day of the Harmony regatta, she'd been in an emotional, reckless state.

Reckless enough to embrace the folly of a rebound affair.

Julian Crane didn't taste like Sam. Or feel like Sam. But his lips were soft and hungry. His arms were strong, his body warm, and his declarations boldly reassuring.

How could she not respond?

When the park loudspeaker finally announced the regatta trophy presentation, Julian grabbed her hand and pulled her forward through the massing crowd.

"Where are Kenneth and Stan?" asked Ivy, glancing around.

"Oh, they had to get back home. They're married men, you know, can't loiter around a park partying all night!"

Ivy laughed as Julian pulled her to the front.

"It's just you and me to claim the spoils," he whispered. "Can you handle that?"

Ivy nodded, a tingling thrill racing up her spine as the tip of his lips touched the lobe of her ear.

The cup was presented and Julian took the microphone on the small raised stage, thanking everyone for their cheers. Then he turned to Ivy—

"And I have for this little crewmate of mine a very special thank you for her help today."

Ivy was grinning from ear to ear. But her grin faded into a stunned line as she watched Julian pull a small velvet box from his loose khaki pants, then sink to one knee.

The entire crowd hushed as he opened the box. The rock was brilliant, flawless—and huge. At least five carats, floating pristinely in an elegant platinum setting.

"I'm sure all of you here must have heard me declare that I love Ivy Winthrop. But you have yet to hear me invite her to become — *my wife*."

Ivy's jaw slackened as Julian took her limp left hand and slipped the diamond on her finger.

"Julian, I—"

The cheers and applause rushed at her like a tidal wave.

No one had assumed that any woman in her position would ever say anything but yes—

But she hadn't!

"Congratulations!"

The Alphas rushed the stage, then her parents, then Julian's arm was around her and he was kissing her again.

With all the attention and fuss everyone made over the proposal, she didn't have the nerve to take it off. Not then.

She had decided to keep it for the night, but in the morning she would find a way to talk to him privately. She'd tell him that she liked him very much. *Very* much. And maybe their relationship would lead to something like this, but she was far from ready for it now.

But when morning came, her mother and father were totally in marriage mode! Julian was ringing the door chimes first thing in the morning, reinforcing his wish to marry Ivy—the sooner the better.

"I don't know. This is all so sudden—"

"Nonsense!" her father insisted to her privately. "You know Julian is the best catch in New England!"

"Oh, yes, Ivy. Your father is right. Don't be hasty to turn down the best offer of marriage you'll probably ever receive."

"That's right. Better not to alarm Julian," Harrison warned. "You don't want his offer off the table. You want to be the one in control, honey. Don't you? You hold the cards. Just spend some more time with him. Your mind will soon be made up, you'll see—"

Ivy thought that sounded reasonable. But she'd never expected the social blitz that followed the public proposal.

Her nights were a flurry of dinners and parties, balls and social events that her parents or Julian's insisted they attend to meet so-and-so or such-and-such, a member of one prominent family or another.

At one party, the question of setting the date came up and before she knew it, her father and Julian's were announcing the date of their nuptials to the papers.

"A short engagement period is a good idea," her father had told her.

With so little time to pull everything together, Mrs. Crane and Mrs. Winthrop threw themselves into the planning. Events began at breakneck speed. Ivy's days were suddenly jam-packed with fittings and flowers, menus and cakes, special shoes, lace garters, rose petals, soloists and photographers.

But in the midst of all this prepping for pomp, Ivy felt herself having second and third thoughts about her intended groom.

Did she really know Julian well enough?

And how well did *he* really know her?

"Mother?"

"Yes?"

"Don't you think we're rushing things? I mean, I've been thinking that maybe we should have a longer engagement—"

She couldn't bear to use the word *mistake*. She couldn't do that to her mother. But maybe if they postponed the wedding . . .

"Nonsense, dear. The Winthrops and Cranes have known each other for ten years. And you've been spending more time with Julian over these past few weeks than with your own family. You know each other, honey. You're just nervous. And tired."

"Maybe . . ."

"Get a good night's sleep, honey, and in the morning we'll stop by the French bakery before your next fitting—I know how much you love fresh croissants."

"Okay, Mother."

"Good night, dear."

"Good night."

Ivy was about to get ready for bed when she noticed someone just outside her door.

"Pilar? Did you want something? I thought you'd left for the evening."

The young maid began wringing her hands, as if she were unsure of whether she should speak. Finally, she did. "Did you know, Miss Ivy, that Sam Bennett came by the house today?"

"What?!" Ivy pulled Pilar into her room and quickly shut the door. "Did you say *Sam* was here? *My* Sam?"

"Sam Bennett, yes, miss. I saw your father come in. He looked very upset, and when I looked outside, Sam was turning from the front window and walking away. Excuse me for saying so, Miss Ivy, but Mr. Sam looked like he'd just lost everything he cared about in the world."

"Pilar . . . I don't understand this! Why would Sam come here? Why? He abandoned me all summer, took up with other women. I didn't think he cared about me anymore. Why would he just show up at the house like that?"

"I don't know, Miss Ivy . . ."

Was there some explanation for his behavior? Ivy wondered frantically. Some excuse for all the women he'd apparently slept with up in Halifax? For his ignoring her latest letter of all to him, which explained that Julian had proposed and she needed to know how he felt?

Ivy shuddered and had a sudden, terrible feeling that she needed to hear *Sam's* side of things. Her feelings for Sam had not changed—she still loved him. She had just assumed he no longer loved or wanted *her*!

Is there still a chance for me and Sam?

On an impulse of hope that Sam still cared, still wanted her, Ivy slipped from the house.

* * *

Sam's callused fingers grasped the loose rock in the wall of Harmony's park. It was his last hope. The place where he and Ivy always left notes for each other.

With a deep, shaking breath, Sam lifted the rock. But there was nothing beneath it. No explanation for why Ivy had abandoned him.

Nothing but dirt.

Choking back tears, Sam knew at once that there was no point in confronting Ivy. She had never answered his letters; she had accepted Julian. What more did he need to get the message? A brick to his head?

There was nothing to be done now but leave Ivy to the path she'd obviously chosen.

His heart breaking, he shakily scrawled a note and left it, along with a gift he bought Ivy in Halifax. With her new life ahead of her, Sam doubted Ivy would even bother to look under this rock ever again.

But he couldn't keep the gift. His heart was breaking now, and the gift would only remind him of this day's devastating pain.

Ivy rushed to the park, but no one was there.

Her heart sank.

She had been wrong to think Sam cared.

She was tempted to look beneath the rock, but she doubted very much that he had left her a note—even of explanation.

It made no sense for him to have ignored her all summer, then leave a note under their rock.

Slowly she began to walk away—

But a jolt of desperate hope made her turn and run back. She lifted the rock. A small box was sitting there. She opened it to find a beautiful little mermaid on a chain. Inside was a note: "To my sea siren."

Ivy's eyes filled with tears when she saw the words hastily scrawled at the bottom of the note. "Good-bye and good luck."

She could come to only one conclusion ... Sam had come to her house today to officially break up with her. To say farewell for good.

He'd even left her a *wedding* present.

Breaking down completely, Ivy sank to her knees and cried.

TWENTY-SEVEN

The Accident

"My baby's gone . . . Oh, my baby's gone . . ."

Eve loved this number. She sang it every night now at the close of each set. Her pregnancy was showing, and she loved to touch her rounded stomach during the song, show the crowd she was singing to her child.

The audience reaction had always been positive. People were moved by the sight, and she'd never heard warmer applause in her months singing at the Blue Note.

As she finished her early set, the house lights turned up a bit, and she glanced into the crowd to thank them for their show of appreciation. Two people weren't applauding, though. And when she got a closer look at who they were, she nearly had a heart attack.

Warren and Tanya.

Her parents were here!

Their faces were full of emotion—pain, anger, and shock.

Eve had written them a letter the day she'd been released from jail. It explained everything that had happened to her: the drug addiction and arrest, her expulsion from Radcliffe, and her pregnancy by a white man who'd since disappeared from her life. *But she had never sent it!* She simply wasn't ready to face them!

With a shaking hand, she gestured to them, waving them toward the backstage entrance. She just couldn't speak to them in public. She prayed they'd follow her and not cause a scene.

"What are you doing here?" asked Eve as soon as she shut the door to her dressing room, a small cinderblock box with nothing more than a standing clothes rack and a battered old vanity.

"We got an invitation," said her mother stiffly.

Even in her obvious state of shock, Tanya appeared as poised and beautiful as ever, her dark brown hair elegantly swept up into a twist, her makeup subtly applied to her flawless light brown face, her pale blue pantsuit tailored to her slender curves.

By her side, her father looked somewhat more unhinged than her mother. His dark forehead was beaded with sweat, and he reached into the breast pocket of his houndstooth jacket to pull out a handkerchief and wipe it dry.

"What invitation are you talking about?" asked Eve, confused. "Who invited you?"

"Here. Look," said her father, handing her a small white envelope. "It was in our pile of mail when we got back from Brazil last night."

Dear Warren and Tanya,
I cordially invite you both to the Blue Note in Boston to hear its hottest new jazz singer. Her name is Eve . . .

Eve read the strange script, but didn't recognize it. Couldn't imagine who would have written such a thing. She was horrified. ❧

Tabby's handiwork, as you recall.

"Eve, how could you have done this to us?" asked her mother.

"Yes," agreed her father. "I just don't understand all this. We worked so hard to raise you right—"

"All the privileges we've *handed* to you—to allow you to achieve great things. To have a bright future. To live an exemplary life. And *this* is how you put those advantages to use—" agreed her mother. "How could you do this to us? To yourself! Singing in this awful place, and . . . and . . . Eve, *whose* baby are you carrying!"

"I know you're angry," pleaded Eve, "but try to understand I'm on track again. I've made some mistakes. But I'm getting counseling now. I'm going to go back to school. And I'm going to be a good mother to this baby."

"Oh, my god, Warren—"

"Calm down, Tanya, calm down—"

"Eve, *who* is the father of your child?" asked her mother a second time. "Are you married to him?"

Eve slowly shook her head.

"Are you *getting* married—"

Eve looked down. "I don't know. He's been in Europe all summer. When he comes back, we'll figure out what to do."

"Oh, Eve," her mother sighed, "I am so disappointed in you. So disappointed."

"We both are," agreed her father.

"I'm sorry, Mother, Father. I really am. I made a wrong turn, okay, I admit that. But I'm getting back on track like I said. I . . . just . . . I don't know what else to say . . . I'm just so . . . so shocked to see you—"

"*You're* shocked!" exclaimed her mother.

"I mean, I wasn't ready for this! I don't know what to say to you!"

"Say you'll give up the child."

"Give it up?" repeated Eve, incredulous.

"Yes, honey. We can arrange for you to talk to someone at an adoption agency immediately. So many couples want babies, Eve, you know that."

"Mother, that was *never* an option. Once I decided to have it, I promised myself that I would protect it, love it. This little life is a part of me now—"

"Eve, dear," said her father gently, "you don't even *know* if the father is coming back. Now calm down and listen to reason. Your mother and I are prepared to forgive you a lot, but there are some things that we cannot allow."

"Allow?"

"Eve, this is beyond what we were prepared for tonight," admitted her mother. "But still, your father's right. We could never approve of you raising an illegitimate child."

Tears spilling from her eyes, Eve shook her head. "I don't care what you *approve*. What you *allow*. I'm sorry if I've hurt you. Shocked you. But I won't give up my child. I won't."

"Then we have nothing more to say to you," said Tanya stiffly. "When you decide to give the child up, call us."

Eve noticed Tanya giving a meaningful glance to her husband. *The signal.*

Eve instantly saw what her mother was doing. This was exactly how she and her father had treated her as a little girl. They were going to pressure her by withholding their help, support, and even their love until she gave in and did what they wanted.

"Good-bye now," said her father. "We'll be waiting for your call."

"Then you'll be waiting a very long time," she whispered, as they walked out the door. "Because I'm *keeping* my baby."

Like a sleek predator, the black Jaguar pulled out of the Cranes' ten-car garage and prowled down the estate's wood-lined drive. Headlights burned through the night as they reached the bottom of Raven Hill, then turned onto the Coast Road in the direction of Boston.

Behind the wheel, Julian smiled. He hadn't a care in the world.

Ivy had accepted his proposal, set the wedding date, and earlier today had even had a shower thrown for her by all of her little sorority sisters. That shower alone told Julian his mission was accomplished.

Ivy would be publicly mortified if the wedding didn't go off now. And Julian knew, after two months of dating the girl, that her prideful reputation with her sorority sisters was her Achilles' heel.

It's a lock, thought Julian, speeding through the dark twists and turns of Coast Road. *Eve, darling, here I come at last!*

When Julian arrived for the Blue Note's late set, however, his high spirits immediately plummeted.

Eve was on stage. Beautiful and radiant as ever and singing a melancholy blues number—"My baby's gone . . ."

The crowd sat in awed silence, more than one of them obviously choked up by the performance. Behind the microphone, Eve's hands ran over her rounded belly as if she were singing to the baby she was quite obviously carrying.

When she finished, Eve thanked the audience without even looking at them, then stepped from the stage and headed straight for the dressing room.

Stunned, Julian took a back booth and sat there alone, unsure of what to do next, other than order a pitcher of martinis.

An hour later, Eve had not reappeared. He wanted her to, he realized. She was carrying his baby.

And he was terrified.

His first impulse was to do the right thing. It was his mother's voice in him, Julian knew . . .

Just calm down and remember how much you care for her. It will be okay. Once you talk to her, this won't seem so terrifying anymore. Just ask her what she needs from you now . . . how you can help her . . .

Another female performer, a blue-eyed blonde, was up onstage singing. Julian had seen her here at the Note before, knew she was a friend of Eve's, but for the life of him, he couldn't remember her name.

He felt her hard eyes find him halfway through her set. Song after song, she continued to stare at him with an increasingly uncomfortable intensity.

When she finished her final number, she'd barely taken the time to thank her audience before she was barreling toward the back of the room, straight to Julian's booth.

"You got my friend pregnant, you lowlife!" she accused him without preamble. "So just what are you going to do about it?"

Julian was pretty drunk now, and he had never liked this brittle singer much. With her cornering him like this, all he could think to do was raise the standard shield of Crane disdain.

"Back off," he told her. "How do you know it's *mine* anyway?"

For a moment, the rage in the woman's eyes made Julian certain he was about to take a blow to the face. But she didn't hit him. She didn't even say another word, just turned on her heel and stormed away.

What a night, thought Julian, rubbing the cold sweat from his brow.

His desire for Eve was doused with the icy realization that his father was going to murder him for this—but Julian knew there was no one else he could go to for help.

Too chicken now to face Eve, especially with a furious singer friend in her corner backstage, Julian left the club.

Drunk, he slipped behind the wheel of the family's Jaguar.

Relaxing in the Crane mansion's library, Alistair Crane heard the doorbell ring and, soon after, loud voices and scuffling.

When he reached the front door, Alistair found a tall, broad-shouldered police officer escorting his son inside.

"Chief Bennett . . . what brings you to my door at this hour?" Alistair asked with cool calm and a raised eyebrow. "Is *Barnaby Jones* not airing this evening?"

"Your son brings me here, Mr. Crane," replied the chief with a stone-cold gaze.

Clearly drunk, Julian slurred his greeting. "Hel-l-lo, Fa-Fa-Father . . ."

"Pulled him over on the Coast Road. His car was swerving, but he didn't *appear* to run over anyone . . . not *tonight* anyway."

"Is that so?" asked Alistair.

"Yes, that's so," answered Chief Bennett with barely contained fury. "*Tonight* he only managed to get caught driving while intoxicated."

"Well, *bad judgement* does happen on occasion with youth, does it not?" responded Alistair, now staring hard at his son, who had collapsed into an antique chair.

Ben Bennett eyed Julian with barely veiled disgust. This was the first time he'd driven his police cruiser to the mansion since last month, when he'd come here to investigate the Russell accident.

The chief had been frank with Alistair then, explaining that when T. C. Russell woke from his coma, he'd given the police a statement about the car that hit him. He'd called it a "silver bullet."

Silver bullet—fast sportscar.

Chief Bennett well knew that Julian drove a silver Aston Martin DB5. And the reason he knew it was because his Harmony officers routinely issued Julian speeding tickets, many of them on Coast Road.

He also knew that Julian had been scheduled to play T. C. the next afternoon in a bitterly anticipated tennis match. And, to top that off, the day after the accident, Julian was seen driving a black Jaguar. The silver sportscar he'd appeared practically wedded to was never seen again.

"Well, Chief, there's a very good reason for that," Alistair had told Ben last month. "Julian's car was stolen."

Alistair had even escorted the chief out to the estate garage to let him see for himself that there was no longer a silver Aston Martin parked there.

All Ben could turn up was a report filed with the Boston police that Julian Crane had claimed his car had been stolen the same night T. C. was run down. The time of the filing was hours before the accident, so Julian had an iron-clad, police-sanctioned alibi.

Chief Bennett could never say so publicly, but he privately confided to T. C. that he questioned the validity of that Boston police report. The *timing* of it, specifically.

The Cranes had a lot of money, enough to buy off some low-paid paper-pushing cop in the Boston Police Department to doctor a report or create a completely false one out of thin air.

Ben wasn't happy about how the Cranes did business. But then, he never had been. He certainly wasn't proud of what he himself had overlooked over the years for the Crane family.

The road to hell is paved with good intentions, he'd told his wife after T. C.'s accident. I looked the other way for the security of my livelihood, the welfare of my family. But I won't do it this time. Even if it means my career.

His wife had agreed. She'd wholeheartedly supported Ben's trying to find evidence against Julian. But Ben had hit dead ends everywhere he turned.

"Julian Crane is a spoiled, reckless, dangerous brat," Ben had told his wife in frustration one night. "Like his father, he's a man without a conscience, and he likely treated T. C. Russell the same way any predator would an encroaching competitor—he ran him down without a hint of remorse, without even looking back."

Yeah, Ben had wanted to nail Julian. But he couldn't make a case that would stick in court . . .

"It was good of you, Chief Bennett," Alistair now asserted, standing stiffly in his mansion's foyer, "to show Julian the way home."

"I *could* have thrown his ass behind bars tonight, Mr. Crane. He's legally drunk."

"Yes, I can see that, Chief," said Alistair with a sigh, his voice not so full of the Crane pride anymore.

"But I'm betting *you'll* straighten him out better than I could."

"And you'd bet right," assured Alistair.

The men stood silently facing each other for a long moment, then Alistair gave the chief the two words he knew the chief was waiting to hear:

"Thank you."

Chief Bennett nodded. "You're welcome."

When the chief departed and the front door closed, Alistair turned to face his errant firstborn.

"You realize, of course, Julian, that I'll have to up the Harmony Police Department's annual budget for this."

Julian cringed.

"Now, son, let's go into my study and discuss what in the *world* could have led you to become so very reckless this evening."

It took less than twenty minutes for a drunken Julian to pour his heart out to his father. By the end of it, he was a defeated ball of sniveling flesh.

"Seems to me, my dear boy, that you are in a great deal of trouble. I mean, in my experience, desperate women do desperate, even *dangerous* things. This Eve Johnson might do almost anything to you," Alistair theorized to Julian, making him squirm even more, and hoping to heaven this night would put Julian under his thumb for years to come.

"*What*, Father? What do you think she might do?"

"Oh, well . . . blackmail, lawsuit, who knows, maybe even hire some nightclub johnnies to perform a strategic act of—well, *violence*—"

Julian gasped.

"We'll have to buy her off, of course," continued Alistair, trying to keep a straight face. "I'll put my private detective on it. Just *stay away* from her, Julian. That's your only hope."

Scared witless by his brush with death as much as by his tyrannical father's terrifying theories, Julian was all too ready to agree.

After Julian departed, Alistair picked up the phone and dialed a familiar number.

"Wilkes, Julian *finally* knows. Good god, it took long enough. I swear, I don't know how I raised such a fool for a son! I can see I have *much* more work to do on him . . .

"In any event, it's time our little problem was taken care of right away. Offer Miss Johnson the bribe, I'm sure she'll take it now that you've told me her parents are out of touch, and I'll need you to arrange something else—a disposal . . . As we discussed, it's not going to be pretty, so get me someone with a spine. . . .

"Watch the girl closely, and remember, when the time comes, she should never once doubt that her baby simply expired of natural causes . . . Given her intake of drugs and alcohol during the beginning of her pregnancy, that's not a stretch . . ."

Hanging up the phone, Alistair sighed. Odds were that his heartless plan wouldn't have to be implemented. Even under the best of circumstances, he doubted Eve Johnson's little bastard would live long enough on its own to take a breath in this world.

TWENTY-EIGHT

The Wedding

Ivy's wedding day dawned bright and clear, with the sort of jewel-toned October sky that's bluer than any other. Everyone remarked on their luck with the weather, but as the day progressed, gray clouds began to gather above the Winthrop house, threatening a storm.

Ivy's father chuckled when he saw the changing sky. He would have thought the Cranes were rich and powerful enough to scare off even the clouds. Maybe they would, too, he mused. But just in case, he personally delivered his giant golf umbrella to the trunk of the stretch limousine waiting to take Ivy and him to Harmony's white-steepled church.

Harrison then climbed the staircase to find his lovely daughter sitting on the same quilt that had covered her bed since she was a little girl, her white bridal skirt spread out around her like a cloud beneath an angel.

Most of her personal items had already been packed up and transported to the Crane mansion, where she'd be living from now on. Yet, despite being dressed for the occasion of her marriage, Ivy appeared far from ready to go.

She was simply sitting there on her bed, gazing longingly

at the inside of a small antique locket, which hung around her neck.

The Crane pearls, priceless family heirlooms that Katherine Crane had sent over this morning, were still sitting untouched on Ivy's dressing table. And her elaborate, cathedral-length veil was still hanging from a hook on the back of the bedroom door.

Harrison Winthrop approached his daughter quietly, his fists clenched. He knew very well whose photo was inside that locket. And he couldn't even guess how many times Ivy had gazed at it when she thought he wasn't looking.

What in heaven's name had this Sam done to gain such a hold on his daughter! thought Harrison. *Even now, on her wedding day!*

Hearing her father approach, Ivy glanced up and quickly snapped shut the locket shut, her face blushing pink at being caught in her daydreams.

"It's natural to be nervous, Ivy," said Harrison after he'd taken a few deep breaths to calm his upset. "And when we're nervous about the future, we often long for the past."

"I know, Father."

Harrison sat down next to Ivy and took her hand. "Julian loves you, honey."

"Yes . . . he's told me often."

"So why don't you take that locket off now. It's time."

Ivy nodded as her father moved to pick up the Crane pearls.

"Come let me fasten these on you."

Sadly, Ivy unclasped the locket, pulled it from her neck, and placed it in the top drawer of her bureau . . . along with the rest of her childhood memories.

Then she shut it.

For the sake of her own happiness, Harrison hoped it was for good.

* * *

Sam wore his best—and only—blue suit. A blue-and-gray-striped tie. He'd shaved so close this morning that he'd nearly cut his throat.

Then again, seeing as he knew what day it was, maybe he'd wanted to.

The Crane and Winthrop families had invited every "important" family in the region, and Harmony's church was completely packed. Sam Bennett, of course, had not been invited. But he had shown up just the same.

It was easy for him to sneak inside. The church's side door had a busted lock the pastor preferred to keep that way. Sam had known that from his years delivering pizza to the reverend's Wednesday-night poker game in the church basement.

Slipping into the end of a crowded pew on the groom's side, he inhaled and exhaled deeply, trying to dispel his nervousness.

When the strings and harp began to play, Sam rose with the rest of the congregation. He watched bridesmaid after bridesmaid traipse down the aisle—a parade of pale violet. Then, finally, came Ivy.

Her dress was a fairy queen cloud of white ruffled satin and intricate designs, with pearls and tiny diamonds stitched to fine white netting that wrapped her shoulders. A pearl-encrusted headpiece graced her golden hair, and a long veil spread out around her like the half-closed wings of a perched dove.

Sam gripped the back of the pew in front of him. Gripped it so hard his knuckles went pale.

"If any man knows a reason why these two should not be joined, let him speak now or forever hold his peace . . ."

Sam bit the inside of his cheek. He wanted to cry out. Was ready to . . . but then he closed his eyes and saw her again—the vision he'd dreamed so many times before . . . Ivy gliding down that aisle . . . so beautiful . . . so resigned.

This is what she wants, Sam reminded himself. *It's what she's chosen.*

"The union of husband and wife in heart, body, and mind is intended by God for their mutual joy . . ."

Sam was aware of the minister's voice, quoting from the Book of Common Prayer, aware that the ceremony was continuing forward, but for the next half hour all sound became a muddled backdrop to the vision of Ivy before him now. The vision of innocence in white.

And then came her voice . . .

"I, Ivy, take you, Julian, to be my husband, to have and to hold from this day forward, for better, for worse, for richer, for poorer, in sickness and in health, to love and to cherish, until we are parted by death. This is my solemn vow."

Sam closed his eyes. If there was a pain worse than this, he'd never felt it.

He had thought it would be okay, coming to see this. Thought he'd needed it for closure—to get it out of his system forever so he would never think about her again.

But he was wrong.

He shouldn't have come.

He wanted to stand up, slip out out the side door again, but he couldn't. He was too devastated, and his body felt paralyzed. He sat there through the exchange of rings and some music. Then finally came the minister's affirmation:

"I now pronounce you man and wife. Those whom God has joined together, let no man put asunder."

I've got to get out now, Sam realized. *For my own sanity*.

He rose to his feet just as the couple turned to face the packed wooden pews. For a moment, Sam was the only one standing. He saw Ivy's head turn toward him, and his heart stopped—

Her blue eyes locked with his.

Sam is here.

Ivy was stunned, unable to think. Unwilling to breathe.

She read his big blue eyes. Saw the emotion there—longing. Confusion. Pain.

My God. Why did he come?!

But the question no sooner flashed through her mind than he'd answered it—

"Be happy, Ivy."

She saw him mouth the words, then the Cranes' guests rose around him, swallowing him up.

Ivy felt her new husband by her side. He was taking her limp arm, wrapping it around his own, coaxing her to step down with him from the altar.

"Ivy? Are you all right?"

She could hear Julian's whispering voice, but she couldn't answer.

Sam is here . . . Sam came . . .

Her maid of honor was pressing the weight of her elaborate cascade bouquet back into her small hands.

Faces were smiling and laughing. Hands were clapping. Applause thundered through the church, greeting the minister's presentation of Mr. and Mrs. Julian Crane—

Then Ivy felt herself being propelled forward, past rows and rows of people—her sorority sisters, his law school buddies, the country club gang, her family's political acquaintances, his family's business associates—

Sam . . . Sam . . . you came to the church? Why?

With all her heart, she wanted to turn back—

But the crowd was too thick.

And no matter how hard she tried, they wouldn't let her find him again . . .

The guest list for the Winthrop—Crane wedding was an exclusive roll call of prominent personages. Captains of industry, important government officials, and old-money families.

Among the very few locals who were invited was, of

course, Tabitha Lenox, Harmony's quintessential queen of clairvoyance.

Mrs. Crane felt compelled to invite her after receiving the wedding gift she'd sent over to the "happy couple"—a priceless antique mirror and frame. The piece was quite something. An appraiser called it "museum quality," and Katherine felt that the woman from town who'd sent it, although the Cranes really didn't know her that well, should absolutely be invited to the wedding and reception.

When the ceremony was over, Tabitha drifted to the back of the church with the other well-dressed guests. As she glided through the receiving line, Katherine Crane grasped her hand with a genteel squeeze.

"I must thank you, miss, for the beautiful mirror and frame."

"Oh, you're quite welcome!" replied Tabby. "You know, I've been looking into that old thing for so *very* long now, I wouldn't be surprised if Julian and Ivy peered into it one day and saw *my* face looking right back out at them!"

Mrs. Crane chuckled, but it was a strained sort of laugh, as if she'd clearly sensed that there was something truly odd about this woman!

After Tabitha had finally "hello-ed" and "you-must-be-so-happy-ed" her way through the exceedingly large wedding party line, she found herself standing on the church's front lawn.

There she was delighted to spot a little golden-haired

Timmy assures you, dear reader, Tabby really had to work some magic to get on the A list of this exclusive party!

"Truly old" . . . now that's an understatement! Actually, Tabby first enchanted that particular antique mirror for Rasputin—one of her many erstwhile suitors. Apparently he used it to spy on the Russian imperial family!

flower girl, spinning in circles on the grass, dancing to music only she could hear.

Across the church yard, a little black-haired boy seemed entranced as he gazed at the girl, who had been dressed in violet ruffles to match the bridesmaids.

Tabitha laughed when Pilar Lopez-Fitzgerald was forced to take the little boy by the hand and pull him, kicking and screaming, toward the parked cars.

"That's all right, little Luis," whispered Tabby. "You've seen her before, and you'll see her again, I guarantee it."

TWENTY-NINE

The Wedding Night

"Your bath is ready, Miss Ivy—Oh! I mean, Mrs. Crane!"

On impulse, as Ivy moved from her spacious new marital bedroom suite to the adjoining marble bath, she hugged her young maid.

She had just helped her climb out of the heavy, intricately designed wedding gown—a feat that required so much balance and bending that it should have earned at least one of them a spot on the U.S. gymnastics team.

"Thank you for all your help today, Pilar."

"Oh, Mrs. Crane, it was my pleasure."

Ivy was so very pleased that Pilar had agreed to leave the Winthrop housekeeping position and take up this new position in the Crane household as her personal maid.

Harrison and Helen had hated to lose Pilar, but they wholeheartedly agreed with the change. A trusted companion would be invaluable to Ivy who would now have to cope with many new social pressures as a young Crane wife.

And Katherine and Alistair Crane were pleased, too. In fact, as a wedding offering to their new daughter-in-law, they had granted Pilar, her husband, Martin, and their two children, Antonio and Luis, free use of the beautiful guest cottage that sat on the rear grounds of the vast Crane estate.

Pilar and her husband were overjoyed. They had been renting the cramped attic of an old, drafty Victorian, but now they could have their very own place, rent-free!

"Are you and your husband all moved in now?" asked Ivy.

"Oh, yes, Mrs. Crane. We are so very pleased with the cottage! It is quite beautiful. And the grounds are immaculately kept."

"Yes," agreed Ivy. "This whole estate is really something."

"I misjudged the Cranes, I must admit now. I was always a little suspicious of them. Of their motives. But I was wrong. I did not know they could be so generous!"

"Yes, they are generous, aren't they?"

"Oh, yes, Mrs. Crane. It looks to me that you will be very happy here with your new family. And you were such a beautiful bride. It was a perfect day."

"A perfect day . . ." repeated Ivy absently.

"Well, you will be wanting to take your bath now. May I help you with anything else tonight?"

"Oh, no, thank you, Pilar. That's all for tonight."

"Good night, Mrs. Crane."

Ivy hugged Pilar again before Pilar left her alone in the luxurious bathroom. Slipping out of her white satin robe, she padded across the Siena marble floor, then eased into the warm, jasmine-scented bubbles. She admired the Tiffany glass bricks lining the walls with rainbows of color, the alabaster side table holding a hand-blown Venetian vase overflowing with fresh hyacinths.

A perfect day . . .

Ivy sighed. Of all the events in her life, she'd expected her wedding day to be the happiest, the richest of all the days that came before. A culmination of everything she had ever wanted.

But at this moment, she knew it wasn't true.

Deep in her heart, a voice whispered that this whole affair was a scam, an exhausting exercise, a theatrical performance for family and friends in which she and Julian were simply the stars.

She closed her eyes, telling herself these awful thoughts sprang from her nerves alone. After all, this was the first quiet moment she'd had to herself in weeks.

The whirlwind of parties and planning, fittings and shopping, dinners and rehearsals—it had gone on and on, nonstop, building to a fever pitch, and now, abruptly . . . it was over.

Somewhere, in the middle of it all, Ivy had realized that the "spectacular" wedding she'd always *thought* she had wanted—the "event" she'd dreamed about since she'd been a little girl—was no longer the wedding of her heart.

In the middle of one particularly long, uncomfortable fitting, she began to fantasize about a small, quiet, romantic ceremony by the ocean. A gauzy white tent at sunset. Lanterns and candles and stars creating the only light. A simple but elegant tea-length lace gown. Champagne, chocolate-covered strawberries, a small white cake, and a bouquet of wildflowers collected from Harmony's hillsides.

But the beautiful day she'd conjured in her mind *wasn't* a Crane wedding, she realized almost upon imagining it.

It was the wedding day she would have had with Sam Bennett.

Why did he come to the church?

Ivy couldn't get the look in his eyes out of her mind. It was a look that said he still cared. That he still loved her. That he was heartbroken—

But it makes no sense. No sense at all.

He'd ignored her all summer, philandered and caroused with other women in Halifax. She'd even written to tell him of her engagement to Julian, begged him for a response, but he'd ignored that, too!

And then here was the unkindest cut of all—the cowardly way he'd chosen to break off their relationship. With nothing more than a *Good-bye and good luck* hastily scrawled on a note left under their rock.

Still, after all the tears and pain Sam had caused her, Ivy

couldn't help remembering those moments of absolutely perfect romance she'd shared with him.

"You know, Ivy, fantasy and reality are two very different things," her father had told her one evening when she finally got the courage to raise her doubts about marrying Julian. *"And the reality is, you'll never find a better offer of marriage."*

Ivy knew her father was right.

She wanted marriage and children. And she saw no point in wasting her life, pining for a lost love until some *less* worthy man than Julian Crane finally proposed marriage.

Julian was handsome, kind, thoughtful, caring—but, most of all, he loved her.

The money didn't hurt, of course, and neither did the society spotlight. Julian's five-carat rock on her finger had at once elevated her, not only among her sorority sisters, but also in every social circle in New England.

She and Julian were the darlings of this year's regatta, and practically every charity ball and fund-raiser they'd attended since as a couple.

But it was the fact that he *loved* her so much that got her down that aisle today. Ivy did care for Julian. She couldn't deny that the man knew how to kiss—and she was sure he'd be wonderful when they climbed into bed together in an hour.

It was just that her own heart still belonged to Sam.

Ivy's mother had counseled her to be patient, share her life with Julian, and she'd see her love for him grow. She'd agreed. Betting on the strength of Julian's love to see them both through.

So that was that.

Gone forever was the small, simple sunset wedding . . .

The Winthrops and Cranes had scores of guests who simply *had* to be invited, of course. The final count was close to five hundred for the ceremony at the church and fifteen hundred at the packed reception and formal dinner.

Ivy couldn't deny that she'd had some very happy mo-

ments today, watching her family and friends laugh and
dance. She'd never forget the joy on her parents faces as
they tenderly swayed together in the romantic candlelight
of the country club's ballroom.

Julian had been a thoughtful bridegroom, too. Sweet
and tender and teasing when they fed each other pieces of
the chocolate-fudge-and-hazelnut-filled wedding cake.

That picture of Julian, tender and teasing and kind, gave
Ivy the courage finally to rise from her jasmine bath — and
put Sam's inexplicable presence at her wedding out of her
mind for good.

Grabbing a big, fluffy towel from the electric warming
rod, she wrapped its luxury around her like the softest
sable.

All things considered, she smiled to herself, *I could get
used to life as a Crane.*

On her marriage bed, Ivy found a gorgeous white negligee,
dripping with lace, which Pilar had laid out. The filmy
nightgown and matching robe had been designed, at
Katherine Crane's insistence, by Pierre Balmain himself, an
exclusive designer whose quietly luxurious creations were
handmade for the aristocrats of world society.

"Do look him up, Ivy," Mrs. Crane urged her a few minutes later when they passed each other in the long hallway
of the mansion. "When you and Julian arrive in Paris next
week, make sure you introduce yourself as my daughter-in-
law, and I promise he'll treat you like royalty."

"Yes, Mrs. Crane, thank you."

"You're welcome, dear." Katherine Crane smiled. Then
her eyes filled with tears, and suddenly she hugged Ivy
close. "I'm so happy to have you as my second daughter,
Ivy. Welcome to the family."

"Thank you," whispered Ivy, touched by Katherine's
warmth and generosity.

"Good night now. Pleasant dreams," said Katherine softly, then turned to head down the long hallway.

Ivy had begun to head for the staircase when she heard Katherine call out to her. "Ivy? Where are you going?"

"Oh . . . uh . . . I thought I'd look for Julian."

Katherine's smile suddenly disappeared, and her brow creased with anxiety. "He's having a *private* word with his father, dear. I wouldn't disturb them just now. Wait in your suite. He'll be along."

"But—"

"Listen to me, dear. I know the Crane men. Better than you. And you don't want to go disturbing them when they're talking privately. Just wait in the suite."

"Yes, of course, Mrs. Crane," she said, but she had no sooner closed the bedroom door before she'd cracked it open again.

Once Ivy was assured her mother-in-law had gone to bed, she snuck back out.

Heavens! declared Ivy to herself, almost laughing out loud. She had never heard of such a thing! Not "disturbing" men when they discussed things "privately." *Please!* Ivy had a good head on her shoulders and had often been present when her father discussed business or politics.

Her new mother-in-law would just have to understand that this was a new generation of Crane women. Ready to hear anything men had on their minds!

Besides, Ivy was simply dying to explore her new home. And searching for Julian, no matter what her mother-in-law advised, was as good an excuse as any.

The Crane mansion was a huge affair, easily three times the size of her father's old colonial. With the place so quiet and dark, Ivy knew it was the perfect time to give herself a private little tour.

In her soft silk slippers and flowing white negligee, she floated like a ghost through the long hallways, admiring the precious original paintings and sculptures, the hand-

loomed rugs, the imported French moldings, and the priceless antique furnishings, polished to a mirrorlike shine.

This tour was such fun, she actually began to believe her
father's whispered words before walking her down the aisle
today . . . *How lucky you are, Ivy, to be marrying Julian
Crane.*

Moving down the staircase, Ivy heard the faint sound of
clinking glasses and male voices in the drawing room. *This
must be that "private" conversation Katherine didn't want
me to hear.*

With the thrill of mischievous anticipation, Ivy tiptoed
toward the arched entryway, careful to remain hidden as
she cocked an ear.

If there was one thing Ivy loved to do, it was eavesdrop!

"It's a great day, Julian."

"Yes, Father."

"Cheers, son."

Alistair handed Julian a heavy crystal snifter with two fingers of the finest cognac in the Cranes' stock. Then he sat
back in his favorite leather chair and lit up a cigar.

"It's an excellent match," praised Alistair. "Ivy's the perfect ornament."

"Yes, she is pretty, isn't she."

"Downright handsome. You hit the jackpot there, son."

"Physically, of course, she's quite distracting. Unfortunately, Father, she's—"

"What she is, Julian, is your *wife.*"

"But you do *know* she lacks passion, unlike Clarissa
Morton."

"Who's that?"

"The raven-haired bridesmaid. Exotic-looking. One of
Ivy's sorority sisters. Did you see how she danced with me at
the reception? Now *that* woman is pure electricity—"

"Forget about Clarissa Morton, Julian. And anyone
else—at least for the time being. Give it a year, son, then
you can take on a mistress with my blessing, as long as you

do it as we discussed—*discreetly*. Despite their wealth, the Winthrops appear to have raised Ivy on middle-class morals, and you know how those people think."

"Yes, I see what you mean."

"You know our plans. With your marriage to Ivy, Harrison has signed over control of Winthrop Marine to Crane Industries."

"Harrison really managed to make a mess of his family's company, didn't he, Father? It's no wonder he went into politics."

"Right you are, son! But not to worry. And as we've discussed, the debts are massive, but the fleet is sound. And with the Asian shipping deals coming together, we'll turn her from red to black in a year."

"That soon?"

"Yes, so listen closely, Julian. There's more work for you to do. I want you and Ivy to concentrate on becoming the glamour couple of the year—on charming all those Wall Street high rollers. If we play our cards right, Crane Industries will go public."

"Yes, Father. I see your strategy. Don't worry, you can count on me."

"Good. You may not love her, but you could do a whole lot worse than the governor's daughter. And from the looks of her, she'll be a hell of a good roll in the hay tonight."

"Yes, I *am* looking forward to that."

"The Crane family will need heirs, don't forget that, either. It's one of the things that keeps a family-run company appearing strong to outside investors."

"Oh, believe me, Father, I'm more than willing to do my duty—which is more than I can say for our little Ice Princess Ivy. But never fear, I'll warm her up soon enough."

"You do that, son . . ."

"Ice Princess Ivy . . ."

In the hallway, Ivy put a hand to her head, then her stomach. She was going to be physically ill.

Julian doesn't love me. Julian never loved me. Our marriage is nothing but a business deal . . .

Backing away, Ivy didn't know what to do, where to go. The front door seemed the nearest escape.

So she took it.

THIRTY

Sam and Ivy

The rustic one-room cabin was a forty-minute drive into the mountains west of Harmony. It was little more than hand-cut logs and a stone fireplace, but Sam's father had built it himself before Sam was even born.

"Are you cold?" asked Sam.

"Not at all."

Ivy answered politely, but Sam could see that she was obviously freezing. Since they'd entered the cabin a few minutes ago, her hands had remained jammed into the pockets of his Castleton College football jacket. He had draped it over her slender shoulders as soon as he'd found her near their wall in Harmony's public park.

Ivy had called him in tears from a pay phone. *"I'm s-so sorry, S-Sam, to b-bother you . . . but I didn't know wh-who else to c-call . . ."*

Sam hadn't asked her one question. Just hearing her voice had been enough to send him rushing out into the night.

He'd swung his rusting Pinto down the park road and pulled in behind the polished bumper of one of the Crane Jaguars. Ivy was slumped inside it, pale and shivering, as if some ruthless animal had swallowed her whole. And it had, Sam realized. The Cranes had chewed her up and spit her out.

She'd told Sam everything on their hour-long drive to the fishing cabin. How her family and friends had swept her up in a whirlwind of wedding plans. How the pressure from her parents had confused her, made it impossible to sort out her true feelings from theirs. How she'd trusted Julian, believed him when he'd said he loved her. And, finally, how she'd overheard the ugly truth from Julian and Alistair this very night—that their union was nothing more than a business deal, a merger.

Sam wanted to ask Ivy how *he* fit into all of this. Sure, he understood her disappointment in marrying Julian. But why, after she'd so firmly rejected him this past summer, had she called him, of all people, for help? But deep down, Sam knew the reason . . .

Ivy just needed another rescue.

Good old Sam the lifeguard, right?

Could she possibly still love him? Still care for him? Sam didn't dare ask her, because if she said no, it would destroy him for sure . . .

Outside, the October wind was picking up. The storm that had been threatening all day moved in on them, sprinkling light drizzle against the windowpanes. The tinkling noise alone made Sam shiver. Or maybe it was the way Ivy looked in the moonlight, so vulnerable and beautiful, still dressed in her wedding-night negligee—except, of course, for his giant wool football jacket still hugging her shoulders.

Sam stepped around the soft fur rug and dropped to one jean-covered knee in front of the fireplace. He crumbled the newspapers he'd brought in from the car and stuffed them beneath the logs for kindling. Then he lit the paper and brought his strong frame back to its full height. Stepping back, he watched the flames leap up and lick the stack of wood he'd split himself not long ago.

As the kindling caught fire, a warm glow enveloped the

small room. Sam turned to face Ivy, and his breath lapsed for a moment at the sight of her in the flickering firelight.

She had shrugged off his jacket and was throwing it over the back of the old couch. As she moved, her long mane of hair seemed to dance with the flames, each strand a silken ray of light.

When she turned toward him again, her porcelain skin, so pale from the cold, began to flush a gorgeous rose in the growing heat. Sam smiled at Ivy and tenderly touched the blossom on her cheek. Then he gestured to the four walls surrounding them—the convertible plaid sofa, the table and chairs in the corner, the various plaques of mounted fish.

"Some wedding night suite, huh?"

Sam's voice was low and teasing when he asked the question, but inside he was a bundle of nerves.

"Oh, Sam, it's perfect."

Despite her sweet reply, Sam exhaled in frustration and ran a strong hand through his chestnut-brown hair. It was thick and long now, the way Ivy liked it, hanging below the collar of his blue flannel shirt.

"You're *crazy*, Ivy," said Sam with a sigh. "It's not perfect at all. It's nothing but a barren little box. You deserve better. You always have—"

Ivy swiftly put her cold, slender fingers over Sam's mouth. "Shhh . . ." Facing him, she dropped her hands to his broad shoulders. "I'm here with you," whispered Ivy. "That's all I care about."

Ivy's hands remained on his shoulders. Her body wasn't touching his, but it was so close that the familiar scent of jasmine tickled his nose. His gaze dropped to her beautifully shaped lips, and he suddenly wished he and Ivy were on their beach again and those lips were once more moving over his body.

Don't go there, Bennett, he warned himself quickly. *Ivy just needs a friend tonight. A friend. That's all . . .*

He forced himself to take in her red-rimmed eyes, her tear-stained cheeks. Forced himself to remember how hurt she was tonight, how vulnerable. *Just comfort her. Make her understand that she's not alone . . . that you're still here for her . . .*

His callused fingers reached out to caress her hair. And her eyes filled with tears again.

"Ivy . . . what can I do?"

"Just hold me," she whispered. "Hold me tight."

"Okay."

Sam pulled her close, into the warmth and softness of his blue flannel. And she began to cry all over again.

"Oh, honey, please don't . . . I can't take it . . ."

He guided her gently backward, into the plaid sofa, and she immediately snuggled into him. Her arms reached up to encircle his neck; her soft breasts, naked beneath the filmy negligee, crushed against his hard chest.

When her lips found his neck, he wanted to bury himself inside her, feel her softness enfold him again. But he couldn't. Despite his desire, she was a married woman now—Mrs. Julian Crane.

A friend, Bennett. Be a friend.

Reluctantly, Sam pulled at Ivy's tightly locked arms, coaxing her to separate. She was gazing at him now with such longing, such affection . . . it clawed at his heart.

"Sam, I know how you feel about me . . . and that you want to be with other women. It's just that I need to be close to you tonight—"

"Other women? What are you—"

"I know you never expected my call. That you broke it off with me—"

"Ivy!" Sam gently shook her shoulders.

Ivy blinked. "Yes?"

"*What* other women are you talking about? And what do you mean, that I broke it off with you?"

"The other women. In the report. From *Yankee Hope*'s captain. My father gets reports on all his ships, Sam, and your captain wrote that you were sleeping with different women on every liberty call—"

"What! That's crazy! I never knew anything about a report like that! And if that's what it said, it's a *lie*. A total and complete lie!"

"It also said you were drinking heavily from the start of the trip—"

"That's another lie. I was one of the two soberest men on that trawler all summer—and Blackie Coombs will attest to it."

"Blackie who?"

"The *other* sober crew member. I'm telling you, Ivy, that report was falsified. It's a lie. And every crewmate will back me up on that. I *never* slept with other women, and I *never* wanted to break things off with you. What gave you that idea? *You* were the one who refused to answer any of my letters. And you were never around when I called your house—"

"You wrote letters? Like you promised?"

"At least fifty."

"What! Sam, I never received even one! And when did you call my house?"

"All summer. Your father always answered. And he always said the same thing—that you were out with a 'young man.'"

"My father? Oh, Sam . . . *My father* . . ."

"What?"

"He put a lock on our mailbox at the beginning of the summer. He said it was because he was expecting so many important financial documents to be sent to him at home. He was the only one with the key. The only one who brought in the mail every day. Oh, Sam . . . do you think my father destroyed your letters?"

"Who else?"

"But you must have gotten mine."

"Your what?"

"My letters, Sam! I wrote you at least thirty!"

"No, Ivy. Not one." Sam shook his head in shock. "I can't believe it . . ."

"What?"

"The captain. All mail to the *Yankee Hope*'s crew members was distributed through our captain—"

"The same captain who wrote that false report about you—"

"Yeah. The same one your *father* employs."

Sam watched Ivy's face crumple, her head fall into her hands. "How could he have done this to me? How . . ."

"How and *why*."

"I think I know the *why*. Julian and Alistair were discussing it tonight. They wanted a painless merger with my father's company. My father wanted it, too. My marrying Julian became the answer."

"So they manipulated you into the wedding—into thinking I no longer wanted you. Oh, Ivy . . ."

"But what about your *Good-bye and good luck* note, Sam?" asked Ivy, lifting her eyes to meet his. "Did you mean it?"

"You *saw* that?"

"Yes, of course—"

"Ivy, I thought you were through with me. I never thought you'd look under our rock again."

"You mean, the little mermaid necklace wasn't a wedding present?"

Sam gazed at Ivy's expectant face. Shaking his head, he cupped her soft cheek with his rough hand. "Sweet Ivy . . ."

"Sam?"

"I had planned to give you that necklace on our beach. Not with that note, but with a shanty Blackie taught me when he heard me call you my sea siren."

"A shanty?"

"An old sailor's song."

Ivy searched his face, waiting.

"She sings the ocean's song . . . My ears forever hear

her . . . A sad, strange sound she brings . . . To roving sailors near her . . . Sing out, sing out, my siren . . . Be not afraid at dawn . . . For where my ship sails onward . . . You're in my heart along."

"In your heart?"

"Always, Ivy."

"Then you still . . . you still *love* me?"

Sam closed his eyes. "I never stopped. I've loved you since the day I pulled you from the water."

"Oh, Sam." Ivy wrapped her arms around his neck. "I still love you, too."

Sam couldn't believe what he was hearing. "Am I dreaming this?"

"It's no dream. And if you still want me, I'll get my marriage to Julian annulled right away."

Sam's hand tangled in her golden hair and he pulled her lips to his in a long, tender kiss. Then he sat back and looked into her blue eyes.

"Marry me, Ivy?"

"On our beach," she whispered, tears streaming down her face as she began to kiss Sam's cheeks, his nose, his chin. "At sunset, with candlelight, and strawberries, and wildflowers—"

"Anything, my love, anything you want—"

Ivy pulled away and stood up. "I want you, Sam Bennett. I just want you."

Stepping back from him, she removed the lacy white robe of her negligee. Beneath it was a sight he would never forget.

"Oh, Ivy . . ."

Sam's body tightened at the vision of her ripe curves, draped with the sheerest mist of delicate lace. She stepped closer and lifted the lace.

"Touch me," she whispered.

Sam did. His hands started at the jasmine-scented skin behind her knees and moved up her silky legs. When he felt the delicate edge of her panties, he tugged on the strip of cloth, slipping the softness down her body. She reached out an arm, leaning on his muscular shoulder as she stepped free of the undergarment.

Then Sam's work-roughened hands returned to her legs again. Swiftly he moved upward to stroke the sensitive inner surfaces of her thighs.

"More," she urged, her breathing coming faster.

His fingers obliged, reaching into her soft folds, parting her, teasing her until she moaned, her eyelids half closing with the feel of his fingers just barely inside her.

"Yes, Sam . . ." she rasped, her head tipping back with pleasure.

Sam guided her closer, coaxing her to straddle his lap and open herself more to him. Her breasts were near his face now, and his mouth and tongue found each one in turn. He enjoyed the way her beautiful nipples responded to him, hardening into dark pink buds through the sheer dampened silk of the negligee.

She rocked against him, her fingers tangling in the thick brown hair at the nape of his neck. But he ignored the throbbing beneath his jeans, the urging for his own release.

"You want *more*, Ivy?" he growled.

"Yes. Oh, yes!"

His fingers invaded her then, just the way she liked it, pushing aggressively past her folds and straight into her dewy heat. She was so ready for him. So sweet. And so ready.

He watched her crest and fall with his movements, like the roll of ocean waves. And when the fury finally broke inside her, she cried out his name. Then she pulled him off the couch and began tugging at his clothes.

She was hungry for him now. Frantic hands worked to remove his flannel shirt, his jeans and briefs, until his body stood naked before her, corded with muscle and tight with need.

Her soft fingers eagerly reacquainted themselves with his contours. Wanting to trace again the breadth of his shoulders, the bulges of his arms, the hardness of his pectorals and abdomen.

It was her turn to touch the most intimate part of him, swollen now with his desire for her. Sam shuddered when she grasped him, then moaned as she began to move her fingers over the length of him.

Her hand felt so soft, so sweet, he thought he was going to lose his mind . . .

"For months on that boat," he whispered, "lying in my bunk, I've dreamed of this . . . of you . . ."

Stepping back, Ivy pulled the lacy negligee completely off.

"Julian called me an ice princess," she whispered.

With a teasing sparkle in her eyes, she cupped her breasts and cooed, "Tell me, Sam. Do I look *cold* to you?"

"Mmmm . . . let's find out."

He pulled her to him and possessively palmed her breast.

"How about we warm you up, Princess?" he growled in her ear as he lowered her to the soft fur rug. Then he knelt between her legs, urging her to open for him.

Gazing into her eyes, he moved over her.

"Say it again," he whispered, teasing her soft folds with his hardness.

"What?" Her breathing was fast, shallow.

"Say that you'll *marry* me."

"Oh, yes, Sam, yes." She put her delicate hands on the strength of his shoulders. "You have my heart forever, Sam Bennett, I promise."

Blue as the sea, her gaze held him, and he plunged into her with all his heart . . . without looking back.

There was a forgetfulness that came with making love to Sam Bennett. Ivy was grateful for that.

The last four months now felt wiped completely clean, her elaborate wedding became a distant mirage, and for hours they had returned to that warm summer night on the beach.

Innocence was theirs again. And the trust they'd shared since the first day they'd met was wholly and completely restored.

It was a miraculous second chance they had now.

And Ivy wasn't going to lose it.

For two hours Sam had made tender, passionate love to her on the fur rug, then he'd pulled her into his arms and wrapped thick, warm blankets over their bare, sated bodies before drifting off to sleep.

The feel of Sam's lips only slightly roused her. It was the clock that woke her completely.

Cuckoo! Cuckoo!

Ivy laughed at the sound of the old bird on the wall crowing two in the morning. Sam had told her that his father had bought the darned thing in the German Black Forest during his years in the army. Of course, Sam's mother hated it, which was why it had been unceremoniously moved to his father's fishing cabin years ago.

"See, Ivy," teased Sam, half-awake, "you've made the clock cuckoo for you."

"Corny, Sam, even for you," she teased, rolling her eyes. "Then again . . ." She threw him a mischievous smile and moved her hand beneath the blanket. "I wonder if there's anything else in the room that's cuckoo for me?"

Her warm, satiny fingers closed over him, and Sam released a sigh of sheer bliss. "I've died and gone to heaven."

"Oh, no, dear. There are definite signs of *life* here."

Sam laughed again and pressed his lips to her neck. Nuzzling her, within minutes he was moving over her once more.

As she felt him enter her yet again, it occurred to Ivy that they hadn't used birth control all night. With their plans to marry, she knew Sam didn't care. And neither did she.

It was a good time of her cycle, she knew, to get pregnant, and she closed her eyes as he moved faster, working toward a swift climax within her.

Ivy knew that once she was carrying Sam's child, there would be no question that they belonged together. No resistance from her family. Her father would *have* to accept her choice. And he'd very likely release her million-dollar trust fund.

Ivy moved her arms around Sam's neck and urged him to fill her again. *Yes, Sam, give me a baby*, she thought with joy. *Our baby*.

More than a living symbol of the love they shared, it would be the key to securing the life they deserved . . .

"Are you sure you'll be okay?" asked Sam, dropping Ivy off at the park near dawn. "Please, won't you let me take you back to your parents' house?"

"No! I told you. I want to handle this, Sam. I'll drive the Jaguar back to the Crane mansion, tell Julian that I want an annulment, then let my parents know what I've decided. Tomorrow morning, it'll all be over. I'll have my things packed and ready for us to drive to Boston. Then we'll finally be together."

"I just wish we could go now. Not wait. Even twenty-four hours."

Ivy nodded. "I know, sweetheart, I wish that, too. But you need to tell your family, too. You need to pack and tie up loose ends."

"I know."

"Tomorrow morning, Sam. I'll see you on our beach."

"Ten o'clock sharp, okay? Don't be late for our new life."

"Sharp!" Ivy kissed him, long and hard. "I promise, my love," she whispered. "Nothing could keep me from you now."

THIRTY-ONE

The Break

Sam waited for Ivy the next morning on their beach as they'd agreed. "Ten o'clock sharp" turned into eleven, which stretched until almost noon.

He thought maybe her family had hung her up, so he took a walk along the shore, always keeping his eye out for her.

One o'clock came and went.

He grabbed a hot dog and soda at a vendor's cart, sat on the sun-warmed sand, and waited some more.

When two o'clock came, he figured that Ivy had just needed more time—another day, maybe. Sam drove to the park and checked under the loose rock in the wall, but there was no note.

He sank to the curb, ran his hands through his hair. *What am I supposed to do here, Ivy? Where are you?*

October was always beautiful in Harmony. The sun was bright, the sky was blue, and the trees around him were red-gold eye candy. Sam sighed under the umbrella of brilliant leaves.

What could have happened?

His heart stopped for a moment when he considered that she might have changed her mind completely—decided not to run away with him after all. But then he remembered how they'd made love last night. How she'd melted into him, called his name over and over, *promised* to marry him, to love him forever.

She *hadn't* changed her mind. She *couldn't* have. On the other hand, the Cranes could be giving her trouble over the legalities of the annulment.

"Time's up," Sam murmured as he picked himself off the curb and pulled open the door of his car.

The Crane mansion looked bigger than he remembered as he drove up Raven Hill. Imposing east and west wings stretched out from the main structure, and an intimidating high-columned portico covered the front drive.

Sam reminded himself not to be too impressed by the place. Its outward grandeur was soiled by the revolting history of its occupants—like some rare flower whose intoxicating smell turned out to be lung-strangling poison.

He parked his car far away from the house, under a particularly beautiful old oak tree. He'd rather that Julian didn't see his rusting little Pinto; and besides, he needed to stretch his legs. Striding up to the front door gave Sam time to settle his jitters and fuel his anger at the Cranes.

Chimes rang inside when he jabbed at the electric doorbell. He shifted impatiently, fists clenching and unclenching.

He supposed he should consider his attire for such an important occasion. Then again, worn blue jeans and an ivory fisherman's sweater were certainly respectable enough for punching Julian's lights out.

Finally the door opened, and a familiar face peered out.

"Hello, Pilar."

"Good afternoon, Mr. Sam."

"I'm here to pick up Ivy."

"She is not here."

Sam exhaled in relief at the good news. His fists unclenched. Obviously, she'd already left Julian. She was probably at her parents' house, still packing.

"Thanks, I'll go over to the Winthrops' then—"

"Mr. Sam," called Pilar as he began to turn away. "She is not there, either."

Slowly, he faced Pilar again, his jaw tensing. "Then where is she?"

With a worried glance back into the mansion, Pilar stepped out onto the portico, pulling the door half-shut behind her.

"Pilar? *Where* is she?"

"She is gone, Mr. Sam. Gone to Paris."

"Paris!"

"She has left on her honeymoon with Julian Crane."

"Champagne, Mrs. Crane?"

"Thank you, no."

The Crane jet's interior was luxurious. Plush seats, thick-piled carpeting, elegant mahogany fixtures, and an impressive selection of audiotapes, magazines, and books. But it was still the last place Ivy wanted to be.

"Come on, Ivy, let's celebrate," purred Julian in the seat facing her. "After all, it *is* our honeymoon. Don't you want to at least get into the spirit of things?"

Ivy glared daggers at her new husband.

"Well, *I'll* have champagne," Julian told the attractive brunette stewardess with a flirtatious smile.

"Yes, Mr. Crane, my pleasure . . . And Mrs. Crane, are you sure I can't get you anything?"

"How about a ginger ale. Maybe that will settle my stomach."

"Of course, right away."

Hitting the recline button on her seat, Ivy leaned back, trying to fight her nausea. She closed her eyes, but that gave her little relief. All she could see was Sam's blue eyes, darkening with desire for her; hear his deep voice, growling how much he wanted her.

Oh, Sam . . . I'm so sorry . . . So sorry . . .

She could only imagine his pain. His devastating disappointment. She knew because she had felt it herself for the last twenty-four hours.

Taking a deep, shaky breath, she tried to control her tears. She'd been crying privately all morning, but Pilar had been there to hold her. Now, en route to a six-month honeymoon, she was on her own, forced to act her part for Julian. The part of the newlywed Crane bride.

She certainly looked it. Her hair was swept up in a sophisticated twist, and her trim white suit was Chanel, part of the trousseau her mother and mother-in-law had packed up for her trip. Platinum and diamond earrings along with a matching diamond bracelet completed the ensemble.

But the only jewelry Ivy truly wanted was her small antique locket. The one still sitting in the drawer of her childhood bedroom. It would be the first thing she retrieved when she returned to Harmony in six months.

Please don't hate me, Sam . . . please don't give up on us . . .

When she'd left Sam, she had thought their plan would work, that the annulment would go off as soon as she demanded it of Julian.

But Ivy had never even reached Julian.

The moment she'd stepped back through the mansion's front door, her father and Alistair had ushered her into the drawing room for a "serious chat."

Apparently, after she'd vanished the night before, Julian and Alistair had searched the mansion for her. When a sleepy groundskeeper had confirmed that Ivy had driven off the property, Alistair sent Julian to bed and swung into action himself.

Phoning Ivy's father at once, Alistair made it very clear that Ivy hadn't just taken *herself* out the front door, she had taken Alistair's global business plans, not to mention the Winthrop good name, along with her.

Harrison Winthrop rushed over to the Crane mansion, and the two men sat up all night, smoking cigars and waiting for Ivy to return. When she walked in, just after dawn, still wearing her wedding-night negligee and demanding an annulment, the two men forced Ivy to sit in the drawing room and listen to what they had to say.

With Julian sound asleep upstairs, Alistair coolly explained that if she ran out on his son now, her family would be ruined. It wasn't just Winthrop Marine that was in trouble, as Ivy had thought, it was Harrison's entire personal fortune, too.

Devastated, Ivy asked Harrison if this were true. His falling face told the story. He had tried everything to keep the company afloat. Cashed in all the family's stocks and bonds, even raided Ivy's trust fund.

Unless a friendly investor came along to pour money back into the business and turn things around, Ivy's family was finished. Washed up. Flat broke.

Without the Cranes' help, Winthrop Marine would sink under its own debts in a matter of months. And Alistair made it abundantly clear that he would offer *no* help to Harrison if Ivy made a laughingstock of his son by running out on him the day after their wedding.

"Make no mistake, you'll be a laughingstock, too, Ivy," threatened Alistair. "Girls like Rebecca Osburn and Clarissa Morton will make you the butt of their jokes at every society soirée. Your entire sorority will mourn you as a pathetic case.

"Stay in the marriage," Alistair smoothly enticed her, "and I'll put three million dollars in your *personal* bank account today. Julian need never know about it."

"You hear that, Ivy!" Harrison exclaimed. "That's very generous of your new father-in-law. Now you can't say no to that—"

"But—"

"Ivy, listen to reason," continued her father. "This is the life you've always wanted. That's why you walked down that aisle yesterday."

"That's right," affirmed Alistair. "You'll be queen of the society page. All those Alpha girls will remain wildly jealous of you. Think of all the Crane influence and power you'll be able to use."

Ivy shook her head, tears slipping down her cheeks. She could still smell Sam's scent on her, could still feel his touch, his kiss. "But I don't love Julian . . . and he doesn't love me . . ."

"Ivy, honey," said her father in the gentlest voice she'd ever heard him use, "I know you *think* you love someone else right now. And I know who. You may even want to run away with him. But think of what it will do to your family. You have to understand now, honey, *really* understand that the money's gone. It's *truly* gone. The Winthrop family is on the verge of a terrible disgrace—ruination after a century of prosperity and pride—and only *you* have the power to stop it."

Ivy's mind was spinning with shock. Disbelief. How could this be happening?

"Don't even think of me and my personal disgrace," whispered her father, about to add the hardest words of all. "But think of your *mother*. You know Helen doesn't deserve it."

Ivy began to sob. It was too much. Too *much*. Alistair and Harrison were making her bear the burden of her family's entire future. Her mother's complete happiness and security.

"Don't you worry, Ivy," said Alistair condescendingly. "Once you get some sleep, you'll wake up fresh and see that this is all for the best . . .

"And when you get *bored* with my son, as I'm sure you will," he added, dropping his voice for sincere emphasis, "there'll be handsome enough diversions around for you on occasion. As long as you're discreet, I don't care. All I want from you, Ivy, by the time you come back from your honeymoon, is the next Crane heir . . ."

Oh, you'll get your heir, Alistair, Ivy whispered to herself on his plane. *Only it won't be a Crane.*

The only thing Ivy could cling to now was the hope that Sam's baby was growing inside her. It was too soon to know for sure, of course, but Ivy had a plan.

Julian was about to discover that his new bride was indeed the little "Ice Princess" he'd labeled her. Freezing him out of her bed with the excuse of illness would work for about six weeks, Ivy calculated. That's when she'd have the test done to make certain she was carrying Sam's child.

And once she *did* know, she'd put on that Balmain negligee and seduce Julian into sleeping with her at last. He'd never know the child wasn't his.

When they returned from their six-month honeymoon in Europe, Ivy intended to find Sam again and make him understand that there was no reason their love couldn't go on the way it had before—in secret.

True, they could never marry, but they still loved each other. And Sam would soon see that their exquisite romantic interludes need never stop.

Ivy had wanted to tell Sam all of this herself, try to explain it before she left, but the Cranes had guarded her every move until she'd finally boarded their private plane to Paris.

I'll love you forever, Sam, she vowed, her lips silently mouthing the words, praying he would know that, no matter what.

"Did you say something, my sweet?" asked Julian, breaking off his flirtations with their attractive stewardess.

Ivy stared at Julian. She had no feelings left for him now. Unless she counted her disgust. Sam was the one who held her heart. And he always would.

"I didn't say anything *you* need to hear," Ivy replied. "But I suddenly seem to have a terrible headache."

The look in Julian's eyes told her that somehow he already knew this would be a refrain he'd be hearing for years to come.

THIRTY-TWO

The Warning

Weeks passed and fall trickled away, draining every drop of life from New England. Trees once bursting with fiery color became drab, leafless skeletons. Grass turned brown, days grew short, and even the bright yellow sunlight became a pale, disappointing ghost of itself.

December trudged in with cold rain and colorless clouds, but with it came the promise of Christmas. And for a few weeks, every home, street, and shop was draped with bold red bows, fresh green pine boughs, and strings of twinkling rainbow light.

When December 24 finally arrived, a heavy snowfall obliterated all color again, covering much of the Northeast with a soundless, seamless blanket of white.

Just outside the remote logging town of Mill Valley, a teenage girl watched the icy flakes fall for hours from inside her family's gray stone farmhouse.

Although Grace Standish appeared delicate and waif-like, with coltish long legs, straight, sand-colored hair, and milk-smooth skin, she was actually a sturdy, active girl with a robust spirit and a pure and open heart.

Grace loved to run, cross-country ski, and skate on the nearby lake. But she also enjoyed nursing injured forest animals, all of whom instinctively trusted her to heal them; growing potted plants, which seemed to thrive no matter how much or little she watered them; and volunteering her time at the old rural church up on Sutter's Mountain, where the elderly and sick often asked her to do nothing more than just sit silently with them and hold their hands.

When bedtime came on this particular Christmas night, Grace blew out the angel-shaped candle in their front window, kissed her mother good night, and climbed the creaking wooden staircase with her twin sister.

According to Grace's mother, the Standish clan had owned this big, drafty house and this rolling patch of farmland for at least two hundred years. And for some reason, down through those years their neighbors had always considered them strange.

"Never do mind those looks we get from them people in Mill Valley," Grace's mother would always say. "Some folks just aren't comfortable with families who like to stick to themselves."

Bad luck, especially with freak fires, had diminished the Standish clan over the years. And much of the farmland had been sold off during hard times.

Grace, her twin sister, Faith, and their mother, Mercy, were the only three Standishes left now. Zachary Sutter, the twins' father, had died tragically years before when a terrible fire swept through his grocery store. The flames very

---

 Yeah, displaying weird psychic powers would make people wonder, all right! Remember what Timmy told you earlier, dear reader, about the Standish women. Well, these are them!

nearly claimed the lives of Mercy and her young daughters, too. But miraculously, they managed to escape.

With the store now gone, Mercy and the girls earned their living through crafts—canning, quilting, baking, and knitting. Their own fields and orchards yielded plenty of food for their own table, with a good deal left over to sell at Mill Valley's farmers' market.

After the fire, Mercy took back her maiden name and became very protective of her twins, even insisting on home-schooling the girls herself. For years Grace and Faith had enjoyed this reclusiveness. It was only lately, as their interest in boys picked up, that the twins had become restless. Grace especially had wanted to attend Mill Valley High, but Mercy wouldn't allow it.

Other than the local library, the family's small black-and-white television was Grace's only window on the world outside. She began to day-dream of traveling beyond their farm, beyond their town, and into a big city.

At the library, she checked out books about places close enough to travel to with a cheap bus ticket—Manchester, Bennington, Boston, Providence.

This summer I'll ask Faith to take some day trips with me, Grace finally decided as she snuggled down under her pile of quilts. *It's Christmas Eve, and tomorrow morning we'll finally turn eighteen. That's old enough to start getting out in the world. I don't care what Mama says!*

Just before the break of dawn, Grace opened her eyes and sat bolt upright. The room was cold and dark. Her twin was in the bed across the room.

"Faith?" whispered Grace into the poorly heated room,

Tim-Tim checked Tabby's diary, and he's sure you can guess who should take the heat for set-ting that little fire!

her warm breath causing the slightest puff of fog to appear in the crisp air. "Faith?"

But Faith didn't stir. Her breathing remained steady, as if she was still deep in sleep.

Funny, Grace thought. *I was sure I heard my name being called.*

She was about to settle herself under the thick covers again when she realized the room was gradually brightening. A light had appeared through the crack in their gingham window curtains — but this light was far too bright to be the pale light of a December dawn.

Grace rose and parted the curtains.

What she saw outside made her gasp in awe.

An angel. A glowing figure, surrounded by the most brilliant white light she'd ever seen, was hovering just outside her second-floor bedroom window. And it was *speaking* to her . . .

"Beware," whispered the angel. "Beware, Grace, for evil is coming . . ."

Grace screamed, turned from the window, and lunged on the lump of covers that cocooned her sister. "Faith! Wake up!"

"What, Grace? What is it?"

But when Grace returned to the window to show her sister what she had seen, the angel had disappeared.

"Go back to sleep," said Faith, yawning and turning over again. "We've got the whole day to celebrate our birthday. No need to start *this* early."

"How I *hate* Christmas."

Harmony's Baroness of Black Arts rose from her bed, crankier than usual, and headed right for the kitchen. Fluffy the cat yawned, stretched, and trotted along behind her. ➤

Looks like Tabby's at it again! (Ditto on the authorial euphemisms.)

"Meow?" asked Fluffy.

"*Why do I hate Christmas?* Because it's nonstop peace, love, and goodness crap!" Tabitha shuddered. "I swear, Fluffy, next year I'm whipping up a potion to let me sleep through the entire holiday week!"

"MEOW!"

"What do you mean, who'll *feed* you? I'll put *you* to sleep, too."

Clearly taking offense at the phrase "put you to sleep," Fluffy turned with a disdainful sniff and trotted away, tail raised high.

"Traitor," murmured Tabby.

"Merry Christmas, Miss Lenox!" came a muffled call from the curb.

"Oh, shut up."

Tabitha had *tried* to sleep right through this wretched day, but the annoying steeple bells had been ringing all morning, and her neighbors were making quite the Yuletide racket, milling around the streets greeting each other on their way to—and then from—the blasted church.

"Black mushroom tea, that's the ticket," muttered Tabby as she put a pot of water on to boil and grabbed a cup and saucer from a shelf near the window. "It's the only thing that might prevent my usual Christmas migraine from starting up—"

Cup in hand, Tabby suddenly stilled.

The sight outside her window made her fingers numb. Her teacup went crashing to the floor.

An angel, a *real* one—not one of those cheesy plastic numbers the Harmony Chamber of Commerce liked to string along Main Street—was floating down from atop the church steeple, reciting a warning . . .

"The light is coming to banish the dark . . . The light is coming to banish the dark . . . the light is coming . . ."

Timmynote to self: Find potion to put Fluffy to sleep—forever!

Tabitha cowered as the angel floated down through the glass window. Appearing as a dark-haired little girl dressed in a blindingly white gown with tall snow-white wings, the angel proceeded to hover right over her kitchen linoleum!

"Wh-what do y-you want?" asked Tabitha, shaking like a wind-buffeted leaf.

"The light is coming . . . change your ways . . . the light is coming . . . turn from evil . . ."

"No!" shouted Tabby, still cowering. "Get out of here! Get out!"

Slowly the angel faded, receding from where she'd come, until the sorceress was alone again. But the event was far from over.

Suddenly the whole house began to shake!

Fluffy ran back into the kitchen, hissing and growling, back arched, tail puffed.

"MEOW!!"

"I don't know, Fluffy, it feels like an earthquake!"

As the house heaved and rattled, smoke and heat began to rise up from beneath the basement door.

After a few minutes, the house finally settled. Then came the ghastly red light. Like an unearthly heartbeat, its rhythmic pulse oozed through the crack at the bottom of the door.

Tabby knew at once that it was *not* her water heater.

"MEOW?!" asked Fluffy, back still arched.

"It seems, Fluffy, that some friends from *down below* have taken a ride *up* and are now camped out in our *basement!*"

"Meow?"

"I don't know why. Not yet."

She ran to the living room and pulled out her tarot cards, shuffled them with an incantation, then swiftly laid them out on the coffee table.

"Oh, no. This can't be. Not *this* soon."

But the cards were clear: A *babe full of light and goodness. Power so strong no evil shall stop her* . . .

"This is bad, Fluffy. Very, very bad. You see, I've gotten a bit distracted with all my little hobbies here in Harmony—

and I neglected to keep an eye on the Standish situation. It seems I've allowed those wretched twins to turn eighteen! My word, time flies!

"Needless to say, the crew down below is not too happy with me . . . so they've sent up some 'friends' to our basement to watch my every move against those annoying Standish women from here on out . . ."

It seemed that the Baroness of Black Arts was really in for it now.

"MEOW!"

"You said it, Fluffy. Talk about bosses from hell!"

"Faith, how long is she going to keep this up?" whispered Grace.

"I don't know."

For hours Grace Standish had been watching in horror as her mother, Mercy, scurried about their house putting up crucifixes on the doors and sprinkling holy water on the windowpanes.

"Mother, stop!" cried Grace, at last.

Together Grace and Faith led their mother to the living room couch, then sat down on either side of her. Mercy had been as attractive as her daughters throughout her twenties, but the loss of her husband twelve years ago had been hard on her. Barely forty, she looked fifteen years older. Her face was creased with worry, and her long, light brown hair was streaked heavily with gray.

"Please tell us what's happening. What's wrong?" asked Faith.

"I've had a vision, girls. A *vision!*"

The wild look in her mother's blue-gray eyes alarmed Grace.

"An angel came to me this morning, girls, and told me that you are both in danger. Evil wants to prevent you from having children!"

Grace glanced nervously at Faith.

Mercy caught the look. "You saw it, too, Grace! Didn't you? Didn't you?"

"I *dreamed* I saw a Christmas angel, Momma. But it was just a dream."

"No! It wasn't a dream, Grace. It was a vision! Listen to me, girls. Listen closely . . ."

Grace was more than a little unsettled by her mother's crazy claims that she and Faith were descendants from a long line of New England Standish women, whose legacy of psychic powers stretched back beyond the time of the pilgrims, back as far as the Middle Ages.

From generation to generation, their powers had been building. But this morning, the angel had revealed to Mercy that one of her daughters would have a child—a baby girl.

That blessed child would have the ability to channel Heaven's very light and essence, bringing goodness to Earth in a way that had not been seen since the saints of olden days.

Grace stared in shock at her mother's ramblings. It was too much! Too crazy!

But her mother insisted it was true. Insisted that her own mother, and her grandmother before her, had passed on this vital knowledge to her when she'd turned eighteen.

"Do you think she's crazy?" Grace whispered to Faith as they worked on a quilt later that day in the sewing room.

"I believe her," said Faith. "Haven't you wondered about your strange feelings? Your visions? I know you've had them, Grace. We've talked about it. And I've had them, too."

Despite Faith's words, Grace refused to believe all this. Watching her mother and sister kneeling and praying together under the Christmas tree angel later that day, Grace got the uneasy feeling that their lives were going to change forever.

"Come join us," urged Mercy, reaching out her hand to Grace.

But Grace shook her head. "I'm going to start dinner."

Later, near sunset, the sound of a baying hound far off in the woods set Mercy off into hysterical motion again, sprinkling holy water. "It's an evil demon! Trying to frighten us!"

She's gone crazy, Grace told herself. *And she's taking my sister with her.*

While she fixed dinner, Grace did begin to pray, but not to ward off evil. She simply asked Heaven to help her mother and sister come back to their senses.

THIRTY-THREE

The Baby

"Merry Christmas, Eve."

Tears streamed down Eve Johnson's face as a pair of gloved hands placed the squalling infant on her light brown stomach.

"Thank you, Doctor," Eve managed between joyful sobs. "It's the best . . . Christmas gift . . . I've ever received . . . the best . . ."

Behind her green surgical mask, the doctor smiled, then carefully cut the umbilical cord.

Eve knew it was traditional for the father of the newborn to do the cutting—but her baby's father was nowhere near this delivery room.

And thank God for *that*.

This beautiful baby boy was hers and hers alone. According to Alistair Crane, Julian had decided he never wanted anything to do with it. And that was fine with Eve, because she wanted nothing to do with him. Ever again.

"He's really something," whispered Crystal behind the surgical mask, still holding tightly to Eve's hand.

Eve glanced into her friend's eyes, usually so hard and jaded. Tears filled them now, and awe—as if the infant she was gazing at shared his mother's beauty, her fierce spirit, and her renewed hope and faith.

Eve stroked her son's tiny head, amazed at the tufts of curly black hair that were already in place. Then she placed the tip of her index finger into his doll-sized palm and watched five perfect little fingers grab hold.

"It's a miracle, Crystal," she whispered. "My baby's a Christmas miracle."

Eve never noticed the masked face peeking through the small rectangular windows of her delivery room's double doors . . .

The young male orderly in surgical scrubs had been loitering outside for an hour, spying with interest on the activity inside. Once he saw that the Johnson woman had birthed a live, healthy baby, he turned and strode swiftly down the drab green hallway.

Boston Metro was far from what you'd call an upscale medical facility. It was understaffed and not very well maintained. This was where you were sent when you had to rely on charity. And the orderly knew exactly who was providing charity to the Johnson woman back there—Alistair Crane.

Smacking a button to open the electric doors between the sterile area and the nearly empty main hallway, the orderly headed for the run-down waiting room. Metro was short on staff as a rule, and with tonight being Christmas, the place was practically deserted.

Good, thought the orderly. *It'll make my job that much easier.*

Digging into the breast pocket of his scrubs, he pulled out some coins and placed a call from one of the few working pay phones.

"Wilkes, it's me. She's just delivered. Yeah, I know what to do . . ."

Eve was back in her room within the hour, nursing her little one.

"You've got to admit it, you're very lucky," said Crystal, perched on the edge of Eve's hospital bed. "Your beautiful baby boy here came with some pretty good benefits."

Eve nodded. Alistair Crane's bribe had been too good to pass up. In exchange for never revealing Julian to be the father of her child, Alistair had deposited a very generous sum of money into Eve's bank account. Enough to take care of her and the child for years to come.

On top of that, Alistair had agreed to foot the bill for her education. She had finally decided to finish college and go on to med school—just as she had originally planned to do before she'd even laid eyes on Julian Crane.

Radcliffe was out, of course, since she'd failed all of her courses last spring. But that was fine with her, anyway. Eve knew she'd be happier attending a school outside the city, where her boy could grow up in fresh air and sunshine.

Alistair Crane had arranged for that, too, promising to help her secure a spot in premed at Castleton College and afterward at the Andrew P. Mott School of Medicine, a small private school near Harmony where Alistair sat on the board.

Eve didn't care what kind of favors Crane had to call in, he owed it to his grandson.

"Your mother's going to be a doctor, sweetheart," Eve cooed. "What do you think of that?"

Eve glanced up at Crystal. "I swear my baby's going to be proud of me."

"He should be already," said Crystal. "I mean, with all that's happened to you—with Julian running out and everything—I wouldn't have had the guts to have this child."

"I used to think that way, too. But it's different when it's yours. When you feel the life growing inside you. He's a part of me, Crystal."

"Well, at least Julian's family is doing right by you."

"I'm just relieved he's healthy. God, I was so scared, you know . . ."

"I know."

Other than being a bit underweight, the baby had miraculously come out just fine . . . so far, anyway. With her drug and alcohol abuse in the early stages of her pregnancy, there was still a chance at vision or hearing impairment, brain function problems . . . but Eve was going to just keep praying that everything would turn out all right.

One step at a time, Eve . . . one step at a time . . .

Eve smiled. Those were her late grandmother Eve's words—loud and clear.

She didn't have her grandmother's gold cross to hold on to anymore—not since she'd sold it back in August to help pay for her prenatal care. But at least she could still hear her grandmother's voice in her heart. It was stronger than ever now that Eve was doing the right thing with her life again.

She could feel the power of her grandmother's spirit, too—and her faith.

The only shadow on this birth was Eve's parents. They'd refused to forgive her for her mistakes, for insisting on keeping the baby. Their silence, she knew, was supposed to make her feel guilty, force her to change her mind and do what they demanded of her.

But Eve was made of tougher stuff than that.

She had vowed not to give up her child. And she wasn't about to go back on it.

And if her parents rejected this baby, then they equally rejected her.

Eve swore she'd never speak to them again. She knew she'd screwed up her life. She knew she'd made a terrible mistake. But this innocent child didn't deserve to pay for it.

If her parents refused to help her—refused to see how important this little life was, this living part of herself—well, then, until they did, they were dead to her.

"I'm proud of having this child," she told Crystal. "I'm proud to take on raising it by myself. He's my whole life now, and I'm going to love this baby with all my heart."

* * *

It was close to midnight when the orderly stopped at another phone booth just beyond the dark alley at the back of the hospital. He'd discarded his surgical scrubs in the locker room hamper and walked out the employee exit in his street clothes—baggy jeans, a black T-shirt, and a cheap green parka.

Glancing around to make sure he was completely alone, he dropped a coin into the pay phone's slot and dialed Wilkes's number again.

"It's done. No one suspects. I did it like you said—just used a pillow. We can show Crane the death certificate *and* a photo. Just make sure I get my money."

Eve was in a light sleep when she felt a gentle hand touch her shoulder.

She opened her eyes, expecting the nurse to be there with her baby again, asking for another feeding.

But it wasn't the nurse.

It was a very young, very tired-looking male doctor. One she'd never seen before.

"Who are you?"

"I'm the on-call intern."

"What do you—"

Eve blinked. Beside him stood Crystal, tears streaming down her face.

"Crystal? What are you doing back here?"

"We called her back in, Ms. Johnson. To be with you."

"I don't understand—"

—but then she did.

"Oh, no. *No!*"

At the same phone booth, the orderly dug into his jeans pocket for a few more coins.

He placed a third call, looking around the whole time to make sure no one was nearby to listen.

"It's Jack. We're in the money, baby. Go ahead and

charge up those plane tickets to L.A. for next week. Yeah, I got enough to pay Griff his twenty thou and eighty big ones left to start over in sunny Californ-eye-ay! Break open the Buds, 'cause we're gonna celebrate tonight!"

Jack felt like a new man as he hung up the phone.

A new man, and a free man.

"No more bedpans. No more sheets. No more mopping toilet seats!" he sang as he waltzed down the sidewalk.

The truth was, he wouldn't have felt even a fraction this good if he'd *really* had to kill that baby. Sure, he needed the money for his gambling debts—not to mention keeping his legs from being broken by Griff's crew. But he sure didn't want to do it by becoming a baby killer.

No way. Especially on Christmas day, for chrissake!

Anyway, luck had truly been with him when another infant had died in the maternity ward. The babe was a foundling. Cops had brought him in yesterday evening, and the poor thing died about an hour after the Johnson kid was born.

Jack had seen that shit happen every week in this place. And boy, was he sick of it.

All he had to do to earn his hundred thou was switch the baby bracelets. He put the dead foundling into the Johnson crib and the live Johnson kid into the foundling bassinet.

And that was that.

Metro was a sloppy operation. Fortunately, he knew just *how* sloppy. They'd shuttle that dead foundling to the morgue without a second thought. No need to check footprints when the kid had a bracelet that said he was Eve Johnson's kid—*and* he was in the Johnson bassinet.

The staff—or what was left of it on Christmas night—would just fill out that death certificate without a second thought.

And as for the *real* Eve Johnson kid, still alive and kicking, well, he would be just fine in that foundling bassinet.

The hospital would put him into the city's social services system and one, two, three, he'd be raised in some new home.

Jack was sorry he had to do that to the mother. But, hey, he didn't know her. And from what he'd overheard, he figured the mother had expected the kid to die anyway, since she'd used drugs and drank during her pregnancy.

So that's that.

Alistair Crane would now believe that his son's little bastard child was dead. And even though he wasn't, no one would ever find out.

Loose ends were tied up, and Jack didn't have to feel guilty about killing some kid on Christmas.

"Yeah, I'm off to la-la land with a hundred grand . . . sun and surf and sand!"

"I'm going to have the nurse give her a sedative."

"What?"

Sobbing uncontrollably in her hospital bed, Eve was oblivious to the conversation going on above her between the doctor and Crystal.

"A sedative. It'll help calm her down."

"No!" cried Crystal, violently shaking her head. "No drugs, Doctor. She'll be all right. I'll stay with her and make sure of it. All night if I have to."

"My baby's gone, Crystal," sobbed Eve, clinging tightly to her friend. "My baby's gone."

THIRTY-FOUR

Good-byes

March 9

Dear Momma and Faith,

By the time you read this letter, I'll be on a bus out of Mill Valley. I'm so sorry to leave you like this, sneaking off while you're both at church, but I didn't want to fight or argue.

For a long time now, Momma, I've wanted to leave home, try my wings, test myself.

Now is that time.

Faith, I'm so sorry to leave you behind, but I know how frightened you've become (and Momma, too) of some supernatural evil you think is coming to get us.

Maybe there is evil out there—but there is goodness, too. I feel it. And I know good is the stronger of the two, and that it will protect me.

I love you both with all my heart, and I'll keep praying that you'll get over your fears soon. Please un-

derstand that I must now follow my own calling, my own path.

May God's love be with you both,
Grace

With a steadying breath, Grace folded the letter and placed it in a small white envelope.

She had tried everything since Christmas. She'd reasoned with them, pleaded with them, even prayed with them, but they'd refused to come to their senses. Hysteria ruled at the Standish farm. "Evil" was coming to get them—and there was no room for any other point of view.

A single tear dropped to the surface of the snow-white envelope, leaving a small dark splotch behind. She set the note gently on her twin sister's bed, then slung her duffel bag over her shoulder and descended the farmhouse's creaking steps.

She'd personally saved one thousand dollars over the years from her quilting and sewing work. It was enough for her to set herself up somewhere, maybe Providence or Boston.

She was very good at sewing, and she intended to find work with a city tailor. She'd been planning this for more than a few months, of course. Dreaming about it, really— exploring the world beyond Mill Valley. And the chance to meet her future husband. She was sure he was out there for her, too.

In six months or so, I'll come back to visit, she promised the house silently as she tugged open the front door.

The March landscape was bleak and brown. Patches of snow and ice were still clinging to the frozen earth, refusing to give up their supremacy.

But winter was ending, Grace firmly reminded herself. And spring's warmth and color were on their way. New life was out there somewhere. She stepped forward to find it, closing the door behind her.

A stinging wind swept down from the high, cold mountain as she moved off the Standish land, striking her face like a slap. It was an angry reminder that life away from her childhood home would not be easy or comfortable.

But the biting cold wasn't the only thing she felt as she began the hike along the main road, her legs pushing forward over the hard, rutted ground.

A strange warmth, like two loving hands, began to caress her cheeks where the wind had struck them. For some reason, it lifted her spirits. Comforted her.

Her logical mind chalked the warmth up to the flush of nervous excitement. But deep inside, she felt that it was somehow coming from something more powerful than herself . . . something that would be with her, no matter where she went . . .

"I'm taking them down one at a time, Fluffy," declared Harmony's witch as she watched Grace's movements from her scrying bowl.

"And since Grace has chosen to separate herself from the little pack, it makes my job *that* much easier . . ."

Fluffy walked closer to look into the scrying bowl, too. Then the cat's pink tongue unfurled to take a drink.

"Fluffy! You've gone and muddled the image!"

"Meow!" said the cat with disdain, and just kept drinking.

"Oh, well," said the witch, "I'm done for the night anyway. I'll pick this up again tomorrow, when I have a clue where the heck Grace Standish is going."

Wherever it was, the witch didn't really care. She was just happy it was away from her more powerful twin sister, Faith, and her mother, Mercy.

Without their protection, the witch was sure, she could kill Grace quite quickly. And there was no question how, either.

Fire was always how she'd vowed to kill the Standish women, ever since Prudence had accused her of witchcraft in 1693, then fanned the flames of the Harmony townspeople to see that Tabby burned.

"MEOW!"

"What's that, Fluffy?" The witch peered back into the bowl and shuddered. "Oh, no . . . no. I don't believe this!"

That blasted angel—the one who'd invaded her kitchen last Christmas—was now following Grace Standish, draping her in a veil of invisible light!

"It's her guardian angel, Fluffy! And it's *protecting* her!" The witch sighed in disgust.

With that angel in place, it could take years of trying before the witch could get a decent shot at destroying the girl. She'd just have to be patient. And keep the fires of hate and vengeance burning brighter than that blasted angel's wings.

THIRTY-FIVE

Old Wounds

Time is a relative thing, especially when one is immortal.

Such was the case with Harmony's resident enchantress.

With three hundred years under her belt Tabitha Lenox barely noticed the passing of four measly little twelve-month cycles, which raced by her faster than her cat, Fluffy, at the sight of a juicy little mouse.

Harmony changed not at all in this brief time period, of course. The ebb and flow of daily life continued as it had for centuries. Children skipped off to school, fishing boats headed out to sea, and townspeople put in their day's work for a day's wage.

Summer brought sunny days and flocks of tourists, and winter ushered in gloomy fog, icy roads, and the general tightening of social circles amid the core town residents.

Three hundred! At least!

Fluffy: noun. Definition: 1. Bloodthirsty creature posing as harmless house pet! 2. Timmy's
worst nightmare.

In this particular four-year span, Tabby's usual meddling hobbies lulled a bit.

With her new "friends" occupying her basement, she felt obligated to pursue the Standishes to the exclusion of all other fun. For a while, she lost complete track of Eve Johnson, T. C. Russell, Sam Bennett, and Julian and Ivy Crane . . .

But one September night, bored with her general research and development on anti-angel spells, Tabby became curious—

I wonder whatever happened with some of that handiwork of mine? What's become of that lovely heartache I so successfully inflicted four years ago?

After strolling to her kitchen, she pulled out her crystal bowl, filled it with water, and gazed into its glassy surface.

"Let's see, Fluffy," Tabby murmured to her curious cat, who sat on the table to peer into the bowl with her, "whom shall I start with? . . . Oh, I know! How about our pathetic little mother? Eve Johnson . . . yes . . ."

Putting her hands to her temples, Tabitha closed her eyes and concentrated . . .

"Show me Eve Johnson . . . Eve Johnson . . . Eve . . ."

The telltale clouding of the water ensued, and a few moments later, visions began to appear from just across town.

"Ah, yes, Fluffy, here we are again! My favorite little Harmony soap opera!

"Hmmmm . . . I see Eve's a medical student now. And my, doesn't she look the part! Straightened her hair, tossed the theatrical makeup, and went back to the conservative wardrobe she'd worn as the 'good girl' daughter of Tanya and Warren. Very interesting indeed! . . . Well, let's see just what this young doctor is up to this evening . . ."

"Nurse. Hey, *nurse!*"

Dr. Eve Johnson walked swiftly past the bellowing man in Treatment Room 3, her hand returning her stethoscope to the deep pocket of her long white coat.

The Harmony Hospital ER was busier than usual tonight, mainly due to a boating accident in the harbor. Seven traumas had been triaged and stabilized in the last two hours, and Eve had just finished splinting a teenage boy's fractured tibia.

"Nurse!"

Eve paused. Room 3 wasn't going to shut up.

She took a few steps to the nurses' station and checked the chart. T. C. *Russell . . . hand laceration . . . plate-glass window . . .*

"Wait your turn, Mr. Russell," she called at the pale green curtain drawn around the Room 3 examining table. "Your injury isn't that bad."

"I've been here two hours, nurse! How *long* do I have to soak this?"

With a tired sigh, Eve stepped into the room and snapped back the curtain. She wasn't sure what sort of guy she expected to see sitting there, but it certainly wasn't a handsome, shirtless black man in red satin boxing trunks displaying an overabundance of dark, sleek muscle.

Eve averted her eyes from the carved chest and focused her attention on his lacerated hand. It was still soaking in a basin of water, stained bright crimson from the combination of Betadine and some of his own blood. One of the nurses must have set him up in here just as the accident victims arrived.

With no major veins or arteries severed and his bleeding under control, this man was last on the list for treatment tonight. Still, two hours was a terribly long time for the poor guy to wait like this. She almost felt sorry for him, until he spoke again—

"Great! At last, some freaking *service*! Can't you people read the sign outside? It says *Emergency* Care. You know, *nurse*—" he began to shout; but when he lifted his dark brown eyes and met Eve's stare, his tongue stilled.

Eve arched a pretty dark eyebrow.

"Mr. Russell, I'm sorry you had to wait, but this is *not* a McDonald's. We do not *service* customers on a first-come basis. We *treat* patients by triage. And there were life-threatening injuries ahead of yours. Got it?"

"Oh, I got it, lady. I've *been* getting it for the last two hours."

Eve's eyes narrowed. The man may have looked like an ebony sculpture, but he had way too much attitude for her ER. Wheeling, she moved to the treatment room's small scrub sink and flipped the hot-water lever with such force that she nearly scalded herself.

Calm down, Eve, you're just tired, she reminded herself, *and so is he.*

After patting dry her hands with a paper towel, she returned to the examining table. With a firm, practiced touch, she lifted the injured hand out of the basin. It was a large, strong hand, attached to a well-developed forearm, bicep, and shoulder. *An athlete for sure.*

Turning the hand gingerly, she took a closer look at the wound.

Knuckles torn up. Angry, gaping gash along the fleshy outside edge. It looks painful. But at least it's clean, and not too deep. No more than a single layer of stitches—

"Room three needs a suture tray!" Eve called out the door to the nurses' station. "Four-oh Dermalon."

"Right away, Doctor," a female voice replied.

"You're a *doctor?*" asked the man.

Eve continued to study the hand. "*Don't* tell me we're going to have a male chauvinist moment here, Mr. Russell. Flex your hand for me."

"It's T. C. And I'm not questioning your sex. I'm questioning your *age.*"

"No tendon damage. Okay, you can stop flexing."

"How *old* are you anyway?" he demanded. "Seventeen?"

"I'm twenty-three. Not that it's any of your business."

"Twenty-three! That's barely enough time to get a bachelor's—"

"Earned my B.S. in three years, and I've got less than two

years left of med school." Eve poked at his hand, around the wound. "Can you feel me touching you?"

"Oh, I get it. You're an intern. With the Mott School, right?"

"Mr. Russell, can you feel me *touching* you?"

The man stared at her for a rather long, uncomfortable moment. Eve was worried for a second that he had neurological damage. That he couldn't feel her fingers on him. But then he shifted and swallowed and said—

"Yeah, sweetheart, I feel it."

"No nerve damage. Good," she murmured, forcing herself to ignore the "sweetheart" comment. Getting into a snippy argument with the man over a sexist term of endearment would do neither one of them any good.

He's in pain and stressed out. Don't bait him, and don't take his bait, either. Try to reassure him, relax him, keep him calm . . .

She'd had more than enough classroom instruction on the psychology of patient care, and now was her chance to apply it. She looked up into his eyes again. They were long-lashed and deep brown. Nice eyes. Full of intelligence—

"You're right. I'm at the Mott School of Medicine. And for the record, I'm an *acting* intern," she suddenly felt the need to tell him. "I won't be a full intern until I start a residency program next year. But I've had plenty of experience suturing wounds, I assure you."

"Well, that's too damn bad you're not a nurse," he muttered.

"Why's that?"

" 'Cause *doctors* ruined my life."

"I'm sure doctors didn't put your fist through a plate-glass window, now, did they?"

The man squinted at her. "Don't patronize me, lady."

Eve gently put the hand back into the basin. "*Doctor* Lady, if you don't mind."

"Sorry . . ." he said gruffly, looking away. "I really don't mean to take all this out on you."

"Oh, yes you do," she said, but her words were light, not accusing. She turned as she said them, stepping toward the door. "Now sit still. I'll be right back . . . *I promise*," she added when she glanced back and saw from his expression that he was on just about his last molecule of patience.

Eve found the attending physician and the triage nurse. After they both assured her that all of the accident patients were either stabilized or sent off to other hospitals for care, she promptly returned to Room 3.

"Okay, Mr. Russell," she said, checking over the suturing tray the nurse brought in. "Let's start stitching."

Eve took a seat on a high stool, repositioned the gooseneck lamp, then snapped on her surgical gloves and settled his hand on the sterile surface of the Mayo stand next to the examining table.

She cleaned the wound with more Betadine, then picked up a syringe off the tray and began to fill it with one percent lidocaine.

"What's that?"

"Mr. Russell, don't tell me you're afraid of needles?"

"Not of needles. Of what's *inside* them."

"You want to explain that?"

"I don't want the shot, Doc."

"It's standard procedure, I assure you—"

"I don't want it. And I *will* not have it."

Eve stared at him for a moment. "Why? You're not allergic. I checked your chart."

"But you don't know my history. No painkillers. Period. Okay?"

Painkillers. Eve studied the man. A cold sweat had broken out on his brow. His shoulders were tense and his eyes looked frantic. *Painkillers.*

Something inside of Eve lurched and shifted. Like a dead thing pushing up from its resting place. It was the part of herself she'd buried four years ago—buried first under numbness, then nonstop workaholic studies—

"My baby's gone, Crystal . . . My baby's gone . . ."

"I'm going to have the nurse give her a sedative . . . It'll help calm her down."

"No! No drugs, Doctor. She'll be all right . . ."

Eve closed her eyes for a moment, felt the shudder rip through her, the sweat slickening the surface of her skin. After all of her intense medical studies, she thought she'd exorcised these memories. This pain . . .

Four years ago, after she'd recovered from the devastating grief of her baby dying, she'd made the choice to continue with her plans to become a doctor.

Alistair Crane had promised to help her, and she'd held him to it. Unfortunately, he'd been unable to pull strings to get her into any other medical school than the one associated with Harmony Hospital.

With her disastrous academic record in undergrad back at Radcliffe, no other med school would take her. She'd had no choice but to make use of Alistair's influence at the Andrew P. Mott School of Medicine up here near Harmony.

She had straightened her black curls, tossed her glitzy wardrobe, and become Dr. Eve Johnson, the efficient, well-spoken young medical student.

No one in their right mind would ever think to associate her with the melancholy jazz singer who'd performed years ago for a few hours one night at the Harmony Country Club.

Eve found it a breeze to resurrect the image she'd carried with her since childhood—the upstanding good girl. Her affair with Julian Crane, her drug and alcohol abuse, her pregnancy, and all the heartbreaking results of it were now buried deep inside her.

She'd vowed never to speak of it to anyone. Not ever.

When Scat had left Boston to perform on the road and Crystal had taken up an offer to tour some nightclubs in England and Germany, she decided she'd never see them again, either. Though she appreciated their kindness, she wanted nothing more to do with that past life. And once she was done training here in Harmony, she intended to leave the area for good.

During her years of study, she'd disciplined her mind to stay focused. Unemotional. And most of the time, she was in total control of everything, inside and out.

But there were times, like this one, when the specter of her past rose up to haunt her anew. And when it did, she always reacted the same way. Just shoved it right back down into its ugly grave, forcing her mind to sharpen again and refocus on the matter at hand—and at the moment, that matter was the man in front of her.

"This is an anesthetic," Eve said softly. "It will just numb your hand. That's all. Like Novocain at the dentist's office." Then she lowered her voice even more. "It's *not* a *narcotic*."

"Oh."

Watching the man's shoulders relax and his eyes settle confirmed what she'd already guessed.

T. C. Russell had been addicted to drugs.

Just like her.

She looked into his deep brown eyes once more. And then she saw it. Pain. Loss. Rage. Defensiveness. A part of herself was in there. She could see it. Right inside his eyes.

"Okay?" she whispered, approaching with the needle.

"Yeah. Fine."

Eve positioned the needle carefully, just under the edge of the skin, and injected the anesthetic.

"It'll be numb in a minute . . . looks like five, maybe six stitches."

"Whatever you think, Doc."

"So, Mr. Russell . . ." Eve opened the Dermalon packet and began to affix the curved suturing needle to the needle holder. "Why did you go and do a fool thing like put your hand through a plate-glass window?"

"How do you know I did that, anyway?"

"It was on your chart."

"Oh."

"So? Why did you—"

"I didn't *know* it was a plate-glass window. I thought I was punching part of the Youth Center's bulletin board."

"A bulletin board?"

"There was a notice up there. Made me crazy."

After testing the wound's numbness, Eve began to take the first stitch.

"Tell me exactly what happened," she urged him, wanting to keep his mind off the procedure. "From the beginning."

"Well . . . I'd finished coaching a few of my students—"

"You're a teacher?"

"PE at Harmony High. I started working with this after-school boxing club, Tuesday and Thursday nights at the Youth Center. Troubled kids, you know? They need a positive outlet for their anger . . . anyway, after the kids left, I started on the bag by myself, and—"

"You're a serious boxer?"

T. C. laughed, but there was nothing funny about it. The sound was harsh, biting.

"I'm not a 'serious' anything. Not anymore. Boxing's just a way for me to get out my . . . emotions."

"Your anger?"

"My therapist suggested it four years ago."

"I see."

"No, you don't."

"Okay, then. *What* don't I see?"

"Forget it."

Eve continued her work, methodically putting in a second stitch, tying it off with three neat square knots, then cutting the blue Dermalon thread with sterile scissors. She needed him to keep his hand steady, and she knew he was aggravated. She'd better keep him talking.

"So keep going with your story."

"And I was on my way back to the locker room when I saw this notice. Turned out the center had so many notices and schedules and paperwork, they just extended the b-board's mess onto the window of the director's office. The window was completely plastered, you know? There was no way to tell it wasn't part of the cork board."

"That must have been *some* notice for you to want to punch it that hard," said Eve, tying off a third stitch and starting a fourth. "What *was* it?"

"Tennis announcement. Had a photo of a guy on it—a former regional champion. You might say I don't like this guy much."

"I see."

"No. You don't."

Eve sighed. This guy was a hard case, all right. Drug addiction. Buried anger so volatile that he'd put his fist through plate glass for what sounded like a trivial reason. She knew it spelled bad news . . . yet there was something about this guy . . . this T. C. Russell . . . that made Eve want to know more . . .

T. C. watched the young doctor tie off the fourth stitch and begin to take a fifth.

He tried not to be too impressed by her. But he was. She looked so young, yet acted so together. Perceptive. Almost wise. He saw it there—living in those bright brown eyes of hers, eyes filled with fire and punch—a thing beyond mere beauty. And that meant everything to T. C.

Beauty approached him all the time. During work, at the market, in the park. Beauty threw herself at him, draped herself over him, lavished him with all sorts of luscious offers. But Beauty, he'd discovered, couldn't stomach ugliness.

Oh, she loved her romantic encounters, her quick, steamy couplings. She even loved the "intimacy" of "sharing secrets"—just as long as those secrets were harmless and petty.

Beauty wanted a happy-go-lucky dude with no problems, no terror, no fury.

She simply didn't know how to handle the kind of wreckage that polluted the dark recesses of T. C.'s soul . . . confusion and helplessness, failure and rage, guilt and self-hate.

This woman. This doctor. She was a beauty: skin as smooth as milk chocolate, inviting lips, a slender, curving figure—from what he could see of her pastel blouse and dark slacks under her open white lab coat. But that wasn't *all* she was.

He could sense the maturity inside her, even though she was younger than him. He could tell she'd seen a lot, and she had a defensive, guarded way about her like the kids in his boxing club.

T. C. studied her, even as she examined him.

He watched how she probed his ragged gash of torn flesh and dried blood. She did it without flinching. Without blinking. She did it stoically, methodically, with tenderness, and even a little bit of humor.

Now she was stitching up this gaping hole in his hand.

And T. C. got to wondering if maybe she could stitch up something more in him . . .

You're nuts, T. C. You're imagining things because you're attracted to her.

Understandable, since he was exhausted and embarrassed by what had happened tonight. But when he'd seen Julian Crane's face smirking at him on that big announcement for an upcoming Crane-sponsored charity tennis tournament, T. C. had just snapped. He'd already thrown about five hundred punches at the bag. It was practically an automatic response to drive his fist through Julian Crane's face.

It was just too damned bad there'd been plate glass behind it.

The endless waiting in this ER had been the hardest part. For two hours his mind had nothing to do but brood about what had happened to him.

The car wreck. His shattered leg and career. His father's devastating disappointment. The inability of Chief Bennett to nail Crane for the crime. His father's heart attacks. His own depression. The addiction to painkillers to make it all go away. Kicking the addiction. The hard physical therapy. Then, finally, just six months ago, his father's death.

Before Dr. Johnson opened the curtain on him, T. C. had just wanted *out* of this place. Out of this room where they'd left him alone with himself and his thoughts. With his anguish.

He still wanted out, he supposed. But a part of him didn't mind being with her. He liked the way she looked at him, spoke to him, touched him.

She made it easier.

But he doubted she'd care to have much to do with him once she found out his history. Shame and guilt suddenly overwhelmed him.

What a loser I am. What a profound loser.

T. C. looked away from his hand and up at the ceiling.

Studying the fluorescent light fixtures, he silently commanded his glistening eyes to dry out.

"Am I hurting you?" she asked in the sweetest, softest voice.

"Nah," said T. C. truthfully. "I can barely feel anything anymore."

After dressing the stitched-up wound and giving him instructions on keeping it dry and clean, Eve sent T. C. Russell off into the warm September night.

She filled out some final paperwork, then approached her boss in the doctor's lounge.

"Dr. Malone, my shift is over. But do you need me to do anything else?"

Malone was a brown-bearded, middle-aged man who was direct and demanding, yet always calm even during the most hectic times in the E.R. Eve had learned a lot working under him, and strived for that same level of cool control in her own approach to emergency medicine.

He was taking his break now, drinking a cup of black coffee. A recent medical journal sat open in front of him on the scratched Formica top of the wooden table.

"How long have you been on today, anyway?"

Eve shrugged. "Sixteen hours."

"Get some rest."

"I will."

"Ms. Johnson—" Malone looked at her from over the top of his reading glasses. "Given any more thought about the residency program here?"

"I hadn't planned on staying in Harmony."

"Too bad." Malone returned his attention to the journal on the table. "You've been one of the best acting interns I've ever had in my ER. You know that, don't you?"

Eve felt a flush come to her cheeks. "I didn't know that's how you felt, Doctor. Thank you."

"Hate to lose you, Ms. Johnson. I hope you rethink your applications."

"I don't know. Maybe. Maybe I will." Eve was about to go when she stopped. "Doctor, do you know anything about the local man who was in here tonight for sutures? T. C. Russell?"

"What do you want to know?"

Eve shrugged. "He said something about my not knowing his history, and I was curious."

"His leg was shattered a few years ago. Nothing we could do here helped. We sent him to specialists in Boston, but . . ."

Malone shook his head.

"I don't understand. He seems fine. I mean, he wasn't even limping. He looks healthy—"

"The leg's fine for average use. But it's too weak for pro tennis. Muscular range of motion is shot, too."

"Tennis?"

"He was a college star four years ago. On his way up. The injury cost him his career."

My god, realized Eve, *that's why he punched the tennis announcement.*

It hadn't been an expression of random, pointless violence at all—his rage had been triggered by pain and loss. She *had* seen all those things in him, the same things she'd felt in herself since she'd lost her son.

"Was it a long recovery?" she asked Dr. Malone.

"Coma for a month. A solid year of physical therapy. Some problems with depression."

"Heavy-duty painkillers, I'll bet?"

"Oh, for sure."

"He have problems with that? The painkillers? An addiction, maybe?"

Malone looked a little uncomfortable, as though Eve was prying into Mr. Russell's privacy. She understood. Harmony was a small town, and rumors, especially when you were a teacher at a local high school, could be a dangerous thing.

"Yes, Ms. Johnson," Dr. Malone finally said. "That's what I heard happened with his treatment in Boston. But he's been through therapy. Not just physical—mental, too. How'd the suturing go?"

"Oh, fine. No problems."

Except for the fact that he was as defensive as hell, thought Eve. *And obviously hates doctors because they couldn't give him back his career. And at least one of them had made him an addict for a time by failing to monitor his abuse of medication.*

"Did you tell him to come back in ten days? To get them removed?" Dr. Malone asked her.

"Yes."

"I'd like you to be the one who removes them. Good for you to see how your sutures healed on the wound."

Eve nodded again, then said good night, privately pleased

that it was now officially part of her job to see T. C. Russell once more.

It's just that he has such an interesting medical history, she told herself repeatedly over the next ten days.

After all, I'm a complete professional now. A woman in control. There's really no other reason, she assured herself, *for wanting that man back on my examining table.*

THIRTY-SIX

Healing

"There you go, good as new."

"That's a cliché, Doc. Once something's been hurt, it's never as good as new."

Eve nodded as she put down the sterile scissors, then brought her gaze back up to T. C. Russell's handsome face. "Guess you're right."

"You know I am."

"But," she added, "wounds do heal. With time."

"Some do. Some don't."

Exactly ten days after receiving Eve's carefully sewn stitches, T. C. Russell had returned to Harmony Hospital's emergency room to have them removed.

Eve was more than pleased with her careful suturing work. The tear in his hand was healing nicely. There would barely be a scar.

As she turned toward the sink to wash up, she heard T. C. behind her, climbing down to the floor from the high examining table.

He wasn't wearing boxing trunks this time. He'd come straight from his teaching job in a crisply ironed pale blue shirt, navy slacks, and a navy-and-gray-striped tie. He was clean shaven, and his sporty, masculine cologne hung in the air.

They'd talked while she'd worked on him. Joked a bit. He'd teased her, even flirted a little. She hadn't discouraged it.

"So. Take care now," she told him, washing up at the sink. "Don't go punching any more tennis announcements, okay?"

"How about if I just promise to make sure they're not posted on plate glass?"

"I guess I can settle for that."

"And how about a nice lobster dinner? Can you settle for that, too, Doc?"

Eve's hands stilled under the water. She shut off the faucet, certain she'd misheard him. "Excuse me?"

"I'm asking you out, Doc. Dinner. Tonight. With me."

Eve hesitated. She grabbed a paper towel and spent a silent moment drying her hands. Then she turned and faced him.

He had rolled down the right sleeve of his pale blue shirt and was now buttoning it up around his wrist. He looked up. His deep brown gaze was steady, almost intense, as he watched her consider his invitation. He added four simple words to it.

"I won't ask again."

Eve knew he wouldn't. He had been through too much to play games.

But, she cautioned herself, a split-second decision about getting involved with a man she didn't know had once changed her life for the worst. How could she possibly consider it again?

"I'm sorry," she said, looking away. "I just . . . I don't know you . . ."

Coward.

That was her grandmother's voice. And it echoed through her entire being as she watched T. C. nod once—

stiffly, unhappily, yet resigned, as if he wasn't at all surprised to have been dismissed so easily by her. Without another word, he turned to go.

Eve chewed at her bottom lip as he strode away. *Am I really done taking chances?* Maybe she wasn't. But she was so out of practice, she wasn't even sure how to take one anymore. There were all sorts of things involved, she knew . . .

Stamina. Imagination. Optimism. Vulnerability.

And faith, her grandmother's voice reminded her. *Faith in your capacity to give, and to receive.*

Work was much less taxing for Eve to think about. And she had plenty of that. There were always more patients to see. More paperwork to fill out. More textbooks and journals to read. She should just forget that his invitation to dinner ever happened.

Refocus your mind, Eve, like you've disciplined yourself.

But for a moment, she couldn't.

She just stood there in the hallway, watching T. C.'s broad back move farther and farther away from her.

A pale blue boat drifting from the dock, heading for uncharted waters. And she couldn't find the courage to call it back.

"Watch your stance, Jay! That's right. Angle your body like I showed you."

Just four days after his stitches were out, T. C. was back at the Youth Center, coaching the kids in his boxing club. Although he couldn't box himself until his wounded hand was more fully healed, he was certainly able to continue his coaching.

Right now he was keeping one eye on the steel stopwatch in his hand and one eye on the two fifteen-year-olds dancing around each other on the springy surface of the boxing ring.

Jay and Antonio were about the same height and weight,

but Tony had a lot more experience wearing boxing gloves, and T. C. wanted to make sure Jay got enough oral instructions to stay in for the entire three-minute round.

"Keep your right up. Protect your face. Footwork! Footwork!"

T. C. smiled. Jay was listening, holding his own.

"Time!" called T. C., clicking off the watch.

The smile on Jay's face gave T. C. more than enough satisfaction for his two hours of work with all the kids tonight.

"I did it!" cried Jay. "He barely touched me. I even got some points on him, didn't I, Coach?!"

"Lucky jabs, man," teased Tony, but he was laughing, too.

Everyone felt good about Jay's progress. The guys around the ring even clapped.

Jay's problems were no different from theirs. He'd been arrested twice for petty theft. Had no father to speak of and a mother who worked three jobs. T. C. knew what this program meant to the kid. To all the kids.

"That's it for the night, guys. Hit the showers and I'll see you on Thursday. Okay, line it up. Let me hear it—"

T. C. knew some of the kids thought it was corny, but he insisted that at the end of every boxing club session each of the boys "touch gloves" with T. C., while promising him to do one thing till they saw each other again:

"Stay out of trouble."

These four words were repeated over and over, echoing through the gym as each of the fifteen kids promised the same thing in turn. T. C. wanted each of them to take the echo of that promise with him no matter where he went, no matter what he did, in the days between their club meetings.

It was that kind of reinforcement that had already kept two of his kids from damaging Harmony shops with graffiti a week ago, and three of his kids from joining a car theft gang in Castleton last month.

T. C. had his own silent four-word refrain when he touched gloves with each of them: *Lord, watch over them*.

When the last kid made his promise and trotted off to the showers, T. C. picked a towel off the ropes and slung it over the shoulder of his gray sweatshirt. As he moved across the center of the Youth Center's gymnasium, he happened to look up toward the doorway about thirty feet away.

What he saw there made him freeze in his tracks.

"Is it too late for the Doctor Lady to change her mind?" *She's out of her lab coat.*

That was T. C.'s first thought as he took in the yellow halter dress, the delicate shoulders, the tiny waist and flaring skirt above long, stockinged legs.

Definitely out of her lab coat.

She was leaning against the doorjamb as if she'd been standing there watching him and the kids for quite a long time. Her dark brown hair was swept up, and she'd even put on ruby lipstick.

"Mr. Russell? Did you hear me?"

T. C. blinked. The knockout had spoken.

Answer her, fool!

"Uh . . . I don't know, Doc. Thought you were all business. Sure you didn't stop by just to check my hand?"

"Oh, I can check your hand if that's *all* you want."

"If that's *all* I want?"

T. C. exhaled a slow, shaky breath as he studied her. Man, he wanted to go to her. Run to her. But he didn't.

"Okay, Doc," he said, standing there in the middle of the gym, deciding right then not to budge an inch. "*Check* it."

He folded his muscled forearms across his broad chest and waited for her to come to him.

That's right, Doc, let's get it straight from the start. I'm not one of your happy-go-lucky, easygoing dudes. Are you really ready to step into my arena?

He watched her hesitate, trying to figure out what his mood was. It was a long, awkward moment, and for a second T. C. was sure she was going to turn right around and run straight back to her little professional refuge at the hospital, where she had all the answers, all the control.

Steady, T. C., he advised himself, watching her. *She's the one who needs to take the steps. So let her . . .*

Finally she did step forward, her long, high-heeled legs moving crisply toward him over the polished wood floor of the gymnasium.

She strode like she was still in the ER, he realized with amusement—tense, professional, acting all in control . . . and uptight as hell.

"Watch it, Doc!" he called suddenly. "Those heels of yours could scuff up my gym floor!"

Eve jerked to a stop. Worriedly, she looked down at the floor, then back up at T. C. She saw his lips twitching.

"Are you trying to make a fool out of me, Mr. Russell?"

No, Doctor Lady, thought T. C., still refusing to budge. *Coach Russell's just testing how badly you want to be here . . . outside your comfort zone . . . outside a world that's safe and small.*

Eve humphed loudly. Refusing to turn back, she placed her hands on her hips, kicked off her shoes, and continued striding toward him in her stocking feet.

"Extra credit for determination, Doc," he teased with a half-smile, "though you've got to loosen up. But don't worry, I'll help with that."

"Let me see it."

"The hand?"

"Of course."

"What do I get for showing you?"

"You get to buy me dinner."

"I see. And what part of my human anatomy do I have to show you for you to *cook* me dinner?"

Eve's eyebrows rose. He knew she could see the humor in his eyes. The teasing. And something else, a message—

I'm a man, sweetheart. A grown man, not a boy. Can you deal with that?

"I'll need time to figure that one out," she told him.

"I see."

"But . . ." she added, mirroring his own mischievous smile, "I'm betting it won't take long."

For the first time since she'd turned him down, T. C. laughed.

The warm, hopeful sound echoed through the gymnasium, more than filling the cold empty spaces around them both.

THIRTY-SEVEN

Second Chances

Despite her early sparring matches with T. C. Russell, it didn't take long for Eve to acknowledge that the chemistry between them was love.

Within five, maybe six weeks, she had recognized how much they shared. A sense of humor and adventure. A fondness for the ocean and small towns. A desire for home, family—children.

They'd spent an intense amount of time together. Almost every weeknight, during her late shifts at the hospital, T. C. would cook a homemade dinner himself and bring it over to share with her in the doctors' lounge.

Whenever she had a free day or two on the weekends, T. C. took her out, flowers always in hand. One Sunday they'd driven through the mountains to enjoy the fall leaves and pick apples; a week later they'd rented a small wooden sailboat to cut a path along the blue rugged coastline; a week after that they'd popped into Boston to join T. C.'s best friend, Sam Bennett, for a late-season Red Sox game.

Sam lived in Boston, a police officer on the force there, and he'd acted overjoyed to meet Eve. "I've never seen a woman make T. C. so happy!"

Eve was pleased because she herself had never met a

man who could be so giving of himself. T. C. gave Eve so much of his time and attention, his help and support . . . and all of it without trying to take something from her.

It was a remarkably uplifting change from what Julian Crane had conditioned Eve to expect from a man.

But Eve no longer wanted plane rides to Bermuda and wild evenings on disco floors. She didn't need diamond chokers or record contracts. What she wanted now more than anything was what T. C. could offer her: A future to build on. A home and family.

The only problem was—he hadn't proposed that yet, even after Eve had dropped a few hints. And she was getting anxious.

Did he have doubts about her? Or himself? Was marriage in their future? And if it was, how long would it take him to decide?

"I just wish my father could have met you," T. C. told Eve one October Saturday afternoon on the beach.

He'd built a campfire, spread a heavy plaid blanket on the sand, and laid out a simple snack. A bottle of California wine, a hunk of Vermont cheddar, and a heavy loaf of homemade Portuguese brown bread. They'd watched the foaming waves for hours, talking, kissing, holding each other.

Fall's cool weather had chased every last dog walker and jogger off the sand by sunset. But Eve and T. C. had both dressed in blue jeans and warm layers, topped with thick cream-colored fisherman's sweaters they'd bought together on their shopping spree in Boston the week before.

"Your father," repeated Eve. "How long ago did you lose him?"

"Seven months."

"I'm so sorry."

"Thanks." T. C. sighed. The sound was profoundly sad. But there was a slight moan of anguish at the end of it. More than a sense of regret. It sounded to Eve like guilt.

She studied T. C.'s strong profile. Early on in their relationship, Eve had confessed to T. C. that she'd asked another doctor about his medical history. She knew that a leg injury had derailed his tennis career. But T. C. refused to talk about it—even to tell her how it had happened. He just repeated that he wanted to stay focused on the present and the future. Forget about the past.

Eve was all too ready to agree. She certainly didn't want to discuss her own past. So that's what they'd agreed to—up until now, anyway.

This was the first time T. C. had brought up his father.

"Doesn't stop hurting, you know?" he said. "They say it never will. I mean—you never stop missing the person you lose. You just cope with it, work it into your life."

"Yes, that's right."

The sun was setting, and twilight was pushing in. Stars became visible in the darkening violet above. T. C. stoked their little campfire, pulled a second blanket from his athletic bag, then sat down next to Eve and wrapped it around them both.

They were completely alone now, the only two souls on the beach.

"You lost someone, too," he said as he put his arm around her shoulders. "I can see the sadness there inside you, Eve. The truth is, I saw it the first day I met you."

"You did?"

"Your eyes told me. I could see you'd been through some hard times."

"You're right," she whispered, surprised that the words affected her so deeply. But no one had ever probed before. She'd never let anyone get close enough to.

"Your parents?"

Eve looked away.

"Gee, both of them. I'm sorry for you, too."

"Loss is hard," she murmured.

In a way, she *had* lost her parents. They'd never even

tried to contact her again after she'd refused to give up her son for adoption. And she certainly wasn't going to call them.

But the hard loss she'd spoken of hadn't been her parents. It had been her child.

With her drug and alcohol abuse, Eve still felt completely responsible for her son's passing. That little, innocent, precious life—she'd as much as killed it with her own hands. She'd never forgiven herself for that, and she'd certainly never reveal it. Not to anyone. Not ever.

It was her own private hell. No one, least of all T. C. Russell with his own slate of problems, needed to be dragged down into sharing that awful pain with her.

"So how old were you?" asked T. C. "Were you very young when you lost your mother and father?"

Eve hesitated. She hadn't expected him to continue questioning her. She shifted uncomfortably.

"Well . . . umm . . . you might say that they left me at a young age to be raised by my aunts."

That was *close* to the truth, she told herself. That's how she'd thought of the succession of elderly sitters her busy mother and father had hired to watch her during her childhood.

"Oh, I see. Your aunts," repeated T. C. "See, I knew I could sense there was a wise old woman living somewhere inside you. Guess they were pretty strict with you, too, huh? I mean, you're so straight-laced and everything."

"What do you mean?"

"You know! Your ethics and your moral standards are so high. I guess it's one of the things I admire about you."

Eve had mixed feelings about his words.

More than anything, she wanted T. C. to believe all those good things about her, because she intended to live up to them—and with his faith in this virtuous image of her, she knew she could.

Things were going so well with T. C., Eve didn't want to

give him any reason to doubt her. Yet a needling little voice inside her accused her of acting a part again—

It's the same thing you did with Julian! Only this time you're pretending to be a good girl, instead of a bad one.

It is not! she railed back. *This is far different. I'm simply going back to the life I'd been living before I'd taken that wrong turn. All I'm doing is wiping that little part of my slate clean again!*

"You know, Eve, so many people take the easy way out. Sink to the lowest, most selfish level of existence; hurt others without a moment's pause. I see it with the kids in my club—parents who neglect them, abuse drugs and alcohol. It just makes my blood boil!"

Eve blinked in surprise as T. C. punched the sand beside him.

Now do you see what you're dealing with? needled that awful voice inside her again. *T. C. better not ever hear the truth about your past. About the drugs. The alcohol. About how your innocent baby died because of your weakness and stupidity . . .*

"Take it easy, T. C.," whispered Eve.

"Sorry. I just . . . I've seen a lot. Been through a lot. I never told you much about my shattered leg."

"T. C., I know it's painful for you to talk about. You don't have to—"

"There are things you should know."

Eve nodded, braced herself.

"I was a cocky kid. But I was also a prodigy. My college coach saw it, Eve. I *knew* I was headed for Wimbledon. Fame and fortune, just like Arthur Ashe, you know? And looking back now, people might tell you that maybe I was. Or maybe I wasn't . . .

"But the hardest damned thing for me to get around is the 'maybe I was' part of the equation. I mean, if I had had my shot and failed, well, at least I'd know, for the rest of my life, that I had done my level best . . .

"You see, at the heart of sport is the journey—the *effort* the athlete makes in achieving. That's what I've tried to teach my students—the young athletes I coach at the high school, and the kids at the boxing club, too. It's that climb to be the best that enriches you. The discipline earns you self-knowledge, self-respect. And the better your competitor, the harder you find you can push yourself, until you've achieved something you never thought possible.

"It's divine, Eve. To me, anyway, the experience felt divine. It elevated my spirit; it nourished me. It was my whole life! So, you see, in the end even if I never made it to the very top, at least I would have had the experience of a lifetime trying . . ."

Eve could hear the emotion in T. C.'s voice. The difficulty at sharing such intimate thoughts and feelings. She knew he was really opening up now—that this was a vital moment for them both.

She had to say something. She knew that. He was silent, expectant, waiting for her response—

"I know what you're telling me, T. C. I understand," Eve whispered gently.

"Do you?"

Eve met his eyes.

"I went through therapy, Eve, but it didn't clean my slate, you know? And I need you to understand that about me. I mean, how do you let go of the rage over a smashed dream? I'm not sure I ever can. Or ever will. I think it's something I'll be living with for the rest of my life."

T. C.'s eyes were still on her. He looked guarded, and she knew he was studying her, waiting for her reaction to his words.

He expects me to challenge him, she realized, *to give him some childish pabulum about how we've all got to move on, leave our pain behind, forget the past . . .*

Eve didn't. Instead, she just took his hand. Continued to stare into his eyes.

"So do you know what I'm saying, Eve?" he whispered.

"I know *exactly* what you're saying. There are some things we just don't get over. *Ever*."

"That's right."

"Some pain we just learn to live with. Like a piece of furniture in the room—the ugliest chair you ever saw. And you didn't bring it into your pretty room. It just got dropped there. And you want to move it, but it's bolted to the floor forever—and that's that. You can maybe drape something over it. Decide not to look in its direction for years at a time. But it will always be there. In a house you can never leave until you die."

T. C. blinked in astonishment. "I've never met a woman who said anything like that before."

"Is that right? What do they usually say, then?"

"Something along the lines of: 'Oh, T. C., honey, you'll get over it. Just keep moving on with your life. You'll forget it soon enough.' And then, of course, they can't understand why I *can't*."

"I know."

"Funny. The night we met. After I put my fist through Julian Crane's face on that tennis announcement. I would have bet you were the type to tell me to just get over it. Get over being so angry that my tennis career, my lifelong dream—and my father's, too—was just smashed to bits—"

"T. C. . . . *whose* face did you say you put your fist through?"

"Julian Crane's."

Eve felt her heart stop. Her lungs still.

"Did you say *Julian Crane?*"

"Yes. I know you don't know who he is, since you didn't grow up in Harmony, but his father sits on the board of your medical school. His father sits on the board of just about everything in this town . . ."

"He does?" Eve's voice became small. The voice of a mouse with its tail in a trap.

"Listen, Eve, I'm sorry I brought him up. He was one of my fiercest tennis competitors. And I guess you could say he's part of that ugly furniture I've been living with. But it doesn't mean I have to talk about him. I don't need or want to bring up his name again. Let's keep the creep in the past, okay?"

Eve nodded quickly.

Urging her to snuggle closer, T. C. curled the muscular arm resting across her shoulders tight around her. She buried her shock and dread in the warm protection of his broad, sweater-covered chest. Then she closed her eyes and listened to the rhythmic crashing of the foaming waves.

But it was the subtle, masculine scent of T. C.'s cologne mingled with the steady sound of his heartbeat that comforted her, settled her own racing heart and ragged breathing. Eve found herself wishing with every fiber of her being that she could just stay right here, in T. C.'s arms, for the rest of her life.

But how could she? *My god, what if T. C. ever discovers that I'd shared a bed with Julian Crane? Conceived a son with him?*

"Eve, I want you to know that after all I've been through . . . with my tennis career ending, the death of my father, a man I let down tremendously . . . I guess I just want some peace back in my life. Some grace, you know? And that's what you are to me, honey. You're a beacon of virtue in this crazy, awful world. Like the Harmony lighthouse over there."

Eve opened her eyes and angled her head toward the rock jetty farther down the beach, where the light turned in a steady, rhythmic pulse, beaming its bright illumination across the dark water.

"You're so good, Eve. So pure and good. I want you to keep me out of the fog and gloom. Keep me on the straight and narrow—"

"T. C., please don't—"

"Don't what?"

"Don't put me on a pedestal like that. I'm just a woman."

"Oh, I know you're a woman, honey."

T. C.'s strong fingers touched her chin, tipping her face toward his. "A warm and passionate one."

His lips were full and gentle as they brushed across hers, soft as eiderdown, sweet as chocolate bark. As it had so many times before, his kiss ignited her.

The intoxicating taste of wine still lingered in his warm mouth, and she drank it in with a soft moan. She pushed her tongue into him, suddenly needing to possess him.

T. C. groaned. He wanted her badly, and she clung to that need within him. *It's so good with him. So good. Please, God, don't let me lose this . . .*

With a touch of desperation, she pressed closer—

And then he suddenly tore himself way.

His breathing was hard, fast. His deep brown eyes were glistening in the dim firelight. Something was wrong.

That's it, Eve! He's sensed you're a liar. You've slipped or something, murmured Julian's name without thinking, done something to make him doubt you!

Eve's heart began to beat wildly. She searched his face, the face of the man she loved. She knew that with all her heart. He'd made her so happy—so very happy. After all the pain and sorrow, all the lies and disappointments, she knew T. C. was her lighthouse now, too. The only thing that could brighten her world, show her the way to having love in her life again.

"T. C.?" she whispered, her voice strangled. "Is something wrong?"

"No, baby. Everything's right."

"Then why did you pull away—"

T. C. studied her for a long moment. Then he reached over, into the outside pocket of his athletic bag, and pulled out a small metal Band-Aid box.

"What in the world is that for?"

"Open it."

With a nervous shiver, Eve flipped open the little tin box. There was gauze inside. She pulled it out, then gasped.

Nestled in the middle of the fluffy sterile cloud was a beautiful marquise-cut diamond ring.

"Wounds heal," whispered T. C. "I believe that now. As long as there's love."

Tears flowed over Eve's eyes, down her cheeks and chin. "Oh, T. C."

"Will you wear it? Will you marry me?"

Too choked up to answer, Eve simply nodded. His thick, strong fingers took the delicate diamond and, with the utmost care, slipped it onto the slender ring finger of her left hand.

"It's so beautiful—"

"You're so beautiful, Eve. *Beyond* beautiful."

She kissed him, her arms curling around his neck, coaxing him closer.

He obliged.

After a quick glance around the dark beach to confirm that they were completely alone, he dragged her into his lap. Then his hands tangled in her hair as he tasted her, pushing past her parted lips to ravage her mouth. The kiss was hungry, aggressive, full of the fire she'd seen in him from the moment they'd met.

It was an incredible kiss, possessive, adoring—it left her weak and dizzy, banished her fears and doubts and replaced them with a passionate resolve.

Julian Crane may have ruined my life once, but I'll be damned if I let him do it again, Eve swore to the winds. *And no man, let alone one as revolting as Julian, is going to keep me from marrying this amazing and extraordinary man in front of me now . . . this man of my dreams . . .*

Eve felt T. C. urging her backward onto the soft blanket, felt his strong, hard legs parting hers, pressing into her as he continued the heady ministrations of his mouth and lips and tongue.

She wanted more of him. God, she *always* wanted more!

When he had her like this, something clicked inside her, and she wanted down off that damn pedestal, wanted him to know there was nothing straight-laced about her when it came to loving him.

Taking his hand, she moved it under her sweater and turtleneck, urged it to move over her skin. The sweater was so thick, she hadn't bothered with a bra this morning. He moaned into her mouth when he found the naked flesh beneath, clearly delighting in the intimate secrets beneath her sweater.

Eve sighed as he feathered his fingers across her breasts, teased their tips the way she liked. She pushed her tongue harder into him as her hand found the tight bulge beneath the zipper of his blue jeans. Shamelessly, she rubbed him.

He ached with sweet agony.

Boldly, she unzipped him, reached inside.

In surprise, T. C. lifted his head and looked into her eyes. "Dr. Johnson . . . what do you think you're doing?"

"I don't know, Coach. What do *you* think I'm doing?" she whispered as her fingers gave him long, lovely strokes.

He closed his *eyes*. "Oh, you can be a *bad* girl, can't you, honey?"

"That's *exactly* what I need you to know, Coach Russell."

"Oh, I got the message . . . mmmm . . . yeah . . . I got it."

"I'm a woman who knows what she wants."

"From this day forward, sweetheart, whatever you want, you're gonna get. I'll make sure of it."

"Good," whispered Eve. " 'Cause I want you, T. C."

"You've got me. I promise. You've got me forever."

"And babies. You can help me with that, can't you?"

"Oh, my darling . . . just say the word."

That same night, far away, a handsome little four-year-old boy blinked in confusion as the nice lady in the dark blue suit took his hand and led him out the doorway of the only small, cluttered home he could remember.

The nice lady came by all the time. She was pretty and kind and he liked her, so he didn't mind going off with her tonight.

The nice lady was the one who explained that he'd been living in a *foster* home. And she told him this place was actually the third one he'd been placed in since he'd been born.

"Why do I have to leave?" he asked the lady. She was carrying his little suitcase in her other hand. And he had his one toy, a worn, stuffed panda, under his arm.

"They can't take care of you anymore, honey. I'm sorry. But we have another place for you to stay."

"Another mommy?"

"Yes, dear. Another *foster* mommy."

The little boy turned and waved good-bye to the lady in the doorway. She'd been nice to him. Fixed his meals and stuff. Though there were so many kids in the house, he felt as though she hardly even noticed him half the time.

Still, she was the only mommy he could remember.

THIRTY-EIGHT

Sam's Rescue

"Step out of the car, sir."

"Why?"

The male suspect was big. Maybe six feet, two hundred pounds, and seriously drunk.

"Step out. *Now*."

Police Officer Sam Bennett was on a night tour alone. Saturday in early May. The Boston bars were letting out, and he was used to this sort of attitude, especially from the college crowd.

This one was about twenty, pristine button-down, driving a BMW. He'd run a stop sign and a red light, nearly hitting an old woman and a young couple. Then he'd started zigzagging over the yellow line, flirting with oncoming traffic.

To top it off, just as Sam was pulling the idiot over, he'd thrown a backhanded slap to the young woman sitting beside him in the passenger seat.

"Hey, look, I'm late for a party. So spare me the lecture and just give me the ticket."

"You're not getting a ticket tonight. *Step out*."

After almost four years patrolling the Boston streets, Sam had to agree with the instructors he'd trained under at the

Police Academy: Drunken college kids were often the most unpredictable suspects to subdue.

Truck drivers and working-class types had been in enough bar fights in their lives to know the sort of colossal trouble that came from wrestling a cop. Unless they were truly bombed, they came along quietly.

Gang members liked to run. They might ambush you down the road, but initially they pounded the ground.

Drunken college males, on the other hand, could do almost anything. With out-of-control egos and little experience in hand-to-hand fighting, they didn't understand how quickly thrown fists could become life-and-death blows.

Youth also made for erratic behavior. And in Sam's experience, few drunken college kids ever displayed anything but disrespect for an officer of the law.

As the car door flew open, Sam stepped back into a bladed stance, his own body angled to the center of the suspect's torso, his holstered weapon away from the suspect's reach.

"Put your hands on the car hood."

"Why?"

"You are driving drunk, almost ran down three pedestrians, and I'm going to arrest you," said Sam calmly. "Now put your hands on the hood of the car."

"Arrest me? Screw you, pig!"

Here we go. Confrontation time.

"Don't be an ass, Hammond!" called the young woman from inside the car.

"Shut up, bitch!"

Sam pulled his baton out of the ring on his utility belt. "We're done talking. Do you *really* want to get hurt?"

The suspect launched, and Sam was ready. An extended shaft circle strike hit his latissimus dorsi and serratus anterior, two major muscle groups.

The guy blinked in shock, stunned that he'd been hit. And hit hard.

Confrontational Situation Training. Ingrained. *When you've got to get physical with a suspect, do it fast. Give him no chance to think and retaliate.*

Sam power-cuffed the idiot in three seconds flat.

"Screw you, pig!"

"Shut the hell up, would you?" Sam patted him down and found a glass vial with about five grams of coke. Street value in the thousands. He held it up to the suspect's face.

"Sorry, buddy. Party's over."

" 'Night, Sam."

" 'Night, Bill."

Another tour over. It was close to one in the morning when Sam trotted down the concrete steps of his precinct house and headed for his parked car.

The Pinto was long gone. He'd been making good money on the Boston force, so after he'd finally completed his criminal justice degree through part-time studies, he'd celebrated by buying the midnight-blue Mustang he'd coveted since he'd turned sixteen.

Actually, if he wanted to be entirely honest with himself, Sam had recognized the mental necessity of ditching the Pinto. It reminded him too much of Ivy and that hideous day she'd sucker-punched him, leaving Pilar to inform him she'd left on her honeymoon with Julian Crane.

Driving away that day, Sam had nearly wrecked that Pinto at the bottom of Raven Hill. He remembered driving it off the road, sitting there in stunned shock, unable to decide what to do.

The pain came later, after he'd driven the thing to the beach and cried at the spot where he'd rescued her years before. Then he'd gotten back behind the wheel and floored it to Boston, just as they'd originally planned the morning after her wedding. The morning after they'd made love all night long and she'd promised, *promised* to leave Julian and marry him.

Well, he'd decided, if Ivy could so easily dispose of him and make a new life for herself, then so could he. Which included the disposal of his damned car.

Over the past five years, Sam had been back to Harmony only a few times. The most recent was for T. C.'s wedding a few months earlier. Man, his friend had really hit the jackpot there. Eve Johnson was a real knockout *and* a doctor.

He'd never seen two people more in love.

It choked Sam up to see them take their vows in Harmony's little white church. He hadn't been back to Harmony since then, but then, his family and friends were used to him staying away. When they wanted to see him, they came to Boston.

Over the last five years, Sam had lied about why it was "so hard" for him to get back to Harmony. At first he was too busy with night school, then police training, and finally extra-duty overtime.

But the truth was, he just couldn't take the pain of the memories back there. And he certainly couldn't stomach news about the Cranes and Ivy.

Simply hearing the gossip that she'd come home from her honeymoon more than a little pregnant had unraveled him. She hadn't wasted a moment jumping right into Julian's bed, that was for sure. The news had been yet another mental blow for Sam to contend with.

That meat grinder by the name of Ivy Winthrop Crane was also the reason he'd avoided romantic relationships like the plague for the last few years. Police work had become his only focus—that and weight lifting, the Sox and Patriots, and the occasional adult magazine.

Oh, he'd had bed partners since Ivy. On the job, cops got lots of offers. And after a period of celibacy in Boston, he finally began accepting those offers. But he'd just never felt anything. Not where it counted—in the heart.

The sex was always empty. He'd lie there after making love to some woman he barely knew, and he'd think of Ivy. Wonder if she was happy. Wonder what kind of mother she was. Wonder if she was lying at that moment next to Julian. Making love to him.

It was pointless to torture himself like that, and he knew it, too. All this wondering was driving him crazy. Making him feel more alone than ever. Like he'd never find what his mother and father had—or what his own best friend clearly had. So for the past six months, ever since he'd been switched to night tours, he'd just about given up on women completely.

Driving now to his one-bedroom rental at Brookline Gardens, Sam silently ran through the contents of his fridge and cupboards. He knew they were skimpy, but he was taking on so much overtime lately he never had time to shop, let alone cook for himself.

He could stop for takeout yet again. But as he passed the Burger Barn, he decided he couldn't even *look* at another French fry or pizza box. Cooking was his only alternative. He pulled into the building's underground garage and took the elevator up to the fifth floor. The halls were empty, as they usually were when he got off this late.

Just once he'd love to see a neighbor. *One* neighbor.

His life was becoming an endless routine of sleep and work. Sleep and work. It was getting to the point where if a person wasn't wearing a badge he didn't have a chance to exchange more than two words—unless, of course, he'd just cuffed him and was reading him his Miranda rights.

Sam stripped out of his uniform quickly, showered, threw on old jeans and a loose cotton shirt, and started dinner, flipping on the radio for company. Dinner was linguine and jarred tomato sauce. Sam hated the blandness of sauce off the shelf, but Fred had showed him how to quickly spice it up with some sautéed onion, garlic, oregano, red pepper flakes, and a touch of rosemary. Smelled good.

Fred Carney was a young fireman with whom he'd shared a cramped two-bedroom apartment during his first year in Boston. And if there was one thing firemen knew how to do, it was cook.

An occupational necessity, Fred had told Sam. *When you've got to take a turn cooking for twenty hungry men, you'd better learn some Galloping Gourmet tricks fast or you're in for some mighty ugly verbal abuse.*

Sam drained the pasta, put it on a plate, ladled on the sauce, and was just about to sit down and eat it when he thought he heard his name being called outside his front door.

He stepped out of the kitchen into the living room and listened. Nothing. No voices. No noise.

Yet a prickly sensation at the back of his neck made him open the front door anyway, just to check. When he did, he immediately smelled it.

Smoke.

He stepped outside his doorway and saw that the other end of the hallway was full of it. He tore back into his apartment to call 911. But the line was dead.

What the hell?

He rushed out into the hallway again and started banging on doors, screaming "Fire!" and wondering what the hell had happened to all the smoke alarms. Not one had gone off!

Helluva way to finally meet my neighbors, thought Sam, banging on yet another door. People came out, saw the smoke, and raced toward the exit.

"Fire! Get out of the building!" Sam continued to yell.

Then he saw it—Apartment 25. Smoke was pouring out from under the door. Sam placed his palms flat against the wood surface. The door was warm but not hot. *Good.*

"Is there anybody in there?!" he yelled, pounding on it with his fist. "Is there anybody in there?"

No response. He backed up, positioned his shoulder, and pretended the door was one of the tackling dummies he used to demolish on the Castleton College practice field.

The thin wooden door was practically ripped off its hinges as he blew through it.

It was a one-room studio, bright with flames. A body was lying under the covers of a bed against the far wall. A young woman. Sleeping or unconscious, he couldn't tell.

"Wake up! Wake up! Are you okay?" he cried as he tore into the room. There was no response, so he pulled her into his arms and raced out again.

He was strong and she was light. He carried her to the stairwell and all the way down to ground level. He didn't release her until they'd reached the front lawn of the apartment building.

With great care, he knelt and laid her on the cool, damp grass. She was slender, with short dark blond hair and delicate features. Maybe twenty. But not much older. The light-colored pattern of her pajamas was grayed from the smoke of the fire.

"Hey, there . . . can you hear me?" he called gently between coughs, trying to clear his lungs of the smoke he'd inhaled. "Can you . . . wake up . . . for me?"

He put an ear to her chest and, thank God, heard a strong heartbeat. A hand over her mouth and nose determined that she was breathing shallowly.

"Did somebody call nine-one-one?!" he cried to the crowd milling around the lawn. They were in pajamas and robes, bedroom slippers and bare feet.

"Nine-one-one was called over ten minutes ago," said a middle-aged man in sweats and a T-shirt. "The phones inside were all dead, but my teenage son ran to the convenience store down the block. He's a track star, faster runner than me. She okay?"

"I don't know."

Sam eyed both corners of the block in frustration. He could hear no sirens, see no lights. *Where the hell is the fire department?*

He turned his attention back to the young woman.

"Does anyone know this woman's name?" Sam called to a few people close by.

"No. Never saw her before," came the replies.

"Anyone know this woman!?" Sam cried more loudly to the crowd.

People shrugged and shook their heads. Finally a plump old woman stepped up. She had short gray hair and wore a pink terry cloth bathrobe with matching slippers.

"She just moved in. Saw her unpacking a few days ago."

"Do you know her name?"

"No," said the old woman. "She always said hello when I passed her, but we never got the chance to talk."

Sam exhaled in frustration, unsure why the young woman wasn't waking up. He bent closer. Put an ear to her nose and mouth, reconfirmed that she was breathing.

"C'mon," he murmured to her softly. "C'mon, miss, wake up. *Please* wake up . . ."

As he peered into her face, it hit him just how lovely she was, and it crossed his mind what a shame it was that they'd never met before this. Sam felt a little frantic. She was breathing, but the smoke inhalation might have damaged her lungs, sent her into a coma.

"Miss, please, wake up, please—"

An odd combination of fear, worry, and masculine interest was playing across his face just as her eyelids fluttered open.

Sam blinked, stunned for a moment by the beautiful radiance shining from her face.

And her eyes—he'd never before seen eyes like that. Around small black pupils, silver-blue irises shimmered and danced as they gazed at him.

It was a shadowy spring night. No moon, and heavy cloud cover. The nearest streetlight was far away, on the corner, and the lighted front entrance of Brookline Gardens provided the only dim light on the dark lawn around them. Yet her eyes were shining up at him like twin silver-blue sapphires.

He didn't know this young woman, had never even seen her before, but her gaze seemed to close gentle fingers around his heart. A rush of pleasure came when he realized that her eyes were filled with joy at the sight of him.

But then her eyes began to dart left and right, up and down. They were looking all around him. It was alarming, and he thought for a moment that something was wrong with her vision.

"Can you see me, miss?" he asked. "Can you see me?"

"Yes, I see you," she whispered, blinking at Sam. "There's a light. A light around you."

Sam was sure she was delirious. The sky was pitch black, and there was no light around him or behind him, not even a streetlight.

"I don't know your name, miss. What's your name?" he asked her gently.

"A white light," she whispered again. "Around you."

"My name is Sam," he told her. "Sam Bennett."

"Sam." She lifted the edges of her lips in a pure and beautiful smile. Then she reached out her hand and cupped his cheek. "Sam Bennett."

Her caress was soft, caring. It warmed his cheek and traveled through him. He swallowed, feeling shaky, moved.

Fire trucks and ambulances, their sirens screaming, finally pulled up to the apartment building. Sam caught sight of his old roommate, strapping, curly-haired Fred Carney, rushing in with other men from his engine.

Sam lifted the young woman in his arms and moved quickly to get her into the hands of the paramedics. He knew them. Bart McGowan and A. J. Foster. He'd worked with them both on the street. They nodded their hellos to Sam as they wheeled the stretcher to meet him.

"What's your name, miss?" asked Bart, a wiry redhead in a white uniform, after Sam eased her down onto the gurney.

"Name. My name . . ." The young woman's brow furrowed, and her gaze looked frantic. Then it found Sam's face again. "I don't know," she told him. "I don't know my name!"

"Calm down, miss," said Bart, slipping an oxygen mask

over her mouth and nose. "Breathe easy. Take slow, deep breaths."

Bart turned. "What's her name, Sam?"

Sam shook his head. "I don't know, either."

Bart and A. J. carefully loaded her into the back of the ambulance, and Sam watched with clenched fists, feeling helpless. Whoever she was, she looked so alone, so afraid. Her eyes continued to look to him, like an injured animal that didn't know what was happening to it.

Sam's heart melted.

"I'm coming with her," he called into the ambulance.

"Yeah, sure, Sam," said Bart. "Climb up."

She couldn't remember anything, this Jane Doe. Not how the fire started, or anything before it. The only thing she could recall was waking up and seeing Sam's face.

"Please, Officer Bennett, can you help me?" she asked him the next morning when he came to visit her, flowers in hand. "I want to know who I am. Please, can you check at the apartment building?"

Sam did. But he found nothing. He canvassed every apartment, but no one knew her name. Even the landlord didn't know her. The building super had sublet the apartment illegally, so there was no lease or paperwork. She'd paid three months' rent in cash and never signed her name to anything.

"Seemed like she was running from someone or something," said the super when Sam interviewed him. "She didn't want to give her name, asked for complete privacy."

Sam's protective instincts immediately went up. Could she be running from an abusive boyfriend or husband? he wondered. Or could she be wanted by the law?

He hated thinking the latter, but he had to find out. With her permission, he took a set of her prints at the hospital and ran it through the system. There was no criminal record that he could find.

The only thing he could turn up was a scrap of paper that had been protected from the fire by a heavy ceramic lamp that fell on top of it. There was only one word on the tiny piece of paper: *Grace*.

He thought it was an appropriate name for her, because that was what she embodied to him. In the face of not knowing who she was, of having every one of her possessions burned to ashes, she'd still managed to keep herself from falling apart.

Over the days that he visited her in the hospital, she was patient and kind, courageous and noble, and even shared a sense of humor with the medical staff around her.

Amnesia was a tricky affliction, he'd learned from Grace's doctor, usually triggered by trauma, sometimes by brain injury or ingestion of toxic substances like carbon monoxide. But Grace's brain scans showed no damage.

Grace was lucid and healthy. She had no trouble with reading, thinking, and short-term memory. She just couldn't remember her name or her identity. Nothing about the first twenty or so years of her life.

"The prognosis for amnesia is variable, depending upon the cause of the memory problem," Grace's doctor told Sam in the hospital hallway during one of Sam's daily afternoon visits. "If the brain has been severely injured, it may take weeks, months, or years for recovery to occur. In some instances, the amnesia never goes away."

Sam knew the doctor could do nothing more for her at the hospital, and he was about to release her. Sam also knew that Grace had no place to stay. No money. And no one to turn to—no one she could remember, anyway.

"Grace, I'd like to offer you a place to stay," Sam quietly proposed to her after speaking with her doctor. "My couch converts into a bed, and I'd be happy to sleep on it for a while. Until you're back on your feet."

"I couldn't do that," said Grace. "It's a terrible imposition."

"No. It's not," insisted Sam. "It's really not."

Grace gazed into his eyes. It felt to Sam as though she was peering into his soul.

"You like to perform rescues, don't you, Officer?" asked Grace with a little smile.

Sam's eyebrow rose. He flashed on Ivy for a moment. Pulling her out of the water, onto the beach. The feelings of affection that followed. But this was different, and Sam knew it.

Back then he'd been a boy, flushed with the infatuation of heroics. Today he was a grown man, reaching out to a grown woman.

There was a calm about Grace. A serenity. A strong belief in God. And even with this bad turn of fate, a profound faith that things would be all right.

She displayed no fear. No anger. No frustration or rage. Just peace and acceptance.

Sam not only admired her for it, he wanted to be around her because of it. And deep inside, he knew he needed to be around her.

His feelings were more than an acute despair over his failed romantic life, more than the weariness of coming home to an empty apartment every night after dealing with the worst parts of society on the job. It was Grace herself. Something about her.

She was the connection he needed.

It might have looked like Grace was the one who needed Sam to rescue her. But the truth was very much the other way around. And deep inside, Sam knew it.

"I'm not offering to rescue you, Grace. Just to help you."

"Really?"

"Really."

"Okay, then. Let's give it a try. But I'll take the couch—"

"No, that's not—"

"You've got a very tough job," she cut in firmly. "You need to sleep in your own bed. I insist."

"Okay, then," said Sam with a nod. "Roommates?"

He extended his hand. She shook it.

"Roommates."

Sam left the hospital in high spirits on his way to his four-to-twelve shift when one word began to echo through his system.

Roommates . . . roommates . . .

Suddenly Sam realized why that word was staying with him. His old roommate, Fred Carney, had been one of the firemen who'd put out the blaze in Grace's room.

After checking in at the precinct and picking up his squad car, Sam drove over to Fred's fire company.

"Do you know what caused it?" he asked.

"No faulty electrical or other accidental cause that we can find," said Fred, pouring Sam a fresh cup of coffee at the engine company's kitchen table. "Looks like arson, but we can't find a direct cause. No smoking gun."

"No lighter fluid? Gasoline? Starter of any kind?"

"Nope. And the damnedest thing about the supposed dead phone lines and faulty smoke alarms was that once the fire was put out, everything was back in working order. No explanations. Smoke alarms had batteries. Worked when we tested them. And the phone company never showed a problem with the lines in the building. Strange. Never saw anything like it . . . and there was one more thing . . ."

"What?"

"Well . . . I haven't told anyone here this or anything . . ."

Fred looked around the firehouse, making sure no one was listening. He was a big guy, not easily intimidated, and Sam was surprised to see him suddenly appearing so sheepish and wary, almost scared.

"What is it, Fred?"

"They'd think I was crazy. Or drunk or something. But you've lived with me, Sam, so you already *know* I'm crazy, right?" he tried to joke.

Sam smiled. "Yeah, right. What? Tell me."

"While I was fighting the blaze, mask on and everything, I swear to God I heard some old bat laughing. Cackling.

Some old lady. Right in my ear. It spooked me, you know? I mean, there was no one around but the engine crew. The floor was empty. And the guys I work with do *not* laugh in the middle of fighting fires. And if they ever did, for sure it wouldn't sound like an old lady."

"Yeah. That's strange, all right."

"Maybe the metal in my mask was picking up a radio signal. Or maybe it was the ghost of your arson perp. I don't know." Fred shrugged. "Whatever."

Sam finished his coffee and bid his old roommate farewell. Slipping back into his squad car, his mind just didn't know what to make of it, but he knew one thing.

If Grace was in some kind of trouble, whatever the hell it was, Sam intended to protect her from it.

Back in Harmony, Tabitha Lenox was cursing a blue streak.

That fire she had conjured was a beauty and should have killed Grace Standish. She'd even psychically teleported herself to the very location just to make sure it got done right!

She was sitting right there, inside Grace's little studio apartment, personally fanning the flames with her magic, when Sam Bennett burst in and saved the wretched Standish waif.

Tabby had tried to use her magic on Sam. Tried to stop him. But it didn't work. That blasted angel was somehow protecting him, and Tabby didn't have the magic in place to get through that damned heavenly veil.

And if that weren't bad enough, now he'd gone and taken much more than a professional interest in her case!

Tabby could see that she had a real problem on her hands.

She'd been trying for four years now to kill Grace, ever since the girl had left the Standish farm. But every time Tabby got close, the girl's ubiquitous guardian angel intervened!

It was only recently that Tabby, with the help of her

friends in the basement, had developed a web of special incantations strong enough to block the angel's protective veil
over Grace, at least temporarily. When the witch had cast
her fire spell on that Brookline Gardens studio, she thought
that would be the end of Grace Standish for sure!

Tabitha hadn't realized that the angel, having already
suspected foul play, had appeared to Grace the week before
with a powerful warning vision.

She'd scared Grace out of her wits. Told her about the
evil that was after her and instructed her to hastily move
into Brookline Gardens by any means possible.

Tabitha had picked up on this warning, but she simply
didn't know what to make of it. She was confident that her
spell could be cast in any building in the city, and the angel
should have known that, too.

Not until Sam Bennett showed his face on the night of
the fire did the witch fully understand.

Obviously, the angel suspected that her own veil of protection could be temporarily torn away by Tabby's potent
spells, so she'd decided to move Grace to a place where a
man like Sam Bennett could be readily called upon to do
the angel's rescuing for her!

Bennett was entirely too willing to risk his own life to
help others. Evil just couldn't get a foothold with a man like
that around!

By now, of course, the angel had brought down some
friends from above to tear away what remained of the evil
web of spells the witch had cast. In doing so, the angel
gained enough ground to begin protecting Grace again
with a vengeance.

It was abundantly clear to the ever-determined witch

As you can well imagine, dear reader, Tabitha
was boiling mad about that little out-of-left-
field maneuver! Perhaps this angel didn't know
with whom she was playing hardball!

that from now on, whenever the angel failed to protect Grace, Sam Bennett would be there to help her instead.

Tabby would just have to come up with a new plan. Perhaps she should abandon Grace, returning to her after she had already struck down her twin, Faith, and their mother, Mercy?

Yes, perhaps this new tack would be for the best.

Now all she needed to do was find those two Standish women.

A few months after Grace had left the family farm, Mercy and Faith had left, too. They were on their way to search for Grace.

Over the course of these last four years, thanks to Tabby, they never even came close to finding one another. When Grace returned to the farm, Tabby made sure that all she found was ashes.

Without Faith and Mercy living there, the house and land were finally free of their irritating goodness. It appeared as if nothing could block Tabby's evil powers, as long as a standard fire spell was at her disposal.

Grace, having found no clue as to what had happened to her family, could only assume the worst.

Serves them all right!, thought Tabitha.

Between the awful Standish women, that annoying Sam Bennett, and the hellish bosses in her basement, rumbling bone-chilling threats at her on a nightly basis, Tabby was nearly at the end of her rope!

"But I refuse to swing from it just yet," she promised her cat. "Sam Bennett or no Sam Bennett, I still have a few tricks up my sleeve for Grace Standish. She hasn't seen the last of me, Fluffy. I swear it!"

THIRTY-NINE

New Life

"Hi, honey, I'm h-o-ome!"

It was the favorite part of Sam's evening—even though it was technically not evening anymore. It was 1:30 A.M. But he was finally off duty and back home.

Home.

When had he started thinking of his one-bedroom rental as home?

The answer was easy.

Curled cozily in the corner of his living room sofa, Grace looked up from her book, her vibrant eyes smiling welcome. Sam unbuckled his heavy utility belt and slung it over a chair near the door, then collapsed on the other end of the couch.

He smiled. Waited.

"Dinner's ready, dear," she said sweetly.

Sam laughed.

It was their *Leave It to Beaver* ritual, and they'd both enjoyed playing at it for the past three months.

Sam absolutely had not expected Grace to begin shopping, cooking, and cleaning when she'd moved in. But she'd insisted on doing something to repay him for giving her free room and board while she tried to reestablish herself in the world.

Sam noticed other little tokens of thanks appearing. Potted plants and vases with flowers, pretty blue curtains framing his stark white miniblinds. Colorful throw pillows brightening his drab beige couch.

She'd had a little bit of trouble functioning at first, after she'd checked out of the hospital, but Sam had helped reacquaint her with the mundane things—dealing with day-to-day life in and around the apartment and getting familiar with their part of Boston.

Although specific memories of her previous life had yet to resurface, her functional memory swiftly returned, and she'd even found some fulfilling work down the block at the local church.

Children and old people responded to Grace's accepting, giving nature, and she'd begun working with the church's day care and homebound elderly programs. It didn't pay much, but she was saving her money and thinking about part-time college, too.

She said she honestly couldn't remember if she had even attended college, but she knew it was something she wanted in this new life. So she'd begun studying for a GED to prove she'd at least mastered high school subjects.

Her mind was always hungry to learn more. Over the past few months, she had voraciously read history books, novels, newspapers, and magazines and was constantly watching television, trying to fill in her spotty memories of the world.

Reruns of old sitcoms especially amused her, and when Sam told her his favorite show growing up had been *Leave It to Beaver*, well, that was it.

She started calling him Ward. He started calling her June. And his nightly dinner conversations—recountings of brushes with perps, scumbags, informants, drug addicts, youth gangs, and various other members of the "up-

standing criminal population," as Sam referred to them —
became their own twisted version of "problems with the
Beaver."

"I would have worn my pearls, Ward," teased Grace,
"but I just *can't remember* where I put them!"

Sam rolled his eyes and tipped his head back against the
top of the couch. "That's not funny."

"You always say that when I joke about it."

"I'm amazed you *can* joke about it."

"Well, I'm not about to *cry* about it. I'm healthy and
alive. That's more than a lot of people can say."

Sam closed his eyes, exhaled.

"What?" she asked. "Problems with the Beav tonight?"

"Gang action."

"Not again. What happened?"

"Fifteen-year-old took a bullet."

"How is he?"

"DOA."

"Oh, no."

"Not the worst part. Worst part was having to book his
younger brother for the shooting."

"His own brother? *Younger* brother?"

"Thirteen. The kid didn't know how to aim a weapon.
He was trying to shoot at a rival gang. Missed."

"Oh, Sam . . . this world . . ."

"It's hopeless."

"No. It just needs a little help."

"More than a little."

"Evil's not going to win with a good man like you out
there."

"Evil?"

Grace nodded. "What else do you call a child with his
whole life ahead of him turned into a corpse on a gurney by
his kid brother?"

"I see what you mean."

"Are you hungry?"

Sam looked at her, his eyebrows rising in a familiar way.

Grace smiled. "I know, I know—you're *always* hungry."

She rose from the couch. "Good thing I'm *always* cooking. Or, rather, *always* trying not to burn things." ⏵

Sam caught her hand as she moved past him.

"What? You can smell the roast chicken, can't you? I swear it's not burned this time—"

"I love you, Grace."

Grace's jaw dropped. She blinked.

"Did you hear me?"

"Yes, Sam—"

"Do you know how you feel? About me?"

Grace took a shaky breath. She stared down at Sam. His big beautiful eyes were looking at her with such affection, such longing. Of course she loved him. Of course she did. She just couldn't say it. Not yet.

"Grace?"

She sat down next to him. Took his other hand in hers, met his gaze in earnest. "Sam, I know you care for me—"

"I *love* you."

"But I'm not sure what you feel is love."

"It is. And I do."

"But—"

"Grace, I'm a grown man. I know what love is. And I certainly know I feel it for you."

"You rescued me. You have a kind heart, but—"

"But what?"

"But you haven't even *kissed* me. And—"

Sam laughed.

"What's funny about that?"

His large, masculine hand cupped her delicate cheek. To Grace it felt like the hand of Heaven. Like the comfort

Residual effects of exposure to a fire spell, so says Tabby!

and protection of the whole world was embodied in this man's warm, strong palm.

"I haven't kissed you because I wanted to give you time. You've been recovering from trauma, Grace. Learning how to function in the world again. The last thing I wanted to do was burden you with confusing emotions to cope with before you were ready."

"What's changed tonight, then?"

"Tonight is about me, I guess. About what I need. And about what I can't stand to keep inside anymore. I'm not Superman. I'm just a man. And I've been wanting to express my love to you for so long now. I've been holding back, trying so hard to wait for the right time. But I felt it so strongly tonight, I couldn't *not* say it anymore. I guess this isn't very romantic, is it? Did I really blow it with you?"

Grace smiled. Her eyes were shining. "That depends. Do you still want to kiss me?"

Sam dropped his callused thumb to brush against her soft lips. Slowly, he leaned forward, his hand moving back to tangle in her soft short hair. Slight pressure urged her toward him. He moved his lips across her own. It was a sweet, feather-light caress. She felt the tenderness, the caring.

She did feel the love . . .

But she also felt the hesitation.

Something was wrong inside Sam. Something was being held back, behind a barrier. Grace could sense it. She pulled away and looked into his eyes.

"Sam, what's troubling you?"

He blinked, clearly a bit stunned that she had once again seen so deeply into him.

"Please tell me. What's weighing on your mind?"

"You," he admitted softly.

"What? My not loving you?"

"No. I know you care for me. I feel it. But . . . I can't get out of my mind what might happen if you suddenly remembered something . . . about someone else . . . another man. I don't think I could stand it, Grace."

She studied him. Someone had hurt him before. Badly. She didn't know the details, but she didn't need to. She just needed to know if he was willing to trust again. Willing to push past the barriers he'd erected—

"You know, Sam, I've thought about all that, too. But you've worked so hard, looked everywhere to turn up something from my past, someone who might have known me—"

It was true. He'd used all his connections with the police force, conducted as exhaustive a search of missing persons as anyone could in law enforcement. But he'd turned up nothing. Zero. After three months, neither he nor Grace knew who she really was, where she'd come from, or whether she might still have a husband, a lover . . . children . . .

"Grace, I'd like to think that any man who may have loved you would be looking for you as hard as I am. But . . . still . . . the truth is, as much as I hate to say it, as long as you can't remember your past, anything could be true of it. Anything."

"I *feel* as though I've never had anyone in my life before you. No lover. No husband."

"You can *feel* it, but do you *know* it? Can you *remember*?"

Grace looked away. "No, Sam, I can't remember. I don't know for certain."

She wanted so badly, so very badly, to reassure this man—*and* herself. But she honestly couldn't.

"Not knowing for certain. That's not good enough for us. Is it, Sam?"

Sam pulled her into his arms, sighed as he stroked her hair.

"Not if we want a future together, free and clear."

In his heart, Sam knew he loved Grace. About that he was certain. But he wasn't so certain of what was in Grace's heart. And truthfully, he felt hesitation in her, too.

Perhaps she wasn't ready to take their relationship to the next level.

And if that was the case, then it was wrong for him to

rush her to the next stage—pressure her into something she might not be certain she wanted.

"What should we do, then?" she asked.

"We'll just have to wait until you can remember."

"Okay, we'll wait."

But for how long? wondered Grace, eyes closing with anxiety. What if she never remembered?

Loving a second time is different.

An hour later, lying in his bedroom, hands clasped behind his head, Sam stared out the open window.

Grace's statement to him, *What's weighing on your mind?*, had stayed with him. Kept him up.

Sam knew he wasn't a complicated man. He felt what he felt, when he felt it. And he expressed it honestly. That was it—period.

But for the first time in his life, Sam wanted to examine not just *what* he felt, but *why* he felt it.

About Grace.

And about Ivy . . .

The August night was warm but not hot, and the moonlight was casting a glow around everything in his bedroom. It was quiet tonight, too. Except for the light sound of crickets chirping on the lawn outside and the occasional silent swish of a passing car, the world seemed completely at peace.

And ever since Grace had come into his life, so was he.

After three months, Sam was glad that tonight he'd finally expressed what was in his heart: that he loved her. He cringed when he thought of how clumsily he'd blurted it out, but he was encouraged that her reaction was mainly positive.

True, her memory loss was an obstacle. But, given time, couldn't they find a way to overcome it? And, given time, couldn't he find a way to overcome what Ivy had done to him?

Ivy . . .

Sam sighed.

Loving Grace was so very different from loving Ivy, he realized lying there.

With Ivy, the love had been full of nervous anticipation, endless wishing. The only constancy about that relationship was the jittery thrill of never knowing when he'd see her again, whether they'd get caught, and whether they'd find a future that they could share happily.

Ivy was longing. Unreachable, unattainable longing.

Sure, their passion exploded every time they saw each other. But afterward, when the fire had died out, Sam had been left with nothing but long, dark periods before they could be together again.

He'd never before understood that those bleak periods of waiting had dug a cold, deep canyon within him—an emptiness he had tried to fill with insubstantial fantasies about their future.

With Grace, that emptiness never came.

Grace gave him a wholeness, a peace he'd never before felt in his life. With Grace, he could glimpse the kind of fulfilling relationship he'd always dreamed of—the chance to share everything with a life partner. A soul mate.

Ivy Winthrop had given Sam affection and *her* version of love. But she'd never really *seen* him. Not like Grace could see him, straight through to his heart and soul.

Grace saw everything that lived inside him—the courage and the doubt, the strength and the weakness. And she accepted all of it. She accepted all of him.

Wasn't it time he did the same for her? Accept the unanswered questions of her past? Wasn't there a way to get past the uncertainties holding both of them back?

The convertible sofa was quite comfortable.

But tonight Grace couldn't sleep on it.

He kissed me. Right here on this couch.

She closed her eyes, trying to conjure the feeling again.

The picture window's blinds were pulled up so she could look at the midnight sky and the evening stars. Lying back, Grace drew a pillow against her body and hugged it close, pretending it was him.

His words replayed and replayed . . .

"Tonight is about me . . . about what I can't stand to keep inside anymore . . ."

Grace felt that way, too. Like she couldn't keep her feelings for Sam bottled up another day. He had guessed that she "cared for" him, but she hadn't really told Sam the truth:

That she loved him.

Loved him for his courage and his kindness. His guts and his strength. His vulnerability, his openness, and his faith.

Not just in God, but in her.

She saw it shining there in his eyes. His faith in her. Shining like a morning star through the darkest night. His love for her gave her strength. And she badly wanted to show him that. Show that she trusted him. Adored him.

Grace turned and tossed in the bed, his deep voice torturing her with its tender honesty: *"I'm not Superman. I'm just a man. And I've been wanting to express my love to you for so long now. . . ."*

She wasn't a superwoman, either.

Grace closed her eyes, trying, trying, trying to remember something, *anything*, from her past.

Please tell me, please, for Sam's sake, she prayed. *I love him so much. I want to reassure him. Convince him how I feel. What can I do? What can I do?*

The dark room offered no answers.

But deep inside her heart, a little voice whispered an idea. It would require some courage on Grace's part—because he might not be ready for what she was about to propose.

He might soundly reject it. And her for suggesting it.

But when it came to loving Sam, well, the man had literally walked through fire for her three months ago. The least she could do was walk from the living room to his bedroom tonight . . .

"Sam?"

The door was open a crack, and she gently pushed it. He was lying there on the white sheets of his large bed, his muscular arms hooked behind his head. Triceps bulging in a way that made Grace's knees suddenly weak.

"Grace? Did you call me? Is anything wrong?"

He bolted upright, looking worried. No shirt. Naked chest. Large, sculpted naked chest.

Exhale, Grace, she advised herself. *Inhale and exhale*.

"Nothing wrong, Sam. I just had an idea."

"An idea?"

Sam was about to reach for the nightstand lamp, but Grace asked him not to turn it on.

"The moonlight's nice," she whispered, moving closer to the bed.

"Yes, it is."

Sam shifted under the sheets, watching Grace move closer to him.

She was right about the moonlight, he realized. The heavenly orb was casting a glow around her that allowed him to make out the feminine curve of her figure in her thin cotton nightgown.

She hadn't worn her robe as she usually did around the apartment, and it was more than apparent that she had no underthings on. His eye caught the loose swaying of her naked breasts, the dusky tips visible beneath the lightly patterned cotton.

He wanted her.

Now.

The need ripped through him like wildfire.

Exhale, Sam . . . Inhale and exhale.

His hands reached to check that the sheet and comforter were still covering his lower body. They were. *Thank goodness.*

He had boxers on, but he could barely control the natural reaction of his lower body to having Grace in his bedroom. In the moonlight. Without underthings.

"Grace, what sort of *idea* did you want to discuss?"

He was trying to keep the edge out of his tone, but he was failing miserably.

"An *important* one."

He watched her step closer and sit on the side of his bed. Tension mounted inside Sam as he felt the slight sinking of the mattress, smelled the subtle, powdery scent of her evening bath.

She's so close.

He swallowed, hardly able to keep from reaching out to her. "Can't it wait until morning?"

"No. It can't wait."

Grace's beautiful silver-blue gaze took in his eyes, his mouth, his chest. She paused as if gathering courage, then reached out and lightly traced her fingers along the broad, hard line of his shoulder.

Sam's sharp intake of breath was the only sound in the room. His hand flashed out to still her fingers.

"Grace! *What* are you doing?"

"Touching you, Sam. Isn't that obvious?"

Sam's eyebrows rose. *"That's* your idea? To come into my bedroom and drive me *insane?"*

Grace smiled. "It's actually the best idea I can *remember* having."

"That's not funny."

"Oh, c'mon, Sam. It's hilarious."

"Grace, am I to understand that you're ready for us to—"

"Yes."

Sam closed his eyes a long moment. When he opened them, he took her hands in his.

"Grace, honey, believe me when I say that I want nothing more than to make love to you tonight. *Right this second.* But what's more important to me than what I *want* is what you *need*. And you don't need to feel rushed, to feel pushed into something you aren't ready for—"

"But I *am* ready."

"Sweetheart, just an hour ago you agreed we should wait. Until you knew for certain about your past."

"But Sam, I suddenly realized something. There is a way for us to solve the problem of my past. Right now. Tonight."

"I don't understand."

"You and I don't know my past. That's true. But I don't know yours either, Sam. Let us from this night forward only look ahead."

Sam moved his hand to caress the soft cap of her hair, shimmering almost like a halo. He could feel the brightness of her spirit in the room. It surrounded him, enveloped him.

"Never look back?" he asked her.

Grace nodded.

He could see what she was trying to do: Illuminate a path to higher ground, a place where they could build a new foundation, one that would never move out from under them. Was it possible to take that path together? Build that foundation? Could they start tonight?

"Grace, are you sure you're ready for this? Isn't a part of you concerned that there might have been someone else in your life? Another man who might want you back in his—"

Sam couldn't finish. He knew what it would be like— *feel* like— if another man laid claim to a second woman he loved.

"You're still not sure," Grace said softly.

"I'm sure about my love for you, Grace. But without knowing your history, there's so much we're not in control of."

"But Sam, don't you see that that's true for both of us? After all, some woman from *your* past might very well walk back into your life someday! Don't you see, we *both* have to let those doubts go. It's our only chance. Every grown person has a past, Sam. I grant you that mine is a bigger challenge than most—it could be a clean slate, or a minefield of complications. I don't know. But one thing I do know is that if we really want a future together, then we have to open our hearts completely. Trust in our feelings for one another. Do you understand that?"

Sam nodded. "Yes. I do, Grace. And I'm ready to."

"Good, because I'm ready, too. And by the way—"

She smiled. Her eyes shined. Blue starlight in the dim room.

"I love you, Sam Bennett. Did I mention that?"

In his heart he'd known how she felt. But hearing her say the words for the first time—God, it was like feeling the warmth of the summer sunlight after a cold, cold winter.

"Come here."

He pulled her into his arms with more than tenderness. Kissed her with more than caring, and Grace reveled in feeling Sam finally release his passion.

There was a sweet pleasure in sensing how badly he wanted her. Grace could feel it in the tension of his body, the low moans when he kissed her, the very vibrations of his spirit. But he did not hurry their lovemaking—and the self-denial of his own pleasure was even more endearing to her.

His tongue coaxed her lips to part for him, and she welcomed the intimate invasion. With patience he encouraged her to return his gestures—using her own lips and tongue, she did.

He angled his head and moved his lips to her jaw, her throat, her neck. His body leaned into her, silently urging her to stretch out beside him on the mattress, allow him better access to her torso.

His strong hands moved over her with masterful skill, her thin nightgown barely a barrier to their tender ministrations. He cupped the swell of one breast, then the other, his palm hot as he fondled them. She gasped when his fingers found a tender peak, and he languorously began to tease the sensitive nipple into a hard bud. She was amazed that his tiny movements could so electrify her body!

"I want to touch you, too," she whispered.

His brilliant smile flashed white in the moonlit room as he gently took her hand in his and spread her fingers across the center of his broad chest. She felt the smooth rock of his pectorals, his abdomen. Fighting her shyness, she reached lower, beneath the waistband of his boxers, wanting to please him, wanting to know him.

He closed his eyes when she found him. So hard and ready.

"Oh, God . . . not yet," he said in a strangled voice.

Then he sat up, pulled her across his lap, and began to touch her again—so sweetly, so tenderly, she nearly cried.

With delicate care, he pulled her nightgown off. She felt the cooler air in the room touch her skin, realized she felt a little nervous about Sam's reaction to her nakedness.

Moonlight was splashing across her curves, and for the first time she knew what it felt like to see her own beauty in a man's eyes. *Sam's eyes.*

She saw the pleasure and love there for her. It was overwhelming. And in an instant any hint of self-consciousness about her body melted in the mounting heat within her.

Then his hands reached up to feel what his gaze had so lovingly caressed, and she sighed.

"Oh, Sam, it feels so good when you touch me."

"Grace, you're so beautiful. So sweet and so beautiful."

He rolled her beneath him, and then his mouth and tongue were everywhere. His desire was growing more urgent by the minute, and she found her own rising to meet his.

"I love you, Grace."

Grace smiled, her eyes dancing. "I love you, too, Sam. It feels like I always have . . ."

Her hands took pleasure in roaming his strong, muscled body. And her heart found indescribable satisfaction in hearing him moan with pleasure at her touch, feeling him shudder at her kiss. What an incredible blessing—to be able to give and give to someone she loved as deeply as Sam.

The realization gave her courage.

Courage to want the next step even more.

"It's time, Sam," she finally whispered. "I need you."

He smiled. Moved away long enough to strip off his boxers, and then he was back in her arms, pausing above her.

"Are you sure, Grace? Absolutely sure?"

She took his face in her hands so he wouldn't miss a word—

"*Yes!* Absolutely. Let's take a leap. Now. Together."

"A leap?"

"A leap of faith. In each other. In our future—"

"Will you *marry* me, Grace?"

"Yes. Will you love me without fear of losing me?"

Could he?

Sam hesitated, looking deep into her eyes.

There was something bright and pure living there. Something that seemed to reach far inside him, past the most guarded place in his soul.

Sam had witnessed and endured so much pain and corruption, so many betrayals and uncertainties in this difficult, disillusioning world, that it wasn't easy to find purity again. Innocence and hope . . . trust and faith . . .

The world's hardships would never go away, Sam knew that.

But in this one moment, he suddenly knew, beyond a shadow of a doubt, that Grace could help him find something more. Something stronger. A way to renew himself again. And he was ready to let her. Ready to open his heart completely once more—

"Yes, Grace," he answered with certainty. "I will."

"I love you, Sam."

"I love you, too."

"Then show me."

He did. Pushing past her awkward innocence, pushing past his last remaining doubts, they both found the love they'd been waiting for all of their lives.

"She's happy, Momma. I can feel it."

Faith glanced into the upholstered bus seat next to her, but Mercy had already fallen asleep. The Greyhound was speeding its way through the dark Rhode Island night. They'd be pulling into Providence soon.

Faith yawned. Over the past few years, she and her mother had been on the move constantly. The life was hard on Mercy. With the Standish farmhouse burned down, Faith knew it was time they just picked a town to settle in and give up the search for Grace—for a while, anyway.

That was fine with Faith. She was tired of running from evil. Tired of searching for her sister. What she really wanted was to meet a husband. Start a family of her own.

Faith missed her twin. But deep inside, she was comforted by an unbroken connection to Grace. At times like this, it almost felt as if they were still sharing the same bedroom.

Joy. Unbounded joy and love filled Faith's heart. And somehow she knew that her twin had finally found the husband she'd been asking God to take care of until she could find him.

"Good night, Grace," whispered Faith, smiling into the darkness beyond the bus window. "Be happy, wherever you are."

FORTY

Regrets

"Good night, Mommy."

"Good night, Ethan, my darling boy. Who loves you best?"

"You do, Mommy. *You* do!"

Ivy smiled at the successfully ingrained response of her son. The firstborn Crane. The heir.

She kissed Ethan's little forehead, slipped out of his nursery, and padded down the long hallway to her private bedroom suite.

An unhappy surprise met her there.

"Good evening, dear."

"Julian."

He was reclining on her bed in his gray silk pajamas, a bent elbow propping his head, a Cheshire cat smile on his face.

"I thought you might like me to sleep in your room this evening."

"What made you think that?"

Julian raised an eyebrow. "You did, my love. I heard you discussing it at the dinner party. You said you wanted more children. Playmates for Ethan. Your child development reading."

"Yes, Julian. That's true. Just not tonight."

Ivy removed the jacket of her peach-colored suit and hung it up, then sat down at her dressing table and began to take off her diamond earrings, her platinum necklace, her jeweled Rolex.

Julian's gaze swept over his wife. Her blond hair was still up from the Hotchkiss party, allowing him access to her creamy, bared skin, covered only by the thin straps of her pale peach camisole.

He moved off the bed, began a light massage of her shoulders. "I can get you in the mood, Ivy. You know how much you enjoy it once I start."

"Julian—"

He bent to press warm lips against her neck. "I've felt the heat in you, Ivy," he whispered. "I've felt you shudder in my arms. You can feel it again tonight. Why don't you let me melt that icy wall of yours—"

Ivy gazed into the mirror. She studied her husband's handsome profile. She saw the desire in his expression, felt the need in his touch. He did want her. She could see that. And he'd have her again, she knew that, too. They were married and there was no escaping it, just . . .

"*Not* tonight."

Julian lifted his eyes to the mirror and met his wife's stone-cold gaze. He almost shivered.

"Have I ever told you, Ivy, that you share many of the same qualities as the Italian marble in our master bath?"

"No."

"You're very beautiful and very costly. But, if you're not careful, you're going to end up just as cold and just as hard."

"Get out, Julian."

He did. Striding down the hall to his own bedroom, he reviewed the possibilities for sexual satisfaction tonight. It was late, but his little black book was filled with private numbers.

Julian sighed as he opened the book and sat down on the

edge of his bed. He'd really have to get a new book. He'd had this one since his law school days.

Suddenly the book fell open to a dog-eared page he had turned to one too many times. His eyes fell on a name . . . her name . . .

Eve.

The phone number was the Blue Note's, he realized. In those months they'd slept together, she'd never given him another. The digits were crossed out, along with her name, of course.

Julian ran his index finger along the line she occupied. He closed his eyes. Could almost hear her voice again, singing that song . . .

"I trusted you . . . you lied to me . . . I cared for you . . . you sighed to me . . . your loving words . . . your loving lies . . . now go to her . . . and break all ties . . ."

His heart raced with the memory, the way it had that night. How she'd displayed her desire for him in that crowded ballroom, her wrenching pain and heartache. Laid it all bare for him.

How he wished he still had that Gucci shoe box full of photos of them together making love in Bermuda. He'd gaze at them this moment if he could.

Unfortunately for him, in a weak moment, he'd obliged Eve when she'd written to him. She said she wanted them back, so he sent them to her by Express Mail. She had no return address on her letter, so he had just sent them to her care of the Blue Note and assumed she'd gotten them. Destroyed them.

Just as she'd destroyed their passion.

Instead of coming to him, she'd kept silent for months.

Then, after the night he'd gone to the Blue Note—drinking himself into such a stupor that Police Chief Bennett had to pull him off the Coast Road and escort him home—she'd blackmailed his father.

"Do you see what your love was traded in for?" Alistair

had chided him. "Hocked for money. One wonders if she'll actually put it toward this medical school education . . ."

God help any patient of hers, thought Julian. *Imagine, a blues singer trying to stumble her way through medical school. Degree in a Cracker Jack box.*

After he'd come back from his chilly honeymoon, Julian had thought long and hard about what had happened with Eve. He had decided that he'd acted too rashly.

He wanted to continue seeing Eve, after all. And he wanted to see his son.

He'd told his father as much, too. But, according to Alistair, the child had died because of Eve's drug abuse. And she'd made it perfectly clear to Alistair, when she took the payoff, that she wanted nothing more to do with Julian.

He supposed he'd never see her again. She'd probably finish up medical school and then blow out of Harmony forever.

"Too bad," murmured Julian, sighing with deep regret. "I guess with some romances, there's just no going back."

Then he lifted his finger from the little black book and turned the page.

From her dressing table, Ivy had watched Julian leave.

Normally, his slamming of her bedroom door would have brought her relief. The quiet and peace she longed for . . .

But not tonight.

After what she'd seen in the *Harmony Herald* earlier today, she didn't know if she'd ever be at peace again.

Ivy reached down and pulled out the drawer of her dressing table. Pushing away a copy of *Town & Country*, her manicured fingers lifted the newspaper clipping hiding underneath.

Social Announcements
Harmony Police Chief Benjamin Bennett and his wife,
Margaret Joyce, announce the engagement of their son,
Samuel . . .

Ivy closed her eyes.

Instantly, the cozy cottage of her dreams appeared in her mind. She knew every room of it now. The fireplace, the kitchen, the den. Every last stick of fantasy furniture, every last pillow and plant had been lovingly picked out by Ivy herself over the past several years.

Sam was there, of course, waiting for her. Bare chested. Ready to hold her, stroke her hair, make passionate love to her. Ethan, their son, was off sleeping soundly in his little bedroom.

Sweet, warm lips touched her ear, and that deep, strong voice filled her being, as it always had: *"Sing out, sing out, my siren . . . Be not afraid at dawn . . . For where my ship sails onward . . . You're in my heart along."*

She was in his heart. *Always.* He'd promised, and she'd never forget. Never.

Opening her eyes, Ivy fixed her gaze on the antique locket in the open drawer below her. She reached in, grasped it, fastened it around her neck, this time with a touch of desperation in her movements.

She happened to catch sight of her image in the mirror. She stilled, leaned closer.

Julian's right.

She hated to admit it, but her eyes were getting harder. Older.

Face it, Ivy, time is marching on. And it's going to march right over you if you don't do something about it . . .

The newspaper clipping didn't say where Sam was getting married. But Alistair Crane owned the *Harmony Herald*, which meant he owned its staff.

All Ivy had to do was waltz right in and corner the society page editor. And if the woman didn't have the answers, then Ivy would just demand she get them — or lose her job.

There was simply no way Sam Bennett was getting married without her being there to see it.

With a furrowed brow, Ivy turned from her mirror. Then

she stripped off her clothes, lit a bedside candle, and stretched out on the large, luxurious bed.

Julian simply didn't understand that she'd rather be with Sam Bennett tonight . . .

All she had to do was close her eyes.

"I'm dying, Alistair. You know that, don't you?"

Sitting in his wife's bedroom suite, on a chair pulled up next to her newly purchased hospital bed, Alistair Crane couldn't speak.

He gazed down at Katherine. She was completely bedridden now. No one yet knew her life would soon be ending. Not their family. Not their friends.

Oh, they knew she wasn't well. That she was weak. But Katherine wasn't even fifty yet. No one, least of all Alistair himself, wanted to face the possibility that she could die.

He'd done everything he could think of. Spent millions on doctors. International consultations, therapy, experimental cures. In Alistair's world, there wasn't anything that couldn't be bought. Everything had a price. And a Crane never lost.

But, for the first time in his life, Alistair had to face the possibility of being wrong. Of losing. Of finally encountering something that could not be remedied with money.

Just this evening, the last specialist—on their long list of specialists—had confirmed what they'd been told over and over again: Her kidneys were failing. The transplant hadn't worked. And the dialysis was so hard on her body that it would soon give out.

There was nothing more to be done. No treatment options left. And the doctor had finally advised Katherine to put her affairs in order . . . *Prepare for the end* . . .

"You've got to face it, Alistair."

"I don't want to," he managed softly. "I love you, Katherine."

Katherine closed her eyes. "Please don't say that—"

"What? Say I *love you?*"

"You know you don't."

"Don't I? After being married to you for almost thirty-one years, how is that possible, Katherine? How is it possible for me *not* to love you?"

"You never loved me. I heard you admit it to our son several years ago—"

"*What?*"

"Outside the terrace that morning. After Julian's graduation party. When you were convincing him to marry that poor child, Ivy. You said that love didn't need to enter into their marriage because it hadn't with ours. With us."

Alistair was stunned into silence. All his life he had bolstered the family's fortunes by saying whatever it took to get what he wanted. He'd learned the strategy from his own father—who'd learned it from his. Didn't Katherine understand that this was all she'd overheard? That it was simply a verbal manipulation?

"Katherine," he finally answered coolly, "after all these years, do you mean to say that you still don't understand how I operate?"

"Oh, I understand how you operate, Alistair. How the Cranes operate. All too well."

"Julian is a weak young man. I manipulate him for his own good. And while it was true that love wasn't the *reason* I married you, I did care for you on our wedding day. And love became something I felt for you in time. I feel it now, Katherine. Don't you know that? Don't you feel it, too?"

Katherine studied her husband. She shook her head. "I can't tell when you're lying, Alistair. I guess I never could. You're just too good at it."

Alistair felt panic seize him. It was an unfamiliar thing to him. A shock to a system that had mastered control. Cool. Calm. But he had never before been forced to face the personal consequences of his verbal manipulations. And he could see that he was losing this argument. And losing it badly—

Leaning forward, he took her frail hand in his. "I'm telling you the truth *now*, Katherine. *I love you.*"

"Why? Why bother to say it now?"

"Because it's true. Please believe me."

"I don't."

"Ask yourself one question, then. What in hell would I have to gain by saying this to you now? In this room, alone with you? *Why* would I lie *now*?"

Katherine shrugged. "A clear conscience."

"Jesus! Is that what you think of me. That I don't have a single honest emotion left to give you?"

She looked away.

Alistair gazed at his wife's profile. Her beauty hadn't faded over time, just matured. Even the ravages of her illness had done little to rob her of the delicate framework of her face, the smooth cream of her skin. Her eyes were red-rimmed, but still blue enough for him to see the young woman he'd married, the young woman who'd given him a male heir, the young woman whom he'd known had fallen madly in love with him on the stairs of her childhood home one night when he'd come to pick up her sister for a date.

Alistair's fists clenched. He couldn't bear to take on the guilt of losing his wife now—the woman whom he'd expected to grow old with him. Couldn't bear to think that maybe her illness had been worsened by her on-and-off depressions that he'd ignored for years.

And so Alistair searched his mind for another reason for his heartache—something or someone else to blame. It came to him in a heated flash—their second child, Sheridan.

She's the reason I'm losing Katherine.

Alistair well remembered telling Katherine not to get pregnant again. But she'd wanted a second child. Wanted it so badly she'd had it against his own and the doctor's orders.

Now look at what's happened.

Katherine was paying the price for her selfish stupidity in wanting another child. And so was he.

And it's not even a boy.

"Katherine, I do love you," he pleaded for the first time in his life.

But she wouldn't look at him, and he could only wonder what was going on inside her mind . . .

Katherine expected her eyes to begin filling with tears. But they didn't.

Perhaps I've already shed too many in the course of my marriage. Perhaps I'm all out . . .

Strange how clear one's vision became when death was near—when one accepted one's fate.

Katherine gazed at the oil on canvas that she'd always loved so much—an original from the Impressionist school. Pilar had been kind enough to think of moving it from her sitting room so she could admire it from bed.

Her life had been like this painting, thought Katherine. A swirl of pastel color. Beautiful people in their beautiful costumes. And looking back on it all now, all the events of her life—so very significant at the time, of course—felt like nothing more than a blur of passing impressions. A dream. Unreal.

Death, the always unreal thing, was the one real thing to her now.

She would soon be a spirit again, as she'd been before her birth. And none of the things around her would matter. Not her clothes or her jewels, not her art collection, or her antiques. She could take none of it with her . . .

Neither could she take her most precious little joy, Sheridan.

A tiny cry of anguish caught in her throat at the pain her little girl would endure after losing her mother.

She closed her eyes, hoping and praying that Julian would remember his promise to look after his younger sister. It was all Katherine could hope for now—because she didn't have the strength for much more.

Death was coming quickly for her. And it would allow her no baggage. Perhaps not even mental baggage, since moving into the next world would mean leaving this one behind.

Perhaps the only thing she could possibly take on this journey was what lived in her heart . . .

"Katherine?"

Alistair's voice is taking on remarkable tones this evening, thought Katherine. *Tones I've never heard before.*

There was pleading. And longing.

Katherine savored hearing both.

If she'd had the strength, she might have smiled.

After years of marriage, this was the first time she'd heard him express anything remotely close to what she'd felt for years—anxiety, neglect, heart-wrenching vulnerability.

You always did have a passion for what lay beyond your reach, didn't you, Alistair? Well, soon that's where I'll be— forever.

Katherine thought of her sister, Rachel. The young bride whom Alistair had pined for during the entire course of their marriage.

Finally, it's my turn, Rachel. My turn to take up that long-coveted spot in my husband's heart . . . move into it for the rest of his life . . .

"Katherine, please. I love you. Did you hear me?"

It was a dark victory for Katherine.

But it was a victory at last . . .

For long minutes her husband stayed by her bedside, but it was too late, and they both knew it.

In the end, Katherine would not turn back to him, and finally Alistair Crane was forced to let go of his wife's hand.

FORTY-ONE

New Wishes

"Dearly beloved, we are gathered here in the sight of God, to unite this man and this woman in holy matrimony . . ."

Sam Bennett heard the words, but he couldn't look at the minister—because he couldn't take his eyes off his bride.

She'd made the lacy gown herself. A "tea-length," she said. Sam didn't care what it was called. It just looked beautiful and delicate and innocent and pure on Grace's feminine curves.

Around her slender neck hung a delicate silver-blue sapphire on a thin rope of freshwater pearls. He'd given her the necklace last week, the night they'd arrived at the romantic Seaside Inn on Massachusetts's scenic Cape Cod, whispering to her that the jewel reminded him of the same blue light he'd seen in her eyes the night they'd met.

In her hands, Grace carried a collection of wildflowers that Sam had gathered himself that morning. She'd said last week that she'd wanted to carry wildflowers as her bouquet, and he knew at once that she should hold something he'd picked with his own hands.

He was going to rent a tux, but Grace said no. The wedding was held outside, in the beautifully manicured garden of the old Victorian inn overlooking the sea. Just fifty or so people at sunset. A small white cake. And plenty of champagne.

It wasn't formal, she said, and he only needed to wear his best blue suit. She bought him the tie, to match the silver-blue color of the sapphire around her neck.

Sam was happy they'd found this beautiful spot where they could hear the ocean waves. Harmony was just as beautiful, of course, and they could have had the wedding there. But too many old memories would have haunted Sam in that town—and he wanted new memories. A new life.

Sam's family and close friends had traveled here from Harmony. They all loved Grace at first sight. It was an incredible gift for Sam. For the first time, he knew what it was to love a woman who *wanted* to meet his friends and family, to weave herself into his life with joy and commitment, without fear or hesitation.

T. C. was his best man, of course. And without any family of her own, Grace had asked Eve to be her matron of honor.

It seemed to Sam, during the ceremony, that the Russells were looking at each other with so much love, so much unbounded affection and joy, that they were getting married, too, right there with Sam and Grace, all over again.

"Marriage is a time of new beginnings," said the minister to the fifty or so people who had gathered around the flower-laced gazebo, where he stood now with Sam and Grace.

"As the Apostle Paul told us in his first letter to the Corinthians, 'When I was a child, I spoke as a child, thought as a child, reasoned as a child; but when I became a man, I put aside childish things.' Now Sam and Grace stand before you today, ready to cast off their pasts, ready to look to their futures. We are here as witnesses to their pledge. And, may I say, they are an example to us all, as we should all ask ourselves to search our own hearts, seek forgiveness of our past mistakes, offer forgiveness to those who have harmed us, and look with clear eyes to our futures—"

Standing near his best friend, T. C. Russell closed his eyes. *Forgiveness to those who have harmed us . . .*

Could he ever do that? Ever have some peace in his heart?

When Julian Crane had taken away his dream, T. C. never thought he'd find a new one. But he had. In Eve. His wife. His love.

She was standing near him now, a vision in baby blue lace, love brimming in her own eyes, too. Love for him.

He heard the minister's voice continue . . .

"Love is patient, love is kind. It is not jealous, is not pompous. It does not seek its own interests or rejoice in wrongdoing . . . It bears all things, believes all things, hopes all things, endures all things. Love never fails."

T. C. closed his eyes, choked back tears.

It was time to let go.

Maybe not forgive. But try to forget.

And thank heaven that the most precious thing in his life had never been tainted by anything as cruel and corrupt as the Cranes.

Eve gazed at her husband.

T. C. Russell was the best thing that had ever happened to her. Marriage to him had become her safe haven, her paradise, her garden of Eden. And she never wanted to leave it . . .

Inhaling the beautiful fragrance of flowers around them, she vowed then and there to forget everything about her past. Forever.

Thank heaven T. C. knows nothing about the Blue Note, the drugs, the baby, and especially Julian Crane.

The Cranes would certainly never reveal what they knew.

And neither would she.

T. C.'s love and respect for her were Eve's whole life now.

She'd do just about anything to make sure she never lost them.

As the minister took Sam and Grace through the exchange of vows and rings, Sam knew he had forgiven Ivy for the pain of their past.

And he hoped to forget it completely in time.

That was one reason he'd agreed to Grace's wish for a wedding by the ocean. Sam had always loved the sea, and he wanted to share that love with Grace, *without* memories of Ivy.

Today he was washing clean those old memories of that secluded Harmony beach and creating brand-new ones—with Grace and their heartfelt vows of marriage to each other.

Grace had taught him that having no memory of a past wasn't such a bad thing after all. It cleaned your slate to live for today. And for tomorrow. For what is and what will be. Instead of what you once wished for, or once thought you wanted.

Forgetting and forgiveness, they were the same.

Today Sam was ready to forget his old wishes and make a brand-new one. A wish for a long life with Grace, and Grace alone.

"I now pronounce you husband and wife. You may—"

The minister paused. Smiled. "Oh, well. I see Sam already knows what to do."

The small congregation of family and friends laughed and applauded. Sam Bennett was a man who needed no prompting to take his wife in his arms.

* * *

At the very edge of the Seaside Inn's back garden, half-hidden by a tall topiary, Ivy Winthrop Crane put down her small, gold-rimmed opera glasses and frowned.

Watching the ceremony had been tolerable until the last moment. Until the kiss. The passion in it had turned Ivy's stomach. That kiss told Ivy far more than she wanted to know about Sam's feelings for his new bride.

But Ivy refused to cry. To be moved. Or to change her way of thinking.

She had heard what the minister said about forgetting the past and moving on. But she couldn't. *Wouldn't.* And everything inside her seemed to harden just a little bit more in that moment: Her heart. Her hatred for Julian and Alistair. And her resolve to someday get Sam Bennett back into her bed.

She didn't care that some other woman was enjoying the wedding of her own secret dreams—near the ocean at sunset, with wildflowers, and Sam as the groom.

No, she didn't care a whit.

Because Sam's true heart was hers. And it always would be.

"Or maybe," whispered Ivy to herself, "maybe his having the wedding near the water *means* something. Yes, it must!"

Sam might have been marrying another woman. But his memories of Ivy were still in his heart. That was why he was having this wedding near the ocean—to be close to his memories of her!

He wouldn't forget her. She was certain of it.

For the immediate future, she knew she would have to live without love. But she could manage that well enough—because there was a new passion burning inside her now: A passion for vengeance.

Vengeance toward Alistair and Julian Crane for what they'd forced her to endure. Forced her to become.

Ivy touched the Chanel bag on her arm, the perfect complement to her custom-tailored kelly-green suit. She had the letter with her even now, the heartfelt letter she'd written to Sam explaining everything to him—*what* had happened on her wedding night, why she had not been able to run away with him, and who Julian Crane's firstborn son really was.

She had more papers, too. Papers revealing Ethan's true paternity. They were hidden in the false bottom of a Dior hatbox in her closet.

This day—Sam's wedding day—held stinging pain for Ivy. But she comforted herself with the knowledge that one day she would triumph. After all, she held the trump card in her pocket—or rather, her pocketbook, she mused, patting her Chanel bag!

She remembered what Julian had told her last year, during a tennis party at the Crane mansion: How the Cranes had foreclosed on the Bennett farm during the Great Depression to build their four tennis courts.

Well, one day Ivy would tell Sam the truth. And wouldn't he be thrilled to learn that his son, the anointed Crane firstborn, was destined to reclaim the very land that was stolen from his grandfather? Wouldn't he rejoice in hearing that Ethan, a Bennett by blood, would one day take over the Crane empire?

Ivy saw that the wedding crowd gathered around the gazebo was now beginning to disperse. With one final look back, Ivy gazed at the man she'd loved so much for so long . . . the man who would, no doubt, continue to fuel her nightly fantasies for years to come—

Maybe Sam had deluded himself into caring for this woman he was marrying today. Ivy could certainly understand his need to rebound from her marrying Julian. But the blissful first blush of married life would surely wear off with time. Ivy had heard that Sam had just been promoted on the Boston police force, but one day, he might move back to Harmony.

And one day, after Ethan was grown, Ivy would be ready to rekindle with Sam what they once had.

Until then, Ivy would devote herself to Ethan. For he had already become her whole life.

Closing her eyes, she conjured his handsome little face. *Oh, my dear, sweet boy. You are the living proof that the love I have for your father is profound and unending . . .*

With tender care, Ivy opened the antique locket around her neck. She wished she could show her young son the picture inside.

Look, my beautiful boy, she'd tell him. *Look how handsome your father is. He's almost as handsome as you.*

"Sam, my dearest love," Ivy whispered on the ocean breeze before turning from the garden and heading back to the Crane Jaguar. "Someday we'll be together again . . ."

Ivy smiled with that new wish. Then she closed her eyes and swore, from the depths of her newly hardened heart, to one day make it come true.

After hearing that new wish bob into her kitchen window on the salty sea air, Harmony's resident enchantress laughed and laughed.

"What a switch, my dear Ivy. What a switch! But then, you were always one to want what you couldn't have!

"Well, don't despair, my dear, it will happen as you wish. I'll see that it will. Not because you want it, but because getting Sam back for you will cause the Cranes pain—not to mention pain for Sam himself and the wretchedly good Grace.

"I even foresee it causing pain for your precious son, Ethan, as well as the woman Ethan will love, Theresa Lopez-Fitzgerald, and all of their friends and family! Ah, yes, delicious scandal and heartache. It's what I live for!"

Tabby was truly in a mood for vowing harm today!

Through the visions in her scrying bowl, she had already been an uninvited witness to Sam and Grace's irritatingly harmonious wedding. She laughed uproariously when she mentally eavesdropped on everyone's thoughts during the minister's sermon—

"Go ahead," she'd cackled to them all, "make your pledges to put your pasts behind you. But remember this: I know *all* your hidden secrets, and I'm not going to let any of you forget them!"

Finally she turned to her cat. "Tell me, Fluffy, what shall I do to make Ivy's new wish come true and bring Sam Bennett back to Harmony?"

"Meow!" cried Fluffy, jumping up on the kitchen windowsill and waving a paw at the house next door.

"Of course! My neighbor! I'll just use my standard inheritance spell!"

The woman next door was old and sickly. Her soul's weakening aura had one, maybe two years left of life on Earth. All Tabby had to do was psychically suggest that she change her will, leaving Sam Bennett her house after she passed.

Sam didn't know the woman, but he'd assume his father, Chief Bennett, had done her a good turn way back when and that she simply wanted to repay him via this gift to his son.

It didn't matter, really, what conclusion Sam finally came to. The witch had known few people to look a gift horse in the mouth. Or in this case, a gift house!

Sam and Grace would likely have their first baby in a year or two. That would make them especially ready to move out of their small Boston apartment for sure. Yes, of course Sam would not want to go back to the memories of Harmony—but with a free house landing in their lap, Grace could certainly persuade him otherwise.

And what bait Grace would be for Tabby!

It would only be a matter of time before her more powerful twin, Faith, would feel pulled toward Harmony, to reunite with her sister.

Yes, the witch would do well to just bide her time and

wait. After all, she *was* getting pretty exhausted with all the scrying and spelling and chasing and conjuring.

This would serve her purpose nicely and conserve her energies, too!

One day, she would destroy all of those wretched Standish women.

Just not today.

Yes, a little vacation was in order. No matter what kind of grief those blasted friends in her basement gave her!

For now, that darned angel and Sam Bennett had won.

But only for now . . . ▼

"So, how do you like being Mrs. Bennett?"

"Mmmm . . . feels good so far."

Sam gently pulled Grace back against his broad, naked chest and wrapped his arms around her.

This romantic Victorian was the perfect place for their wedding night. The balcony of their suite opened over the water, and the fresh Atlantic breeze cooled their heated skin.

After making love all night, Sam pulled Grace out into the morning air. He said he wanted them to see the first sunrise of their married life together.

Grace leaned against his chest and smiled. She knew her body, her cycle. She knew what making love all night could give them . . .

It pains Timmy to tell you, dear reader, that Tabby made a serious error when she decided to take her little vacation from fighting the Standishes. By the time Grace's twin sister came anywhere near Harmony, Faith had already given birth to a daughter named Charity. Now Tabby's up against the most powerful force for good she's ever encountered in her very, very, very (did Timmy say *very*?) long life!

"Think we made a baby?" she whispered.

"Yes, Grace." Seeing the first colorful streaks of the new day's promise, he kissed the soft cap of her hair. "I think we made a life."

APPENDIX

Timmy

SHERIDAN CRANE'S PAST
LIFE WITH LUIS LOPEZ-FITZGERALD

Tabby's Vision of the Revolution

July 5, 1776

"Sarah, what are you doing?"

"Reading, Father."

Sarah Crane stopped the movements of the rocking chair and held up the book in her hands so that her father could read its title.

"*Fancy Stitchery*," he read aloud, standing in the doorway of the Crane library. "Good. 'Tis a *proper* book for a young lady. No more of that other nonsense, do you hear?"

"Yes, Father."

"Our guests have arrived. Come at once to greet them."

Nineteen-year-old Sarah Crane nodded obediently at Alfred Crane as he turned haughtily on his imported English heel and left the library. Then she closed the covers of the stitchery book, making sure Thomas Paine's *Common Sense* was well hidden inside.

" 'The sun never shined on a cause of greater worth,' " Sarah quoted in a whisper.

Her father had been furious last week when he caught her openly reading Mr. Paine's beautifully written treatise, a fifty-page pamphlet that called Americans to declare their independence from Britain. He'd ripped it to shreds in front of her, calling it traitorous bilge.

Sarah had been forced to borrow this copy from a middle-aged woman in her spinning bee. The spinster, Miss Tabitha Lenox, had a bit of an eccentric, flighty nature, except when it came to her distaste for the British. And on that subject, Sarah and Tabitha agreed completely. ☞

For well over a year now, the bee had been meeting three days a week to spin cloth for the town poor, whose numbers had been increasing at an alarming rate since the British began occupying Harmony eighteen months ago.

"Sarah!"

At her father's impatient call, Sarah hurried through the carved oak door of the mansion's library. She had hoped to hide out for a good deal of this party. Hearing the distant

---

Are you perhaps wondering, dear reader, why Tabby was no Tory? Timmy found the answer in Tabby's diaries.

For a solid year Tabby was forced to house and feed two British soldiers in her spare bedrooms. They not only ate her out of house and home, but also made it virtually impossible for her to cast spells, conjure spirits, or do almost any scrying with their suspicious little soldier eyes always about.

"Hell's bells!" she wrote in early 1776, "I am less concerned they would jail me as a witch than hang me as a patriot!"

And all along, while these British were sucking the towns-people of Harmony dry of sounds of arriving guests, chattering voices, and clinking glasses, she had thought for a little while that she had succeeded, but clearly her father had other ideas.

Sarah's delicate kid slippers made no sound as they padded along the hallway's thickly loomed rug. Finally they reached the arched entryway to the drawing room—and stopped dead.

The wall of red before her sent her back a step in shock. She had expected a few British officers, but not this many!

Gossamer skirts of pink, white, and pale blue rustled among the laughing, drinking Redcoats. The overly dressed daughters of the area's wealthiest merchants had been escorted here by their mothers and fathers. Sarah recognized the Winthrops, the Osburns, the Higgenbothams, the Motts, and a dozen other fine families.

In shame, Sarah bit her bottom lip. She was just as overly dressed as these other young women. A pretty doll ready for display.

For three days, her father had insisted that the maids attend to her, preparing her for this evening. Her face had been washed with buttermilk to make her skin soft. Lemon juice had been applied to her freckles to bleach them out.

------

their stores, Alfred Crane (a descendant, by the way, of that no-good magistrate William Ephraim Crane, who sentenced my princess to burn in 1693) had been working to convince the Redcoat officers that the people of Harmony wanted them in the town, and would even defend them against the Continental army!

Well, that was just too much for Tabby! The first thing she did was slap a copy of Thomas Paine's *Common Sense* into the hands of Alfred's eldest child, Sarah. Tabby was hoping not only to gain an ally, but also to give old Alfred apoplexy while doing it! And as for the next thing she did . . . well, just keep reading!

And this morning her father had insisted she wear a white-powdered wig over her beautiful yellow hair. Sarah had point-blank refused, but the three-hour standoff had finally ended with her father winning.

"Sarah, you must be dressed *properly* for this party," he'd argued. "Do you not wish to make these British officers feel at home in Harmony, so they may continue to protect us from that rabble about the country who call themselves Patriots?"

"Father, have you not heard of the Boston Massacre? Innocent Americans slaughtered by the British soldiers! Or the burning of homes at Lexington, or the harsh assaults and whippings and the two unjust hangings, right here upon our own Harmony neighbors!"

"Do not discuss politics, daughter, 'tis not ladylike."

"But, Father—"

"Enough, Sarah! A Crane always finds the advantage in a situation, and befriending these soldiers is far more agreeable a prospect than fighting them. Now! As for your attire . . . would you rather these officers come to our home and *look down* upon your simple colonial appearance?"

Sarah bristled at the idea of Redcoats looking down upon any colonial woman, so she'd obeyed her father's wishes. But now, as she forced herself to enter the large drawing room in her French gown, a delicate confection of dusty rose silk, Sarah wanted to scream.

One of her garters was slipping, her corset had definitely been tied too tightly, her bosoms were practically exposed by the daring neckline, and she simply hated the bulky hip pads and layers of petticoats needed to give the proper bounce and movement to the skirt of the fashionable gown.

"Ah, *here* she is!" her father announced as she moved to join him. He was decked out himself tonight in royal-blue silk breeches and as fine a waistcoat and jacket as any European aristocrat's.

Beside him, Sarah's aunt Jane smiled sweetly. "You look lovely, dear girl," she whispered. "Now *smile* at the officers."

When Sarah's mother had died of fever ten years before, her mother's sister, Jane, had come to live with them to help raise Sarah and her younger brother and sister. It was no surprise that Alfred had married Jane within a year; this was a common enough occurrence in other families.

Jane was a kind woman, but Sarah was often vexed that Jane didn't wish to think beyond what Father told her to.

Sarah mustered a half-smile at four tall, uniformed men—a colonel, a major, and two lieutenants—and tried not to cringe as they looked her up and down, then settled their gazes on her immodestly exposed bosom.

"Good evening, *gentlemen*," Sarah pronounced with a practiced air of Crane disdain while trying her best to ignore the hot flush of embarrassment at having four pairs of male eyes staring openly at her barely covered breasts.

The officers wished her a good evening, and their expressions turned more respectful, yet a possessive look remained. It unsettled Sarah.

"Please excuse me," she said quickly, "but I see my girlfriends across the room, and I should like to say hello."

With barely a curtsy, she turned and fled.

"Drink, miss?" asked one of the house servants thirty minutes later.

Sarah nodded and removed the crystal goblet of the newly imported French wine from the engraved silver tray. She would need the drink to get through this horrid evening.

She'd tried to engage her girlfriends in conversation, but every last one of the pampered heiresses was more interested in entertaining the damned Redcoats!

Finding an empty corner of the drawing room to hide in, Sarah gazed silently out the window and considered Harmony's situation. Her father had long ago declared himself a Tory—staunchly loyal to the English monarchy. But the reason why, it seemed, had little to do with his love of fat King George's crown and everything to do with the British half-crown.

Profits had skyrocketed for the Cranes' Harmony-based

shipping business since the British had closed Boston's harbor two years ago, and Harmony had become one of the few ports of trade in this area of the country not blockaded and thus legally able to receive European shipments.

This had made Alfred Crane a very happy shipping merchant. But Sarah was increasingly concerned about the less fortunate members of the town, who had been forced to house and feed the British soldiers.

To add insult to injury, these troops had been ordered not only to keep the port open for British ships and supplies but also to enforce the British Parliament's restriction on fishing—a punishment to the colonists for their rebellions, one that was robbing New England's fishing families of any way to earn their living.

Sarah knew her father barely tolerated any expression of her own views, but she did *have* her own views. And she'd read enough of Mr. Paine to believe that the Sons of Liberty and the Minutemen were all correct in their opinions. The British crown had taxed and bullied the American colonies beyond what was just. America *must* declare her independence.

"Well, well, Miss Crane, I see you are in need of company."

Sarah jumped at the sound of the deep British voice that tickled her ear from behind. It was the major from the group of four to whom her father had introduced her.

The officer was tall, blond, and quite handsome, except for the smirking arrogance that so plainly wrote itself across his aristocratic features.

"May I say that you are quite above the average looks of the *common* colonial woman."

"You *may* say it, sir, if you wish to be an insensitive oaf," Sarah snapped, then quickly turned her back to him.

To Sarah's chagrin, however, instead of respecting her chilly message and leaving her in peace, the British officer simply moved to stand in front of her again!

"You *are* a feisty one, aren't you?" he said with a raised blond eyebrow. "I pegged you right from the start."

"Pardon me?"

"It's that rough-hewn colonial blood, I suppose. But what else can one expect from families who have lived among the savages for a hundred years. A shame that with all this shipping going on about you"—he gestured at the expensive furnishings and draperies, the fancy carpeting and elegant clothing—"your father did not see fit to ship *you* back to England for some proper instruction in polite behavior."

"I act like a lady, sir, when I am in the company of a *gentleman*. Good evening." Sarah heard the officer's laughter as she stepped hastily away from him.

She found her aunt Jane after that, and remained close by her for the rest of the evening.

Hours later, the guests were just finishing the platters of baked beef, roast goose, crowned pork, cheese and fruit pies, warm loaves of bread, and bricks of chocolate that had been set before them at the large dinner table. Sarah thought the indulgent spread obscene in the face of the want she'd witnessed in many Harmony homes.

Slipping away, she instructed the cook to quickly divide the abundance of leftovers into packages. Tomorrow morning Sarah herself would deliver the food to the neediest families in the town.

When she returned to the party, she saw that the guests had left the dining room and had begun to scatter themselves throughout the first floor's hallways and parlors. In the music room, one of the guests sat down at the pianoforte, and music filled the air.

Sarah noticed that some of the officers were beginning to pair off rather demonstrably with the merchants' daughters—while the parents purposely gave the couples privacy by absenting themselves in the music room.

Wanting nothing to do with these goings-on, Sarah padded down the long hallway and slipped into the library at the back of the house. It was the perfect hiding place for the rest of the evening, and she could finally finish reading Mr. Paine in peace!

After lighting the room's candles, she had barely had time to ease into her favorite rocking chair when she heard footsteps by the closed door. When Sarah looked up, she found the tall blond major entering the room.

"Giving me the grand tour of your home, sweet one?" he asked, swiftly closing the door behind him.

His face was flushed as red as his coat, his breath carrying a distinct aroma of a drink more potent than French wine.

"You are drunk on rum, sir!"

"Yes, of course! It *is* a party, miss."

"Leave this room at once!" cried Sarah, leaping to her feet and pointing to the door behind him.

To Sarah's horror, the officer merely smiled and turned the key in the lock with a shockingly determined click.

"Did you hear me, Major?"

Sarah wanted to flee, but the man was larger than she. And despite his drunken state, he appeared braced to intercept her should she attempt to run his blockade of the door.

"Your prudish act does not fool me," said the officer as he took a step into the room, removed his coat, and draped it across the back of a nearby chair. "My eyes were upon you all night. You knew it. That is why you led me here."

"You are quite mistaken, sir! I deplore your being here. In this room! In this house! And most of all, in my country!"

Ignoring her protests, the blond officer moved in on her. "Hear me, miss, there is *no need* to continue your little teasing game. I am quite caught. Now let us enjoy ourselves. Come and kiss me."

Sarah was outraged. So outraged that she waved the *Fancy Stitchery* book at him like a flag. "You are in my country, I say!"

"What's that?" he laughed. "The country of bobbins and needles?"

"No!" With her right hand, Sarah pulled Thomas

Paine's pamphlet free of its hiding place and waved it under his nose. "The country of all those who value liberty!"

The Redcoat's eyes narrowed, and the laughter in them was replaced with something much harsher. He moved quickly, closing his fingers around the wrist waving the patriot's pamphlet.

"You are a foolish little girl, playing at a dangerous game in the king's land, do you realize that?"

"The king is a tyrant," she charged in outrage, "and he has lost his just rights to govern this land!"

"Very well, Miss Crane, play your game, and so shall I. *My* way—" Tightening his grip with bruising force, the major forced Sarah to drop the pamphlet.

"Stop this!" she commanded.

"Why? Shall I not show what the king's soldiers *do* to female traitors?" he growled in her ear, his breath stinking of rum as he crudely squeezed her breast. " 'Twill not be gentle, but I am happy to oblige—"

Sarah tried to swing the heavy stitchery book in her left hand and strike the side of the Redcoat's head, but even drunk the soldier was too fast for her. In one lightning move, he'd knocked the book down, twisted her left wrist behind her, and shoved her swiftly backward.

With all her might, Sarah fought him. Her white powdered wig fell to the floor in the struggle as she tried to pull herself free of the officer's harsh grip. She kicked out, but the layers of petticoats made it impossible to swing her leg more than a few inches.

In seconds, she was trapped by the officer, a solid wall of shelves at her back. "Stop this! At once, I say!"

But the officer would not stop. He was quite skilled, in fact, at keeping her from wriggling free as he pinned her hands helplessly against the bookshelves.

The noxious stench of alcohol and sweat, combined with the man's vile assault, was making her sick.

"Help!" Sarah shrieked when she realized at last that she could not help herself. "Help!"

"Who do you think will help you?" The officer laughed.
"Do not you comprehend why you were paraded before us
at this party? Do not you see you are part of the payment for
our protection of this pathetic little town—"

"Someone help!"

"Be still and enjoy it," commanded the major, pressing
his lower body into her skirts. "Or must I treat you the way
I've been treating the wenches from Harmony's *less* privileged families?"

Sarah shrank back as the officer raised his large hand
above her head. Closing her eyes, Sarah braced for the blow.

The sharp crack came loud and angry, but it did not land
on her.

Opening her eyes, Sarah gasped in shock. The blond officer was no longer pinning her. He had fallen at her feet.
Looming over her now, not far from the library's open window, was a tall American woodsman of about twenty years,
with hair so brown it was almost black, and a pair of eyes as
sharp as a raven's.

On his broad shoulders hung a wheat-colored homespun tunic. Strapped to his waist was a wide leather belt that
defined hips so narrow they made his shoulders appear massive. On his long, strong legs he wore rough brown
breeches, and his knee-high boots were dusty enough to
have been riding the countryside for hours.

In his raised hands he held the blunt end of a musket,
and tucked into his wide leather belt were two loaded pistols.

"Good evening, miss," he said, then bent to check on the
major.

"Still breathing," he pronounced with a hand over the
major's mouth. Then he leaned closer. "And enough rum
to pickle a barrel of cukes, I'd say."

Sarah was in a state of panic, her heart galloping faster
than the hooves of her favorite mare. She glanced at the
door. It was still closed and locked. Then she looked back
toward the wide-open window and shuddered as she realized that this dark-haired intruder must have been lurking
right outside.

I have traded one attacker for another! she thought in horror.

While the intruder was still bending over the officer, Sarah grabbed a heavy volume off the shelf behind her, raised it high, and slammed it down.

"YOW!" cried the dark-haired man as the book bounced off his skull. Sarah instantly fled for the door.

Unfortunately, far from rendering the man unconscious, the book trick did little more than annoy the tall stranger. He jumped to his feet, grabbed Sarah by the shoulders, and plopped her down into a nearby chair.

"Be still, if you please!"

"Help! Hel—" Sarah began to yell, until the woodsman put a large hand over her mouth.

"Be quiet, miss! I am not here to harm you!"

Sarah eyed him. Though his hand was still covering her mouth, it was gently applied and, she realized, had rather a pleasant smell of worn leather and the fresh outdoors about it.

"Will you promise to keep quiet?"

Sarah paused before answering. Despite his gentle touch, the man appeared very strong, with an almost feral look about him. She didn't doubt that he was capable of all kinds of ungentlemanly conduct.

I could bite his fingers and attempt to flee . . . But in truth, she doubted the act would do more than perturb the woodsman, who looked as though he'd had a good deal of practice snagging game rabbits faster than she.

It truly galled Sarah to give in to anything or anyone, but she felt it was her best course of action until she thought of another. Meeting his dark eyes, she nodded her agreement to his demand.

For a moment, he seemed to weigh whether or not to trust her pledge—which in itself made her blood boil. Then, finally, he lowered his hand.

"Who *are* you, sir?" she demanded at once in her most disdainful tone.

"Luke Fitzgerald, miss, a captain in the Massachusetts militia."

"A *Minuteman*?"

"Aye, miss."

Sarah blinked in astonishment, and immediately hid any trace of admiration. After all, the man could be lying. For her own protection, she maintained her mask of chilly Crane arrogance.

"Well, Captain, if what you *say* is to be believed, I'll have you know that I am Miss Sarah Crane, daughter of Alfred Crane, master of this house, and I demand to know what you mean by breaking into a private home like a common criminal?"

Luke narrowed his eyes on Sarah. "I save you from that fool Redcoat snoring on your floor there and *this* is the thanks I get?" he muttered, irritably rubbing the spot where Sarah had beaned him with a volume of French poetry.

Sarah folded her arms. "The major has nothing to do with it."

The captain sighed. "Miss, it makes no difference to me if that officer was your attacker or your betrothed—"

"My what!"

"—I have a mission to fulfill and your caterwauling in the arms of that officer was about to jeopardize it."

"I was being *attacked*, sir! I assure you!"

"If you say so—"

"I do say so. You may have saved me from ravishment, but your methods scared the stuffing out of me—sneaking up like some sort of savage! You made no sound at all!"

"I take that as a compliment."

"Why, in heaven's name?"

"Because I'm a *scout*, miss, and I'm here for a purpose."

"What purpose?"

"The Continental cannons have chased the British out of Boston. We've sent them running north to Halifax, and this detachment of British soldiers here in Harmony is the king's last foothold in a New England port. We are here to free this town of its British occupation and claim it for the government of these United States."

"These *what* . . . ?"

Luke Fitzgerald stared at Sarah as if she suddenly couldn't understand English. "These *United States*."

Hearing the words after so many months of waiting, hoping, praying . . . it seemed impossible. "Do you mean to say they did it? They've declared—"

"Independence. Yesterday, miss, in Philadelphia. Have you not heard?"

"We have been British-occupied and we . . . no, Captain . . . we have not heard. No one in the town has . . ."

Overwhelmed with emotion, Sarah's voice trailed off, her head bent, and tears filled her eyes. For a moment, in the soft quiet, she began to sob.

The sounds of the snoring Redcoat, the summer crickets outside the open window, even the pianoforte at the other end of the house . . . all faded in her head as the deep, resounding echo of this Minuteman's words filled her being: *these United States . . . these United States . . . these United—*

The warm pressure beneath her chin brought her back to her surroundings. The patriot's fingers were rough, yet his touch was gentle as it coaxed her face to turn up toward him.

Wet streaks dampened her cheeks as Sarah's head tilted back, and she realized that the tears that had been brimming in her eyes were now spilling down her cheeks.

"Do not be sad, Miss Crane."

His voice was deep yet surprisingly tender. "Liberty can seem a frightening thing at first, I grant you. 'Tis often easier to rely on others to rule us, to make our decisions for us—like a child wanting always the safety and riches of its parents' household. But choosing privilege and safety over liberty robs us of our ability to chart our own destinies, live our own lives. Liberty, you see, is worth the price of safety. And we Americans have finally made the choice to govern ourselves. No more tyrant king. We will be better off. You shall see, miss. So, please . . . do not cry—"

As he spoke, Sarah gazed at this rugged man with new eyes. Finally she allowed herself to admire the strength in his square-shouldered build, the sturdiness of his lantern jaw and prominent cheekbones, the kindness in his long-lashed eyes, so handsomely set beneath dark, masculine brows.

"Captain Fitzgerald," she said at last, "you misunderstand my tears."

"You are not saddened by this news?"

"No, I am not," said Sarah, rising to her feet. "I am overjoyed by it."

Confusion crossed the captain's features, until Sarah pointed at the floor. He looked down. A pamphlet was lying there.

"*Common Sense*," he read with the lift of an eyebrow.

" 'The sun never shined on a cause of greater worth,' " quoted Sarah, a broad smile finally splitting her pretty tear-stained face.

This time it was Luke's turn to look at Sarah with new eyes. His dark gaze seemed to caress her cheek, her lips, her throat, then return with more than a glimmer of admiration to her bright blue eyes.

"Now what is the daughter of a Tory like Alfred Crane doing with Mr. Paine's pamphlet?"

"Well," said Sarah with a half-smile. "I *tried* to get our snoring major over there to read it, but he simply was not interested."

"Imagine that," said Luke with a laugh. "It seems to me that you are quite the patriot, Miss Crane. Welcome to our cause."

Sarah Crane's face beamed with undisguised pride, not to mention the gratefulness she had been withholding from this man since he'd brained the Redcoat with his musket.

"Thank you," she said at last.

"You are quite welcome."

"No. I mean, thank you for . . ." She gestured to the major.

"Oh . . . oh, aye! You are quite welcome," said Luke with a slight bow and the faintest blush of humility. "But I am afraid that lout is only a small part of this night's work, Miss Crane."

"Please call me Sarah," she said softly.

"Sarah," Luke said.

His dark eyes sparkled as he gazed at her, as if he enjoyed saying her given name. Then his mind clearly turned to more serious thoughts, and the sparkle faded.

"Most of the Continental volunteers have gone south to join General Washington. I was about to leave myself when I received an odd message two days ago in Boston. About your father."

"An odd message?"

"Aye, 'twas delivered by a strange sort of little man. He said his name was Timmy and that he was a spy for the patriots of Harmony."

"Timmy?" muttered Sarah. "There is a Timothy Reese, who works sometimes on the Bennett farm, but Mr. Reese is at least six feet tall—not little. So it could not have been him. I wonder who this Timmy is?"

"Well, whoever he was, this little man came to visit me this morning in Boston. He told me that Alfred Crane was holding a party this night in his Raven Hill home to entertain every British officer stationed in the Harmony area."

"What did you do?"

No! I cannot believe it. This could not possibly be another version of me!

I know, dear reader, that you are probably asking yourself how Revolutionary War Timmy happened to appear to Luke? Well, Timmy has found an answer in Tabby's diaries!

Apparently when Tabby heard about Alfred Crane's big bash for the British officers, she decided to sew up a brand-new Timmy doll and send him off to Boston to fetch military muscle.

"I took the little spy to my commanding officers. There was not enough time to move artillery or troops into place, so I asked for a detachment of militia. They agreed to give me only ten men, then they warned me not to act until I'd confirmed the little man's claim." ⟁

"Well," said Sarah, "I do assume you have peeked in our windows and seen the rest of the officers in the drawing room, have you not?"

"I saw them earlier and have already dispatched a man under my command, Hancock Bennett, to bring back reinforcements. I'm afraid we are on our own until daybreak. Now I am down to nine men, three of whom I have already sent to alert the townspeople to arm themselves." ⟁

"This all sounds so dangerous. Mere townspeople defending themselves against seasoned soldiers—"

"I know, Sarah. That is why I have returned to your home."

A little judicious scrying in her crystal bowl revealed that the best bet for Timmy's contact was a young man named Luke Fitzgerald. Two years before, Luke left his family's farm in Harmony to join up with the Minuteman and was eventually stationed in Boston with the Continental army.

Tabby sent Timmy to convince him to come back to Harmony and kick out the Redcoats. Or, at least, give it his best darned pistol shot!

Hmmm . . . interesting little choice on Luke's part. After he gets a peek at Sarah in the Crane mansion window, he chooses Hancock Bennett to send back to Boston! Timmy does believe Hancock is a previous life of Sam Bennett's brother Hank! And it also looks to the highly astute Tim-Tim as if Luke wasn't going to take any chance on Hancock charming Sarah before *he* could!

"Why?"

"To come up with a plan. A way to capture the Redcoat officers and convince them to evacuate with as little bloodshed as possible."

"And how will you do this?"

Luke sighed. "Sorry to tell you, miss, but I'm still thinking."

In the quiet of the mansion's library, Sarah Crane listened to Luke Fitzgerald's concerns. He was drastically outnumbered in the Crane household. He had exactly six tired and hungry Minutemen waiting in the garden outside, while twenty-four rested and well-fed British officers were scattered throughout the first floor's parlors.

How could Luke possibly capture the officers without discharging weapons and endangering Sarah's family and friends?

"I have an idea," said Sarah.

The plan she laid out was dangerous for her. If it failed, she could be hanged. But Sarah insisted that it was their only option. Luke could think of no better way to avoid bloodshed, so he agreed and signaled his six men.

Until one of them spoke, Sarah would have thought them ghosts for the soundless way their silhouettes slipped through the library window and into the candlelit room.

The men were of vastly different ages, and all were dressed the same as Luke, with homespun tunics, roughly made breeches, and well-worn leather boots.

The last of them, the youngest, caught Sarah's attention, primarily because he looked like a much younger version of Luke himself.

"Pssst, Mickey, come here," Luke whispered to the fifteen-year-old boy.

"Ah, Miss Crane, may I present my brother, Michael," Luke whispered awkwardly in an obvious effort to offer Sarah a modicum of civility, even in the midst of a rebel invasion. "Say hello, Mickey," he added, poking his brother in the arm.

"Oh, uh . . . pleased to meet you, Miss Crane," said a blushing Michael with a polite bow, one that appeared to include a sharp elbow to his older brother's ribs for embarrassing him.

"Please to meet you as well, Mr. Fitzgerald," Sarah returned, trying her darnedest not to laugh at Luke's contorted face at the momentary loss of air to one lung.

All the men around Sarah were well armed with muskets and pistols, and Sarah exhaled a nervous breath. She would have no pistol or musket to defend herself. But she did have *one* thing . . .

Her white powdered wig still sat on the floor where the major had knocked it off. She nearly laughed out loud when she realized that this woman's wig would serve the Patriots' cause more powerfully than any man's pistol or army's cannon.

Thank you, Father, she thought, amused as she picked it up and repinned it to her yellow hair. *Since you insisted that I be "properly" dressed tonight, I am sure to make the British officers feel right at home!*

Adjusting her skirts and pinching her cheeks, she glanced at Luke.

"Be careful, Miss Crane," he whispered.

"Keep your muskets loaded, boys," she advised the men with a wink.

Luke's eyebrows rose in amazement when the rough-hewn men around him nodded obediently at Sarah.

"Looks like we've got ourselves a new commanding officer," he remarked with a half-smile.

"I can shoot straight, sir," asserted Sarah.

"Just as long as you're not aiming at us," replied Luke.

By the way, Michael (a.k.a. Mickey) is a past life of one of Pilar Lopez-Fitzgerald's sons (due to be born a few years after Luis), Miguel Lopez-Fitzgerald!

The men laughed softly, and Sarah did, too.

"Do be careful, Sarah," Luke said again, and this time she saw the serious concern in his eyes.

Sarah nodded, encouraged by his own returning nod of confidence, the sort of respectful gesture she'd seen officers give soldiers under their commands. It pleased her that he thought her capable of this . . . entrusting her with such a frightening and important task.

Inhaling with determination, and casting one last look into Luke's eyes, Sarah pulled open the door and ventured out of the library and down the long hallway.

The British officers were scattered about the house's first-floor parlors. Since there were more men than women at the party, it was easy to find one or two officers without benefit of female company. These lone Redcoats were more than happy to see Sarah approach them with flirtatious eyes and bubbling laughter.

By ones and twos she lured them down the long hallway toward the library—of course, the "surprise" she had promised them was not exactly what they expected!

The Minutemen subdued each officer one by one, gagging them, tying their hands and feet, then laying them side by side like caught fish on a Harmony dock.

When Sarah had cleared out the unattached officers, she began to approach the kissing couples. "You two look as though you could use a little more privacy," she whispered. "Follow me."

When it was nearly over, they had managed to tie up sixteen of the officers while Sarah handled the eight young women, half of whom swooned the moment they faced the business ends of six American muskets.

The remaining eight officers surrendered without so much as a yip. With guns at their backs and the news that reinforcements were on their way, the Redcoat officers were forced to listen to Luke Fitzgerald's terms: Flee Harmony at dawn, or wait for the Continental army to take the officers prisoner for the duration of the war and blast the hell out of the rest of their troops.

The decision was an easy one—the British officers agreed to withdraw immediately.

Armed with axes, pitchforks, and the occasional musket—hidden after the British ban on Harmony households stocking firearms—all of Harmony's families took to the streets at daybreak to ensure that every last Redcoat followed that decision.

With Sarah by his side, Luke Fitzgerald and his men happily watched the British sails depart from the top of Raven Hill.

" 'Tis our Harmony now," said Sarah with joy. "And our country."

"Though not yet in Britain's eyes," said Luke somberly. " 'Tis a long fight ahead of us still."

"But we shall win. I feel it, Luke."

"Do you now?" Luke asked, turning to take her in his arms. "And what else do you feel this fine morning, Miss Crane? Anything else?"

Sarah reached up a hand and caressed Luke's face, her fingers tracing the outline of his broad smile. His strong jawline was rough with stubble, but it was just about the most wonderful thing Sarah Crane had felt in all her nineteen years.

"I feel the pleasure of a man," she whispered.

"Aye," said Luke. "And what would the pleasure of this woman be?"

"A kiss," said Sarah simply.

Luke obliged her. With all his heart.

Much to her father's dismay, Sarah Crane invited Luke's dust-covered detachment of Minutemen into the elegant Crane dining room for a hearty breakfast while they waited for their reinforcements to catch up to them.

By that evening, Sarah found her father pacing the drawing room, questioning what he should do now that his ships had lost their protection.

"What shall I do? What shall I do?" he muttered.

Every last British officer was likely to believe that Alistair himself had set them up for capture—and they would likely be on the lookout to blast any Crane ships they spotted out of the water should he try an Atlantic crossing.

"If you please, sir, I would like a word."

Sarah watched Luke Fitzgerald's broad-shouldered form stride across the expensively furnished drawing room of the Crane mansion, his worn leather boots starkly out of place on the immaculate Chinese needlepoint rug.

Alfred Crane's eyes could barely contain their disdain—and fury.

"What could *you* possibly want?" he demanded.

"I have a letter of marque here from the Massachusetts Assembly, Mr. Crane."

"And why should I have any interest in such a document?"

"A letter of marque, sir, gives me the right to privateer. I've had a word with my commanding officer and he's given me leave to approach you with a plan."

"What sort of plan?"

"With the aid of your ship captains, the Continental army can outfit your ships with guns and marines so that you may continue your trading under the protection of the United States government."

"I see. And where's the rub?"

"The rub, as you put it, sir, is this: Any English ships we see, we shall overtake. Legally."

"Legally?"

"Aye, sir. We shall claim the ship and any cargo for the United States. You and I shall split the booty with the army."

Mr. Crane raised a pleased eyebrow. "Pirating? This United States government will legally sanction pirating?"

"*Privateering*, sir. A standard practice in times of war."

"Well, well, well . . . I should say this independence scheme may not be such a very bad idea after all!"

" 'Tis not a *scheme*, Father!" exclaimed Sarah, who had been listening closely to every word.

"Say what you will, Sarah. But in my opinion, this Patriots' cause is no different than the king's. 'Tis about riches and booty and taxes, in short, what makes the world revolve—*money*."

Sarah was about to respond, but Luke beat her to it. "On the contrary, Mr. Crane. Our cause may require money for arms to defend it, but it is in no way simply *about* money or even might. 'Tis about our destiny and who will decide it for us."

"Not ruled by a king, Father, but by ourselves," said Sarah.

"Your daughter is right," said Luke, his grateful gaze briefly finding hers. "For we are not merely *another* country, sir. We are the very *first* country to declare a self-government."

"All right, already!" cried Alfred Crane with a dismissive wave. "As I've always said, the Cranes survive by choosing the most agreeable course. And at the moment, Mr. Fitzgerald, *yours* appears to be it."

"Aye, sir, and so it shall be," affirmed Luke with a happy wink of thanks to Sarah. "And one day you shall see. Independence, 'twill make a difference in this country— and in this world."

Sarah smiled with such pride in Luke that her heart filled nearly to bursting.

The next morning, Sarah followed Luke out the mansion's front door to say farewell.

The day was cloudless, with a bright beating sun that made many parts of Harmony overly hot. But up on Raven

Hill the ocean's breeze sent a cooling kiss to the young couple as they stopped beneath the swaying shade of Sarah's favorite old oak.

For a moment, it felt to them both like an oasis of perfection, a bubble in time that, if it were completely up to them, would never be broken.

With a suddenness that surprised Sarah, Luke dropped his musket and pulled her into his embrace.

"How good you feel," whispered Sarah, running her hands along his muscled arms to link them behind his strong neck.

"And you," said Luke, his fingers stroking Sarah's unbound hair, lifting a few strands to watch them dance and swirl on the sea's breeze.

"I shall take this image with me, my darling Sarah. Your beautiful hair, natural and free at long last."

Sarah wryly lifted an eyebrow. "You mean to say, sir, that you do not prefer my white powdered wig?"

Luke laughed. "I say we burn it at the first opportunity."

"How about our wedding night?" asked Sarah boldly.

Luke was silent a long moment. "Would you *have* a man like me for your husband?" he asked softly, his voice hardly steady.

"*Like* you?" asked Sarah. "No. I would have *you*. Period, Mr. Fitzgerald."

With a burst of joy, Luke picked Sarah up and twirled her around. "Heaven help me! She will be my wife!"

"I will! I will!"

"Is it possible to feel this much love?" he asked, setting her down, his dark eyes radiant with bliss.

"It is. For I do."

"Then let me go to make my fortune, win you this war— and I swear, Miss Crane, we will be together for the rest of eternity."

"I can think of no promise that could make me happier."

The kiss was beyond powerful. Beyond joyful. It locked

them in a moment of time so sweet, so perfect that neither of them, for the rest of their lives, would ever mark time without thinking of this moment . . . of this hour . . . of this day.

"Come back soon, my love!" called Sarah, running to the edge of the hill to wave him off.

With his musket slung over his broad shoulder, Luke tossed a breath-taking smile at his betrothed and promised, "As soon as the wind will carry me!"

Addendum: Now, you may wonder what happened to these two lovers. Well, the truth is not so happy, Timmy is sorry to tell you. Tabby's diary reveals that Luke Fitzgerald's ship was lost at sea. Sarah Crane never married. She lived out her life on Raven Hill, every day looking out to the turbulent Atlantic waves for her love to someday return. Tim-Tim found this entry in Tabby's diary that even marked the occasion of her passing . . .

July 5, 1816

Dear Diary,

I am sorry to tell you that Sarah Crane passed away today, sitting beneath the very oak tree where she had last seen her betrothed exactly forty years ago this month.

Now I swear to you, dear Diary, that I had nothing to do with Luke's disappearance.

Timmy was quite upset when he heard about it, and I had to assure him over and over that young Luke went down on the Crane ship during a terrible storm — his last thought, of course, was of Sarah.

" 'Twas a freak accident. No spells involved!" I swore repeatedly to Timmy.

Many suitors attempted to court Miss Crane years after Luke disappeared at sea, but she refused every one of them, clearly feeling tied forever to Mr. Fitzgerald.

A few times, Timmy even asked me to cast a love spell over a promising suitor. But it never worked—quite simply because the spell of Luke was stronger.

Miss Crane remained a spinster the rest of her life, continuing her volunteer work around the town, attending her spinning bees, and helping to raise her younger brother's children in the Crane mansion on Raven Hill . . . until her own death today.

It is quite a tragic case, I must admit. Even brings a tear to my eye . . . and having already seen so much in this world, that is not easy, I assure you, Diary.

Not that I have ever felt any love for the Cranes, mind you, but I must say that in her girlish years, Sarah did display quite a bit of courage.

It is my professional opinion that Miss Crane and Mr. Fitzgerald have become a classic pair of "star-crossed lovers," which in supernatural terms means that their spirits will most assuredly come back again and again, until they get it right.

I shall keep an eye out for these two souls, for they are bound to play out at least one of their future meetings in Harmony.

The question for me now is this: When and if I ever do see them again, shall I help them, as Timmy urges me?

Or, as my friends downstairs would always prefer, shall I bring them heartache?

I think, perhaps, that Timmy is right this time. After all, I do owe these two a little thanks for helping me rid Harmony of those pesky Redcoats.

Don't you agree, Diary?

Really, as long as it does not interfere with my other evil plans and schemes, what's the harm in casting a little love spell over their spirits to help them along? Especially if their love ends up vexing a descendant of William Ephraim Crane—or even jeopardizes the Crane fortunes! Yes, that would be rich indeed!

I will tell Timmy not to be too sad today.

He should think of us as members of an audience, waiting for these two souls to reappear on our stage sometime in the future—and undoubtedly star in yet another affair of the heart!

APPENDIX II

Timmy

THE LOST LOVE LETTERS
SAM AND IVY'S FATEFUL SUMMER

Dear Reader,

What can Timmy say but OOPS! While snooping through Tabby's private things (a truly scary thing to do, I assure you!) Timmy discovered these lost letters, written between Sam Bennett and Ivy Winthrop Crane more than thirty years ago. If Timmy had found these letters before Tabby's publisher went to press with the first edition of *Hidden Passions*, Timmy certainly would have included them for you to read. Aren't you lucky Timmy was able to publish the letters now in this paperback edition! These heartbreaking notes are not to be missed! They certainly complete the story, showing in Sam and Ivy's own words just how closely the two young lovebirds came to spending their lives together. Timmy wonders what would have happened if just one of the letters had actually gotten through. According to Tabby's diaries,

most of the letters were destroyed by Ivy's father. So how did Tabby get her mitts on them?
Timmy asked his princess, but all Tabby would
say was "a sorceress can't reveal all her secrets in one book!"

Enjoy!

Yankee Hope
June 12

My Darling Ivy,

*When I left Harmony, I thought I'd be writing you
romantic letters of life at sea. How I wish I could tell you
about cloudless days, soft sea breezes, and the upstanding character of my fellow crewmen. But, honey, you
know me. I'm always honest, and the honest truth is:
there's nothing the least bit romantic about working on
one of your father's trawlers!*

*Three days out of five are foggy; there's not a damned
thing soft about the cutting sting of the north wind; and
the crew (with the exception of the 50-year-old captain
and an even older salt named Blackie) is a rough, unhappy group of borderline alcoholics whose vocabulary
consists mainly of four-letter words. This is not game
fishing. It's hard, back-breaking labor. And the truth is,
they are all here, like me, not to experience the romance
of the sea but to earn stacks of the filthy green stuff.*

*We're in the Grand Banks tonight, hundreds of miles
off the Newfoundland coast. It's foggy again. Not a sin-*

gle star shines above. We've been baiting longline for
endless hours. Almost 500 hooks in the water. Just finished wolfing down dinner in the galley before falling
into my bunk. It's near midnight. And the airhorn will
wake us before dawn. I should try to get some sleep, but I
can't stop thinking of you, my love. So I picked up my
notebook and pen because it's the only way I can reach
out for you . . .

The dull green of these banks goes on forever (350
miles), but it's the place to be for fishing. The shallow-
ness of the water here lets sunlight penetrate, so the cold
Labrador current is rich with plankton. Little fish feed
on the plankton. The warm Gulf Stream runs up the big
fish, then we fishermen hook them. So there you have it:
the 500-year old recipe for wealth (as Winthrop Marine figured out): plankton to fish to fishermen to
cash. Treasure handed over from one bank to another.

For much of the crew, that's the extent of their goal: to
earn cold hard cash. And from the sound of all the stories I've heard since I stepped aboard—stories of drinking
and gambling and womanizing—it seems these guys toss
their pay as easily as they toss gutted bodies of big-eye
tuna and occassional shark into the ice-packed hold
below. Well, that's not what I have in mind, and I even
told them so when they asked. That flimsy green paper
is worthless to me in its own right. What use is the stuff
unless it's to buy you and I a start?

My lovely Ivy, I can see our future as clearly and
certainly as I can see my own hand holding this pen
and scrawling these words. We'll live in a quaint Harmony cottage. Our home will be small, much smaller

than the beautiful Colonial you grew up in and no
more than a servant's house to the likes of the Cranes'
mansion. But the place will be ours. Well-kept and
well-loved. I'll plant ivy all around the walls to remind
me of you. It will climb the stone and every time I come
home from work, it will be the first thing I catch sight of
from the road.

I can almost smell dinner cooking as I race up the
walk, the scent of baked bread mingling with Harmony's
fresh sea air. And there you will be, standing in the
doorway, smiling and waving and opening your arms
to me. Our little children will be sleeping in their beds.
They'll have your beautiful bright eyes, your warm intelligence and graceful good looks. And they'll have my
stubborn chin (the Bennett chin)—the surest sign
they're ready to take every dare that comes their way.
And give some right back, too!

I'll light the fire and after dinner take you to the
large feather bed in our room. I'll make love to you for
hours. We'll have little girls and little boys too, sweetheart. And they'll be as gorgeous as their mother. How
about four children total, two of each! What do you
think? Can you see our home with me, Ivy? Our little
piece of Heaven on Earth? The dream of our hearts? It
hardly seems possible that a small stack of dirty green
paper can be transformed into a treasure like that. But
it can. It can. And it will. I promise you.

Men like Julian and Alistair Crane, who've built their
whole lives around wealth for wealth's sake, will never
understand the way people like you and I see things.
But I'll never, as long as I draw breath, see any better use

for my pay than to build a life with you, my love.
Flimsy green paper transformed into a home and family, now that's the recipe for real riches. I know you feel
the same way, Ivy. That's one reason I love you so much.
So much . . .

My bunk is narrow and hard. From it, I can hear the
constant hum of the diesel engine, the uneven slap of
waves against the steel hull. But, darling, I'm not really
in this bunk tonight or on this creaking trawler. When
I close my eyes, the dank air in this cabin becomes a
Harmony breeze, the slapping waves become the sandy
surf, and I'm in our cove again with you, feeling you . . .
your warmth and softness under our beach blanket.
Seeing you . . . the tiny smile of happy dreams on your
lovely lips.

Are you surprised to hear that I watch you when you
sleep? I've never told you before, but I do. After we make
love, I lie very still and listen to your breathing, waiting until it becomes steady. (Did you know it sometimes
matches the same steadfast rhythm as the Harmony
surf? It's like you're part of the ocean—or something out
of it.) And then I pull away just enough from the pillow to gaze down at the sweet look of contentment on
your angelic face.

You are my very own sleeping beauty to wake, if I
choose, with a kiss. But I don't wake you. I stay as still
as I can, holding my breath and taking you in as if
you're all the breath I need . . .

I can almost hear you now as you read these very
words. You're asking, "Sam, why in the world do you do
that? Watch me while I sleep?"

I don't know, baby. Or maybe I do . . . maybe it reassures me that you're real. Our lovemaking is so incredible sometimes I just need to know that I didn't dream it . . . that you're really there beside me. I mean . . . a girl like you with a guy like me? Who'd believe it? Sometimes I hardly can.

You make me so happy, honey. You are everything that's pure and sweet and innocent and beautiful. You are all I'll ever want. You are my life . . . that's why being apart from you is so painful to me.

I lied to myself the night I left, telling myself the days would pass quickly. I was an idiot. Time was at a standstill while we motored up to Halifax. I spent torturously slow days watching the crew do nothing but drink and play cards.

Every day I wrote to you, and then when we docked, I dropped the stack of letters into the Canadian post. Did you get them? It's been almost two weeks so you must have them by now. Did you read them?

The evening we were docked, I called your house, hoping to reach you, but your father answered. It shocked me into silence for a few seconds. I mean, Pilar is the one who always answers your house phone. I didn't hang up though. I wanted to speak to you so badly, to hear your voice, that I asked if you were available to come to the phone. Don't worry, honey, I didn't give him my name! I just told your father I was "a friend."

He said you were out with "a young man." That shocked me into a second silence, but I didn't ask any more questions because I was sure he would press for my name. So I got off the phone fast.

Ah, but, sweetheart, now I've got to ask you: Who is this mysterious "young man"? One of your cousins? Or some snobbish son of one of your father's business associates that you couldn't get out of going to dinner with at the Harmony Country Club? Or . . . hmmm . . . are you already trying to make me jealous?

I'm just kidding, honey! I know I can trust you!

But darling, make no mistake, I do want to hear from you, so please write to me. We'll be docking again in just a few days, almost to the day I estimated in my first batch of letters to you, so I'm expecting you'll be at home in the evening like I asked, and then I can finally hear your sweet voice when I call this time.

When I talk to you, I'll tell you more about our docking schedule and you can always find out from the Winthrop Marine office, too (just to be sure you'll be home when I call from now on).

Please be sure to pick up the phone, honey. It's tearing me up to wonder daily what you're doing, what you're feeling. I'd rather have a steel hook rip through my heart than hear you're having second thoughts about me . . . about us . . .

I don't know why I even wrote that. Guess I'm just tired and sad to be missing you so much. I mean, I know you love me. I know you must be missing my touches, my kisses, as badly as I'm missing yours.

I can hardly wait to hear your voice on the phone. To read your letters. The captain picks up the mail at the harbormaster's office and distributes it among the crew. I can hardly wait to see his face when he has to lug the stack that I'm sure you've written to me by now!

Getting very tired, honey. My mind's drifting back to our cove . . . . Did you know you look younger when you sleep? I can almost see the little girl you must have been. The pint-sized, sun-kissed child with peaches for cheeks and bright blue eyes. I wonder what you were like then. Giggling and happy? Carefree? Or shy? Earnest and quiet?

My arms are wrapped around you now Ivy. Can you feel them? The scent of Jasmine from your sweet neck fills and satiates my entire being. You're like a golden spring day, lush and new, full of living promise. I listen to your breathing, hear it once again slip into the same slow and steady pattern as the nearby surf.

You are part of the sea now. You surround me. Cradle and hold me. . . as I hold you.

Drifting off. Cannot keep eyes open.

I carry you in my heart.

Yours forever,
Sam

Yankee Hope
July 9

Dearest Ivy,

We rode out a storm yesterday. Had the lines out overnight and the weather service misjudged the speed and direction of the gale. The captain woke us with an airhorn hours before we were due to rise. We stumbled up from our bunks and started hauling in the line at 4 AM to save it from damage. Waves started washing over the deck. The captain was in the wheelhouse trying to ride out the swells and keep us from getting slammed broadside. Then just as dawn broke a man went overboard.

Blackie was the fastest, throwing a lifesaver, but the man seemed dazed, like he'd been struck in the head, and never even grabbed for it. Everyone froze as he began to sink down. I didn't even pull off my boots. No time, just dived off the deck. Brought him to the surface, snagged the lifesaver, and the crew hauled us in like part of the catch.

Hours later, sipping coffee in the galley with a blanket over me, the captain came down and sat with me, told me I'd done well. That surprised me because the captain has said very little to me during this entire trip.

Cap's in his late forties or so and has fished most of his adult life in Winthrop Marine vessels. Wears a full brown beard that's graying, a balding head but a solid, stocky build. Used to play football.

The captain seems like a good enough man. I know he cares about this crew. And I know he was grateful I saved one of his men. Well, after he thanked me, he looked at me for a long silent minute, and I got the strangest feeling that he wanted to tell me something but couldn't.

Then he just put a hand on my shoulder and told me the sea at times is like life and love—without mercy. "Waves beat the big hulls same as the small, the best men same as the worst. But remember, Sam," he said, "it's all survivable."

I argued with him. Not about life treating us without mercy. I've seen my own father withstand some hard knocks, and I've taken a few myself. But I could not agree with him about love being that way.

How could he say that? How could he compare love to a volatile, viscous, near-fatal gale? He's obviously the sort who's never known a love like ours. Or a woman like you. Our love is sturdy as steel. I know you know that. I know you'll wait for me . . .

Won't you, darling?

Just seven more weeks, Ivy. I know it's hard on you to have me gone. I know you can't tell your family and friends about me yet . . . but honey . . . I have to tell you . . . when I tried to call you again just before July Fourth, your father answered and told me you were out with Julian Crane.

Honey, you haven't written so far this summer. Not one letter. Not one line on a single postcard. For some reason you haven't stayed at home during those few times when we've docked, so you could take my phone calls. And now your father is telling me something I can hardly believe. I mean, I expected you might be pressured into a few evenings at the Country Club just to please your parents, but going out with Julian Crane . . . of all people . . . I'm so sorry. I know it sounds like I'm accusing you . . . doubting you. Maybe it's just the stress of the storm and then the captain's strange words: Not just what he said, but what he didn't say . . . or wouldn't say. And he seemed so . . . I don't know . . . guilty about something . . . but it just makes no sense . . .

My god, I'm not making any sense in this letter!

It's late and I'm tired. Sweetheart just write to me and

I'll understand . . . if only you knew how much I need you right now, this moment . . .

You know, I'm the only one on this ship who never complains when the sixteen-hour days of work stretch to twenty. It's grueling, but it mercifully distracts me from the pain of wondering about you. Wanting you . . .

Truly, the hardest part of my day is hitting the bunk at night. God, Ivy, even when I'm completely exhausted, I still want you so badly it hurts.

How I want you now, tonight, with me in this bunk. What I'd do to you . . . how you'd enjoy it . . . I can almost hear you calling out my name . . . almost feel you touching me, caressing me . . .

Never forget our passion, Ivy. It will be ours again. I promise it will.

> All my love,
> Sam

Yankee Hope
August 8

Dear Ivy,

It's a calm afternoon, and I'm writing to you during my shift in the wheelhouse. Sitting in the skipper's chair now, watching the autopilot, monitoring the radio and weather bulletins, checking the radar. No fog today. I can see for miles and miles. But it's not exactly a beautiful sight. The dull gray-green of the Grand Banks are nothing like Harmony's glittering shoreline, where sunlight is always flickering on the deep blue waves. The water here is dense with plankton, and the waves seem to swallow the light rather than reflect it.

These currents are fascinating to watch though, always shifting and changing. Yet the far gray horizon itself never changes. Day in, day out, it is always the same. Vast and empty. Empty and vast.

Keeping watch on a trawler is very different from keeping watch as a Harmony lifeguard. Even on a cloudy day when the beach was empty I could hear the squawking gulls, catch sight of a distant tanker or a yacht's snowy sail. I never before realized how much comfort there was for me in just those little signs. How it reassured me with a sense of belonging . . . of being connected . . .

But now I'm at sea, Ivy.

I feel so alone, so completely cut off . . . as if I'm floating in a dismal purgatory. And, well . . . what I'm trying to say is that it's not just the vast emptiness around me. It's the emptiness inside me.

Oh, Ivy, how can I tell you this . . . it's so hard . . . but I have to try . . .

I've been tossing and turning since we last docked. By chance I happened to see your photo in one of the Harmony newspapers. The Winthrop Marine home office had sent it so the crew could catch up on local news. The photo was of you, arm and arm with Julian Crane, and the caption talked about how you've been seen with him socially for some time now. It called you a "couple."

The word cut like broken glass.

Ivy, my dearest love, you are my life. There is no day forward without you in it. No place at the altar without you there in white . . .

I know you feel the same about me. That's why I don't understand what's happening. I've sent you so many letters, tried to call you all summer . . . yet you haven't answered one of my calls . . . haven't made the effort to write one little postcard.

If you knew what I've been going through each time we dock: how I watch the captain distribute the mail . . . how he hands me a few letters from my father and mother . . . a few more from my college friends . . . but nothing else. Nothing from you, my one and only love. Nothing!

If you could understand how it makes me feel . . . how lost . . . and empty . . . and worthless . . .

Oh, god . . . just write me an explanation, honey, and I promise I'll understand. Was there some string of parties, some engagements you couldn't get out of? Please, just tell me, sweetheart . . . just write me . . .

Is your father pressuring you? Is he guilt-tripping you? What is it?

At lunch today, Blackie told a sea story about a siren who lured a ship of Newfoundland sailors onto the rocks of Sable Island . . .

While he was talking, I had a vision of you that way. Beautiful, naked, golden hair swirling around your curves; sweet lips whispering promises, tempting me to step off the deck one night into the damned Banks fog. Will I find you there beyond it? Will you reassure me that our lovemaking wasn't just some glimmering mirage that I'll never experience again?

Oh, my love, not to have it again . . . that would be the nightmare. The descent from this purgatory to a true

hell, an emptiness vaster than even this desolate sea.
Please write. Explain. Help me to endure this.

With hope and love,
yours always,
Sam

Dear Sam,

It's well past one in the morning. I'm lying on my bed. My evening gown has become a wrinkled, tear-stained rag because I've been crying over you for the past two hours — No, that's not true. The truth is, I've been crying over you all summer long.

When I think back on what we shared in our cove just three months ago, I never, ever would have guessed I'd be writing you a letter like this one. No girl in her right mind would waste her time. No girl in her right mind would deny the obvious message you've sent through your three months of silence. But then again, I'm not in my right mind, so here goes . . .

I've been searching my heart tonight to connect with what I truly feel, digging deep into my very soul, and, Sam, the truth that lives in me is this: Even after everything I've learned about you — your despicable behavior all summer aboard my father's fishing boat; the drinking; the brawling; and worst of all, the sleeping around with every woman you could get your hands on wherever you docked — even after all of it, I still want you, Sam. I still love you.

I'm sure you've read all fifty or so of my gullible letters, telling you how much I've missed you, how much I've wanted you, how much I've longed for your strong hands and soft mouth to be on my body again. And I'm sure you've read the desperate note I fired off weeks ago when I first heard about your behavior from one of my father's Winthrop Marine log reports. I pleaded for an explanation from you, begged for some word, but still you chose silence. The same silence you've inflicted on me all summer.

I thought I knew you, Sam Bennett. Knew what you were and, more importantly, weren't capable of. I never thought you capable of betrayal, or deliberate cruelty. But I've never seen you tested before, tested away from me.

Maybe you thought I'd never find out about the women. Maybe that's part of the reason you never wrote me all summer. Maybe, in some perverse way, your silence was how you thought you'd remain true to me — you didn't want to write lies, didn't want to pretend that everything was okay when it wasn't so you simply refrained from writing at all. Maybe there's some other explanation you can offer that will make more sense — something beyond all my pathetic attempts to defend you in my own mind, something believable even in the face of the mounting evidence against you . . .

The other day while I was sitting by the county club pool, Rebecca, one of my Alpha sisters, tossed off some words that I still can't get out of my mind. "Men want sex. And they'll do anything to get it."

Rebecca never used to think like that, but she's changed quite a bit this summer. She says that the Clarissa Morton and Jonathan Hotchkiss affair have "opened her eyes" to the truth about the "transaction" that takes place between a man and a woman.

"If you know what he wants," says Rebecca, "then you know just how to get what you want. And what he wants — what he always wants is sex. That's pretty clear."

Her ugly words have stayed with me, Sam. I don't want them to be true, but I think of us, and I think of those terrible words, and I feel them eating away every good thing that I ever believed about you . . .

Is that all you ever wanted from me? Sex? A good time? And when I was no longer available, is that why you fell into other women's arms?

Oh, Sam, I can't face the idea that you used me—

No. NO, it can't be true. The way you looked at me, the way we planned our future. How can it be true? . . . Oh, god, Sam, I know that you love me . . . or at least that you loved me when we were together . . .

God . . . I can't think straight tonight . . . everything's so confusing . . . the summer's been so long, and I need so badly to hear your voice, if only in a letter. One letter.

Please, Sam. Please . . .

It's as if you've left me hanging over some terrible dark chasm, and I'm looking down into it, barely able to hold on anymore.

I need to hear the words, Sam. Tell me. Am I truly being a fool? Do you really want to be rid of me? Or . . . do we still have a chance? Are you silent because you are so ashamed I found out the truth about your behavior? Is there some further explanation? There has to be because I have something to tell you tonight, something very, very important. Something that will change my future, and yours, forever—

Julian Crane has asked me to marry him.

Oh, Sam, I honestly don't know if this news is a shock to you or a relief. I didn't actually say yes to him. But I didn't say no, either, and everyone (my parents, my friends, my sorority sisters) is assuming that I will accept . . . well . . . that I'd be insane not to. So, of course, they're pretending I said yes!

This ruined gown I'm still wearing is one of a dozen new ones my mother insisted I buy for the social whirlwind that's already begun around me. The Cranes have put the word out that Julian and I are to marry, and everyone from New York to Newport wants to celebrate by throwing us a party.

But, Sam, I don't care about all that, don't you see? What I care about is you. And that's why I'm crumpled up on my bed tonight, shedding tears on this stationery, ready to forgive you anything, ready to take you back — because I still do love you.

Oh, god, it's your wife I want to be. Not Julian's!

You have to answer me soon, Sam, because I'm almost out of the strength to hold on to us. Don't you see, it not only means fighting them but it means fighting the logical parts of my own mind. It's so hard to keep believing in you when every shred of evidence says I should give you up, just let you go . . .

But letting go . . .

Oh, god.

I know what letting go will mean. It will mean facing that chasm below, that dark pit without your love, your touch, without even the hope of you . . .

Write, Sam, please. Before the chasm consumes me. Becomes me. Eats away at every last good thing inside me and leaves me completely empty.

Tonight's darkness feels so bleak, so black. It's closing in on me, even as I lie here, because I know in the light of day, with my parents and friends rallying for Julian, even I won't be able to hold out any longer. To hold on.

If you read these words and choose not to respond, I guess I'll be forced to accept the obvious. Your silence will mean you're through with me, and if you truly want to be rid of me, Sam, I'll let you go. I'll cry, but I won't cry forever . . . even though I'm sure to remain in love with you for that long.

With hope,
Ivy

All you who read these words
a spell is cast on you
to forget in Harmony
that every word is true!

Like a dream you won't recall
all my secrets you've read here
they will fade from memory
keeping my neck in the clear!

-Tabby

BOOKS BY KASEY MICHAELS

Can't Take my Eyes Off of You

Too Good to Be True

Love to Love You Baby

Be My Baby Tonight

This Must Be Love

This Can't Be Love

Maggie Needs an Alibi

Maggie by the Book

Maggie Without a Clue

Published by Kensington Publishing Corp.

Kasey Michaels

Maggie Without a Clue

KENSINGTON BOOKS
www.kensingtonbooks.com

KENSINGTON BOOKS are published by

Kensington Publishing Corp.
850 Third Avenue
New York, NY 10022

All Kensington titles, imprints, and distributed lines are
available at special quantity discounts for bulk purchases for
sales promotion, premiums, fund-raising, educational, or in-
stitutional use.

Special book excerpts or customized printings can also be
created to fit specific needs. For details, write or phone the
office of the Kensington Special Sales Manager: Attn. Special
Sales Department. Kensington Publishing Corp., 850 Third
Avenue, New York, NY 10022. Phone: 1-800-221-2647.

ISBN 1-57566-884-X

First Kensington Hardcover Printing: August 2004
First Kensington Mass Market Printing: August 2005
10 9 8 7 6 5 4 3 2 1

Printed in the United States of America

To Stan Gorzelany, with thanks.

The past lies like a nightmare upon the present.
—Karl Marx

Don't look back. Something may be gaining on you.
—Satchel Paige

PROLOGUE

I've decided to keep a journal. Maggie says a lot of writers do, except she doesn't because she can't see the point of writing anything if she can't sell it. But, as I am not a writer by vocation, I suppose this isn't a complete frittering away of time for me, so here I am, penning my first entry.

The weather remains warm here in Manhattan as we move through September. The park is delightfully sparse of school age children and I can sit here, my scooter resting against the bench as I write. I should describe the scene in more detail, I suppose, as Maggie told me people tend to wax poetical in their journals, but it's a park. Trees, flowers, paths. What else is there to be said about a park?

My name is Sterling Balder, by the way, in chance hundreds of years from now someone discovers this journal tucked away inside an ice floe or some such thing, and wonders who I might have been. Until a few months ago I lived inside the pages of Maggie's mystery novels, along with my dearest friend, Alexandre Blake, the Viscount Saint Just. He solves crimes in Maggie's books, and I, as I once overheard her refer to me, am the Comic Relief. Oh. Maggie's books are set in England, Regency England to be specific about the thing. I probably should have already said that.

For several years Saint Just was fairly content to exist inside Maggie's head, as it were, until he decided he was sufficiently versed in how to properly comport himself in Manhattan. At that time we . . . we . . . well, we *poofed* out of Maggie's head and into her apartment. That probably sounds more difficult (and possibly painful) than it was. Really. Learning to zip things? Now *that's* difficult.

Saint Just is Alex Blakely to everyone here except me, and Maggie introduces us as her distant English cousin Alex and his friend Sterling, on whom she patterned her mystery series, using both our names and our physical . . . attributes, I believe she terms them.

Things have been wonderfully interesting ever since. We've met a multitude of people. I suppose I should say who they are, and then the journal won't be a hodgepodge and all of that. Very well.

Maggie is Maggie Kelly, although she used to be Alicia Tate Evans when she wrote historical romances and now she's Cleo Dooley as she writes her marvelously successful Saint Just mysteries. That's clear, isn't it?

Bernice Toland-James is Maggie's editor at Toland Books, and her very best friend, although Tabitha Leighton, Maggie's literary agent, is also a boon companion.

After Maggie's publisher was murdered we became acquainted with Lieutenant Steve Wendell. The good lieutenant continues to wander in and out of Maggie's life, which depresses Saint Just more than he will admit, although the two gentlemen seem to have formed a bond lately, much to Maggie's surprise and, I believe, dismay.

There's Snake and Killer, of course, and Mary Louise. They're all cousins, and little more than children, really. Once denizens of the street, they have become the nucleus of Saint Just's ever-expanding group of Street Corner Orators and Players, one of my friend's endeavors to become financially solvent without dirtying his hands with trade or anything even vaguely smelling of the shop.

Oh, dear, that sounds cruel. Saint Just is a marvelous man, truly. A trifle high in the instep at times, granted, but a good one for all of that. If only he wouldn't persist in believing himself a wealthy viscount from 1811 who is also a master at mystery detecting. He dove right into the fray when Maggie's publisher was murdered, and just again a few weeks ago he deliberately insinuated himself into a rather muddled affair of pranking and murder at a writers convention we all attended.

Once again, Saint Just had been looking for a way to pad his pocketbook, and he found that at this same convention by entering a cover-model contest which he did not win. He did, however, manage to be noticed by Mr. Pierre, who has taken up both Saint Just and Mary Louise to tout his perfumes.

Mary Louise is still much the urchin, but she cleans up extraordinarily well.

This new endeavor of simply being himself as he poses for photographs is important, because now Saint Just and I have enough blunt to vacate Maggie's condominium and relocate ourselves across the hall to Mrs. Goldblum's apartment while she visits with her sister in Boca Raton, where we are about to install a most wonderful large screen television machine.

I am to be in charge of the apartment, by my own wishes, and because Saint Just may be a champion detective, but he wouldn't have the first idea on how to go on with anything as complicated as a motorized can opener. He'd much rather continue to excel at what he does best. That, dear journal, would be in being Saint Just.

Is that it? No, there's one more, isn't there? Felicity Boothe Simmons. May I say—shudder! Miss Simmons used to be Faith Simmons, and one of Maggie's best friends, but then she became *NYT*—whatever that is—and dropped Maggie like the proverbial hot potato. Maggie is also *NYT* now, and Miss Simmons cannot forgive her for her even greater success (this is Saint Just's explanation at any rate). Although, now that Maggie has very recently saved Miss Simmons from a Dire Fate, it would appear the woman is attempting to worm her way back into Maggie's life.

Maggie is not best pleased by this turn of events. Saint Just says Maggie tends to be prickly in an effort to keep from having herself hurt. Did I mention that he fair dotes on her? Not that he wishes that sort of thing bandied about, of course.

Now I'm done, I'm sure of it. I hadn't realized journaling could be quite so difficult. I seem to have been scribbling for hours, and I would dearly like to toddle over and purchase a flavored ice. It's Saturday, so I am allowed a blue one. Saint Just limits me to two blue ices a week, as he seems to be inordinately put off by blue lips and tongue. As I said, he can be a bit of a stickler, although his heart is pure.

You see, I have deduced—Saint Just is not the only one who can deduce—that as Maggie invented Saint Just, Saint Just is partly Maggie, and the other way round. They are different, and yet they are alike. Sometimes enough alike to disconcert each other mightily.

I'm still wondering if the same can be said for me.

Have I forgotten anyone? Should I mention Doctor Bob? I've yet to have the pleasure, but Doctor Bob is Maggie's confidante and advisor, much to Saint Just's disgust. Maggie refers to the gentleman as her *shrink,* but as I've already said, I've yet to meet the fellow, so I myself won't comment on his size.

I've also yet to be introduced to Maggie's parents, most especially her mother. Maggie mostly talks to Doctor Bob about her mother, and about Dame Nicotine, the most persistent bane of the dear girl's existence.

And Socks! How could I forget Socks? He's really Argyle Jackson, doorman of our building, but we know him as Socks, aspiring actor. He's also my friend.

So that's it, finally. We're here, and we're enjoying ourselves immensely. I've purchased a few tomes on something called feng shui, and hope to devote myself to arranging Mrs. Goldblum's apartment in tune with nature and the environment and serenity and good health and wealth, and all of that.

Now if only Maggie would stop stumbling over murders, I should think everything will be just as I'd hoped it would be when Saint Just first proposed coming here. A Most Edifying Adventure.

Respectfully,

Sterling Balder

P.S. Did I mention Henry? I don't think I mentioned Henry. Where is my head? Henry is my mouse. His nose twitches and he enjoys running on a wheel inside the cage Maggie purchased for him. It's so good to have someone else to care for, don't you think?

CHAPTER 1

Maggie sat hunched at her computer desk in the living room, staring at the screen. She'd been staring at the screen for five minutes, wishing the words displayed on it to change, reassemble themselves in a more pleasing manner, but it wasn't working. They were still there, damning her.

"Amazon.com? *Again?* Really, Maggie, self-flagellation is so unbecoming," Saint Just said, leaning over her shoulder to press a Post-it note on the edge of the computer. "There. Does this help?"

Maggie took off her computer glasses, threw them to the desktop, and grabbed the note. " 'The trade of critic, in literature, music, and the drama, is the most degraded of all trades.' Mark Twain."

"You seem to enjoy him," Saint Just said when she turned her chair to glare up at him. "I've become a bit of a devotee myself. A pity he wrote after the Regency. I would dearly love to quote the fellow in our books."

Maggie crumpled the note and threw it into the garbage can. "Mark Twain didn't have to put up with these damn reader reviews."

"Maggie. Dear Maggie. There are, at last count, seventy-three reviews posted there on our most recent opus. A star-red review from *Publishers Weekly,* a quite flattering review from *Booklist,* and *Kirkus* was its usual damning-with-faint-praise self. Add to that sixty-seven unremittingly marvelous remarks from readers."

"And three one-star rips," Maggie said, reaching for her nicotine inhaler. "They drive me nuts. I can't answer them, I can't do a thing about them. Why in *hell* would a Web site that wants to sell books show reviews that say a book is the worst piece of drivel they've ever read? And this one," she said, turning her chair to the screen once more. "See this one? It gives away the murderer, for crying out loud."

"That would be the reader from Iowa? The reference was oblique at best. I wouldn't say she spilled all the gravy. Mostly, she complained that if you knew anything at all, you'd know that English gentlemen of the Regency era did not swear or take the Lord's name in vain."

"Yeah, right. We invented all that in the last fifty years or so. I can hear Wellington now." She dropped into a British accent. *" 'Please, my dear fellows, if the spirit so moves you and I'm not interrupting your tea break, might you redirect that lovely cannon over there, as I do believe the Frenchies are advancing up the hill at us in a rather sprightly manner.' "*

"God's teeth, woman, if I might further depress the hopes of our Iowa reader with some mild swearing, would you please *stop* obsessing? And your accent is atrocious."

Maggie wasn't listening. "And this one. This guy said he figured out the murderer halfway through the book. That's not good, Alex. That's really not good."

Saint Just leaned closer. "And does it also say that he most likely peeked at the ending before he began to read?"

"You can't know he did that."

"You can't know he did not do that. You can't know if he's just another frustrated—what are we not supposed to call such people? Oh, yes, another frustrated wannabe. That's it.

Can't do, so he attempts to rip apart those that can. Anyone with a computer and a modem—and an axe to grind—can submit a review on these things. Now, are we quite done with this morning's descent into the pits of self-pity?"

"No, we're not. This last one's the worst. She says you and Leticia weren't together enough. You know what that means, don't you, Alex? It means there wasn't enough *sex* for her. The 'together' enough bit is a tip-off. So's 'I wish there had been more emotion.' And 'It was a little light on the romance.' There's a dozen ways they say it, but they all mean the same thing. Didn't feel the romantic tension, the characters didn't connect enough, on and on. They're all buzz words. What they mean is there wasn't enough nooky for them. Not enough hot, sweaty, jungle sex. Why don't they just say it? Why don't they just say, Hey, lady, put them in bed on page three and keep them there? Better yet, have them do it in public. On horseback."

"Well, my dear, speaking as the hero in question, may I say it's not—minus the horse—an entirely unpalatable idea."

"If I wrote soft porn, no. I'm writing mysteries, damn it. I'm writing about people, not positions. I'm writing characters, not fifty ways to screw your lover. Can't they just get subscriptions to *Playgirl* and stop pretending they're looking for anything more than a cheap thrill?"

Maggie sank against the back of the chair, inhaled deeply, and blew the air out on a sigh, her bravado gone, to be replaced by her usual insecurity. "Maybe they're right, Alex. Maybe the books need more sex."

"Do I get a vote?" Saint Just asked, waggling his eyebrows.

"No, you don't. And maybe you shouldn't say 'Christ on a crutch' anymore."

"I shouldn't?"

"No, maybe you shouldn't. Or 'God's teeth.' "

"Perhaps, just perhaps, I should be all things to all people. Has anyone ever succeeded in that sort of lofty endeavor?"

"Only until after they win on election day. Whoops, can't talk like that, either. Democrats and Republicans. Saint Just's Whigs and Tories. You name it. You saw the e-mails I got. There are people out there who'd like me lined up against a wall and shot for treason and heresy, just because I uttered one little opinion on free speech at the WAR conference and that reporter ran with it."

"Ah," Saint Just murmured. "We Are Romance. The mind still boggles over that unfortunate name."

"Yeah, yeah. Back to me, okay? I'm in pain here." Maggie clicked the mouse over the SIGN OFF menu. "I'm nuts, aren't I? Bernie says I'm nuts. Hell, Bernie said if I ever talk to another reporter *she's* having me shot."

"Never be afraid to speak your mind, Maggie. You simply tend to worry overmuch about everyone else's opinion," Saint Just said, holding out a hand to her as she rose from her chair. "It's a failing you mercifully did not pass along to me. Simply stop obsessing."

Maggie pushed a hand through her recently clipped and streaked hair. "I am not obsessing. I do not obsess. Really. I'm not obsessing." She flung herself inelegantly on one couch as Saint Just gracefully lowered himself onto the facing couch. "Okay, okay, stop grinning at me. I'm obsessing. Just a little. Why do I even *read* these reviews?"

"Again, dear love, you're insecure. You are, in fact, the greatest mass of insecurities I have ever encountered, and I have resided with Sterling. Oh, wait, you know that. You created him."

Maggie looked at her nicotine inhaler, then at the pack of cigarettes on the coffee table. Would she really sell her soul to the Devil for a cigarette? Good thing that so far all her imagination had managed to dredge up was Alex and Sterling. If she could summon a guy with horns and hooves and a tail, she'd be in some serious trouble. "Poor Sterling. I think I gave him all my more vulnerable traits."

"Yes, and gifted me with everything you wish yourself to be, and could be if you'd only believe in your own considerable worth. Now, having said that, you might notice that I am holding a key in my hand."

Maggie felt her stomach do a small flip. Was this it? Was this really the big day? Was she ready for the big day? "Mrs. Goldblum's key?"

"Until recently, yes. But, as of this morning, all mine. Mrs. Goldblum wasn't to leave for another few weeks, but her sister took a tumble on the shuffleboard court or some such place and fractured her hip, as she informed me last evening. Mrs. Goldblum rushed off at first light, leaving us full access. In quite a dither to be gone, poor woman. We'll be transferring the remainder of our belongings as soon as Socks arrives. What will you do without us, Maggie?"

She tipped up her chin (the better not to see the pack of cigarettes on the coffee table). So this was it. Mrs. Goldblum had (verbally—she put nothing in writing) subleased her apartment to Alex and Sterling while she left for a lengthy, open-ended stay with her sister in Boca Raton. "You're moving across the hall. I think I can manage."

Saint Just crossed one long leg over the other. He was the picture of sophisticated elegance, even in modern-day clothing, although in her mind's eye, he was the perfect hero when dressed, by her, in Regency costume.

She'd made him perfect, at least her idea of perfect. The man every woman drools for, to be honest. Handsome, with Val Kilmer's sensuous lips. Physically long and lean and muscular, like Clint Eastwood in those old spaghetti westerns women still sighed over on cable. Eyes blue, Paul Newman in *Hud* blue. Tanned skin, smile lines, a tumble of ebony hair. The voice of a young Sean Connery as James Bond—that Scottish burr mixed with an English accent that had been melting feminine knees for decades. Peter O'Toole's aristocratic nose. To die for; that was the Viscount Saint Just.

She'd made him self-confident, which she was not. She'd made him witty, which she could only be on paper, and so seldom in public—having lived her life as one of those people who wake at two in the morning to say, *"That's* what I should have said when she made that crack about my hips!"

She'd made him brave, to cover her own fears, made him independent of his parents because she was still fighting to saw through a cast iron umbilical. She'd made him daring, witty, cuttingly sarcastic, deliciously sophisticated.

The perfect hero—perfect Regency hero, that is.

And then she'd given him a few flaws, because a totally perfect person would be nothing more than a stereotype; plastic, unbelievable. The sort of flaws that would make him more real, and yet weren't really flaws in Regency England, where the gentlemen ruled and the ladies poured tea. She'd made him arrogant. A tad selfish. A bit domineering.

A know-it-all.

Which had been all well and good, as long as he stayed between the pages of her books, solving crimes and bedding the ladies. Having the perfect hero live in her apartment? That had proved problematic.

Maggie knew she could leap into this man's arms and yell, "Take me, you gorgeous man, you!" If she were that sort of girl, which she wasn't. If she didn't worry that he might one day poof out of her life as unexpectedly as he'd poofed into it. If she was the chase 'em down and tackle 'em type, which she most definitely wasn't.

Although, right now, at this very moment, he was looking pretty damn good . . .

"Maggie? Maggie, please be so kind as to at least pretend you're paying attention."

"What? Oh, sorry, Alex. What were you saying?"

"I was saying, I think Sterling and I should celebrate our

first evening in our new home by escorting you to dinner. I've already taken the liberty of making reservations at Bellini's, as a matter of fact. For eight o'clock. Unless you'd rather remain here all day and night, punishing yourself with other people's opinions?"

"I'm not going to read any more reviews, all right? Ever. Because you're right. They don't help me, do they?"

"Not unless you can be convinced to allow me another romantic tryst per book, no, I would say they aid none of us."

"Okay, okay, give it a rest, you made your point. I really have to write today. What time is it now?"

Saint Just looked at the small clock on the table beside the couch. "It's already gone ten. Sterling was up and about early, for his daily constitutional in the park. He should return soon, with shining eyes and dreadfully blue lips. Why?"

"Because I want to call Bernie. Or hadn't you thought about inviting her?"

"The reservation is for four people, yes, allowing you a guest of your own choosing. Bernice would also have been my choice."

"Ten, huh? I'll wake her up if I call now. You know how she is on Friday nights."

"Drunk and Disorderly, I believe was the charge last month. There's a lot to admire about our dearest Bernice. And one recent development in her life to lament. That would be her ever-increasing affection for the grape."

Maggie leaned over the arm of the couch and snagged the portable phone. She hit the speed dial button and punched 1, for Bernie. "She doesn't have it easy, Alex. Kirk left behind a mess when he was killed, and she's still reorganizing. Damn, I got her machine. She never checks her machine. I'll call again later. In the meantime, what can I help you carry across the hall?"

Saint Just blinked. "I beg your pardon?"

"Carry. Across the hall. Your things?"

"Me?" He pressed both hands to his chest in mock dismay.

"Oh, cut it out. Of course, you. What? You were going to hire movers for some clothes and a few boxes?"

There was a knock at the door, and Saint Just rose to answer it. "Ah, Snake, Killer. And you, the most estimable Socks. Just in time, in the nick of time, actually. The boxes are stacked in the bedroom on the left, directly down that hall. Yes, there you go. Have a care with the clothing in the closet, if you please."

Maggie watched as Snake (unfortunately christened Vernon), Killer (handsome in a downtrodden, Byronic sort of way), and Socks headed for the hallway. "You hired all three of them, didn't you? No, wait, scratch that. They *volunteered.*"

"Absolutely. Vernon and George no longer labor on Saturdays now that they've been elevated to management in our small enterprise."

"Your street corner orators. I still can't believe you turn a profit."

"Minimal, I agree, but an opportunity is an opportunity, and it pleases me to have found a legitimate device for George and Vernon to pad their pockets. I should think you'd be proud of me. Now, if you'll excuse me, I do believe I will adjourn to my new apartment, to direct the placement of my belongings."

"Yeah, yeah, you do that," Maggie said, waving him away as the phone rang. "Hello?"

"Maggie? *Maggie!*"

"Bernie? I just called you to—"

"Maggie! Ohmigod, Maggie! I was sleeping! The phone rang! I had to pee, so I—he's dead, Maggie. Sweet Jesus, Buddy's dead!"

Maggie closed her eyes, hugging the phone close to herself. Oh, yeah. Her friend had tied on a big one last night. "Bernie, calm down. Buddy's dead. Yes, he is. He's been dead for a long time, honey. What were you doing last night?"

"What? He's *dead,* Maggie! It's terrible!"

Maggie was already on her feet, heading across the hall to motion to Saint Just. "Bernie, I want you to calm down," she said, raising her eyebrows to Saint Just, who followed her back into her apartment and took the second portable phone she handed him.

"Keep her talking," Saint Just said, then lifted the phone to his ear.

Maggie did her best, even as her hands shook, because this one was bad, very bad. "Do you want to talk about Buddy, Bernie?"

Had Bernie gotten some bad drugs? She only snorted a little cocaine a couple of times a year, for dietary purposes, Bernie promised, but the woman also drank like a fish. In these past weeks? Like a whale. Maggie felt tears stinging her eyes; why couldn't she do something to help Bernie?

Saint Just was moving his hand in a circular motion, urging her to keep talking.

"Bernie, honey, Buddy went out on his boat seven years ago and he never came back. He's dead. We know that. *You* know that. A couple more weeks and it's officially official. He's dead. What happened, honey? Did you have a bad night? Bernie? Stop crying, honey. Talk to me."

"I . . . I don't know. I don't know. I don't *remember.* I— damn it, Maggie, he's *dead*! I woke up, and there was this *blood.* All over. Blood. And . . . and there he was. God, look at all this blood! I'm blood all over! Help me, Maggie. What do I do?"

"Bernice," Saint Just said and Maggie looked to him in relief. He sounded so calm. "Bernice, darling, this is Alex. Now, you're at home?"

"Alex, thank God! He's in my bed. Alex! Buddy's dead in my bed!"

"Call nine-one-one," Maggie suggested, earning herself a frown from Saint Just. "No. Stupid idea. Scratch that, Bernie. Don't call nine-one-one. Alex?"

"Bernice," Saint Just said soothingly, even as he took the phone from Maggie and hit the Off button. "Maggie and I will be with you in ten minutes. In the meantime, exactly where are you?"

"In . . . in the living room. The blood, Alex. It . . . please come! Maggie, I need Maggie."

"We're already on our way. I want you to sit down, take several deep, cleansing breaths, and await our arrival. Do nothing. Touch nothing. We'll be right there, and you will let us in, and then we will see all this blood. All right?"

"Blood? What blood? Who's seeing blood?"

"Not now, Socks," Maggie said as the doorman stood in the living room, half of Saint Just's wardrobe over his arm. She grabbed her purse, checked to make sure her cell phone was in it. Tossed in her cigarette pack; there was a time to abstain and a time to suck in that nicotine for all she was worth, damn it. "Just drop that junk and run down to hail us a cab, okay?"

"Correction. Place my clothing back where you found it, and then go downstairs and secure a hack for us. Oh, and I'll take the blue jacket, if you don't mind," Saint Just said, crossing the room to pick up his cane (the one with the sword in it—when Maggie wrote fiction, she wrote fiction she liked, and fiction she liked had her hero a whiz with weapons).

"Alex, we don't have time to—"

"Maggie, dearest, there is always time to be properly attired. That, in case you may be wondering, is offered in the form of a polite hint. Ah, thank you, Socks," he said, taking the jacket. "Now, please hold the elevator for us. We're right behind you. Maggie?" he asked, extending his arm.

"What do you think, Alex? Is she drunk? High on something? She sounded so *scared*. And Buddy? God, she hated him. Why would she dream about Buddy? Let's go. Damn it, let's just *go.*"

Saint Just motioned for Maggie to enter the elevator ahead of him. "There is such a thing as a nightmare, Maggie. Now, I'm afraid I'm woefully uninformed about this Buddy person. Please correct that lapse."

"Okay, okay," Maggie said, dashing out of the elevator, only to have Socks pass her as he jogged to the front doors and the street. "Buddy is—was—Buddy James. Bernie's second husband, after Kirk. Bernice Toland-James, remember? I never met him."

"Interesting," Saint Just said, waving to Sterling, who was scootering toward them, his lips distressingly blue to anyone who didn't know his proclivities in confections, a large red-covered book tucked under his arm. "Come along, Sterling," he said. "Give the scooter to Socks and join us. It would appear Bernice is having a bit of a come-apart."

Maggie stood back so that Sterling could enter the taxi first, then crawled in after him, only then noticing that she was wearing her pajama top with her shorts. Had she combed her hair? No, she couldn't remember combing her hair. But she had brushed her teeth after drinking her morning orange juice. That had to count for something.

She looked at Saint Just as he issued calm commands to the driver, at his neatly creased slacks, his expensive sport coat, his pristine white shirt. "I could hate you."

"A gentleman is always prepared for any circumstance," he said, smoothing down his slacks. "Now, Buddy?"

"I don't know his real name. After Kirk dumped Bernie for ten or twelve younger versions, she went for the first guy who was as far from Kirk as she could find. Buddy James.

They married, bought a house somewhere in Connecticut. Near the water. He wasn't in the business. Sold insurance, I think."

"Fascinating man, I'm sure, but perhaps we can move on? The marriage was a happy one?"

"Sure, until Bernie got sick of the commute, and being domestic. Bernie was born for high-rises and doormen and limousine service. Sailing made her hair frizz. Just being near the water in Connecticut made her hair frizz. After a while, just looking at her gardens and her snazzy kitchen and weathered clapboard and anything that looked remotely like an Early American antique made her hair frizz. She was planning to divorce Buddy when he took his boat out one day. A storm came up, and they never found him. Not even the boat. Just some wreckage of some sort."

"A boating tragedy. I see."

Maggie nodded, then leaned forward and knocked on the glass. "Hey, you up there. Cut through the park, all right?"

Sterling was still attempting to fasten his seat belt, as well as trying to catch up. "I don't understand. Bernie married a buddy? A friend?"

"In good time, Sterling, in good time. Now, Maggie. How long ago was this boating mishap?"

"Seven years ago. Well, almost seven years ago. Buddy left behind a pile of debt, but Bernie had no proof he was dead, so she couldn't even get his life insurance money, and he had a bunch of that, because he was an agent, remember. She's been paying off his bills for years. I think she's planning to have a party next month, when he's officially dead. A Bury Buddy party, she calls it, or something like that."

"And yet, according to Bernice, he's dead now. In her apartment. In her bed."

"What?" Sterling abandoned his search for the end of the seat belt and grabbed at the hand strap.

"Obviously Bernice had a difficult evening last night, Sterling," Saint Just said, patting Maggie's hand.

"Don't pat my hand," Maggie said, drawing away, holding her spread fingers out in front of her. "I'm hanging on by a thread here. I never heard her sound like that before. You think she's hallucinating? God, Alex, what are we going to do? Should I call Doctor Bob?"

"For you? Never. For Bernice? It is a tantalizing prospect, as she'd eat him alive. But no, Maggie, we'll handle this. Hopefully. Ah, here we are, and I'm afraid I am not quite as prepared as I believed. Maggie? Pay the gentleman, please?"

Maggie glared at him, then searched in her purse, coming up with a ten-dollar bill. The fare was four dollars and eighty-five cents. And she knew she could wait for change until hell froze over.

"Perfect," Saint Just said, snatching the bill from her as the taxi pulled to the curb on Park Avenue.

"Yeah, yeah, I know. The last of the big tippers. Just get a receipt."

"Of course, as you are the last of the cheeseparers." Saint Just helped her out of the taxi and, with Sterling following behind, still looking bemused, they gave their names to the concierge. As they were all named on Bernie's list of allowed visitors, they then were imperiously directed to proceed to the elevator that would take them to the penthouse condominium.

CHAPTER 2

"Wait," Maggie said, stopping in front of the elevator. She began digging in her purse for her cell phone.

She looked so frazzled, and yet so incredibly beautiful. A tall, slim woman wearing wrinkled shorts and a robin's-egg-blue pajama top with little grinning white sheep on it. A woman with uncombed hair and no makeup. A woman who wore her insecurities on her sleeve, almost as a badge of courage, as she did her best to convince the world she had worth; she really did have worth.

Saint Just felt his heart squeeze, and immediately struck a nonchalant pose. Maggie wasn't the only one who felt it safest to hide embarrassing vulnerabilities.

"My dear girl, whatever is wrong now? You've suddenly remembered that you're still *sheep-clad*?"

"Very funny. Just be happy I'm wearing shoes, okay? But maybe we shouldn't be doing this. Maybe I should call Steve, have him go up with us? I mean, cripes, Alex, what if Bernie isn't hallucinating?"

Saint Just refused to react, although he'd been harboring much the same thought. Bernice was a dear of a woman, but she could be a tad . . . unpredictable.

"Maggie, you have to make up your mind. Either Bernice is hallucinating as a result of ingesting some substance, legal or otherwise, or she has a dead Buddy in her bed and blood on her hands. Either scenario, do you really think we need the New York police at this moment?"

She pressed her hands against her head, her fingers curling into her hair. "I don't know. I'm panicking." She gave her hair a pull as she added, "I *hate* panicking."

"Come here," he said, pulling her against his chest as, neatly, efficiently, he employed the tip of his cane to depress the CALL button. "It's all right, Maggie. Everything will be fine. I'm here."

Maggie wrapped her arms around him and clung. Just for a moment. Then she pushed herself free, saying, "Oh, brother. That was a terrible line. And a terrible lie. If Bernie's in trouble, it doesn't matter who's here."

"I'm here, too, Maggie," Sterling said, gently patting her shoulder.

Saint Just winced. Sympathy from Sterling? He reached into his pocket and extracted a clean square of folded linen, handing it to Maggie as she let out a subdued yet unnerving wail.

"Never sympathy, Sterling. Not from anyone save me, because she knows that, at heart, I'm only offering comfort in order to make her angry enough not to dissolve in a moment of crisis."

"I'll never understand you, Saint Just," Sterling said, stepping into the elevator and holding the door open for Maggie, who was wiping her moist eyes. "I'll never understand either of you. Like you well enough and all of that, but understand you? Never."

Saint Just glared imperiously at the concierge, who was looking at them questioningly as the doors slid closed, then began examining the elevator as it rose to the top floor. "Is this the only elevator? The only access?"

Maggie blew her nose in his handkerchief and dared to try to hand it back to him. "I suppose so. I've only been here a couple of times since Bernie moved in. No, wait. There's probably some sort of service elevator, too. And a stairwell, in case of fire. Why?"

"Nothing. I was just thinking. If Bernice entered her penthouse with a gentleman in tow last night, someone would have seen her, probably someone much like that suspicious gentleman we encountered just now in the foyer. And, that person would have to sign in as we did, even if he arrived with Bernice, I would suppose. I should have requested a peek at the register. Sterling, we'll have to see to that."

"Absolutely, Saint Just."

Maggie held up one finger. *If* she came in with Buddy. That's what you're saying. But she couldn't have come in with Buddy, because Buddy was fish bait seven years ago."

"I really wish you'd stop saying things like that, Maggie," Sterling said, wincing. "I can't swim, you know. Never could."

"Hush, Sterling. Yes, Buddy is supposedly dead, as you say, Maggie. That is problematic, I agree, but not an insurmountable obstacle to sweet reason, if applied correctly."

"Uh-oh, there he goes," Sterling said, looking at Maggie. "He's detecting."

Saint Just ignored his friend, choosing instead to examine the control panel in the elevator. Passengers went all the way up, or all the way down, with no buttons listing the other floors. "Kirk lived well," he said, arching an eyebrow at Maggie, knowing that this had been Kirk Toland's penthouse until his untimely and rather spectacular demise not that long ago.

"I know," Maggie said. "Bernie had to give up most everything else, but she's keeping the penthouse. Forgetting to change his will after the divorce was the only decent thing that man ever did. Guess he thought he'd live forever."

The car stopped, the doors whispered open, and Saint Just stepped directly into a black-and-white marble foyer complete with twelve-foot ceilings and thick white marble pillars. A towering arrangement of fresh flowers sat on a round table. Obviously the very tasteless Kirk had hired a decorator. "Sterling, if you'll keep Maggie here for the nonce?"

"No way! I'm coming with you. Bernie! Bernie, it's Maggie! Where are you, honey?"

Maggie's words echoed in the large foyer, but there was no answer.

"Oh, God, she's not answering. That can't be good," Maggie said, trying to break free of Sterling's grasp, but Sterling had been given a commission by Saint Just, and he held on tight.

Saint Just proceeded slowly, grasping his sword cane midway down in his left hand, leaving his right hand free. Ordinarily, he would be pretending not to be impressed by the opulence unfolding before him as he passed through the foyer and into an immense cavern of a room, the furnishings of which could have graced Buckingham Palace, even Versailles. But he was impressed.

"Bernice?" he called softly, searching the dimness, for heavy drapes hung in front of floor-to-ceiling windows, banishing the sunlight. "Bernice, darling, it's Alex."

And then he saw her. She was crouching in a corner, her knees drawn up to her chest, her head buried against those knees. Her glorious long mane of Titian curls tangled like a bird's nest. Her lime green satin pajamas had an odd design. . . .

"Bernice?"

Bernie looked up at him, her eyes wide. She moaned low in her throat.

"Bernice, darling. Maggie's here, too. And Sterling. You wouldn't want them to see you like this, would you?"

Bernice Toland-James was a beautiful woman. She worked

at remaining a beautiful woman as she ventured more deeply into her forties (at least that's the decade she claimed), via cosmetic surgery, liposuction, Botox injections, starvation diets, a couture wardrobe, and a hair colorist who had to be a genius.

She was brilliant, both in her coloring and in her mind. She was kind, generous, amusing, a loyal friend; Maggie's loyal friend, as well as her editor. She was now sole owner and publisher of Toland Books.

She had become, in these past weeks, something else: a dedicated—and seemingly happy about it—drunk.

"Alex?"

Bernie's voice was little more than a whisper.

"Yes, Bernice. That's right. Alex. Here, allow me to assist you to a chair." He held out his hand and, slowly, definitely reluctantly, she took it. As she stood up, the design on her pajamas became clear. There was no design at all. There was blood. Quite a bit of blood. Still wet, definitely sticky. More blood was on her hands, on her face. Even matted into her hair.

"Alex? Buddy . . ."

"Yes, my dear," he said soothingly, wishing Maggie at the other end of the earth, but as she was here, he knew he had to call her, gain her assistance. "Here you go. Just sit down on this lovely couch, and I'll fetch Maggie. All right?"

"Maggie," Bernie said, swallowing hard. "Yes . . . yes . . . Maggie. I called Maggie. I remember."

Saint Just looked down at his hand, saw the blood on it, and wished back his handkerchief. Instead, he tucked his right hand into his pocket so that Maggie wouldn't immediately see the blood on him, mentally putting paid to his favorite jacket, and returned to the foyer.

"Is she all right?" Maggie asked, standing quietly, without Sterling's having to restrain her. "I heard you talking to her. She's still hallucinating?"

"Unfortunately, no," Saint Just said, looking to Sterling. "Maggie, I need you to be very brave. There could be a problem. There's blood on Bernice's pajamas, a rather copious amount. Mine was only a cursory examination, but I think I am safe in saying it is *not* her blood. Now, I want you to go to her, don't ask about the blood, and just sit with her. Possibly fetch her something restorative to drink. Sterling, come with me, if you please. Touching nothing, as *Left*-tenant Wendell will have to be summoned at some point, I'm sure."

Maggie had already brushed past him, so that when he and Sterling reentered the living room, it was to see the two women on one of the immense couches, hugging each other, Bernie sobbing soundlessly.

"There are stairs, Sterling," Saint Just said, pointing toward another hallway and the landing he'd already seen. "We'll assume the bedchambers are up there. Come along. Again, touch nothing."

"Do you think there's a body, Saint Just?"

"Conjecture seems rather pointless, as we're soon to find out definitively, but yes, Sterling, I'm very much afraid we will shortly discover a body."

He stopped at the head of the broad, winding staircase, confronted with a long hallway lined with several doors. Then he looked down at the Oriental carpet and saw the blood. There also were three bloody hand prints on the wall, as if Bernie had repeatedly staggered against that wall as she escaped the bedroom. Poor terrified woman.

"Sterling, if you would be so kind?" Saint Just stripped off his jacket and handed it to his friend—perhaps it could be saved—then unbuttoned his shirt and removed it.

How he enjoyed these moments, this clarity of sight he felt when put to the test. He had been born for this. Well, *made* for this, at the least.

Using one shirt sleeve as a glove, ineffective as that was, he stepped carefully, avoiding the blood, and then pushed open the already slightly ajar door that was second on the left.

"Oh, gracious," Sterling said from behind him as they both proceeded into the dimly lit bed chamber.

"Indeed," Saint Just said, raising the bulk of his shirt to his nose, the better to cover the sour-sweet smell of blood, of bodily fluids. "I don't know who that is, Sterling, but the gentleman in question is most definitely quite dead."

"All that blood, Saint Just. On the bed, on the ceiling, on the walls. Everywhere. Just like *The Case of the Lingering Lightskirt*. Only that was a woman, of course, and this is most definitely a man. He's so white, Saint Just. The parts that aren't bloody, that is."

"Exsanguination, Sterling. Our victim bled to death." Saint Just moved closer, mentally cataloguing all that he saw, as he feared that once Wendell was on the scene, he would be banished from the room. The man's neck had been cut, ear to ear, transecting both carotids. "See the wound?"

"Uh . . . no, that's all right. As I said, we saw something very like this is *Lightskirt*, and I distinctly remember Maggie's description of the wound," Sterling said, already backing from the room.

"Very well, you may wait downstairs with the ladies. The less we disturb the scene the better, I suppose. No need to summon Maggie, as she never had the acquaintance of Mr. James. We'll have to believe Bernice, unless she was too muddled to be certain of her identification. Poor thing, to awaken to this. I'll only be another few moments."

He thought about Sterling's observation. The scene was rather reminiscent of *Lightskirt*, Maggie's third Saint Just mystery. The victim had been female, of course, and the first of four dispatched in such a way until he, Saint Just, had solved the murders and apprehended the titled and powerful miscreant. *Lightskirt* had ridden the *New York Times* best-seller list for three months.

But this? This was not fiction. This was fact.

And he, Saint Just, was once more on the case.

He could move no closer, not without stepping in blood. But he was close enough to see where Bernie had been lying on the far side of the wide mattress, her body crudely outlined by blood spatter. Close enough to see the naked man's exposed and slit windpipe; a stronger hand with the knife, and the man's neck would have been completely severed. Close enough to see the very large knife lying tangled in the sheets.

Retracing his steps, Saint Just pulled the door shut and headed down the hallway, in search of a bathroom. After washing his hands, he retrieved his jacket from the stair post, where Sterling had left it, and extracted his cell phone, punching in memorized numbers.

"Alex?"

He turned quickly, blocking Maggie's sight of the bloody wallpaper. He slipped his arms into his shirt, buttoning it. "There's a body, yes. I'm phoning *Left*-tenant Wendell now. Please rejoin Sterling and Bernice in the living room."

"Oh, God! Sterling just nodded when he came back downstairs and I thought . . . but I didn't want to ask in front of Bernie. It's Buddy?"

"That I don't know. Please, Maggie. Bad news doesn't improve with keeping, and I want Wendell here rather than anyone else." He turned away from her and spoke into the phone. "Yes, Wendell, so happy you're answering your phone at last. Blakely here. I was wondering, would it be possible for you to come by Park Avenue? The Bernice Toland-James residence, to be precise. Excuse me—Maggie? The exact address? Ah, thank you."

He repeated the address to the lieutenant. "Yes, very near the museum as a matter of fact. Lovely neighborhood, quite a step up in the world for you, so you might wish to brush the doughnut crumbs from your shirt before joining us. What's that? No, no. No problem. I'm always delighted to provide sartorial advice to those in need."

He flipped the cell phone shut.

"Why didn't you tell him?"

"I didn't tell him, Maggie, because I'd rather he didn't enter leading a parade of his compatriots. He expects me to be snarky, to descend to your vernacular for a moment, and I was not about to disappoint him. He's a copper and, friend or nay, he thinks like a copper."

"Okay, I guess, although he's going to be angry."

"How relieved I am to have your approval. Wendell's displeasure is merely an added gift, isn't it? You do know you're now fairly well covered in blood? I fear we'll be waving a fond, final farewell to the sheep upon our return to our domicile. But enough of joy, how is Bernice? And how are you?"

"Bernie's sipping scotch and spazzing out about her bloody pajamas. I know you said restorative, and you probably meant a cup of Earl Grey tea or something, but, well, it's Bernie. And I washed her hands. I know I shouldn't have, but she was really starting to freak out about them, so I washed them for her. And her face. Me? I . . . I'm fine."

"Really?"

"No, not really. Not even close, or I would have been able to think up something snappy to say to you about my pajamas, that I *like,* damn it. God, Alex, what's going on?"

"There is a very dead man in Bernice's bed, there is blood virtually everywhere, there is a knife most conveniently lying on that bed, and Bernice is even more conveniently covered in blood. Her fingerprints, I'm convinced, will be on that knife. Other than that? I missed breakfast this morning because Sterling was in a rush to get to the park, but I do believe I can now forgo lunch without any great personal sacrifice."

"Oh, God." Maggie sat down on the top step. Collapsed onto the top step. "I asked her what happened last night, and she says she doesn't remember. All she remembers is waking up with Buddy next to her—like you said. Bloody and dead. Everyone's going to think she did it."

"Most assuredly."

"Well, she didn't! You know she didn't. I know she didn't. Bernie wouldn't hurt a fly."

"On the contrary. If I were to go into battle, I would very much appreciate having the valiant Bernice guarding my back. She's an exceedingly strong-willed woman who has, if you'll recall, on more than one occasion declared herself capable of killing without a blink, if she felt herself threatened. And, much as it pains me to remind you, Bernice was a prime suspect in the murder of her first husband not that long ago."

"But we know who killed Kirk, and it wasn't Bernie. And Buddy disappeared seven years ago. You know what? It can't be Buddy. Bernie's just so strung out, she thinks it's him. I saw a photograph of him once. How about I take a look?"

"Not if you clutched the hem of my garments and begged," Saint Just said as Maggie got to her feet. "And, now that Wendell is on his way, we cannot in good conscience disturb the scene. We might even destroy evidence that would exonerate Bernice."

"Really bloody, huh?" Maggie wrinkled her nose. "That's what you're saying."

"The deceased is also nude. It would not be proper for you to view a nude male body."

Maggie rolled her eyes, as he knew she would. "Oh, bite me, Alex. Like I haven't seen a nude man before."

"Not in my presence, you haven't. Come along downstairs. Wendell was already in his vehicle. He'll be here in approximately a half hour, traffic permitting. Have you seen the kitchen?"

Maggie rubbed at her forehead. "No. I used the powder room to get a towel and washcloth for Bernie. Why?"

"I would like to see Bernice's knife collection, if that is what it's called," he said, retrieving his sport coat. "Such as the block of wood filled with knives you have on the counter in your kitchen?"

Maggie followed behind him as he returned to the first floor, stopped a moment, then headed to his right, around the staircase, through a magnificent dining room, and pushed through a swinging door. "There you go," she said. "One kitchen. One big-assed kitchen, too. But I thought we weren't supposed to disturb anything. Oh, and if it isn't too much trouble, would you mind telling me why you took off your shirt?"

"Because I didn't think to bring rubber gloves with me?" Saint Just offered, walking around a large center island topped in butcher block, stopping when he noticed that one side of the island sported a slotted piece of wood holding a dozen knives.

And one empty slot.

"Ah, our murder weapon. I recognize the handles. Convenient."

Maggie pushed him aside and took a look. "I know you hate when anyone states the obvious, but there's a knife missing. You think it really is the murder weapon? That's at least something, Alex. I mean, that makes it seem a crime of opportunity. Just the sort of thing Bernie might do if she was suddenly confronted with Buddy, who she thought was dead. Wished was dead. But at least there's a chance of second-degree, not a first-degree charge. Maybe even involuntary manslaughter? You can get bail with those, I think."

Saint Just arched a brow. "You've convicted her already? Your best friend?"

"No, of course not. But it looks bad, Alex, and if she's charged, I want her able to get out on bail. I told you she doesn't remember anything, right? She was drunk. Hell, she's even been having some blackouts lately, which is why I've been begging her to see Doctor Bob, get some help. Go away somewhere. Do the Betty Ford thing. Something. But she says she can't, because of everything going on at Toland Books."

"Just as you say you'll stop smoking once you've made your next deadline. Or was that when you've lost five pounds? Or perhaps it was after you've gotten your apartment back and Sterling and I are on our own? I know you well enough to be fairly positive you've made a list of excuses and refer to it from time to time. Which is it this week, Maggie?"

"Go to hell."

"That's my girl. Now, no more thoughts of Bernice being dragged away in chains. I know you like to think out loud, but this is neither the time nor the place. Who is her solicitor?"

"Her lawyer? Oh, right." Maggie took a deep breath. "Sorry. But I'm pretty creeped out here. I've never been in the same place as a corpse, unless you count my Uncle John's wake, and he was wearing a suit and the mortician had put a smile on his face, so he sort of looked happy about being dead. My mind's been racing. Bernie's lawyer, you said? I don't know. He's corporate anyway, I'm sure. Bernie needs a criminal lawyer. But Steve won't like it if we call a lawyer before he's had a chance to talk to her."

"My condolences to the *left*-tenant, of course, but Bernice will not speak to anyone unless there is a lawyer present. Not a single syllable. To the good cop, or to the bad cop."

"Watching all those *Law and Order* reruns again, aren't you?" Maggie said, then nodded. "Okay, you're right. Definitely right. She'll look guilty as sin, though."

"My dear girl, she looks guilty as sin now. How much blacker can prudent silence paint her? Now, where do you suppose her telephone directory is located?"

"I think she keeps everything on her Palm Pilot. Shall I go get it?"

Saint Just nodded, even as he opened drawers, on the hunt for the Manhattan phone book. He wished to keep Maggie busy, but didn't want the name of Bernie's corporate lawyer. He wanted a shark. A big one. He wanted a lawyer who had no life, who worked on weekends, who would devote himself to one Bernice Toland-James. If he couldn't get all of that, he'd settle for anyone he could get for the moment, and find his shark later.

Locating the phone book, he hefted its weight onto the counter and paged through it until he found the listings for attorneys. Those listings were a small book on their own.

He ran his finger down page after page, curiously inspecting the large individual advertisements, until he saw the one for J.P. Boxer, Criminal Law. There was an ink drawing of a teeth-bared boxer dog in one corner of the small ad, and a telephone number. That was it, other than a Park Avenue address, one not three blocks away. It seemed providential.

Saint Just called the number. The phone was answered on the first ring.

"Boxer here. Talk to me, because if you're calling on Saturday, you've got as little life as I do on weekends, you're in deep shit, and you need me bad," said a gruff voice made even worse thanks to the poor connection on his cell phone.

"I also need you now," Saint Just said smoothly, already halfway to being satisfied with J.P. Boxer. He recited the address, promising to meet the lawyer in the vestibule. "Ten minutes, or I call someone else. Oh, and the name is Blakely. Alex Blakely."

"Yeah, yeah, good for you. And I don't take cases unless I like them."

"Good. I don't hire barristers unless I like them. Nine minutes, my good fellow. The constabulary is already on its way."

"You called them first? I don't work with idiots. What is it? Your wife ran up her charge at Tiffany's and you beaned her with your squash racket?"

"Eight minutes," Saint Just said, and flipped his cell phone closed, already heading for the living room as he slipped his arms into his sport coat. "Maggie? You needn't look further. I'm going downstairs to await the arrival of the lawyer. Kindly call the concierge and pretend you're Bernice, tell him that J.P. Boxer is allowed up."

"I'll do it myself," Bernie said, getting rather unsteadily to her feet, Sterling quickly moving to take her elbow. "Really. I can do that."

"Of course you can," Maggie said soothingly as Saint Just hit the button for the elevator, the gold-veined mirrored doors opening at once.

He stood in the vestibule, smiling as the phone rang and the concierge spoke into it, shooting him curious looks as he listened.

Five minutes later, Wendell still not on the scene, the doorman held open the door for an Amazon.

Saint Just's eyelids widened almost imperceptibly as J.P. Boxer employed a baritone growl to announce herself to the concierge.

The woman was dressed in bright green sweats with blue stripes running up the outside of each pant leg. She was at least two inches over six feet tall. Her hair, what there was of it, was cut to within a half inch of her well-shaped but quite large skull. Her ankle-high sneakers were orange, the laces untied. She was a garish rainbow, and seemed to be quite proud of that fact.

"Blakely? You look like you sound, Englishman," the woman said in her gravelly voice, slipping off her mirrored sunglasses.

"Boxer?" Saint Just responded, still rather nonplussed.

"Yeah, that's me," she said, grabbing a pen from the desk and signing her name on the guest register. "I'm big, I'm black, I'm ugly. I'm fifty-six and hormonal, and I'm your best friend or your worst nightmare, depending on whether or not I came running up here for nothing and left my onion bagel to get stale. Let's get to it."

"By all means," Saint Just said, motioning for her to precede him into the penthouse elevator. "Your client is—"

"Not yet, gorgeous. Wait until the doors close."

"Of course." Saint Just kept a smile on his face as, inwardly, he was reconsidering his choice. "There, alone at last. Now, as I was saying, your client is Bernice Toland-James."

"Know her, know her, this is good," J.P. said, nodding her head. "Classy redhead. Don't let your eyes bug out, Englishman. We travel in the same circles, we just don't look like it. I've seen her around. Who's the stiff?"

"I beg your pardon?"

"The stiff, the body, the victim. This is murder, right? Saturday calls have to be murder. Who is it?"

"We're not certain," Saint Just told her, and Boxer reached out, slamming her palm against the STOP button.

"You're not *certain*. What are you *certain* of, bucko? Are you sure there's a body? My bagel, remember?"

Saint Just believed it was time he took charge. And, if he had the faintest idea how to do that, he would. As it was, he knew himself to be outgunned and even outbullied. By a woman. It was disconcerting.

He did his best to fill her in, including the fact that Wendell was on his way.

"Wendell. Know him, too. Tough. But decent. Dresses like a bum, but that's all an act. Likes to play Good Cop. Who else is up there? You look like the sort that wants an audience. I don't like surprises."

"Really? I would think you rather enjoyed them. Handing them out, that is."

"Funny man." She glared at him. "I hate funny men. Who else?"

Saint Just told her.

"Don't know them. A writer, huh? I hate writers, too, especially crime writers. They never get their facts right. But you're all friends of my client? How much has she said to any of you? You'll be subpoenaed, you know."

"Bernice hasn't said much of anything, claiming to know nothing, except to say that she awoke this morning to discover the deceased in bed with her. She believes the body to be that of her husband, Buddy James, who supposedly was lost at sea seven years ago. And yes, there he was."

"You shitting me?" Boxer grinned. It was an unholy grin. She hit the STOP button again, and the elevator began to rise once more. "Oh, Blakely, you beautiful, beautiful man, this is going to be *fun*."

"How edifying for you, I'm sure," Saint Just said, at last discovering some empathy for Maggie and her tendency to retreat in the face of large, blustering, supremely assured people. A woman? God's teeth!

CHAPTER 3

Maggie heard the soft swish of the elevator doors, handed Bernie a fresh tumbler of Scotch, and headed for the foyer. "Alex?" she said, looking at J.P. Boxer.

"This the crime writer?" J.P. asked, hooking a thumb at Maggie. "Stay out of my way, sweetcakes."

"Excuse me?" Maggie said, stepping back a pace. "I'm Bernie's best friend."

"Good for you. I'm her lawyer. Quick, who does she need right now? Oh, wait, I know. *Me*. Where is she?"

"In . . . in there," Maggie said, stepping back even more. It was either that or be mown down by this huge woman in orange sneakers. "Alex?"

"It's all right, Maggie. Miss Boxer—"

"*Ms*. Boxer, Englishman," J.P. called over her shoulder. "Better yet, *Attorney* Boxer. My mama scrubbed a lot of floors just so I could say that. You can start writing it that way on my retainer check. That would be a two and a five, gorgeous, with three zeroes on the end."

"Who . . . who *is* that woman?" Maggie asked Alex. "She's *horrible*."

"Exceedingly and, I have no doubt, purposefully so, yes,"

Saint Just agreed, taking Maggie's arm. "However, she's here, and as Wendell will also be on the premises very shortly, we'll simply have to muddle along. You did bring your checkbook, didn't you, my dear?"

"Traveling with you? I'd have to, wouldn't I?" Maggie said irritably. "Come on, we can't leave Bernie alone in there with that woman."

"She's not alone. Sterling is with—ah, yes, I see your point."

Maggie was still shaking, both inwardly and outwardly. Wishing herself stronger for Bernie's sake, doing her best to keep herself in check, to not start screaming or crying. She reentered the living room and approached one of the chairs.

"Don't sit!"

"I beg your pardon?"

"I said, don't sit," J.P. commanded. "Don't sit, don't touch, don't breathe deep. This whole place is evidence. Go over there and stand with your chubby friend in front of the fireplace, like good little soldiers."

"Maggie?" Bernie held out her hand. "I want you here, with me."

J.P. grabbed the tumbler of scotch out of Bernie's hand. "Say bye-bye to Johnny Walker, Ms. Toland-James. From this moment on, you're officially on the wagon."

"But . . . but . . ." Bernie's panic was palpable.

"Oh, screw this," Maggie said in exasperation that overcame her insecurities, quickly heading for Bernie and sitting down beside her. "It's okay, sweetie. It's okay."

"I said—"

"Good day, Attorney Boxer," Saint Just said, stepping up behind her. "So sorry for your inconvenience, but we won't be needing you after all."

J.P. turned to face him. Looked him up and down. Slowly. "You don't like me, do you, Englishman? That's good, because I work at being unlikable. But you know what else? I'm good at what I do. I am fucking excellent. So excellent I can see the blood all over my client here. You called me, but from here on out, I call the shots. Now, if you can't live with that, if you want some namby-pamby to hold her hand, hold all your hands, and try to get her to cop a plea in exchange for ten to twenty upstate, that's no never mind to me. Otherwise—like it or not, I'm Big Mama here, even if that means playing rough with your cute little writer girl-friend. So, what is it? I stay, or I go?"

Maggie bit her bottom lip as she watched Saint Just. His blue eyes gave nothing away, but she could see the slight tic working in his left cheek, just beneath his eye. The Viscount Saint Just did not take orders.

"You stay," Saint Just said, and Maggie could hear Sterling's sigh of relief. "You stay, Maggie is allowed to render moral support, *and* Bernie gets her drink. Other than that, we're yours to command. You see, I am not above sensible compromise."

J.P. stuck out her hand. "I guess I'm not, either. But we detox her before the trial. Like I said, I've seen her around."

"Trial?" Bernie moaned low in her throat and grabbed Maggie's hand once more. "I have to have a trial?"

"Maybe," J.P. said, all her attention on Bernie once more. "We'll get there when we get there, okay? For now, tell me what you know."

Bernie gripped Maggie's hand even harder. "I don't know *anything*. I went out last night. It was Friday, right?" she asked Maggie, who nodded, blinking back tears. "I woke up this morning, and Buddy was . . . Buddy was . . ."

J.P. had pulled a pad and pen from her jacket pocket. "Went out. When? Where?"

"Um . . . there was a party. Yes, a party. At Binky Halstead's brownstone. You know Binky, Maggie. She used to be married to Walter Yeager, the financier? He's . . . *upstate* now, for insider trading. Oh, God, and we were *laughing* about it, and now I—"

"Charming circle of friends," J.P. said, scribbling. "I'll need her number and address later. Where else? Did you go anywhere else?"

Maggie used her free hand to rub Bernie's back. "Think, Bernie, honey. Anywhere else?"

"I . . . I came back here. Yes, I came back here. In the limo. But then I didn't want to come upstairs yet, so I walked a little and . . . I think I went to Brenda's. You know? Two down, around the corner, three over?"

J.P. scribbled on the pad. "Brenda's. I know the place. High-toned watering hole. They'd remember seeing you. Anywhere else?"

Bernie shrugged. "I don't know. Maybe. I'm not sure. Binky was handing out tequila shooters."

"Ah, Bernie, you should have come to me," Maggie said. "If you were lonely or something."

"Were you lonely, Bernie?" J.P. asked, dropping all formality. "Were you alone?"

Bernie turned her head toward the stairs. "I couldn't have been, could I? I mean, I don't remember. God, Maggie, *I don't remember*!"

The elevator doors opened and Maggie stiffened, knowing Steve Wendell had arrived. "Bernie, let go. Steve's here."

"I'll handle this," J.P. said.

"Actually, no, you won't, not just yet," Saint Just said silkily. "Maggie, go fetch the good *left*-tenant before he becomes hopelessly lost, saying little, if you please."

"Thanks, Alex," Maggie said, and hurried out to the foyer, to see Steve standing there in his usual rumpled khakis and knit shirt and ill-fitting jacket, his sandy hair blown by the wind, glad to see her, his smile warm—and quickly disappearing.

"Maggie? Is that blood?" he asked, pointing to her pajama top. "Are you all right? Are you hurt?"

"Oh, Steve, I'm so glad to see you. She didn't do it. I know she didn't do it."

He took her hand, bent to kiss her cheek. Good old Steve. So reliable, so without his own agenda. So unlike Alex, who maddened her, intrigued her, *bothered* her so very much. Steve was comfortable, safe . . . as long as she didn't think about the dangers of his job . . . as long as she fought down her attraction to an imaginary character who could disappear from her life just as she'd be telling him she loved him.

"Who? You're talking about Bernie? She didn't do what?"

"Kill Buddy," Maggie said. "Her husband. He's dead, if it's him. Somebody's dead upstairs. She called us and told us. But she didn't do it. You know Bernie. You know she didn't do it."

Steve held up one hand. "You're telling me there's a body in here? Jesus, Maggie, why didn't Blakely—"

"He thought . . . I thought . . . we thought it would be better if you came first, took a look around. That would make you primary, right? You'd be in charge of the case?"

"Technically. But probably not. I know Bernie personally, remember? I might be pulled off. Where's Blakely? More important, where's the body? Where's Bernie?"

"We're in there," Maggie said, pointing to the living room. "Except the body. That's upstairs, in Bernie's bed."

"In her bed? I'd say heart attack during sex then, if it weren't for the blood on you, Maggie. Why is there blood on your clothes?"

"I hugged Bernie. She's covered in it. Alex went upstairs to see if there really was a body, and he said the bedroom was covered in blood too, and—"

"He went upstairs? He disturbed the scene? Damn it, Maggie. Next he'll be giving me his cockamamie ideas on who did it."

"Well, he has been giving that some thought," Maggie said quietly.

"Keep him away from me, Maggie, I mean it. If Bernie didn't do this, I'm her best friend."

"Wrong, Wendell, that would be me," J.P. said, entering the foyer. "If you two are quite done, maybe you want to call the crime scene guys and get the stiff out of my client's house? You know how it is, they start to stink after a while."

"J.P.," Steve said, rolling his eyes. "Gee, my day just keeps getting better and better. Still chasing ambulances for your supper?"

"Only if you're in 'em, sweet knees," J.P. said, winking. "Now, before you call in the dogs, what do you say we all go upstairs and take a look around."

Steve laughed, but he was clearly not amused. "Oh, yeah, sure, let's do that. Hey, call out for pizza and we can make a party of it."

"Forever droll," Saint Just said, already heading for the stairs. "But, being reasonable, Wendell, something you may have just a fleeting acquaintance with, you really should be sure in your own mind that there is a body upstairs before you call in reinforcements."

"I hate when he has a point," Steve said. "You stay here, Maggie. You too, Sterling, Bernie."

"Are you nuts?" Bernie said, and took a deep drink from her tumbler. "I'm not going back up there. I didn't like looking at him when he was alive."

"Nice, real nice. Anyone want to hear my vote as to whether or not Red over there takes the stand in her own defense? I didn't think so. Lead on, Wendell," J.P. said. "Have you got any extra gloves?"

"Not in giant size, no," Wendell said, and Maggie bit her bottom lip. She waited until they were all upstairs, then followed after them, to stand just beside the doorway, the better to hear anything anyone said. After all, if Alex could be there, so could she.

"Yup, that's a body, all right," Steve said. "Blakely, keep back."

"In these shoes? I should most certainly say so. Do you see the knife? Wonderfully convenient, don't you think?"

"She was probably drunk."

"Never assume, Wendell," J.P. said. "Little weenie, ain't it? Pitiful. All shriveled up and all."

What followed was silence, and Maggie had to cover her mouth, so as not to laugh out loud as she pictured Steve blushing and Alex—well, God knew what Alex was doing. Probably keeping himself busy sticking his quizzing glass to his eye.

"We'll have a tough time separating bodily fluids in this mess."

"Sperm, Wendell. You can say it around me. Sperm. Little swimmers. Very little swimmers, I'd say. Guess it is true, what they say about you white guys. You want a rape kit? What will you give me to get it?"

"We're not playing *Let's Make a Deal* here, J.P. This is a crime scene."

"And Ms. Toland-James is my client. Now, what will you give me? I know what I want. I want the sexual assault team here. No hospital. You get her clothes, you get access. But she stays here. And I want it now, so she can get a shower. The woman's covered in blood, for cripes' sake."

"I get to talk to her?"

"Oh, Englishman, do you hear the man? He dreams. Wendell, she talks to you when I say she talks to you. Pretend I've got the police commissioner's ear, Wendell, which means I've got your ass in my hands. Figuratively."

"I liked you better when you were a cop, J.P."

"If we might return our attention to the clues, leaving this descent into personalities and sentimental waxing over times gone by to some other more appropriate moment?"

"Jesus, Blakely, you're talking clues? And stop saying clues. It's evidence. *Evidence.* We have a body, we have a wound, we have a knife. We've got a suspect downstairs. I think that's enough to start with. What else do you want?"

"I want, *Left*-tenant, to know how this gentlemen came to be dead in Bernice's bed. I want to know how he arrived here, with whom, when. I want to know if it was self-defense. I want to understand why there is an imprint of Bernie's body on the far side of the mattress, outlined in blood."

"She slashes him, then passes out right after, while he plays Fountain Man," Steve suggested.

"I don't know, Wendell," J.P. said. "That's one hell of a slice. I could make it, I'm a big strapping kind of gal, but I don't think Twinkletoes downstairs could have done it. Especially drunk."

"Who says she was drunk?"

"I thought you said Wendell knows her," J.P. said, obviously talking to Alex.

"Okay, okay, I get your point. But this guy was invited in. There's no sign of a struggle here."

"No, Wendell, there's not," Saint Just said. "You know what else there isn't? There are no items of male clothing here. Now why, do you suppose, is that?"

"They're somewhere," Steve said, and Maggie heard his voice trailing off as he moved farther from the doorway. "I see three doors. Closet, bathroom, something else."

"Sauna," Maggie said, then clapped her hands over her mouth, her eyes opened wide. "Oops."

"Margaret," Saint Just pronounced in taut, even tones. "Shame on you."

Maggie stepped into the doorway, trying to peek past J.P.'s large frame, to the bed. "I'm her friend, too. And who do you think really solves all those murders, anyway? You? I mean—um, never mind."

Man, she'd almost blown it, almost said that Alex Blakely was really Alexandre Blake, Viscount Saint Just, the perfect hero of her imagination come to life here in Manhattan, and not just in her imagination anymore. Oh yeah. Sure. That would have gone over big.

"Some small hysterics," Saint Just was saying. "My American cousin writes fiction, you understand, but we have, together, stumbled over two bodies in the past little space, at which time I stepped in and solved both cases. With nominal help from her, I agree, as I am a magnanimous man."

"And I'm supposed to care? Be impressed? Don't hold your breath, handsome," J.P. said. "Wendell? I want a full report as soon as you get it. Hair, fibers, fingerprints, blood type, fluids. Rape kit. The whole magilla. I know you love to share. Are we done here?"

Maggie watched as Steve pulled out his cell phone and flipped it open. "We're done here, yes. I'll meet you all downstairs. Don't touch anything."

"Gee, and here I was, about to go to the kitchen and make myself a sandwich. Come on, Englishman. Let the man call his little friends. We've seen enough."

Maggie got one good look at the bed, which was more than enough for her, and quickly preceded J.P. and Alex down the stairs, back into the living room.

Bernie, Maggie noted, was looking better, even wearing those blood-soaked pajamas. The booze had helped, having her friends here had helped, but Bernie had also helped herself. She was a strong woman, something you had to be if you wanted to swim with the sharks in the publishing world, and win. "Maggie? Is it Buddy? I'm sure it's Buddy."

"Ah-ah, you talk to me, Bernie, not little Mary Sunshine here. You sure this is your dead husband?"

Bernie looked to Maggie. Maggie looked to Alex. Saint Just said, "Approximately six feet tall, muscular build going to fat. Thinning blond hair, eyes brown, teeth capped, at least in the front. Rather large brownish mole approximately three inches below the left shoulder blade. Healed incision on the left knee. Flat feet."

"You saw all that?" Maggie was impressed. "In all that blood, you saw all that?"

"Simple observation by a trained eye, my dear. May I suggest your next corpse have his eyes open and fixed, his jaw slack? It's quite a dramatic image."

"Dead a while, long enough for the eyes to start to cloud a little," J.P. added. "I'm impressed, Englishman."

"Alex. Please, call me Alex. And of course you are. I am nothing if not impressive."

"All right. Alex. God, you're weird. Almost as weird as me. But you missed the good stuff."

"Really? By the good stuff, I imagine you're referring to the bruising around the body's wrists and ankles, and possibly also the faint hint of what could be adhesive residue on his right cheek?"

"Damn. Okay, Alex, weird or not, you can join the team. Everybody else? Out."

"I need Maggie," Bernie said, grabbing Maggie's hand and unceremoniously pulling her down onto the couch. "I'm hanging on by a thread here. Don't leave me, Maggie."

"I won't," Maggie promised, glaring up at J.P. Boxer, then sparing a little of that glare for Alex, who was preening now. Definitely preening, the bum.

"And I'll just be leaving," Sterling said, before anyone could throw him out. "Pausing downstairs to slip a few Andrew Jacksons to the concierge for a peek at the guest register, isn't that right, Saint Just?"

"They watch a lot of television," Maggie offered weakly to J.P. "My purse is over there, Sterling."

"Okay, one gone," J.P. said once Sterling had entered the elevator. "Now, who's Saint Just?"

"That would be me. Maggie borrowed our names for characters in her book, and gifted me with the title Viscount Saint Just. Sterling finds it amusing to address me as Saint Just. He's a simple man. A good man."

"You're all nuts, that's what I think. Okay, Bernie, we'll do this again, from the stiff on. Does anything we've said sound like Buddy?"

Bernie nodded furiously. "He had knee surgery about six months before he disappeared. Had me waiting on him hand and foot, the louse."

"There she goes again. Word of advice, babe. Newly deceased spouses, especially those found murdered in your bed, are not referred to as louses by the suspect. Drowned, right? I got to tell you, Bernie, that corpse upstairs looks in pretty good shape to have been in the water for seven years. Tell me about the boating accident."

Bernie shrugged. "What's to tell? He took his boat out. We lived in Connecticut, right near the water. Buddy was always taking that damn boat out. This time there was a storm, and he never came back. They found stuff, the Coast Guard. A few life preservers, some other debris. It will be seven years in two months, six days, and a couple of hours. Maggie? What date did I reserve the Rainbow Roof for, do you remember?"

Maggie grinned weakly. "Bernie hired the Rainbow Roof at the Waldorf for her Buddy's Officially Dead celebration. That isn't going to sound good if the newspapers get ahold of it, is it?"

"I'm not doing handsprings," J.P. said, rolling her eyes. "You fell into a lot of bucks when your first husband was murdered, didn't you, Bernie? Toland Books? Lots of press, as I remember, especially when you were a suspect. Lot-a-lot-a press."

"And a lot of debt. The papers never mentioned that. Oh. Wait a minute. I think I see where this is going," Maggie said. "You're thinking Buddy wasn't really dead, that he faked his death, and he heard about Bernie inheriting everything from Kirk and then came around looking for his share? Because it isn't seven years yet and they're still officially married?"

"And Bernie didn't want to share. Yes, that's one theory, if the stiff really turns out to be James," Steve said from the hallway. "Bernie? Was Buddy in financial trouble when he took the boat out that day?"

Bernie snorted. "He was—"

"Zipper it, Bernie. Wendell, I told you. She doesn't talk to you. If you overheard anything, you overheard privileged conversation between lawyer and client and I'll have your scrotum and its contents bronzed and on my mantle if you try to use any of it."

Saint Just, who was standing behind the couch, leaned forward slightly to whisper to Maggie, "I grow to appreciate this fairly obnoxious woman more with each breath she takes. Crude, but definitely effective."

The elevator opened again and suddenly the living room was crowded with uniformed cops, technicians dressed in blue jumpsuits and lugging large metal suitcases and cameras as Steve jerked a thumb toward the stairs, a female uniform escorting a middle-aged man carrying a medical bag.

Steve had stuck his flip-badge into his belt, and looked every inch the cop. "I want the bedroom, any adjoining rooms. This room, the elevator, the kitchen. Hallway and stairs. Any access in or out. Anything I didn't think of. Get it all. Don't touch the body. M.E. should be here any minute. He goes first. By the book, people."

"Wow, some digs," one of the techs said, turning in a full circle before following after the rest of his team.

"There's another bedroom, Bernie?" J.P. asked as Steve followed after the techs, redirecting two of them to the kitchen. "You'll have to be examined."

Maggie couldn't be sure, but she believed her metatarsals were "kissing," Bernie's grip on her hand suddenly became so fierce. "It's okay, Bernie. They . . . they want to check you over, make sure you're all right. Since you can't remember. I'll stay with you, I promise."

"Just a minute, Bernie," Steve said, turning over a page in his notebook as he reentered the living room. "You say the deceased is Buddy. Buddy James? Buddy's his first name?"

"That one you can answer," J.P. told her.

"Willard. Willard James. But he liked Buddy."

"There's no accounting for tastes," Saint Just murmured, picking up his cane. "If I'm no longer needed?"

"Oh, you're needed, Blakely. You've all been all over this place. I need all your prints, to rule them out. Where's Sterling?"

"I'm sorry, Steve. Sterling left. But he didn't touch anything. Alex told him not to touch anything. He just stood next to the fireplace, with his hands in his pockets. I mean, he's very . . . obedient. I'll bet he kept his hands in his pockets when he went upstairs. Didn't he, Alex?"

"He went upstairs? Is there anyone here who *didn't* go upstairs?"

Saint Just looked at Maggie. "No, I think we all wandered up there at one time or another, Wendell," he said. "My apologies."

"Yeah, like you mean it. All right. I'll be a few hours, but then I'll come over and get Sterling's prints. Sorry, Maggie, but it could be late. I'm going to be pretty busy here."

"I understand. As long as you promise to keep an open mind, Steve, because even if it looks bad, we all know Bernie didn't do this."

"Maggie?"

Maggie hastened to follow after Bernie, who was being led away by the female uniform cop. "Here I come, Bernie."

They went through the dining room and into another hallway that led to several rooms, including a large study Maggie remembered from her last visit to the penthouse.

The room was forest green, with immense white moldings and miles of bookshelves. The couches were burgundy leather, the fireplace was brick, and Kirk's temperature-controlled cigar humidor table still took up one corner of the room. Bernie enjoyed the occasional cigar, when she was feeling macho.

Bernie looked at the couches, but Maggie turned when she heard voices, to see a litter being wheeled into the room, the sort used by ambulance crews.

"That . . . that's for me?"

"Star treatment, dearie," the female cop said rather sarcastically. "We need fibers, hair, blood, fingernail scrapings, mouth swabs, any trace. Those pajamas. And the sexual assault kit. Lieutenant Wendell says your friend can stay with you. We'll try to make this as painless as possible."

Bernie's eyes went wide and she began to tremble. "This is real, isn't it, Maggie? Oh, God, this is *real.*"

CHAPTER 4

Socks hastened to open the cab door and helped Maggie onto the sidewalk. "Something's up, Maggie, Alex. You'd better go upstairs."

Saint Just handed the taxi receipt to Maggie and looked at Socks. Was it possible the young man was pale? Yes, it was. His lips seemed rather bloodless, his eyes wide and anxious. Just the image he wished Socks to project at his audition next week, for the Mel Gibson movie set to film in Queens in November.

Not that he'd have much time to closely manage Socks's acting career, not with Bernice's troubles being necessarily moved to the front burner of his increasingly active life. Assisting Socks with his career, including that book-cover-model contest he won at the WAR conference, managing the Streetcorner Orators and Players, signing a contract next week for Mary Louise and himself with Fragrances by Pierre. And now Bernice.

For a gentleman of leisure, Saint Just was an inordinately busy man. If Sterling harbored any love for him, he'd not choose this moment to tumble himself into a briar patch.

"What is it, Socks?" Saint Just asked, as Maggie seemed

fully occupied in sucking on her nicotine inhaler. He decided to be hopeful, and believe Sterling was not involved. "You're experiencing a difficulty of some sort and wish to speak to me upstairs?"

"Not me," Socks said, pressing his hands to his chest. "And I didn't see anything, because my shift was over and I was upstairs, moving the rest of your stuff, and Snake and Killer took off, so it was just me." He blinked. "I haven't seen you wear that yellow shirt. You know, the *Dior,* the one with the tapered sides? It would be bitchin' with my—"

"Yours. Done and done. Now, what happened that you didn't witness? And please don't tell me Sterling decided to take apart the plasma television machine to see how it works."

"No, no, nothing like that. And it didn't fall down, either. It's good and bolted to the wall; I watched them install it while you were gone. But Sterling . . . Sterling had some company."

Maggie, who had been slipping a new nicotine cartridge into the holder and making rude comments under her breath about how sucking air and pretending it was a real cigarette was like standing outside a bakery and hoping the smells would fill her belly, said, "Sterling had company? Who?"

Socks looked to the curb, where another cab was pulling up. "Duty calls, sorry. Go ask Sterling. He'll tell you all about it."

"Maggie?" Saint Just said, offering her his arm. "Unless you'd rather we take advantage of that now unoccupied hack and proceed to the airport. I've yet to fly, you may recall, and purchasing a ticket to Anywhere But Here seems a viable option at the moment, don't you think?"

Maggie used her key card to open the interior security door to the building. "Oh, cut it out. I couldn't leave Bernie. And neither could you. You want to solve the murder. Admit it."

"True. Although I could leave Ms. J.P. Boxer with few regrets, we cannot desert Bernice. Or Sterling, whatever problem he seems to have stumbled into in our short absence. And you wonder why I fret, watching him scootering off alone to the park."

But Maggie still wasn't giving him her full attention. "I'm so glad J.P. said no to Steve when he asked if Bernie would go with him, to make a formal statement. How long do you think she can keep her away from the cop shop?"

"I beg your pardon?"

"The cop shop. I think that's what they called it in some movie I saw. The precinct. The station. The guard house? Does that help? Anyway, how long do you think J.P. can keep Bernie away from the cops?"

"That depends on the evidence, I would imagine, and how well Ms. Boxer's blustering protestations concerning *Miranda* rights and chains of evidence and compromised crime scenes carry her. Right now," he said as they entered the elevator, "I suggest we take comfort in this one small victory. Bernice has yet to be hauled off to the cop shop in bracelets."

"Bracelets? Now who's using cop show words? And you don't mind if J.P. brings her over here later? I mean, she isn't being allowed to stay at . . . at the crime scene, and she's too messed up to check into a hotel alone. Socks seems to think he's done moving you and Sterling out of the guest room. I mean, it should work, right?"

"It depends. Do you know a liquor establishment that delivers? By the gallon?"

The elevator doors opened just as Maggie was glaring at him. "Bernie's been a pretty heavy social drinker as long as I know her, but I won't say I haven't noticed how bad it's been getting lately. I'm going to help her quit."

"The lady says as she rummages in her purse for her lighter," Saint Just said, because Maggie already had a cigarette between her lips. He extracted a lighter from his sport coat pocket. "Here, allow me. Shall we go inspect my new, definitely not destined to be smoke-free quarters?"

Maggie drew almost desperately on the cigarette. Her eyes closed as she then exhaled a thin blue stream of smoke. "The real thing. God, that's good. And only my second today. Or my third?"

"I tip my figurative hat to you, my dear," Saint Just said, slipping his key into the lock of his new door, which led to his new home. The sense of independence this gave him was immeasurable, and he'd have enjoyed the feeling to the top of his bent had it not been for his worry about Bernice. As it was, any celebration he and Sterling decided upon would necessarily be muted.

"Sterling? Where are you hiding?" he said as Maggie entered the apartment ahead of him.

"Oh, wow. I've never been in here. Look at all the antiques." Maggie frowned. "And she has a separate dining room? Damn. How many rooms are there?"

"Six," Saint Just said. "This room, the aforementioned separate dining room, kitchen, two bedrooms, and a small secluded room behind the kitchen I shall employ as my private study. Oh, would you care to see our view? We have one, you know."

"So do I," Maggie muttered. "Of a brick wall and somebody's windows. You know, Alex, I can sometimes hate you. You just seem to fall into good luck, you know?"

"What can I say? I am the man you made me," Saint Just said, smiling at the plasma television screen that now held pride of place above the working fireplace, Mrs. Goldblum's rather uninspired oil landscape presumably having been banished to the depths of a closet. "Although I prefer to think of myself as capable of seizing opportunities, rather than being merely lucky. Sterling? Front and center, if you please."

Maggie slid her fingertips over the shiny black top of the baby grand piano, on her way to the Louis XV credenza propped against the wall. "Hiya, Henry, nice piece of lettuce," she said, bending down to peer in the cage at Sterling's pet mouse, a small white creature with a constantly twitching pink nose and a rapidly expanding waistline, thanks to Sterling's doting attendance. "Where's your owner?"

"Oh, no, Maggie, I don't *own* Henry. We're friends," Sterling said, entering the living room.

"Sterling, whatever are you wearing?" Saint Just asked, looking at *his* friend.

Sterling pushed his spectacles back up his nose and grinned sheepishly as he looked down at the bright blue bib-apron on which was sewn, in Day-Glo pink, KISS THE COOK. "You like it? It's my housewarming present from Socks. Along with a cookbook. An English cookbook at that. I'm preparing a pudding even as we speak, and must get back to it. Yours is a box of very thin cigars. It's over there, on the coffee table. How's Bernie?"

"Coming along, coming along," Saint Just said, sparing a moment to cast his gaze over the cigar box on the table. "Socks, however, seems to think you might have experienced some sort of problem?"

"Me? No, I don't think so. I was a little worried, I admit that, but I'm sure it's all right now. Just a mistake."

"On whose part was this mistake?"

"Why, on the part of the gentlemen who came here, of course. And possibly Mrs. Goldblum, if that doesn't sound ungracious. I had nothing to do with it."

"Let me," Maggie said, walking over to Sterling. "From the top, Sterling honey, okay?"

"The top of what?" Sterling asked, clearly perplexed. "The top of the two gentlemen? Well, if you really want to know, they wore hats. Black hats. But I don't see—"

"You made him this literal, my dear," Saint Just reminded

Maggie as she dropped into a chair, grabbing a crystal candy dish and dumping out a few decades-old hard candies, to use the dish as an ash tray. "You thought it amusing."

"I thought I made you the perfect hero, too," Maggie said. "Am I excused if I admit I was wrong?"

"If I could get back to my pudding? I'm nearly at a critical stage, I believe."

"Not yet, Sterling, if you don't mind. You said you had visitors. Shall we begin with opening the door to the men in hats, and you can take it from there?"

"Very well. You just had to say so."

Saint Just ignored Maggie's snort of amusement.

"Thank you, Sterling. I'm most appreciative."

"I heard the knock on the door—"

"Hold it, Sterling. You heard the knock on the door? Nobody buzzed you, to ask you to buzz them in?"

Sterling frowned. "Uh . . . no, Maggie, there was no buzzing, by anybody. I suppose they just slipped in, when someone else opened the door? Is that all right? I do it sometimes, when the door is already open for somebody else. Especially when I have my scooter with me."

Saint Just was no longer amused. "Go on, Sterling."

"As I said, I heard the knock on the door, and I opened it to see two gentlemen standing just outside, in the hallway. They were very large gentlemen, even if they removed their hats, although they didn't, not even when they came in."

"You invited two very large strange men into our domicile?"

"Well, actually, Saint Just, I did not, so there's no need to cut up stiff about it and all of that. They rather walked in without invitation, asking to see the old lady. That's what the bigger one said. The old lady. I assumed they meant Mrs. Goldblum, they said yes, and I told them she was away, on an extended vacation. They weren't best pleased about that, I'm afraid. Unhappy."

Maggie lit another cigarette. "Define unhappy, Sterling."

"Well, they . . . um . . . one of them, that is, rather grabbed at me." Sterling put a hand to his throat. "Here. At which point he asked where it was. When I told him I had no idea what *it* was, the second gentleman took umbrage and became rather volatile. I hope it wasn't a valuable vase, or one with sentimental value."

Saint Just cast his gaze around the room, stopping at the Sheraton writing desk. He remembered a rather inferior blue and white vase he had already decided to banish to the closet along with the landscape. But it was already gone. "What happened to the vase, Sterling?" he asked with deceptive calm.

"It's beyond repair, I'm afraid. As I said, volatile. But now it's all explained, and they've gone, and there's nothing to worry about."

"I need some aspirin. About six of them," Maggie said, and disappeared in the direction of her condo. "Get the rest of this, will you, Alex, and feed it to me in one go when I get back."

Saint Just watched her leave, then followed Sterling into the kitchen. "What exploded?" he asked, looking at the mess that seemed to cover every counter.

"Oh, this? It's just me, cooking. Did you know that you should turn off the blender before you add more ingredients? And I think I should probably have taken out the little stopper and poured through there, rather than remove the entire lid. Ah, well, we learn as we go on, don't we, Saint Just? I'll get the ceiling later."

Saint Just looked up, wished he hadn't. "I'll leave you to it, then, once I understand everything that happened with your visitors."

"Mrs. Goldblum's visitors," Sterling corrected, carrying bowls to the sink. "It's just as I said, Saint Just. They were under the impression that they had an appointment with Mrs.

Goldblum this afternoon, to pick up *it*. I still don't know what *it* is, but when they realized that Mrs. Goldblum was gone, they finally left."

"I see," Saint Just said, still not seeing, not at all. "Then they won't return?"

"I shouldn't think why. Mrs. Goldblum isn't here. We're here. Really, Saint Just, I would have thought you'd realize that. You're usually so sharp."

"Thank you, Sterling. Carry on," Saint Just said, gratefully departing the kitchen.

Maggie was in the living room when he returned. She looked tired, worried, perilously close to frazzled. "So?"

"I don't know," Saint Just said honestly. "Mrs. Goldblum had an appointment with those two men who frightened Sterling and broke a vase. You know, Mrs. Goldblum departed in quite the hurry when she received the news about her sister's accident. Perhaps she forgot the appointment?"

"And perhaps not? Right? Because you're wearing your skeptical face."

"Am I that obvious? Perhaps I'm seeing mare's nests, and there's a simple explanation for everything. The questions remain, however. Who were these men, and why, if we are not wrong to be suspicious of her hasty departure, did she take such pains to avoid them?"

Maggie shrugged. "You could call her, I suppose. She's got to be there by now, it's after four o'clock."

"She did leave a number when I suggested it, in the event of some emergency," Saint Just said, walking over to the desk to pick up the scrap of notepaper Mrs. Goldblum had placed there.

He thought back to his meeting in the hallway yesterday with Mrs. Goldblum. She'd told him she would leave in the morning, she'd all but shoved the key to the apartment into his hand, and he'd had to inquire twice before she agreed to leave a number where she could be reached. It had all seemed the nervous anxiety of an old woman worried about her sibling. Now, however, it seemed more like panic, and a crushing need to be gone in a hurry.

"Alex? You're just standing and staring. How about you let me make the call? You know, woman to woman? Mrs. Goldblum's an old lady, and you wouldn't want to frighten her."

"As you say," Saint Just said, handing Maggie both the paper and his cell phone. "I would very much like to know the identity of our visitors. Duns, do you suppose?"

"Bill collectors, you mean. Nobody calls them duns anymore. They dun, yes, but they aren't . . . aren't dunners. Okay? And could be. Maybe they'll be back Monday with an eviction notice. No, that's my luck, not yours. Besides, look at this place. I didn't realize it, but Mrs. Goldblum is *rolling* in it. Now hush, this is a lot of numbers to push."

Saint Just took up his seat on the facing couch and waited, listened.

"Yes, hello. Would you repeat that, please?" Maggie asked, looking at Saint Just. "I'm sorry, and your number is . . . ?" The frown deepened. "Yes, yes, I must have the wrong number. Thank you."

She shut the cell phone and tossed it back to Saint Just.

He slipped the cell phone into his jacket pocket. "You didn't dial incorrectly?"

"Nope," Maggie said, reaching for a cigarette, then sitting back again, leaving the cigarette in the pack. "I dialed correctly, if I wanted to talk to somebody at Hartman's Drug Store in Boca." She crumpled the note in her hand. "She gave you a bogus number, Alex. I don't like this. I don't like this at all. And how are you supposed to pay her? She just gave you a telephone number, no address."

"You . . . that is, I recompensed her for six months rental before she departed for Boca Raton. Now, now, don't climb up into the boughs, my dear. I sign that contract with Mr.

Pierre on Monday, at which time all debts will be paid in full."

"I don't care about that," Maggie said, waving him off. "Oh, all right, I do care, but we've got more important things to think about right now. This could be bad, Alex."

"Already weaving a scenario in that agile, yet fiction-oriented mind of yours, Maggie?" Saint Just asked, shaking his head. "Surely not. I mean, this is Mrs. Goldblum we're talking about, correct? Nice old tabby?"

"That nice old tabby was supposedly married to a lawyer for the mob, Alex. Remember me telling you that?"

"The mob." Saint Just considered this. "What, precisely, is the *mob?*"

Maggie spread her hands. "The *mob*. It's the *mob*. It's . . . okay. I'd say it's a bunch of Italian guys running around doing illegal things, except that now there are a lot of mobs, and they aren't all Italian. Sicilian. Whatever. Anyway, they do illegal things, like loan sharking and protection rackets and prostitution, money laundering, and drugs—lots of them are into selling drugs these days, I think. And one mob hates the other mob and sometimes there are wars, and they go to the mattresses and then pop out to go around shooting each other."

"I'm sure you think this is helping," Saint Just said, taking out his quizzing glass and dangling it from its black grosgrain ribbon.

"I'm not really making this clear, am I? I mean, except for watching *The Sopranos* and that old *Untouchables* movie, I really don't know what they do. They're just the mob. Organized crime."

"Yes, it does all sound rather organized. And, unforunately, as clear as mud. Suffice it to say, these are violent men?"

"Oh, yeah. Cement shoes, swimming with the fishes, bullets to the head while eating a plate of pasta, you name it. Not nice guys. Not the sort who say, Okay, she's not here, sorry, we'll go now, please excuse the intrusion."

"And you think the two men who visited Sterling are representatives of this mob?"

"I don't know," Maggie said, pushing her fingers through her hair. "I mean, I only *heard* that Mrs. Goldblum's late husband was a lawyer for them. I don't know it for certain. But remember how she didn't want to sign any sort of sublease with you guys? How she said her husband—what was his name? Oh, yeah, Harry—told her never to put anything in writing? Lawyers kill forests every day, for all the paper they use. So, what kind of a lawyer was Harry?"

"I can see your highly inventive brain is percolating. Pray, continue," Saint Just said, steepling his fingers in front of his chin.

"Okay. Let's say, for the sake of discussion, that Harry Goldblum *was* a lawyer for the mob. How did he die? When did he die? And, did he have something that could put some big cheeses in the mob behind bars for the next seventy years if the Fibbies got hold of it?"

"We'll soon need the services of a translator, I'm afraid. And these Fibbies are—?"

"Federal agents. FBI. Writers always seem to call them Fibbies. I think they're the ones who go after the mob. And the IRS—that's the tax collector. The IRS got Al Capone for filing false tax returns or something. Couldn't get him for anything else, the murders and that kind of thing, but they got him for tax evasion. But accountants keep financial records, not lawyers."

"And you're certain the late Mr. Goldblum was a lawyer?"

Maggie frowned. "Yeah. No." She sighed. "I really don't pay a lot of attention to my neighbors."

"Now there's a revelation. You don't pay much attention to anything but your work, Maggie, ergo that muddled definition of gangs."

"Hey, I write historicals. Ask me about the Bow Street Runners and I can give you chapter and verse. And it's 'mobs.' Gangs are different."

"I stand corrected, and humbly beg you decide not to further enlighten me. That said, if not for Sterling and myself, you'd soon be a recluse, walking around all day in your pajamas and talking to your cats."

"Ha. Ha. I've got a life."

"So does Henry over there. But, the sad state of your existence to one side, only recently made better by my decision to come into your life and give it—shall we say, *life?*—how do we go about learning more about Mr. Harry Goldblum? And Mrs. Irene Goldblum, for that matter?"

"We could start with Socks? He was already here when I moved in two years ago."

Considering this a splendid idea, as well as their only idea, Saint Just used the intercom to call down to Socks and request his presence.

Two minutes later, looking nervous, Socks entered the apartment, peering around curiously. "They didn't come back?"

"No, we're quite alone," Saint Just said, motioning the doorman to a chair. "We'd appreciate some information, Socks, about Mrs. Goldblum. What can you tell us?"

"About Mrs. Goldblum?" Socks asked, looking at Maggie. "I don't know. She's a nice old lady. Good tipper at Christmas. Oh, you want more than that, right? Okay. I don't know when she moved in, but I do know that until it got changed, the name plate over her mailbox had her name on it and her husband's, but his was crossed off. So I guess they both lived here, until he died."

"Interesting," Saint Just said, slipping his quizzing glass back into his pocket. "Continue."

"Yeah, sure. This place is rent controlled, if you can believe that. Last unit in the building that is, since it started going condo. Me, I don't really believe it, but Mrs. Goldblum told me it is. Do you think she's lying about the rent control, that she really bought the place, you know, like

Maggie bought hers? I don't think she has that much money, you know? But why would she lie about that? Is that what you want to know? Because I don't know anything else."

"Oh, but on the contrary, Socks, you do, you do. For instance, did Mrs. Goldblum have many visitors?"

"Visitors?"

"Socks, please concentrate on what I say, and then on answering the question, not repeating it, all right? Yes, visitors."

"You know, I don't think so. She goes away, sometimes for months at a time. Probably to see that sister in Boca, right, the one she's visiting now? I take in her mail then, save it for her. I take it in a lot, actually. Okay, all the time."

"Ah-ha, we progress. Socks, do you remember what sort of mail Mrs. Goldblum receives?"

Socks shrugged. "What kind of—oh, sorry. Bills, mostly. Doctor bills, lots of those. She gives me fifty dollars every couple of months, to bring her mail to her, even when she's here, and it was mostly bills, and her Social Security check once a month. Sometimes a postcard. You know, one of those 'wish you were here' picture postcards."

Maggie came to attention. "Oh, that's good, Socks, that's very good. You read the postcards, right? People always read postcards."

"I don't . . . oh, okay, Maggie, yeah, I read them. But they all said the same thing. Like I said, 'wish you were here.' I remember one in particular. It showed a castle, one of those big old stone ones? And it had an arrow drawn to one window, and it said 'my room.' It wasn't, though, because it was just a printed postcard. Funny card."

"Anything else?" Saint Just prodded. "Any other pretty pictures?"

"Hey, I didn't really look. You're not supposed to look, you know. I mean, maybe while I was in the elevator I might have looked a little, but . . . Paris. There was one from Paris.

And Greece, I think. One of those islands over there. Everything was over there, now that I think about it. Europe, you know? I have to get back to work."

"Yes, thank you, Socks, you've been most helpful. If you recall anything else you feel might be pertinent, please let Maggie or me know at once."

The door had barely closed when Maggie was on her feet, pacing. "He isn't dead, he's just hiding, and she sticks around, going to him when she can, like she's going on vacation. But the mob gets wind of it, comes knocking on her door, wanting secret books or records of some kind, and she hands the keys to you and splits, leaving you and Sterling holding the bag. And what are you going to do about it? Nothing, that's what. You have no lease, no papers, no receipt, no proof. You're just squatting here. After a while, she calls you, sees if the coast is clear, and then she comes back. It works. It really works."

Saint Just applauded softly. "A great mind at work. Perceive me as wonderfully impressed."

"Oh, shut up. What's wrong with it?"

"You mean other than the fact that, as Buddy James has just come back from the dead to die again, your brain is automatically resurrecting Harry Goldblum as well? I forgive you that, as it is a logical conclusion, considering what has already occurred today. But, what's *wrong* with your scenario, my dear woman, is Mrs. Goldblum's continued occupation of this apartment. Why not simply leave the country, travel with her husband as he avoids this mob of yours?"

"It's not *my* mob. And I don't know. Maybe Steve will know more about Harry Goldblum?"

"Don't you believe the good *left*-tenant has more than enough on his plate at the moment, with Bernice's woes? Chasing down one of your flights of fiction seems rather unimportant."

"You're not worried? Those guys broke a vase, Alex. One of them picked up Sterling by the *throat*."

Saint Just was well aware of that. He was aware that hidden deep inside him was an anger that, if released, could be A Most Terrible Thing. Especially since, at least for the moment, he had no target. So he beat down his anger, and looked at Maggie levelly, intent only on keeping her calm.

"And then they left. Obviously Sterling, a very credible man and a terrible liar, convinced them that Mrs. Goldblum is no longer in residence. Whatever they wanted, mob or dun or whomever, whatever, they now know it is not here. She is not here. And Sterling, dear man, seems none the worse for wear. Alas, if only I could say the same for our kitchen."

CHAPTER 5

Maggie closed the door behind her and looked around the living room. Her empty living room.

Well, not empty. Napoleon and Wellington were in the room, Wellington draped over the back of one of the couches, shedding black hair everywhere, and Napper contentedly curled up on her desk chair, obviously after having typed a million lines of *zzzzzzzziidooooeeffffsssssuuuuu22222ktt34-dxnkkkkkkhhh* onto Maggie's computer screen. That was one way of adding pages to her manuscript.

The ridiculously large, and really pretty ugly vase of flowers Faith had sent over two days ago was still there, on the coffee table, some of the lily petals dropping off and making what was going to be a big mess in another two days.

She liked Faith better as a former friend. She didn't like her as what she was attempting to become, which was a born-again friend, or whatever.

Faith Simmons, now known as Felicity Boothe Simmons, had once been Maggie's friend. But then Faith had hit the big time and forgotten she knew Maggie, until Maggie hit the big time too, which was when Faith decided that she hated

Maggie. Saint Just had told her that Faith couldn't forgive her for being a success; Maggie just thought Faith was a jerk with a bad boob job.

But now, ever since the We Are Romance convention two weeks ago, and ever since Maggie had stupidly pushed Faith out of harm's way and, okay, maybe saved the woman's life, Faith had been calling and stopping by and sending presents.

Like these fugly flowers.

Maggie picked up the vase and carried it into the guest room. Maybe Bernie would appreciate them. Bernie liked exotic. Maggie would have preferred daisies, something simple. And Faith knew that.

"And I know she knows it," Maggie said, giving the single bird-of-paradise topping the arrangement a last disapproving look.

Then she stripped the queen-size bed and fitted it with clean sheets from the linen closet, checked the dresser drawers and closet to be sure they were empty, and pulled the drapes, darkening the room, pretty sure Bernie wouldn't be in the mood for sunlight.

"Dinner," she said, heading for the kitchen. There'd be no celebration at Bellini's tonight, she thought, mentally waving good-bye to delicious garlic, rosemary, and sage chicken, and lemon ice for dessert.

She opened the refrigerator and frowned at the contents. A half dozen eggs. An open pack of bacon. Orange juice; six half gallons, because orange juice had been on sale. Well, at least she was ready for Sunday breakfast.

"Soup," she said, closing the refrigerator and opening the cabinet next to it, standing on tiptoe to look inside. "Chicken noodle, chicken rice, chicken with stars, chicken vegetable, chicken broth. Damn, I eat a lot of chicken soup."

"You also talk to yourself quite often, another very valid reason for my more substantial entry into your life."

"Alex!" Maggie whirled around, nearly losing her balance. "Don't *do* that. And stop just barging in like you're freaking Cosmo Kramer and I'm Jerry Seinfeld. You don't live here anymore. I am alone again. A-lone. Remember?"

"You'll be wanting your key returned?"

"No-o-o, I won't be wanting my key returned," she sniped angrily, opening the refrigerator and yanking out a bottle of spring water. "I'm sorry, Alex. I'm just . . . just on edge. Bernie, and now Sterling? Have some pity here, okay?"

Her eyes widened as Saint Just stepped forward and pulled her into his arms, pressing her head against his strong chest. She hadn't been in his arms, *really* in his arms, since that night at the WAR convention. She'd been trying to forget that momentary weakness . . . even as she replayed the memory about five times a day.

"This . . . this isn't quite what I had in mind," she said, her words sort of slurred, because her mouth was pressed against his shirt.

"I should let go?"

"Shut up," Maggie said, sliding her arms around his waist. "Just shut up and hold me."

"My pleasure," Saint Just said, lightly stroking her back. "Everything will right itself in time, Maggie, I promise. Bernice will be exonerated, the true culprit will be apprehended, and Sterling will be safe in his kitchen, unless he persists in wearing that most atrocious apron, upon which time I shall myself threaten him with bodily harm."

Maggie laughed against his chest, then lifted her head to look up into his face. "I think he looks cute. Just a cuddly teddy bear."

"Precisely as you made him, my dear, and I thank you for that. Now, don't you think it time you showered and got out of this dreadful creation?"

"It's not that much blood. Do you think it can be saved? I mean, I like this pajama top." Then she closed her eyes. "No, don't answer that. I could never wear it again, not without thinking of Bernie today. Alex, you should have seen her when they explained what a rape kit was and what they wanted to do to her. She . . . she made a joke, a really terrible joke, but I was holding her hand, and it was shaking. *She* was shaking, all over. I just—"

His mouth closed over hers, cutting off what she might say next, even if she knew she'd run out of words and was rapidly being taken over by her emotions.

He kissed her once, twice, then trailed a string of kisses across her cheek, into her hair. "You were very brave today, Maggie," he whispered into her ear. "I was extraordinarily proud of you. I am always proud of you."

Maggie sagged against him, her arms still tight around his waist. "I was so scared."

"You were a Trojan, a brick. And you will continue to be so, for Bernice's sake. Now," he said, his hands on her shoulders as he held her slightly away from him, "why don't you go shower and change, before Bernice and Ms. Boxer arrive. I'll phone Bellini's and add the amazon to our table. The reservation is at eight, remember?"

"You . . . you don't really think Bernie will want to go out for dinner, do you?"

"I have no idea what Bernice desires. I do know what she will do, and that will be to do what she normally does, with no change in her routine. She is, after all, innocent. She should behave as such."

"With her criminal lawyer in tow?" Maggie asked, wondering if there was some way she could wrangle another kiss . . . and then wondering why she'd want to, since she told herself every day that she had to keep her distance from this man who was, after all, a figment of her imagination . . . with a very solid-feeling chest.

"Ms. Boxer lends cachet, my dear. Now, I've got telephone calls to make, and you've got to attend to your toilette." He dragged her close and kissed her once more, a definitely hard, definitely tongue-probing kiss, then let her go. "Oh, and I'll be borrowing a few towels, as we seem to have forgotten to purchase any as yet and Mrs. Goldblum's are all, well, they're Mrs. Goldblum's towels. I'm sure you won't mind."

"Uh-huh. Sure. Anything you need," she said, lifting a hand to wave weakly at his back as he headed for the door. "God, I'm *so* easy, and he knows it, damn it," she said, talking to herself again, and went off to take a long, cold shower.

She was dumping ice into the bucket in the living room, having checked the level on her scotch bottle and unearthed a fresh one from underneath the drinks table, when her houseguest arrived, lawyer in tow.

"I've got a message for you from Wendell," J.P. said, kicking the door shut behind her, as her arms were full of luggage. "He'll be busy tonight, attempting to lynch my client, but will come by tomorrow to roll Sterling's prints."

"Oh, okay. Thanks, I think. Bernie, how are you?" Maggie asked, hugging her friend even as she dragged her over to the couch.

"How am I? You mean after being poked and prodded and fingerprinted and generally violated? Oh, and after being bled on by Buddy. Let's not forget that part. I don't know. How should I be?"

Maggie nearly said *devastated,* but bit the word back in time. "In need of a stiff one?"

"True, true," Bernie said, winking at her. "But I'll take a drink instead."

"And that, Bernie," J.P. said, settling her large frame in the facing couch, "is exactly the way you are *not* going to talk from here on out. I thought we settled this."

Bernie flipped back her curly mane of bright red hair. "It's only Maggie."

"Who can be subpoenaed," J.P. said, folding her arms beneath what could only be called her generous bosom. No, magnanimous.

"I'd never repeat anything like that," Maggie said, handing Bernie a tumbler one-third full of scotch and ice.

"That's my girl. Loyal. I love you, Mags."

"Oh, cut me a break. What are you two looking for, adjoining cells?"

Maggie picked up the pair of large suitcases J.P. had carried into the room and took them down the hall to the guest room, where she stopped, took three long, deep breaths, then returned to the living room. "I thought you were getting Bernie off?"

"Oh, good. An optimist. Little Mary Sunshine is an optimist. Get her off? I'd love to. But this one isn't going to be easy. Wendell wants her, wants her bad."

"Steve wants me," Bernie said, raising her empty glass. "How about that, Maggie? Your guy's after me."

"Actually," J.P. said, "he's after the truth. Wendell's a good guy, as cops go. Let's just hope he can find it without us."

Maggie sat down next to Bernie. "We're not going to help him?"

"No, Little Mary, we're not. We're going to help our precious booze hound here. And we're going to start by taking away her hootch. That's it, Bernie. No more."

"Oh, God," Bernie said, sinking low on the cushions as Maggie took the glass from her hand.

"Um . . . J.P.? Do you think we could start tomorrow? Alex wants us all to go to Bellini's for dinner tonight."

"The Englishman? Is he out of his—wait a minute. That could be good." J.P. got up and began to pace, nearly stepping on Wellington, who hurriedly hid underneath the computer desk. "Make her public, make her visible. Keep her visible. She's innocent, right? Innocent people don't hide. I think I like it."

Maggie considered this for a moment. It only took a moment. "And you want her doing this cold turkey?"

"I'm doomed. Doomed," Bernie said, falling over onto her side, her hands clutched to her chest.

J.P. looked down at her client. "She's never sober?"

"I . . . I really don't know," Maggie said honestly. "She's just Bernie. I think she has a . . . a capacity."

"She's a drunk. Rich, so she's a poor distressed soul with a problem, but she's still a drunk. A functioning drunk."

"Well, she was," Maggie said, wincing.

"Meaning?"

"I'm doomed, doomed. . . ."

"Shh, Bernie, it's all right," Maggie said, rubbing Bernie's hip. "Lately . . . lately she's not been so good. Since Kirk was murdered, I'd say. He left her everything, the company, the penthouse, all his toys. But that's not as great as it sounds. He had a lot of debt. And then there was the money Toland Books lost thanks to—"

"Yes, I remember that. So she's had problems."

Maggie nodded. "She's been reorganizing the company, selling off Kirk's toys. The place in the Hamptons, his plane, stuff like that. But when Buddy's life insurance comes to her she'll be—oh, God."

"Doomed . . ."

"Hello? Am I missing anything? Has the ladies' sewing circle convened without me?"

"Alex!" Maggie got to her feet and motioned for him to close the door behind him. "I just realized something."

"Doomed . . ."

"Yes, and now she's going to share, isn't she?" J.P. said, seating herself in Maggie's desk chair (a sin punishable by death, but Maggie was too upset to think about that).

"Buddy's insurance, Alex—J.P." Maggie pushed her hands through her hair. "He sold insurance, remember? That meant he wrote a lot of it for himself while he was at it.

Cheap. The premiums, not the policies. I think he was insured for about three million. Bernie? Is it three million?"

"Doomed . . ."

"Stop saying that!" Maggie looked at J.P., who wasn't looking ready to do cartwheels at the news. "When Buddy disappeared Bernie said insurance investigators were haunting her, for months and months, sure Buddy had either faked his death in some plan with her, or that Bernie had poked a hole in his boat—or something. Isn't that right, Bernie?"

"Mmmmm," Bernie said, having passed beyond doom, into complete inarticulation.

"I should have asked for a larger retainer," J.P. said, spinning the computer chair in a circle, then bracing her feet on the floor and glaring at Maggie. "Let me get this straight. Seven years ago— almost seven years ago, let's not forget the Hip Hip Hooray, Buddy's Dead party—insurance investigators thought Bernie might have killed husband number two. Husband number *one* dies a little bit back, and she's suspected of killing him, too. Now husband number two is dead. Really dead this time. And our gal over there stands to rake in three million in insurance payoffs? Beautiful. Maybe I should be the one downing the hootch."

"It does look bad, doesn't it?" Maggie asked Saint Just.

"It could be problematic, yes. If her inheritance would banish the last of any financial embarrassment, and Willard were to resurface just as the funds were about to come due, one could suppose Bernice's . . . displeasure. Her reluctance to share."

Silence descended on the room, not broken until Sterling burst in, all excited, as only someone without a firm grasp on the severity of events could be. "I say, everyone, turn on the television machine. They're going to talk about Bernie after the commercial."

Maggie grabbed the remote. "What station, Sterling?"

"I'm not sure. But it's that nice Fox lady."

"Miss Holly Spivak, Maggie, Fox News," Saint Just told her.

"Got it," Maggie said, and turned up the volume as everyone, even Bernie, focused on the screen, watching some demented woman dance with a floor mop.

And then there was the anchor's smiling face and a quick segue to Holly Spivak, just another in Alex's strange coterie of acquaintances, and a pretty decent investigative reporter:

"Thank you, Jim. As you can see, I'm standing outside the Park Avenue building containing the Toland penthouse, home of the late Kirk Toland, the socialite and businessman who was murdered not quite two months ago, and the residence of his ex-wife, Bernice Toland-James."

"She's making it sound like Bernie lived with Kirk," Maggie said, only to be shushed by everyone else in the room. "Well, she is."

"In a Fox News exclusive, this reporter has learned that police were called to the Toland-James penthouse before noon today and discovered the body of one Willard James, a.k.a. Buddy James, Toland-James's second husband. And here's the kicker, Jim. James supposedly died at sea seven years ago."

Spivak nodded, an obvious signal, and suddenly they were looking at a tape recorded earlier, with Spivak talking over the tape.

"The litter containing Willard Buddy James is being wheeled out behind me, his body, according to my source inside the police department, discovered nude and mutilated in the bed of Bernice Toland-James, his wife, now his widow. James, who had been reported lost at sea nearly seven years ago after taking his boat out in a storm off Connecticut, had been presumed dead until this afternoon, when he was positively identified through photographs taken from the Toland-James residence."

"You kept pictures of the guy?" This question, directed at Bernie, came from J.P.

"Wedding pictures," Bernie said, clutching a cushion to her breast. "I looked good in them. Wore a Vera Wang."

The camera panned up the building, all the way to the fifty-fourth floor, the penthouse, then trailed down again, zeroing in on the black bag being loaded into the coroner's SUV.

"Ms. Toland-James," Holly Spivak's voice droned on, as tape of Bernie and J.P. leaving the building was shown, "refuses all comment at this time and police are investigating."

"Damn, they're good. I didn't even see a camera," J.P. said. "They got the sneakers, too. Looking good. This goes to trial, maybe I can get an endorsement fee, if I wear them to court."

Maggie tossed her a dirty look.

The tape ended and Holly Spivak's smiling face was back on the screen. "One thing more, Jim, taken from the Fox News archives. A statement made by Ms. Toland-James during the investigation into her *first* husband's murder."

Tape rolled again, this time a clear close-up of Bernie speaking into a phalanx of microphones and tape recorders outside Toland Books.

She looked beautiful, her smile vibrant, her glorious hair tangling around her shoulders, a lock blowing across her face. She was wearing that damned black and white striped pantsuit she'd worn as a joke, saying she wanted to get into the mood for prison uniforms. Sure. Designer prison stripes.

But it was when she spoke that even Sterling said, "Oh, dear. Oh, dear me," for what she said was: "No, I didn't kill him. But I could have. Him and my second husband, both. Man, can I pick the losers."

"Off the cuff? An amusing anecdote? Or a foreshadowing of this morning's violence? Needless to say, Jim, we'll be following this story closely." Holly Spivak was grinning—

flat-out grinning—into the camera as she ended, "Back to you, Jim." Maggie switched off the power.

"My big mouth . . ." Bernie said, falling onto her side again, this time to cover her head with the pillow.

J.P. stood up, began to pace. J.P. pacing was rather like a tiger looking for a way out of its cage, and with a pretty good chance of finding one. "Somebody get her a drink," she said, hooking a thumb at Bernie. "Get me one, too. A double."

"I'll do it," Sterling, always helpful, said, hastening to the portable bar.

Maggie lit a cigarette with trembling hands.

Saint Just took out his quizzing glass, draped it over his head, and began swinging the glass from its riband.

Everyone was very busy being very busy.

"At least they don't know where she is," Saint Just said at last. "Unless . . . ?"

"I don't think anyone followed us," J.P. said, taking the glass from Sterling.

"You didn't see Ms. Spivak's cameraperson," Saint Just pointed out, heading for the windows that overlooked the front of the building. "Nobody's down there. Not yet, at least. That's in our favor."

"But it won't last," J.P. said, and Bernie, still under the pillow, groaned.

"What we can't avoid, we embrace," Saint Just said, looking at Maggie. "Isn't that right, my dear?"

Maggie mulled this for a moment. "Oh. *The Case of the Pilfered Pearls.*"

"Exactly."

"Do you really think it could work?"

"Possibly. I might even be able to solicit assistance from Miss Spivak, if we were to grant her—what is the term? Oh, yes. An *exclusive* interview?"

"Okay, you two, a moment here," J.P. said, stepping between them, her hands held up in the age-old time-out signal. "What am I missing? What do pearls have to do with anything?"

"Oh, not just pearls, Miss Boxer," Sterling said, beaming at Saint Just. "Pilfered pearls. One of Maggie's books about Saint Just. *The Case of the Pilfered Pearls.* Very good book. And a brilliant bit of detecting by our Saint Just. But that's all I know. I don't understand what they're talking about now," he ended, stepping back, out of the way again.

"It's relatively simple, J.P.," Saint Just said. "In my . . . in Maggie's book, a jewel thief cum murderer was skulking about London, and it was Saint Just's mission to ferret him out."

"So, since he seemed to always be after the best jewels, I had Saint Just arrange for a demi-rep ball—"

"The cream of the demimonde. Ladies of negotiable affections to you, my dear," Saint Just interrupted.

"Pros," J.P. said. "Go ahead."

Maggie began again. "I had Saint Just give this ball. You could do that in Regency times, you know. Gentlemen would host pretty outrageous balls that were for their friends and their mistresses. Anyway, all the females were to wear pieces of the famed Saint Just collection. The murderer took the bait, couldn't stay away."

She turned to Saint Just. "Is that what you meant?"

"Something like that. What I actually meant was that if we are as public as possible Bernie will not be chased, hounded by the press. What is easily accessible is never as tantalizing as what is hidden."

"You've never seen a full-fledged feeding frenzy from the press, have you, Englishman?"

"Actually, I have had the pleasure," Saint Just said, winking at Maggie, who remembered how they'd met Holly Spivak in the first place. "And I still put forward that hiding Bernice away here in Maggie's apartment will only fuel the press to further outlandish behavior such as the airing of that rather unfortunate statement we just saw."

"Yeah. She can make *more* unfortunate statements for them to air. No. She stays locked up here. No press, no exclusives. It's a bad idea. Stupid book, too."

"Oh, yeah? It went to number two on the *NYT,* lady, and stayed there for a long, long time. And the paperback—"

"Calm yourself, Maggie, my dear," Saint Just said, patting her arm. "Consider the source. Amazon.com, remember? You know your own worth, and you're no longer reacting to criticism."

"Thank you, Doctor Bob," Maggie said, reaching for another cigarette. "And now make me believe it."

"If you two are done?"

"Pardon us, J.P.," Saint Just said, bowing slightly. "Artistic temperament, you understand. Now, where were we?"

"I was putting the kibosh on your harebrained idea of parading Bernie around the city like some pet pony, that's where we were. Tonight's one thing, but not a steady diet of it, okay? However, I'm beginning to like the idea of an exclusive interview with this Spivak dame. The cops will go nuts when Bernie talks to her instead of to them—you know, the JonBenet Ramsey case? Her parents talked to everybody but the cops. It could sway public opinion in Bernie's favor."

She turned to look down at Bernie, what was visible of her now that she'd pulled two more large cushions on top of her body. "So, now that you've given it some thought, how is she better, on or off the booze?"

Maggie looked at Saint Just. "I'll lay in more scotch?"

"Splendid idea," Saint Just said, swinging his quizzing glass. "I'll phone Miss Spivak and arrange a meeting here at Maggie's. Is Monday morning too soon?"

J.P. sighed. "Just do it."

"Excuse me, now that this is all settled," Sterling said, "but I'm afraid I have some bad news. The pudding, Saint

Just? It . . . it wasn't quite a success. I'm so sorry. Shall I toddle down to Mario's for some meat and salads?"

"No, Sterling. We'll all be going to Bellini's later. Isn't that what you said, J.P.?"

"Yes. I must be out of my mind, but yes. I'm that desperate, considering how bad things look now. What was it? 'What we can't avoid, we embrace'? What a bunch of crap that is. This had better work."

"I'll see that you get a copy of the book, J.P. Autographed, of course," Saint Just said, and Maggie wanted to hug him.

CHAPTER 6

Saint Just awoke early, happy to be in his own room and no longer sharing a bed with a softly snoring Sterling. He quickly showered in his private bathroom, the one holding his toiletries and a lingering scent of lilacs, Mrs. Goldblum's fragrance of choice.

He dressed in black slacks and a soft black knit pullover, slid on his favorite Hessians—brought with him when he stepped out of Maggie's imagination and into her life—and used the pair of silver-backed brushes on his ebony hair.

He penned a quick note to Sterling and taped it to the man's favorite appliance, the toaster oven, then picked up his sword cane, slipped Raybans over his startling blue eyes, and departed the apartment.

Mario's opened early on Sunday mornings, serving the bagel and coffee and Sunday papers crowd, and Holly Spivak was already seated at one of the impossibly small tables Mario's wife had ordered set up at the rear of the store, in hopes of attracting more customers.

Saint Just accepted a cup of coffee, black, from a grinning, bowing Mario, and headed for the tables.

Holly Spivak was Fox News–blonde, wore too much red

lipstick, and either lived on air and water or exercised for hours each day, because her five-foot frame couldn't be carrying more than six stone.

"Miss Spivak, so good to see you again."

"Holly, Alex, remember? Call me Holly. And it's so good to see you again, too. God, you're gorgeous in those sunglasses," she said, lifting a hand for him to bow over. Saint Just had learned that, far from being a customary greeting, bowing over a woman's hand had the power to melt a generous majority of them into jelly. And what he knew, he invariably used to his advantage.

"Holly, my dear, you are too kind, and ravishing, as usual," he said as he sat down, leaning his cane against the back wall. "And how very good of you to meet with me."

"Yes, and how very naughty of you to throw out hints like that. I barely slept last night, wondering what I'm going to receive in return for this," she said, leaning down and removing a file from a lizard-skin briefcase.

Saint Just eyed the folder. "Am I going to be happy, Holly?"

"I don't know how you're going to be, because you're not going to see any of it until you tell me what you've got to trade. You said it was big."

J.P. Boxer would hate him for this. Maggie, being more dramatic and yet, bless her, pragmatic as well, would have his liver and lights for not letting her in on what he was about to do.

But he was Saint Just. And he did what he did.

"I have Bernice Toland-James, my dear, and am now dangling her, tantalizing you with her in point of fact. Do you want her? Exclusively?"

Holly, to be crude about the thing, instantly began to drool with excitement. "You've got Toland-James? You've really got her? Don't play with me, Alex. That wouldn't be nice."

"I am not always nice, I fear, but I am rarely untruthful. Yes, I've got her, as you put the thing. Safely tucked away and ready to talk. To you. As already mentioned, exclusively. On camera. If you're a good girl."

"Oh, I'm a *very* good girl, Alex, and I can do a whole lot more for you than this bunch of old news," she said, leaning her elbows on the folder. "Why don't we go back to my place?"

Saint Just took her hands in his, pressed a kiss against her knuckles. "How you tempt me, my dear."

"But no, right?" Holly said, pulling her hands free.

"For my sins, yes, you're right."

Holly slapped her forehead. "You're gay, right? I told myself. I mean, I knew it. All the good ones are gay."

By now Saint Just had become accustomed to this entirely unreasonable reaction to what to him, a gentleman of the English Regency, were only common good manners, a precise way of speaking, and an attention to his toilette that was only, well, only gentlemanly. "Think what you wish, my dear, as I would not so demean myself as to launch a protest if your deduction pleases you, but I very much need the information you've collected for me."

Holly recovered quickly, instantly on the attack again. "Why? It's like I said, old news. Unless you know something I don't?"

"Always the reporter," Saint Just said, smiling. "Much as I'd like nothing more than to prostrate myself at your feet, telling you all, it is, alas, not my secret to divulge. I do promise you—what is it called? Oh, yes, first dibs, if anything should come of it."

"You'd damn well better," Holly said, pulling a notepad from her briefcase. "Now, back to the Merry Widow."

"I beg your pardon?"

"You didn't see it? That's what the papers are calling her this morning. The Merry Widow. I think it's pretty lame, but they'll come up with something else by tomorrow. They always do. Of course, that something else will be my tag line. I'm calling it the Twice Dead case. Like it?"

"Not particularly, no," Saint Just said. "I won't condone a circus, Holly."

She sat back in her chair. "Well, excuse me, Mr. Perfect. What do you want?"

"Decorum would be a start, and quite refreshing, actually. A man is dead, Holly. A terrified and totally innocent woman is fast becoming the target of a media intent only on selling newspapers and raising television ratings. For shame, trading on tragedy."

"Yeah, right. Wait here, I've got to run back to my place and get into my sackcloth and ashes, repent for all the media who are *only doing their jobs,* Alex. It's the public's right to know."

"Yes, I believe I've already heard that ludicrous excuse. Tell me, if the public wanted to know about *your* private life, would they have a right?"

"If I killed my husband, yeah."

"Ah, but therein lies the rub, as well as the gaping hole in your logic, if I may be so blunt. *Did* Bernice murder her husband? You can't know that, and yet you, meaning the media in its entirety, not just you, dear lady, are already citing the public's right to know as your excuse to exploit poor Bernice. I find that contradictory."

"They found him stiff in her bed. Considering her as the prime suspect isn't much of a stretch, you know. What do *you* think?"

"That is immaterial. But what I most fervently hope, Holly, is that your American law, your marvelous Constitution, although admittedly under assault, remains quite firm on the concept of innocent until proved guilty. Why is it, do you wonder, that the media is always so happy to seek out guilt, but never innocence?"

"You don't understand market shares, Alex, that's for sure, never mind the First Amendment. Do you know how long we'd last if we played this down while every other station in town is in a feeding frenzy? If we refused to let the talking heads loose on Toland-James's carcass every night of the week and twice on Sunday, now, and all the way through the trial? If we said, hey, she's innocent until proven guilty, there have been no new developments and won't be for months, and now we'll hear from Gerry about the forecast for a sunny weekend? Give me a break. Toland-James is a gift, Alex. A *gift.*"

"I see," Saint Just said, retrieving his cane. "In that case, I'm very much afraid that this discussion is closed. Forgive me for calling you out so early on what is proving to be a fruitless errand."

"Whoa! Wait a minute, Alex. Sit down, sit down. Nothing's written in stone."

"Including your Constitution, I would say, at least since nine-eleven. Bernice's right to privacy to one side, did you ever wonder how much *you* might lose when you begin giving up someone else's rights and freedoms? Good day, Miss Spivak."

"Holly. Call me Holly, remember? Look, no sermons. I don't make the laws. And I may be part of the media, but I don't control it. What's going to happen to Toland-James is going to happen with or without me, so don't go all ACLU on me for trying to do my job. Cripes, you British make our media look like a Sunday school class. Sit down, Alex. Please. I know we can deal. Tell me what you want."

Saint Just replaced the cane. This was going well. First a well-baited hook, and then the demands. "Having spent most of the night researching high profile murder cases on the Internet, commentaries on the garish and often biased reporting of such cases, I have come up with a few, shall we say, guidelines."

"You mean ground rules."

"Another term, yes, if you wish. First, you will bring a single cameraperson with you."

"Agreed."

"Second, you will allow Bernice to answer any question in full, and not edit her words in any way in order to—again, I'm struggling with these new terms—in order to *spin* them in any one direction."

"Next you'll want me to show you the tape before it airs. Is that what you're saying? I don't do that, Alex. I'm a reporter. Hard news. I don't do puff pieces."

Saint Just smiled. "Never assume, my dear. No, I shan't demand to view what you've done. I trust you to remain true to any promise you make here, now. I trust you not to set out deliberately to show Bernice in a bad light, or any light at all other than that of impeccably fair and impartial reporting. I trust you to ask intelligent questions, and allow ample time for her answers."

"What if I ask her if she killed him?"

"I most sincerely hope you will."

Holly shrugged. "All right. What about her lawyer? Will she be there?"

"In the room? I would imagine so. As a part of the interview? Definitely not. Oh, and one more very small thing."

"Here we go," Holly said, flipping her notebook shut. "Go ahead, shoot. You already know you've got me."

"That's high praise indeed, thank you. Very well. You will not advertise the airing of the interview every five minutes by showing highly volatile excerpts and telling the viewing audience in what the dear Maggie would term a *snarky* tone that Bernice is denying killing her husband."

"Damn, you must have been reading my mind. Okay, what the hell am I supposed to say?"

"I'm not a scribe or a reporter, Holly. However, since you are so kind as to have asked? I would most sincerely wish that you simply tell the viewers that there will be an in-depth, exclusive interview with Bernice Toland-James on your network, and then announce the time."

"That's boring," Holly said, then grabbed Saint Just's forearm as he reached for his cane. "Okay, okay, I'll do it. But she did it, right?"

Saint Just inhaled deeply, sighed. "Holly, dear Holly, you are a journalist. You don't have opinions, correct?"

"You're a real pain, you know that, Alex? Do you want this file or not?"

"Oh, I want it, most assuredly. Is there anything not in it that you can tell me?"

"Not much. Just that no one was ever charged, but that's not unusual. Are you going to tell me why you want this stuff?"

"As I said, Holly, all in good time. Until tomorrow morning? Let's say at nine, as Bernice cannot neglect her responsibilities at Toland Books."

"She's still going to go to work?"

"Innocent, dearest Holly. Innocent people continue with their lives as the wheels of justice grind slowly but inexorably toward the truth. And exoneration."

"With your help, right? I remember that horseback rescue, you know. And that WAR business. A thing of beauty—both of them were. What are you up to this time, hero man?"

"Why, simply being heroic, of course," Saint Just said, getting to his feet and saluting Holly Spivak with the cane before departing Mario's, picking up copies of each of the Sunday newspapers as he went. Mario would put the cost on Maggie's bill, as always.

"Good morning, Socks," he said as he approached his building. "When did you begin working on the weekends? I thought you were studying for your audition."

"I'm filling in. Paul's got a toothache. I see you saw the newspapers. It's bad, isn't it?"

"It's typical of your sensationalistic culture, Socks," Saint Just said, readjusting the thick papers under his arm. The move secured the newspapers, but the file folder slipped to the ground, opening, and papers were quickly set scattering by the morning breeze.

"I'll get those, Alex," Socks said, bending to pick up the pages, then piling them back into the folder. He held onto one of them, his eyes wide. "Oh, damn. Would you look at that? I think my breakfast is knocking at the back of my throat."

Saint Just took the paper, realizing that it was a photocopy of a photograph. He saw a body lying in what looked to be a garbage-strewn alleyway. A body, but without its head and hands. Holding the paper closer, he could make out a stamp on the bottom of the photograph stating that it was an official police photo.

"Hmmm, it would appear Miss Spivak has very good sources. Socks, you are to forget you saw this."

"Sure, Alex, like that's going to happen in the next twenty years. I think it's burned into my retinas. What *is* that?"

"That is, or should I say *was,* one Mr. Harry Goldblum, or at least I presume so," Saint Just said, replacing the photocopy inside the folder.

"Mrs. Goldblum's husband? Oh, now that's just gross." Socks wiped his hands on his uniform. "And I touched it."

Saint Just flipped through the reassembled pages. "There are more, Socks. Would you like it if I stood out here with you and shared them?"

"No thanks, no way, not hardly," Socks said, backing away.

"Very well. I think I know of someone who will want to see this."

He rode the elevator up, still trying to balance the newspapers, his cane, and the open folder as he attempted to scan all of its contents, and didn't have to feign surprise when the doors opened and Maggie was standing there, her arms folded as she tapped her foot.

She was wearing blue knit shorts, a pullover top of bright green sporting the message IN YOUR DREAMS, and a pair of bright pink fuzzy slippers. Her hair spiked all over her head, and her expression could only be called dangerous.

That was his Maggie. Definitely a morning person.

"My felicitations on your ensemble, Maggie, my dear. Aren't you up bright and early."

"Stuff it, Alex. Yes, I'm up early. I'm up early because I couldn't sleep because I'm worried about Bernie. Who snores, by the way. *Loudly.* Tonight I close both our bedroom doors. So you know what I did? Huh? I'll tell you what I did. I got up, and I wandered into the living room, and I looked out the window. I don't know why, I just did. And what did I see out there? Huh? I'll tell you what I—"

"Maggie, my dearest girl, please stop, you might strain something vital. I know what you saw. You saw a white automobile with the words 'Fox News' on the door parked at the curb. You saw me. You put two and two together and got—"

"Holly Spivak. How could you do that, Alex? I wanted to talk to her. She's got to understand that she can't come in here and—"

"Done and done, my dear," Saint Just said, motioning with his cane for her to precede him down the hall, to his apartment. "I've something to show you."

"Oh, yeah? Maybe I don't want to see it. I would have liked to see a bag holding some bagels and coffee, but I'm not seeing those, Alex."

"Ah, we're going to be mulish, I see. Such feigned reluctance is not becoming, my dear."

"I don't care." She opened the unlocked door, then turned to look at him. "Yes, I do. What do you have? I see the newspapers. What else?"

"We'll leave the newspapers for later, as I'm sure they'll

be depressing," Saint Just said, closing the door and placing the newspapers on a table. "What I have that is definitely more interesting is all of Holly Spivak's information on one Harry Goldblum."

"You have—that folder is about—oh, God, Alex, you're sneaky. You traded Bernie for Harry, didn't you? That's cold." She grabbed the folder. "And *brilliant.*"

"It was rather inspired, I agree, and the interview, in case you don't think to ask, is set for nine tomorrow morning in your apartment, which, I might add, could probably do with a dust and brush up, especially your desk area," Saint Just said, waiting for Maggie to sit down on one of the couches, then sitting down beside her. "Perhaps we could look at this together? There are a few rather . . . disturbing photographs."

"Like what?" Maggie asked, paging through the half-inch stack of papers. "Oh, *eeeuuuwww.* Like this one?"

"Precisely. Perhaps I'd better take the papers, and keep the rest of the disturbing photographs hidden?"

"Ordinarily I'd say I could see anything you could see, but I think I'll make an exception in this case. There was no head, was there?"

"And no hands."

"Oh. Missed that." Maggie pulled her nicotine inhaler out of her shorts pocket. "Glad I missed that."

Within a half hour, they had pieced together the entire story. First, because both were the sort who could readily sift and distill facts, pertinent information; and second, because there wasn't all that much of it.

Harold Goldblum had been an attorney with a flourishing practice made up of thieves, thugs, and various other undesirables, including some rather high-profile members of one of the local mob families.

Nine years ago Harold disappeared, although his wife did not report him missing. She said nothing, actually, even denying his absence when the police came to her with the possibility that the headless, handless corpse recovered from a vacant lot in Hell's Kitchen could be that husband.

She said nothing until a package containing Harold's head and hands was delivered to her, and then she spoke up only to ask for the rest of the corpse in order to bury Harold all in the same box.

There had been a fluttering of media attention, some rousting of the usual suspects, but in the end, no one had been charged. Harry's name had been scratched off Irene's mailbox and life went on, or, for Harry, didn't.

"So why now?" Maggie asked as Saint Just closed the folder. "Nine years, Alex. If the mob was going to go after Irene, they would have done it by now, right?"

"True," he said. "Unless something new has occurred to once more pique their interest in the woman."

"Like what?"

"I have no idea, my dear," Saint Just said, sliding the folder beneath the couch, out of sight, as Sterling's sensibilities would not be best pleased to see those photographs. "But, clearly, something has changed."

"It," Maggie said, sucking on her inhaler. "Sterling said they were demanding he hand *it* over." She pressed her hands on the couch cushion and pushed herself up, her head and shoulders swiveling to look all around the living room, rather like a hunting dog going on point. "God, Alex, there's something in this apartment, isn't there?"

"I doubt that," Saint Just said, having already considered and discarded that possibility.

"Oh, well, then I'll just have to forget the whole idea, won't I? Silly me. *Duh.*"

Saint Just patted her hand. "Don't fly into the treetops, my dear. But do you really think, if this *it* exists, and Irene Goldblum was aware that some very bad people knew *it* exists, and that they had contacted her and planned a visit to collect *it,* that *it* would still be here?"

Maggie made a face. "Okay. So she took it with her?"

"My thought, yes."

"So we've both agreed that there is an it. A journal, do you think? Something detailing Harry's exploits with the mob? Or maybe just a collection of incriminating evidence?"

"Sterling's visitors said *it,* which makes me believe that we're speaking of one thing."

"Unless the one thing is a file, like the one you got from Holly Spivak. A file can have a lot of *its* in it."

"I believe we're traveling in circles, Maggie, not to mention drowning in *its.* What's clear is that we have no idea what those men wanted."

"True. But they'll be back. Count on it. You two have to get out of here."

"I don't think so," Saint Just said, reaching into his pocket for his quizzing glass, then rubbing it as he would a talisman or a worry stone.

"Oh, right. Saint Just doesn't run. Saint Just is the big bad hero type. But what about Sterling?"

"I should imagine he'll make his own decision, given what we know, once we share it with him."

"I could hate you. You know damn full well Sterling will go where you go, even if you planned a swan dive straight into the mouth of hell."

Saint Just sat silent for long moments, moments in which he didn't quite care for himself very much (a novel experience on its own). It was all so much easier in his books, where he was assured, because, after all, he was a continuing series, that no matter how dire his position, he and Sterling would survive to adventure again another day . . . in another book.

It was Sterling who had discovered that no matter how he exercised since his arrival in New York, he did not lose weight. And, no matter what he ate, he did not gain weight. Saint Just had a scar from a pistol ball on his shoulder, but Maggie had put that there, describing it in one of her books. They were what Maggie had made them, how she had created them, and would not age, sicken, or die, unless she wrote about it.

Hence her occasional jokes about writing him a wart on the end of his nose.

Still, he was safe. Unless coming to life had changed things. Not the little things, but possibly the big things? Like their possibility of mortality? And could he take that chance? He could, for himself. He was, after all, a hero, and could not imagine himself in any other role, no matter how, in small ways, he had felt his attitudes *evolving* in his new surroundings.

But not for Sterling. He could not take that chance for Sterling.

"Well? Aren't you going to say anything?"

Saint Just shook himself back to attention. "I will not, I cannot, in good conscience remove myself from this building, desert my post, leave you ladies to fend for yourselves. I'm no white feather man, and you won't turn me into a sniveling coward, or Sterling, who has more backbone than you seem to imagine."

"You're such a—"

He held up a hand, cutting her off. "That said, we will, however, return to the hospitality you have shown us on the morrow, or as soon as Bernice is allowed to return to her own domicile."

"Boy, that really torked you, didn't it, saying all of that? And don't think I didn't notice that you got a few swipes in there as you were giving in. But good for you, Alex. You're doing the right thing. Now, how about you let me search this place? You know, humor me? I've always loved treasure hunts."

"If you must. I'm sure Sterling will be happy to assist you. Do you think Bernice has awakened for the day? I should begin preparing her for her interview."

"J.P.'s coming over at eleven to do that. Although I'm betting she doesn't realize you could actually set it up for tomorrow. And I guess I have to tell you, I was pretty impressed at how you handled J.P. last night at Bellini's. Do you think it was the wine, or is she really letting you be in charge of Bernie's publicity?"

"You doubt my powers of persuasion?"

"No, not me. You've persuaded the world you're real, you know. But we had a free ride last night. Nobody knew anything yet, or not enough to start stalking Bernie. Today, and from now on, it's going to be a different story. The barracudas are going to be circling."

"Knock knock. Yoo-hoo, are you in there? Olly-olly-umstead-free."

"Oh, shit," Maggie said, sliding down on the couch. "Speaking of barracudas . . ."

Saint Just stood up and smiled at Felicity Boothe Simmons. "Good morning, Miss Simmons. I hadn't realized I left the door unlatched. How remiss of me."

"Bernie told me you probably were over here. I know it's still early, but I rushed right over, as soon as I saw the morning papers, to lend my support," Felicity said, advancing into the room, bringing her strong floral scent with her. "Wow, very nice. Maggie, you could learn something from the way Alex decorates."

"Bite me," Maggie said, but only loud enough for Saint Just to hear her, then added, "How did you know Bernie was here?"

"You haven't seen the papers? There's a photograph of you, Alex, leaving Bernie's building yesterday. You were *unidentified man.* I think you're there, too, Maggie, but luckily all that's visible are your legs. I recognized those skinny ankles."

"Hold me back, Alex, or I'm going to kill her."

"Shhh," Saint Just soothed, sitting down beside her once more.

"Anyway," Felicity said, crossing her long legs and reaching into her purse for a tissue she then used to dab at the corners of her mouth, "I put two and two together and figured out that if Bernie wasn't under arrest and she couldn't stay at the crime scene, she had to be here, with you. Is that a Steinway?" she asked, pointing at the grand piano. "I play, you know."

"How wonderful for you," Saint Just said, the better to cover Maggie's low growl. "So you raced right over? Tell me, are there many members of the press camped outside?"

"Only two or three," Felicity said, frowning. Then she brightened. "But I told them. I told them all."

Maggie sat up, would have stood up if Saint Just hadn't grabbed her arm. "What did you say, Faith? Damn it, can't you ever walk past a camera or a microphone without sticking out that pair of silicone marvels and opening your big mouth?"

Felicity smiled, a soft, sympathetic, *you poor flatchested thing* smile. "Maggie. Maggie, Maggie, Maggie. I know how you loathe public speaking, what with that way you have of speaking too quickly, or mumbling, but some us of know the value of self-promotion."

"You were promoting yourself?" Saint Just asked, wondering if it would soon be time for Maggie to hold *him* back.

"No," Felicity said, waving her manicured hands to wipe away that impression. "Of course not. I was just speaking generally. But to use poor Bernie's tragedy to promote myself? My dear editor? My very good *friend*? How could you think such a thing?"

"Easy. I know you, remember," Maggie said, sucking on her nicotine inhaler.

(There was much to compare and contrast between Maggie and Felicity, Saint Just thought. One of those things would be how Maggie had heard from Bernice and raced hotfoot to her aid still clad in those unfortunate sheep, while Felicity would doubtless have taken a good hour with her toilette, and shown up prepared to face the cameras.)

"Always making jokes, aren't you, Maggie? But that's just because you're so loyal. Loyal to Bernie, and definitely loyal to me, saving my life that way. I'll never forget it, Maggie. I really won't."

"Try. Please," Maggie said, and Saint Just busied himself with his quizzing glass, carefully keeping his features blank.

"Don't be silly. Oh, I forgot. I brought you something. Just a little something I saw in Tiffany's the other day."

"Faith, you've got to stop this. Really. I don't want any more presents."

"They weigh heavily on her, you understand, Miss Simmons. Presents, any expression of kindness or even praise. She is much more comfortable when ignored," Saint Just explained as Felicity pulled a Tiffany blue box from her large purse and tossed it to Maggie, who missed it, because she was glaring at Saint Just.

Saint Just retrieved the box from the floor and handed it to her.

Maggie slid off the ribbon and opened the box, lifted out a soft Tiffany blue cloth holder and slipped out the small silver pen within. "Pretty."

"Say thank you," Saint Just prodded.

"Thank you, Faith."

"I knew you'd like it. I saw you using a Bic at the WAR convention. It's really time you displayed some cachet (she pronounced it *catch-it*), Maggie, now that you've been lucky enough to make the list. I had it engraved. Look."

Saint Just took the pen and squinted at the necessarily small letters. "'Maggie Kelly, heroine.' How . . . how very thoughtful."

"I know. I wanted *heroine extraordiniare*"—Saint Just visibly winced at that pronunciation—"only it was too long, and we weren't sure how to spell it. You like it, Maggie? You really like it? You can use it at autographings. Oh, wait, you don't do those."

"Yes, I do. Sometimes I do," Maggie said, looking at Saint Just, obviously in the hope he'd rescue her heroine self.

"Ah, yes, that's done now, isn't it? Now, please tell us what you said to the reporters downstairs?"

Felicity openly preened. "I was brilliant. I told them that nobody who knows Bernie, *really* knows her, would ever believe she'd kill anyone, even if she certainly had a good reason. Oh, and that I was convinced that nowhere in the length and breadth of this great country will she receive such a fair trial as right here, in my beloved Manhattan."

Maggie pressed a hand to her forehead. "Jesus. She's already got her arrested and going to trial."

"Maggie's right, Miss Simmons. Bernice is yet to be charged, you know."

"Oh, well, that's only a matter of time. But I'm sure it was self-defense."

"Out," Maggie said, getting to her feet before Saint Just could stop her. "I mean it, Faith. *Out.* And don't call, don't try to see Bernie again, and for God's sake don't let her see you once *she* hears what you said."

"I . . . I don't understand," Felicity said, grabbing her purse and holding it in front of her as she rose and backed toward the door, Maggie stalking after her. "What did I say wrong? Did I really say something wrong?"

"Your choice of words could be termed . . . unfortunate," Saint Just said, stepping in front of Maggie and escorting Felicity to the door.

"I didn't mean them to be. I thought they were good words."

"Yeah, you think that about your stupid books, too," Maggie said, and Saint Just quickly shoved Felicity out and closed the door, just as the pen hit it. "Damn, Alex, with friends like Faith, Bernie doesn't need any enemies."

"No, she doesn't. Although, if we're correct and Bernice is innocent, she certainly has one."

CHAPTER 7

Maggie was torn. Part of her wanted to rip into Mrs. Goldblum's apartment, looking for journals taped on the underside of drawers or hidden behind paintings. But another part of her knew she had to be, as Saint Just would have said, a "supporting prop to Bernice in her hour of need."

It was that part of her that stopped only long enough to peek behind the very uninspired oil painting of a dark cavern on a dark day in hopes of finding a wall safe, before crossing the hallway to reenter her own apartment . . . to see Bernie sitting on the couch, dressed in a turquoise silk blouse and black slacks, her makeup in place, one foot propped against the coffee table.

The foot was bare. There was cotton between the toes. And the apartment reeked of nail polish.

"What are you doing?" Maggie asked, not sure if she was disappointed not to see Bernie lying on the couch in a fetal position, overcome with dread, or just unhappy with the smell of nail polish. Who said smokers didn't have sensitive noses?

Bernie dipped the brush in the bottle, coming out with

fire engine red, and concentrated on painting the nail on her big toe. "Well, Maggie, it's like this. Either I curl up and die, or I fight back. Or didn't you figure out that someone did this to me?"

"Well, actually, Alex and I did come to that conclusion. But I thought you said you couldn't remember anything."

"I didn't. I don't. But I didn't kill Buddy. Turn him over to the cops for faking his death, sure. Turn him in to the IRS because the forgetful little bugger hadn't filed in five years before he took his hike—we filed separately, I insisted on that, and the pre-nup. But kill him? I'd rather see him in jail. I could go visit him once a month, and bring him prunes. He hated prunes."

"Right," Maggie said, sitting down on the opposing couch. "That sounds like you. A long, slow torture, right?"

"Absolutely. Besides, why would I kill him in my own house? It doesn't make sense."

"It does if you wanted to use the defense that it doesn't make sense," Maggie said, watching as Bernie, hands as steady as the proverbial rock, put a first coat on the second toe of her right foot. "But you're right. You wouldn't have— wait a minute. You had Buddy sign a pre-nup?"

Bernie used her free hand to push back her tangled curls. "Um-hmm, everyone was doing that back then. It had cachet."

"Or *catch-it,* depending on who's saying the word," Maggie said, pulling out her nicotine inhaler and taking a deep drag of unsatisfying chemicals. "So, Buddy would have gotten nothing if you divorced? If you died?"

"Right. He sold insurance, Maggie, and not very successfully. He even had to take a second job, once the bloom was off the rose and I took away his allowance. Kirk was a worm, but he was pretty fair in our divorce. I mean, I was able to buy that house in Connecticut. It's in my name."

"Still is?"

"Uh-huh. Damn! Get me a tissue, will you, Maggie. I'm all smudged."

Maggie grabbed a box of tissues from the end table and held it out to Bernie. "I'm shocked. I thought I knew everything about you. You still own a house in Connecticut? Why?"

Bernie shrugged, smudging another nail. "Because everyone in town thought I'd killed Buddy and buried him in the backyard, that's why. So I kept my backyard, just to drive them nuts." She looked up at Maggie. "You do know me, Maggie. I'm a nasty woman, right?"

"One of the reasons I love you. Is it leased?"

Bernie looked at her right foot, sighed, and reached for the bottle of polish remover. "Can we change the subject? I was doing great until we started talking about this stuff."

"In a minute. Is it leased, Bernie?"

Bernie sat back, sighed. "Yes, it's leased." Then she sort of rolled her eyes. "I think it's leased. It used to be leased by the week, you know, in the summer. You know, Maggie, I don't know. I really haven't been paying attention. I go through an agent, you understand."

"Call him," Maggie said, grabbing the portable phone and holding it out to Bernie. "Call him now."

"Why?"

"I don't know. But if Buddy wasn't dead, and he wasn't, maybe when he came back he went first to Connecticut, thinking you still lived there. The realtor can ask the people leasing the house if anyone came sniffing around, looking for you. If the house was leased, that is. Oh, just call."

"And this would be in aid of . . . ?"

"Buddy tracking you down. He heard about Kirk, wherever he was hiding, heard about your inheriting and taking over. He was getting a little tired of Mexico, or Brazil, or wherever the heck he'd stashed himself, and decided to come back, hop on the gravy train. It would be logical for him to go first to your house in Connecticut, right?"

Bernie finished wiping off the newly applied polish. "I hope you're happy now, Maggie. I have to face the world with bare toenails. You don't wear Ferragamos with bare toenails. It's sacrilege."

"Bernie, honey, concentrate. If Buddy showed up at the Connecticut house, that proves he was after you, not the other way around."

"Nobody has opined that Bernice was hunting Buddy," Saint Just said from the doorway. "Only that they so obviously found each other."

"I gotta remember to lock that door," Maggie said, sucking on the inhaler. "Either that, or we buy out the other two condos on this floor and just use the whole place."

"An interesting idea, but four kitchens would be a tad superfluous, don't you think? Actually, two are superfluous, unless you're planning on cultivating a heretofore hidden talent, my dear."

"Bite me," Maggie said absently. "And you're right, Alex, nobody has said that Bernie was hunting Buddy. Crime of opportunity, crime of passion, that's what they'll be saying."

"They, that nebulous they, are already saying just that," Saint Just said, holding up the front page of one of the newspapers.

"The Merry Widow?" Bernie slammed down her bare feet and headed for the portable bar. "Cut me a freaking break. That's so cliched."

"Miss Spivak plans to go with Twice Dead, I believe."

"Better," Bernie said, gesturing toward him, empty tumbler in hand. "If it was a book, it could be *Bumping Off Buddy.*" She lifted the top of the ice bucket. "Maggie?"

"Bernie, nobody has scotch for breakfast."

"I already ate a health bar I had in my purse. Now I want

a drink. J.P. said I could, at least for a while. Don't harp on me Maggie, please. I only look like I'm holding on." She held the bucket higher.

"Going," Maggie said, giving Saint Just a look before taking the ice bucket and heading for the kitchen.

Once there, she stood in front of the open freezer door, rethinking her reasons for learning about the Connecticut house. They didn't change, not if she put herself in Buddy's shoes. Even if he'd had access to the Internet, all he'd get from that would be that Bernie had an apartment in the city, and a house in Connecticut. He'd think she lived in town during the week, went to Connecticut on the weekend.

Or at least he *could* think that way.

He could have been there, lying in wait like a snake in the grass. But, when she didn't show up? Next move— Manhattan. It made sense. She thought it made sense. Maybe it made sense. . . .

Maggie filled the ice bucket and returned to the living room, to see Saint Just sitting on the couch she'd vacated, leaving room for her. He stood at once, because he was a Regency gentleman, then motioned to the couch as if beckoning her to join him, because he was arrogant and bossy and just assumed she'd want to sit next to him. *Here, girl. Sit.*

Man, she was feeling snarky. But, then, she'd been awake for only about ninety minutes, and it wasn't looking like it was going to be a great day to be happy.

She put down the ice bucket and headed for her computer chair, then glared at Saint Just.

He smiled back at her, just as if he knew that she wanted to be sitting next to him, which was why she wasn't sitting next to him. How could he read her so well? No, scratch that. She knew why he could read her so well. Because she'd given him parts of her, just as she'd given Sterling parts of her, never thinking that one day she'd look at the two of them and see herself.

The self she was; the self she wished she was; the self she hoped she could be; stronger, smarter, more daring, more "I want it, so I'm going after it."

More Saint Just, less Sterling.

"Maggie? Bernice and I were discussing Connecticut, and I believe you have a very valid idea."

"You do?" she asked hopefully, then cleared her throat and said, "Well, duh, of course you do. It's a good idea. A brilliant idea."

"Oh, my dear, I wouldn't go quite that far," Saint Just said, and she recognized the twinkle in his eyes. He was deliberately trying to make her angry.

It was working.

"Bernie? What's the name of your realty company? I'll look it up on Google, get a telephone number. Realtors always work on Sundays. My mom was a realtor, for all the vacation condos in Ocean City. Sundays were good days."

Five minutes later, Bernie was speaking to one Lureen O'Boyle, saying yes, of course she remembered her (even as she made a face and shook her head at Maggie), saying yes, she wished she had time to summer in Connecticut (while rolling her eyes), and finally snapping her fingers for Maggie to hand her pen and paper so she could scribble as she said, "Uh-huh, okay, thanks, Lureen. And say hello to Gordie for me. Oh, he did? Isn't that just like a man? Bye now."

She clicked off the phone and took a sip of her drink.

"Well?" Maggie asked impatiently.

"Well, what? Oh, Gordie's gone."

"Who? Oh, your realtor's husband? He left her?"

"He died."

Saint Just looked at Maggie, who was mouthing, " 'Isn't that just like a man. . . .' "

"J.P. does have a point, doesn't she, about putting a muzzle on our dearest Bernice?"

"Oh, yeah," Maggie said, glaring at her friend. "Bernie,

you have to stop saying stuff like that. I think you're funny, Alex here thinks you're funny, but the rest of the world could think you're being . . . flippant."

"Good, because I was being flippant. Gordie got me backed into a corner at the annual let's all pretend we're hicks celebration, or whatever it was. I had to knee him, which I enjoyed." She waved the note. "Do you want to know what Lureen said?"

"I don't know," Maggie said, dropping her head in her hands. "I'm beginning to wonder what it was I wanted to know."

"Have a cigarette, Maggie. Trust me, the vice of your choice will go a long way toward keeping you sane."

"Right up until the moment it kills you, I'd imagine," Saint Just purred, earning himself another dirty look from Maggie.

"Anyway, Lureen says my last tenant left the end of July. She'd been trying to rent it, but she swears the economy is keeping everyone at home this year. So, Maggie, my house is empty. I forget. Is this supposed to help me or hurt me?"

Maggie looked at Saint Just. He inclined his head slightly, allowing her the floor. Not that she wasn't capable of taking it on her own, although it might be better if she knew what she wanted to say.

She'd have to wing it. "Okay," she said, "the house is empty. Has been empty since the end of July. So, since we can't find out if Buddy came there at any time, looking for you, that idea's shot. However, that doesn't mean he wasn't there."

"And . . . so what?" Bernie asked, sipping her scotch.

"So," Maggie said, and then hesitated. "I don't know. Alex, do we need to know if Buddy was there? I mean, would that help Bernie or hurt her? Like, if the cops thought she knew he was there and visited him there, maybe? That he could have been trying to hit her up for money or something? Part of the insurance money, at the least, even if he didn't know about her inheritance from Kirk?"

Saint Just steepled his fingers in front of his chin. "Go on."

"Okay. The timing makes sense on the insurance money, I'd say. Like, he'd promise to stay dead if she split the insurance with him? But that would mean that maybe Bernie knew that no blackmailer bites once and then goes away, so that then maybe she lured him here, and murdered him? Wow, why do I keep making cases *against* Bernie?"

"I hate scenarios," Bernie said, pulling cotton from between her toes.

"Or," Saint Just said, "Buddy returned, hid at the Connecticut house in order to prepare himself for coming to the city to confront Bernice, demand money from her? He may have felt safe there, although I would think the first place he'd be noticed and remarked upon would be in the area in which the two of them resided. You know, Maggie, I think we've come to a dead end. Unless, purely for purposes of discussion, and in an attempt to track Buddy's movements before his death, we at some point decide it necessary to explore that avenue."

"At some point? You've got another street to travel?" Maggie asked, still trying to figure out why she'd thought this was such a good idea. But that was like looking for a motive for Buddy to want to get himself murdered, and she was pretty sure that idea wasn't going to get off the ground for anyone but the prosecution.

"In point of fact?" Saint Just said. "No, I don't have any other streets to travel. Not yet. Not until J.P. extracts as much information as possible from the good *left*-tenant. And, speaking of J.P., remember that she'll be arriving shortly, to prepare Bernice for her television debut, which will make us fairly superfluous for most of the day. Bernice, would you happen to have a key to the Connecticut house with you?"

"No," Bernie said. "I haven't been there, oh, for at least four years. But Lureen has to have one. Why?"

"Oh, nothing," Saint Just said, speaking to Bernie, but looking at Maggie. "I just thought, as there's little else for us to do today, Maggie, Sterling and I could drive to this Connecticut and inspect the house."

"For clues," Maggie said, shaking her head. "I mean it, Alex, for clues, right? Not just to humor me?"

"Or to keep you out of the way while J.P. preps me," Bernie said, then winced. "Sorry, Mags. I am using your place, aren't I?"

"No, no, that's okay, Bernie," Maggie said, already heading down the hall. "Alex?" she called over her shoulder. "Let me shower and get dressed. You can go collect Sterling, he likes taking rides. Oh, and call Socks, see if we can borrow his car. I'll be ready in twenty minutes."

Twenty minutes stretched to thirty, and when Maggie exited the foyer of the building it was to see Saint Just and Socks standing together, talking. "Where's Sterling?"

Saint Just held open the car door on the driver's side. "Sterling is upstairs, aligning his bedroom in harmony with the elements. To that end, he and Socks will be shopping this afternoon, as Sterling has put forth a desire to visit Chinatown, where he plans to purchase some brass amphibians he calls three-legged money frogs, of all things, plus a quantity of Chinese coins tied with red ribbon that he intends to employ in a way I was not interested enough to linger and listen to, I'm afraid. Oh, and brass elephants with their trunks raised."

"Very important, Maggie, that the trunks are pointing up," Socks said, holding the door as Saint Just walked around to the passenger side. "Sterling's really into this feng shui stuff, Maggie. We're going to stop by my apartment first and pick up my bagua. That helps you figure out which part of your place is the wealth area, which is the health area, which is the—"

"Thanks, Socks," Maggie said, starting the car, trying to ignore the fact that the key chain was in the shape of a naked man, waist down, and anatomically correct—perhaps more optimistic than correct. "Tell Sterling to make sure he locks up before you two go shopping, okay? And thanks for the loan of the car. I'll make sure to fill it up before I bring it back."

Socks grinned. "You might want to fill it up before that, Maggie. The gas gauge doesn't work, but I'm pretty sure you'd be running on fumes before you made it to the FDR. Oh, yeah, do you know how to go? Alex printed out directions from MapQuest, so that should help."

Maggie turned to look at her co-pilot and navigator. "This ought to be good," she said, putting the 1984 Chevrolet in gear and pulling away from the curb as Socks hurriedly slammed the door.

It wasn't easy to find a gas station in Manhattan, so it was another half hour before Maggie had merged onto the FDR Drive North ramp, and straight into heavy traffic.

"Very good, my dear. There's nothing to do now but drive until we reach the exit that takes us onto something called the Deegan Expressway. At which time you'll allow me to take over the wheel?"

"Oh, yeah, that's going to happen. You don't know how to drive."

"You do, my dear. Ergo, I should be able to do it."

"Chauvinist pig," Maggie said, wondering how offended Socks would be if she had Saint Just take the fuzzy dice off the rearview mirror. "Oh, wait. You mean you think you learned how to drive by osmosis or something?"

"Alas, probably not, as Sterling and I never left the apartment during the time we confined ourselves to living in your mind. No, I think I was being a chauvinist pig, actually. I mean, *you* can do it. If a female can do it, I don't see why a reasonably intelligent man couldn't—"

"You're driving me crazy on purpose, aren't you? Why?"

"Perhaps to keep my mind free of the thought that my life

is in your hands? Although I will say that you seem much more competent than Tabby, if you'll remember the small trip Sterling and I took to her summer home. Ah, Exit Eighteen. See it, Maggie? We're heading for the Deegan Expressway now. Very neatly accomplished, my dear."

"That's because you didn't look in the mirror on your side," Maggie said, ignoring the middle-finger salute coming from the driver's seat of the car she'd just cut off. "Next time, Alex, don't leave it until the last second. What's next?"

"Hmm, it appears slightly complicated here. FDR Drive N (and he pronounced all of the letters, to Maggie's mingled amusement and chagrin) has been followed by the Willis Avenue BR—I believe that means bridge—as we head right onto the bridge, which becomes Willis Avenue, then a right onto Bruckner Boulevard, then the Bruckner Expressway, the exit for New Haven, *back* onto the Bruckner Expressway somehow, and that becomes I-95, portions toll, for, oh good, 38.71 miles. I've taken fewer turns traveling from London to John O'Groats."

"Just give me that," Maggie said, snatching the printout from Alex and reading it as she drove. "God, these directions are nuts. Look, Alex, just play with the radio or something, and let me drive, okay?"

And he did. He played with the radio. Incessantly, looking for the Mets game until he realized it didn't start until two.

Maggie figured she'd ground down at least one millimeter of tooth enamel before they finally entered the small town that sat on the water, one wrong turn and a good thirty minutes after the fifty-five-minute drive time decreed by some guy at MapQuest who'd probably never driven in New York traffic.

"Pretty," Maggie said, driving slowly, on the lookout for a restaurant.

"Picturesque," Saint Just agreed. "Bernice informed me

that her house overlooks the water, so I would think we're traveling in the correct direction."

"We will be," Maggie said, turning into a gravel parking lot beside a small cafe bearing the sign Rosie's Place. "First, we eat."

"And then we toddle over there and procure the key," Saint Just said, pointing to the realty office directly across the street. "Ah, smell that air, Maggie. Pure ambrosia."

"It is nice," Maggie said, the smell of the water taking her back to her childhood in Ocean City, New Jersey, where her parents still lived . . . which made it not an entirely pleasant recollection. "Let's go. Hamburgers and fries sound good?"

"Not quite as tempting as a good joint and pudding," Saint Just said, at which time Maggie reminded him, yet again, to add the words "of beef" to "joint," before he got himself in trouble.

Maggie was just paying their bill when the door opened and a short, plump woman of indeterminate years with a very bad dye job came into the restaurant, at which time the man behind the cash register said, "Hi, Lureen. The usual?"

"Yeah, Joe, thanks, and to go, all right? I've got some nimrods coming up from Manhattan to look at the James house. Look, not rent. I'm not going to retire on that kind of commission—*none.*"

"Excuse me," Saint Just said, bowing to the woman as Maggie retrieved change from a twenty. "Allow me, dear woman, to introduce myself. I am Alex Blakely, here to see Ms. Toland-James's house. And you, I trust, are Mrs. Lureen O'Boyle?"

"Oh shi—shoot," Lureen said, offering her hand, which Saint Just bowed over, turning the woman's pale complexion to rosy red. "I'm . . . I'm . . ."

"Eager to turn over the key and direct my good friend here, Maggie Kelly—Maggie, say hello to Mrs. O'Boyle—to the James house?"

Maggie took the key Lureen fished out of her pocket, listened to the woman's garbled directions, and allowed Saint Just to bow her back out onto the pavement. "Sometimes," she told him as they got into the car, "just sometimes, I really love watching you politely rip idiots to shreds."

"Me? Don't be silly, Maggie. I merely rescued Mrs. O'Boyle from her own folly. We're turning here? Ah, is that it? It's nothing like Tabby's summer home."

"That's because my dear agent's place in the Hamptons is all glass and . . . heck, I think it's all glass, and yellow curtains, thanks to Sterling. This is Connecticut, Alex, and small-town Connecticut goes more for gray Shaker shingles and clapboard, whatever that is. It's pretty, but I can't imagine Bernie living here."

"Neither, it would appear, could Bernice, at least not for any great space of time. Shall we go inside?"

Maggie handed Saint Just the key as he helped her out of the car and he opened the door, letting out damp, musty air and the smell of rotting food. "Hit the lights, Alex, it's dark in here with all the drapes closed."

"I am here only to obey," Saint Just said, and the next moment the living room of the rather small house was bathed in artificial light. "How . . . quaint."

"It's pretty ugly, isn't it? While I was getting dressed Bernie told me she took out all her good stuff and had it replaced with renter type stuff," Maggie said, walking into the room, taking in the faded chintz couches, the maple tables, the overhead light that looked as if it was made out of an old wagon wheel.

She proceeded through the dining room, and opened the drapes on the back wall. "Oh, wow. There you go, Alex, that's what you pay for up here. Look at that view. I think you can see all the way across to Long Island."

"And I can see all the way to the kitchen, and evidence

that either Mrs. O'Boyle hasn't inspected the premises since the last tenants vacated, or someone has been living here."

Maggie followed Saint Just's voice into the kitchen, and saw about a dozen Brennerman's pizza boxes scattered on the countertops. Alongside the beer cans. "Buddy. He was here. That explains all the closed drapes. He was here, hiding out. For a while, considering this mess. Sonofagun, Alex, does this help Bernie or hurt her?"

"It does nothing, if we don't tell anyone what we've discovered until we know how such knowledge might affect the case," Saint Just said, heading for the staircase.

Maggie followed, and after peeking into two small bedrooms, found more evidence in the third one, the master bedroom probably, as it had its own bathroom.

"Don't touch anything," Saint Just said, using the tip of his cane to flip open a rather battered suitcase lying on the bed. "Coming or going, Mr. James?" he asked the room at large as Maggie peeked around him to see that the suitcase was half-filled with socks, underwear, and a small plastic bag she was pretty sure contained marijuana.

Maggie got a washcloth from the linen closet in the dirty bathroom and used it as a glove as she opened the closet doors. "Did he spend the last seven years in Hawaii? Look at these shirts, Alex. Pretty flashy."

"Bernice was married to a man who would wear those shirts? The mind boggles. However, I think I've discovered something much more interesting."

Maggie followed him across the room, to what must have been Bernie's makeup table. There, spread out on top, were newspaper clippings, about Kirk's murder, about Bernie's days as the prime suspect, about her being exonerated, the real murderer found, and Bernie having inherited Toland Books and Kirk's private estate.

"He knew," Maggie said as Saint Just poked at the clippings with the tip of his cane. "That's why he came back. He knew, and he wanted in, wanted his share. Damn it, Alex, we can't show this to anyone. It gives Bernie a motive to get rid of him."

"On top of another very reasonable motive, that being the three million dollars in insurance money she would have collected in a few weeks. I'm convinced he would have demanded at least half. Bernice really is much better off with Buddy James dead."

Maggie looked up at him mutely, wishing they both hadn't been thinking the same thing.

"However," he said, "I believe Bernice, if she were to contemplate murder, would have found some other way to dispose of the man. After all, everyone already believed him dead. Who would know?"

"You're right! Why didn't I think of that? Alex, you're brilliant."

"That being the case, I may drive us back to the city?"

"You're not *that* brilliant," Maggie said, heading for the stairs, eager to get back to the city while J.P. was still at the apartment.

CHAPTER 8

The drive back to the city was uneventful, with traffic increasing as they went because the president, they learned via the radio, had come to town for a fund-raiser. Although his visits always snarled traffic, today they included a gift—a total absence of media in front of Maggie's building.

"Socks, there you are," Saint Just said as he helped Maggie from the car. "I have a boon to ask of you."

"I don't know, Alex. I don't have any Boones. Got a couple of Crocketts, and they say my Bowie's pretty sharp."

Saint Just looked at him blankly.

"Ah, come on, that was funny."

"Wrong country, Socks," Maggie said, patting him on the back. "But Alex does a great Beau Brummell impersonation."

Now Socks looked blank. "The Beau Brummells? Hey, I know them. I listen to the oldies station. They're ancient, from the sixties. *Laugh, Laugh. Just a Little.* Bitchin', Alex. I didn't know you could sing."

"No, Socks, not the group, the—never mind," Maggie

said, giving up. "Have you been here all day? Is J.P. still up there?"

"The Wicked Witch of the West? No, she's gone. And the lieutenant was here and left again. We weren't here, but Ms. Toland-James told me when she called down to ask if I knew when you were getting back, and to tell me not to buzz up any visitors for at least an hour because she was going to take a bubble bath. That was about ten minutes ago. Oh, and Sterling really scored in Chinatown. A two-for-one sale on lucky bamboo."

"So Sterling is upstairs?" Saint Just was attempting to get all his ducks, as it were, in a row.

"No, he's at Mario's, storing up on Twinkies. Now I have to go move the car."

"Oh, right," Maggie said, handing him the keys. "Nice key chain."

"Sorry about that. It was a gift from my mom. She's got some really weird ideas about gay people, you know? But she tries. Oh, here comes Sterling. Hey, bro, don't forget you've got all those bags in the corner of the lobby."

"Sterling," Saint Just said, inclining his head toward his good friend, who had half a Twinkie sticking out of his mouth.

"Mmmmfff . . . hullo," Sterling said, then licked sugary white filling from his lips. "Home again, home again, jiggity-jig, right?"

"Sugar high," Maggie whispered to Saint Just.

"Shall we head upstairs?" Saint Just asked, swiping his key-card in the slot and then holding the door open for Sterling and Maggie. "I'll get those," he told Sterling, whose arms were already laden with groceries . . . if sugar and fat and artificial flavors could be called groceries.

"We'll deposit all of Sterling's booty in our apartment, Maggie, and then join you and Bernice," Saint Just said as they exited the elevator.

"I'll get the door. See my new key chain?" Sterling said, holding up a key ring that included a small brass elephant, trunk raised.

"Different animal, same upward gesture," Maggie said. "I guess maybe Socks's mother thought it was good luck?"

"Contain yourself, my dear," Saint Just said, waiting for Sterling to open the door.

"Oh, gloomy hour."

"It is? What's wrong, Sterling?" Saint Just asked, pushing past his friend to enter the apartment.

The living room was a mess. An unmitigated wreck. A disaster of epic proportions.

Couch cushions were on the floor, cut open. Pictures were stripped from the walls. Tables were overturned, their drawers pulled out.

"Henry?" Sterling called out, dropping his packages and heading for the sideboard, which had been overturned. "Henry? Where are you?"

"Ohmigod, Alex," Maggie said, squeezing Saint Just's arm. "If they hurt Henry . . ."

Saint Just was listening but, selfish man that he was, just barely. He was rather involved at the moment, looking from the bare space above the mantle to the floor and his completely destroyed plasma television machine, to the bare space, to the desecrated screen, to the bare wall, to the screen . . . and he had yet to even watch a Mets game on the thing.

"Did you find him, Sterling?" Maggie asked, stepping over a couch pillow.

"Be careful where you step, my dear," Saint Just said, coming back to attention, and to what really mattered, and Henry mattered to Sterling. Very much. "He may have broken out of his cage."

"Oh, damn, didn't think about that one," Maggie said, backing up. "I like Henry. I really do. But I like him in his cage."

Sterling was on his hands and knees, trying to lift the heavy sideboard. "Henry? Henry?"

"Here, Sterling, let me help. But, before we lift this, I must remind you that you are an Englishman. Whatever we discover, you will not flinch," Saint Just said, taking hold of one end of the sideboard.

"Oh, God, Alex, do you really think he's under there?"

"Henry!" Sterling shouted as he put all his weight into it, almost single-handedly lifting the sideboard, so that it fell against the wall with a thud. *"Henry!"*

"I can't look. Alex?"

"The cage is rather smashed," Saint Just said as Sterling dropped to his knees and picked up the cage. "But, wait . . . yes, there he is. Sterling, can you get him out? He's fine, Maggie."

"Henry," Sterling said, standing up, holding the misshapen cage in both hands. He turned and headed for the hallway. "Thank God, you're all right."

"Where's he going with Henry?" Maggie asked, picking up a small silver candy dish, an effort that made little difference in the shambles that had once been Mrs. Goldblum's quite lovely living room.

"He has a second cage in his bedroom that he uses for Henry while he's cleaning the larger cage," Saint Just told her. "And, now that Sterling's world is right again, perhaps you could spare a moment's silence for the demise of my plasma television machine?"

"Oh, Alex," Maggie said, carefully making her way across the room to look down at the broken set. "That was just mean."

"Yes, I do believe that was the point of the exercise, once our visitors realized they hadn't found what they were looking for."

"It."

"Correct. It. I imagine it is no longer feasible for me to

try to fob you off with any notion that I have ever considered our visitors a small problem. Shall we inspect the remaining rooms? I doubt their appearance will be much improved over this one."

"We should call Steve."

"Oh, most definitely. Good man. I had no idea he divides his time between *left*-tenanting and housekeeping."

"Wiseass," Maggie said, reaching into her purse for her cell phone. "This is a crime, Alex, it has to be reported."

"On the contrary. This is my problem, and I will solve it."

"So will I," Sterling said, coming back into the living room. He stood straighter, walked taller, and the set of his jaw, and both his chins, was almost impressive.

"Sterling? Henry is all right, isn't he?"

"All right? How can you say that, Saint Just? He had to have been terrified. What sort of monster would do such a thing? I vow, Saint Just, I won't rest until the miscreants are incarcerated!"

"The mouse that roared," Maggie said, picking her way through the debris to hug Sterling, kiss his cheek. "I love you, Sterling."

"Yes, I know," Sterling said, and Saint Just smiled as he watched embarrassed color run up his friend's face. "Like a brother, I remember. Thank you very much, and I apologize for being so fierce. But I am very angry. Exceedingly angry."

"Do you wish to turn over the investigation into these blackguards to Steve Wendell, Sterling?" Saint Just asked.

"What? Not avenge Henry myself? No, Saint Just, I won't have anyone else interfering when I find these horrible people. I want them horsewhipped." Then he frowned. "How are we going to find them, Saint Just?"

"Good question, Sterling," Saint Just said, remembering that he had slid the folder beneath one of the couches. "Maggie? Do you see the folder?"

"Uh-oh," Maggie said, always so wonderfully acute when

it came to deducing possible trouble. "Do you think they saw it?"

"Saw what?"

"Shhh, Sterling, and help me move these couches, if you please," Saint Just said, already tossing ruined pillows toward a corner of the room.

Ten minutes and some intense searching later, Saint Just dropped his quizzing glass over his head and rubbed the grosgrain ribbon between his fingers. "I think we can safely deduce that the folder is gone."

"That's probably not good," Maggie said, righting a reasonably intact Chippendale chair and sitting down on it. "I mean, now they know we know about them."

"We do? Isn't that above everything wonderful? What do we know?" Sterling asked, opening a Twinkie. "All I know is that someone broke in here and nearly killed Henry."

Saint Just and Maggie exchanged looks.

"Sterling, I've learned a few things about Mrs. Goldblum and her late husband. Rather disturbing things, and I promise to elaborate on all of them later, as we straighten this mess."

"I looked in the kitchen as I went by, Saint Just. All the cabinets were open and empty, and the floor was full of spilled flour and the like. You'll really help me clean up?"

"Of course I will," Saint Just said, ignoring Maggie's snort of disbelief. "Oh, very well, I'll be phoning Killer and Snake, and possibly even Mary Louise, if you must know."

"What, not Socks, too?"

"I'll have another mission for him," Saint Just said, and went off to inspect his bedchamber.

He stood in the doorway, his hands clenching and unclenching.

"Ah, Alex, all your pretty clothes," Maggie said, touching his arm as she went past him, into the room. "Did they have to throw all your clothing on the floor? Look, I know this is a shock to your . . . your sensibilities. Why don't you go call Mary Louise and I'll hang up everything, put everything back into the closet."

"I'm not going to fall into a sad decline, Maggie," Saint Just said, looking at his Weston designed jacket, the one he'd worn to his "debut" into Maggie's world. One sleeve was torn, and someone's very large feet had stomped all over it, leaving waffle-like treads on the fine fabric. "What was that quote you mentioned to me the other day? 'Don't get mad . . . '?"

"Don't get mad, get even," Maggie said, gathering up a half dozen crisply starched neckcloths that were now rumpled, and wet with the contents of a broken bottle of Obsession for Men, Saint Just's newly acquired favorite scent.

"Yes, that's it. It's not quite enough, is it? I fear I wish to get very much more than even. Considerably more. Stay here, I'll fetch a towel to wipe that up."

Picking up slacks and shirts and, surreptitiously, underwear, Saint Just pushed open the door to the bathroom.

He smelled the boot black before he saw the message written with it on the mirror above the sink: *Your dead.*

"They spelled *you're* wrong," Maggie said from beside him.

Saint Just, left eyebrow raised, looked down at her.

"Well, not that the grammar is important," Maggie said quickly. "I mean, it isn't important, right? What's important is that I think you're the *you* in that message. Or Sterling. Both of you. They must know two people are living here, having seen the bedrooms. And the you're dead business has to be about the file they found. I'm going to go call Steve. Don't say no again, Alex, because I'm going to call him. And I've got to check on Bernie."

Saint Just let her go, returning his interest to the message on the mirror. It was an empty threat. After all, no one killed the person from whom they needed information, needed *it*. What good would that do? It simply wasn't logical.

Then again, none of this was logical.

"Your chamber, too, Saint Just?" Sterling said, looking into the room. "Mine is a shambles."

"Yes, I'm sure it is," Saint Just said, escorting Sterling out of the bedchamber and closing the door behind him before his friend could see the bathroom mirror. No need upsetting poor Sterling further, as he had already advanced several yards beyond Incensed. "Maggie is phoning the *left*-tenant, so I suggest we vacate the premises, not touch anything else."

Sterling frowned, punched his glasses back up on the bridge of his nose. "But I thought we weren't going to ask for his assistance, Saint Just."

"I have reconsidered, to soothe Maggie, you understand. You know females, Sterling. They can be overly volatile at times like this."

"I've never had a time like this, Saint Just," Sterling said, then retreated to his room, quickly emerging with Henry. "However are we going to fix Mrs. Goldblum's furniture? She'll be that displeased."

"But not overly surprised, I imagine. However, she'll be considerably more than displeased when I locate her, Sterling, and ask her a few pertinent questions about her deceased husband, and about *it.*"

"Oh, yes. You were going to tell me something, weren't you? You didn't want to tell Maggie, right? I can understand that. Some things are simply too terrible for females, and all of that, as you said. Will you tell me now?"

Saint Just debated about correcting Sterling's misconception as to just whom he might be protecting, but decided against it. He slung an arm around his friend's shoulders. "Come along, Sterling. Henry will be safe enough here now, for I doubt the baddies will return any time soon. Let the two of us adjourn to Mario's for something to eat, and a little talk."

"But . . . but where will we sleep tonight, Saint Just? We can't sleep here, not if you won't let me straighten this mess, and if Lieutenant Wendell puts up that yellow tape the way they do on television programs, barring us from our own door."

"A very good question, Sterling, and one for which, sadly, I have no answer at this exact moment," Saint Just said as they stepped into the elevator.

He did, of course, have one possible answer by the time the elevator reached the lobby.

"Socks, just the man I wanted to see."

Socks looked at Saint Just with widened eyes. "Now what? You look a little . . . and Sterling, you do, too. Are you guys mad at me?"

"On the contrary, my good fellow," Saint Just told him. "Quite the contrary. Now, while Sterling and I are at Mario's, filling our bellies, I fear, I would like you to contact Mary Louise, who will then alert Snake and Killer to report here at, oh, seven o'clock this evening?"

"Sure. Is that all?"

"Not quite. Socks, tell me, how does your mother feel about overnight guests?"

"Huh?"

"Yes, I was afraid so. Probably a sad lack of extra bedchambers? Oh, well, then there's nothing else for it but for you to assist the others as they set the apartment to rights once the police are gone."

"I'm missing something, right?" Socks asked, looking at Sterling, who was still frowning as he stared intently into the middle distance, as if contemplating mayhem at any moment.

"I would say yes, you're missing something. Or, rather, that Paul missed that something while he held his post here, if he took your place this afternoon. A return visit from Sterling's two hatted gentlemen, as a matter of fact, or others of their ilk. They . . . redecorated our new apartment in our absence."

"Redecorated? Oh, jeez. You mean trashed, don't you?"

"They nearly killed Henry," Sterling said, his hands drawn up into fists.

"Henry? Oh, gosh, Sterling, I'm sorry. But he's all right?"

"Much better than my new television machine which, alas, you no longer will be able to use for that small soiree you and Jay were planning. A celebration of Judy Garland movies, I believe?"

"You knew about that?"

"I make it a point to know most things, Socks. Also, I saw Jay the other day when I was out for a stroll, and he not only thanked me for volunteering my new plasma television machine with its DVD player and surround sound, he also wondered if I preferred jalapeño to onion dip, as he is in charge of procuring refreshments."

"Oh, boy. I was going to ask you . . ."

"I'm sure you were. Mary Louise, Socks. Please contact her as soon as possible."

"Absolutely. Right away," Socks said, heading inside to make the call.

"How do you know everything, Saint Just? Did you really just see Jay-Jayne while you were out and about? I mean, it's a very large city."

Saint Just turned to head for Mario's. "You become unusually astute when agitated, Sterling," he said with a smile. "No, it wasn't a coincidence. Actually, Jay stopped by Maggie's the other day while you were out scootering, to ask if we also had a VCR machine, as some of his July Garland movies were in that format. I think he said format. But don't tell Socks. I'd much rather he think I'm omnipresent."

"All right. I don't think I'm hungry, Saint Just."

"In that case, order us each a cup of tea, if you please.

Earl Grey, as I've convinced Mario to provide it. Go on ahead of me, Sterling. There's something I forgot to mention to Socks."

Sterling nodded and continued on to Mario's while Saint Just retraced his steps to the canopy over the front of his building. He smiled, just slightly, in the knowledge that, by the time he joined Sterling, the man would have ordered a Reuben, his new favorite sandwich, and a diet root beer, as he liked the flavor of diet soda. Who could hear that last bit of information and not understand that Sterling Balder was actually a very complex creature?

"Socks?" he asked, reentering the lobby just as the young man put down the phone. "Did you reach them?"

"They'll be here. All but Snake. He's visiting his mother."

"Ah, yes, the dear creature who gifted her child with a switchblade knife, even going so far as to engrave his name on the hilt. Vernon. How could I forget? Where does she reside?"

"For the next eighteen months, she's in jail. Snake visits her once a month."

"I must be nicer to that boy," Saint Just said, shaking his head. "I have one more favor, if you don't mind?"

"Sure. And, you know, you guys could crash at my place, if you don't mind sleeping on the couch. I called Mom, and she said it was okay."

"How very kind of your mother," Saint Just said with a slight bow of his head. "I think we will be able to muddle through, however, now that I've considered the thing. Although I do have another favor to ask."

Socks struck a pose (a Saint Just pose). "I am yours to command, of course." Then he grinned. "How was that? For the audition I'm hoping to snag next week. I thought I'd give the guy a British accent. Soap opera fans like that kind of stuff. It's classy."

"So I've heard," Saint Just said, hoping his smile was gracious, appreciative. Encouraging. "And then there's your paperback romance cover model appearance, which will go a long way toward making you more attractive to prospective employers."

"It's one little paperback book cover, Alex," Socks said, jamming his hands into his pockets.

"Yes, and from little acorns, I'm told, mighty oaks grow."

"But don't give up your day job, right, Alex?" Socks said, running to open the door for Mrs. Yates, from Six-B. She handed him the plastic bag containing the deposit her poodle, Mr. Pinky, had made on the city sidewalk, and kept on going.

"She's a good tipper at Christmas," Socks said, shrugging. "What else did you want me to do, Alex?"

"After you dispose of that, you mean? What I'd like is for you to keep an eye on Sterling. And when I say I want you to keep an eye on him, I really mean both eyes, and I mean around the clock. Is it possible for you to ask Paul or someone to take your place here for a few days?"

"I suppose so. Why? What's wrong with Sterling?"

"Nothing that I can think of, other than a propensity to believe he's a chef. I will be fairly well occupied with Bernice's affairs, I'm afraid, and I'd like to assure myself that Sterling will be in good hands."

"In case those guys come back?"

"Precisely. I would like you to go to the park with him, to Mario's with him, to anywhere he decides to take himself. I want you to stay as close as sticking plaster to the man. Keeping to the maxim that there is safety in numbers, you understand. I don't ask that you protect him. Just that you grab hold of his arm and remove him from the scene of any possible trouble."

"At warp speed. I remember that picture of Mr. Goldblum, you know," Socks said, nodding. "And I can get Jay to help. Days. He's got a really sweet gig uptown this week. He's on stage as Judy Garland at a private club. Great costumes. And you should hear him sing. He almost makes you forget Judy wasn't six feet tall."

Saint Just had nothing to add to that, remembering Jay's flamboyant and quite convincing appearance as Jayne at the WAR costume competition, so he returned to the street and headed for Mario's, to give Sterling a highly edited version of the life and definitely messy demise of one Harold Goldblum.

CHAPTER 9

"Are you sure you're all right, Bernie?"

"Only until I explode because you keep looking at me as if you think I will," Bernie said, sliding her knees up beneath the hem of her satin caftan as she lounged on one of the couches.

Her eyes were wide, a little wild, her movements jerky, uncoordinated. "No, really, I'm fine. Strong. Recovered. Confident. Whatever you want, kiddo, I'm it. I'm back up to fighting strength, whatever that means. No more being scared out of my mind. I don't like me scared, you know? Not exactly the image I want to project."

"But you haven't had a drink since I got back here," Maggie said, not happy to be bringing up the subject, except that somebody had to, didn't they? But she'd keep quiet about the wild eyes, the jerky movements, and the way Bernie's words nearly tumbled over themselves as she spoke quickly, too quickly.

Maggie was getting nervous. She didn't think Bernie would explode, pop like a balloon. But she could.

"You're counting my drinks now? Oh, wait. Is that where you're going? You want to talk about my friend Johnny

Walker? I'm not on the wagon, if that's what you're hoping. I'm . . . I'm on the cart. Cutting back. Slowly. I get another drink in," she squinted at her watch, "five minutes. No, four and a half. That's it, four and a half. Four now. My watch is slow."

There was so much tension in the room, so many uncomfortable vibes. Like a pot of Angry, simmering, ready to boil. Maggie bit her lips between her teeth, then said what she had to say. "I don't think that's going to work, Bernie. Tapering off. You've got . . . you've got a problem."

"Yeah, and his name is Buddy James," Bernie said, reaching for Maggie's pack of cigarettes, which was on the table between the couches. "God, and I thought he was trouble the first time he was dead." She dropped the pack, slipped her bare feet onto the floor, and stood up. "Okay, hour's over. I mean, close enough. Johnny, baby, here I come."

"No."

Bernie turned her head, pushed back her flamboyant red hair and said, "What? What did you say?"

Maggie felt the ground shifting under her feet. "Um . . . it was no, Bernie. I said no. I don't think you should have another drink. J.P. said—"

"That was the phone call you took in the other room? My attorney? Operative word in that interrogative sentence, Maggie—*my. My* attorney."

Maggie would have very much liked to be able to pick up one of the throw pillows, to hide behind it. Bernie was looking just a little dangerous. And her voice was getting louder, even faster. Maggie hated raised voices, just hated them. Had hated them all her life. She hated confrontations, period.

But she couldn't back away, back down, hide. This was her friend.

"Bernie, please. J.P. said you might be arrested in the next few days. If that happens you'll get bail, she promised, but if the D.A. wants to be a prick—her word, not mine—he won't arrest you until it's too late in the day to get bail set before the next morning. You'll be locked up, Bernie, and Johnny Walker isn't allowed to visit. So . . ."

"So?" Bernie said, looking rather menacing in her green satin caftan, rather like she was ready to swoop on something. Maybe on Maggie. And, although Bernie was tall, she suddenly seemed bigger. Large, loud, domineering, all the things that set Maggie's insecurities into Red Alert Mode. But she pushed on.

"So, you've got to try to stop, now, before—not that it's really going to happen, but it could—before you're arrested. There, I've said it."

"Well, bully for you." Bernie chewed on the insides of her cheeks, her eyelids narrowed, her stance aggressive. "So you're saying I can't have another drink? Bottom line, Maggie. Redundant as that might be. Is that what you're saying?"

Maggie whimpered, but silently. "Yes, honey, that's what I'm saying. No more scotch."

"Fine, glad you clarified that. It's what I always tell my authors: clarify, clarify, clarify," Bernie said, heading for the drink cabinet. "You have any orange juice to go with this vodka? Never mind, I'll drink it straight."

"Stop showing off. You're not the town drunk, for crying out loud." Maggie clambered off the couch and grabbed the bottle from her friend's hand. "No. No more booze. J.P.'s on her way over with a plan to help you, and I promised her—"

"Oh," Bernie said, backing away, her chin sort of hiccuping as she went. "So that's it. J.P. She your new buddy, Maggie? Are the two of you *chums*? Two good *chums,* with a *plan.* Gee, next thing you'll be exchanging fucking friendship rings—while I'm getting fucked by some Fat Sadie in prison. Or, no. Not prison. A detox, right? You think you're going to lock me up in some detox? *Like a common drunk?* "

"Bernie, don't say the *f* word, please," Maggie said, wishing she herself hadn't said anything at all. It would have been so much easier to let Bernie have one more drink. Just one more, until J.P. got here, until Alex got here, until *somebody* got here. "Please, honey, don't do this."

Bernie grabbed up Maggie's cigarette pack and held it over her head. "How about I toss these in the toilet, Mags? Oh, look, little Maggie flinched. Got to you, didn't I? Poor Maggie, just as hooked as Bernie. They planning on locking you up, too?"

"Not yet, but I'll bet that day is coming," Maggie muttered, trying to marshal her thoughts. "Okay, Bernie, listen to me. You know you have a . . . a problem. I used to think it was social drinking, but since Kirk died and you had to take on so much at work and all—well, you drink all the time now. I'm your friend, you know that, but you're in trouble. You have to get sober."

"I *am* sober," Bernie said. Shouted. "I'm as sober as I want to be, damn it! Now leave me the fuck alone!"

Maggie wanted to back off. Oh, God, did she ever want to back off. The memory of her mother screaming at her, bullying her, dripping her special brand of sarcasm all over her, and over her father and the whole family, set off all the old feelings of just not being quite good enough.

But this wasn't her mother; this was Bernie. This wasn't an increasingly vicious contest of whoever yells the loudest wins, as it had become when her brother, Tate, had hit his teens and started screaming back. And she had to help her friend, not hide in her room, or in a book, or in some fantasy world of her own making. Bernie needed her. "I can't," she said with all the bravado she could muster. "I love you, so I can't leave you alone."

Bernie's shoulders slumped. "Damn you, Maggie. You're such a dweeb. 'Please, Bernie, don't say the *f* word.' Dweeb. This is killing you, isn't it? I love you, too."

Maggie collapsed onto the couch, vodka bottle in hand. "Because I'm a dweeb?"

"No, because you're gutsy," Bernie said, her bottom lip quivering. Bernie hated showing fear, had never shown it, not to this intensity, not in Maggie's memory. It was as if Bernie were more afraid of losing her Johnny Walker than she was of being arrested and sent to prison.

So Maggie tried to let her off the hook, tried a small joke, hiding behind humor when the going got too tough, as she always did. "Because I'm gutsy? I always thought you said it was because I'm neurotic, just like you."

Bernie smiled. "Oh, right, that too." Then her face sort of crumpled. "I need a drink, Mags. I'll admit I'm an alcoholic, if that's what it takes. I'll climb the twelve steps, whatever the hell that means. Give me the knee-jerk phrase and I'll repeat it, sing it to you if you want, for crying out loud. But one more, Mags. Just one more? You have to let me say good-bye, right? I'll just die if I can't have one last drink. My swan song. Maggie, please. I'm begging here."

She'd fought the good fight, maybe even gotten somewhere. But Maggie knew that Bernie wasn't going to be cured or broken or whatever the heck the right word was in one small moment, some melodramatic epiphany. Not with J.P. on the way, J.P. and her *plan*. "Okay," she said, getting to her feet. "Just a small one."

"Dweeb," Bernie said, already heading for the drink cabinet. "I scared you there for a minute, didn't I, Mags? But I knew I'd get to you. You're so easy." She grabbed up the bottle. "Come to Mama, Johnny."

Maggie felt something snap inside of her. Sort of go *sprrro–o-ing!* She shot from the couch like a missile out of its silo. "Give me that damn bottle," she said, capturing the Johnny Walker. "That was low, Bernie. How dare you push my buttons that way, get all loud and bullying, then all soppy and sorry and saying what I wanted to hear—do just what you knew would work on me?"

"Because I'm a desperate drunk?" Bernie asked, tossing

back her hair. "Because I'd do anything, even to my best friend, to get a drink? That I'd *kill* for a drink? Is that what you want to hear?"

"I don't think so," Maggie said quietly. "It can't be a good idea to let people think you'd *kill* to get what you want."

"Maggie, put a case of scotch on one side and a million dollars on the other, and I'd go for the scotch, every time. I didn't kill Buddy, Maggie. I don't remember, but I *know*. I did *not* kill that slimy little bastard. And I'm not a drunk. I'm just . . . drinking." She grabbed the bottle and retreated to a corner, like a squirrel off to hide a nut.

"Well, that one line would make one heck of a headline, wouldn't it? 'I did not kill that slimy little bastard,' " Maggie said, then closed her eyes in gratitude as Socks buzzed on the intercom. "Got to get that."

A minute later, J.P. Boxer was in the condo, taking it over, making it her own as she paced the carpet in her orange sneakers and black fleece jogging outfit with the white stripes up the sides.

"Drink up, Bernie," she said matter-of-factly as Bernie held the bottle protectively against her chest. "I want you listening to me, not trying to figure out how to get the next drink."

"I am not a drunk," Bernie said, pouring scotch into a tumbler. "You know how insulting you people are? I drink. Okay, I drink. But it's my problem, not yours, and I am *not* a drunk. Drunks talk to themselves and lie in gutters and drink Ripple. I have a life. I have a very important job. I *function*."

"Right, you're a functioning alcoholic. When you're not blacking out. When you're not waking up with a stiff next to you and can't remember how he got there," J.P. said, rolling her huge eyes. "But you're not a drunk. Why not make that a double, Bernie?"

"Oh, shut the—just shut up," Bernie said, filling a tumbler and all but slamming herself down on the couch. "Maggie says you have a plan. Let's hear it."

"Gladly," J.P. said, pulling out Maggie's desk chair and turning it to face the couches. When she sat down she still was tall, and big, and very imposing, but for some reason Maggie knew she'd never understand, she wasn't the least bit nervous around the woman. "Let's start with the bad news, shall we?"

Bernie saluted the lawyer with the tumbler, then said, "Is this where I get so scared straight I'll listen to any bullshit crap you tell me to do?"

Maggie rallied again. "Bernie! Cut that out. J.P.'s only trying to help. We're all only trying to help."

"Sorry, J.P.," Bernie said, pulling her legs up under her. "Maggie could tell you that I broke a nail earlier and I'm in a bad mood. You know how that sort of thing can screw up what was otherwise a perfectly great day, right?"

"Am I missing something here?" J.P. asked, looking at Maggie.

"We were discussing Bernie's drinking before you got here," Maggie told her. "I'm afraid I was pretty hard on her."

Bernie sprayed scotch and began to choke. "Hard . . . *hard* on me? Yeah, like being beaten to death with marshmallows. J.P.? Allow me to introduce you to my best friend, the Terminator. R–i–i–i–ght . . ."

"Oh, shut up," Maggie said, reaching for her cigarettes, then hesitating.

"Go on, Maggie. To each her crutch, that's what I always say."

"Thanks, Bernie, but maybe not."

Bernie's eyelids narrowed again. "Take one, damn it! I'm not the only addict in this room."

"Don't call me an addict."

"Why not? You do. Maggie Kelly, the happy nicotine addict."

"It's different."

Bernie downed half her drink. "In a pig's eye, it is. You're hooked, I'm hooked, all God's chillun is hooked on something. It's what makes the world go round. Nicotine, sex, caffeine, junk food, Xanax—booze. Pick your drug of choice, because we've all got one. You know," she said, waving the drink about, so that it sloshed over the rim, "what this world needs is less pointing fingers and more damn *mirrors*. Cripes, that was profound. I am so good. Aren't I, Maggie? I'm right, admit it."

Maggie glowered at Bernie, who glowered back.

"My, my, my, aren't we having fun," J.P. said, getting to her feet. "You two do these chummy sleepovers often? I don't know how to break it to you, but some girls paint each other's nails and talk boys. You two? You're beauts, you really are."

Okay, so maybe Maggie didn't like J.P. all that much. Didn't the woman understand *friendship?*

"Never mind us, J.P. Maggie and I never played well with others, but we understand each other, and that's all that counts. Now, what's your bad news?" Bernie asked, sipping her scotch once more, as Maggie lit her cigarette.

"His name is Dettmer. Chad Dettmer."

Maggie sat up, blew out smoke. "The D.A.? That guy with the pompadour hair weave and the rouged cheeks? He's in on this? *Already?"*

"Are you kidding?" J.P. said, shaking her head. "He's in up to his neck, and happy as a pig in slop. The election's in two months, remember, and good old Chad is having wet dreams about charging Bernie, putting his face in front of the cameras 24/7. You're a gift, Bernie. A high profile, too rich, sensational-headline-producing gift."

There was a knock on the door, and Maggie went to answer it. Obviously the person was someone she knew, and Socks had just buzzed him through.

"I think this is where I go back to saying *doomed, I'm doomed,*" Bernie said, then tossed back the remainder of her drink.

"So this Dettmer guy is going to arrest her?" Maggie asked, looking at Bernie as she opened the door.

"I can answer that one," Lieutenant Steve Wendell said, kissing Maggie's cheek as he entered the living room. "And that answer is, yes, as soon as he's got things nailed down a little tighter. Hi, J.P., and before you toss me out as a spy, I'm off the case."

"What do you mean, you're off the case? Bernie's case?" Maggie took his hand and led him toward the couch. "Why?"

J.P. said, "Let me count the reasons for you. Wendell is friends with the prime suspect. Also—nope, that's probably enough."

"Enough for what? Maggie, my dear, I could hear you yelping from the elevator," Saint Just said, closing the door behind him. "Sterling is downstairs with Socks, waiting for our jolly helpers. Hello, *Left*-tenant. J.P., you're looking well. What am I missing here?"

Maggie returned to the couch. "Steve is off Bernie's case, Alex," she told him, caught in what was becoming a familiar dilemma. Who did she go to, trust more, need more—Steve or Saint Just? Right now she—and Bernie—needed them both.

"Really," Saint Just said, looking at Steve. "How unfortunate. However did you manage that?"

"We already covered that one, Alex. The D.A. tossed him for conflict of interest," J.P. said. "How far off, Steve?"

He sat down beside Maggie, ran his fingers through his shaggy hair. "About as far as I can get. Dettmer suggested I use a couple of weeks of vacation I've had hanging for about a year now. He suggested it real strong, you understand."

"Pissed him off, did you?" J.P. asked.

"You could say that. He doesn't understand why I don't already have Bernie cooling her heels in an interrogation room. And he wasn't exactly pleased to hear you're on the case, J.P. I'm not saying you're not on his Christmas card list, but I don't think he likes you much."

J.P. snorted. "I'm a traitor, according to Chad. Left the good guys to defend the scum of the earth, and all for the money."

"That would be me. Scum, paying the money, all of it," Bernie said, hoisting her empty glass to Maggie in a sort of salute.

"Right," J.P. said, nodding. "But mostly it's because I win more than I lose. Steve? Did he threaten you, or did you just take the hint before it got that far?"

"You know how it is, J.P. First the suggestion, then the threat of unpaid leave, a whiff of I.A.B. waved in my direction. Internal Affairs would have had a field day. I will admit, the crime scene was a circus. I didn't come off looking too good, giving out favors, practically having a tea party in the suspect's living room. Doing tours through the crime scene. I'm not proud of any of that."

"You were being a good friend," Maggie said, squeezing his hand. "Besides, you know Bernie didn't do it."

"What I know, Maggie, is that we've already got the results from the crime lab on the fingerprints on the murder weapon."

"Bernie's?" Maggie asked, her stomach doing a small flip.

"Bernie's."

"Ah," Saint Just said. "Exactly as I predicted. Our murderer is so very obvious."

Wendell looked at Saint Just, shook his head. "Dettmer wanted me to bring her in, but I told him she'd already lawyered up and it went downhill from there, especially when he found out J.P. was on the scene before I got there.

But he's holding off because fingerprints aren't enough, not if we don't find more, and if Bernie can keep refusing to talk to him."

"But I don't remember anything. It's true, Steve. Maggie, tell him about the blackouts."

J.P. held out her hands. "Wrong. Don't tell him about the blackouts. Blackouts are not a defense. Steve, you tell me something, because I'm not buying this. Why isn't Dettmer here with a warrant?"

Saint Just, Maggie noticed, was being unusually quiet, just standing on the edge of the carpet, watching.

"Because the techs found blood in the shower drain, for one. Until we get results on that, there are still more questions than answers, and Dettmer may be a jerk, but he isn't a joke. He won't move until he's got more than fingerprints."

"Like motive," Maggie said. "Does he know about the insurance policies on Buddy?"

"It's Sunday, so he's still pretty limited. But he will tomorrow. What will he know, Maggie?"

"Well, you see—"

"Shut it, Little Mary Sunshine," J.P. said, stepping in front of her. "Why are you here, Steve?"

At last Saint Just spoke. "To help, of course. I vouch for the *left*-tenant personally, J.P."

J.P. looked around the room. Bernie nodded. Maggie all but preened. Saint Just returned her look levelly, then winked; Maggie felt a tingle down to her toes at that wink. Only Steve appeared the least surprised, and he, too, was looking at Saint Just.

"Okay," J.P. said at last. "As long as we don't have to hold hands and sing 'Kumbaya,' I guess we've got a team. Just don't make me regret this. Spill it, Sunshine."

Maggie sat forward on the couch cushions. "Buddy has about three million in life insurance that becomes Bernie's when the seven years are up, except that they don't have to be up yet because now Buddy's really dead, and Bernie gets the money right away to help Toland Books become really, really solvent again after that mess with Kirk, unless she goes to jail for killing him, but the D.A. will definitely see a motive because if Buddy came back to either get cut in on some of the money Bernie inherited from Kirk, or to make her split the three million, which he would have to have been planning all along, and which doesn't exactly exonerate Bernie anyway, because the two of them could have been in on the whole thing together for seven years but then Bernie got greedy at the last minute—is anyone else getting this?"

"We've got motive," Steve said, patting her hand. "Got ya, sweetheart."

The room was quiet for some moments before Saint Just spoke again. "Explain the blood in the shower drain, Wendell, if you please. Are you saying that the murderer committed his crime, then bathed?"

Steve nodded. "Which makes no sense, because Bernie was covered in blood when you guys first saw her—sprayed with it—and you don't get covered in blood, arterial blood, once the victim is dead.

"Unless she killed him. A slice to the throat, then quick lying on her side while Buddy . . . *spurted,* so that you could see the outline of her body in the blood. Then she took off her pajamas, showered to get rid of the worst of it because it was really disgusting, got back into the pajamas, smeared some blood on her face and hands, and then called us. But why would she do that?"

"Sunshine, stick to fiction," J.P. said, standing behind the facing couch, her beringed hands on Bernie's shoulders. "Most women don't like blood all over them and I'm pretty sure Bernie here is no exception. But that's pushing it. You don't shower to wash off blood, then cover yourself with it again. Nope, there has to be another reason for the blood. No wonder Dettmer isn't here yet, cameras in tow. When he arrests her, he wants to make sure it's going to stick, and that I won't be able to paper his office with motions to dismiss. Steve—did they find the victim's clothes yet?"

Steve nodded. "We did. In the bathroom, all folded and stacked neatly on a stool. Why?"

"My turn, if you don't mind," Saint Just said, perching himself on the arm of the couch, beside Maggie. It was like being between particularly appealing bookends. "I can think of no one, including myself, who would, in the throes of or anticipation of—forgive me, ladies—*passion,* who would take the time to neatly fold his or her clothing. Therefore—"

Maggie held up a hand. "Unless he was in Bernie's bathroom when she came home, waiting for her after sneaking in somehow, and just about to take a shower when she found him there, naked? Argue, argue, sex, sex, sleep—sneak downstairs and get a knife. And he's dead?"

"I would not have sex with that bastard," Bernie pronounced tightly. "Drunk, sober, blacked out, sane or crazy as a loon. I would *not* have sex with Buddy James. And fold his clothes? Buddy? First he'd have to get lessons."

"Steve?" J.P. asked. "The rape kit?"

"Nothing's back yet, not officially."

"Okay, unofficially."

"I'm off the case, J.P., but I'm still a cop. Sorry, but you're going to have to go through channels."

"Ah, a man of honor. How refreshing. And they also performed a tox screen, correct? Although those results are undoubtedly still pending as well?"

This was from Saint Just, and Maggie looked up at him in surprise. "Did you say *tox screen*? Oh, wait. Cop shows. I keep forgetting."

"Actually, my dear, the Learning Channel, as well as the History Channel. But we won't nitpick. So, this Dettmer fellow, hot as he is to arrest Bernie, is still awaiting results from the crime lab that would cement his position, although his intent seems already to be chiseled in stone. How long do we have, J.P.?"

"To solve the crime, or to stash Bernie?"

"Excuse me?" Bernie, who was in the midst of pouring herself another scotch, turned to look at her attorney. "This is happening? Are you really going to stash me somewhere?"

"That's dicey, J.P.," Steve warned her.

"Not with voluntary commitment papers, it isn't. She hasn't been charged. She hasn't even been interviewed. Nobody's pulled her passport. She's as free as you or me, and I'm going to make sure she stays that way. Sort of," J.P. said, opening her attaché case and pulling out some official looking forms. "Alex, you were right. Good call. The man's a sleaze, but he's well known, and hot to get his name in print. He jumped at the idea."

Maggie narrowed her eyelids and looked up at Saint Just. "Who's well known? Who jumped? Cripes, Alex, when do you find the time to get into so much trouble? What did you do?"

"Come on, Bernie," J.P. said. "You won't need luggage, so just throw on some clothes and we're off to see the good doctor and get these papers signed. There was no press when I came in, but that isn't going to last much longer. I want to get out of here without a tail."

"Maggie?" Bernie asked, her voice quavering.

"In a minute, Bernie. Alex? Who jumped? Are we talking Doctor Bob here? *My* Doctor Bob? We are, aren't we?"

Saint Just only smiled at her, then crossed to the other couch and sat down beside Bernie. "We're going to protect you, Bernice," he said in a tone that, even to Maggie, inspired trust. "And Maggie guessed correctly. You remember Doctor Bob, don't you? Maggie's psychiatrist? You published his book, *Love Well, Live Free*?"

"Ah, Jesus, Alex, you're going to have me *committed*?"

"Legally tucked away, my dear," Saint Just corrected. "Doctor Bob, it would seem, carries considerable influence, and he has already made arrangements for you to be a guest at a very lovely establishment in something called the Catskills."

Maggie was stunned. He'd sent J.P. to Doctor Bob? He ridiculed Doctor Bob every chance he got, tried to get her to stop her every-Monday visits to the man's office. And now he'd contacted him? Was *using* him? She didn't know if she should be surprised, disgusted, or damn proud he'd thought of it.

"Still New York State, Bernie," J.P. interrupted. "You won't be crossing state lines, the D.A.'s office is only told you're a patient, and nobody can touch you. It's legal, Bernie, marginally, and I want you out of here almost as much as I want you sober."

Maggie blinked at tears stinging her eyes as Bernie seemed to collapse in on herself, suddenly the small, frightened child sitting where the supremely confident, wisecracking, sophisticated woman had been.

"But . . . but what about my interview with Holly What's-her-face?"

"Canceled," J.P. told her. "I wasn't going to mention it, but now that you've brought it up I might as well tell you. Fox wouldn't go along with Alex's demands for a straight interview, no opinions, so that's done. Fox is interviewing Dettmer instead. You know, Alex, it was a good idea, until it backfired. Now Spivak will be saying how she tried to interview Bernie, give her a chance to tell her story, but that Bernie insisted on controlling the interview, so that, as a *real* reporter, Spivak had to say no. This is *not* going to play well to the jury pool, let me tell you. Now go on, Bernie. Get dressed."

"I'll help you," Maggie said, following a slump-shouldered

Bernie into the guest room, then pulling her into her embrace while her friend shivered.

"I don't know, Mags. I don't know what scares me more—being arrested or going cold turkey. I might not make it through this."

"Sure, you will," Maggie said, sniffling. "You're my hero, remember? The bravest, most ballsy woman I know."

Bernie pulled away from Maggie, wiped her streaming nose with the sleeve of her caftan. "I am, aren't I? Ballsy." She took a deep, shaky breath, let it out slowly. "Okay. Okay, Maggie, let's do this."

CHAPTER 10

Saint Just opened the door to Tabitha Leighton, Maggie's agent, and stood back as the woman swept past him, blonde hair moving through the breeze of her quick step, the scarf around her neck floating. He nearly missed the large, soft-sided suitcase she all but tossed into his arms.

"Where's Maggie? She must be devastated! Do you know there are about a dozen reporters outside? What a mess; I had to fight my way through. I was in the Hamptons all weekend, incommunicado on something very important, but then I finally turned on the television and saw it and I've been calling ever since. Doesn't anyone answer a phone here? Maggie—*yoo-hoo!* It's Tabby!"

"Maggie's not here," Saint Just told her, gesturing that she should have a seat. "Although I am assured she would be grateful to know that you have rushed here to be a supporting prop in this, Bernice's hour of need."

"Maggie's gone? Gone where? Oh, no. She's down at the jail, isn't she? They've arrested poor Bernie. I knew it, I just knew it. And *now*, of all times."

"Actually," Saint Just said, depositing the suitcase on the floor beside the couch, "Maggie and Bernice and J.P. Boxer, she would be Bernie's solicitor, are on their way to an undisclosed location where Bernice will be receiving remedial training, shall we say."

"Remedial . . . huh?"

"She's going to get help with her drinking problem."

Tabby nodded her head a single time. "Oh. Well. Good. About time, don't you think? But . . . but isn't she going to be arrested?"

"Only if I have not discovered the true murderer before she is, as they say, dried out, and released. She was not best pleased with the plan, but we managed to convince her of its efficacy. Actually, Maggie should be well on her way home by now, Bernice safely tucked up and neatly tucked away."

"Oh, wow. I'm glad I wasn't here when you were talking her into it. So I guess we won't need the suitcase just yet."

"I don't understand," Saint Just said, looking down at the thing.

"Clothing. I brought clothing for Bernie. Just threw a few things into a bag. You know her wardrobe, Alex. Flashy, expensive. Juries hate that. So I brought her a small selection of outfits."

Saint Just looked at Maggie's literary agent, who was dressed, as usual, in flowing scarves, an ankle-length soft skirt, and a quite sedate blouse. Tabby tended toward natural cottons, pastels, clothing that, to be charitable, was serviceable, if usually two sizes too large.

Bernice, on the other hand, dressed with a flamboyance that complemented her fiery hair, her vivid makeup, and her general arrogant carriage. "Versace versus Laura Ashley" was how Maggie had explained the thing to him.

"That was exceedingly thoughtful of you, Tabitha," Saint Just said, then walked over to the answering machine. Earlier he had turned off the ringer on the telephone, not that many knew Maggie's unlisted number.

But when he'd checked her America Online account (a

habit he should break but was loath to do, as he not only de-
plored the amount of penis enhancement and Viagra-clone
spams she received, but did the occasional housekeeping
that removed all but the most flattering fan mail), he had discovered three hundred and eighty-two messages received via
her Web site.

A cursory check had revealed that the majority of e-mails
were from various reporters, inventive little cretins that they
were. Now, he supposed, it was time to discover how many
of them had found a way to procure her telephone number.

"Excuse me for a moment, my dear," he said, and pushed
the PLAY button, as the message indicator was flashing.
There were three messages from Tabby, one from the head of
the condo committee tersely demanding that she remove a
murder suspect from the premises and rid their formerly
quiet building of the masses of reporters outside, and two
others:

"Maggie? Maggie, it's Virginia. I saw the news on television and I just had to call. This is terrible, just terrible. Poor
Bernie! I'm sure she didn't do it. Gosh, and to think we were
all just together at the WAR conference, and so happy. Well,
happy, but not really happy, what with the murder and all,
huh? Oh, I hate talking to machines. Call me, Maggie, okay?
I know it's stupid, and selfish, but do you think this means I
won't get a contract with her like she said? Oh, scratch that.
I shouldn't have said anything so stupid. I don't care, really I
don't. Okay, so I do. I'm shallow, I admit it. Call me, okay?
Oh, and the baby is just great. I'll e-mail a photograph to you
next week. Call me!"

Saint Just hit the STOP button. "Virginia Neuendorf," he
said as Tabby nodded. "Quite a mix of concern and selfish-
ness, not that I blame her."

"I've already got the contract on my desk to go over,"
Tabby said. "She's safe."

"Good," Saint Just said, and pressed the PLAY button again.

"Margaret? Margaret, I know you're there. This is your mother, Margaret. Can't you stop? I pick up the newspaper and what do I see? That Bernice woman, that's what I see. A murderess! Well, that's it, Margaret. This it your third strike, young lady, and you are *out*. Your father and I insist that you sell that horrible New York apartment and come home where you belong. Can't you people go more than two weeks without killing someone? I have a reputation here, young lady. How can I hold my head up when you keep trampling our faces into the mud? Never, never have I seen such tawdry— what? Evan, if I say Margaret comes home, she comes home. And stop pushing those chocolate things into your mouth. I swear, you're going to clog every artery in your heart and— what do you mean you're not interested in living forever? Was that supposed to be a dig at me? It was, it was a dig at me. You know what? She's just like you, Evan. Smart mouth. Weasely. Sly. It's all your fault. Heaven knows I tried. Margaret? Margaret, you listen to me. Tate already called, all upset, and Erin and Maureen are embarrassed to be your sisters, what with those artsy-fartsy people you run around with in the city. Your own siblings, ashamed! Must you be such a black sheep, always hurting me? It's that writing you do, all that perverted sex and smut. I always knew that Bernice person was trouble. That hair? And she's got a smart mouth. Didn't surprise me she killed her husband. I still think she killed the other one, I don't care that you say someone else did it. Class will tell, Margaret, and that wom—"

"Now there's a bit of luck. It would appear the machine ran out of space before Mrs. Kelly ran out of invective. Shall we just erase this?"

"Oh, God, yes," Tabby said, hugging herself as she shivered. "Come home? Maggie would rather have someone shove bamboo slivers under her fingernails. You know, Alex, I deal with crazy publishers and crazy writers, day in, day out, but that woman scares me."

"She is unique," Saint Just said, holding down the DELETE button. "There, all gone. Do stay and visit until Maggie returns, and that won't be long. I was just collecting some additional cleaning supplies for Sterling, however, and have to return to my own apartment."

"Cleaning supplies? You?"

He picked up a blue bucket holding a plastic bottle of something called Spic and Span, and several sponges. "As I said, for Sterling. Join us, please. We've located one chair that is still reasonably intact."

He opened the door and bowed a frowning Tabby across the hall, then let her into the shambles that was once his apartment. The bedrooms and his private study were nearly back in order, and most of the kitchen, but the living and dining rooms were so far untouched.

"What . . . what on earth happened here?"

Saint Just ushered Tabby to that one intact living room chair. "A long story, not really worth telling. Suffice it to say we have come to the conclusion that the previous tenant has something someone else seems to very much want, and that someone else decided to look for that something themselves."

"A robbery," Tabby said, nodding her head. "No. Not a robbery? Alex, what's going on? And Steve? You're here? *Cleaning*?"

Steve, his sleeves rolled up, a large, bulging white garbage bag in his hand, nodded to Tabby. "Like Alex said, long story. Alex? This place was tossed by pros. You do know that, right?"

"Pros?" Tabby looked from one man to the other. "I'm confused. Does this have something to do with Bernie?"

Seeing that there was nothing else for it but to explain, Saint Just did just that, while Killer and Mary Louise, having proved themselves to be quite accomplished workers, began picking through the debris in the living room and dining room.

"The mob?" Tabby said at last, looking around her rather frantically, as if deciding whether or not to bolt for the nearest exit. "But they're dangerous. Maybe even crazy."

"And most definitely messy," Saint Just agreed as Mary Louise began picking up bits of a broken lamp. "But we'll soon have it all to rights."

"You're going to *stay* here? Tell me you're not going to stay here. They might be back."

"Yes, they might, as every room in the apartment was searched. Unless the last place searched was the one in which they discovered what they were after, I would say our visitors left with their hands empty." He frowned slightly, remembering the folder Holly Spivak had given him. "Mostly empty."

"But not before writing that note," Steve said, having just returned from dropping the garbage bag down the chute in the hallway. "I got a call on my cell while I was dumping the garbage, Alex. That friend I told you about? He says we're probably dealing with the Totila family. Enrico Totila. Minor league, nowhere near a John Gotti. Goldblum was their mouthpiece, but Enrico, the head guy, was upstate on a weapons charge when Goldblum was offed, and nobody could get anything to stick to him. He's out now, been out for about six months. He's our guy, count on it."

Tabby got to her feet. "I . . . I think I'd like a glass of water. And I could help in the kitchen. Really." She grabbed the bucket, then picked her way through the living room.

George, who persisted in going by the name Killer even as Saint Just tried his utmost to bring the boy up to snuff, enter him into the business world (i.e., The Streetcorner Orators and Players), surfaced from behind one of the couches, large pieces of a broken vase in his hands.

Killer was a thin, almost pathetically weasel-like lad with a good heart, the brains and courage of a particularly dense doorstop, and the bladder control of an infant.

"Did he say Enrico Totila?" he asked, dropping the pieces into a previously empty metal waste can, where they broke into even smaller pieces.

"Yes, I do believe that's exactly what the *left*-tenant said, George. Why do you ask? Do you know the man?"

"Me?" Killer's small eyes grew almost large in his head. "No. Not me. Don't know him. Oh no."

"Calm yourself, George," Saint Just soothed as the boy backed up three paces, colliding with the wall. "Hang on to your bladder, remember?" Then he sighed, as Killer remained one of the regrets of his life, a youth he could reach at some levels, but not really effectively change. "No, not literally, George."

"You're from up around Morningside Heights, aren't you, George?" Steve asked as Killer dropped his arms to his sides, blushing. "The Totila family doesn't operate up there."

"No, sir. But his aunt Isabella, she lived next door to my grandma, and Mr. Totila, he'd visit her. He spit on me once."

"How utterly charming. Thank you for sharing that, George. And now, I think perhaps you should toddle off to Mario's for some of his marvelous sandwiches and salads, to reward everyone for their kind assistance. Oh, and do *not* speak to any of the reporters who may remain outside on the flagway."

"Okay," Killer, ever obedient, said, taking the money Saint Just handed him and all but bolting for the door.

"Now," Saint Just said, turning to Wendell. "Where do I find this Enrico Totila person?"

"You don't," Steve said, shaking his head. "He finds you. Hell, he's already found you. What we have to do is find what he sent those goons to find."

"And you don't mind that I've refused to call in your cohorts?"

"Normally, yeah, I'd mind. I'd mind a lot. But let's just say I'm not too happy with my cohorts, as you call them, right now. Besides, this one would go straight to Dettmer, and he's too happy as it is, with Bernie. Plus, I have a feeling you want a piece of these guys. You know, the TV set?"

"I would be a liar if I disagreed. Even Sterling, as you said, would want a piece of them. You can have them after we're done, if that's all right."

"Just don't leave me out of the loop. I'm giving you some rope, I'm not giving you the whole damn lasso."

"Whatever that is. So, you'll help us find the perps and then make the bust yourself after we're done with them?"

"Maggie's right. You watch too much television. We don't say perps. TV cops say perps."

"Really? What do you call them, then?"

"Bastards, pieces of—well, I guess they can't say that on TV, huh?"

"I don't think so, no."

"Cable. They can do it on cable. And movies." Wendell righted an end table. "You know, Blakely, we're sort of getting along here."

"Yes, I had noticed that," Saint Just said, picking up what had to be a hand-crocheted doily. "Rather odd, considering we're in competition."

"Maggie, right?" Steve ran a hand over his hair. "She told me you're not close cousins."

"Very distant, yes," Saint Just said. "I'm quite . . . fond of her."

Steve grinned. "I guess then we can rule out flipping a coin for her, huh? Just kidding. So, you're staying? Not going back to England?"

"No, I've no plans to return to . . . my estates any time

soon. I've been longing to come here for some years, you understand."

"Okay, it was worth a shot. So we're in competition. I can handle that. Doesn't mean we can't be friends, or work together."

Saint Just struck a pose. "Oh, *Left*-tenant, that had to hurt."

"You got that in one. But, hey, we're doing all right, so far. I mean, working together. If we could only keep Maggie from sticking her nose in, that is."

"That adorable little nose is a problem, and I agree that we should collaborate in keeping that nose out of trouble, even while we acknowledge that our intents are the same and our hopes vastly different," Saint Just said.

"If you just said that we protect Maggie, keep her out of trouble, but we're both free to . . . well, go after her, then you got it."

"How very wonderful, and allow me to express my condolences at what I am convinced will be your undoubtedly futile attempts to *get* her. Now, having cried friends, if we might return to the problem at hand? With Bernice safely out of the picture, Maggie will consider herself free to insert her inquisitive nose, not only in the investigation of Buddy James's demise, but also in the small problem we've encountered with this Totila person."

"Who?"

Saint Just closed his eyes, then slowly turned around, to see Maggie holding on to the doorknob. "Back so soon? How delightful. And is Bernice settled comfortably?"

"Are you kidding? I have imprints from her fingernails on both forearms. Want to see? But J.P. finally peeled her off, and we left. Nobody can visit her or call her. Not even J.P. So, what have I missed? Who's Totila?"

"Like I said, we work together," Steve said quietly to Saint Just.

Saint Just inclined his head a mere fraction in acknowl-edgment of Wendell's whisper. "Enrico Totila, my dear Maggie, was the late Harry Goldblum's client, his only client, estab-lishing him as our prime suspect in this wanton destruction of my property. The plasma television machine, remember."

"Oh. The mob boss who ordered this place trashed to find whatever it is Harry had and Irene's got? I got it. So? We confront him?"

"Heaven preserve me from females possessing the world's most undesirable trait."

"Here we go," Maggie said, glaring at him. "And what would that be?"

"Pluck," Saint Just said, lifting his quizzing glass to his eye and looking at her through it, knowing his eye was now enlarged by the glass, knowing that she'd love to, in her words, "bop him one" for using that glass on her. "Yes, pluck. It's vastly unbecoming to the gentler sex, whose role in life is to defer, stand back, admire, and then applaud their gentlemen."

"Okay, consider me off the team, at least for now," Steve said, backing up.

"Would you stop, both of you? I'm not going to be in-sulted, and I'm not going to be diverted, or whatever it is you two have dreamed up between you."

"She heard us," Steve said to Saint Just.

"Yes, I believe I've already deduced as much, thank you, Wendell. Maggie? The *left*-tenant and I have, as you've al-ready heard, joined forces. In Bernice's behalf, and to ferret out whatever is going on here in my apartment. We have also cried friends in protecting you from . . . well, from you, my dear. Which means, behave yourself and don't get into trouble."

As Maggie stood there, jaw dropped, he turned to Wendell and said, "This is where she says *bite me.*"

Maggie closed her mouth, then opened it again to say, "No, it's not. I understand. You want me thinking, helping, but not acting. Not doing anything on my own, getting myself in trouble."

"Or possibly shot at, yes," Saint Just said, patiently waiting for the other shoe to drop. Because this was his Maggie. He'd lived inside her head. He knew the girl, bless her.

"Yeah? Well, you can both go to hell, okay? Bernie's my friend and she needs help, and if that means I end up sticking my neck out for her, then that's what happens. And the same goes for Sterling. You?" she said, pointing to Saint Just. "You just take care of yourself. You, too, Steve. Now, I'm going to bed."

"The moment she's finished looking up Enrico Totila on Google, although I doubt the mob lists its addresses in their directory pages," Saint Just told Wendell, wiping his quizzing glass on his shirt sleeve as Maggie turned to leave the apartment.

"I could seriously hate you sometimes," she said, turning back to glare at him.

"Maggie? Maggie, is that you?"

Saint Just watched in some amusement as Maggie attempted to hide a wince at the sound of Tabitha Leighton's voice. Maggie liked Tabby, very much, but the agent did have this annoying way of saying all the wrong things at precisely the wrong time.

"Hi, Tabby," Maggie said, waving weakly.

Tabby, wearing Sterling's KISS THE COOK apron and large yellow rubber gloves, picked her way across the cluttered floor and put those gloved hands on Maggie's shoulders, brushed cheek against cheek. "How's Bernie? Have they locked her up tight? She must feel as if she's already in prison. I saw the news before I came here, and they're calling her the Black Widow. She shouldn't wear black to the arraignment. I brought her some clothes, but all of that can wait. I've got the most *fabulous* news!"

Such as now, Saint Just thought, shaking his head.

CHAPTER 11

Maggie wanted a shower, a long, hot one. She wanted something gooey, preferably chocolate. And she wanted to be alone. Completely alone. She wanted to shed a few tears for Bernie, who had looked like a frightened child as she and J.P. had left her at the clinic with a kindly enough woman who also had the build of a fullback and one hamlike hand wrapped tightly around Bernie's arm.

She wanted to look up Enrico Totila on Google, exactly as Alex had said. She wanted to change the sheets on the guest room bed again, and make sure both Sterling and Alex promised to sleep there tonight.

She wanted a cigarette. She'd kill for a cigarette. No, scratch that. Not a good choice of words. But she wanted one, desperately. An hour up to the clinic, an hour there, an hour back—three hours without a cigarette. The thumbnail on her left hand was already bitten down to the quick—a habit she thought she'd lost at twelve.

But Bernie couldn't have a drink. If Bernie couldn't have a drink, then she couldn't have a cigarette. It wouldn't be fair. Not that anyone got locked up because they smoked. Yet.

Maggie stared at her reflection in the bathroom mirror. "I am an addict," she said quietly, forcing out each word. "I am a . . . damn. Nicaholic? No, that's stupid. Try again, Maggie." She lifted her chin. "I am addicted to nicotine."

Her brother Tate had gone to military school, and for some reason a snippet of something he had to repeat to upperclassmen when he was a plebe—freshman—snuck into her mind now. "I am a worm, sir, a wiggly worm, sir. . . ."

Maggie lowered her head, shook it. "Maybe tomorrow," she said, and headed back to the living room, which was pretty much stuffed to the rafters with people she currently wished would all find somewhere else to go.

"Tuna's fine, thanks," Steve Wendell was saying, accepting a wrapped sandwich from Mary Louise as he straddled one of the chairs at the game table.

Killer was sitting in Maggie's favorite spot, the window seat, dangling string cheese into his gaping mouth with all the dexterity of an octopus in boxing gloves.

She looked behind her, to see that Sterling and Alex were conferring in a corner of the kitchen, and Sterling didn't look very happy.

Tabby, spreading a napkin in her lap, her sandwich waiting for her on the coffee table, didn't see her, so Maggie retreated from the living room and went straight to Alex and Sterling.

"What's up?"

Sterling, bless him, immediately looked at the ceiling, before recovering with a sheepish grin. "That's not really what you meant, is it, Maggie? Sorry, and all of that."

"That's okay, Sterling. Hey, I like your gloves."

Alex did one of those highbrow English *tsk-tsk* things and said, "Please don't encourage him, Maggie. Sterling, take those things off. I'm begging you, which is something I don't ordinarily do, but you must know you look ridiculous."

Sterling held up his hands, still encased in bright yellow

rubber gloves. "But I still have to clean the bathrooms and Tabby says it's important to protect one's hands when one is . . . oh, all right."

"Bless you," Alex said, then turned to Maggie. "Bernice is really settled in and fine?"

Maggie felt quick tears sting at her eyes. "No," she said, almost whined. "And I'm such a lousy friend. If she's going to dry out, then I shouldn't light up, right? Support her, you know?"

"It's a laudable idea," Alex told her kindly, then added, "but I do believe you have to stop smoking for *you,* not for anyone else."

"Yeah, that's what Doctor Bob says. I see him tomorrow morning."

"Ah, yes, our every-Monday-morning session with the good doctor. You wouldn't consider giving up those sessions for *you,* would you?"

"I know you don't like that I go there."

"Always the mistress of understatement."

"But I think I'm finally getting somewhere, Alex. I mean, I really don't want to smoke. Besides, I want to thank him for helping out with Bernie when you asked. He didn't have to do that."

"No, he didn't," Alex said, nodding his head. "By the way, you owe him five hundred dollars."

"I . . . he . . . you're *kidding.* He did it for money? He's a *doctor.* How could he have done it for *money*?"

"I believe he termed it a consultation fee," Alex said, inspecting his fingernails.

"Oh," Maggie said consideringly. "I guess that makes sense. Five hundred dollars?"

"A pittance compared to what you've paid the man over the years."

"Would you stop? He's helping me."

"Really? Your mother phoned earlier, left a message.

She'd like you to move back to New Jersey, tuck yourself under her protective, maternal wing. Demanded it, actually."

"Sweet Jesus," Maggie said, maybe pleaded, as her stomach hit her toes and her knees buckled slightly.

Alex touched a hand to her cheek. "Yes, Doctor Bob has been such a tremendous help. It's so obvious. Maggie, my dearest girl, you're rapidly approaching three and thirty years of age. Isn't it time you stood up to the woman? Faced her down, informed her that you are an adult now, and in charge of your own life?"

"Sure," Maggie said tersely, but not moving, because Alex was touching her, and his comfort, his hand, felt good. "I'll do just that. Right after I can stand up to the dry cleaner when he tells me it's my fault he lost my blue coat. Can we talk about something else?"

Alex smiled at her. "We could *do* something else, to take your mind off all your varied worries."

"Um . . . excuse me?" Sterling said, gulped. "I think I'll go wash up your bathroom, Saint Just, if that's all right with you? I mean, if you're going to be romantical, and all of that. Snake has come back from visiting his mother and he's still over there. He was going to throw out your television machine, Saint Just. I'm so sorry about that. I'll take him a sandwich and we'll keep on straightening up. I can't abide the shambles, I'm afraid. Maggie? Did you know you made me neat? Isn't that amazing?"

Alex was looking at Maggie as Sterling rambled on. Maggie was looking at Alex. Maggie was forgetting that there was anyone else in the room, in the world. She allowed herself to start leaning forward, her eyes on Alex's mouth.

"No!" she said suddenly, stepping back, grabbing onto Sterling's arm. "Alex, tell him no."

"It's all right, Sterling. You may go, since you're so hot to find reasons to wear those atrocious gloves. Remembering your waistcoat, I'd say it's probably the yellow that holds the attraction. Say hello to Vernon for me, if you will, and give him my thanks for his help."

Maggie watched Sterling leave the room, then turned on Alex. "Are you nuts? He'll see the threat on the mirror."

"Actually, no, he won't. It has already been taken care of, removed. Now, as we've put it off long enough, and Tabitha has doubtless finished her sandwich, I suppose it's time we heard her *fabulous* news."

"I could have choked her for that," Maggie said, sighing. "I mean, she means well, but tonight? How can there be any good news tonight?"

"Slap me down for saying so, but I thought we might have been making some *happy* progress a moment ago," Alex said, extending his arm, so that she took it. "Now, to listen to Tabitha and then usher her out. Usher all of them out."

"Stop that," Maggie told him, leaning against his arm. "You don't really think I think sex is the answer to all my problems."

"No, but I thought you might want to consider it."

"Bite me."

"Ah, an invitation. I'd be delighted, my dear. Nibble, that is."

Maggie's stomach tightened. "Cut that out. You're just trying to get me all flustered and make Steve think something was going on in the kitchen. That is so low, Alex."

"Not if it had worked," he said, dropping his arm as she let go of it and headed for the couch, to plop herself rather inelegantly next to Tabby.

"Okay, let's have it. What's this fabulous news?"

Tabby patted her mouth with her napkin and replaced it on her lap. "Maybe this isn't the time?"

"Good," Maggie said, slapping her knees and getting to her feet. "Because you're right, Tabby, now isn't the time. I've got Bernie on my mind, news hounds at the front door, the mob after Alex and Sterling, my mother on my back, and—"

"We sold to the movies."

Maggie stood, mouth still open, and blinked. Blinked again. *"What* did you say?"

Tabby openly preened. "I've been working on this for months, Maggie, with my agent associate in Los Angeles. I didn't want to tell you, get your hopes up, but this weekend cinched it. We've sold your first three books for television movies. Now, I know it's not the big screen, but it's a start, and a good one. Someone else will write the scripts, but we've got approval—that took some doing, let me tell you— and they've even invited you out there to watch the whole thing. Cast selection, you name it. I worked hard, Maggie. I really did."

Maggie sat down. It was either that or fall down. "We . . . we sold to the movies? Ohmigod . . ."

"Hey, Maggie, that's great," Steve said, sitting himself on the arm of the couch and leaning over to give her a kiss. She blinked again. Her ears had begun to buzz.

Tabby took Maggie's hand in hers, patted it. "I didn't get everything I wanted. It was a package deal, the first three, but I figure that it's better to get less up front for three than just take our chances with one. We have to build an audience, although they're counting on your readers tuning in. And I got some substantial bonus clauses written in, as well as the possibility that, if the ratings are good enough, the third one goes to the large screen. Or, and this could be even better, they turn it into a series. They've even agreed to put your name on them. You know, like *Cleo Dooley's Viscount Saint Just Mysteries—The Case of the Misplaced Earl*. It's long, but having your name there is big, really big. Maggie? Say something."

So she did. She said the first stupid thing that entered her head: "I can't fly to California."

"Oh, jeez," Mary Louise said, grabbing up her purse and motioning for Killer to follow her. "See? Told you she was weird. Come on, let's get out of here. I've got class in the morning. Hey, Maggie, you don't care if I keep the purse, right? You know, the one you loaned me for the conference? I kind of like it."

"I can't fly to California. I just can't."

"Right. Knew you wouldn't mind. See ya, Vic," she said, waving to Alex. "We see Mr. Pierre tomorrow at one, right? Gotta sign on the dotted line."

Vaguely, Maggie heard Alex agree to meet with Mary Louise. She heard Mary Louise, but she didn't seem able to form either the words "I didn't give you that purse, Alex did, and I want it back, damn it!" or "Don't call him Vic. It's Viscount, *Viscount.*"

Alex. Alexandre Blake, the Viscount Saint Just. Her Alex Blakely. He'd heard what Tabby had said. He had to have heard, even understood. Yet he hadn't said anything. Why hadn't he said anything?

"Alex?" she said, leaning forward to see past Steve, to see him standing there, fingering the grosgrain ribbon on his quizzing glass. "What do you think?"

"I'm considering the possibilities, actually. Very good, Tabitha, procuring script approval. And we'll be able to weigh in on who is to play the characters in the books? I should not wish anyone I did not approve of pretending to be—Saint Just."

Maggie rolled her eyes. Oh, this was going to be good. One fictional character casting another fictional character. Casting himself. "Maybe you want to play the role, Alex?" she asked, then immediately wished she hadn't.

"It's another of the possibilities I've been contemplating, yes."

"But . . . but he can't do that. He's gorgeous, and I know you based your Saint Just on him," Tabby said, tugging on

Maggie's arm. "But they want real actors. Maggie? Tell him."

"She's right, Alex," Maggie said, grinning at him. "They want real actors, not real characters. Not that it matters, because we're not going."

"Because you can't fly to California," Alex said, inclining his head slightly. "Yes, we've heard. Might we now inquire as to why?"

Maggie looked from one to the other, to Tabby, to Steve, and at last, to Alex. "Because they have earthquakes out there, that's why, and you damn well know it. I don't like to fly anyway, but the minute my plane's wheels hit the tarmac out there, count on it—*bam,* the big one will hit. Next thing we know, Nevada is beach front property. Not that I'll care, because I'll still be strapped to my seat in a tin can, three miles under the ocean and a couple of million pounds of California."

"Quite the verbal picture," Alex said to Steve. "She's a writer, you know. Chock full of imagination."

"Maybe you can talk to Doctor Bob about this tomorrow," Tabby said. "I know he's helping me with David. I'm doing affirmations now. You know. I am a good person, a worthy person, a good, worthy person deserving of love. Really, Maggie. Affirmations."

"Tabby, David sleeps with anything he can catch. How do affirmations change that?"

"I don't know," Tabby said, sounding hurt. "But I know I don't deserve it, because I'm a good, worthy person."

"No, you don't deserve it. You don't deserve David catting around, Tabby. Bernie doesn't deserve to be blamed for Buddy's murder, Alex and Sterling don't deserve to have that apartment over there trashed and their stuff all ruined, and I don't—well, I guess I'm doing okay, aren't I? I'm sorry, Tabby. You're right, this is great news. Me, selling to the movies."

"Made-for-television movies," Tabby corrected. "Wait until Bernie hears about this. She'll be hot to repackage your earlier books, maybe even with photographs of the cast on the covers. Saint Just, in the flesh. Can you imagine the *god* they're going to have to get to be your perfect hero?"

Maggie shifted her gaze to Alex with an unspoken "don't you say it, don't you say a word" flashing in her eyes.

Steve bent down and kissed Maggie, then got to his feet. "Congratulations, Maggie. I'd better get going, though. Alex?"

"Steve," Alex said, and Maggie shook her head. She didn't know why, but she was pretty sure she'd liked it better when they'd addressed each other as Wendell and Blakely. She did not need the two men in her life liking each other. She definitely didn't like them planning ways to keep her in the dark about Bernie's case, about this Enrico Totila guy.

"Hey, where are you two going? If you're going to talk about Bernie or the mob, you can talk right here, damn it."

"Yes, you do that, just as Maggie says," Tabby said, gathering herself and standing up. "I'll just clear away all this food, all right? I really don't want to be involved, you understand. It's not that I don't care, really it isn't. But it's frightening."

Maggie waited until Tabby had loaded plates and glasses on a tray and escaped to domestic bliss in the kitchen before saying, "So? What's next? Start with Bernie."

Alex gave a wave of his hand. "Oh, go ahead. She'll never let us rest, elsewise."

Steve went back to the straight-back chair, straddled it once more. "Okay, here's what I've got. Maggie? You already know about the blood in the drain."

She nodded.

"Okay, but that wasn't all there was."

"It's a shower drain," Maggie said. "There's got to be a lot of stuff in it, right?"

Steve rubbed at the back of his neck. "Yeah, right. The

blood. I'll find out when they get an ID on it, through my source, count on that. And . . . the rest of it. Man, this is why I don't like working with women."

"Gee, thanks," Maggie said, looking at Alex. "No wonder you two like each other."

Steve was still rubbing at the back of his neck, and avoiding her eyes. "They found hairs, too. It was easy to identify Bernie's—red, you know? But four others."

"Four other hairs," Maggie said, nodding.

"Four other, um, *donors,*" Steve clarified, his cheeks reddening. "Maybe more. Four different ones so far."

"Oh," Maggie said, looking down at her hands. "Well, she is single, you know. Is that it? Is that all you know?"

"Pretty much, yeah. Nobody signed in as Bernie's guest, I know that, so either she snuck Buddy in the back way, or he got in on his own."

Maggie sat up. "If he got in on his own, so could somebody else."

"Damn, Maggie, I've already got Bernie and Buddy. Don't add to the mix."

"We have to, Steve, unless you think Buddy committed suicide in Bernie's bed, holding Bernie's hand to the knife while he sliced his own throat, and nobody would believe that. So, somebody else could get in if Buddy got in on his own?"

"Anything's possible."

"Not anything, Steve," Alex said, pocketing his quizzing glass. "It is not possible that Bernice murdered Buddy James."

"Wrong. It is possible. I agree, she would have had to be really strong to damn near cut his head off like that, but she could have done it. Crime of passion. And, once Dettmer gets that stuff about the insurance? He's going to see a slam dunk here. I wish I could trace James's steps, backtrack on his moves. I could maybe get something there."

Maggie felt Alex's gaze on her, but wouldn't look at him. "Oh, why not?"

"If you insist, my dear. Steve, it may be possible that Maggie and I have discovered the recent whereabouts of Buddy James."

"Damn. I should just turn in my shield and pack groceries or something. Where?"

Maggie filled him in quickly about Bernie's Connecticut house and the evidence they had found when they drove up there, Alex adding, "The man was a bit of a slob, with a decided appetite for what you call fast food. Pizza in particular. There were bags and boxes everywhere, along with some of his personal belongings. I would deduce that he had been in residence at least a fortnight and, as the bills I saw scattered about included a delivery charge, remained hidden in the house and had his meals brought to him."

"Dettmer has to be told about this."

Alex stiffened, and Maggie fought an urge to duck. "I beg your pardon?"

"Withholding evidence, Blakely. I can't do that."

"Ah, Wendell, but I can, and you're on holiday. We are friends here, talking, and anything we say is in confidence."

Maggie hid a smile. They were back to Wendell and Blakely. Good. "Guys, guys, think about this. So Buddy was at Bernie's house in Connecticut. So what? I mean, face it, Steve, you have to know that Alex and I went through the guy's clothes and everything. There's nothing there for Dettmer to find. Is there, Alex?"

"Don't answer that, because I think I'd have to start yelling if either one of you is naive enough to think contaminating yet another possible crime scene, or at least a scene connected to a crime, is like your good deed for the day, or something. Oh, and you can do a better job examining evidence than the lab boys. Sure you can." He got to his feet and slammed the chair back under the table. "Cripes almighty, I can't believe this."

Alex perched himself on the arm of the couch. "A trifle perturbed, the good *left*-tenant, wouldn't you say? Tell me, Maggie, do you find him more or less appealing this way?"

"Shut up," Maggie hissed at him, then got to her feet and went to Steve. "We're sorry. But it wouldn't be good if you went to Dettmer with this, would it? I mean, now Alex and I have our fingerprints all over the place. And the real estate agent is sure to remember us, come to think of it."

"Aiding and abetting, concealing evidence, corrupting a crime scene, hiding the prime suspect—anything else you two? Or are you all done now? Never mind, I'm on vacation. I don't want to know. Maggie—tomorrow."

Once the door had closed behind him, slammed behind him, Maggie blew out a breath and sat down again. "That wasn't good."

"I agree. He's of no use to us now."

"What? Is that all you can think about? That he won't be of use to us? What about him? What about Steve? He's really mad, Alex."

"No, he's in a snit. He'll move beyond it. He did say he'd see you tomorrow. Now come along, let's roust Sterling and Snake out of the apartment and get some rest."

Maggie looked at the mantel clock; it was almost midnight. "Good idea. These have got to have been the two longest, most screwed up days in my life."

She didn't resist when Alex slid his arm around her waist as they walked to the door, and then across the hallway to the apartment. The door was ajar, but that didn't mean anything.

The note on the floor just inside the door, however, did.

Alex picked it up, Maggie immediately feeling icy panic sliding down her spine as she saw the cut out letters that made up the message:

Tern It over or the littel guy Dies

Below the cut and pasted letters was another line, hastily scribbled: *And the other one to.*

Maggie ran toward the kitchen calling, "Sterling! Sterling! Snake, where are you?" She knew it wouldn't help, that they were gone, but she had to try. From the kitchen to the hallway, into the bedrooms, calling out their names until Alex caught up with her and pulled her close against his chest.

"Oh, Alex, what are we going to do?" She pushed herself free of his arms. "Steve. He just left. Maybe I can still catch him."

She turned to race to the elevator, but Alex took her arm, held her. "He's already gone, Maggie. Go back across the hall and I'll be right with you, after I lock this door."

"But . . . but . . ."

"Now, now, calm yourself. In a situation like this panic, my dear, aids nothing. And I might suggest that we can divest ourselves of Tabitha's presence."

Maggie took a deep breath, which didn't do much to calm her. "Good point. But I'm waiting for you."

CHAPTER 12

"Well, that's all done," Tabby said, entering the living room just as Maggie and Saint Just closed the door to the hallway. "You know, Maggie, it would be a lot less expensive to buy the meat and bread separately and make up your own—what's wrong? You're really pale, Maggie. Something else is wrong, isn't it? Do I want to know?"

"No, you don't," Maggie said, holding her hands to her head. "You don't want to know. Go home, Tabby. Go home, and I'll talk to you tomorrow, okay?"

"That was certainly well played, my dear, although perhaps not quite as subtle as I might have liked. Still, you did restrain yourself from making *shooing* motions with your hands," Saint Just whispered, busying himself with leaning his sword cane, just rescued from the apartment, against the wall.

"You can do better?" she whispered back.

"Go home? Well, it is late." Tabby looked at Saint Just. "Alex?"

He stepped forward and took her hand, bowed over it. "I cannot begin to express my gratitude at your stunning success in settling Maggie's books so nicely, Tabitha. And thank you so much for all your concern, as well as your splendid housekeeping. However, the hour is late, and Maggie, dear girl, is not quite herself. The commotion over Bernice, you understand. Now, might I escort you downstairs to have Paul hail a hack?"

"Show-off," Maggie muttered on her way to the couch.

Tabby frowned. "Um . . . okay." She picked up her sweater, then looked at Maggie, who was sitting and staring at . . . actually she was simply staring. "Get some sleep, honey. I'll call you tomorrow. Ba-bye."

By the time Saint Just returned to Maggie's condo, she had kicked off her shoes and was sitting cross-legged on one of the couches, smoking like the proverbial chimney. To help her think, he knew. "Paul saw nothing, in case you might have thought to ask. As I had to wake him to make my inquiry, I had already fairly well deduced that he'd be no help to us."

"Damn. Socks would have seen something. Okay, okay, let's forget that. I'm calmer now. Here's what we have to do. We have to call Steve," she said, not even looking up at him. "He'll call in the FBI and they'll set up a task force or something in here, waiting for the call from the kidnappers to arrange the drop, and we'll . . ."

"Sterling isn't real, Maggie," Saint Just reminded her, sitting on the opposite couch, neatly crossing one leg over the other. "Thanks to Mary Louise and her inspired forgeries of all the necessary papers, Sterling and I *appear* real, but a closer inspection would prove that the pair of us arrived from nowhere only a few short months ago. Do you really want that? The FBI, and eventually, the media, probing into Sterling's life? Oh, and Wendell, of course. You'd have to tell him. Dear Steve, sit down, I have something to tell you. Alex and Sterling are real, you can see them, they're really here, but they didn't get here in the usual way. They popped out of my head."

"Shit," Maggie said, which Saint Just took to mean *no,* she didn't want that. "So what do we do? That note was so stupid. We still don't even know what *it* is. And you and Sterling might be fictional, Alex, but Snake isn't. And neither are these goons. They *kill* people."

"I am aware of that," Saint Just said tersely. He was holding on, attempting to project an air of calm. But, inside, he very much longed to throttle somebody.

How dare they! How dare they go after Sterling, a completely lovable, guileless, and, unfortunately, often clueless Sterling Balder? If they injured him, if they frightened him, if they harmed a single hair on the man's balding head . . .

"Alex? Alex, I'm talking to you."

"Pardon me, my dear," Saint Just said, only then realizing that his hands had clenched into fists. This wouldn't do. The Viscount Saint Just was the epitome of calm at all times, in any storm. A veritable brick in a crisis. The Viscount Saint Just held all the answers, all the solutions, and possessed all the derring-do necessary to save any day. With aplomb.

Except that, he was realizing more and more, the Viscount Saint Just had Maggie Kelly making sure all the miscreants failed and her perfect hero triumphed in the end. Damn. Damn and blast. The whole thing was quite lowering at best, and at worst it was dangerous.

"Alex? Don't apologize. And stop looking so far away, okay? Talk to me."

Maggie Kelly as Cleo Dooley, setting up problems for her hero to solve, giving him the leading role, the brilliant mind, the inventive ploys, even the current heroine—and most definitely the happy endings. It came from Maggie. Everything came from Maggie. He was a fraud, a fake, a . . . a paper thin creation. Could he really allow Sterling's fate, Vernon's fate, to rest in the hands of such a sham?

But this was no time to lament truths he'd only just realized, or to attempt to play the hero at Sterling's expense. It was lowering, yes, depressing—and, dear God, totally out of *character*—but there it was. He needed help.

Saint Just blinked. "Perhaps we should contact the good *left*-tenant."

"Really? Wow, what hit you?" She grabbed the phone from the side table and punched in the numbers. Then waited. "He's not answering. I'll try his cell." More number pushing, more waiting. "He has it turned off. Man, he must really be mad at me. Now what do we do?"

Saint Just took his quizzing glass from his pocket and placed it over his head, began fingering the ribbon as the glass swung at the end of it. Perhaps this mindless activity, one of his trademarks courtesy of Maggie, would help him think.

After all, he was more than a cipher, a figment of her imagination. He had gotten himself here, hadn't he? With no help from Maggie. He had, in his arrogance, solved two murders since his arrival.

So why the apprehension? Why this sudden, inexplicable fear? He'd never felt fear, not in any measurable amount.

"I hope Sterling is behaving himself," Maggie said, putting down the phone.

And there it was. Sterling. His Sterling. His friend. His very good friend. Sterling held all the answers to this sudden bout of insecurity and, yes, self-pity.

Because this wasn't a lark, this wasn't an intellectual exercise. This most certainly wasn't fiction. This was Sterling, alone, possibly injured, and with the threat of death hanging above his head unless he, Saint Just, could save him. Knowing Sterling, he also knew his friend depended on him, expected him to arrive on the scene in full rig-out and complete glory to effect a rescue—preferably a flamboyant rescue. He could not, he *would* not let him down.

"I'm sure Sterling is fine, Maggie," Saint Just said, getting to his feet to pour them each a glass of wine. Taking charge, taking command, because that was what he'd been born to do, even if he had only been "born" six years ago, in Maggie's fertile imagination. "As for us? I fear there's little we can do save to wait for some communication from his captors. That, and locating this ridiculous *it* they seem to crave."

Maggie accepted one of the glasses and took a sip. "Yes, you're right. That's what we need to do. I'll call Steve back, leave messages on both his phones, and tell him to call me on my cell. Where is it? I want to take it with us while we search the apartment again."

"You do know that it would be reasonable to assume that whatever these thugs want departed the apartment with Mrs. Goldblum?"

"I know. But we've got to come up with something. Even a fake something. Something we can say we have so that they agree to meet us and we can see Sterling."

"I concur," Saint Just said, putting down his wine glass. "Shall we?"

Maggie beat him to the door and across the hallway, into the apartment. "Wow, it looks a lot better. They did a good job."

"Yes, they did. Now we must do a better one."

For two hours they searched, knocking on walls, stamping on floorboards.

"Alex, come here," Maggie called from the living room as he contemplated pulling the refrigerator away from the kitchen wall. "I've found something."

He hurried to the living room to see her sitting on the floor, pulling a multitude of crumpled papers out of the bottom of a very large brass pot. "What is it, Maggie?"

"Old bank statements and canceled checks. She must have used them to stuff this pot before she put the plant container in it. You know how old people can't stand to waste anything."

"Actually, I don't. But do go on."

"Shut up and look at this one," she said, holding up one of the statements.

"I don't . . ." He sighed. This being imperfect rather than perfect was beginning to prove a strain on his sensibilities. "Explain, if you please. I'm convinced you're all agog to do just that."

Maggie got to her feet, took the statement from him. "They're from 1995, all of them. I guess she figured she was safe to toss them after seven or so years. IRS, you know."

"Nine years, Maggie. Nineteen ninety-five would mean nine years. And the same year, I believe, her husband was murdered."

"Hey, right. This is good. Anyway, she shows a deposit, third of every month from March on, for a cool fifteen thousand. Was he murdered in February, do you remember? Oh, well, never mind. Ten thousand of that goes out later in the month. She uses a check payable to cash so I can't tell where it goes, but it goes in like clockwork on the third. I'll bet it still does."

"Blackmail? Ill-gotten rewards from illegal activities?"

"I don't know, but I doubt it. I don't think the mob works on the installment plan, Alex. It could be some sort of income Harry set up before he died, was murdered. Something perfectly legal and legitimate. No matter what, Irene wasn't a poor little old lady living on some meager fixed income. She wasn't loaded, but she was plenty comfortable."

"And this aids us how?"

"Wait, I'm not done. You know what I didn't find, Alex?"

He wanted to get back to the refrigerator. He felt certain he could move it if he just found the proper leverage. "You didn't find anything the mob might want."

"No, I didn't. But I also didn't find any canceled checks for rent on this place. Or a monthly condo fee, like I pay. She owns this place, Alex. She owns it and nobody knows. I'll bet Harry made some private arrangement when they bought it, some under the table deal with the seller. Why would they do that?"

Saint Just shrugged. "I'm afraid I must admit my ignorance. To save herself the monthly condominium fee?"

"Or Harry bought the place with those ill-gotten gains you mentioned. Paid cash. Mob money, you know? Under the table bucks the IRS never got to hear about? With some extra bucks for the seller so he kept his mouth shut."

"I believe I'm getting the headache. All this unbecoming cant."

"Slang is slang, and you watch enough TV to know what I mean." She threw down the papers, the checks fluttering to the recently cleaned hardwood floors. "Yeah, well, it is interesting, and I'd love to get my hands on Irene Goldblum and ask her a few questions. Just not right now, huh? We keep looking?"

"We continue looking, yes," Saint Just agreed, sparing a moment to look at the bare space over the fireplace, where his marvelous plasma television machine had so recently hung in all its glory. "Maggie?"

"Hmmm?" she said, having replaced the small ficus tree and in the process of shoving sphagnum moss around the top once more.

"The landscape. I put it in one of the closets, but Sterling took it downstairs, to the storage area."

"You're kidding. How big is it?"

"Quite large. Quite homely. Shall we? It may mean nothing, but perhaps the area holds other secrets."

"We'd need the key to Mrs. G's bin."

"I saw some keys in one of the kitchen drawers," Saint Just said, already heading that way. He was progressing, doing something, and it felt good. *Remain calm, Sterling, good friend. I will not let any harm come to you.*

Dear Journal,

I'm not really writing this because my hands are tied behind my back, tied to Snake's hands, actually, and the two of us are sitting in a dark room somewhere, but I am writing this inside my head because Saint Just always says that it is helpful to talk to one's self about problems in order to discover workable solutions.

I feel rather silly talking to myself. So now I'll talk to you, inside my head, and see if a workable solution presents itself.

Let's see. First, dear Journal, I opened the door, which, Saint Just would tell me, was not only my first action but my initial mistake. What could I have been thinking? Oh, I remember. I was thinking that perhaps it was Saint Just come to help us finish straightening the apartment. My, perhaps I wasn't thinking but only imagining hopefully. Dear Saint Just. He wasn't created to be domestic. It isn't his fault. He was created to give orders, not take them.

I, on the other hand, was created mostly to listen to him when he speaks, and make comments he can then answer. But still he talks to himself inside his head, which is a wonderment. Saint Just is quite complicated, as is Maggie. They are so alike, and yet so different. Saint Just will rail and say something witty at me once we are rescued, and Maggie will kiss my cheek and give me a hug. Then she'll rail at me. I don't suppose I would want Saint Just kissing my cheek, so that's all right.

Snake is being terribly quiet, but then, so am I, which has to do with this rag stuffed into my mouth. Quite an ill-bred, ill-mannered pair of captors, if I must say so myself.

But here we are, my having opened the door and those two large men having pointed wicked looking pistols at us and obliging us to leave the building with them without calling out or otherwise bringing any attention to our dilemma.

Not that Paul, who is manning the doors tonight in lieu of Socks, would have noticed if we'd left the building with our hair on fire. The man, as Saint Just would say, is next door to a yahoo, and with the brains of a flea.

And so here we are, dear Journal, Snake and myself. In the dark. Trussed up like chickens, our mouths stuffed shut, and without the faintest idea what will happen next, except to know that Saint Just will be exceedingly put out when he discovers we're gone.

But not to worry. Saint Just will find us, I know that. Snake, poor boy, does not, so he might well be terrified, while I am only mildly upset.

Moderately upset.

But I do know my place in all of this. That place is to sit still, sit quietly, and await rescue. Because rescue is not my job, it's Saint Just's. He is the hero, after all . . . and, oh dear.

You can't see it, dear Journal, but someone is removing my bonds. Is that a good thing or a bad thing? Shall I ask? If that someone removes this horrible rag I could . . . "Well, thank you. That wasn't entirely hygienic, you know. Could I please have a drink? Something diet? And perhaps a light? It's terribly dark in here."

"Shut your pie hole, jerk. Come on, youse and me are gonna go make a movie."

"A movie? Isn't that a coincidence? Tabitha Leighton—I don't believe you've been introduced—told me earlier as we were cleaning up that mess you made—no offense—that we're going to be a movie. Saint Just and myself, you understand. Well, not really *us*. It's rather complic—oh, a light. Thank you. Snake, we have light. Open your eyes, Snake."

"No way, no how, no fuckin' *way*," Snake said, his eyes squeezed shut. "Can't kill you for what you don't see."

"Oh," Sterling said, looking at his captor. "But I'm afraid I have to point out the error in your reasoning, and all of that, because we have already seen—um, never mind."

"Shut up and come here, fatso."

"No. I think not," Sterling said, backing up, backing into Snake. "Saint Just would not obey orders from a—ah, excuse me. I was very nearly brave there for a moment, wasn't I? That's because of what you almost did to Henry, you know. You should be ashamed of that. Truly asham—"

As Sterling lay on the floor, five-pointed stars circling his head, he thought to himself, *Dear Journal. I am a fool. . . .*

"Anything?"

Saint Just looked over his shoulder, his head nearly colliding with Maggie's. He'd taken a knife with him to the basement storage area, and used it to slice open the back of the ugly landscape. "Just this rather odd key," he said, holding it up.

Maggie took it. "That's a safe deposit key. Damn it, Alex, she put the stuff in a safe deposit box. There isn't even a bank name on the key, just some numbers. They don't want a key they can't use—they want what's in the box. This is no help at all."

"I was afraid you might say something along those lines," he said, getting to his feet and brushing down his slacks. The floor was exceedingly hard, and quite dusty. "I am not by nature a violent man, but I have this recurring thought that has something to do with sliding my hands about Mrs. Goldblum's neck and—"

"You're not the Lone Ranger in that one," Maggie said, pocketing the key. "Now what? Do you want to keep looking?"

"We are here," Saint Just said, looking around the small wire mesh cage at the plastic bins, five of them, that were stacked there. "I'll lift one down for you."

"Thanks." Maggie pried off the lid of a deep purple container. "Oh, photograph albums. They're no help. Although

I'd like to see a photo of Harry. One with his head on, I mean."

Saint Just lifted layers of clothing from a second container, scattering small white and rather smelly balls over the floor. "What on earth?"

"Mothballs," Maggie said. "My grandmother always smelled of them. Oh, look, here's one of Irene and Harry at their wedding."

Saint Just ignored her and went on to the next container, and the next, and the next, his frustration growing at each new failure. Sterling and Snake were in danger, and he was on his knees, picking up balls for moths. Frustration did not begin to express how he felt.

"Um . . . Alex?"

"All done here, Maggie," he said, more than ready to quit this depressing area and go upstairs, move that blasted refrigerator and hope there was some sort of safe built into the wall behind it. A wall safe he understood. He did not understand basement bins and little white balls that smelled like grandmothers.

"No, Alex, look. I think we've got something. It might not be the something those guys are after, but we've got something. Look—here's a photograph of Enrico Totila. See? It's labeled. You see who he's standing with? Oh, wow."

"A rather well dressed man, in a flashy sort of way. Is that a wig?"

"I don't think so. But you're right, he's well dressed. That's John Gotti, the Dapper Don." She turned the page. "Oh, wow, here's more. And they're all labeled . . . Totila and Gotti . . . the date . . . the place. You know, Gotti's dead now, but he was the big guy. Not a good thing, having your picture taken with him, though, not if you keep saying you're not in the mob. Harry must have taken these photographs, don't you think? He's not in any of them." She turned another page. "Oh, wow."

"Would it be at all possible for you to stop saying *oh, wow?* What do you see?"

"Totila. See him? Now look behind him."

Saint Just leaned in closer, the better to focus on the photograph. "I see pants legs, shoes."

"Yeah. Pants legs and shoes lying on the ground. And the caption, Alex. It says here, *'Enrico Totila and Biggy Two-Ears Mordini. Outside Trenton, August 14, 1989.'* How much do you want to bet that Mordini is dead, and that Totila was posing over him like a hunter over a six-pointed buck?"

"Now I do need a translation," Saint Just said, taking the album from Maggie and helping her to her feet. "May I suggest we adjourn to my apartment, in the faint hope those two imbeciles who absconded with Sterling and Snake might have thought to copy down Mrs. Goldblum's telephone number?"

"Okay, sure. Oh, wow, Alex, wait until Steve sees this. He's going to go *ape.* I mean it. I'll bet, with these dates and everything, they'll be able to put this Totila guy away for a long, long time."

Any trepidation, any sense of not being quite sure of himself, faded in one brilliant instant as Saint Just turned to look at Maggie. "Steve does not see this."

"Why not?"

"He has a commendable sense of honor and respect for the law, Maggie. In other words, if this is some sort of compelling evidence, and you seem to believe it is, the good *left*-tenant will feel it his duty to take it to his superiors, leaving Sterling and Snake very much in the lurch. I repeat, the *left*-tenant does *not* see these photographs."

"But . . . but the mob guys probably don't even *know* these photographs exist, Alex. They'll be delighted to get them and—oh, damn."

"Exactly. We will have given them something they don't know they need in exchange for Sterling and Snake, still leaving them without the something they think we have that they actually want. In other words, these photographs serve no good purpose. Unless . . ."

"Unless what? What are you thinking?"

"Shh, Maggie, I'm concentrating. There must be a way to employ these damning photographs, dangle a few of them in front of Mr. Totila's henchmen in order to be allowed to see—and therefore rescue—Sterling and Snake, *and* some way to use them to assist Bernice."

"Bernie? What do the photos have to do with Bernie?"

"I don't know. Not yet. But I am under the impression that the good District Attorney Dettmer is the sort of man who would relish a coup. These photographs, these days and names, would you consider them a coup?"

"Oh, yeah," Maggie said, rubbing her hands together as they rode up in the elevator. "Steve can take the photographs—some of them—to Dettmer, and we can wave the rest of them in front of the goons when they contact us, and—no. This isn't going to work."

"Really? Why not?"

"I don't know. But it's too easy, especially when you think about the mob end of it. Those people carry guns, Alex. And Steve would have a lot of explaining to do to the D.A."

"You keep assuming that Wendell will be meeting with this Dettmer person. You could not be more wrong."

"You're not . . . *you're* going to . . . ?"

"It's Sterling, Maggie. I will be in charge of everything, every move, every ploy, every stratagem. Had you a single doubt?"

"Me? Damn right I—wait a minute. *You* told me we needed Steve."

Saint Just lifted his chin. "You must have misunderstood. Ah, here we go, our floor. Get a good night's sleep, my dear, for what remains of it. I will adjourn to the apartment in the off-chance the kidnappers phone early in the morning. You may tell Wendell, when he finally is done with his snit and phones you, that you are terribly sorry for having gone sleuthing without telling him and will never do so again. That should delight him down to his badly shod toes."

"I . . . my head hurts. Alex, what are we doing? We're breaking the law, I think."

"How? By not giving away Mrs. Goldblum's personal belongings? After all, are they ours to give? I think not. Go to bed," he said, lightly touching her cheek as he stepped close to her, lowered his mouth toward hers. "I'm here, Maggie."

"Oh, brother," she said, rolling her eyes. "That was so B-movie, Alex." But as he lifted one brow in question, and made to back off she grabbed his shoulders. "Come here."

This was different. The female as aggressor. A part of him found it quite improper . . . while another part of him firmly told the starchier, Regency Era part of him to, well, to take a hike.

He slanted his mouth against hers, accepting the invitation of her parted lips, sliding his tongue against hers, smiling slightly as she eagerly began a duel that could, should, at least in his stories, end with the two of them in his bed.

"I'm sorry you were scared there for a while, Alex," Maggie said, having pushed herself free of him before he could think to hold her close. "No, don't deny it. You were scared. I was scared. I'm still scared. But you're not, are you? You're over it. You're ready to act. Man, I made you brave. Or very, very arrogant. I'll see you at eight, right before I go to Doctor Bob, unless the goons call. I won't stay for the full hour, but I need to talk to him about Bernie. G'night."

Saint Just stood, the photograph album tucked under his arm, staring at Maggie's closed door, wondering why he'd thought, even for an instant, that he, such an accomplished lover, and with an acknowledged insight into the workings of her mind, understood anything about this particular woman.

CHAPTER 13

M aggie knocked on the door a second time. Pounded on it this time. Counted to ten, then heard the dead bolt turn and, before the door had opened more than a few inches, demanded, "Tell me again why you have a key to my place and I don't have one to yours."

"And a pleasant good morning to you, too, my dear," Alex said, stepping back to wave her inside. "And, so that you might not waste your breath, no, I have had no communication from the mobsters. No, I have not discovered anything else of any consequence in the apartment, although it might please you to learn that, yes, I can be injured without your first writing that injury into one of our books. Meaning, refrigerators are heavy as well as cumbersome, and gentlemen were not meant to move them about willy-nilly without assistance. Oh, and I have not as yet partaken of my morning coffee, as I do not possess any, unless I wish to go down to the basement and scoop some out of the garbage gathered up after our, again, mobsters destroyed the kitchen. And how are you?"

Maggie shrugged, pretending not to notice his wince as he turned to close the door and the way he grabbed involuntarily at his back. She also pretended to ignore how absolutely gorgeous the man looked in a pristine white dress shirt still open at the neck, form-fitting black slacks, and, oh God, bare feet. Nor would she notice his disheveled, shower-damp ebony hair, his bluer than blue eyes slightly bruised from lack of sleep, the somehow yummy smell of Dove soap that clung to his tanned skin.

She didn't have time for any of that. Too bad.

"Gee, now I know why you usually don't crawl out of bed until ten," she said, adjusting the strap of her purse on her shoulder, because she needed something to do with her hands that didn't include helping to boost her up as she climbed the man, grabbed him by the ears, and let him get a taste of the coffee she'd just finished as he plunged his tongue into her mouth and . . . Okay, that was enough of that, too.

"I'm assured the mobsters—must we call them mobsters?—will be contacting us sometime today. Although I discovered, unfortunately only a few minutes ago, that both phones here in the apartment have had their cords ripped out of the wall. Is there some establishment nearby where I can purchase new equipment?"

Maggie reached behind the end table beside the couch pushed against the wall, and came out with a cord that no longer had that little clip thingie at the end. "You don't need new phones, Alex. I can fix this. I'm sure I have some of this stuff somewhere."

"Good. Where?"

"I don't know. In my desk? I'll go look."

"No, I will. You'll be late for Doctor Bob, remember?"

"Oh, right," Maggie said, in no rush to keep her appointment. "I don't know if I should be thanking him or asking if he takes MasterCard or Visa. Although I already know the answer to that one, he takes both. You know, maybe it's wrong of me, but I can't believe he actually charged five hundred bucks to help Bernie. I mean, she's his publisher, for crying out loud. I'm the one who gave his manuscript to Tabby, so without me, and without Bernie, who bought it, where would he be? Not on the talk shows, I'll tell you that much. I had no idea he was so cheap."

"Isn't that strange? Like usually has no problem in recognizing like," Alex said, and she threw a pillow at him as he left the apartment, then looked at her watch. She still had plenty of time. Maybe even time enough to take another look around the apartment, hoping for a miracle.

There was a large walk-in closet located in the hallway that led to the bedrooms, and Mrs. Goldblum had transferred all of her wardrobe there before running away. The clothing had almost all been ripped from the rods, but Mary Louise, or someone, had replaced them. There were shoes on the floor of the closet and purses stacked on shelves above the clothes rods.

Nothing much to look for, nothing much to see, but Maggie had the time, and it still bugged her that they'd found nothing useful in the apartment.

A second glance told her that these were all winter clothes, with no summer clothes, sandals, or straw purses anywhere. Everything summery was gone. Obviously Mrs. Goldblum hadn't headed for Nome, and she didn't pack light.

One by one, she pulled down the huge old-lady purses, looking through them. Scented hankies, crumpled tissues— "Ick!"—wrapped peppermints, a few loose pennies, a bus schedule, a passport, an emery board, a small roll of antacids, a—"A *passport?*"

Maggie flipped the now empty purse on the floor and opened the passport, winced. "Man, nobody looks good in these things, but they don't usually look like they've been dead for three days," she said, then pressed on. It was a current passport, with one stamp in it, for Freeport, in the Bahamas. "She left in a hurry. I wonder if she's missing this right about now."

Ignoring the mess she'd made on the floor, Maggie went looking for Alex, who should have found the cord by now. Holding up the passport like a trophy, she crossed the hall and pushed open the already ajar door to her own condo . . . and stopped dead.

Alex was sitting in her computer chair, reading something. Several typewritten pages held together at the top left corner with a staple. What did she have that was stapled?

And why did he look like that? Sorrowful. Yes, that was it. Sorrowful. His shoulders almost slumped, his entire posture speaking most eloquently of some unhappiness she'd never seen him show, never had thought to allow the character of the Viscount Saint Just to show. Yet he wore even sorrow well, almost elegantly, with just enough reluctance to feel whatever emotions were filling him to be achingly attractive, curiously vulnerable.

"Alex? What's wrong? What do you have?"

He looked up, his eyes clouded for only a moment before he blinked, flipped the pages over and replaced them in the drawer she'd hadn't noticed had been pulled open. "Nothing important. I found the cord. Several of them, actually. They're fairly well tangled but I believe I can manage to fix that."

"Uh-huh," Maggie said, watching as he stood up, tangled cords in hand, and brushed past her, into the hallway. He was gone approximately one-and-one-third seconds before Maggie had tossed the passport on the desk, yanked the drawer open, and was pulling out the pages.

She frowned, flipping them over quickly. "This . . . this is the character description I wrote about him when I first thought him up," she said out loud. "What's in here that would make him . . . ? Hair, black, eyes, killer blue, height, six foot two. Gee, it rhymes. Slender face, can lift his left eyebrow in amusement or as an insult. Bullet scar on his left shoulder. Right. I added that after I had him shot. Lives in Grosvenor

Square mansion when in London, right. Quizzing glass, right. Estranged from father, mother died having him. No siblings."

She frowned, scanning the rest, which was nothing more than scribblings she'd added from time to time as she developed his character more fully, like putting in that bit about the young Clint Eastwood slashes in his cheeks.

"There's nothing here that—no," she said, looking at the door to the hall. "He couldn't actually . . . Alex?" She headed back across the hall. He was on his way to the kitchen, a telephone cord in his hand. "Alex? Hold it right there a minute, okay? You were looking at your character description, weren't you? What upset you? This stuff about your parents?"

He looked at her levelly. "Is that so amazing? That I should mourn a dead parent, perhaps even mourn the estrangement from the remaining parent?"

Maggie blinked. "Uh . . . no, I guess—wait a minute. You don't *have* parents. I made them up. I made *you* up."

"True, but you didn't make me heartless," Alex said, running the cord between his fingers.

"No, I didn't make you heartless. But I've never written a single thing about your parents, not in six books. That was just information I needed for me. How can you feel what I haven't created you to feel?"

His jaw set as he looked at her. Maggie nearly backed up a step. "Yes, you created me. I am a figment of your imagination, or at least I was. Until I took charge, took control of my own destiny, which, as it happens, brought me here. You made me, Maggie, and now I am making me . . . more."

Maggie looked at him for long moments, moments during which her heart pounded, her throat went a little tight, and she thought, just for an instant, she might actually faint. "But . . . but you can't do that. You're Saint Just."

"Part of me is, yes. A majority of me. But now there is

also Alex. *I* am also Alex. I didn't fully realize that, Maggie, not until a few minutes ago. It is rather staggering, isn't it, and explains how I've been reacting since Sterling's disappearance. I am . . . evolving."

Maggie didn't know what to say. She sure couldn't think. And then the phone rang.

"Get that!" she said, pointing at the phone.

Alex approached the phone leisurely and lifted the receiver to his ear. "Good morning, Alexander Blakley here," he said, then listened, nodding to Maggie, who wished the extension was working. "Might I remind you that if you had not rendered our telephone machines inoperable in your needlessly overwrought and even wanton destruction of the apartment, I could have answered your earlier calls. Far from me to point out the obvious, my good fellow, but you and your thug cohort might wish to consider that eventuality, when next you are running about destroying personal property."

Maggie clapped her hands to her ears and hissed, "Jeez, Alex. Don't piss him off."

He waved her back into silence. "Yes, I quite understand. Yes, we have *it*. We will, of course, expect verification that the gentlemen are unharmed." Maggie watched as he frowned. "I suppose that shall have to suffice. And precisely when would that—?" He looked at the receiver, then replaced it. "He disconnected. He's not a very polite man, and with a remarkably intense disposition."

"Yeah, I got that."

"I'm ashamed of myself, as Sterling and Vernon must be my primary concerns, but I have to tell you, Maggie, I'm going to enjoy bringing these people down."

"Yeah, I got that, too. What did he say? You should have asked to talk to Sterling."

"There wasn't time. According to our caller, we will be able to see for ourselves how Sterling and Vernon are faring

when a package is delivered later today. Until then?" He
shook his head. "I imagine you'd better go. It wouldn't do to
keep the great doctor waiting. Besides, he'll charge you."

"And Steve? We need him, Alex. These guys are going to
want us to turn over what we've got and tell us we'll be able
to pick up Sterling and Snake on some street corner in
Hoboken or something later tonight. But how do we know
they'll keep their end of the bargain? We need an experienced negotiator to talk to these guys, set up cops all around
the drop area. All that stuff."

"I'll consider it, yes. But not until after this package arrives and we know exactly what we are forced to deal with,
all right? My conversation with that man has given me new
hope, as he may have been angry, but he didn't sound in the
least intelligent. Why else would they be called *thugs*? Now
go, I must finish preparing myself for the day."

Maggie backed toward the door, picking up her purse as
she went, her eyes still on Alex. "I . . . I'll be back soon," she
said, then turned and ran for the elevator.

Her hands were still shaking as the cab headed up the avenue, and she didn't even bother to yell at the driver when he
ran a red light and nearly took out a bicycle messenger.
Tossing a five at the guy, she bolted from the cab and into
Doctor Bob Chalfont's office a full minute before the good
doctor started his meter running.

"Margaret, how are you this morning?" Doctor Bob
asked as he opened the door to his office as if he'd been
standing behind it, listening for her. "And Ms. Toland-
James? She's all settled?"

"Yeah, yeah," Maggie said, collapsing into a chair. "Can a
person change on their own?"

Doctor Bob sat himself down at his overlarge desk chair
and steepled his fingers beneath his nose. "You think Ms.
Toland-James could have stopped her alcohol addiction on
her own? I can't discuss another patient, Margaret, you

know that. I will say that few people are strong enough to change, to evolve, completely on their own. We all need some help from time to time."

"Strong enough," Maggie repeated, nodding. "Okay, that makes sense. I made him strong."

"Him? I beg your pardon. I thought you were referring to Ms. Toland-James."

"Ah . . . that is . . . did I say *him*? I didn't mean to. I meant . . . so, you think Bernie could have kicked the drinking without this clinic thing?"

"Margaret, I cannot—"

"Right. Let's talk about me. Just for a minute, though, because I really can't stay. I decided that I'm a nicaholic—a nicotine addict—and even though I say that all the time, I've decided now that I really, really want to stop smoking. That's good, right?"

"Is it?"

Maggie curled her top lip back over her teeth. "Don't do that. Don't answer my question with the same question except it comes out of your mouth. Yes. Yes, it's good that I really, really want to quit. I mean, the smelly clothes, the cost—pretty soon crack cocaine is going to be cheaper, if it isn't already. I can't light up in ninety percent of the places I go. I should quit. I want to quit. I mean, if Bernie can quit, I should be able to quit, too. But can I do it on my own?"

"Margaret, you are not alone. I'm here, remember?"

"No insult intended, Doctor Bob, but you've been here for a while now, and I'm still smoking."

"Because smoking, Margaret, is not really your problem. You know that. Smoking is your crutch. You hide behind it, you use it in lieu of expressing yourself verbally anywhere except inside the pages of the books you write; you pretend you will lose your creativity without it. But, in truth, it's your rebellion, begun in your teens, and now you are physically, psychologically, and most definitely emotionally addicted.

You are an interesting case, although not unique. With many, I merely have to help the patient over the chemical addiction. With you? There are other considerations."

Maggie began to reach for the box of tissues on the table beside her, then caught herself in time. She'd come here for two reasons. To ask about Alex and Bernie, and to do just a little bragging. "I did something yesterday. I told Bernie she had to stop drinking. She . . . she went a little nuts on me, yelled at me, but I didn't back down. I'm learning. I'm learning to stand my ground when someone starts yelling. So maybe I'm ready to quit smoking, too? And," she added, thinking about Alex, "maybe I can do it on my own."

Doctor Bob removed his new half-glasses and made a big deal out of polishing them with a small blue cloth. "Has your mother phoned since the stories about Ms. Toland-James appeared in the news, Margaret?"

Damn the man. He might be a pain, but he was also good. Very good.

"Yes," she said, sticking out her chin.

"Did you talk to her?"

The chin lowered slightly. "I was out. She left a message."

"And did you, knowing that she had to be quite put out at the news she'd read, return her call?"

Maggie stood up. "I'll see you next week. Charge me for the full hour."

"Yes, I thought so. You're making strides, Margaret. *We* are making strides. If you work hard the day will come when you need no crutches, neither the nicotine nor me."

Maggie bolted from the office, stopping once she was back on the sidewalk, where she stood and took deep breaths of the polluted air; rather like smoking, if you were hooked on exhaust fumes.

So she'd made Alex strong, given him all the strength she would like to have, but didn't. She gave Sterling all the heart, because balance was necessary. And yet Sterling had gotten as close to violent as she imagined he ever could when he'd thought Henry had been hurt, and Alex had shown emotions, including sorrow and, yes, fear, she'd never written for him.

She'd made him everything she'd ever wanted to be. Witty, arrogant . . . and yes, brave. And he and Sterling both had taken what she'd given them a step farther. Growing. Evolving.

She could do it. If Alex and Sterling could do it, she could do it.

Deciding to walk home, she reached into her purse and pulled out her pack of cigarettes and her lighter. "But not today. I'm not a total idiot."

By the time she got back to the condo the media had set up camp for another day.

"Hey," one of them yelled at her as she put her head down and tried to reach the door before any of them saw her. "Aren't you Cleo Dooley? Toland-James's friend? She up there? What did she tell you? She did it, right?"

Maggie turned, to see that the reporter who'd yelled wasn't the only one coming at her. Television camera lights went on, flashbulbs popped, and now everyone was yelling at once.

Socks burst from the foyer, arms spread, and placed himself in front of Maggie.

"You, fag boy, out of the way!"

Maggie had been so grateful to see Socks, and hiding behind him until the two of them could sort of shuffle toward the door had seemed like a good idea.

But if not today, when? If not for Bernie, for Socks, then for who? Whom? Oh, hell, she had to do it.

She pushed herself past Socks's outflung arm and stepped in front of him. "Who said that? Which one of you cretins said that?"

"Maggie, it's okay," Socks said, tugging on her arm.

"No, Socks, it's not." She took another step forward, as did one of the reporters. It had to be him. He was smirking like it was him.

She stepped right up to him, poked a finger in his chest. "Look. One, this is my friend, so keep your homophobic mouth off him, okay? Two, Ms. Toland-James is not here. She is, however, totally innocent, a victim. Now go chase a fire truck or something."

Someone else yelled: "What about the D.A., Ms. Dooley?"

"That's Kelly. Maggie Kelly," Maggie said, still glaring at the reporter in front of her. "And what about him?"

"He was on TV this morning saying an arrest was imminent, that Toland-James is a stone cold killer. What about that? Any comment?"

Maggie couldn't see the lights. She was too busy seeing red. "Sure, I've got a comment. The D.A. needs to lose the makeup and get a new hair stylist. Now go away, because two of my windows overlook this sidewalk and I'm thinking of boiling up some pitch. And in case you're going to say it, yes, that rhymes with bitch, so *back off.*"

It wasn't until she was in the foyer that her knees began to wobble a little and she remembered that the cameras had been rolling the whole time. "Oh, God, what did I do?"

"You were bitchin', Maggie," Socks said, all but dancing in his excitement. "That was Rob Bottoms you were poking. Nobody likes him. You're going to be all over the noon news. Man. Bitchin'."

"Stupid. That was stupid. I should have just mumbled *no comment* and kept going."

"Bottoms got you mad," Socks reminded her.

"Oh, right. You okay, Socks?"

"I'm fine. But my mama might send over an apple pie to thank you," he said, leading her toward the elevator.

She stepped inside, waving at Socks and trying to smile

as the doors closed, then leaned against the wall. "Man, I do pick my times. *That's Kelly, Maggie Kelly.* Good one. Mom's gonna blow like Vesuvius."

Alex was gone when she entered her condo, a Post-it note stuck to her computer screen. Two of them actually, as Alex's note, written in his lovely copperplate, was more of a message than a note, though damn cryptic:

No more calls, don't expect any until the delivery. Gather Socks, Killer. Assemble here at three. Mary Louise, self, to Pierre at noon. Other errand in the meantime.

The second Post-it was shorter: *If at all possible, fob off Wendell until after we've seen whatever is going to arrive.*

He'd signed it *Saint Just.*

"What the . . . ?" Maggie crumpled the notes and looked around her living room in frustration. "We're waiting for the kidnappers to contact us and he goes off to sign a damn modeling contract? He needs to be here. We need to talk. I didn't even show him the passport yet, for crying out loud."

Then she smoothed out the first note, read it again. *Other errand in the meantime.* What did that mean?

She went into the kitchen to open a can of soda, then wandered back into the living room, feeling about as useful as a snowplow in Miami—where had that one come from? Was she losing her mind?—and saw the photograph album on the coffee table.

"Might as well look at the rest of them," she said, picking it up and laying it in her lap. She turned one page, two, then frowned. "Where's the dead guy? I'm missing Biggy Two-Ears Mordini."

She paged back to the beginning and looked again, saw the four white photo corner holders minus the photo. Saw the caption with no photograph. Checked the entire album quickly, found more empty spots.

"Alex, what are you doing?" she asked, looking at her watch. He wouldn't be back until at least two, and she could either sit here and stew or she could do something. Something brave.

She lit a cigarette (she wasn't that brave), picked up the cordless phone, hit a speed dial number, waited.

"Hello, Mom? It's me, Margaret. Um . . . do you watch Rob Bottoms on the news?"

CHAPTER 14

Saint just had prepared himself as best he could, discarding the black slacks he had hastily donned that morning when Maggie had all but beaten down the door while he was dressing. He exchanged the dark pants for tan slacks that had remarkably retained their knife-sharp creases and resisted wrinkling, even though they'd been tossed to the floor, along with the remainder of his wardrobe.

He'd kept the white dress shirt, one of his favorites and newly returned from the laundry, topped it with yet another navy blazer, eschewing a formal necktie but strapping a tan belt around his waist. Butter soft tan shoes and matching socks. His hair combed into its usual windswept style, his quizzing glass around his neck, the glass itself tucked into the breast pocket of the jacket.

It wasn't a jacket by Weston, supple buckskins—putting paid to any faint hope of cutting a dashing leg—nor his favorite Hessians, but the ensemble would do.

All that was missing was his sword cane, and he felt vaguely naked without it. But he was aware that security in official buildings included metal detectors, and explaining away his cane would cause undue attention. Perhaps even confiscation.

Still, his free hands seemed to itch to hold something, so he stopped on his way and purchased a bumbershoot—umbrella—at a small, exclusive shop that seemed to understand that such things should be black, should be large, and should include a solid, curved handle and a long point at the opposite end.

There wasn't a cloud in sight, but he felt better now. More himself.

Once inside the building he examined a large directory, then set out to confront his quarry.

"Good morning, Miss Angela Perkins," he said, quickly reading the nameplate on the desk of the young woman who sat in an anteroom outside the main office of that quarry. "I am, of course, Alexander Blakely, here to see Mr. Dettmer. You will kindly apprise him of my arrival?"

"Who?" Ms. Angela Perkins said, obviously caught between staring at him in expected admiration and paging through the appointment calendar in front of her without looking at it. "I don't think . . ."

"Of course," Saint Just said smoothly, inclining his head in a deferential bow. "How silly of me. I forgot to present my calling card." He reached into the inside pocket of his sport coat and extracted a thin white envelope. "If you would only be so kind as to take this to the esteemed gentleman, I believe he'll recall our appointment."

"Uh . . . um . . ." Miss Angela Perkins slowly stood up, holding out her hand.

Saint Just caught it, as he caught her gaze with his own, as he bowed over that hand, brought it to his lips, kissed her fingers. Then he folded those fingers around the envelope. "What a marvelous mouth you have, my dear. You must become weary of the constant compliments."

"Uh . . . uh-huh," she said, still holding out her hand as she backed from the desk, nearly upsetting her chair. She kept backing away, until she encountered the door behind her, then turned and ran into the next office.

"Who the hell are you?"

Saint Just turned to notice the three gentlemen sitting on leather chairs, looking at him as if they wanted to eject him from the room via the nearest window.

"Is there some problem, gentlemen?" Saint Just asked, gracefully leaning on the handle of his umbrella.

"Yeah. I have the ten o'clock," one of the gentlemen said.

"You? No way. I have the ten o'clock," said another.

"I've got the nine-thirty, so I'm ahead of both of you. And we're all ahead of *him*."

"Mr. . . . Mr. Blakely?"

Saint Just raised one eyebrow as he smiled, then bowed to the men before turning around, tucking the umbrella under his arm. "Yes, Miss Perkins?"

"You can go in now," she said, plastering herself against the open door, fingers to her lips as he strolled past her into an office at least three times the size of Maggie's very generous living room.

"You brought these?"

"Indeed," Saint Just said, bowing to the large, red-cheeked man of medium height and expanding build just then coming out from behind a desk that, set with china, could have served twelve comfortably, with room for candelabra, etagere, and the family silver salt cellar.

District Attorney Chadwick Dettmer waved the photographs at him. "What the hell are these?"

"I thought that would be obvious," Saint Just said, strolling across the expanse of carpet to visually examine and then avoid the pair of chairs on the opposite side of Dettmer's desk. They were low chairs. His was a much more substantial chair. Saint Just wasn't worried about the size of his consequence, but Dettmer obviously needed to feel an advantage over his visitors. Saint Just was not about to give it to him.

So he took himself over to the small sitting area to one side of the office, stopping only to admire some photographs on a cherrywood credenza.

Dettmer with the mayor. Dettmer with the president. Dettmer and the obligatory family photo; wife, daughter, son. It was this photograph that Saint Just picked up, gazing at it admiringly.

"Ah, what a lovely family. You must be quite fond of them."

"You threatening me?"

Saint Just blinked. "Why, the thought had never occurred. I was merely making a comment. Is that a beach I see behind you, outside the window?"

"Yeah. A beach."

"Your daughter is quite lovely." Saint Just restrained himself from adding something along the lines of how grateful that child must be, how she must go down on her knees nightly, thankful that she resembled her mother and not her father. "And this is your son?"

"Put that down."

"A . . . sturdily put together lad, much like yourself. And what's that he's got written on his shirt?" Saint Just held the photograph closer as he reached for his quizzing glass and raised it toward his eye. "I think I may be able to make it out if I might just—"

Dettmer grabbed the photograph by its silver frame and set it back in place on the credenza. "Angela said your name, but I didn't catch it."

"Blakely. Alexander Blakely," Saint Just said, giving the photograph one last look, then replaced his quizzing glass and took up a seat in the conversation area—the best seat— negligently propping the umbrella against it.

Dettmer didn't seem to notice, but just stood there, waving the photographs his secretary had given him. "Now, what's this all about? I'm a busy man."

"Oh, dear. No polite conversation? No idle chit-chat? No offer of refreshments? It's this hurly burly world we live in, I suppose. Very well then, straight to the point. You know who all is depicted in those photographs, I'll assume?"

"Totila. It's Totila, standing with a couple of the family foot soldiers. And this one, with just Totila and—what the hell? Whose legs are those? Where are they? When was this taken?"

"What unseemly impatience, sir. That will come, that will come . . . as will several dozen more photographs even more, shall we say, interesting. Once we've discussed terms."

Dettmer finally sat down, his beady eyes narrowed. "Terms? You're an informant? An *Englishman*? In the mob? You want to make a trade? For what?"

Saint Just pondered the word informant (as well as the man's overweening stupidity) for a moment, then decided to dismiss it. "I am here, my good man, in order to negotiate a sort of exchange, yes, although I would prefer to term it an agreement between gentlemen."

Dettmer held up the photographs, waved them. "These are evidence. I can take them right now."

"True, you could. But then, alas, you will not know exactly what you have, will you? Not the dates, not the places, both of which could lead to . . . interesting conclusions. Just those photographs, my good sir, and no others, and they are copies. I did not count each and every photograph, but I do believe I have in my possession approximately fifty, spanning the course of perhaps three decades."

Dettmer glared at him.

"Then, again," Saint Just said, getting to his feet, "I understand that Enrico Totila, with his assorted gang of thugs, is only a minor player. A small but irritating thorn in your side now that some earlier district attorney, not you, laboring with federal authorities, I presume, disposed of John Gotti, Senior—forgive me if my information is fuzzy, as I am, as you say, English. You probably don't want Totila anyway. Not much of a feather in your cap in the ongoing struggle against what is known as organized crime? Although thus far, alas, in this election year, you have none."

"Sit down."

Saint Just looked at the District Attorney, smiled. "Oh, I don't think so. Good day."

Neatly tucking the umbrella under his arm, Saint Just bowed, then headed for the door.

He had taken only two steps when Dettmer said, "Name your terms."

Saint Just took two more steps, then turned around to bow once more to the man who had at last begun to show at least a flicker of common sense. "A gentleman of reason. I applaud you, figuratively, of course. Shall we ring for those refreshments now? No, I suppose not, as by the look of that scowl on your face I doubt we're about to become bosom chums. Very well. I happened to catch your television performance with Miss Holly Spivak earlier this morning."

Dettmer tugged at his suit lapels, did some rather odd moving about of his bull-like neck and chin. Could it be preening? "So?"

"I didn't appreciate it," Saint Just said. "I'm sorry, that was blunt, wasn't it? And yet truthful. I have a friend who tells me you were making political hay on Ms. Toland-James. A quaint term. Is that correct?"

"Toland-James? This is about *her*?"

"Oh, most definitely about her, my good man. This business of being a stone cold killer? Your supposedly open and shut case against her? How *do* you Americans come up with these colorful sayings? Especially as, in this particular case, they are not true."

Dettmer got to his feet. "They damn well are."

"Really? Why, then, is Ms. Toland-James not under arrest? Wait, let me make a supposition. You don't have sufficient evidence to arrest her, do you? Which, I fear, begs the question—how much are you going to flog that innocent woman's reputation in the media in order to shore up what I also have heard is your flagging run for reelection?"

"She's a friend of yours?"

"How minimally incisive of you. A very dear friend, yes, and it pains me to see you, or anyone, attacking her character the way you did this morning, in the manner I am assured you intend to continue flogging her good name in order to— What is the term? Oh, yes. Procure airtime. For shame."

Dettmer waved the photographs again. "So what's the deal?"

"You haven't guessed? Careful, sir. If the remainder of Manhattan realized how very thick you are, those poll numbers might take another tumble. But I am happy to explain, in words of the fewest syllables."

"You're walking a thin line, buddy."

"Again with the colorful phrases. Ah, yes, it's above all things wonderful. If you will but promise to not rush hellbent to arrest Ms. Toland-James until and unless you have sufficient evidence, not just hopeful dreams of your own prominence, and if you will order your underlings to pursue all avenues of investigation into the identity of the *actual* killer, then I will turn over the originals of those photographs and all previously mentioned particulars, so that you may gain the evidence to arrest a *real* criminal, thus according you the same media interest. Understood? Or shall we review this again?"

"Oh, I understand. You're telling me to back off your girlfriend in exchange for some pictures."

"Merely a suggestion. A bird in the hand, my good sir,

has always been preferable to one in the bush, or so I've heard. Ms. Toland-James is not guilty, as the evidence will prove in good time. Mr. Enrico Totila most assuredly is guilty of, ah, so many sordid and terrible things. Which, I would ask, is of more importance to a crime-fighting gentleman like yourself?"

"Get out."

Saint Just, who really believed he had been making progress with this ignorant lout, was surprised again by the man's blatant stupidity, his short-sightedness in the face of all reason. He allowed that surprise to show. "I beg your pardon?"

"Damn right you do. Obstructing justice, hindering an investigation—blackmail threats. I should get you and that bitch adjoining cells. And I would, if these photos meant spit without supporting evidence."

"Supporting evidence which you do not desire?"

"Which I don't think you've got, or you would have shown it to me. And if you think I'm calling your bluff, calling you a liar, then you're right. No deal. That woman's a killer."

"Oh, she is not, and you know it as well as I," Saint Just said, waving his umbrella up and onto his shoulder. "But very well. This was, in many ways, a courtesy call. Since you have refused my offer of assistance, I shall simply have to do everything myself."

"What everything? You can't do that. It's interfering with police business, and if you do that I'll have your nuts in a wringer. Besides, you'd never get anywhere."

"Ah, a challenge. That was a challenge, wasn't it, mixed in with the crudity? How delightful. Very well. I make you this promise, sir. I will exonerate Ms. Toland-James of any involvement with the murder of her husband *and* deliver sufficient evidence to the media to arrest, convict, and return to prison one Enrico Totila, and perhaps most of his gang of thugs, even whilst I ponder why you would so readily give up that bird in the hand."

He raised a hand to his hair. "I should probably think about a visit to my barber, don't you think? I wouldn't wish to look shabby when the media calls. Again, good day. Oh, and you may keep those. They're merely copies, as you know, and I have more."

"I'm not kidding. I see you getting in the way and you're going to jail," Dettmer called after him. "Got some big boys there who'd love to make you their bitch, pretty boy."

Saint Just softly closed the door, smiled at Miss Perkins and the now five gentlemen awaiting audiences with the district attorney, and exited the building. He walked only a few steps before standing himself against a decorative indentation in the marble wall and peering around that wall to watch the busy entrance.

And then he waited. Not five seconds later a young man dressed in a suit much better than Saint Just would have expected (and the standard unlovely, heavy-soled police dress shoes) came running out, to stop at the head of the wide steps, looking left, looking right. Then he spoke into his sleeve. "Sir? You said blue blazer? Umbrella? No sir, I don't see him. He must have beat me to a cab. Yes sir. Sorry, sir."

The young man, looking disappointed, reentered the building.

Saint Just twirled the umbrella in one hand, then tucked it beneath his arm as he strolled off to meet Socks around the corner.

"You look kind of mad, Alex," Socks said as he fell into step beside Saint Just.

"Really? I'm foaming at the mouth? How rude of me."

"Okay, not mad. Angry. What's up? I told you he'd throw you out. If he didn't lock you up."

"He should have locked me up, Socks. I hadn't quite realized that when I entered his office, but he made that quite clear. He could have ordered my arrest."

"But he didn't. So that's good, right?"

"In some ways, yes. But he also refused to exchange some courtesy to Bernice for what you and Maggie have already assured me would have been a tremendous coup for the man. He wants Bernice, Socks. He wants her perhaps even more than he wants this publicity you say he craves. Remarkable, and quite unexpected. Now why, do you suppose, is that?"

Socks shrugged. "Because he figures he can get Bernie, *and* the stuff you've got."

"Really? Would you take that chance? With a person you don't know? I could have given him a false name. I could burn the photographs, Socks, or sell them to the media. I could contact Enrico Totila and exchange them for a good deal of money. So many, many options. Can the esteemed district attorney be that certain that I wouldn't exercise any one of them?"

"No, I don't suppose so. You're right. He really should have arrested you."

"Yes, and that was dicey for a few moments, I must tell you, as I should be of no help to Bernice or Sterling from the guardhouse. I really have to study your American law more thoroughly. Maggie would not have appreciated having to secure my release."

"She'd have killed you," Socks said, nodding. "So now what? You and Mare still going to meet that Pierre guy for lunch?"

Saint Just pulled his watch from its place in his jacket pocket, opened it, and frowned as he considered the time. "Not lunch, Socks, not any more, although Mary Louise was quite put out when I informed her of our change in plans. Instead, we'll meet at noon at the offices of Fragrances by Pierre, simply to sign the contracts. I am very shortly to be delightfully solvent, Socks. I believe Maggie is caught between consternation at losing monetary control over me and doing handsprings in her delight that I will no longer be a drain on her pocketbook."

"And Mare can stop worrying about money and finish college. It's good, Alex. It's really good."

"Yes, we were fortunate. As were you, in procuring that cover model contract when you performed your impromptu performance the final night of the WAR convention. Fortune often favors the brave, as well as those who happen to do nothing more than happily stumble into the right place at the opportune moment."

Saint Just stopped, ran what he'd just said through his mind once more. And thought about his recent visit to the office of D.A. Chadwick Dettmer.

"Hail us a hack, Socks. As I wasn't with the good district attorney above a quarter hour, I believe we have sufficient time to visit Miss Holly Spivak before my appointment."

"You don't want to go back and see if the kidnappers have sent what they're sending?"

"Maggie is perfectly capable of monitoring that, although I don't believe I mentioned to her that the thug who contacted me said that the package would arrive at two. Do you think I should have told her?"

"Not now, I don't," Socks said as he held open the back door of a cab and Saint Just proceeded him inside before telling the cabbie to head for the headquarters of Fox News.

"An address, buddy. It's a big town. I'm supposed to know everything?"

Saint Just leaned forward and gave the address, as he did know most everything.

Socks struggled to fasten his seat belt as the cab pulled back into the traffic. "Aren't you worried? About Sterling and Snake, I mean."

"No, not really. Concerned, definitely. We are at an impasse at the moment, both with Sterling and Bernice, each side wishing to gain what the other has and fearful of making too many moves, lest one of them be wrong. In addition, Socks, if I cannot outwit some thick-as-planks thugs and one overbearing, overweening, definitely *overconfident* district attorney? Why, that isn't even conceivable. Now hush, if you please. I have to think. Something happened while I was in Dettmer's office. Something important, but I can't quite put my finger on it."

"That you got out in one piece?" Socks suggested.

Saint Just waved him to silence, then mentally retraced his visit, settled on something. Yes, that had to be it. Wasn't life odd? Chock full of coincidences . . . and those that doth protest too much. But he was not the sort to go off half-cocked, and although his word was bond, and highly respected by the characters in Maggie's books, he was now in New York, and had to play by the rules here. Those included a multitude of solid evidence, not merely his famous insights and suppositions.

"We're here," Socks said as the cab pulled to the curb.

Five minutes later they were being ushered into Holly Spivak's cramped, crowded office.

"Alex?" she said, getting to her feet. "I didn't expect to see you for a while. You've got something for me?"

"Other than a firm reprimand for putting your career above the rights of the innocent and a reminder that ethics is more than a word? No, I think not. Although I do have a request. Unless you don't wish to be back in my good graces?"

"You've still got Toland-James stashed somewhere and I still want her. So stow the insults and name the favor. But first, did you see the bulletin we just flashed? No, guess not, not if you were on your way here. Toland-James is as good as locked up. You might want to get her to talk to me, Alex, before they slap the cuffs on. You know, tell her side of the story, cry a little, soften up the jury pool."

Saint Just pressed thumb and forefinger to the bridge of his nose. "I am quite certain you know precisely what you're nattering on about, my dear. Now, if we might be similarly enlightened?"

"The bartender," Holly said, sitting down once more and reaching for a VCR tape. "Watch."

Holly inserted the tape and the small television screen immediately filled with her cheerful, only slightly feline-looking face:

"I'm here in front of Brenda's, the upscale watering hole frequented by Bernice Toland-James. With me is Mr. Ray Givens, who was behind the bar Friday night. In an exclusive to Fox News, Mr. Givens has come forward to tell us what he witnessed that night. Mr. Givens?"

Roy Givens squinted into the camera, grabbing at Holly's microphone to pull it close to his mouth. "That's right, Holly. I called Fox News as a good citizen, to tell what . . . um . . . what I witnessed perpetrated that night."

Holly, still smiling, attempted to retrieve her microphone. "And what was that, Mr. Givens?"

He pulled on the microphone again, turning his head to face the reporter, while keeping his gaze directed at the camera. "She was in here, Holly."

Holly leaned into the frame, to get closer to the microphone. "She, Mr. Givens? Could you be more specific?"

"Her. Johnny Walker Red. Oh, jeez, I shouldn'ta said that. I mean Mrs. Bernice Toland-James, Holly. It was her. She comes in a lot."

With both of them holding onto the microphone, Holly said, "And when did she leave, Roy?"

"She, um, she departed the premises at one, one-thirty, Holly." Roy smiled at the camera. "And she wasn't alone, neither. She left with this *guy*. Hanging all over him."

"Hanging all over him?"

"Yeah." He turned to grin at the camera. "She was pretty smashed, Holly."

"Really? And did you recognize this gentleman?"

"Naw. Never seen him up to that night." Roy stood up straight, obviously excited now to get out the rest of his story. "But I can tell you what he looked like. I seen that picture of the dead guy you showed when you were talking to the D.A. on the tube this morning, and the guy was this Buddy James guy. Yeah, that picture you're holding up now. Stack of Bibles, he was him, Holly. You know, the guy she killed."

Holly hit the remote control and sat back in her chair, grinning at Saint Just. "Game, set, match. Now, what was it you wanted me to do, Alex? I mean, right after you bang your gorgeous head against the wall for trying to tie my hands so I could interview Toland-James the way you wanted me to. Softball? I don't play softball, Alex. I play hardball. What do you have to trade now? It had better be good."

Fortunately, as he hadn't planned to see Holly Spivak today, Saint Just had happened to reserve some of the copied photographs he'd removed from the album. He'd thought they might be his trump cards if Dettmer proved reluctant. But as he wasn't, Holly Spivak's suggestion to one side, the sort who banged his head against walls, he hadn't used them. Taking the copies from his pocket now, he carefully placed them on top of her disorganized desk.

Holly kicked her chair front and frowned at the photographs. "These aren't file photos. Looks like an amateur took these. Copies, too. Where's the originals? There's Totila, still with his hair, so this one is an old picture, and a bunch of his goombahs with him."

She leaned back again, doing a very good impression of a woman completely unimpressed. "They were probably going out for spumoni. So what?"

"I showed a pair of similar copies to the district attorney, along with informing him that I possessed enough evidence to possibly arrest Mr. Totila again, if he were to agree to relax his clutches on Bernice and pursue other possibilities, delay his arrest of Bernice until more information is learned."

"That took guts, or a total lack of brains. And . . . ?"

"And he turned me down," Saint Just told her.

"Didn't arrest him, either," Socks put in, then stepped back, bowed his head. "Sorry."

Holly waved the photograph again. "You say you've got more?"

"Many more, in addition to documentation of names, places, and dates. I would imagine that comparing these snippets of information with crimes committed in the mentioned areas might be of some importance?"

"Damn straight. At the least, it could make a lot of news. But Dettmer didn't bite?"

"Not so much as a nibble. Interesting, yes?"

"No. That's nuts," Holly said. "What's one woman slicing up her husband over getting to take credit for nabbing Totila, maybe turning him, offering him a deal if he rolled on a bunch of others?"

"My question precisely, although I do believe the man had second thoughts, as he sent some underling chasing after me as I departed the building. Poor fellow, I imagine he got quite a dressing-down for having missed me."

"He was trying to put a tail on you?" Socks said. "You didn't tell me that."

"I rarely tell anyone everything, Socks. Now, Holly. As Dettmer doesn't seem to want those photographs, or the many others I have, along with the documentation as to where they were taken and when—perhaps you might?"

"Are you kidding? I'd bang you for them, Alex. Hell, I'd bang you anyway if you weren't gay."

"But he's not—"

"Socks, hadn't you said you were thirsty? Why don't you toddle off to locate a vending machine somewhere and then meet me on the flagway in, say, five minutes?"

"Oh. Okay," Socks said. "Sorry. I'll see you outside."

"Now," Saint Just said, taking the photograph from the desk before Holly could grab it, "how long will it take an excellent, hardballing, ethical reporter like yourself to assemble comprehensive biographies of Chadwick Dettmer and Willard James, and have them delivered to the apartment of my good friend, Maggie Kelly, hmmm? By, say, seven this evening? There's a dear."

CHAPTER 15

"Where the hell were you?" Maggie asked as Alex opened the door and walked into the living room carrying a small brown bag showing a grease stain at the bottom.

"Out and about, on the strut. But I've brought a peace offering," he said, raising the bag. "White cream, not custard filled."

"Gimme that," Maggie said, snatching the bag and opening it, sniffing its contents. "You are *so* lucky. Now, where were you?"

"Signing my contract with Mr. Pierre, of course, as he leaves for Paris tomorrow for an extended stay, and I could not fob him off. A bird in the hand, Maggie. Don't you think that's a sound choice? The bird in the hand? Ah, well. Has the package been delivered as yet? I saw nothing waiting in the foyer with Paul, or sitting outside my door. I arrived half hoping I'd see some hired street urchin approaching the building, package in one hand, a fiver in the other."

"Nothing. I'm going crazy here. Oh, and J.P.'s coming over. And Steve. I couldn't fob—head them off. They'll both be here soon." She dug in the bag for a doughnut. "Do you realize all that's happened since I got up Saturday morning? And you know what I've been thinking? I've been thinking that my life started going crazy right after you showed up. Like you brought trouble with you. I used to have a quiet life, Alex, a calm life, a—"

"A boring life?"

"Shut up, I'm on a roll here. Back to the last couple of days, okay? Saturday morning. All I wanted was to be a slob all weekend, maybe get some writing done. I mean, I don't ask for much. Then Bernie called. Then we saw a body. Then we drove all the hell the way up to Connecticut. Then your apartment got tossed. Then Sterling and Snake got kidnapped. Oh, and we're going to my parents' house for a family Thanksgiving dinner, and don't try to get out of it because this is partly your fault."

"My fault? Really? And how is that?"

Maggie bit into one of the doughnuts, closed her eyes as the sugary white cream hit her tongue. Barely noticing that, when she squeezed the doughnut and then licked more of the cream filling, Alex lowered his head, began inspecting his cuffs. But definitely noticing. After all, she *had* seen *Tom Jones*.

"Parents, Alex. Subconscious motivations. Evolving, growing, changing, whether we want to or not. You name it, it's in there, and you're all over it."

"Fascinating," Alex said, taking a seat on the facing couch. "Do go on. Although you might first remove that bit of cream from your upper lip and . . . ah. Of course, why employ the napkin?"

"Pay attention," Maggie said, running her tongue over her bottom lip, too, just for good measure. She'd been sitting at her computer, playing Snood for the past few hours, and thinking. Letting her mind drift, land where it wanted.

She'd already figured out that she'd subconsciously given the Viscount Saint Just his quizzing glass and sword cane so he'd have things to fiddle with, keep his hands occupied, use as props, even as defenses (hence the sword in the cane). Much as smoking kept her hands occupied, gave her something to do, even had the happy side effect of keeping away people she didn't want close. But that revelation, although stunning to her, could wait. "I created you."

"We're in agreement so far. Do go on," Alex said, pulling out his quizzing glass and polishing it on his sleeve.

She closed her eyes for a moment. Was he on the defensive? Perhaps even a little nervous? Good. She sort of liked this particular revelation. "But then something happened, after you got here. You began to change. You're still Saint Just, but you're also . . . I don't know."

"Ah, yes. May I quote Jane Welsh Carlyle and say, 'I am not at all the sort of person you and I took me for'?"

"You, too? Right, I guess we're both confused. Because, yes, you've started creating *more* of you."

"Unknowingly, yes."

"Right. It's that unknowingly bit. Now shut up and listen. When I sat down to make you up, a blank piece of paper in front of me, I wanted to make you the perfect hero. I did that." She looked at his gorgeous face, and winced. "Cripes, did I do that. But then I had to give you some flaws, to make you more real."

"I don't care for broccoli, and Sterling is saddened by my penchant for disposing of damp towels on the bathroom floor. Guilty as charged."

"Knock it off, I'm being serious here. I made you arrogant, sarcastic. Women love that, if you do it right—and, before you ask, I'm not really loving it right now. But I also had to make you human."

"And my most sincere congratulations on that head, my dear, as you obviously did just that. Perhaps we should both rise, take bows?"

"Stop it, I want to get this out. I gave you a father you're estranged from, and a dead mother, a woman you never knew. You know, the obligatory dysfunctional family, the lousy childhood."

"And then neither mentioned nor used said parents in any of our books."

"True. When I research, when I do character descriptions, I need all this information for me, to maybe use someday, or maybe not to use, but just so I know it, know the character, what he or she has had to overcome. With you, what I did was give you all the junk that I wish I had. Then added some of the bad stuff."

"Such as?"

Maggie fought a cringe as she remembered her explosion in front of the media. "Well, like being brave. That was a good thing. I try to be brave, but I'm really not, except sometimes I just sort of . . . sort of *blow*. You got all the rest of it. And my parents. You got them, too. That was the bad stuff."

Alex sat forward, looked at her intently. "I beg your pardon."

Maggie held out her hands. "It fits, Alex. You're estranged from your father. Pencil in my mother. Your mother is dead, you never knew her. My father is alive, but he's nothing more than . . . than a cipher. I don't know him at all. It's like he's not really there, you understand?"

She blew out a breath. "Man, and I always swear I don't put anything of myself into characters. I've learned a lot since you got here, Alex, and I'm not exactly sure I couldn't have lived without the information."

Alex looked at her levelly for a few moments, then said, "And Thanksgiving dinner?"

"Your fault. I got brave. Told myself I was getting brave—evolving—and called home. But you've got most of the brave, I only got a little, and it ran out about five minutes into Mom telling me what an ungrateful child I am. So, like I said, your fault."

"And so I'm now sentenced to Thanksgiving dinner. You have such an interesting mind, my dear, at times almost frightening," Alex said, then stood up and skirted the coffee table, to sit down beside her. "But you do know that I am not you, and you are not me."

"Parts of us are."

"True. And we'll include Sterling, if you will. But we are not all the same person." He slid an arm behind her on the couch, settled his hand on her shoulder. Cupped her shoulder. Pulled her closer to him. "It is the opposites in us that attract."

Maggie tried to swallow, but her mouth was suddenly too dry. "You know, Alex, I don't think I'd like anything more right now than to just grab on to you and let you make love to me so that I don't have to think about Bernie or Sterling or Rob Bottoms or my mother or—"

"Shhh, sweetness," he said, lowering his head toward her. "Worries can always wait." He hesitated. "Rob Bottoms? Who or what, pray tell, is Rob Bottoms?"

"Did I say him? You'll find out, but he isn't important now."

"Good."

"Yeah. Good," Maggie said, closing her eyes.

And then he kissed her.

And Maggie melted.

And someone knocked on the door.

Alex sighed. "If you don't mind another quote that has just leapt into my mind, I will tell you that it was Michael Drayton who said, 'These poor half-kisses kill me quite.' "

"Michael whoever has a point," she said, pushing at his shoulders. "That's either J.P. or Steve."

"Both of whom I would happily consign to the devil at any other time," Alex said, kissing her one more time before heading for the door.

"Did you see it?" J.P. asked, brushing past Alex, tossing

her briefcase at him. "Got anything to eat? I skipped lunch to get here and this magnificent body of mine needs fuel." She threw her bulk onto the couch. "Damn. Talk about your *presents*. So? Did you see it?"

Maggie and Alex exchanged shrugs. "No," Maggie said. Could J.P. be talking about Rob Bottoms? "What did we miss?"

"The bartender," J.P. said, toeing off her orange sneakers and curling her legs up under her on the couch. "One photo. Spivak showed him one photo. Not an array, not any kind of variety—here's a photo lineup, do you see anyone you recognize? Nope, not Spivak. She shows him just one, Buddy. Blows the bartender as a witness. Completely corrupts his testimony. Plus, dollars to doughnuts, they paid him. His credibility is shot. Totally shot." She raised her head, sniffed the air. "Speaking of doughnuts?"

"Here, go wild." Maggie tossed her the bag. "What bartender?"

J.P. explained while Alex played host, got them all cold drinks.

"So the prosecution won't be able to use him?" Maggie asked when J.P. was done.

"Oh, they'll try to use him, but I'll rip him to shreds on the stand. Were you paid to appear on television, Mr. Bartender? Really. How much? I'm telling you—that's one witness we don't have to worry about."

"Yes, but what he said is still interesting," Alex said, then took a sip of soda. "Bernice was seen with another man, seen leaving the watering hole, visually intoxicated, with that man. And, the next time anyone sees Bernice, she's covered in blood and a man is dead in her bed."

"Yeah, well, Tonto, one victory at a time, okay?"

"J.P.?" Maggie said, almost able to feel the wheels turning inside her head. "Is it possible the man she left with is the killer?"

"What? Oh, wait. You're thinking she got picked up by some serial killer, took him home, and damn, there's Buddy back from the dead, choosing that night of all nights to show up and claim his share of the three million in insurance? That's too pat. Plus, a serial killer would have knifed her, too."

"I guess so," Maggie said, looking to Alex. "Well? You have any ideas?"

"Several, my dear, but none I wish to share at the moment. J.P.? Have you been able to learn how Bernice is faring?"

"That's the other reason I'm here. Gloating about how Dettmer's going to be pissed about the bartender isn't all of it. I got that Doctor Chalfont to call up to the clinic, and he found out Bernie's behaving herself, not asking for a drink, saying nothing's wrong, she's fine, so can she get out of there."

"No horrible withdrawal symptoms?" Maggie asked. "That's wonderful. Or maybe it's too soon for that?"

"Chalfont says they're beginning to think she was on a binge. Didn't you say her drinking got worse after her husband—first one—was murdered?"

Maggie nodded. "Bernie drinks. She always did. But not like she did when Kirk was killed. Since then? It's been pretty bad. So she isn't an alcoholic?"

J.P. shrugged. "Beats the hell out of me. Could be one doozy of a bender, and that could mean she's also an alcoholic, or maybe she's just depressed and it was easier to get alcohol than Prozac. I just know she's being good, and wants out."

"And can she get out?"

"She signed herself in voluntarily. That's all Chalfont and I could get her to do. Three days, according to the rules at this clinic, and she's free to leave. Maybe sooner. Chalfont was kind of vague on that one."

"So she could be coming back to the city—when? Wednesday or Thursday? I mean, maybe they don't count Sunday, because she checked in so late? But she'll be arrested."

"Possibly. Probably. If she even comes back here, which I'm sure she will. She's not stupid enough to run, and I've got her passport. Anyway, I wanted you all to know, and to watch for her if she shows up, let me know right away. But I've got court starting tomorrow, so I can't baby-sit her."

"Alex?" Maggie looked to him for support. "What do we do if she shows up?"

"Ridding this apartment of spirits would be my first suggestion, although that could prove embarrassing for her. Oh, and pray the few media persons remaining on the flagway will have disappeared by then. Other than that?"

"Other than that," J.P. said, "I'm outta here. Oh, and Mary Sunshine? You did great today. Bottoms deserved every bit of it. Just don't do it again, okay?"

Maggie sat and examined the contents of her glass while Alex escorted J.P. to the door, handed her the attaché case.

"Bottoms? I've heard that name before, haven't I, Maggie? What did you do?"

"Nothing," she said, taking a sip of Pepsi. "Well, not exactly nothing. Rob Bottoms is a reporter for one of the stations, I forget which. He shoved a microphone at me when I was coming in and I told him Bernie was innocent or something like that. J.P. must have seen it on the noon news." She shrugged. "That's about it. Nothing big."

"Big enough for you to have mentioned his name in your litany of complaints," Alex pointed out, because he probably hated her and wanted to watch her suffer.

"Okay, okay, so he said something nasty to Socks when Socks tried to keep me off-camera and I . . . I went a little nuts."

She waited, still not looking at him.

"I see," he said at last. "One of those impossible to hold back moments of bravery. You may not stand up for yourself with enough regularity to please me, but you are a tiger for your friends. My congratulations. Did it feel good, Maggie?"

She looked up at him, grinned. "You mean until I realized what I'd done and started to shake? Yeah. It felt good."

"In that case, my dear, hold up your head and let the world know you not only did it, you're prepared to do it again, in a heartbeat. A good third of brave is actually bravado, I've always found. Now, that must be the good *left*-tenant. Are you ready for him? Chin lifted?"

"Oh, open the damn door," Maggie said, giving straightening her spine her best shot.

"Maggie. Blakely," Wendell said as he entered. "The doorman gave me this to bring upstairs."

"Ohmigod, the ransom stuff!" Maggie said, leaping off the couch, ready to grab the package out of Wendell's hands.

But he reacted quickly, holding the package above his head. "You were expecting this? And you didn't call me? Do I have to remind you that I'm a—"

"Oh, cut line, Wendell, we know who you are," Alex said, neatly divesting the man of his prize. "I merely wanted to inspect the thing myself, before calling you in. Maggie had nothing to do with it. Here you go, my dear," he then said, tossing the box to her.

"So much for fingerprints on the packaging," Wendell said, sitting down beside Maggie. "Okay, sweetheart, this is what we do. You open it, but slowly, touching it as little as possible. Unless you want me to take it downtown?"

"No time for that, Wendell," Alex said. "And might I remind you, speed in recovering Sterling is of the utmost importance right now. You may obtain fingerprints directly from the kidnappers once we've apprehended them."

"Speaking of fingers . . ." Maggie hesitated. "What . . .

what if Sterling's little finger is in here? They do that sometimes, Alex. Kidnappers. You want proof, so they send you fingers, and ears, and—here, you open it."

Wendell shook his head. "You two are a real pair."

"Ah, you've noticed. How remarkably observant of you, *Left*-tenant," Alex said, retrieving scissors from Maggie's desk and cutting the string that held the brown paper wrapping over the contents, then pushing back the paper with the tip of the scissors. "We were discussing exactly that before your arrival, as a matter of fact. Well, hello. I believe we have a videotape."

"Handle it by the corners, Maggie."

Maggie, who'd had her hands over her eyes, lowered them slowly, to press them against her cheeks, then looked at the thing in her lap. "They made a tape?"

"I have to take that downtown, Maggie. I mean, I can't believe I'm letting you two talk me into what I've done so far. Why am I letting you do this?"

"Because you don't trust the FBI not to screw it up and get Sterling and Snake killed, and because you hate Dettmer and don't want him to get the glory," Maggie reminded him. "You're as bad as we are, and that's why we like you so much. You just pretend to go by the book."

Alex chuckled, then inserted the tape in the VCR and picked up the remote control. "Here we go. Ah . . . Sterling, there you are, my friend."

Maggie bit her lips between her teeth as Sterling's face appeared on the screen. "Where are his glasses? Freeze that, Alex. Oh, look. He's got a black eye, and his glasses are missing."

Alex had paused the tape and continued to stare at Sterling's frozen image even when Maggie was eager for him to start it again. "Alex?"

As if it took him a moment to understand that she'd said

his name, Alex gave a small start, then composed himself, although Maggie could see a muscle working in his cheek. "Yes, of course. Forgive my small lapse."

"Alex, it's okay. It's a black eye. Sterling's okay."

"For now," Wendell said tersely. "Are you sure you two don't want to rethink this?"

"Even less so now than before, thank you, Steve," Alex said quietly, and picked up the remote once more.

"Got you, Alex. Play the rest of the tape."

Maggie grabbed a notepad and pen from the coffee table, ready to take notes.

Sterling seemed to be listening to someone off-camera, squinting at someone off camera. "Oh. Oh, yes. You did say for me to do that, didn't you? Sorry, I'm feeling a bit befuddled, which is not all that out of the ordinary for me, as Saint Just might tell you. Like this?" he asked, raising a newspaper in front of him, holding onto both edges.

"Today's paper," Wendell said. "So we know they were alive this morning. Sterling, at least."

"Shhh," Maggie said, leaning closer to the set.

Sterling put the newspaper down and looked off-camera once more, nodding several times as he heard what was to Maggie no more than a mumble.

An arm appeared on the screen, shoving a piece of paper at Sterling, who took it. "And now this? Not that I wish to complain, far be it from me to do any such thing, but don't you think this is all rather dramatic?"

There was another rumble of a deep voice and Sterling sighed. "That wasn't very nice. Snake becomes frightened when you say such things, don't you, Snake? And Saint Just won't be best pleased, I should warn you of that. Oh, and if you could step back with that camera? The light is blinding me."

More mumbling.

"I wish we could hear what that bastard's saying," Wendell said, and Alex raised the volume.

The camera panned back, showing more of the room Sterling sat in, his hands free, his feet trussed together at the ankles.

Sterling squinted at the paper. "Do . . . what we dish? No, wish. Wish. Do what we wish—or less . . ." He looked off-camera. "You might have meant *else* here, not less. E-l-s-e. Just a friendly observation. And I'm having a deuce of a time reading this. You broke my spectacles, remember? Perhaps it would be better all round if you read the message yourself?"

The screen went dark, then there was Sterling again, with Snake sitting beside him, his ankles also tied, and now Snake held the paper, which shook in his hands.

" 'Do what we wish—or else.' " Snake looked at the camera, his handsome face pale. "Or else what?" he asked.

"I don't think you want to pursue that train of thought, Snake," Sterling said, speaking out of the corner of his mouth. "Just read that, if you please. These two lovely gentlemen who are not that far away have promised us lavatory privileges once we've performed for them, as it were, remember? Yes, performed for them, that's the word I want. To return to my current dilemma? That door back there, with the light over it? I don't wish to be crude, but I believe that light is calling to me, and all of that, and it's not that far away. And I'm feeling quite peckish, what with smelling the air filled with the aroma of Chinese food. I particularly enjoy wonton soup. Now, finish it, Snake."

Snake visibly swallowed, nodded. "Bring what we want to the Staten Island Ferry at midnight tonight . . . or the . . . *they* are both dead." Snake looked at the camera, blinked. "Oh. That's what else. Fuckin' A."

And that was it, the end of the tape.

"I want to know who delivered that tape," Wendell said, and was out the door before Maggie could tell him that Paul was on duty, which meant he was wasting his time.

Alex rewound the tape, then put down the remote controller. "Bless Sterling. What a brick in a crisis," he said, shaking his head. "I am truly overwhelmed by his genius."

"Clues, you mean?"

"Most definitely. They are being held near, beside, or above a Chinese restaurant."

"Yeah," Maggie said, rolling her eyes as she reached for her cigarettes and lighter. "Only a couple of those in Manhattan. Should be a snap. God only knows why I was worried."

Alex silenced her with a look. "He also talked them into moving the video camera back so that we could see more of the room. What did you think of it?"

"That it was pretty shabby-looking?" Maggie offered, shrugging. "And there were two bathrooms, one marked MEN, the other WOMEN. So they're holding them somewhere normally used by the public, not an apartment or house. The room was big, and pretty empty—there was almost an echo. Did I miss anything?"

"There are still only two kidnappers."

Maggie looked down at her notes. "Oh, right. Boy, Sterling *is* good. Another case of evolving, right? I wrote down everything he said, word for word, so we can go over it again, for more clues."

"Sterling was always highly intelligent. He just has had no opportunity to remove his light from beneath the bushel basket of his more subservient role in our books."

"Okay," Maggie said, pretty much deciding she'd been an unwitting genius when she'd created Sterling and Saint Just, and then looked up as Steve reentered the room. "Anything?"

"Nothing. Jackass says he was emptying a trash can and came back to see the package addressed to Saint Just and

Maggie Kelly—Sterling must have given them the names. From the smell on him, I'd say he'd been out back with a reefer, but I'm homicide, not narcotics, so I don't give a crap." He nodded toward the television. "Did you play it again?"

"No, not yet. There's really no need," Alex said. "Tell me about this Staten Island ferry?"

"Forget it," Wendell said, sitting down beside Maggie and taking her hand in his. "From here on out, it's my ball game. Maggie, you do understand that, don't you? I'm a professional. Sterling and Snake are in real trouble, and they need professionals."

"I agree totally," Alex said. "You'll probably want the tape?"

Maggie's head jerked around so she could goggle at Alex. Now what was he up to? It was getting so she couldn't tell the players without a scorecard.

Steve looked at Maggie. "Yeah . . . I need that. What the hell is going on inside that head of yours now, Blakely? I—"

"Here you go then," Alex said, handing over the tape, the wrapping, even the string. "We are counting on you to do your utmost. You or one of your compatriots will, I am assured, be clad as me when you prepare to make the exchange? Do make sure he isn't wearing ugly shoes. I have my reputation as a gentleman of good taste to consider."

"You . . . you don't want in?"

"Passionately. But Maggie has convinced me that this is no time for me to insist upon taking charge. I know you have to be off now, so don't let us detain you. Please keep us apprised."

"God, I'm crazy. All right. You know, we still don't even know what it is that they want. I'll just have to fake it when they show up."

"You?" Alex sighed. "Definitely other shoes. And perhaps a haircut?"

"Every time I start to like you . . ." Wendell said, then kissed Maggie on the cheek and left the apartment.

"And what the *hell* was that all about? Why didn't we tell Steve about the photographs?"

She watched as Alex moved to her desk and sat down, put his hand on the mouse controller of her computer. "Because we may need them. I have every confidence that I will be the one to effect Sterling's rescue, and long before midnight. However, if I have overestimated myself, it would not do for the police to bollix such a delicate exchange and lose what we have. Now, to get to work on Sterling's clues."

Maggie leaned over his shoulder as he searched Google for *restaurants Chinese Manhattan.* "Have you been to Chinatown, Alex?"

"No, I don't believe I've as yet had that pleasure."

"I didn't think so. You'll never find Sterling that way. I'll get that. Cripes, we've got Grand Central Station here today."

Maggie opened the door and Socks, Killer, and Mary Louise straggled in. When Killer asked if they'd found Snake yet Maggie shook her head, and waved them to the couches.

"All we know is the kidnappers want us to bring what they want to the Staten Island Ferry at midnight. Presumably, that's when we'll get Sterling and Snake back," she explained as Socks took her place leaning over Alex's shoulder.

"What you looking for?"

"Chinese restaurants."

"Can't help you. I hate the smell of those places."

"Ah, yes, the smell," Alex said, then turned the chair to face the room. "Thank you all for coming here this afternoon. We've had a communication from the kidnappers that consists of a videotape of both Sterling and Snake that proves they are still in good health."

"Aces," Killer said, raising a fist, sticking up his thumb. "Now what?"

Maggie looked to Alex. *Now what? Good question.*

"Now, George, I am afraid we do nothing. *Left*-tenant

Wendell and New York's finest will take things from here. Although I'm certain Sterling would appreciate it if you were to go across the hall and feed Henry?"

"Sure," Killer said. Alex flipped him the key, and he was gone.

"Good move, Vic," Mary Louise said, munching on a pretzel from the bag she'd taken from the kitchen. "He's been driving me nuts. 'Snake's in big trouble.' 'Snake's gonna be killed.' 'Snake's gonna die.' I was thinking about buying the guy some Depends."

Maggie coughed into her hand.

"So you're really looking for Chinese restaurants?"

"Yes, Socks," Alex told him. "Sterling was brilliant enough to try to lead us to him by way of some clues he mentioned in the tape. In addition to those he so outstandingly laid out for us, he has proved to us that the thugs holding him and Vernon are dumb as red bricks—something good to know. But Maggie here tells me that locating one Chinese restaurant in Manhattan is a fruitless exercise."

"Man, I'll say so. What did Sterling say about a Chinese restaurant? Is that where they're holding him?"

"Possibly," Alex said, reaching into his jacket pocket for a cheroot. "But that was only one of several clues Sterling managed to give us with his captors none the wiser. It is quite lowering, really, that two such unintelligent buffoons could have us so thoroughly baffled."

"Now you know how I felt when Paul got promoted to head doorman over me," Socks said, nodding. "What other clues? I mean, we're here, right?"

"Very well. Maggie?"

Maggie picked up the notepad she'd scribbled on earlier. "Two kidnappers. Snake and Sterling in old, straight-back wooden chairs. You know, like the kind institutions use. Schools. Ankles tied. Sterling's with rope, Snake's with something that looked like a really thick drapery cord. You know—deep maroon, shiny, like two pieces of cloth wrapped around each other."

Alex held up a hand. "This was impromptu, not well planned out," he said, looking happier. "They took them in daylight, close to dusk, but still in daylight. They could have put them in a vehicle with tinted windows or the like and taken them anywhere, but I doubt they wanted to move them too far, as they'd still wish to watch us. And I believe that most especially because Sterling said very nearly those very words, twice. *Not that far away.*"

"Somewhere between here and the Staten Island ferry, is that what you're saying?" Maggie asked. "That narrows the search a little, but it's still a lot of Chinese restaurants. If that's what Sterling smelled."

Alex closed his eyes. "Pessimism is not helpful at this point. We're making progress. Please continue. Every word Sterling uttered could be another clue."

Maggie shook her head. Poor Alex. He couldn't help himself, he had to be a hero, not understanding that *she* planted all the clues for him in their books. God, she was even starting to think of them as *their* books. Pitiful.

Or did he know all of that, and still he pressed on? What would that make him? A real hero? Yeah . . . it would.

She brought herself back to attention. "Okay. First the rest of my notes. The room was pretty big, really bare. Echo in there, in fact. Wood floors. Dark. In fact, the only real light beyond that from the video camera came from the light Sterling talked about, over the restrooms. It was red, and kept blinking. You know, not regularly, but like there was something wrong with the bulb. That's it."

Mary Louise, bag of pretzels still in her hand, stood up. "That's nothing. I'm going to go help Killer."

Alex turned back to the computer. "Maggie? Is there a way to narrow this search to the area between here and the ferry port?"

"I don't know," Maggie said, putting down her notes, which Socks immediately picked up. "I guess we can give it a shot."

So Alex and Maggie surfed the net, and Socks read Maggie's notes, her word-for-word transcription of everything Sterling had said.

"Um . . . Alex?"

"Yes, Socks. You want to help us search?"

"No . . . and this is going to sound really screwy, but . . . but I think I know where they are."

It all got a little weird after that. . . .

CHAPTER 16

There is a lot to be said for dumb luck, as Maggie would call it, Saint Just thought as he and his coterie of eager assistants stood at the curb a full block away from Maisie's Chinese, waiting for Wendell to arrive.

"You know," Maggie said now, seemingly having some trouble speaking around the large amount of chewing gum in her mouth, "I'm really not thinking about this as any kind of fun, or some adventure or something. I'm thinking about Sterling. Really. But it is exciting, I have to admit that. And then there's—Mare? That's my purse."

"Yeah. You said I could keep it."

"Bull! That's Coach. I did not. When did I say that?"

"Let it go, Maggie," Saint Just said, taking her elbow and guiding her away from the curb. "Are you sure you want to do this?"

She blew a small bubble, let it pop. "Are you kidding? You're doing it. Killer and Mare are doing it. Socks is doing it. I'm supposed to wait on the curb? I don't think so."

"Wendell is not going to be best pleased."

"Yeah. And don't think I didn't hear the two of you planning to keep me out of trouble from here on out. Do you have any idea how insulting that is? I can do anything you can do."

"You are rather necessary to the plot," Saint Just agreed, adding, "especially if you could . . . is the word hike? Hitch?"

"Hike up my skirt? Again? You're kidding. It's already two inches above my knees. I roll the waistband any more and I won't have a waist."

"It was only in the way of a suggestion."

"I can open another button on my blouse."

Saint Just sighed. "I suppose that will have to do."

"What's the matter with my—with me?"

"Not a thing, my dear. You are perfection."

"But you like my legs best."

"My dear, I am a Regency hero. Bosoms were always on display. Gentleman of my era, however, were regularly enticed and all but rendered stupid by the merest glimpse of an ankle. Why, I'm amazed I haven't as yet swooned at the sight of your legs."

"Oh, shut up." She leaned forward, looking up the one-way street. "Steve should have been here by now. Are my legs really that good?"

"A lady doesn't fish for compliments. But, yes, they are outstanding," Saint Just said, adjusting his cuffs. "Now, I am counting on you to stay with Mary Louise, completely out of the way except to perform as I've asked you both to do."

"We're the diversion. I know. Oh, here comes Steve. Get ready for fireworks."

Saint Just watched as Wendell climbed out of the front seat of what he had learned was called a "black-and-white," followed by the uniformed driver.

Steve spared a look for the others, then headed for Maggie, hooking a thumb over his shoulder. "What are they doing here? And where's the costume party?" Then he looked more closely at Maggie, frowned. "You, too? Oh no.

Absolutely not. Whatever you've got cooked up, I don't want to know about it and you're not doing it anyway, so I don't care what it is."

"Tch, tch, *Left*-tenant," Saint Just drawled as he lit a cheroot. "Have you forgotten that you are here as an invited guest?"

"On what's probably a wild goose chase. Whose idea was this?"

"Actually, Socks is the one who put all of Sterling's clues together. Socks? Toddle over here a moment, if you please."

Socks crossed to them, rubbing his hands together. "What's up? We ready to move? Curtain up, light the lights?"

"Jeez Louise," Wendell said, looking at Socks. "Are you wearing make-up?"

Socks closed his eyes. "Just a trace of shadow. And some blush. Why?"

"Hey, no reason," Wendell said, rolling his eyes. "But I repeat, you all know this is probably a wild goose chase, right? There have to be a couple of hundred rehearsal halls in the city."

"With a blinking light over the bathrooms, right across from the stage? Do you know how hard it is to concentrate on being a tree in a windstorm with a red light flashing at you? And the Chinese food? I used to have to go home after my lesson and take Pepto-Bismol, and all I did was *smell* the stuff. That was about six months ago, and they've closed the place, I heard. But that's it, I'm one hundred and ten percent positive."

"Yeah, yeah, okay," Wendell said as Saint Just merely stood back, allowed the man to have his moment.

"Jake and I have already gone around the block for a look-see. There's a back door, and Jake will cover that. I couldn't call anyone else in or I'd have the brass all over me for a—hey, why not say it again—a damn wild goose chase. But, because you'll go with or without me, I'm here. Socks, you've been in the place. What's it like through the front door?"

Socks lifted his chin, smiled, obviously now enjoying *his* moment. "Let me see. We enter through the front door. Narrow hallway, flight of stairs. Steep flight, up to the rehearsal hall. Anteroom first, office to the right, coat rack to the left. Door straight ahead, into the hall. Stage on the right, bathrooms on the opposite wall. Two windows, but they're blacked out. Oh, and there's a short hallway at the back, on one side of the windows, I don't remember which side. Anyway, that leads to a door and more steps that go straight to the street."

"Probably leading to that back door you mentioned," Saint Just said when Socks was through, and all but taking a bow.

Wendell scratched at a spot just behind his ear. "Okay. If you're right, and we all know you're not, they probably have Sterling and Snake in the rehearsal hall. Or in the office, and moved them to the rehearsal hall to make the tape. We can't know which. Blakely, you've had more time to think about this. What's your plan? And tell me it includes Maggie and Mary Louise out on the street, waiting for you to do your big rescue."

"I told you not to call him," Maggie muttered under her breath.

"Maggie? Are you chewing bubble gum?"

"Our plan, Wendell," Saint Just said, as the man looked at Maggie, frustration evident in his expression, "is to enter the building as if we are a troupe of hopeful thespians and their teacher."

"Let me take a wild shot at this. You're the teacher?"

"I'm hardly suited for the role of ingenue, *Left*-tenant," Saint Just said, fingering his quizzing glass. "If the small foyer is unguarded, we will proceed into the rehearsal hall, quite casually, while you stay back to inspect the office

Socks mentioned. If it's occupied by Sterling and Snake, you will release them while we cause a diversion in the rehearsal hall. If Sterling and Vernon are not being kept in the office, we will know that when we enter the rehearsal hall, and you will follow us, to gather up the baddies once the ladies and gentlemen, and myself of course, have confused and diverted them. You are, I presume, armed?"

"I shouldn't be. I should be locked up somewhere. Okay, you said there's only two of them. I'm not even going to ask how you know that one. Now here's how it goes. Jake gets inside, up the back steps, ready for anything. I stay in touch with him by radio—don't ask, Alex, I can do that, okay? We go in the front, *I* go into the rehearsal hall while you grab Sterling and Snake from the office. If they're not in there, I'll have already drawn down on the kidnappers and called Jake in for backup. Everyone else?" Wendell glared at Maggie. "Everyone else damn well stays here. Either that, or I call for another squad car now, because I'm not putting civilians in harm's way."

"You're letting Alex go with you," Maggie pointed out, blowing another bubble. The girl was obviously, as Socks explained when he himself did it, "getting herself into the role."

Wendell looked at Saint Just. "You still got a sword in that thing?"

"Need you ask?"

"Right. Look, I walked out on the prep for the exchange at the ferry, saying I was following up one last lead, and they're soon going to be looking for me. Let's do this."

Wendell patted the small bulge in the side of his ill-fitting jacket, motioned to the uniformed officer, and started off down the street, Socks, Killer, and Mary Louise just about skipping after them.

"He's only one cop," Maggie said as she and Saint Just hung back, strolled more than skipped or stomped (Wendell did the stomping). "One person. And that Jake guy looks about twelve. I like your idea much better. The more people that come crashing into the rehearsal hall, the more confused those two goons will be, the less they'll be apt to pull out their guns, and the better our chances. Besides, I want to do this."

Saint Just grinned down at her. "Yes, I'd already sensed that. It is fun, isn't it? Danger, derring-do, the flamboyant act, the ingenious rescue, the brilliant capture. Serious business, I grant you, but Sterling would expect no less of me. You've written it, Maggie, many times. Now it's your turn to shine."

"You're doing this for me? Because . . . because I don't think I'm brave?"

"In part. Why, docs that upset you?"

"If you think we're maybe putting Sterling and Snake in more danger, yes. But . . . but if you really think I can do it?"

"I know you can do it, my dear. I, after all, am a hero, and you created me. Ergo—"

"We're talking fiction here, bucko," Maggie said as they joined the others outside the door to the rehearsal hall. "This is real life. I can't go back and rewrite it if it all goes belly up."

"Yes, yes, of course," Saint Just said, stepping closer to Wendell. "Shouldn't you go with the officer? Just to make certain the door isn't locked? I mean," he said, lowering his voice, "I believe I still see the dew on that boy's chin. I wouldn't wish to see him come to grief. We'll await your return, once the lad is in place."

Saint Just then looked pointedly at the uniformed cop, to see him gripping a baton with white-knuckled fingers as two red flags of color stained his peach fuzz cheeks.

"So very young," he said, sighing. "And you're quite sure he won't shoot himself in the foot?"

"You're such a pain in my—Jake. Follow me." But first he jabbed a finger in Saint Just's chest. "Wait for me."

Saint Just brushed at his shirt, to be sure there were no wrinkles, and waved Wendell on his way. "Well, that was simple. It is so lamentably easy to mislead an honest man," he said, opening the door to the rehearsal hall and bowing for the ladies to precede him into the small foyer.

Which smelled of Chinese food, almost more so than the air on the street.

"What about the lieutenant?" Socks asked, closing the outer door softly. "Aren't we going to wait for him?"

"He'll catch up. Ready, ladies and gentlemen?"

Killer, his face as white as his shirt, raised a hand. "Uh . . . I gotta go."

"Oh, for crying out loud," Mary Louise said, rolling her eyes. "Didn't you go before we left the apartment? I *told* you to go."

"Sorry, Mare." Killer hung his head. "I forgot?"

"Very well, George. When nature calls, what use are we to deny the summons? You're excused."

"Oh, great. Thanks. I'll bet there's a bathroom next door, at the restaurant. I'll be right back."

The door opened and closed once more.

"Moron. Great big *ma-roon*," Mary Louise said, one hand on the bannister. "Are we really going to wait for him?"

"Hardly," Saint Just said, tucking his sword cane beneath one arm as he surveyed his troops one last time:

Mary Louise, lamentably but, at the moment, fortunately clothed in her more usual garb. He had dressed her for the cover-model contest, which gained the naturally beautiful young woman her own contract with Fragrances by Pierre, but this afternoon she had chosen to dress herself: what Saint Just had recognized as cowboy boots. A pair of shorts that began two inches below her navel and ended approximately eight inches later. What could only be a large handkerchief tied around her small bosoms. But she had agreed not to color her hair pink, and had left out all the facial adornment save five earrings, all of them most mercifully in her ears.

Mary Louise, Saint Just knew, remained a work in progress.

Socks, bless him, had ingeniously dressed himself as exactly who he was, a doorman and hopeful actor and now cover model who still lived with his beloved mother, could impersonate Barbra Streisand with remarkable accuracy and range, counted a female impersonator as one of his closest chums, and in his off hours had proven himself to be the proud possessor of at least a half dozen pair of extremely slim black imitation leather slacks and twice as many skin-tight black T-shirts. He had a lean and hungry look about him, as well as a most endearing vulnerability.

He looked, in short, exactly like someone who had come to the rehearsal hall to . . . rehearse.

And then there was Maggie. The lovely body most often hidden beneath too-large clothing and depressingly uninspired pajamas, showed very much to advantage in her current too-short skirt, high strappy heels, and knit blouse. She'd tousled her artfully streaked hair, wore at least one too many pieces of jewelry, and even now she was pushing yet another stick of pink chewing gum into her mouth, past her overly red lips.

If the thugs upstairs weren't diverted, they were either eunuchs or blind. Or Socks. Hmmm . . . no, he didn't think so.

Saint Just started up the stairs, careful not to touch the railing, which appeared to be rather sticky, his troupe following behind. A bare bulb hung at the top of the stairs, illuminating a second foyer, and the door to the office.

Motioning for everyone to remain quiet, he drew his sword and then signaled for Socks to open the door.

Socks did, pushing it in even as he kept his back to the wall, and Saint Just stepped through into another room lit by a bare bulb. There were two chairs. There was evidence of lengths of rope, lengths of satin cords on the floor. There was nothing else.

He exited the room, shook his head, and replaced the sword. "They've been moved, but hopefully are still on the premises. Stage in this direction, correct, Socks?"

Socks nodded, his eyes wide. "I was right, they're here? Wow."

"In full throat, people," Saint Just said as he heard the door to the street open and heavy footfalls on the stairs. Clearly Wendell was on his way up, and with all the finesse of a charging bull. *"Now."*

Saint Just flung open the double doors to the rehearsal hall, his arms remaining spread wide as he visually sized up the interior and its occupants before he turned to everyone and said, "Ah, my young thespians, here we are. Home of the muse. Haven of the artist. The cathedral of sweet creation. Step lively, my lovelies, and we will commence. As Abelard said, 'What a King, what a court, how fine a palace!' "

Still with his back to the room, sure he could feel an angry glare boring between his shoulder blades, he continued to move backwards, waving his fingers to encourage everyone else to follow him, even as he kept his eyes on Maggie. Tightly on Maggie. "Come now. Come, come."

Maggie inclined her head to the left, then turned to her right and could not suppress a smile.

Yes, he already knew that. Thugs to the left, Sterling and Snake to the right. A rather loud, obviously laboring fan running somewhere, most probably inside one of the bathrooms. That could turn out to be a stroke of luck.

Mary Louise took up the dialogue, as she'd volunteered to go first, and had the only real rehearsed lines. The rest would be, as Socks had termed it, improvisation. "Oh, wow, a real stage! I haven't been on a real stage since high school. I was Eliza. Well, her understudy. Hey—who are these guys?"

Curtain up.

Saint Just turned around, but not before seeing Wendell at the door, and waving him back into the shadows. The man was set up well enough to look the actor, but he also all but screamed *copper.* It was imperative he remain out of sight until Sterling and Vernon were safe.

"Youse! Who the hell do youse think youse are? G'outta here."

Saint Just wheeled about. "Enunciation, my good man, e–*nun*-ciation. *You,* not *use. Get out of.* Three distinct words. Clearly, and from the belly, speaking to the balcony." Then he frowned, added: "I say, are you here to join our group?"

As the man blinked and glared, Saint Just got his first clear look at the enemy's face. One of them, at least. Pitiful creature. Overweight. Huge, but soft. And with egg noodles trailing down his shirt.

Maggie and Mary Louise, as earlier directed, now hastened past Saint Just, all the way across the large room, to the wall near the hallway to the rear door.

Wendell might have wished to know that Socks and Saint Just had tended to that door an hour earlier, making sure it was unlocked, so that Maggie and Mary Louise could have an easy escape of it if necessary, if the moment became truly dangerous.

Now Saint Just was in front of the stage, Socks to one side of the room that had to be at least forty feet square, the ladies far to the other side. Too many places for one man, even two, to look at the same time.

A perfect flanking maneuver, if he did say so himself, even with George and his nervous bladder absent.

The thug was at it again, advancing on Saint Just, his arms hanging away from his body, rather like an ape on the move. "I said, youse get out. Youse can't be here. This here's private."

Saint Just frowned at the thug. "I beg your pardon? Are

we early? I was certain I was promised use of this hall from five to seven."

"Yeah, well, Twinkletoes, youse *don't* got it," the man said, his hands balled into fists the size of hams. "Now get out."

"Oh, but he can't get out, Bruno." Sterling's voice came from behind Saint Just, from the near dark of the stage. "You see, it's exactly the way I told you. He's—"

"Oh, wonderful. More students. Bruno, you say? Wonderful name," Saint Just said quickly, placing himself in front of center stage, where Sterling and Snake sat perched on the edge, surrounded by opened white boxes of Chinese food.

Snake, never the brightest star in any galaxy, still had a plastic fork halfway to his mouth, dripping noodles. "Uh . . . hey, hi, Al—"

"Yes, students!" Saint Just said, cutting him off. "Come, come, everybody. Today we begin *Macbeth.* 'Macbeth shall never vanquish'd be until Great Birnam wood to high Dunsinane hill shall come against him.' Tell me, children, what does that mean?"

"Oh, I know that one," Sterling said, raising his hand. "Great Birnam wood was near Macbeth's castle, and the attacking army cut off branches and put them on, then advanced on Dunsinane. Macbeth thought it couldn't happen, but it did. Because the soldiers pretended to be trees and—oh."

Wonderful. Sterling understood. He, Saint Just, and the rest of his small entourage, were Birnam wood, and had come in disguise to conquer Dunsinane.

Saint Just, his back to the stage, pretended to count heads, using the tip of his cane to do so, while actually checking on everyone's positions. Maggie and Mary Louise to the right, a lovely diversion. They were to preen, pose. Stay out of the way, even as their mere presence made them very much in the way.

But Mary Louise seemed to wish to enlarge her role. "Louise?" she said, stroking Maggie's arm. "How 'bout we practice that lesbian kiss again while we're waiting?"

"Okay, we could do that, *Thelma*," Maggie said, not missing a beat. "But not so much tongue this time. You're not Madonna."

"You're no Britney yourself. Now, open up."

Bruno's attention was instantly diverted, and Saint Just motioned toward the bathrooms. "Logical, yes?" he said quietly, and Socks nodded, then started across the room.

"Saint Just? *Pssst,* Saint Just?" Sterling whispered, leaning front on the stage. "I knew you'd come. I told them you'd come. I told them you're a hero and—"

"Yes, yes. Hush now. Sterling, Vernon, hop down from there and start for the door. Now, while Socks diverts the man. I have your backs."

"Gotta piss," Socks said loudly, rolling his shoulders as he went.

Bruno, who seemed to have his attention and his hopes elsewhere, belatedly sprang to attention. "Hey, you. Where do youse think you're goin'? I told youse all, youse gotta go," the man called Bruno growled.

"God, man. Didn't I just *say* that?" Socks said, giving his head a little slap with the heel of his hand. "Duh. Be right back, dude." Then he hesitated, put a hand to his hip, looked Bruno up and down, winked. "Unless you want to come along, sweetbuns?"

"Go screw yourself."

"How boring," Socks said, and kept going, breaking into the chorus of "It's Raining Men" as he went.

Bruno watched Socks for a moment, then turned back to Maggie and Mary Louise, then back to Socks again. Poor fellow. So easily confused.

But Bruno wasn't *that* stupid.

"I don't think youse jerks are getting this. We've got the

room. Youse get out," Bruno said, advancing toward Saint Just again, hitching up his pants by pressing both forearms against his waist and hefting at his protruding stomach. "Else somebody's gonna get hurt."

"Oh, I know that one. That's from *Guys and Dolls,* right?" Maggie asked brightly. "I'll just bet that's where it's from."

Saint Just turned to see that she was on the move, blister it, ignoring his strictures, advancing on the thug, perilously close to getting very much in the way.

"Mag . . . er, Louise? Return to your place, please."

But the dratted woman had the bit between her teeth now, and wasn't to be turned away.

"Say, you're kinda cute," Maggie said, then pointed at Bruno. "Didn't I see you in that Swiffer commercial last month? Sure, I did. Hi, I'm Louise. What's your name again?" Then she blew a bubble.

"Sterling, Snake," Saint Just hissed. "I'll most certainly throttle her later, but don't waste this. *Move.*"

"In a twinkle, Saint Just," Sterling said. "I knew you'd come. I was just telling Bruno about how you foiled that attempt to assassinate Prinney by—um, Saint Just? The jig is up. Bruno has pulled out his pistol."

"Alex, watch out!" Maggie yelled at much the same time.

Saint Just, who had calculated distances and possibilities earlier, anticipating just such a move on Bruno's part, swung about with one graceful motion, wielding his cane like a club, so that it slammed against Bruno's forearm. The man's weapon skittered across the floor and Mary Louise snatched it up, held it in both hands as she aimed it at Bruno.

"I got him, Vic. Is this cool, or what?"

"Socks!" Saint Just called out. "The door! Close the door!"

The door to the men's room was opening, and Socks kicked it shut again, the second mobster's hand caught between the door and the wall, the gun he had in that hand falling to the floor. Socks picked it up, grinned at Saint Just.

The entire adventure had lasted no longer than two inspired minutes.

"Unbelievable," Wendell said, stepping into the room with his own weapon drawn, even as Jake came through from the back. "Un-freaking-believable. I had the drop on him the entire time you bunch of clowns were fooling around out here, you know," he said, looking down at Bruno, who was rolling from side to side, moaning, "My arm, my arm. Youse broke my freakin' arm."

"There was never a doubt in my mind, *Left*-tenant. Perhaps you'd care to assist Socks now? I believe he's having some difficulty keeping our second thug contained."

Wendell did a head tip thing toward the bathrooms. "Jake. Handle that."

"My arm! My arm!"

Wendell bent down. "Hey, bozo, you have the right to remain silent. Use it." Then he grinned up at Maggie. "I've always wanted to say that, just like a TV cop. Why should you guys have all the fun?"

"Inspired, *Left*-tenant. Wasn't it, Bruno?"

"Screw you," Bruno said, then looked up at Wendell. "You're a cop? Youse is all cops? Cripes, he's gonna kill me. I'm a dead man."

"Who's going to kill you?" Wendell asked, leaning closer.

Saint Just picked up one of the small white containers, sniffed it, then put it down again. "I believe the gentleman may be referring to one Enrico Totila, don't you?"

Bruno moaned.

The second mobster, a near clone of Bruno, his hands cuffed behind him, his trousers pooled around his ankles, was being half shuffled, half dragged toward the group, Jake on one side, a grinning Socks on the other, holding the man by the elbows.

"Shut it, Bruno," the man warned. "We say nuthin'."

"He broke my arm, Nick. He freakin' broke it."

"Call for the wagon, Jake," Wendell said, motioning for Nick to sit down beside his partner. "Makes no never mind to me, boys. We already have Totila nailed. But, first one of you who decides to help, hey, I'm not making any promises. Just think about it."

"A pity they're both incapacitated," Saint Just said, then sighed. "I really would have liked to pummel them. I had been quite looking forward to it, actually."

"And me," Sterling said. "You know, Saint Just—Henry, and all of that."

"Ah, well, we'll have to comfort ourselves that we carried off our plan so wonderfully. Shall we take our bows and depart?" Saint Just took out his handkerchief and lightly rubbed at Maggie's too-red lips, then motioned for everyone to leave the building.

Maggie nearly danced as she walked. "We were all wonderful, weren't we? We were all wonderful! Sterling? How's the eye?"

"Not so bad. Did anyone think to bring my spare spectacles?"

Mary Louise opened her purse and pulled them out. "Here you go, Sterl-man." Then she grinned at Snake. "Come here, you big jerk," she said, and opened her arms to him.

"Maggie, wait," Wendell called out, jogging over to them all just as they neared the stairs. "I'm going to need statements from Sterling and Snake here."

"Later, Wendell, if you please," Saint Just said, and Sterling, who believed Saint Just's word to be law, waved to the lieutenant and headed down the stairs.

"Yeah, all right, later. I've got to go call off the stakeout at the ferry anyway. I'm telling you, that was nuts in there, and if you ever try something like that again I'll—"

"Never complain about success, Wendell," Saint Just interrupted. "But thank you so much for your assistance. Truth to tell, I saw your participation in this exercise as being one of, well, cleaning up after us."

"Why, you—"

"Steve, please. All I want to do now is go home and wash my face. And take off these shoes. Is there anything else, or can it wait?"

"Yeah, there's something else. About Bernie." Wendell waited until Socks took the hint and went down the stairs, then said, "As long as I was at the station anyway, I checked the lab, pulled in a favor, and got something new for us to think about."

"And . . . ?" Maggie prodded when Wendell didn't say anything else.

"J.P. has to find out through channels, okay? My ass—my neck is already in a sling over Bernie's case, and now I've got to explain what happened here. I'll be lucky if I don't end up walking a beat at the Staten Island Ferry. You don't mind if I sort of twist what happened here around a little, so I don't look like a complete jerk?"

"Understood. Our lips are sealed," Saint Just said. "But I take it this is good news for us, and unfortunate for Dettmer?"

"I think so, but who knows? Blood work on Bernie came back. Alcohol level? She was up there. But they also found Rohypnol."

Maggie staggered where she stood and Saint Just reached out to steady her. "Was she raped?"

"No. No assault. Just the Rohypnol."

"Excuse me?" Saint Just said. "Loath as I am to admit such a thing, I find myself adrift here."

"Oh, God, I'm sorry, Alex. Rohypnol," Maggie told him. "They call it the date rape drug. Right, Steve?"

"Right. It makes you look really drunk. A guy can pour

some in a drink, and next thing you know he's walking the victim out of the bar. She'll do anything he wants, and remember next to nothing the next morning. It's a bitch. And, if we don't get the blood fast enough, we can't even trace it. Bernie's must have been one hell of a dose."

"So she's innocent," Maggie said, and Saint Just squeezed her hand. "I mean, we always knew she was innocent, and it's terrible that somebody slipped that stuff into her drink—but she couldn't have Rohypnol in her system and cut Buddy's throat, too. Could she?"

"I doubt it. Time of death establishes that Bernie was full of the drug at the time. But, that's up to the experts, and I'm sure there will be plenty on both sides. Personally? No way. No way in hell."

CHAPTER 17

Maggie dragged herself into the apartment, aimed her body at one of the couches, and dove in, her nose buried in the pillows. "I've never been so exhausted in my entire life," she mumbled.

"Yes, so you've said. In the hack, in the elevator, and again now," Alex said, placing his cane against the wall beside the door. "Am I to assume that your excursion into playing the heroine is one you don't wish to repeat?"

"Not any time soon, no," Maggie said, turning onto her back, to look up at him. "But we were great, weren't we?"

"I know my performance bordered on the superb, but that was only to be expected," he said, grinning at her as he walked over to her computer, brought up the screen and her America Online account.

"I'd have a comeback for that one, but I'm too tired. Catch me tomorrow, after a good night's sleep, and I'll zing you with it. What are you doing?"

"Eliminating your spam, of course."

Maggie closed her eyes, too tired to get up, stagger to the desk, bop him over the head. "You're doing *what*?"

"I see no need for you to read so much as the subject

headers of some of the garbage you receive. Ah, another one. And we bid a fond farewell to *Size does matter.*"

Maggie giggled. "Are you deleting those for me or for you? What's the *matter,* Alex? Do those messages embarrass you?"

He ignored her, his hand still on the mouse, obviously still deleting like mad.

"There, done," he said at last. "Only six from journalists begging interviews. In a city this size, it would appear that Bernice is rapidly becoming yesterday's news."

"I'm sure she'd like nothing better, but I doubt you're right," Maggie said, stretching her arms over her head. "Where's Sterling?"

"Safe as houses in our own apartment, now that we've so thoroughly routed the baddies. You do know that Wendell could have put a period to our little adventure at any time? And yet he didn't."

"I know. And then he did that bit about the creeps having the right to remain silent. He had fun, didn't he? I mean, he broke darn near every rule in the cop manual, or whatever it is, and he *enjoyed* it."

"And now we must reward him. This could prove difficult."

Maggie pushed herself up against the cushions, bent to unstrap her shoes. "Why? We give him the photographs, he's a big hero all around, the mayor pins a medal on him, and Enrico Totila is hauled off to jail. Where's the problem?"

Alex poured them each a glass of wine, handed one to her, then sat down on the facing couch. "For one, I do believe I remember promising the photographs to Holly Spivak."

Okay, she wasn't tired anymore. "You *what*?! What in *hell* were you thinking?"

He shrugged. "A moment of madness? And, I'm hopeful, one that will bear fruit very soon. And it's not as if Wendell knows we've discovered anything, remember. As far as he knows, we have been dealing with an unknown, undiscovered *it*. Fortunately, we have managed to discover two *its*. Tell me, do you think Wendell would be satisfied with the key we found behind the landscape?"

Maggie blew out her cheeks, shook her head. "I doubt it, not once those photographs hit the news. Would Spivak? No, wait, never mind. She can't do anything with a safe deposit key. The cops can. Except, you know, none of this stuff is ours to give to anybody. It all belongs to Mrs. Goldblum."

"Who is not here. Who departed rather precipitously and may never return. I'm not too well versed in your American law, but doesn't this mean that the person in possession of the photographs, the key, is the one who is in charge of same?"

"Meaning you?"

"I would be my first choice, yes. At the moment, the coppers know that Sterling and Snake were kidnapped, held for some sort of ransom, and then rescued. Hopefully, Bruno and his friend will be singing—is that the word? singing?—to them about their employer, how they were merely following his orders."

Maggie sipped from her glass. "It could . . . no, wait. The goons know, don't they, and that's what they'll tell the cops when they try to make their deals? Even if they don't know, if Totila didn't tell them what they were supposed to pick up, if they only trashed your apartment as a warning or something, when those photos hit the news Steve is going to know just how they got there. We can't get out of it, Alex. We have to turn them over, first thing tomorrow, or sooner if Steve insists."

"Miss Spivak will not be best pleased."

"She'll be pissed," Maggie agreed. "Boy, Alex, you really screwed up this time. Shame on me, but some small part of me is laughing like hell."

"Anything to amuse you, dear lady," he said, executing a flawless "leg," as a formal Regency bow, complete with arm flourishes, was called. And he'd pulled it off beautifully in twenty-first-century clothes. Man, she'd given him panache, in spades.

"Gee, thanks, but this isn't funny. We have to give the album to Steve, no question. Look how Spivak messed up that bartender interview. We don't want her messing up this one. I don't want anyone else coming after Sterling."

"Nor do I," Alex said, and Maggie felt a tingle skip down her spine at his tone. Gone was any hint of his usual good humor, and even sarcasm. His tone had gone flat, and definitely dangerous.

"Alex? You okay?"

"Right as a trivet," he said, smiling. "Then it's settled," Alex added, getting to his feet. "The photograph album goes to the coppers tomorrow. Wednesday at the latest. As they don't know we have it, they also won't know when we first recovered the thing."

"The police, Alex. Stop saying coppers. You sound like an old movie."

He smiled. "I'm so glad you agree. It goes to the *police.* And now, if you'll excuse me, I wish to go check on Sterling now that his undoubtedly emotional reunion with Henry is over. May I suggest you go wash your face?"

"You can suggest it," Maggie said, getting up and padding after him, barefoot. "I want to give him another hug."

When Alex opened the door the sound of a piano reached them as they stepped into the hallway.

"Piano? Sterling doesn't play the piano," Maggie said, putting her ear to the door. "Who's playing the piano in there?"

"Well, my dear, we have two avenues to pursue on that head," Alex said. "We could stand out here and discuss possibilities, or we could open the door and find out."

"You're really starting to get on my nerves," Maggie said, turning the knob and stepping into the apartment. "And this should be locked. Why isn't this locked?"

"Probably so that you won't feel it necessary to knock it down," Alex suggested as they both turned to see who was playing the baby grand. "Felicity?"

"Faith?" Maggie added, blinking.

Sterling either saw or heard them, because he came running over, smiling. "Isn't she wonderful? She was here when I came home. That's Mozart she's playing now. We should be quiet, not disturb her."

"What's she—" Maggie hesitated, because Sterling frowned at her, then lowered her voice to an angry whisper, began again. "What's she doing here?"

The music stopped abruptly and Felicity stood up, her hands still outstretched, her manicured fingers curved over imaginary keys. "Hello, Maggie. Alex. I told you I played."

"Bully for you," Maggie said, grabbing a spot on one of the couches. "Who let you in here?"

Felicity sat down at the piano once more and idly ran up the scales as she said, "A very nice young man. Paul, I think. When I told him I was expected he escorted me up here, let me into this lovely apartment that I so wanted to see again." She frowned. "It looks different somehow. Wasn't there more furniture? Oh, well, I couldn't wait at your apartment anyway, Maggie. He didn't have a key that fit yours."

"And now you know why," Maggie said as Felicity's fingers cascaded over the keys to the opening of "Autumn Leaves." "Yeah, yeah, we're all impressed. Now cut that out."

"Maggie's had a very long day," Alex said, his hand on the keyboard cover, ready to slip it back into place as soon as Felicity removed her hands—which she did with some alacrity. "Delighted as we all are to see you, Felicity, is there some special reason you're here?"

Felicity shrugged her shoulders, swiveled around on the

bench to face the room. "I came to see Bernie, of course. But she isn't here. I have a present for her." She then smiled at Maggie. "And one for you, of course," she added, her nose all crinkled up as she spoke as if to a child who might otherwise pout. "I could never forget *you.*"

Maggie glared at her, because that was all she could do. "You are so lucky I'm beat, Faith."

"Yes, you are, aren't you? This is a new look for you. I wasn't going to say anything, but you do look . . . oh, dear, *hard* is such a nasty word."

"Sterling," Maggie said, still glaring at Faith, "take a note, will you? Kill Faith. Pencil it in for, oh, Thursday?"

Sterling patted at his pockets. "I . . . I don't have, that is . . . I'll remember, Maggie. Oh, wait. You didn't really mean that, did you?"

Felicity laughed, a sound halfway between a bray and a trill. "So? Where is Bernie? You've hidden her somewhere, haven't you? I mean, you said she wasn't here the last time I tried to see her, but I knew you just had her in a bedroom or something because, well, you'd do that sort of thing, wouldn't you, Maggie?"

Maggie stood up, hugged Sterling. "I'm going home. You guys can stay here. Have a sing-along or something."

"No, wait," Felicity said, reaching into her oversize bag. "Don't forget the presents."

"Maggie . . . ?" Alex said quietly, and her shoulders sagged. "There's a good girl."

Maggie turned to Faith, held out her hands. "Okay, okay, give me the presents."

Felicity handed them over; two envelopes, each tied with a large pink bow. "I just think they're the neatest things. I mean I was with Jerold today—he's my broker—and it hit me. The perfect gift. Enjoy!"

"Wednesday," Maggie muttered under her breath. "I don't

think I can hold out until Thursday." But knowing Alex would just prompt her anyway, she smiled and thanked Felicity for the gifts. "Bernie will be delighted," she said, figuring that was close enough to a thank you.

"Oh, you're angry, aren't you? You never could be graceful about these things, could you? I remember when you won your single Harriet. Was that at the Detroit conference? I think it was. 'Romancing Detroit.' WAR always comes up with such innovative names for the convention. You just mumbled, then got off the stage. I've had prepared speeches for *all* of my Harriets. Of course, now that I've been installed in the hall of honor in my category, I'm not eligible for the the the contest anymore."

Maggie was just standing there, tapping her foot. "Done now?" she asked, smiling brightly. "Good. Faith, Sterling and Alex are gentlemen, so they won't boot you out of here, but we've had a long couple of days, so . . . ?" she ended, turning to look pointedly at the door.

Felicity gathered up her bag and light jacket. "You will tell Bernie I was here? And that she's in my thoughts? I leave tomorrow morning for a whirlwind tour for the new book, but she *is* in my thoughts."

"We'll tell her," Maggie said, opening the door, then closing it almost on Felicity's heels. "In her thoughts. Right. At least Bernie won't be crowded for space." Then she counted to three, turned and looked at Alex. "What?" she said, spreading her arms. "What did I do wrong? I thanked her."

"You won't allow her to be grateful, Maggie. That isn't kind. And, if I might put forth a theory, until you gush and gurgle and ask her to possibly go to the shops with you or share a suite at next year's WAR convention, I would say she will continue knocking on your door—or ours."

Maggie considered this. "You're saying she'll keep coming around, giving me presents, until I start *liking* her again?"

"Exactly," Alex said, rolling his head on his shoulders, obviously feeling weary himself. "Then, and only then, will she be able to snub you once more. It's fairly obvious."

"That's sick. Twisted." Maggie bit her lips between her teeth. "And *so* Faith." She looked down at the pair of envelopes. "I wonder what she got me this time."

"Yes," Sterling said, stepping closer. "Open it, Maggie. I like to see presents."

Maggie looked at the envelopes again. "Tomorrow, okay? If she did something dumb I'll just get angrier, and I need to get some sleep. What time is it, anyway?"

Alex pulled out his pocket watch. "Not quite seven."

"Seven? It feels like midnight. How can I be so tired? I can't go to bed yet. Steve is probably coming over to take statements from Sterling and Snake—who isn't here, by the way—and I haven't even had dinner. Only seven?"

"Yes, and with Holly Spivak on her way, if she has gathered everything I want. A decision, Maggie. Do we want the information or not?"

"Well, now, there's a question," Maggie said, stepping out into the hallway, looking both ways, to be sure Felicity wasn't still there, hunkered down behind a potted plant and ready to spring. "What information?"

Alex opened the door to Maggie's condo and ushered her inside. "I'd rather not raise your hopes merely to dash them," he said, picking up his wineglass once more, "but I believe the information will go a long way toward solving the murder of one Buddy James."

Maggie, who had snatched up and begun downing the last of her wine, sputtered and choked. "It . . . it *what?* What is it? Don't do this, Alex, don't keep secrets. We're *partners,* remember?"

"That we are, my dear. But I would rather be more certain of my suppositions before involving you."

"Your theory's full of holes, right?"

"Rather large, gaping ones, yes," Alex said, taking her wineglass and refilling them both. "You will allow a gentlemen some small latitude until he feels more certain?"

"I guess." Then she held up a hand. "But there's a limit. How much latitude?"

"Enough to tell Wendell that we still don't know what *it* is?"

"And here we go round the merry-go-round. Again. I'm getting pretty tired of playing devil's advocate here, but I think I should point out that he'll want to bring people in to search the place."

"Will he? He does, after all, know that Bruno and—Nick, was it?—didn't find anything when they performed their search. Why would he expect to find what they did not?"

Maggie rubbed at her forehead. "I'm too tired, because that sounds logical. But not too tired to know there's a stiff penalty for withholding evidence."

"Which we will not do," he said, and Maggie could tell that he was thinking even as he was speaking. "What we will do when next we see him is tell Wendell nothing, agreed? He goes away frustrated, no unfamiliar feeling for the dear man, and we show the album to Holly Spivak when she arrives, telling her she'll have photocopies of each page as soon as possible."

"Then, after Spivak hands over what you want from her, we give the album to Steve, saying we found it . . . Where did we find it?"

"I would suggest behind the refrigerator," Alex said, touching the small of his back.

"So why don't we go right now, photocopy the damn thing, and give it to him tonight? Get this over with?"

"One, time constraints. I expect Holly Spivak at any moment. And two, I may wish to employ it again before Wendell takes possession."

"Employ it for what?"

"Nothing to worry your head about. Now, perhaps you'd like to shower before the good *left*-tenant arrives? Are you hungry, my dear? I can phone out for a pizza or two. I think Sterling would like that."

"Yeah. Eat Chinese, you're always hungry an hour later," Maggie said, and put down her wineglass. She stood up, felt her head go light and her knees weak. "Wow. One and a half glasses of wine, and I'm feeling it. I do need to eat. Okay, I'll shower, you get the pizza. Give me a half hour."

"Done," Saint Just said, just as the telephone rang. "Would you like me to—"

"I'll get it," Maggie said at the same time, and picked up the portable phone. "Hello?" She covered the mouthpiece. "It's Steve."

Alex picked up the extension:

Steve: I'm not going to make it there tonight, sweetheart. It's all going to hell here.

Maggie: What's wrong? Did they find out about us being there?

Steve: No. Jake's cool on that. But our boys clammed up immediately, and then their mouthpiece showed up.

Alex: Explain, please.

Steve: Cripes, Blakely, you're on here? You're always around.

Alex: And a veritable thorn in your paw, Wendell, yes. Now, what is a mouthpiece?

Maggie: Lawyer, Alex. Bruno and Nick already have a lawyer. Bet it's Totila's lawyer.

Steve: Bingo. And he's already arranged bail. It's not a done deal. They have to be arraigned at night court, but they're getting out before morning, Maggie, and everyone here knows it. Unlawful restraint, they're calling it unlawful restraint, not felony kidnap. So they get bail. Can you believe that? Who says the mob doesn't own judges anymore?

Blakely? Stash Sterling and Snake someplace safe, okay? Unless you want me to take them into protective custody?

Alex: I'll do just that, thank you. So we won't be seeing you this evening? Aren't you finished the moment the thugs are locked behind bars?

Steve: Are you kidding? I'll be writing reports until midnight. And here I am, the guy who never took creative writing. Anyway, they'll be back on the street and I'll be here. Like they say, there's no justice.

Maggie: Awww, Steve . . .

Alex: Yes, well, I believe I'm done here and will hang up now. Feel free to bill and coo.

Maggie: Damn it, Alex, don't—

She covered the mouthpiece again. "Don't *do* that. Go home. *Your* home. And call for that pizza. Jeez. . . ." She turned her back to him and headed down the hall to her bedroom, holding on to the phone with both hands.

CHAPTER 18

Saint Just waited until Maggie had closed her bedroom door behind her before picking up the photograph album and his cane and heading across the hall.

"Sterling? Is it all arranged as I requested?"

Sterling nodded. "Mare and Snake will meet you at Mario's as soon as Miss Spivak leaves. Oh, and Mare dropped this off, saying you'd asked for it." He handed over a cell phone. "Saint Just, exactly what are you planning?"

"Nothing you need to worry your head about, my friend. Have you been putting ice on that?" he asked, looking at the purple bruising around Sterling's eye.

"This? Oh, yes, yes. But with my glasses on, I can't put the ice bag where it's needed, and with my glasses off, I can't see past the tip of my nose. It's a conundrum."

"One easily solved," Saint Just said, leading Sterling to one of the couches, the one with the cushions placed there upside down so the slashes in the fabric didn't show. "Lie yourself down and I'll fetch the ice bag."

"You're so good, thank you," Sterling said, toeing off his sneakers and pushing them onto the floor. "Oh. Mrs.

Goldblum phoned. Did I tell you? Such a nice lady. I didn't have the heart to tell her what happened to her apartment."

Saint Just had stopped dead; he slowly turned to face his friend. "She phoned? When?"

"Let's see. We've been so busy. Ah, I remember. Just before Miss Simmons played the Mozart. I was going to come find you, but I couldn't be a neglectful host, and you arrived only a few minutes later and—was that all right?"

Saint Just fetched the ice bag and returned to the living room. "It was fine, Sterling. Just fine." He sat down on the facing couch. "So. Is Mrs. Goldblum enjoying her vacation?"

Sterling put the ice bag to his eye, then winced.

He did not see Saint Just's hands close into white-knuckled fists.

"She didn't say, actually. She just wanted to know if everything was fine here and I told her it certainly was, right as rain, because she's dead old, Saint Just, and I wouldn't want to shock her."

"You've a good heart, Sterling."

Sterling eased back against the cushions. "And a very sore head. She'll be here tomorrow evening. Yes, that's it. Tuesday. That's tomorrow."

"I beg your pardon. She's returning to the city?"

"Only to pick up something she forgot. Some passing thing? I really couldn't hear her, as there was a lot of noise in the background. Bells ringing, voices, music. She wants to talk to you when she arrives, Saint Just."

"And I her," he said, feeling his jaw tighten. "I'm going to phone for some pizzas to be delivered to Maggie's in about an hour or so. Why don't you rest until then?"

Sterling sighed, then smiled. "Yes, that sounds wonderful. You'll come get me?"

"Someone will, Sterling, in the event I'm still out and

about on my errands," Saint Just said before returning to Maggie's apartment to use her telephone. He listened for a dial tone, which was rather unnecessary, as he could hear her shower running, then used the speed dial to order pizza, and some of Sterling's favorite cheese sticks. Poor man; he was too overset to remember those himself, but Saint Just was certain he'd miss them if they were not there.

Then he was off again, the photograph album tucked under his arm, his cane in his right hand, to wait for Holly Spivak in the foyer of the building.

She was already late, but by seven-thirty she was walking into the building, carrying a large brown manila envelope.

"We meet again," she said, holding up the envelope. "Where do we go to do this?"

Saint Just motioned to the single faux leather couch in the foyer and Holly sat down, patted the seat beside her. "You first this time. Show me."

For a good quarter hour Holly Spivak grinned and gasped and several times descended to a variety of expletives a gentleman pretends not to be hearing pass a lady's lips.

Besides, he was fairly well engrossed reading the material she had brought to him. He uttered a few expletives himself, but only in his mind, and manfully refrained from uttering a "huzza!" when he discovered what he'd been hoping would be there; that nebulous thing that he did not know to look for, but would recognize if he found it.

The gaping holes in his hopeful theory began to draw in on themselves like a noose.

At last Holly closed the album, laid the palms of her hands on the cover. "I'm going to *own* that station, Alex. Where did you get this?"

Saint Just carefully extracted the photo album from her grasp and placed it beneath the envelope. "That, my dear, is information you neither need nor want. Suffice it to say that copies of each and every page of the album will be yours to do with as you please . . . Wednesday. Perhaps sometime to-morrow, but Wednesday at the latest."

She made a grab for the album. "No. No! I want it now. You have to give it to me *now.*"

"My dearest Holly," he said, holding out a hand and helping her to her feet. "What you have just seen is evidence, correct?"

"Damn straight, it is. Totila goes down hard with that stuff, and so do a bunch of other wise guys. Stefano Tiberio, to name one big wise guy. Nasty son of a bitch."

"Wise guys?" Saint Just shook his head. "Never mind, my dear, I'm sure I'll be able to figure that out on my own, eventually. But, back to the album. In its original form, it is evidence, and the police will doubtless confiscate it immediately, as well as ask you some very pointed questions."

"So? I'm a reporter. I don't reveal my sources. They can put me in jail, but I won't talk, won't give them your name."

"How gratifying, I'm sure. However, if the police were to come into possession of the original, and doubtless announce what it contains, but not publish any of those contents for public consumption . . ."

He paused, waiting for her to pick up the thread. Which she did, as she was not a stupid woman.

"Then I can show the copies and say I was sent them anonymously, hint that they came from the cops themselves—and I'm home free."

And here it was. He either stopped now or was committed to going forward. There was no real decision; nobody was safe until and unless Enrico Totila and his group were removed from the board.

"I believe I would be happier if you hint that the photocopies came from Enrico Totila himself."

"Really? Wow, he'd be dead meat if I did that—turning on his own, maybe making a deal to inform on his buddies. But I like it. Totila will sing like a bird to the cops once I show the photocopies, he'd have no choice if he wanted to stay alive. I mean, not that I'm worried he'd try to come after me, but he could. God, Alex, you're a genius. A real fucking *genius.*"

"Modesty to one side, yes, I do believe I am. So? You're pleased?"

"Absolutely. When do I get the photocopies again?"

"No later than Wednesday. We must be certain the original album is already in police hands before you present your copies on the air, hinting that you believe they came to you courtesy of one Enrico Totila. Timing, you will agree, is fairly crucial."

Holly nodded. She pulled a card from her purse. "Here. Here's my home address. Send them there. I don't want anyone else at the station seeing them before I have my hands on them. I owe you, Alex. That stuff I gave you? Bunch of junk, all of it."

"Possibly. Did you reserve a copy of everything for yourself?"

"Do fish swim? You get anything out of that mess, and I'll be able to figure it out, and use it. Man, am I going to be the fair-haired girl at the station. Love you," she said, kissed his cheek, and ran out of the foyer on her high heels.

Saint Just picked up the album and his cane, and was off once more. Next stop, Mario's.

Mary Louise and Snake were sitting in the back, sharing a large cold roast beef sandwich, a soda bottle in front of each of them. "Hiya, Vic," Mary Louise said, waving him over to the table. "Mario put this stuff on your bill, okay?"

"Certainly."

"You get the phone?"

"I did. And it is untraceable?"

"Use it and lose it," Mary Louise said, grinning.

"Splendid."

"Not really. Anybody can get one."

"And modest with it all. Very well. You have the numbers?"

Mary Louise chewed several more times, then swallowed. "Give them to him, Snake."

Snake reached into his pocket and pulled out two crumpled slips of paper. "Killer's aunt Isabella's daughter Annuziata who lives where his Aunt Isabella used to live before she croaked got it from Totila's cousin Concetta who lives where his grandma used to live because Annuziata told her that her nephew Maurizio got stiffed by his boss and he wants to ask a favor of Totila. Like cracking a couple heads."

"These intricacies truly boggle the mind," Saint Just said, pocketing the papers. "How did you procure the second one? I have managed the address through another source, but not the telephone number."

Mary Louise grinned around a mouthful of sandwich. "I did that one. I know this cop, see? Started talking to him about how high and mighty the big guys live, while the cops who do the *real* work are out there holding the thin blue line, taking the bullets. Said I bet our guy lives in some mansion somewhere. And he told me where. The rest I got from this cross-directory I just happen to have. Sometimes it's just too easy, you know?"

"Easy enough to abandon, I pray, now that you've got your contract and a considerable step up in the world?"

"Hey, I told you I'm retired. You're the one asked me to do it. Shame on you, Vic."

"Too true. I am corrupting the easily corruptible. I should be, and am, ashamed. And now, thank you and farewell. Oh, and Mary Louise?"

"Here it comes," she said, rolling her eyes. "What is it this time, Vic?"

He reached into his slacks pocket and pulled out several large bills. "Go shopping, if you please. Our initial photography session is in less than two weeks."

Snake laughed. "Yeah, Mare, go shopping. Maybe then guys won't be walking up to you and asking how much."

"At least I'm not like Killer. I don't spend half my life walking with my legs crossed."

Saint Just left Mario's, a smile on his face. A smile that faded quickly.

Busy. Busy. And so very grateful for all the attention he had paid previously to both the Learning Channel and various police dramas.

Once away from the deli, he extracted the cell phone from his pocket, found the number he wanted, and punched in the numbers:

"Dettmer residence. Who is calling, please?"

"Alex Blakely for District Attorney Dettmer, concerning our meeting earlier today."

"I don't think—"

"How wonderful. Are you paid to do that? Not think? Please give my name to the gentleman. I'll wait."

Saint Just continued to stroll along the flagway, nodding to passersby who for the most part ignored him. How he adored New York.

"Blakely? Dettmer here. I'm in the middle of a dinner party. How the hell did you get this number?"

"And a good evening to you, my good fellow. I won't detain you. I'm only calling to ascertain whether or not there has been a change of heart on your part and you are now interested in the proposition I forwarded this morning."

"Pictures of Totila."

"Indeed. I have them with me now, even as we speak, and would be happy to meet with you, make you a gift of the whole lot. In exchange for a more, shall we say, civilized treatment of Ms. Toland-James."

"No deal. She's guilty and we're bringing her in. Like we don't know where she is? The hell we don't, and Boxer better

start worrying about her license. I'm giving her name to the review board."

"Boxer, you say? I don't believe I know the name."

"Bull. And don't pull that crap about those pictures again. They're fakes. They've got to be fakes."

"Are they? Is your zeal to arrest Ms. Toland-James so intense that you can take that chance? I must ask myself, Dettmer—Why is the man so hot to have her under lock and key?"

The phone went dead.

"And now I'm certain," Saint Just said, smiling thinly.

He took out the second number, made yet another call.

This one took longer, but when it was done and a meeting arranged, he strolled to the corner, crossed the street, and walked a good three blocks to the south and another three to the west before stopping.

He wiped down the cell phone, smashed it beneath his heel, and then tossed it into a large dumpster before hailing a hack to take him to the nearest Kinko's, where he photocopied the entire photograph album, returning to Maggie's condo just as the pizza delivery van pulled away from the curb.

Timing is all. Timing is everything.

And Saint Just was always in the nick of time.

"Saint Just, there you are," Sterling said as he picked out a slice of pizza and aimed it toward his mouth.

"Sterling. Maggie. Shall I procure napkins from the kitchen, or would you rather simply pretend you're at the trough?"

"Nice try, Alex," Maggie said, expertly using her tongue to whip a string of pizza all the way into her mouth. "I will not be diverted. Where were you?"

"Off to see the wizard?" he suggested, having been forced on the occasion of a previous pizza-devouring gathering to sit through *The Wizard of Oz* while Maggie explained the plot to him and Socks sang along with Judy Garland.

"You mean the witch, don't you, or didn't you meet with Holly Spivak?"

"I met with her, yes."

"And you took that album with you."

"So observant. Have you also noticed that I've brought it back? I thought I might have more need of it this evening, but as it turns out, the party wasn't interested. And, before you ask, I have photocopied the thing for Holly Spivak, so you may feel free to phone the good *left*-tenant and apprise him of the fact that, goodness gracious, we have discovered *it* behind Mrs. Goldblum's refrigerator. He can then turn the album in to his superiors and receive a pat on what they will doubtless consider his fair head."

"Stop trying to score points off Steve, okay? Sit down and eat, and tell us what Spivak said. Did she go for it? I guess she did, right?"

"She saw the wisdom of my plan, yes," Saint Just said, selecting a slice, holding it slightly aloft over the box while oil drained off onto the cardboard. "Did Sterling inform you of his telephone conversation with Mrs. Goldblum?"

Once Maggie was done coughing, Saint Just explained the call, hoping she might know what a "passing thing" might be.

"Oh. Oh! I found it in her closet." Maggie unfolded her crossed legs and headed for her computer desk. "Where is that?" she asked, rummaging through the perennial mess that made up her corner of the writing world. "Okay, here it is. Her passport, Alex. She's coming back for her passport. She can't leave the country without it."

Saint Just took possession of the thing, paging through it, manfully not wincing at the photograph that should, by rights, have had Irene Goldblum challenging the photographer to pistols at dawn.

"She also wants to speak with me," he said as he handed the passport back to Maggie, who wiped her hand on her shorts, then took it, stuck the thing in her pocket.

"Maybe she wants to sell you the apartment. Remember, she does own it. We learned that much. Oh, and you can't afford it. Neither can I, so don't ask."

"Not even as an investment?" Saint Just asked, mostly because he rather enjoyed watching Maggie's green eyes flash in anger.

"Forget it. Although . . ." she added, biting her lip. "You know, it beats the hell out of the alternative."

"Oh! I know that one. Having us move back in here. That's the alternative," Sterling supplied, then dropped his chin. "Sorry, Saint Just. I lost my head there for a moment."

Maggie giggled.

"That's quite all right, Sterling. But to return to Mrs. Goldblum, if we might? According to Sterling, she will be dropping by tomorrow evening."

"You know what I don't get?" Maggie said, waving around a slice of pizza. "If Mrs. G. has been blackmailing Totila, why did she go overseas to do it? If that's what those trips were about. Why the postcards? And why in hell would she come back now, after Totila figured out it was her blackmailing him? Wouldn't she know that she's still in danger?"

"One would assume so, but then again, we all know the danger in assuming things."

"I don't think we have any other choice," Maggie said. "Until she shows up, that is. Man, do I have a bunch of questions for that woman. I think I'll make a list."

"Yes, I agree. Mostly, I'd like to know where she made her mistake, so that Totila discovered her. Indeed, there are still ends to be tied up there, even as we progress to other things."

"Other things being Bernie."

"Exactly."

"You're not going to tell me what you're thinking yet, are you?"

Saint Just got up, removed the manila envelope from the small pile that included the photo album and the photocopies, and tossed it on the couch. "Here you go, my dear, bedtime reading. We'll talk again tomorrow. For now? Well, I think best while walking, so if you'll excuse me I believe I'll take a stroll, breathe in some clear night air before turning in. Sterling, you also should be heading for your bed."

"It's eight-thirty, Saint Just. Isn't that early to be crawling into bed?"

Saint Just looked at Maggie, who was yawning behind her hand, even as she held up the envelope, squinted at it. "Whatever you wish. I have my key, Sterling, so don't wait up, although I won't be long."

And then he picked up his cane, patted his pocket to be sure he had everything he needed. He opened the door, pausing to look at Sterling, at Maggie. They'd be fine, the two of them. Safe. And they would remain so.

He, Alexandre Blake, Viscount Saint Just, was going to see to that.

CHAPTER 19

Maggie opened her eyes and rolled over, looked at the bedside clock. "Seven o'clock? It should be at least ten."

Throwing back the covers, she stumbled to the bathroom, made a face at her reflection in the mirror, stripped, and stood under the shower for five minutes before she had the energy to wash herself.

Teeth, brushed. Hair, too damn bad. Clean underwear, a pair of jeans, T-shirt.

Good to go.

Bacon and eggs. Bacon and eggs sounded good. And Sterling deserved a nice breakfast. Alex? Okay, he could eat, too.

Bacon draining, scrambled eggs on a plate and topped by another one so they'd stay warm, Maggie put two slices of wheat bread in the toaster and padded barefoot through the living room, opened the door to the hall.

"Alex?"

His back was to her as he was inserting his key in the lock. "Ah, good morning, Maggie," he said, slowly turning around to face her, the morning newspaper tucked beneath one arm, the ever-present cane tucked there with it. He raised one eyebrow. "Been in a contretemps with a garden rake?"

Maggie pushed her fingers through her still damp hair. "Bite me." She stepped closer, squinted up at him. "You didn't shave yet. And aren't those yesterday's clothes?"

"Sadly, yes. I fell asleep on the couch last night, and decided to visit Mario's for my morning tea. Shame on me."

She thought he looked pretty good in a morning beard, but she wasn't about to say so. "I made bacon and eggs. I was just coming over to get you and Sterling. Mostly Sterling," she added, because the man looked entirely too good, rumpled. She could imagine waking next to him, his head on the pillow, a slow, sleepy smile on his face. "Do you want some or not?"

"How could I possibly refuse such a gracious offer? Let me see if Sterling has stirred yet."

Maggie followed him into the apartment, pulling the newspaper out from under his arm as she went. "Wasn't he up before you went to Mario's?"

"My, so many questions. And one answer, I don't know. This apartment is so large, you understand, so much larger than yours, that he may have been awake and I simply did not hear him."

"You don't have to get snarky," Maggie said, stung. "Man, and I thought I didn't get enough sleep."

"You didn't," Alex said, grinning. "Now, if you'll excuse me for a few moments, I'd like to splash some cold water on my face and clean my teeth. Sterling."

"Oh, hullo, Saint Just." Sterling entered the living room, the left side of his face and his eye a rainbow of ugly purples, reds, and yellows. "Good morning, Maggie."

"Sterling," Maggie said, tipping her head to one side. "Oh, does it still hurt? It looks like it still hurts. I cooked breakfast for you, sweetheart."

"Thank you, Maggie," Sterling said, and when Alex returned to the room, the trio crossed the hall together.

Sterling and Saint Just sat at the table and Maggie served them, feeling extremely domestic, a feeling that would probably evaporate in a rush when she had to wash the dishes.

"Did you have a chance to read the information Miss Spivak provided, Maggie?" Alex asked, patting his mouth with the cloth napkin he insisted upon rather than paper napkins, then neatly folding it and placing it on the table.

"Some of it. Bios of Dettmer and Buddy. So what? What's the connection?"

"Are you going to eat that last piece of toast, Saint Just?"

"No, Sterling, you may have it with my blessings. Read all of the information, Maggie. I think you'll understand."

"Go ahead, Maggie. I'll clean up here," Sterling offered, and she didn't wait for him to say it twice.

"I left everything in my bedroom," she told Alex. "You go sit down, and I'll get it."

By the time she entered the living room Alex was sitting at his ease in front of her computer, probably deleting spam again. For some reason this made her feel all soft and fuzzy for him, because he cared enough to shield her from what he had to think was information not suited for the eyes of a gentle lady.

"Cut that out," she said, because he expected her to, then sat down, slipped on her reading glasses, and pulled everything out of the envelope. "Okay, what am I looking for here?"

"You really want a hint? That's not very sporting."

"Yeah? Well I don't *feel* very sporting this morning."

"Very well," Alex said, seating himself on the facing couch. "You know that I paid a call on District Attorney Dettmer yesterday morning? Oh, wait. I don't think you do."

"I do now," Maggie said. "Why would you go to see him?"

"As a supplicant? I had hoped to appeal to his better instincts, so that he would be . . . less aggressive in his condemnation of Bernice."

"Oh, wow. You're lucky he didn't lock you up."

Alex lifted one hand, visually inspected his fingernails. "So I've been told. At any rate, while I was in his office—"

"You actually got in? Wow. Oh, oh, I'm sorry. Keep talking."

"Thank you. While I was in his office—rude man, he didn't even offer refreshments—I happened to notice a family photograph. He has a wife and two children, one boy, one girl. Teenagers."

Maggie narrowed her eyelids, shook her head. "So?"

"The photograph was taken in a room, the background of which was rather . . . shall we say homely? You know, Maggie. Rather like Bernice's home in Connecticut."

"Early American," Maggie said, nodding.

"Definitely not recent," Alex said, and Maggie bit back a smile. "Also, behind them was a very large window looking out over a beach, the ocean."

"They were on vacation. I don't get it."

"Dettmer was rather unhappy that I was inspecting the photograph, which could have been simply because he is not, I would think, a happy man by nature. But he did agree that a beach was part of the photograph."

"If you're going to drag this out any more I may be reaching for my cigarettes, and it would be your fault."

"A beach, Maggie. We'd just been to the beach, you and I. You know how deeply I believe in coincidence?"

"There are a lot of beaches between here and Connecticut, Alex."

"True, which is why I had Holly Spivak gather information about our friend Dettmer."

"And Buddy."

"And Buddy," Alex agreed. "Now, would you care to read over that information again, or shall I simply tell you?"

"How about I just guess? The beach behind Dettmer and his family is in Connecticut?"

"Very good, Maggie. Yes, it is. Dettmer is separated from his wife of twenty-seven years, but not yet divorced, perhaps for the sake of his political career, perhaps because he is lazy. That's one piece of information. Another is that before Dettmer moved to Manhattan to take up his political career, he practiced the law from his home. In Connecticut. His wife and children still reside there."

Maggie reached for her cigarettes without even thinking about it. "Where in Connecticut? In the same town as Bernie and Buddy? Bernie never mentioned it."

"Bernice never bothered to meet her neighbors," Alex said.

"True." She frowned. "Dettmer made D.A. here in only ten years or so?"

"He left Connecticut fifteen years ago, actually, long before Buddy disappeared. Although I will admit that his political star did rise quite rapidly. If you'll read Holly's report, you'll see that he was very well financed in his bid for election."

"I have to write this down," Maggie said, grabbing a pen off the coffee table and using the envelope to write on. "Okay. Dettmer and Buddy both lived in the same town in Connecticut. Dettmer left fifteen years ago. Buddy disappeared seven years ago." She looked at what she'd written. "Nope. I still don't get it. So they once lived in the same town. So what?"

Alex crossed one long leg over the other. "They did more than live in the same town. They both sailed, both belonged to the same sailing club, as a matter of fact. On the last page, Maggie, you'll see that they often sailed as a team, and won trophies together. They were lifelong chums, friends."

Maggie paged through everything until she came to the last page. "So why didn't he say that when he gave that stupid interview to Holly Spivak? He really could have milked that, you know, and all to his advantage. What's he hiding?"

"Oh, dear, you got there more quickly than I'd thought. That is the problem, Maggie. I don't know what he's hiding. But he is hiding something. I offered him the photographs, if you must know, if he would desist in besmirching Bernice's good name in the media, and he refused."

Maggie sat up straight. "You offered *him* the album? Cripes, Alex, is there anyone you *didn't* offer that thing to? We could have put it up on eBay and made a bundle."

"You'll be contacting Wendell this morning?"

"Right. He's the lucky winner, and let me tell you, I'll be glad to have that thing out of here. Once the police have it, Totila and his goons won't bother us anymore, don't you think? I mean, they might be mad, but they won't be back. You agree?"

Alex got up, walked over to the table and retrieved the pink bow-tied envelopes. "I see you haven't opened your present from Felicity."

"Huh? Oh, right. Do I have to? I want to think about this Dettmer-Buddy connection some more."

"Very well. If you'll excuse me, I'm going to go clean up my dirt and change into fresh clothing."

"Okay, sure," Maggie said, still frowning at the pages and pages of information.

She was still at it an hour later when Socks buzzed her to say that J.P. Boxer was downstairs.

"And so begins another day in Cloud Cuckooland." Maggie sighed, and told him to send her up.

"Have you heard from Bernie?" Maggie asked, waiting in the hallway as the elevator doors opened and she saw not only J.P. but also Steve. "Oh, hi."

"Hi yourself," Steve said, kissing her on the mouth. "Ummm, you taste good."

"Bacon," Maggie said, smiling up at him. He was so

good, so kind, so sweet. So *not* Alex. It would be so easy if only she was half as attracted to him as she was to the dangerous, yes, dangerous personality of her no longer quite so imaginary hero.

"To answer your question," J.P. said once they were in the condo and she was sitting on the couch, facing Maggie, "Bernie is fine. As a matter of fact, she's so fine that they're going to allow her a personal phone call. Only one, which is why I'm here—I wrangled a continuance on my case for court. You talk to her, I talk to her, anyone who wants to talks to her, and then she's incommunicado again for another week. Okay?"

Maggie blinked back sudden tears. "That was so nice of you, J.P., to have the call come here. When?"

J.P. looked at the man-size watch on her left wrist. "Any time now. What are those papers? Anything to do with Bernie?"

Maggie looked down at the papers strewn beside her on the couch. "Uh . . . well, maybe. We're not sure."

" 'We' meaning our English friend? Where is he, anyway?"

"He lives across the hall. He'll be here soon."

Steve picked up the papers and started looking through them, and Maggie was torn between being glad he was interested and wondering if she should snatch them away from him. Which was stupid. He was on their side.

It was just that she really wanted to be the one who solved the crime, made the final connection, cleared Bernie. And Alex, of course. He'd already found some connection between Dettmer and Buddy.

Hoping to distract Steve, she said, "Ohmigosh, I forgot. Steve? We found what Totila's men were after."

Well, that worked. He put down the papers at once. "What? Where?"

Maggie fetched the photo album and dropped it into his

lap. "Don't worry about fingerprints. I think half of Manhattan's are on there."

"What?"

"Never mind," she said, sitting down again, watching as he paged through the album. "Alex found it behind Mrs. Goldblum's refrigerator." Then she decided to play dumb, because that seemed safest. "What do you think? Is it important?"

"Important? This . . . this is . . . I've got to get this downtown. Maggie, J.P.? I was going to break it to Alex that I had to send a team out here to search, but this is—I have to go." He blew out a breath, squeezed the album between his hands. "Wow. I mean, *wow.* Thank you." He grabbed Maggie, kissed her hard on the mouth. "Gotta go."

"I've always liked him," J.P. said as the door closed on Steve's back. "Doesn't even pretend to be hard-boiled. Costs him when it comes to moving up the ladder, but he's one of the good ones. What was that anyway, Sunshine?"

"Nothing important," Maggie said, picking up the envelope with her name on it. "I guess it's time I open this."

"And I guess it's time I mind my own business," J.P. said, slapping her hands on her knees.

"Oh, I'm sorry," Maggie said, sitting down again. "It's just . . . well, I have this . . . acquaintance. Yes, this acquaintance, and she keeps giving me expensive presents, even when I ask her not to."

"I should have such problems. Open it."

Sighing, Maggie did just that, sliding off the pink ribbon, then ripping open the envelope. She removed a single sheet of scented note paper as well as a second piece, typewriter size and of good quality.

She unfolded the larger paper first, scanned it quickly. "I don't believe this. I think she's giving me *stock.* Why would she give me stock?"

J.P. grabbed the paper out of her hand. Whistled through

her teeth. "Five hundred shares of Johnson & Johnson? Interesting friends you have, Sunshine."

"Are they worth a lot?"

"Enough. What does the note say?"

Maggie fought down an insane urge to correct J.P., because the note didn't *say* anything; Faith had written something in the note. But that was just her writer self, and she pushed away the urge.

"God, one more curlicue and nobody could read this," she said, squinting at Felicity's florid script. She retrieved her reading glasses from the coffee table, slid them on. "Hey, at least she doesn't dot her i's with little hearts. I should be grateful for small favors."

"Does this person know you can't stand her?" J.P. asked. "Because if she's looking for a new friend . . . ?"

But Maggie wasn't listening. She was reading. And fuming.

"I don't believe this. I do not freaking *believe* this. Listen to this. 'Dearest Maggie. Just in case the writing falls through, so you won't have to take a second job. Ha-ha. Love, Felicity.' God, how I *detest* that woman. She can't do anything nice without putting a dig in it. Second job, my sweet—"

She shut her mouth. Blinked. Second job? That rang a bell. Why did that ring a bell?

"Something wrong, Sunshine?" J.P. asked, aiming herself toward the bowl of M&Ms perpetually on Maggie's computer desk.

"I don't know," Maggie said, reading the note once more. "Second job. Second job . . . don't eat the blue ones. I save those for last."

"And I thought my orange sneakers were eccentric," J.P. said. "So? What's bothering you about a second job?"

Maggie crushed Felicity's note in one hand and got up to pace. "Second job, second job. Don't make enough money, you take a second job. Moonlighting. No, not moonlighting, just a second job. If you need the money. If you can't get by on the job you have, you take a second job. . . ."

"God, this is scintillating," J.P. said, shoving more M&Ms into her mouth. "You belong to Mensa? The weird ones usually do."

"Shh!" Maggie ordered with a wave of her hand. "Second job, second job. Got it! Oh, wow, I've got it! Be right back."

Alex was in his bedroom, still bare to his waist. Long, lean muscles running across his shoulders, down his arms. Six-pack stomach. Good enough to eat, or at least crawl all over, but she'd already pretty much decided to add that on her To Do list. "I've got it! Alex, I have *got* it!"

"My felicitations," he said, removing a navy silk pullover from his closet and sliding it over his head, then smoothing his hair once more. "Are you going to share it?"

"Buddy. He had a second job," Maggie said, pacing once more. "I remember Bernie saying so, that she wouldn't mingle—that's the word, right? mingle?—she wouldn't mingle their finances. He sold insurance. Buddy sold insurance. But he needed a second job, too. Maybe to afford that boat of his, right? Especially since Bernie could care less about boats, and wouldn't help him there."

Alex put a hand to his forehead. "No, sorry. I don't know where this is going."

"Good. Because I do. I'll bet, I'll just bet, that Buddy worked for Dettmer. Part-time."

"Lawyering?"

"Paperwork? Research? I don't know. Just go with me here. He worked for him, and he found out something on him and—no, I'm still thinking blackmail. Why am I thinking blackmail?"

"Possibly because the former tenant of this very apartment dabbled in that particular pot?"

"Yeah, right," Maggie said, sitting down on the edge of

his bed. "It felt so *right,* you know? Bernie—ohmigod, Bernie's going to be calling, any minute now. Let's go."

J.P. was talking on the phone when they entered Maggie's apartment, and waved them to silence. "Absolutely, Red. No, I'd tell you if I knew. You can stay put, so do it. I can wangle you at least another week, ten days, no problem. Okay, here's your friend."

Maggie grabbed the phone. "Bernie? How are you?"

"Thirsty," Bernie said, and Maggie grinned.

"But it's going okay?"

"It's going great. I can't tell you who else is here, but I think Random House is going to be majorly pissed the next time a certain author's contract comes up. J.P. says I can stay."

"I know. And Alex and I, and Steve, we're working to find the real murderer, so you'll be able to stay as long as . . . as long as you need to stay."

"Ah, the Three Mouseketeers. I don't know why I was worried. Look, Mags, this is a public phone, and believe it or not—and I can't, not for what this place is costing me—everyone has to use the same one. There's a line, so I have to go."

"Okay," Maggie said, holding on to the phone with both hands. "I miss you. Oh—wait, don't hang up. Buddy, Bernie. You said he had to take a second job, remember? What was it?"

"Why?"

"No reason. We're just . . . just gathering information. Do you remember where he had that second job? Like maybe it was for Dettmer?"

"Who? Hey, Blue Eyes, I'm trying to hear here. Thanks. Man, Maggie, I feel like a prisoner sometimes. But I'm handling it."

"I know you can handle it, honey. You're a brick. Now. Dettmer. The D.A. He used to live up in Connecticut, too. You never met him up there?"

"No. I prided myself on not meeting anybody *up there*. The mob is getting restless, Mags, I have to hang up."

"The job, Bernie. What was Buddy's second job?"

"Tax collector. Can you imagine that? Bye."

Maggie hit the OFF button, tossed the phone on the couch.

"And?" Alex prompted.

"He was the tax collector." She looked at Alex. "What the hell can a tax collector do that might make him want to fake his death? That might get him killed?"

J.P. snorted. "Oh, Sunshine, let me count the ways. Slip me some cash and I'll look the other way while you go delinquent for three years. Skim some off the top at tax time, cook the books. And the ever popular blackmail."

Maggie's head jerked up. "Blackmail?"

"Sure. You want to sit down? I'll tell you about one I know about."

Maggie sat, and Alex sat down beside her. She grabbed his hand, and didn't say a word when J.P. extracted a blue M&M from the bowl and popped it into her mouth.

"Okay, you're the tax collector in some small town. For a lot of years that didn't mean all that much. Part-time work, small salary, busy once or twice a year, no big deal. Nobody even hated you for being the tax collector. But then it started. The federal government started cutting taxes."

"The federal government doesn't set local taxes, property taxes, that kind of thing," Maggie said, confused.

"Button it, Sunshine. No, it doesn't. What the federal government does is cut taxes, which is one surefire way of getting reelected. But—big but here—lower federal taxes means not as much federal money going to the states. What does go to the states is a list of unfunded mandates."

Maggie raised her hand. "I know that one. The federal government looks good, yelling about education, cheaper prescriptions, the environment, all that good stuff, but when they pass the laws for all of it they don't give the states any money to help fund any of it. Unfunded mandates. They sound good, noble, but no bucks. Mama, pin a rose on the President and Congress."

"But with plenty of penalties for the states if they don't live up to the mandates. Okay, onward. The states have less money, right? That means less state money to the towns, the cities, the boroughs, you name it."

"So local taxes go up," Maggie said, feeling as if maybe they were getting closer to something important.

"Along with state taxes, right. But the states try to be helpful to their towns, and so they don't have to raise the state taxes too high and get themselves booted out of office come election day. So they send out helpful hints on how the towns can make money on their own to take up the slack. New fees, higher fees, new kinds of taxes. A whole raft of new fees and taxes. And the beauty of it is, by the time the taxpayer figures out he's going broke, there's nobody to point a finger at, no big federal or state government to vote out of office, nothing. Instead of screaming where the screaming, and voting, will do some good, what you've got is a bunch of disorganized taxpayers, all hit by parts of these fees and new taxes, and with no clout, no way to mount any kind of ballot box rebellion. It's like being nibbled to death by ducks, and it's getting worse every year. Tax cut? Watch your wallet. Oh, and watch services decline while you're at it—education, after-school programs, senior citizen benefits, aid to the poor, clean air and water, you name it."

Alex squeezed Maggie's hand, then let it go, stood up. "I may be wrong, and correct me if I am, but I believe we've just witnessed a soapbox oratory."

"Yeah, okay, I get carried away sometimes. It's the bleeding heart in me, I guess."

"Nevertheless, I believe I'd like to borrow your eloquence for a small enterprise I oversee here in the city."

"Oh, good grief," Maggie said, rolling her eyes. "Can we get back to the point of this?"

J.P. held out her hands, fingers spread. "What I'm saying is, there are a lot of new nibbled-by-ducks taxes out there, on the local level. And, with those taxes and fees, a lot of new regulations, including, in a lot of small towns, the right for the tax collector to audit anyone, any business he wants to audit. For no reason at all, with no recourse for the taxpayer or business owner. He can go anywhere, look at anything. Inventory, equipment, all the books."

"Without reason?" Alex sat down again.

"Totally without reason. And with the very real threat of audit. I had this client when I was practicing in—well, we'll leave the state out of it. I was only there for a year before I knew I had to get back to New York, where at least when someone spits on you, you can spit back. Anyway, the town passed one of these new taxes, but nobody really knew about it. My client moved into the town, set up shop, paid all the taxes he thought he had to pay, only to find out ten years later that he'd missed one, the new one. A nibbled-by-ducks one; but get enough ducks together and those nibbles become big bites."

"Ignorance of the law is no excuse," Maggie said. "I've always thought that was stupid. I mean, if you *meant* to do something wrong it's one thing, but if you didn't know? At the least, the law could cut you a break."

"We'll get to that later, all right? One outrage at a time. Anyway, he paid all his other taxes, so the tax collector knew what he did for a living. But he never told the guy, just let it slide for ten long years. Then he pounced."

"Pounced how?"

"Demanded an audit, ten years of audit. A real fishing expedition. I read the ordinance, and my client didn't have a prayer. The ordinance let the tax collector do anything, no statute of limitations, nothing. My client was looking at ten years of back taxes, fines, plus monthly interest, monthly penalties—compounded over those ten years—plus the threat of some pretty substantial jail time. But it was the audit that really spooked him. The town had hired on a private auditor who could, either ordered by the tax collector or on his own—remember that, on his own, and then worry about the state of our government—could demand audits going back to the dawn of time if he wanted to. The IRS is in a straitjacket, compared to what these guys can do."

"Excuse me," Maggie said. "This is still America, right?"

"Ah, the dewy-eyed innocent. It's all legal. That's bad. What's really bad is when the auditor and the tax collector get together and go around threatening audits—unless the target comes up with some bucks under the table. The law lets them in, and greed does the rest."

"Blackmail," Maggie said. "I knew it. I knew it all along. Buddy was blackmailing half of his town, I'll bet you, and one of them scared him enough that he took a hike. Then he came back, was seen, and one of them killed him. God, I'm *good.*"

"Yes, my dear, you are. It is a very workable theory, and I'm sure at least some of it fits the criteria we've considered as motive. And we even know who, don't we? Now all that is left is to ascertain *how.* Shall we put our heads together?"

J.P. winked. "Let me tell you, handsome, that's the best offer I've had all month."

CHAPTER 20

The press conference was called for three o'clock, on the steps of the building housing the District Attorney's office.

Saint Just ushered Maggie ahead of him into the small crowd of reporters and other interested onlookers, heading straight for Holly Spivak, who was checking shooting angles with her cameraman.

"Good afternoon, my dear, how nice of you to meet us here," he said. "Delightful day, isn't it? The sun in the sky, not a cloud to hide it. Your complexion shows well in sunlight."

"Alex," Holly said, turning around and grabbing him, giving him a hug. Holding him close, she whispered, "You sent it over, right?"

An actor friend of Socks's, a very large, very Italian-looking gentleman who worked days filleting flounders in a fish market, had been given the job of delivering the photocopies to Holly's doorman, in case anyone decided to ask that man for a physical description of the messenger.

"Everything is proceeding according to plan, yes. But, alas, I fear I need another favor."

"Name it, handsome. I told you I owed you one. Maybe three or four, but don't push it. I'm about to be a very, very big deal, you know. Today New York, tomorrow the nation, the world." She squeezed him again. "Oh, I love you."

"Pardon me," Maggie said, talking to the cameraman. "You have a barf bag around here anywhere?"

"Maggie, behave," Saint Just said as Wendell joined them on the flagway. "*Left*-tenant. Thank you for apprising us of the time of Dettmer's hour upon the stage. Although I would have thought you'd be on the dais along with our esteemed district attorney, sharing the glory."

Wendell scratched at his cheek. "Yeah, you'd think so, wouldn't you? My captain decided to stand in for me, take the credit. Oh, and not put me up on charges for the sloppy way I handled this whole thing."

"Politics," Holly Spivak said, shaking her head. "It's everywhere. What did you do, anyway? I take it you're a part of this?"

Saint Just took Holly's elbow, walked her a distance away from the crowd. "I do believe the good *left*-tenant desires his anonymity in this entire matter, as do I."

"But—"

"That favor, my dear." He extracted a folded paper from his pocket and slipped it into her hand. "When Dettmer calls for questions, I'd like you to ask him this one. And follow it quickly with the second and most definitely the third one. They're written out for you. It is not my usual denouement in the parlor, with all the suspects gathered 'round, but it will have to do."

"Huh?" Holly tried to open the note, but Saint Just squeezed her hand shut.

"When the time is right."

"If you were anyone else . . ."

"Ah, but I'm not, am I? Thank you, my dear."

The sound of feedback had them both looking toward the

top of the wide marble steps, and Holly quickly ran back to her place in the small crowd as Dettmer and four heavily braided and gilded uniformed officers approached the tangle of microphones.

"Good afternoon," Dettmer said, his florid face pressed close to the microphones, setting off another round of screeching, until he stepped back, smiled at his audience.

He pulled a folded page from the breast pocket of his suit and shook it open, began to read. "I am here to announce a major breakthrough in my administration's concentrated war on organized crime in this city. Through months of hard work by the people behind me, coupled with my personal involvement in each and every stage of the investigation, my office is now in possession of irrefutable physical, photographic evidence implicating the heads of two crime families in the crimes of murder, extortion, and other crimes whose details I will not go into at this juncture. Suffice it to say that warrants have been issued for thirty-seven members of organized crime, most notably one Stefano Tiberio and one Enrico Totila, and the roundup of these individuals and their underlings by my personal task force is underway even as I speak to you."

He grinned, turning this way and that for the cameras. "That is the end of my prepared statement, copies of which will be available to the press. As duty calls, I'll only be able to take a few questions."

"You'd better have a damn good reason," Holly whispered, then grabbed her microphone. "District Attorney Dettmer!" she called out loudly, getting her question in first. "Holly Spivak, Fox News. On another matter, sir, if I might. Is it true that you were personally acquainted with one Willard James, recently murdered in this city? And I have a follow-up."

Dettmer frowned down at her. "I scarcely see where that—this press conference was called to report on a major victory in the war against organized crime, and I—"

"Yes, sir," Holly interrupted. "My congratulations, sir, on a job well done. Is it true that not only were you and Willard James acquainted but that you were friends? That you sailed together when you both resided in Connecticut? That your zeal, sir, in proclaiming James's widow a stone cold killer comes from personal motivations?"

Saint Just smiled at Maggie. The crowd had stilled, until a person might be able to hear the proverbial pin drop. Or, when it dropped, and it would, the other shoe.

"Sir?" Holly called out, after referring to Saint Just's note. "One more thing, learned from an anonymous source, if you'll forgive the melodrama."

The district attorney leaned closer to the microphones. "I don't give credence to anonymous sources, Ms. Spivak."

Saint Just stepped closer to Holly, and gifted Dettmer with a jaunty salute, then faded into the crowd once more. After all, a man should know his accuser.

Dettmer went pale behind his rouge.

"Almost done, sir, and again, that anonymous source. Is it also true that additional evidence that will exonerate Bernice Toland-James is expected to be discovered at Willard James's Connecticut home?"

"And now he knows what we know," Maggie whispered. "Or, what we want him to think we know."

Dettmer turned to one of the uniformed officers. "Take over," he said, and then returned to the microphone. Smiled. "Buddy James and I were friends, yes. He was a good man, a good sailor, a good friend. But that has nothing to do with the pursuit of justice, especially in a crime so vicious and hideous, so callous, as that perpetrated on Buddy James. I welcome any and all evidence that might aid in convicting his killer. Captain O'Hara will take over now, as I've got criminals to catch."

One more smile for the cameras, and he was gone.

Holly lowered the microphone as other reporters yelled

out questions. "Oh boy. It's a good thing I've got those photocopies, or my ass would be grass back at the station. I looked like a jerk."

"You were magnificent," Saint Just said, and lifted her hand to his lips. "Thank you, my dear."

"Thank her for what?" Wendell asked. "What am I missing here?"

Maggie took his hand. "Come on, Steve. Show us where Dettmer parks his car."

"What? Why do you need to know that?"

Saint Just sighed. "Because the good district attorney is doubtless about to depart shortly for Connecticut. I thought that would be self-explanatory."

"Yeah, well, it's not. What are you two doing?"

"Shut up and move," Holly Spivak said, motioning for her cameraman to follow as well. "Something's obviously going down, and I don't want to miss it."

"He's got a driver," Wendell said as he led the way around the rear of the building, heading for a five-floor, open-sided parking garage.

"I doubt he'll avail himself of the convenience," Saint Just said, standing back so that Maggie could precede him up the cement stairwell, moving fast in her worn sneakers.

"Hey, wait up," Holly Spivak called after him, slowed by her very high heels. "Damn it, these are steep. Don't wait for me, follow them, I'll catch up," she told her cameraman.

By the time they'd reached the third floor Holly had caught up. Minus her shoes. The woman was truly dedicated.

Wendell stopped on the fourth floor, motioned for everyone to wait while he checked the deck, returning a minute later to say, "I see his Lincoln, on the far left, near the outside wall. And now, if nobody minds, what the hell are we doing? I've already been lucky enough to have my ass pulled out of one wringer, I don't want to have to do it again. Sorry, Maggie."

"We're waiting," Saint Just said, leaning on his cane. "Although I would prefer to be closer, with Miss Spivak and her companion tucked neatly out of sight, but positioned so as to be able to record everything."

"Everything *what?*" Steve asked, and this time it was obvious he wasn't going to be fobbed off.

"Very well, as we seem to have time." Saint Just paused behind one of the large cement pillars, and smiled at Maggie. "Would you care to begin?"

She made a face. "You know I want to. Steve, it's like this. We're not one hundred percent sure, not even fifty percent sure, as a matter of fact. . . ."

"I probably should not have suggested you begin," Saint Just said, sighing.

"Shut up, I'm trying to be honest here, and to be honest here, we don't know a heck of a lot. But—*but*—we do know that Buddy James was the tax collector before he faked his death seven years ago, and we're betting that he faked his death because he'd been playing fast and loose with his perks as tax collector, either skimming off money or blackmailing people. Probably both. One of his victims threatened him, and he took off."

"Dettmer," Steve said. "He knew James, lived there, was friends with him. You think James had something on Dettmer? Wait a minute. James disappeared seven years ago. Dettmer was an assistant D.A. by then, probably getting ready for his run for D.A. If he had some kind of monkey business in his past he sure wouldn't have wanted it brought up."

"Or he was tired of paying so it wasn't brought up," Maggie suggested. "Except that he had a very well financed campaign, so I'll bet he was part of the blackmail scheme, not a victim. So we decided to go with the second one."

"Could you guys talk a little louder? Joe's barely getting this."

"Holly," Saint Just said, shaking his head. "Did I say you could film our discussion?"

Maggie leaned against the post. "Sometimes I feel like I'm in an old *Seinfeld* episode. Maybe the one where they get lost in a parking garage. All I need is a plastic bag with a goldfish swimming in it."

Steve smiled. "Only if I'm Jerry. Alex can be Kramer. He does live across the hall, right?"

Saint Just ignored them, as he didn't understand them, and was fairly certainly he wouldn't appreciate their humor if he did. And then the large metal door opened and Dettmer was striding across the garage, on his way to his car, and there was no time for anything but the Plan.

"Heigh-ho? Dettmer?" he called out brightly, stepping out in front of the D.A., blocking his path. "Delightful running into you here. I have a question. Does your son enjoy his employment at Brennerman's?"

It was a gamble, because he'd not been able to read the imprint on the boy's shirt, not clearly, but a gamble he had to take.

Dettmer had backed up three paces. "I don't know what— get out of my way."

"No, no, please," Saint Just said, extending his cane, even more effectively blocking Dettmer from his vehicle, unless the man wished to dance about and make a complete ass of himself, trying to dodge Saint Just and his cane. "You'll remember that I admired that photograph of your lovely family yesterday, in your office? I was most taken with the fact that the photograph had been framed in front of a beach—I so love the beach, don't you? It wasn't until my mind was jogged by . . . shall we say *other* things, that I realized what else I had seen. Your son's shirt, Dettmer. The wording on that shirt. Brennerman's Pizza."

"So?"

Saint Just smiled. He really was very good at this detecting business.

"So," Maggie said, stepping out from behind the pillar, "when we drove up to Bernie's house in Connecticut we found Buddy James's suitcases and a bunch of bags and boxes from Brennerman's Pizza."

"Yes, I can imagine it now," Saint Just said, sensing Holly Spivak and her cameraman edging in closer. "A visit to Connecticut, perhaps to drop in on your children, perhaps to take a sail. You love to sail, don't you, Dettmer? You speak with your son, ask him how he's coming along, and he tells you that he's fine, and did you know that someone's living in the James house again? Perhaps he tipped well, or perhaps your son mentioned the man because he did not tip well? Or the man looked familiar. Or he was simply making conversation. But he told you, didn't he?"

"I'm not going to stand here and listen to this."

"Please, feel free to leave. Miss Spivak? Could you possibly ask your assistant to record the flight?"

"He's not going anywhere." Maggie pointed a finger at Dettmer. "You knew he'd come back. Didn't you? You knew Buddy was back."

Wendell, who had been keeping silent, added his mite to the conversation. "Buddy's back. That has a nice ring to it."

This called Dettmer's attention to his own lieutenant. "Arrest these people. Her, too," he said, pointing to Holly Spivak.

"On what charge, sir?" Wendell asked.

"On . . . on . . . just arrest them, damn it."

"But this is public property of a sort, sir. They're allowed to be here. And I heard this gentleman say you were free to leave at any time."

Dettmer set his jaw, glared at Wendell. "You were always a troublemaker. That's why you're not going anywhere. You're too damn *cute*."

"Handsome, in a faintly bucolic way," Saint Just interrupted. "But I wouldn't say cute."

"He doesn't mean it that way, Alex," Maggie said, grabbing at his arm, shaking it. "We're losing steam here. Do something."

"Dettmer?" Saint Just said, and the man turned to look at him. "If we could return to the matter at hand? We have a theory, if you don't mind. A theory that includes your friendship with one Willard James, and a plan the two of you implemented several years ago. A plan to line your own pockets through the threat of James's office of tax collector."

Dettmer shifted his gaze to the cameraman, then back to Saint Just. Said nothing.

"At first, I thought perhaps Buddy—you don't mind if I call him Buddy, this good friend of yours? At first I thought he had found a way to blackmail you for something you'd done in your position as lawyer. But then I remembered that you two were bosom chums, sailing together. It made much more sense that the two of you, perhaps after chatting while sailing, decided that, together, you could relieve quite a considerable number of your town's residents of a portion of their income."

Maggie stepped forward. "He'd threaten to audit them, they'd come to you, the lawyer, to get out of it, and you'd arrange the deal. It was perfect. Perfect! What happened? When you decided you wanted public office Buddy threatened *you*? Threatened to expose you? Even if he didn't, could you afford to have Buddy as the skeleton in your closet?"

Saint Just watched Dettmer's face, attempting to gauge how much of their theory had struck the target.

He pushed on, for what was the mind of a sleuth for, a fiction writer for, if not to formulate theories?

"Buddy feigned his own death because he knew you were out to eliminate him before you could feel safe in declaring yourself for office, or you sabotaged his boat and he escaped, then realized the benefits to being assumed dead. Does it matter which is correct? Not really. What matters is that Buddy came back. You must have been horrified, poor man. All your hopes, all your dreams, so nearly within your reach, just to have them all snatched away by the dastardly, damned inconvenient Buddy James."

"Isn't that almost a line from one of my books?" Maggie asked, then shook her head. "Never mind. Keep going."

"So how did he get Buddy to Bernie's penthouse? That's where this is going, right?"

"Correct, *Left*-tenant. That is precisely where we are going. Having discussed all of this today with Miss Kelly here, and attorney J.P. Boxer, we have come up with a possible scenario. Would you care to hear?"

Dettmer took two steps to his left, moving away from Saint Just, who extended his cane once more, blocking him.

"His son told him about the man living in Bernie's house, and he went to check, found Buddy, and pretended he was happy to see him," Maggie said, her words nearly tumbling over themselves in her excitement. "Buddy told him he'd come back to get the three million in life insurance from Bernie now that the seven years were just about up and he was declared legally dead—plus more money from Toland Books, because he knew Bernie had inherited the company. He had newspaper clippings all over the house. He *knew*. Alex?"

"Happily. You, Dettmer, convinced Buddy that you were his friend, delighted to see him again, and would assist him in his quest. You brought him to the city, in secret, to help him confront Bernice."

"Wait a minute," Wendell said, holding up a hand. "Dettmer got him into the penthouse? That works. We have bypass keys for elevators. It would explain how they got in, probably through the freight elevator. And the Rohypnol?

The evidence locker. He could get it from there. It fits. Damn, it all fits."

"Yes, it does, doesn't it?" Saint Just said, feeling rather proud of himself, even if he knew most of the more technical explanations, the business of the pass keys, the evidence locker, had come from J.P. Boxer, and Maggie. "Once Dettmer had Buddy's confidence, he sent him off to Brenda's, to slip the dastardly Rohypnol in her drink and fetch her back to the penthouse. Either he slipped it into her drink without her taking notice of him, then sat back and waited for the drug to work, or he wore a disguise. We'll have to ask the bartender, won't we?"

"This is crazy," Dettmer said.

"Not really, if I might continue. Thanks to your department's investigation into Kirk Toland's death, you already knew much about Bernice's habits, including her proclivity to social drinking. To continue? You had Buddy James drug her, then help her home, upstairs via that same freight elevator. At that point, you subdued Buddy James. How, I'm not sure as of yet, but it will come to me."

"I can help with that," Wendell said. "I didn't tell you, but the medical examiner found a hell of an egg on the back of Buddy's head. Blunt force trauma, he said. Dettmer knocked him out."

Maggie raised her hand, and when she wasn't "called on," spoke up anyway. "Cold-cocks him, strips him, tapes his wrists, mouth, and ankles. Undresses Bernie, re-dresses her in her pj's, plops her unconscious body on one side of her bed, Buddy on the other. Except Buddy's awake now. That's why his eyes were open, Alex. The man saw everything. *Euuuwwww.*"

"You're all insane," Dettmer said. But he was sweating. Sweating, and shivering.

Holly Spivak ordered her cameraman to do a close-up.

Maggie kept going; she was on a roll now. "You killed

Buddy, pressed Bernie's hand around the knife, for fingerprints. Then you cleaned up, took a shower to get the blood off you, and left. Oh, and on your way out you put the tape in the trash that was picked up early Saturday morning, which is why no one found it."

She turned to grin at Wendell. "Hey, it's a possibility. I called Bernie's building to find out when the garbage was picked up. We've been very thorough. And Dettmer's been very bad."

"Yes," Saint Just said. "What did you call it a few minutes ago, Dettmer? Oh, yes. 'A crime so vicious and hideous, so callous.' "

Steve added his mite: "Even folded James's clothing, so it looked like he was some sort of invited guest, taking a shower before crawling into the sack. I kept trying to figure out why the clothes were folded."

"Hey, good one, Steve," Maggie said. "We hadn't thought about that one. So Bernie wakes up the next morning, covered in blood, Buddy's on the bed beside her, dead, and she can't remember anything." She pointed a finger at Dettmer. "Oh, and we're betting you cut yourself at some point, because murder's messy, isn't it, even if you wear rubber gloves, and it's your so far unidentified blood that was found in Bernie's shower drain. But that can be proved very easily. DNA, Dettmer, DNA from the DA. It wasn't the perfect crime, bucko, and they would have gotten your sooner or later. We just made it sooner."

She raised both hands, grinned. "Ta-da! Hey—where's he going?"

Saint Just, who had been enjoying Maggie's enjoyment, turned just a moment too late to stop Dettmer, who had taken off across the garage, Maggie in hot pursuit.

"No!" she yelled. "Don't you jump! You have to tell the truth! Don't—"

Saint Just winced as Maggie positively *launched* herself

at the running man, bringing him down by the simple expedient of wrapping her arms tightly around one of his legs.

Dettmer fell forward onto the low cement wall that caught him across the thighs, grabbed at the wall with his hands and attempted to boost himself over . . . Maggie still holding onto his leg . . . Saint Just and Steve running to help . . . Holly Spivak and the cameraman right behind them.

While Steve grabbed Dettmer at the shoulders, Saint Just pried Maggie loose and took hold of the man's legs, and the DA was pulled to safety and then almost immediately cuffed.

Saint Just helped Maggie to her feet as she winced in pain.

"Oh, boy, my knees. Look at my knees. They're bleeding. Why did I wear a skirt? I had to stop him, Alex. If he jumped, Bernie might still be in trouble."

"You must insist on playing the heroine, mustn't you?" Saint Just said, lifting her hand to his lips, turning it over and placing a kiss in her palm. "Don't do that again."

"Okay," she said, her voice small and her eyes wide as she saw the camera pointed in her direction. "Oh, God. My mother's going to *kill* me."

"Not until you spend at least a few hours giving statements," Steve said. "All of you."

CHAPTER 21

A few hours turned into four hours, and it was only when Maggie begged Wendell to be allowed to go home and take a shower that they were freed to leave.

Sterling greeted them at the elevator, doubtless alerted by Socks. "I saw it. I saw it all, on the television machine. You were magnificent, Saint Just. You, too, Maggie. I was so proud. And Bernie will be that thrilled," he continued as Saint Just pointed his cane toward their own door.

"Thank you, Sterling. Now please tell me we haven't missed Mrs. Goldblum's arrival."

Sterling shook his head. "I've kept the door open to the hall so I would see her, but she hasn't appeared."

"Good," Maggie said, dragging herself into her apartment. "I'm heading for the shower. If she shows up, hang on to her. Tackle her if you have to."

Sterling watched her go. "Poor thing. Being a heroine is difficult work."

"Yes, I do believe that realization came to Maggie, probably as she propelled herself across the parking garage like a shot from a cannon. Shall we adjourn to our domicile? Oh, and if there might be anything to eat?"

"I had Mario make up some sandwiches, yes," Sterling said. "Oh, and I set up a small drinks table. Would you care for a glass of wine?"

"Yes, thank you, I—I'll get a glass for both of us. It's time we nip this notion of yours that I am in charge and you are somehow somewhat less than me. We are friends, Sterling. Equals."

"I know that," Sterling said, raising his chin. "But I do what I do and you do what you do. I prefer it that way, Saint Just, I truly do."

"I don't value you nearly well enough, my friend," Saint Just said, knowing that he was feeling maudlin, for all his success earlier today. "But I will say that I am honored to be your friend."

Sterling blushed to the roots of his hair, held out a plate. "Liverwurst?"

There was a knock on the door, more of a pounding, and Saint Just said, "We really must give her a key."

Sterling let Maggie in and she sat down beside Saint Just, picked up half of his sandwich. "No potato chips? I like to crush potato chips on top of the liverwurst and then squeeze it all between the bread slices. Stop making faces. Never mind, I'm starving, I'll eat it like this."

"Have you brought your list?" Saint Just asked a few minutes later, when Socks buzzed to alert them that Irene Goldblum was on her way up.

"Right here, next to the passport that she doesn't get until she answers all of our questions," Maggie said, patting her jeans pocket. "Bring her on."

Sterling stood sentry at the door, opening it even before Mrs. Goldblum could knock, then escorted her to a chair as Saint Just, ever the gentleman, stood and bowed his welcome.

"Oh, so glad you're all right—I mean, so glad you're home," Mrs. Goldblum said, smiling at Saint Just. "I'm only here for a few moments. I forgot something, you understand. Honestly, I'd forget my head if it wasn't attached. Oh! I shouldn't say that, should I?"

Saint Just and Maggie exchanged glances.

"How's your sister, Mrs. Goldblum?" Maggie asked, dragging her notes out of her pocket.

"My sister?"

"Yes, you know. The broken hip?"

"Oh! Oh, the broken hip. Of course. I—" She stopped, sighed. "You know, don't you?"

"That you've been blackmailing Enrico Totila for the past ten years and you left town when he got onto you and left Alex and Sterling here to take the fall for you? Is that what you mean?"

Mrs. Goldblum frowned. "What? Enrico Totila? That horrible man? You think I was *blackmailing* him? I should be so stupid."

Maggie said it all again, adding, "Sterling nearly got killed because of you."

Mrs. Goldblum pressed her heavily ringed fingers to her ample breast. "Me? Truly, I didn't think anything would happen if I was gone." She looked at Saint Just. "I didn't know what he wanted."

Maggie snorted. "Yeah, right."

Saint Just put his hand on her thigh. "I believe her, Maggie. She truly doesn't know what we're saying." He smiled at Mrs. Goldblum. "Perhaps, as you've realized now that we have earned the right to be curious, you will tell us about these past ten years? The postcards? The trips that were *not* to visit your sister? Your abrupt departure Saturday morning?"

Mrs. Goldblum put a hand to her mouth. "First Mildred, and now you. Well, I suppose there's no reason to keep secrets any more, is there?"

"You're right, Alex," Maggie whispered. "She's either really good, or she's got a whole other something else going on here."

Sterling offered Mrs. Goldblum a cup of tea, an offer she gratefully accepted, and Sterling escaped into the kitchen, obviously unnerved by the woman's upsetment and off to do what he believed might help.

"Where do I start?" she asked, looking around the room. "Oh. You got rid of the landscape. Thank you. You know, Harry bought it for me, telling me that some day it would be worth a lot of money, but I've always hated it."

"That's it," Maggie said, shaking her head. "She really doesn't know. Mrs. Goldblum? Where have you been since Saturday?"

"Hmmm?" Mrs. Goldblum, who had continued her visual inventory of the room, undoubtedly counting up all the lamps and vases that were no longer there, said, "Oh. Atlantic City. We always go to Atlantic City. To the Taj Mahal. Isaac prefers poker, you understand, and there's a lovely poker room there. I like the slots, myself. Those new nickel slots? They're such fun! Stripping chickens, dancing hats—even Lucy, from *I Love Lucy*. I always liked her—have you been?"

Maggie rubbed her forehead. "I wonder if it's okay for me to take more aspirin yet."

"Headache, dear? I'm so sorry. But I should tell you everything, since I seem to have caused so much trouble. I mean, now that Mildred knows, I imagine there's no reason to keep secrets."

"Certainly not," Saint Just said encouragingly. "Please, start at the beginning, and tell us everything."

Mrs. Goldblum opened her large purse and extracted a packet of tissues, one of which she used to dab at the corners of her mouth, where her very red lipstick had begun to leak into the creases. "At the beginning? Well, I suppose that would be two years or more before Harry . . . died. I'd always been very partial to his brother—Isaac, you understand—but as Harry became more secretive, more *standoffish,* I found myself confiding more and more in dear Isaac."

She blew her nose. "Mildred is Isaac's wife. Horrible woman. But Isaac said it was easier to keep our . . . our love a secret."

Saint Just nodded his head. "So he'd go overseas every now and then, send you a postcard, and you'd join him?"

"Heavens, no. Why would we do that? The postcards were our signal. Whenever one arrives, I take the bus to Atlantic City. He always sends such lovely postcards. You know about the postcards? I suppose Socks told you. Didn't he mention that they are all postmarked Chicago? Isaac drops one in the mail as our signal, even though I always know the date of our next rendezvous anyway. Isaac likes to be silly and romantic. Such a dear. We were to meet in two weeks, this time for a full six weeks, as Mildred had planned to visit her daughter. From her first marriage, you understand. That's why I thought you could stay here, to keep an eye on the place. I was going to return the bulk of your rental fee. But then I had to leave early."

"You always met Isaac in Atlantic City?"

"Yes, Alex, always. I don't like to go far away from my doctors, you understand. My cardiologist, my internist, my rheumatologist. Oh, and my podiatrist, of course. I have these most awful corns, and—"

"So you were never blackmailing Enrico Totila?"

Mrs. Goldblum pulled herself up straight. "No, Miss Kelly, I most certainly never was doing anything of the sort. An adulteress, yes, even a hussy, shamed as I am to say it, but a blackmailer? Never. Besides, he's not a nice man."

"So you've met him."

"Only once, Miss Kelly, just last week. He was not, after all, welcome at Harry's funeral. I saw him on the street and said hello, because politeness demands such things. He stopped, asked who I was and if I wanted anything from him, and I told him no, thank you, you gave me quite enough through Harry. Then he asked me if I'd recognized him from his photographs in the newspapers and I said no, not in the newspapers, but that Harry kept this rather extensive photograph album that I only discovered after his unfortunate death—I was very daring, wasn't I, speaking of Harry's death?—and said that I recognized him from many of the photographs."

"You said that?" Maggie asked, wincing.

Mrs. Goldblum frowned. "Yes, I'm sure I did. I was very, very nervous, knowing I shouldn't have said hello in the first place, so I was sort of jabbering, running on and on. I told him that Harry had written all the names and even dates and places beneath every photograph, so that was how—oh. Oh, dear, is that what they wanted? Well, why didn't they just say so instead of saying all those horrible things to me on the phone? I would have given it to them. What do I want with all those old photographs? I put them in the basement."

Maggie made a rather rude sound in her throat. "They didn't have to do it. They didn't have to threaten Mrs. Goldblum and send her running. They didn't have to trash this place, or kidnap Sterling. If they'd asked, she would have handed it over. If they'd done nothing, no one would ever have known. If they'd just left well enough alone. Amazing. Freaking amazing."

"Mind-boggling, I agree."

"But you're all fine, yes?" Mrs. Goldblum asked, taking the cup and saucer from Sterling. "Thank you. You're such a dear. Oh, and that's the other thing. Alex?"

He was still sorting through everything in his mind. "Yes?"

"Mildred found out. Isaac and I were going to meet in Atlantic City in two weeks, as I said, but when that horrible man called on the telephone and said he was coming to get something from me in the morning and I'd better have it ready for him, or else . . . well, I called Isaac in a panic and Mildred listened in on the extension. She's like that, horribly suspicious. So, Mildred knows."

"We all have our problems," Maggie said, fingering her nicotine inhaler. "I can't believe this comedy of errors, because that's what it is. It is. Really. Except it's not funny. But, hey, I'm sorry, Mrs. Goldblum. What happened with Mildred? Oh, and here's your passport," she ended, fishing the passport out of her pocket and handing it over to the woman.

"Thank you, dear. Isaac wants to celebrate, fly to Freeport for a few days, and I may need this. Lovely casino in Freeport. But I left in such a hurry. I mean, between that awful man, and Isaac being so upset that Mildred had found us out . . ."

"You've had a trying few days, Mrs. Goldblum," Saint Just said, wishing the woman's story over, wishing her gone. Because Wendell would be showing up sooner or later, probably sooner, and he needed to have all of his wits about him.

"I have, Alex, I most definitely have," Mrs. Goldblum said, then smiled. "But it's all settled now, if you'd be so kind as to agree to purchase this apartment. You see, Mildred has moved out, gone to Palm Springs to live with her daughter permanently, and Isaac has invited me to come live with him. Living in sin. I'm seventy-three, and about to live in sin. Isn't that delicious?"

Maggie sat forward. "That was the other thing. Thanks for reminding me. Mrs. Goldblum, why did you keep it a secret that you own this place? That rent control business?"

Mrs. Goldblum fingered the pendant on her necklace. "That was Harry, dear. He purchased this place in a . . . a rather unorthodox way, and told me never to say anything. After all, dear, if people believe you to be poor, they're less apt to rob you. Alex? Would you like to buy the apartment? You can have everything, even all this lovely furniture, as I won't need it."

Saint Just gave a moment's thought to "all this lovely furniture," knowing much of it had to be replaced. "Maggie?"

"You'll have to pay me back."

"Fragrances by Pierre," Saint Just said quietly.

"That, and not wanting to go back to having the top left off my toothpaste. Okay, okay. Mrs. Goldblum? How do you want to do this?"

"Oh, I'll just call down to have Socks send Isaac up here. He's very good at that sort of thing. He's a lawyer, you know."

Maggie coughed into her hand. "Corporate?"

"Criminal," Mrs. Goldblum said, smiling. "Just like his brother. It's very lucrative. Tell you what, dear. It's late. I'll wait for Isaac at the elevator and we'll go to a hotel, come back tomorrow."

Saint Just quickly agreed, before Maggie could say anything else, and Mrs. Goldblum and her passport were reunited with Isaac (the spitting image of his late brother), and sent on their way while Sterling lingered behind to feed Henry and Saint Just and Maggie retired to her apartment.

"We had it wrong. We had it all wrong," Maggie said, sinking into the couch cushions. "And we still ended up smelling like roses. Alex, you're the luckiest man in the world."

"I consider myself fortunate, yes," he said, crossing to answer the knock on the door, admit Wendell. *"Left*-tenant. How is District Attorney Dettmer this evening?"

"No longer running for reelection, for one thing." Steve took three steps into the living room, and stopped. "I'm on a quick dinner break. I can't stay, but I wanted you all to know that you guys don't have anything else to worry about. It's over."

Saint Just closed the door, kept his back to the room.

"Over? What are we talking about here, Steve?" Maggie asked. "Dettmer, or the other?"

"The other, Maggie. Dettmer's pleading not guilty through reason of diminished capacity—says he's nuts—but that'll get tossed. I'm talking about Totila."

"You found him?"

"Yeah, you could say that. We picked up Bruno, too, not Nick, but we'll find him, or he'll turn himself in. He'd be nuts not to. The task force rounded up an even dozen of Totila's men, along with about the same for Stefano Tiberio's guys. We just didn't get them in time. I'm trying to feel sorry about that, but I can't do it."

And here it was, Saint Just knew. He seated himself on one of the couches. Took out his quizzing glass, held on to it halfway up the ribbon, began swinging it lazily. "In time for what, Wendell?"

"In time to keep Tiberio from putting out a hit on Totila. Word travels fast, and we figure Tiberio found out about the photograph album and blamed Totila. Who knows, maybe Nick went to him, looking to cut a deal when he figured his boss's boat was sinking. Anyway, a uniform found Totila about an hour ago in an alley, behind a dumpster. He'd been dead for a while, we think, maybe since late last night. Somebody put a knife clean through his heart."

"Totila's dead?" Maggie looked at Saint Just. "Wow."

"Yeah," Wendell said. "Tiberio's screaming he didn't order the hit, didn't do it, that he didn't know anything about any photographs until we showed them to him. But that's a crock, we know he did it. He's been getting away with murder for years, but not this time. Anyway, I've got to get back. We're going to be interviewing and booking all night, but I wanted to let you know. Nothing else to worry about. It's over."

"Over," Saint Just repeated. "Yes, it is."

Steve kissed Maggie, who stood up, walked him to the door.

"Oh, one more thing. Totila must have been planning

something when he was killed. We found a safe deposit box key in his pocket, and we're betting it's loaded with cash because he was about to leave town, or maybe even evidence he'd been gathering to protect himself in case he ever had to make a deal with us. Either way, it's going to be just more proof that Totila was dirty. We'll know in the morning. G'night."

"Thank you, Wendell," Saint Just said, replacing the quizzing glass in his pocket. He'd had to leave the key with the body. Totila had to be found with incriminating evidence in his possession. If it couldn't be the photograph album, it had to be the key.

"Good night, Steve," Maggie said, slowly closing the door, even more slowly turning to look at Saint Just. "Alex?" Her voice was low, tremulous.

"Some things must be done," he said as he got to his feet. He looked straight into her eyes. "To protect those we care about."

Maggie swallowed down hard, stumbled to her desk chair and collapsed into it. "You . . . you *killed* him? Last night . . . you went out. You . . . you were just coming home when I saw you. That's why you hadn't shaved. You'd been out killing somebody. And then you sat down and ate bacon and eggs? Just like that?"

"Not *somebody,* Maggie. Enrico Totila, a man who very much deserved to be dead. I could not trust your welfare, or Sterling's, to anyone or anything less than myself," he said quietly, firmly. "And it was a fair fight, even if I admit to having instigated the thing. The man was armed. But I am who I am, Maggie, and I do what I must do. Surely you understand that."

She didn't say anything. She just kept looking at him.

"Maggie. He's not the first man I've been forced to kill."

Her eyes went wide. "I . . . get out, okay?" She raised her hands in front of her, her fingers spread. Her hands shaking.

"Just . . . I need time to . . . I mean, *I'm* responsible. I taught you how to kill, Alex. I *made* you."

"And I have made me more, so rid yourself of guilt," Saint Just said quietly, but in a firm voice filled with the conviction he felt, which he hoped she'd come to understand. "At the heart of it, my dearest love, at the bottom of it, I am Alexandre Blake, the Viscount Saint Just. And the Viscount Saint Just takes care of his own."

"Oh, my God," Maggie said, closing her eyes. "I have to think. Alex? Go home now, okay? I have to think. . . ."

He retrieved his cane, ignoring her wince as he picked it up, and let himself out into the hallway. Sterling would want to talk to him and he wasn't ready for that, not just yet.

He turned toward the elevator, pressed the button, and stepped inside when the car came, his back to the wall. As the doors closed he wondered . . . wondered if he really had made himself more, now that he was also Alex Blakely. More . . . or less?

EPILOGUE

Dear Journal, I've been neglecting my duty to you these past days, although I did speak to you in my mind. Which probably doesn't count for much, but I will say that I am glad you were there during a difficult time.

Has it only been a few short days since last I took up my pen and prepared to record the events of my life? It seems so much longer. Years longer.

So much has happened. Dear Bernie was in a very bad way for some moments, accused of murdering her dead husband, but that has all worked out, thanks to Saint Just. Oh, and Maggie. Not me, certainly, as I was rather occupied with other things.

Saint Just has told me I am a hero and I suppose I am, of sorts. Being a hero is not everything one might suppose it to be, by the way, and I am going to strive very hard not to be a hero ever again.

Oh, Bernie has gone away, to "dry out," Socks says, and I think Maggie must miss her very much, because she looks quite sad, and is barely even speaking to Saint Just, which he says is nothing to worry my head about, even though I do.

They had been rubbing along together so well that, I will admit it, I had begun to harbor High Hopes in that direction.

But I must get busy. Saint Just is purchasing Mrs. Goldblum's lovely apartment that is not so lovely now but will be once we have bought new furnishings. I have taken over that chore for the most part, having convinced Saint Just that we must incorporate proper feng shui to promote harmony, serenity, good health, and all of that.

He is for the most part fine with that, as he is a kind and generous man, but he tells me that he draws the line at wind chimes hung just outside his bedroom window. I read in one of my feng shui books that wind chimes only bring good luck when they are not annoying to others, so I have returned the wind chimes to the shop, exchanging them for a lovely brass elephant for the coffee table. Trunk pointing up, of course.

That's for good luck, Dear Journal, and I must say we seem to be in frequent need of that particular commodity. Let me tell you about these past few days. . . .

Please turn the page for an exciting sneak peek of

Kasey Michaels's next Maggie Kelly novel

MAGGIE GETS SOME DIRECTION

coming in November 2005!

Dear Journal,

Once more I take up my pen to record the happenings of my life and of those around me. I must admit that I have been quite remiss in my entries this past six weeks or more, but I have been much occupied in assembling our apartment after the shambles it had become thanks to those horrible gentlemen I told you about not so long ago.

But everything is all right and tight now, and properly done up according to Feng Shui guidelines. (Mrs. Tabby Leighton has corrected me, and it is not Feng *Shoo-ee,* as I had thought, but Feng *Schway*—isn't that interesting? Saint Just says it isn't.)

My only problem now is that Mrs. McBedie, whom Saint Just has engaged to look after us, will persist in facing the three-legged money frog in entirely the incorrect direction whenever she dusts the Wealth corner of our main saloon. (Which Maggie calls a living room, which I think rather eerie, as who wants to lounge about in a *living* room?)

Unfortunately we don't have much time to enjoy our new apartment, which now legally belongs to Saint Just, who is quite happily solvent now that he is half of the photographic modeling pair of him and our own Mary Louise, posing for magazine and even billboard advertisements for *Fragrances by Pierre.* It is, I must admit, rather disconcerting to see Saint Just twenty-five feet tall in Times Square.

And we have just baskets and baskets of lovely toiletries now, courtesy of Mr. Pierre, but Saint Just persists in favoring *Brut.* Maggie finds this amusing.

Saint Just has been toiling night and day at this new venture that, he told me rather proudly, entails considerably more work than he had supposed when he agreed to pose. Mary Louise has been able to forego any other employment (and more nefarious document counterfeiting dealings), and is now a student only, completing her last year at what she calls NYU.

It's lovely to see so much progress since our advent onto this plane of existence just a few short, exciting months ago.

Saint Just still oversees the Streetcorner Orators and Players (or however he says it—I keep forgetting the order), with Mary Louise's cousin and houseboys in charge. The enterprise has grown to include forty-seven street corners. Just imagine. Saint Just now calls himself an entrepreneur, which also makes Maggie laugh. I like it when she laughs.

Because even all this to-ing and fro-ing by Saint Just does not explain the Decided Coolness I have observed between him and our Maggie, friend and creator of both Saint Just and myself. I only hope that she is not so put out with us that she decides to stop writing about us, because I am not sure if we can continue to exist outside our books once Maggie has turned us off inside her head.

That's the problem with being imaginary characters come to life: this tenuous existence. Saint Just says he is working to ensure that we evolve, grow, and become more of own persons, thereby enabling us to create our own, completely-separate-from-Maggie identities, so perhaps this is why she seems to be sulking. I think Maggie likes to be Needed.

She has completed her new book in record time, a full three months early, which is explained by the fact that she has been all but living in front of her computer seven days a week. Regardless, she is now officially on vacation for the next month before beginning her research for another Saint Just adventure, but has yet to put on an All Done party as has been her custom in the past. Then again, considering what occurred after the last All Done party, I suppose she has her reasons and all of that.

But back to what is happening now, dear Journal, not what

is already past. After all, I believe this journaling business is supposed to be a chronicle, not a history, yes?

Bernie has returned from her drying-out place, and seeing her editor and very good friend again has put the roses back in Maggie's cheeks, just a little bit, although I'm still concerned for her. She so badly wanted a cigarette the other night that she asked me to "light" the pretzel she'd been munching, poor thing.

But, as Saint Just reminded me, the weeks have passed by and the day is rapidly approaching when we must all travel to a place called Ocean City, in a state called New Jersey (quite unlike our own English Jersey, I fear), to partake of Thanksgiving dinner with Maggie's parents.

I know very little about Mr. and Mrs. Kelly, save that Maggie studiously avoids them whenever possible. That, added to the fact that Maggie has explained Saint Just and myself to all in New York as the distant English relations she patterned her Saint Just books on in the first place could prove a tad sticky, as her parents are unaware of our existence.

Saint Just volunteered to have us remain here, safely out of sight in Manhattan, but Maggie looked at him with such *daggers* that he quickly rescinded that offer. Besides, we leave for England directly after the parental visit, invited guests of the film company that will be turning the very first Saint Just Mystery into a movie made just to fit television machines. I wonder who will portray me. I hope he isn't pudgy and balding; then again, I *am* pudgy and balding.

My Henry will be well taken care of by Mrs. McBedie, who has quite a fondness for mice, thank goodness, although she will insist upon thinking of him as a hamster, a species she considers a more domesticated animal. I am happy to report, also, that I discovered the most lovely new home for Henry, with lots and lots of tunnels for him to run through, and a wheel for him to run on, and a. . . . But I digress. It's a failing.

Bernie will meet us there—in England, dear Journal—along with Tabby, who says an agent's place is at her author's side. Saint Just calls that a tax deductible hum meant to give Tabby a vacation overseas, but he smiles almost indulgently when he says it. Saint Just, you see, is greatly enamored of something called loopholes in the American tax codes.

Socks, my very good friend who has taught me all about the Duties of a Doorman, will remain here in Manhattan, to celebrate this uniquely American holiday with his mother, and to toil nightly in the off-off-Broadway play he auditioned for after his paperback-romance-cover-model debut proved less than auspicious. I shall miss him, and I have told him he is free to borrow my motorized scooter any time he wishes.

Lieutenant Steve Wendell also sadly will not be a part of our entourage, and I will admit to you, dear Journal, if not to Saint Just, the trepidation I feel at his absence

For, as you already know, dear Journal, we often seem to have need of a representative of the constabulary.

Respectfully,

Sterling Balder

Grab These
Kensington Mysteries

Mischief, Murder &
Mayhem – Grab These
Kensington Mysteries